A WARRIOR'S PENANCE

THE CASTES AND THE OUTCASTES
—VOLUME THREE—

DAVIS ASHURA

A WARRIOR'S PENANCE

Copyright © 2016 by Davis Ashura

Cover art by Andreas Zafiratos
Cover Design by Andreas Zafiratos and Davis Ashura
Map illustrations by Roger Speer
Interior design by Mikey Brooks (mikeybrooks.com)
Interior illustrations by Mikey Brooks

DuSum Publishing, LLC

Printed in the United States of America.

Paperback Edition 2018

ISBN: 10: 0-9997044-9-4
ISBN 13: 978-0-9997044-9-3

DEDICATION

To my two sons.
What wonderful gentlenerds you've become.

ACKNOWLEDGMENTS

Like all things of worth, this book would not exist without the help of some truly wonderful and generous people. First, as usual, comes my wife, Stephanie, who once again allowed me the time to write this book. Next, my sister. Without her absolutely invaluable input, the books of *The Castes and the OutCastes* would have been immeasurably worse. I also can't forget Mike Weaver, all around great guy, wonderful friend, and fabulous reader.

To all of them, I once more offer my most humble thank you.

And again, if the book is not your cup of tea, it's entirely my fault.

OTHER BOOKS BY DAVIS ASHURA:

The Castes and the OutCastes

A Warrior's Path

A Warrior's Knowledge

A Warrior's Penance

Omnibus edition (available as eBook only)

Stories of Arisa — Volume One

The Chronicles of William Wilde

William Wilde and the Necrosed

William Wilde and the Stolen Life

William Wilde and the Unusual Suspects

William Wilde and the Sons of Deceit (available Spring 2019)

William Wilde and the Lord of Mourning (available Summer 2019)

TABLE OF CONTENTS

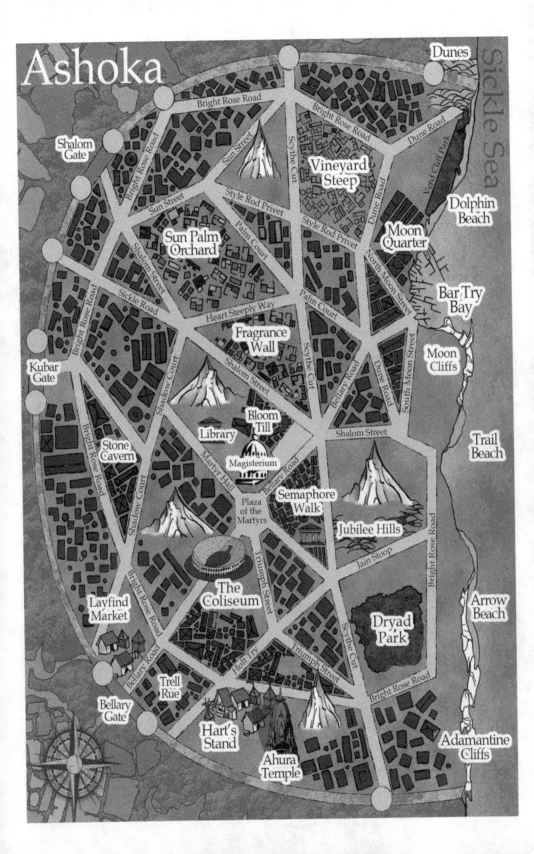

THE TRIAL SO FAR

The Trials are the means by which Humanity maintains a fragile link between their far-flung city-states. It is a holy mission, and most often carried out by Caste Kumma, the warrior Caste, and all who accept such a weighty obligation understand that it might lead to their deaths.

The Trial from Ashoka to Nestle is no different, and it is also Rukh Shektan's first. He is a Virgin to the Trials, as is his cousin, Farn Arnicep; Keemo Chalwin, a fellow Kumma and close friend; and Brand Wall of Caste Rahail. Rukh, however, is unique. He is the current Champion of the Tournament of Hume. His sword is said to be the finest in generations.

Disaster eventually overtakes the Trial. It is discovered by a large band of Chimeras and destroyed en masse. Few Ashokans survive, and among them are Rukh and his friends. They escape the ambush, but the means of their survival is considered anathema: they learn Talents not of their Caste. It is a situation that leaves them dismayed and horrified.

But they are also warriors of Ashoka, and they know their duty:

their home must be warned of what has happened. They know that this many Chimeras gathered together at one time might indicate that Suwraith, the Sorrow Bringer, has deadly intentions toward their home, the city of Ashoka. Rukh elects to send several warriors back to Ashoka in order to carry word of the Nestle Trial's fate, while he, Farn, Keemo, and Brand track the Chimeras to their staging area.

Their plans proceed, and as they follow the Chimeras, all four men seek to master their newly acquired, but unsought Talents. Brand learns to Shield and quicken his movements like a Kumma, while Rukh and the others form Blends, a perfect means of camouflage.

It is a situation that leads to great unhappiness, and Farn wonders if they would have been better off dying amongst their brother warriors in the Trial. He worries they are naaja—Tainted—or worse, ghrinas, children of two Castes. His fears are not without foundation, but Rukh will not hear of it. They have a mission to accomplish, and if Talents not of Caste Kumma are the means by which they complete their assignment, so be it. He demands that they put aside their fears for the future and accept whatever punishment is due them, *after* they find where the Chimeras are staging.

His orders are reluctantly carried out, and by the time they finally track down the Chimeras, all four warriors have a better understanding of their newfound Talents.

Rukh, Farn, Keemo, and Brand reach the Hunters Flats and discover the leaders of the Chimeras, the bull-like Baels, conversing privately with one another, far away from the bulk of their army. The Ashokans see an opportunity to destroy their hated enemies. But before they can launch their attack, Suwraith arrives in a storm of wind and terror.

The Ashokans hide, Blended as hard as they can. And while the

2

Sorrow Bringer is amongst the Baels, they learn of Her plans for Ashoka: their home is to be destroyed.

Suwraith eventually leaves, and just as Rukh and the others are about to attack the Baels, they listen in astonishment as the bull-like commanders argue on how best to disobey Suwraith—to actively oppose Her and protect Humanity. It is a stunning revelation, and one not easily believed.

Rukh decides to speak with Li-Dirge, the Bael commander, who is now alone after sending his brethren back to rejoin the rest of the army while he meditates.

Before Rukh can approach the Bael, he captures a Blended woman who suddenly manifests by his side. Her appearance is staggering. Women do not ever join the Trials, so she should not be in the Wildness. But even more shocking is the woman's features. She is obviously a ghrina, a child of two Castes. No such individual has ever been known to survive to adulthood since they are universally banished from the cities upon birth. They are thought to die in the Wildness, but given this woman's presence, it is obviously an incorrect assumption.

Some of the confusion is cleared when Rukh is finally able to speak to Li-Dirge. From the Bael, he learns of the great Kumma warrior, Hume, and the death of Hume's home, the city of Hammer. Rukh discovers how Hume had instructed Suwraith's commanders in the ideals of fraternity, and in the centuries following, the Baels had worked as best they could to disrupt Suwraith's plans.

And the ghrina woman, Jessira Grey, turns out to be a scout from Stronghold, a hidden city of her kind—OutCastes as they call themselves. She and her brothers, Cedar and Lure, had also been tracking the same Chimeras that had destroyed the Trial to Nestle.

During all this, Suwraith finds a way to rid Herself of Her

madness. The unceasing complaints of Her dead Parents and Mistress Arisa, a terrifying voice that only She hears, are silenced. The Queen pours Her insanity into the minds of Her children, the Chimeras—all except the Baels. By doing so, Suwraith regains Her sanity, realizes the truth, and discovers Her betrayal at the hands of Her commanders. She sees them speaking to Humans and is enraged.

However, before She can act, She notices Her Chimeras killing one another in violent abandon. It is because of Her madness poured into them. Reluctantly, the Sorrow Bringer takes back Her insanity and as a result, loses Her memories and regains the unwanted voices of Her dead Parents and the fearsome Mistress Arisa. Confusion overwhelms Suwraith's mind, but She remembers enough. She still knows the truth about the Baels, and She thunders from the sky, intent on destroying them.

Li-Dirge and his brother Baels are gathered with the Humans, joyful that the ideals to which their ancestors had held, are finally being realized. Rukh believes them. For the first time since Hume, a Human understands the truth of the Baels' situation. It is a momentous event, and Li-Dirge even tells Rukh about the location of the Chimera breeding caverns—the place where Suwraith helps birth Her hordes. All the breeds of Chimera require Suwraith's direct intervention in order to procreate—the cat-like Tigons, dog-like Ur-Fels, snake-like Braids, and elephant-sized Balants. Only the Baels, born mysteriously and unexpectedly from the placid, dull Bovars, do not require Suwraith's touch. However, in the midst of their jubilation, the Baels realize that Suwraith has discovered their centuries-long deception.

Suwraith comes to annihilate all Her Baels, but just before the Sorrow Bringer carries out Her attack, Rukh and the other Humans are urged to flee. They do so, escaping Suwraith's clutches by the barest of margins, but Dirge and his fellow Baels—the entire command of the Eastern Plague of Continent Ember—are destroyed.

Before Rukh and the others can take stock of their situation, they are attacked by two Shylows, the giant, deadly cats of the Hunters Flats. In the ensuing battle, Jessira's brother Lure, and Rukh's friends, Keemo and Brand, are killed. Farn is gravely injured and he and Cedar, Jessira's other brother, go missing. Rukh escapes with a young Bael, Li-Choke, and an injured Jessira.

Meanwhile in Ashoka, Rukh's brother, Jaresh, is accused of murdering Suge Wrestiva, a thug and degenerate who also happens to be the only living son of Hal'El Wrestiva, the ruling 'El of House Shektan's most bitter rival. The situation is even more clouded because Jaresh is of Caste Sentya but was adopted by Dar'El and Satha Shektan into House Shektan. Such an adoption is unprecedented and many Kummas are still troubled by the situation.

As a result, when Hal'El calls for a tribunal to have Jaresh judged with the Slash of Iniquity—a death penalty—his petition is granted by the Chamber of the Lords, Caste Kumma's governing body. During the ensuing trial, Jaresh's sister, Bree, discovers that Suge was secretly a snowblood addict and convinces the Chamber to decide in Jaresh's favor.

Later, a meeting of the Sil Lor Kum, the Hidden Hand of Justice—Suwraith's Human worshippers—is convened in Ashoka. The SuDin, their leader, tells the other members of the Council of Rule, the MalDins, of Suwraith's plans for Ashoka. He displays the Withering Knife, a mythical weapon said to steal *Jivatma*. It may also be the means through which the Sorrow Bringer can overcome Ashoka's Oasis, the mystical barrier around the city that has proven impenetrable to Her might for two millennia.

Shortly after this meeting of the Council of Rule, the first murder utilizing the Withering Knife is discovered. The victim is Felt Barnel, and his corpse is withered and desiccated, as if all the water was removed from his body.

Dar'El is deeply troubled by the murder and tasks Jaresh, Bree, and Mira Terrell———the daughter of one of House Shektan's councilors—with discovering the truth about the Withering Knife. In the course of their investigations, another victim is found murdered. This one is of Caste Cherid, Aqua Oilhue. Rector Bryce, a member of the City Watch, realizes that the murderer has to be of Caste Kumma, and he joins the other three in their search for information on the Withering Knife.

Jaresh is paired with Mira, and the two of them search the Cellar, the City Library's lowest floors where the oldest records are kept, while Bree and Rector look for the information in other locations. The work proves frustrating and drags on for weeks. Eventually, it is Jaresh who discovers a code within the journal of a caravan master— a leader of a Trial—and a known member of the Sil Lor Kum. The cypher confirms the existence of the Withering Knife as well as the physical markers it leaves on its victims. They are identical to those found on Felt Barnel and Aqua Oilhue.

During all this, Rukh and Jessira, having been thrown together, are forced to overcome a lifetime of prejudice and indoctrination as they make their way to Ashoka. They come to share a deep friendship, but Jessira's wounds from the battle with the Shylow are stealing her life. The wounds fester and grow infected. Jessira is dying, and can only be saved if she can teach Rukh her knowledge of Healing. It is another Talent not of his Caste, one mastered by Shiyens, and he is unable to learn what Jessira tries to teach him.

It is then, as Jessira lies dying, that another Shylow, a female calico named Aia, walks into their camp. Rukh is prepared to lay down his life in Jessira's defense, but the cat simply stares at him, and *speaks* into his mind. It is a shocking revelation, and at first, Rukh fears he is going mad. Aia convinces him otherwise.

She is rare for her kind, able to speak to those who aren't Kesarins—the name Shylows call themselves—and as a result, quite curious about Humans. She is especially fascinated by Rukh. Aia has been following him and Jessira since before they had exited the Hunters Flats, wondering as to why he was taking such exquisite care of someone who wasn't close kin.

His notions of brotherhood and compassion captivate Aia, and she asks why he doesn't Heal Jessira. When she learns that Rukh lacks the knowledge, the Kesarin reaches into Jessira's mind and shares it with him. Aia leaves then, vowing to see Rukh again.

As a result of the Kesarin's help, Rukh is able to stave off Jessira's infected injuries, and the two of them continue on to Ashoka where she is fully Healed of her wounds. Afterward, they make their way to the House Seat where Rukh is joyfully reunited with his family. He makes a full report on what has happened to him, including his Talents of Blending and Healing to the House Council. Also present during Rukh's account is Rector Bryce, who has always been unforgiving and certain of that which he considers immoral. Rector is unwilling to accept Rukh's new abilities. As a result of his attitude, Dar'El and the rest of the House Council re-examine the Watch captain's role in the search for the Withering Knife murderer.

Rukh's account of his actions in the Wildness is also explained to the Magisterium, Ashoka's governing body. Though few of the Magistrates are willing to believe the Baels are their allies, the decision is made to act upon Li-Dirge's information and send an expeditionary force to the Chimera caverns. Their goal will be simple: the extermination of all Chimera breeders. Rukh is chosen as one of the warriors for the coming expedition, and he throws himself into his work.

As the preparation for the expedition continues, the SuDin of the Sil Lor Kum turns out to be Hal'El Wrestiva. He and his Rahail lover, Varesea Apter, a fellow MalDin in the Sil Lor Kum, share a sinful relationship, one that would call for their execution were it ever discovered. But Varesea and Hal'El are undaunted. They love one another, and they decide to kill her abusive husband, Slathtril Apter, with the Withering Knife as their first step in being together.

Rukh is able to examine the site of Slathtril Apter's murder and realizes that *two* people were involved in the killing. He recognizes that the victim knew his murderers, and that the Kumma in question had to have come from one of three Houses.

As for Jessira, she is alone in the city but comes to view the Purebloods in a more positive light. Always before, she had been dismissive and sneering of Rukh's people, but seeing the beauty and culture of Ashoka, she begins to change her mind. And in some ways, Jessira's presence stimulates a change in the city's own harsh attitudes toward the OutCastes, those traditionally called ghrinas. It is a subtle difference.

Meanwhile, unbeknownst to Rukh, forces conspire in the shadows to have him declared Unworthy and exiled from Ashoka. Dar'El senses these hidden enemies and knows they will likely learn of Rukh's Talents—it was a mistake to trust Rector Bryce—and bring Rukh down in order to hurt House Shektan. Dar'El concocts a scheme to keep Rukh safe: have him go with Jessira to her home of Stronghold rather than simply be cast out in the cold.

In order to do so, he needs Bree's help to trick both Rukh *and* Jessira. His plan works, and Rukh and Jessira, friends already, are seen in public in what might be considered a romantic circumstance. Rukh's fate is sealed by a late-night stroll with Jessira through Dryad Park.

The time approaches for the expedition to the caverns to leave the city, and a few days beforehand, Rukh learns of Jaresh's possible romantic feelings toward Mira Terrell. Ironically, Rukh is unaware of his own perceived relationship with Jessira, and he confronts his adopted brother and orders him to break off all contact with Mira.

Jaresh does so, telling Mira they can't work together anymore. She hears what he's really saying and surprises him by kissing him on the lips. Given the prohibition against a man and a woman of two different Castes even touching one another, her expression is a bold declaration of her feelings for Jaresh—as well as a sign of farewell.

Rukh's departure to the caverns takes place, and early on, he tells the commanders of his new Talents. They are disgusted by what he can do, considering him a naaja—Tainted—and the information spreads to the rest of the warriors, who share their commanders revulsion. The expedition travels through the Hunters Flats, and Rukh's diminished status dims further when Aia enters the camp and Rukh is forced to explain her presence.

There are too many changes for the other members of the expedition to accept, and Rukh is essentially thrust out of the brotherhood of warriors. He is forced to work alone, left intentionally vulnerable and exposed with no one to guard his back. Rukh perseveres, but even in the caverns—which are exactly where Li-Dirge said they would be—he is left to fend for himself.

His situation is dire, but somehow Rukh survives. He even comes across Li-Choke and the last few Baels of the Eastern Plague to survive Suwraith's pogrom. He leads Choke and the others to safety where they can make their way to the Hunters Flats and, as promised by Aia, find shelter amongst the Kesarins.

Following the battle, Rukh's ability to Heal proves essential. He is able to keep dozens of warriors alive during the long march back to Ashoka. His selfless devotion to the lives of others slowly changes the opinions of his fellow warriors. They acknowledge his service with gratitude, and even Rukh's greatest enemy amongst them, his direct commanding officer, Lieutenant Danslo, comes to appreciate and respect all that Rukh can do.

After weeks of emotional toil, Rukh finally sees hope for the future. If his brother warriors of the expedition can look past their prejudices and accept Rukh, then why not all of Ashoka?

It is a short-lived hope.

Days after leaving the city, the Chamber of Lords had met and—just as Dar'El had feared—judged Rukh Unworthy. He is to be exiled. Jessira learns of this just prior to her own departure from Ashoka, and she agrees to delay her leave-taking. She will wait for Rukh's return and lead him to Stronghold.

When the expedition to the caverns returns, she meets it a day short of Ashoka and informs Rukh of what has happened. He will never be allowed to enter his home again.

Rukh is heartbroken and prepares to leave with Jessira for Stronghold, but before he can do so, the warriors of the expedition honor him the Champion's salute. It is their apology for what they now recognize as their wrongful treatment of him during the long march to the Chimera caverns.

Jessira leads Rukh away from the expedition. Later, she apologizes for her role in his situation and reaches to console him. They share a deep, but confusing, kiss before she pulls away, and Rukh follows her west.

That evening, as they set up camp, Jessira is conflicted by what she has done. She feels the kiss was a mistake because she is engaged to Disbar Merdant, someone she's known since childhood. While she likes Rukh, any feelings she has for him can't be acted upon. Thankfully, Rukh feels the same way. He understands her situation, but just as importantly, Kummas don't infringe upon someone already in a serious relationship.

As they begin their travels, Jessira tells Rukh about Stronghold. He learns that the city was founded by fifty-five survivors of Hammer's Fall, a small group of Sentyas, Duriahs, Cherids, Shiyens, Murans, and Rahails, but no Kummas. More surprising, though, is the fact that the survivors of Hammer's Fall were saved by Hume, the legendary warrior who would go on to teach the Baels of fraternity. As a result, the OutCastes revere him, even holding a martial tournament in his name—the Trials of Hume.

The fifty-five eventually founded Stronghold within the heart of Mount Fort in the Privation Mountains. It is a city like any other with certain occupations holding greater status than others—such as farmers and craftsmen being valued above simple laborers. However, there is one important distinction: Stronghold doesn't have an Oasis. As a result, the OutCastes prize secrecy above all else. They have to if they wish to survive

Rukh takes all this in and hopes that he can find a position in Stronghold's army as a warrior, something Jessira assures him will not be a problem.

Weeks into the Privations, Rukh and Jessira are tracked and attacked by a band of Chimeras—a nest of Ur-Fels and a claw of Tigons. Rukh's thoughts go black during the battle. He takes reckless risks, essentially courting death and willing to die.

Jessira, initially furious with his actions, quickly comes to recognize the deep depression Rukh has fallen into. She's experienced something like this herself, and she tells Rukh a personal story of horrifying betrayal by someone she trusted. Rukh listens, knowing all the while that he can't go on as he has and eventually speaks of his own pain.

And watching the battle is a young Tigon named Chak-Soon, the leader of the Chimeras that had attacked Rukh and Jessira. He witnesses the carnage from a nearby bluff, and after the clash's conclusion, he begs for Suwraith's attention, the being he knows as Mother Lienna.

She answers Chak-Soon's call. When She learns that a single Human had killed a claw of Tigons and a large nest of Ur-Fels, She is convinced that it must be the acts of Hume, the dreaded warrior of Hammer. How the Sorrow Bringer had learned of him, is unknown, but Her mind, briefly sane when She had learned of Her betrayal at the hands of Her Baels, is obviously confused and cluttered once more. Suwraith orders Chak-Soon to scour the Privations and kill Hume. She promises to supply him with all he will need to carry out this task.

After the meeting with Chak-Soon, Suwraith continues to find Herself deluded. She cannot distinguish the past from the present, and the lamenting cries of Her Mother and Father persist, as does the needling horror of Mistress Arisa. It reaches a boiling point, and once again, Suwraith pours Her insanity into Her children. This time, She finds a means to permanently banish much of Her madness.

For the first time in millennia, She is able to plan.

First, Suwraith sends a blizzard scouring through a valley in the Privation Mountains. It is meant to kill the Human who Chak-Soon had seen. Next, She sends for Li-Shard, the SarpanKum of the Western Plague and orders him east to assume control of the Eastern Plague. After Her murder of Li-Dirge and his Baels, the Eastern

Plague had been turned over to the incompetent command of the Tigons. It is about to tear itself apart.

And finally, Suwraith recaptures Li-Choke, the Bael who had escaped the destruction of Dirge's command and, through Rukh's help, the abattoir of the Chimera breeding caverns. He and several other eastern Baels had been living quiet lives in the Hunters Flats. All of them but Choke are ripped apart by Suwraith, and She offers him a simple choice: serve Her or see every Bael in Arisa destroyed. Choke bends knee and, by Her orders, takes command of Chak-Soon and a number of Chimeras. They are to journey to Hammer and kill the Human who destroyed Chak-Soon's Tigons and Ur-Fels.

Meanwhile, back in Ashoka, Rector Bryce thinks himself noble. It was he who exposed Rukh's new Talents to House Shektan's foes. Rector learns to his folly that Dar'El Shektan is a man who will swiftly repay such betrayal. Dar'El knows a secret about Rector's family, one that would see them ruined: Rector's great-grandfather had been of the Sil Lor Kum. To keep such devastating information secret, Rector reluctantly agrees to do as Dar'El orders: spy on House Shektan's greatest enemy, Hal'El Wrestiva, and find a means to ruin him.

Rector is paired with Mira and is expected to report any findings to her. It is a situation neither of them like. Rector thinks Mira is arrogant and possibly Tainted while Mira thinks Rector is a self-righteous hypocrite. Nevertheless, they end up working well together.

Dar'El also has plans beyond Hal'El's ruination. He has every intention of finding a means to bring Rukh home. Dar'El is a member of the Society of Rajan, a near-mythical organization whose members are all high-ranking personages in Ashoka. With their help, he hatches a scheme that will see Rukh's conviction overturned. However, not all is as it seems. A member or the Society, Ular Sathin, one of Dar'El's closest friends, is also a high-ranking member of the Sil Lor Kum.

And none of them know that Hal'El Wrestiva is actually the SuDin of the Sil Lor Kum or that he and his Rahail lover, Varesea Apter—also of the Sil Lor Kum—are struggling with their own terrifying problems. The people murdered with the Withering Knife sometimes whisper in their minds. Despite this terrible turn of events, upon Suwraith's orders, Hal'El kills one last time with the Knife, a Rahail named Van Jinnu.

During all this, Rukh and Jessira press on toward Stronghold. The dark depression he hid from even himself is now gone for the most part, but a new threat arises. As they traverse a narrow gorge, Rukh is thrown from his horse and badly injured—his leg is broken and his right arm hangs useless at his side. Even worse, a freak blizzard takes them by surprise. The storm was presaged by a lightning-laced, bruise-colored cloud crisscrossing the sky—Suwraith.

Rukh and Jessira find shelter in a nearby cave where they ride out the storm, but a hidden injury nearly kills him. In her fear for him, Jessira lets slip the truth of her feelings for Rukh. She names him 'priya', a word that means beloved in Ashoka. Later, after Rukh recovers, they press on toward Stronghold. When Rukh asks Jessira about the meaning of 'priya', she dissembles. She claims that priya means close friend, but in Stronghold, it actually means 'only beloved'.

When they finally reach her home, Jessira reunites with her family. Her cousin, Sign Deep, is the first to greet her. Her brother Cedar made it back home as well, bringing Farn with him. Rukh, though, is briefly held prisoner until Stronghold's Senate decides to grant him asylum.

Afterward, he is sponsored by Court Deep, Sign's brother, and along with Farn, the three men share a flat. However, Court is a warrior while Farn has been relegated to work as a laborer. Rukh's cousin had suffered a head injury and until recently had been unable to walk for any length of time without stumbling.

In addition, Stronghold isn't as Jessira described. The OutCastes have their own form of bigotry. The two Kummas face discrimination. They are bluntly told that Purebloods—the Stronghold aspersion for those who aren't OutCaste—come from a culture that is inferior to that of Stronghold's and that the OutCastes are inherently better and more civilized. This attitude, combined with the lingering effects of Rukh's injuries, ensures that he will not be allowed to demonstrate his Talents as a warrior. He, too, must work as a laborer.

Nevertheless, Rukh settles into the city as best he can. He even finds someone to Heal his damaged arm, and he and Farn began training once more. Rukh's cousin plans on returning to Ashoka as soon as he can, even willing to brave winter's winds in order to leave Stronghold. While Farn admires what the OutCastes have built for themselves, their superior attitude has long since grown too grating to tolerate.

Unknown to Farn, Rukh also plans on leaving Stronghold. He reckons that after his cousin's departure, he will be all but alone in the city. While Court and Cedar have become good friends, as have some laborers, it isn't enough. Rukh, too, is tired of Stronghold's bigotry. In addition, he has purposefully put distance between himself and Jessira. If her people ever discovered the depth of their feelings for one another or learned of the kiss they shared, it might ruin her reputation.

Jessira is incensed by the decision Rukh has made regarding their friendship, but she has little time to challenge him over it. Her work as a scout keeps her too busy. Plus, she has struggles of her own. She is disgusted by the attitude and behavior of her people toward Rukh and Farn, but whenever she brings the matter up to her family or friends, it is only Cedar and Court who understand her revulsion. No one else recognizes the problem. To most people of Stronghold, their home is a paragon of equality and refined thought.

Matters aren't improved when Jessira truly gets to know her fiancé, Disbar. He is clutching, controlling, and calculating—on his word, his cousins spy on Jessira to ensure she doesn't contact Rukh. His loathsome conduct becomes too much for her to bear, and she ends their engagement. It is a scandalous action, but Jessira doesn't care. She can't live a lie.

Later, after returning from weeks of maneuvers in the Wildness, Jessira learns that Farn has left Stronghold and that Rukh, Healed and hale once more, plans on entering the Trials of Hume.

No one else gives him a chance at victory. The OutCastes discount Jessira and Cedar's accounts of what Rukh can do. They reckon that the supposed Talents of the Kummas are likely nothing more than an exaggeration. Stupidly, they've not even bothered to ask Rukh for a demonstration. The one time he had offered to do so, he was vulgarly dismissed. He is also attacked on multiple occasions by masked assailants. The situation has him disgusted, and Rukh plans on carrying through with his decision to leave the city and never return.

The Trials of Hume arrive, and just as Jessira predicted, Rukh devastates all the warriors he faces. It is a stunning display that leaves all of Stronghold in silent shock as he leaves the arena.

Rukh's feelings toward the OutCastes softens somewhat at the Champion's banquet when many individuals come to express their sincere regret over their behavior and actions. The Governor-

General, Mon Peace, even goes so far to give Rukh an officer's commission in the Home Army and his own flat.

However, Rukh is still insistent on leaving Stronghold. In the final letter his nanna had sent to him, a reference was made to *The Book of First Movement*, the supposed journal of the First Father. *The Book* is said to be in Hammer, and it is there that Rukh chooses to journey. But Jessira decides to accompany him, something to which he is categorically opposed.

While they set off in their travels, back in Ashoka, the search for the Withering Knife murderer continues. Information comes to Bree and Jaresh, but in the course of their investigation, they are attacked. In a narrow alley, they fight for their lives. Bree, who had never given proper seriousness to her martial training, is almost frozen in panic. She does enough to stay alive, but for the most part, it is Jaresh who defends them both. The attack is thwarted, and the only surviving assailant escapes but only after nearly killing Bree.

Rector learns of the assault, and he is able to deduce the location of the surviving attacker. From him, he learns that the one who initiated the assault was a Rahail woman, a MalDin. The same woman who was likely seen by several of the Withering Knife murder victims. She may also be a silent partner at the Wrestiva warehouse that Rector oversees.

As House Shektan prepares to investigate this new information in greater detail, Farn Arnicep returns to Ashoka. His miraculous homecoming allows Dar'El to push forward with his proposal to have Rukh's ruling rescinded. The Society of Rajan helps him, and with their aid and Farn's testimony, the Council of Lords decides in Rukh's favor. He is no longer Unworthy. He can return to Ashoka if he wishes.

Immediately, further plans are initiated. Farn will command a

Trial to Stronghold, and Jaresh will go as well.

And far to the south, Li-Choke meets Chak-Soon for the first time. It is not an auspicious beginning. Discipline amongst the Chimeras has fallen precipitously since Li-Dirge's death. Choke almost has to kill Soon in order to force the Tigon to accept his mastery. However, after Soon bends knee, the other Chimeras fall in line as well. Nevertheless, even after their submission, Choke is still forced to institute harsh penalties for even the most minor of infractions. The Chimeras suffer, and Soon surprises Choke when he offers to accept everyone else's punishments if the other's will no longer be harmed.

The Tigon's willing sacrifice is stunning, and Choke eases off the punishment and teaches Soon of fraternity, who becomes the first Tigon in history to become so aware. There even comes a moment when Chak-Soon realizes that Suwraith is mad. He recognizes the folly of this quest that She has set them upon: to find Hume in long dead Hammer—the Bone Place, as the Chimeras call it.

During all this, after their months of turmoil in Stronghold and during their own travels to Hammer, Rukh and Jessira rekindle their love. It requires patience and understanding, but eventually they come to forgive one another for whatever hurts they suffered on the other's behalf. Rukh even agrees to return to Stronghold.

However, while camping on the famed black cliffs north of Hammer, the sound of Braids on the hunt drives them into the city. They huddle in a crumbled building and are shocked when Li-Choke and Chak-Soon burst into their sanctuary. Wolves on the hunt had driven the Bael and Tigon to seek shelter, but their respite is brief.

Rukh runs Soon through before Choke can explain their presence. Jessira Heals the Tigon, and the pursuing wolves leave of their own accord. Afterward, with Soon still unconscious, the three of them recount their journeys to Hammer. Choke also explains Chak-Soon's importance and agrees to help Rukh and Jessira recover *The Book of First Movement*. He already knows where it is, a secret known only to the Baels. *The Book* is hidden away in the Library of Hammer, and after they retrieve it, they quickly exit the city.

Eventually, Chak-Soon awakens, but now a new challenge awaits him. He has been instructed since he was a cub that Humans are evil. Yet, one of them Healed him, and according to Li-Choke, *all* Humans are Soon's brothers. The young Tigon eventually comes to accept this truth.

The four of them travel east and go their separate ways on the banks of the Soulless River. Choke and Soon return to the Eastern Plague while Rukh and Jessira make their way to Stronghold. However, the two Humans are careful to never reveal that there is, in fact, a city in the Privation Mountains. The Chimeras are led to believe that the Humans mean to return to Ashoka.

Later that evening, Rukh, overcome by curiosity, cracks open *The Book of First Movement*. The pages are blank just like all the stories say. However, a blue light overwhelms his senses, and he finds himself reliving the last night of Linder Val Maharj, the First Father.

All the stories are true. The First Father and the First Mother had a single child, Lienna. That child would go on to murder Her Parents with the Withering Knife and become the being known as Suwraith. But somehow before He died, Linder was able to create the Oases and *The Book of First Movement*.

As Rukh lies entranced by Linder's last moments, Suwraith, drawn by what She thinks is Her Father's *Jivatma*, seeks out the source of what She senses. She races to where Rukh and Jessira had been camped, and the two of them barely escape Her wrath.

The rest of the journey back to Stronghold is tense, except for an evening when the Kesarin, Aia, and her brothers, Shon and Thrum, briefly reunite with Rukh and Jessira.

As for Choke and Chak-Soon, they make their way back to the Eastern Plague, where the new SarpanKum, Li-Shard greets their arrival with acclaim. What Choke has accomplished—befriending a Human—is the longed for dream of all Baels. The fact that he could open Chak-Soon's eyes to the truth of fraternity is another stunning blessing.

Their glad celebration is short.

Suwraith informs Choke that he is to take a full Shatter of Chimeras and follow Her north into the Privations. There, he will assist Her in eradicating a city of Humans. Choke is certain this must be Jessira's hidden home, the one she never spoke of, but which he was able to infer must exist. He and Li-Shard plan for how best to thwart the Queen's plans.

And back in Ashoka, Dar'El discovers the truth about Ular Sathin. His friend, a member of the Society of Rajan, is also the Muran MalDin. However, before Dar'El can extract any information from the traitor, Hal'El tracks Ular down first. In the confrontation with Hal'El, Ular ends up taking his life, and by doing so, all his secrets as well.

Days later, a journal—Ular's—arrives on Dar'El's desk. It contains everything the Muran MalDin knew of the Sil Lor Kum . . . but it's written in cypher.

That same day, Rector and Mira, through a great deal of investigation, separately learn the true name of the SuDin: Hal'El Wrestiva. Mira is about to relay the information to Dar'El, but before she can do so, she is abducted by Hal'El, who had been watching her movements and monitoring what she had been doing. He takes her back to the secret flat that he and Varesea share.

Rector had been on his way to meet Mira, and he catches a glimpse of her with Hal'El. At first, he isn't sure it's her, and before he can act on what he's seen, she's gone. He's further distracted when Satha and Bree Shektan ride up to him. After hearing what he's learned, and what he's just witnessed, Satha returns to the Shektan House Seat to gather warriors, while Rector and Bree go after Mira.

They burst inside just as Hal'El strikes Mira. In the ensuing battle, Varesea is killed and Mira terribly injured. Hal'El, however, manages to escape.

During all this, Rukh and Jessira manage to make their way back to Stronghold. Shortly thereafter, they are married. Any damage to Jessira's reputation when she broke off her engagement to Disbar is long since washed away, especially when the wedding ceremony is performed by none other than the Governor-General, Mon Peace.

Their honeymoon, however, is short-lived.

Several weeks after their wedding, Suwraith arrives at Stronghold. Rukh and Jessira, along with Sign, Cedar, and Court, watch helplessly as the Sorrow Bringer eradicates the OutCaste city. Only a handful manage to escape the destruction.

Also arriving at Stronghold on the same day as Suwraith is Farn, Jaresh, and the rest of the warriors of the Trial from Ashoka to Stronghold. They, too, are witness to Suwraith's wretched evil as is Aia, Shon, and Thrum.

Li-Choke, who has brought his Shatter of Chimeras north, does his best to save the survivors. He and Chak-Soon had managed to haul a number of canoes up to River Gaunt, which the OutCastes can hopefully use to escape. Choke tells Rukh, newly reunited with Jaresh and Farn, about his plan and promises to do all he can to keep the Chimeras away from where the boats are to be launched.

A tearful trek makes its way north. Out of Stronghold's original forty thousand, a little more than one hundred remain. Nevertheless, through luck, courage, and skill, all of the survivors—Strongholders and Ashokans alike—make it to the River Gaunt and the promised boats.

They push off into the water, but in the ensuing, frenetic escape, a Fracture of Chimeras discovers them. The battle that follows is horrific, and none would have survived if not for the timely intervention of Aia and her brothers. The Kesarins had been tracking their Humans—Rukh and Jessira—back to Stronghold. During the battle, they pass on all of Rukh's Talents to the OutCaste warriors fighting for survival.

By the barest of margins, the new abilities prove just enough to hold off the Chimeras, and it is left to a ragged and weary Jessira and Rukh to lead the other survivors to safety. They push their canoes into the water, hauling on the oars as they hurl them into the river's rapids.

PROLOGUE

When a city is destroyed by Suwraith, Hope itself becomes a victim.

—*A Concise History of Arisa* by Kalthe Mint, AF 1839

Rukh watched as Jessira sat alone by the banks of the Gaunt River. Her knees were clutched to her chest, and she stared across the water wearing a distant expression of shell-shocked weariness. Her air of grief and exhaustion was one that was mirrored by rest of the OutCastes, all of whom sat about in small clusters of huddled misery and mourning. Their losses were incalculable. From a city of over forty thousand people, there were now but one-hundred twenty-nine survivors of Stronghold's destruction. The OutCastes were people at risk of extinction.

Rukh glanced over at the small encampment of Ashokans. Fifty warriors had journeyed from the city of his birth to Stronghold, and they too, had suffered grievous losses. There were now a little more than thirty Ashokan warriors remaining. They mourned their dead alongside the Strongholders and appeared every bit as drained. Most of the Ashokans leaned against one another, bone-tired and dozing, while a few of them remained alert and kept watch. Jaresh and Farn were amongst those who remained awake.

Rukh shook his head. He still couldn't believe his brother and his cousin were actually here. It was like a waking dream, and he would have been overjoyed to see them, except for the occurrence of yesterday's events. So many terrible tragedies. So much loss. So many dead. Too many. Rukh bit his lip, refusing to let the tears fall as he remembered Cedar and Court.

His gaze shifted and fell upon the people grouped along the river's bank. Some of them were angry with him. After the rapids, when the water had leveled out and calmed, some of the OutCastes had called for a halt. They wanted to stop and grieve, but Rukh wouldn't allow it. He knew they had to push on. They needed distance between themselves and Stronghold. The Sorrow Bringer was probably still seeking them.

While Li-Choke could promise that his Fracture of Chimeras would not be patrolling the Gaunt River, he couldn't make the same vow on behalf of the Queen. She would almost certainly be on the hunt for them, and if She succeeded, they were all dead. According to Choke, Suwraith had discovered a new Talent. She could somehow sense a person's *Jivatma*, even through the tightest of Blends. It was apparently the reason why no word of Her imminence had been carried back to Stronghold by the Home Army's scouts. The Queen had killed them all.

If Choke was right, the news was disastrous, not just for those huddled here but for everyone throughout the world. The Trials might no longer be possible. They relied on Blends to hide from the Sorrow Bringer's sight, but if She could see through them, then no one entering the Wildness would ever be safe.

Art and learning—so important in rebuilding civilization after the Days of Desolation—would suffer as each city was cut off and left as an isolated island alone. The loss of communication and sharing would lead to stagnation, decay, and a slow-motion death for each city.

Word of this potential calamity had to be carried as quickly as possible and . . .

Rukh sighed, cutting off his thoughts.

Tomorrow would have to take care of itself. Right now, all of them—Ashokans and Strongholders alike—needed to get going again if they were to make it through the rest of this day.

He stood and stretched before turning to face the river. After last night's harrowing ride, they'd beached their canoes along a flat stretch of water. A broad valley spread out around them, enclosed on all sides by the Privation Mountains. A sandbar cupped the curve of the water, and a morning mist wrapped the world in silence.

And Jessira remained seated on a plank of driftwood next to the river, as still and unmoving as a statue. She continued to stare out over the water and as Rukh approached her, he did his best to set aside his sorrow. His wife didn't need his tears. Not now anyway. Maybe later when they could properly grieve. Right now, she needed his support, his strength, his clear-eyed judgment to see them safe until they reached Ashoka. But as he studied her empty expression, he immediately knew he was wrong. Jessira needed his strength and support, but she also needed his comfort, even if it was nothing more than his quiet presence.

Rukh sat down next to his wife and pulled her close. She didn't resist, and she rested her head on his shoulder.

They sat silent, quiet and still and seemingly alone despite all the others nearby.

"We have to get going soon," Jessira said, breaking the quiet.

"You heard what Li-Choke said about the Queen?"

"She can sense a person's *Jivatma*," Jessira replied, her voice uncharacteristically flat.

Rukh kissed the top of her head. "We have to get to Ashoka as quickly as possible," he said. "Will the river be the swiftest means to do so?"

Jessira nodded. "Traveling downstream, it is," she answered.

"But not upstream?"

"No."

"Is that why we didn't just follow the Gaunt to Stronghold when we left Ashoka?"

"Yes. We would have had to climb too many cliffs and waterfalls," she replied, a bit of life to her voice. "It would have taken weeks longer."

"But even going downstream, we'll have to hike down those same cliffs and waterfalls," Rukh reminded her, glad to hear her take an interest in what they had to do next. He had worried that she might not; that she'd retreat into a bitter shell.

"It will be difficult, especially for the children and those unaccustomed to the hardships of the Wildness," Jessira mused.

"But it should be a little easier since we'll know what to look for." At Jessira's look of confusion, Rukh explained. "Farn just made the journey we're about to take. He can tell us what to expect."

"His experience will be invaluable," Jessira said with a nod. "I'll let my people know we have to get going."

She made to stand, but Rukh held her down. "Our people," he reminded her.

She held a hand to the side of his face and offered a brief, wan smile. "Thank you."

Rukh kissed her fingertips as he sought to buy some time. He didn't want to tell her the final piece of information.

"What is it?" Jessira asked.

"Disbar survived," Rukh answered. "After everything he did— setting his cousins to attack me—he was stripped of his rank and forced to work as a laborer at East Lock. He escaped Stronghold's destruction, but during the ride on the river, he was thrown from his canoe and battered by the rocks. He won't live very long." Rukh hesitated. "He wants to talk to you."

Jessira sighed in what sounded like a mix of regret, sorrow, and disappointment. "I'll go see him."

———◦———

The canoes provided by Choke and Chak-Soon had carried the survivors of Stronghold's demise far in the past week. Though ugly and rough-hewn, they were also rugged and durable, and Rukh was grateful for them. They were holding up well. Only a few easily repaired leaks had been required to keep them afloat.

"Everyone sure is quiet," Jaresh observed as he took a seat next to Rukh.

"Would you expect any different?" Farn asked, walking alongside the other man.

Jaresh shrugged. "I suppose not."

Rukh glanced about.

They'd stopped for the day near a series of rapids and falls, and from them came a plume of mineral-scented mist. The exuberance of the water was a sound not reflected by those who travelled upon it. As usual, the camp was somber. A few muted conversations could be heard, but otherwise, the OutCastes and Ashokans quietly moved about their tasks. Some had prepared the evening meal while others readied the bedrolls or inspected the canoes.

"Do you mind if I eat with you?" Lieutenant Altin Danslo interrupted, sounding diffident as he handed a plate to Rukh. "I noticed you hadn't had your supper yet."

Rukh motioned for Altin to sit down. He still had trouble believing that this was the same lieutenant who had hounded him so mercilessly on the expedition to the Chimera caverns. That man had hated Rukh with a deep, dark passion, willing to see him dead, no matter the means. But in the end, that man had also apologized to Rukh, and according to Farn, as soon as the expedition for Stronghold had been announced, it had been Danslo who had been the first one to volunteer. He'd even been willing to change his House affiliation if that was what required to join the Trial.

Apparently, many of the Kummas who had journeyed to Stronghold had similar stories to tell. Rukh's selflessness on the brutal return to Ashoka from the Chimera breeding caverns had won him the admiration of a number of warriors who felt they owed him a lifelong debt. Farn said hundreds of them had leapt at the chance to see Rukh home. They claimed to have sins that needed expiation, and while their gratitude was humbling, it was also something for which Rukh felt wholly unworthy.

"We lost another OutCaste today," Farn said, gesturing to the rapids. "It's the fifth so far. She jumped off the falls. We found her body downstream."

The group fell into a reflective silence, and Rukh shook his head in disappointment. With everything the OutCastes had been through, it wasn't surprising that some of them would take their lives, but it was still heartbreaking.

"How do you suppose we should get past those rapids?" Jaresh asked, changing the subject.

"It's too treacherous to try the canoes, even during the day," Danslo said. "We'd be better of portaging overland until we reach a quieter stretch of water."

Farn grunted. "It might cost us a lot of time, but dying would cost us even more."

"I think we've all had enough near-death experiences on this journey to last a lifetime," Jaresh responded with feeling.

"Then it's a good thing you weren't on the Trial to Nestle," Farn said.

"Or the one to the Chimera caverns," Danslo added.

Jaresh looked between the two men before rolling his eyes. "And I'm sure in both Trials, the warriors waded through knee-deep snow and a howling blizzard in both directions."

"No snow," Farn said, "but with the Nestle Trial, we did fight uphill the entire way."

"And in the expedition to the Chimera caverns, we fought in pitch black." Danslo grinned. "A blizzard would have been easy. All the Chimeras would have died of frostbite."

"And surviving a blizzard *is* easy, especially if a beautiful woman keeps you warm." Farn nudged Rukh. "Isn't that right?"

The other three men laughed. They all knew the story by now, and Rukh chuckled with them.

On the road to Stronghold, Rukh's horse had thrown him. He'd broken his leg and badly injured his shoulder and lungs. Then had come a freak blizzard, and Jessira had snuggled close to Rukh and kept him warm. She'd Healed him, saved him, and called him 'priya' for the first time.

He caught sight of Jessira just then. She was heading out in the same direction he had seen taken by Jaciro Plume just minutes before.

He frowned. He knew all about Jaciro Plume. The one time he'd confronted the man, it had taken all his self-control not to beat him within an inch of his life. What Plume had done to Jessira was unconscionable, unforgivable. Plume should have been castrated and cast out of Stronghold for the hurt he'd done to Jessira.

But to see her following him, the two of them far away and alone, and the knife-edged anger Rukh sensed from his hot-tempered wife . . . He had a bad feeling. Rukh made his pardons to the other three men and set off in pursuit. He had to catch up with her before she did anything rash.

Luckily, it wasn't hard to find Jessira. Somehow Rukh could feel her presence. He always knew exactly where she was.

As he approached closer, Plume was nowhere in sight, but Jessira was marching on. Rukh followed after her with a frown. What was happening? From Jessira billowed a wave of icy fury, cold as cruelty and heartless as a grinding glacier.

Rukh continued to shadow her trail, careful to keep far enough back that she wouldn't see him. When he finally found her, he watched her confrontation with Plume, and after a few minutes, he turned aside and returned to the camp.

The survivors of Stronghold's death sat huddled about small fires that shed thin streams of quickly dissipating smoke. The crash of the nearby rapids overwhelmed most conversations, but every now and then, softly spoken words caught Jessira' attention. They were words of disbelief and denial; of anger and accusal; of sorrow and suffering; but sometimes of prayer and belief.

Was Devesh truly up there in the heavens listening to the devotions of His people?

Jessira hoped so, but she was no longer so sure. Still, even now, despite her fragmented faith, she continued to pray. She lifted her face to the heavens and prayed for her parents, for her family, for all the people she loved. She prayed for herself, for strength, for courage, for forgiveness. She even prayed for Disbar Merdant, her once fiancé. Their final conversation still haunted her.

"Passion can drive a man to stupidity." Disbar had wheezed. His face had been a purpled wreck, bruised and broken just like his body. *"And I wish I could have been the man I should have been."* He hesitated, and a wistful smile, a fleeting look of regret had stolen across his face. *"Tell Rukh I'm sorry. Tell him I hope he remains a better man than I was."*

Disbar had died later that morning, but Jessira liked to believe he'd achieved a state of grace before his passing. She hoped so anyway. She *prayed* so.

It was in that moment, when she returned her gaze to the camp, that she noticed Lake Wren walk into the nearby woods. She looked to have been crying. Jessira's heart ached for the younger woman. Lake's entire family was gone. She had been married with three small children, but they were all dead now.

Minutes later, Lieutenant Jaciro Plume left the camp as well, and Jessira's hackles rose. Plume's path carried him along the same route as the one recently trod by Lake.

Well did Jessira remember the lieutenant and what he had taken from her. She stood and followed him.

A quarter mile away, in a secluded space of boulders with a curtain of aspen, she found him.

Jessira's mind hardened with fury. But her anger, usually hot and raging, was frozen this time. It was a bitter, biting thing, like an icy spear. It left Jessira in a strangely wicked mood, chill and hollow. In that moment, she knew herself capable of all sorts of cruelty, and it was this recognition that caused her to pause. She reconsidered if this was truly who she was, who she wanted to be.

Jessira forced herself to reach past the coldness, back to the person she was. Molten rage, controlled and potent, filled her. It was better than the cruelty that had been icing her veins moments earlier.

She unsheathed her sword and stepped forward. "Let her go," Jessira growled.

Plume jerked his head up, panic flashing across his face. "Jessira—what are you—I saw Lake wander away from camp. She looked ill, and I was concerned." He gestured to the unconscious woman. "I found her like this. She must be injured or sick."

"I saw what you did to Lake," Jessira said to him. Her blade was level with his heart. "Stand up and move away from her."

Plume slowly rose to his feet. "This is all a misunderstanding," he said. "I was just trying to help—"

"Like you helped me?" Jessira interrupted. "Is that why I was unable to remember what happened to me that night?"

Plume's face twisted into a sickly smile. "I know you feel differently, but for me, our night together was special," he said. "I'm sorry if you later came to regret your decision but . . . " He shrugged.

Some of the earlier coldness returned. "Strip off your clothes," Jessira ordered. When Plume hesitated, she moved. Quicker than he could follow, she sliced him across the face, just below his right eye. "I don't want to kill you, but I will if you leave me no choice."

Plume wiped at the blood trickling down his cheek. "You are making a mistake," he vowed darkly. Nevertheless, he began unbuttoning his shirt.

Jessira didn't bother responding to Plume's words. "Remove your pants and your boots," she ordered.

"I can help our people," Plume entreated, even as he followed her orders. He soon stood naked except for his undergarments.

"Fold your clothes and sit on them." She kicked his belt to him. "Tie your hands with this. Tighten it with your teeth."

"I'm one of the few warriors we have left," Plume continued to implore even while he tied his hands with his own belt. "Who else can you trust to protect us? The Purebloods?" He sneered. "They aren't all like your husband. They'll slit our throats when it suits them."

Jessira didn't pay attention to his statements. She wasn't here to convince him of the righteousness of the Ashokans or defend their honor. She was here to protect her people from a predator.

"You cannot come with us," Jessira intoned. "The lives of my people—"

"*Our* people," Plume hissed. "I'm no less a child of Stronghold than you!"

Jessira shook her head. "Not anymore. You lost that honor several years ago, and tonight, after what you almost did to Lake, judgment will be rendered."

"Why are doing this?" Plume cried. "Lake wouldn't have remembered a thing. It would have been as though it had never happened. No one would have been hurt."

"The fact that you believe so is the reason you cannot come with us," Jessira replied. "Hold your knees against your chest."

"Why?" Plume asked suspiciously, even as he obeyed her command.

Jessira stepped forward and kicked him in the side of the head.

His eyes rolled back, and his legs stiffened. He keeled over with a groan.

Jessira checked to make sure his belt was as tight as possible. Good. It would take him some time to get free. She stuffed one of his socks in his mouth and used his bootlaces to bind his feet together.

Plume would live, but never again would he be allowed amongst her people.

It was justice—justice long-delayed and long-deserved.

———————◆———————

Rector Bryce waited outside Dar'El Shektan's study with a brooding sense of foreboding. Given what had occurred the last time he had been here at the Shektan House Seat—Rector's forced enrollment into House Wrestiva as a spy—it was an understandable fear. In fact, the only reason he had managed to muster the courage to ask for today's meeting was because of the words Mira Terrell had spoken before she'd died.

"Your honor is as you see yourself, not as you wish others to see you. See yourself truly." Those had been among Mira's final statements as she had slowly bled to death in a drab dwelling in Stone Cavern.

Rector swallowed back grief that was like bile in his throat.

When he and Mira had first been forced to work together, he had held a very poor opinion of her. She had struck him as arrogant and conceited, full of herself despite the minimal accomplishments to her name. Add in her possible immoral relationship with Jaresh Shektan, and there had been little reason for Rector to have ended up respecting, much less liking, Mira Terrell. But something about her rugged perseverance, her inner strength, and core of dedication had struck a chord with him. Mira had never offered sympathy for Rector's plight—she had expected him to deal with his circumstances without becoming mired in self-pity—and in return, she had never once asked, nor expected, forgiveness for her own situation.

Their conversations, so heated early on, had eventually softened into friendship. Rector came to know and respect Mira, finding her to be insightful and fiercely loyal, and even though she had never admitted it, he knew she *had* loved Jaresh Shektan. Her struggle to reconcile her emotions with what she knew to be moral must have been difficult, but ultimately, she had remained true to her Kumma heritage and the teachings of *The Word and the Deed*. She had never acted upon her feelings. Mira had remained upright and virtuous.

Her admirable example had pushed Rector to become a better man himself, a more understanding one. In the face of her unrelenting courage, how could Rector have continued to wallow in his self-pity? And as her friend, how could he have hated her for the simple act of loving?

Mira had been a special person. She had deserved so much more than the ending she had received: murdered by Hal'El Wrestiva, the SuDin of the Sil Lor Kum.

Rector's fists clenched in fury. Even now, weeks after the fact, Mira's murderer had yet to be captured. The fragging bastard had escaped from the Stone Cavern flat he had shared with his Rahail lover, Varesea Apter, and had managed to elude the justice he so richly deserved.

Of course, news of Hal'El's infamy had thrown all of Ashoka into upheaval. His actions had been unprecedented, and the resultant shockwave, especially through Caste Kumma, had been unlike anything Rector had ever known of or experienced. The outrage over Hal'El's betrayal had been overwhelming, and House Wrestiva had lost all standing. Even their allies had been ensnared in the riptide of anger and excoriation.

No one wanted to be associated with such a disgraced House, and that included Rector Bryce. It was another reason why he sat waiting outside Dar'El Shektan's office. House Shektan was his birth House, and most of his family were still members of it. What better place for him to turn to than the honorable House that had exposed Hal'El's evil? More importantly, Rector had once promised Mira that he would try and reconcile with Dar'El. It was a vow he had made while she had lain dying, and it was a vow he was determined to keep.

He knew it wouldn't be easy, not after what Rector had done to Rukh, and it was likely that Dar'El had yet to forgive him, but still, he had to try.

Eventually, the call came for Rector to enter Dar'El's office, and he rose to his feet. He closed his eyes and took a cleansing breath, seeking to control his nervousness. One more breath, and he was ready. A servant ushered him into the office where he found Dar'El sitting alone behind his desk. The door to the room closed, and Rector had to keep himself from glancing back at it.

Dar'El didn't bother looking up from his work. He waved vaguely at a chair on the opposite side of his desk. "Have a seat," he ordered.

Rector took the indicated chair and waited. The room was silent except for the scratching of Dar'El's pen. Rector held still, not allowing himself to shift nervously.

Minutes passed before Dar'El set aside his work with a satisfied grunt. "What did you wish to discuss?" he asked as he finally looked up.

"I wish to rejoin House Shektan," Rector replied in what he hoped was a clear, even tone as he met the older man's gaze.

Dar'El gave a grim shake of his head. "That seems an unlikely proposition given your actions the last time you were a member here."

"I was wrong to have acted as I did," Rector replied. "And I offer my sincerest apology for what I did to Rukh and to your family."

"Your sudden remorse is certainly convenient given House Wrestiva's fall," Dar'El said, viewing him with narrow, suspicious eyes. "But since Mira spoke in your defense, I'll hear you out. What's changed your mind about this House with which you were once so greatly displeased?"

Rector smiled briefly as he thought of Mira. She was who had changed his mind. With her dogged determination and sarcastic questioning, she'd changed many things. "I had notions of what was right and moral, but events since then . . ." Rector shrugged. "I've learned some hard lessons. Rukh's friendship with Jessira, much less his Talents, should not have resulted in his being found Unworthy."

"And Hal'El's relationship with Varesea Apter?" Dar'El asked, staring at him with a measuring, cunning gaze.

Rector shrugged again, discomfited. "That man should be executed for many crimes far greater than whatever kind of relationship he and Varesea might have shared."

"But they were lovers. Does that not count as a sin?"

"So it is said in *The Word and the Deed*," Rector began uncertainly. "But I'm no longer sure we can afford to unquestioningly follow that book, not when there is a more ancient creed, one that is more generous." He hesitated. "I think generosity is going to be sorely needed in the future."

"*The Book of All Souls?*"

"Yes."

Dar'El templed his fingers beneath his chin."I'm impressed," he said sarcastically. "A politician could not have provided a smoother, more convincing answer."

Rector gritted his teeth, forcing himself to remain quiet in the face of the older man's insult. A politician was another name for liar. Rector tried to hold his face as unexpressive as a plank of wood.

"But trust, once lost, is hard to recapture," Dar'El continued. "How can I ever trust you after you betrayed me so terribly?"

Rector stared at a point over Dar'El's shoulder, trying to come up with an answer to the older man's impossible question. "I hope that my recent actions in exposing Hal'El might serve better than any words I can offer."

Dar'El studied him for a stretch of silence before suddenly sighing. "You did what you could, and in doing so, you kept my daughter alive. I only wish you could have preserved Mira as well," he said as a fleeting look of sorrow passed across his face.

"So do I," Rector whispered.

"As I said, toward the end, Mira spoke in your defense," Dar'El continued. "I trusted her judgment when she said your . . . conversion wasn't merely one of convenience, but I must confess"— he leaned back in his chair—"I find it hard to reconcile the man I see before me who so humbly asks for forgiveness with the man I once knew, the one who was so certain that it was only his moral compass that pointed unerringly to the truth."

"That man was an arrogant fool."

"On this we are agreed," Dar'El agreed. He leaned forward suddenly, the look of a raptor on his face. "I'm told you found a small book amongst the possessions of the Sentya MalDin, Moke Urn. What information did it contain?"

Rector scowled. He had hoped he wouldn't have to bring this up. The information in that slim volume would be disastrous if it ever came to light. "It was a history of the Sil Lor Kum, especially the SuDins. There was one name that was of particular relevance: Kuldige Prayvar."

"The founder of House Shektan," Dar'El said, appearing

unsurprised. Instead, he looked like he had been expecting the answer.

Rector realized Dar'El must have already known about Kuldige, and he mentally grimaced. Was there anything of which the man was unaware?

"Knowing this, the sin at the heart of House Shektan, are you sure you still wish to rejoin us?" Dar'El asked.

Rector nodded. "The sins of the fathers should not pass on to their progeny." He coerced conviction into his voice.

"And if I still deny your request," Dar'El said. "What will you do then?"

Rector kept his face impassive. "I won't release the knowledge about Kuldige if that has you concerned," he replied. "I'll just have to find a different House to take me in."

"And if the knowledge about Kuldige became available to everyone?"

Rector tried to remain impassive in appearance even as he hid a shudder. It would be a disaster if the truth about Kuldige became public knowledge. "Then House Shektan will have a problem."

Dar'El stared at Rector with a discomfiting gaze. "You'll have my decision in the morning," he finally said.

"I look forward to it," Rector said, schooling his features to a serenity he didn't feel as he rose to his feet.

The next morning, Rector was summoned back to the House Seat. There, in the presence of an enigmatic Dar'El and a glowering Durmer Volk, he was oathed back into House Shektan.

Rector left the House Seat with a sense of stunned elation. His life was his once more. No longer did he have to pretend allegiance to the Wrestivas. All the lies binding him to that fallen House could be shed. He was once more of his birth House, able to offer it his steadfast and unrestricted support.

He walked with a bounce in his step and an easy grin on his face. His smile fell when he purchased the morning's broadsheet. It had just been published. On the front page was an exposé, a list of all the known Kumma members of the Sil Lor Kum dating back over the past several hundred years. Prominently displayed was the name of Kuldige Prayvar.

Rector swallowed an oath as he crumpled the paper.

———————— • ————————

Hal'El Wrestiva hid within the shrouded recesses of a corn field. He wore a dark cloak that blended with the surrounding shadows, and his hood was thrown forward, hiding his features. Nevertheless, even if he had chosen to walk the streets of Ashoka with his face uncovered, he doubted many would have recognized him through his layers of grime and weeks-old stubble. Given his grubby, pathetic appearance, no one would have taken him for the ruling 'El of House Wrestiva.

He scowled.

The *former* ruling 'El of House Wrestiva. He had been deposed several weeks ago when his membership in the Sil Lor Kum had been exposed, including his role as the Withering Knife murderer. All it had taken was a single disastrous night for his entire life to come undone. It had all started when he'd captured Mira Terrell and ended with Rector Bryce and Bree Shektan breaking down the door to his flat in Stone Cavern. They hadn't managed to save the Terrell girl, but they had done something far worse: they had murdered Varesea.

Hal'El worked to suppress his pain. It had been weeks since Varesea's death, and he still had trouble accepting that she was gone.

He missed her.

Since that awful night, Hal'El had been forced to hide in his safe house, one that only he knew about. Years ago he had prepared it, all in case his membership in the Sil Lor Kum ever reached unfriendly ears. Not even Varesea had known of it. The safe house had been stocked with enough food and water to have lasted Hal'El for months. Of course, what to do after the supplies ran out was a concern he had never been able to properly answer.

Thus, with little thought of the future, Hal'El had simply hidden himself away in the safe house, not knowing what to do next. After all, he was thrice cursed with a death sentence. He was a murderer, a member of the Sil Lor Kum, and a ghrina.

All Ashoka knew it.

Despite his isolation, though, news of the outside world had still reached Hal'El. A daily broadsheet, easily stolen from a nearby stand, told him what was occurring in the rest of the city. Unsurprisingly, House Wrestiva was nearly ruined, while House Shektan was widely lauded for their role in unveiling such a heinous evil living in the center of Caste Kumma.

Hal'El cursed at the memory.

It was intolerable that the man responsible for Varesea's death should be so extravagantly praised. Dar'El Shektan had forever been a thorn in Hal'El's side, foiling his plans at every step, and setting his House in opposition to Hal'El's. After all, it had been Dar'El's instructions that had set Mira, Rector, and Bree to ferreting out Hal'El's secrets. He'd even found a means to keep his cursed 'son', Jaresh, from facing proper punishment for murdering Suge.

Hal'El cursed once more.

Dar'El Shektan should have shared the same fate that Hal'El had managed to apply to Mira Terrell.

Indeed, immediately after Varesea's death, it had been Hal'El's intention to seek out the death of his hated enemy. He had gone to the Seat of House Shektan with a simple scheme to see his bitter nemesis ended. Nothing would have stopped him, and his plan would have worked, except for the interference of one singularly stupid woman.

As Hal'El had approached the Shektan Seat, barring further passage to the front gates had been the Hound, Sophy Terrell, Mira's amma. Even though Hal'El had been Blended, she had sensed his presence and confronted him. There had been a pregnant pause when Hal'El had revealed himself.

Then Sophy had run away, howling like a madwoman for help.

Hal'El had meant to kill her quickly, but she had been surprisingly agile, sprinting and screaming while she threw Fireballs at Hal'El to slow him down. She had even formed an unexpectedly strong Shield. In the end, though the chase was short-lived and Sophy's life shortly stilled—the Knife had quieted her cries—by the time Hal'El had managed the task, a dozen Kummas had converged on their location. Hal'El had been forced to beat a hasty retreat to his safe house.

There, he'd hidden away, trying to come up with a plan out of his predicament. The first few days after had passed in hours of morose, unaccustomed self-pity with Hal'El had curled up in a ball of misery. Everything he had loved and worked so hard to protect had been stolen away from him, and during those moments, he had reckoned that his life couldn't sink any lower.

He had been wrong.

The true horror of his situation quickly became manifest soon thereafter.

"Fool," a voice whispered in the vaults of his mind.

Hal'El flinched. He'd come to know and dread that voice all too well. Whereas Felt Barnel, Aqua Oilhue, and Van Jinnu had all remained relatively quiescent following their deaths, only muttering and murmuring now and then, Sophy Terrell had burst into his mind like a thunderclap, raging like an inferno at what he had done to her. She rarely remained quiet for longer than a few hours at a time before beginning again with her screamed vilifications and dire threats of retribution. Worse, the others—Felt, Aqua, and Van—had begun following Sophy's example. During such moments, Hal'El felt like his mind was going to tear apart from the cacophony of bloodcurdling oaths and howled promises.

To make matters even more chaotic, last night the Queen had visited Hal'El's dreams. He had explained what had happened, told Her why he couldn't kill anyone else. After his recitation of what—even to him—sounded like incomparable incompetence, rather than react in fury, the Queen had surprised Hal'El. She had been understanding. She had quietly ordered him to find a way to leave Ashoka, promising him safety amongst the Chimeras.

With no better plan in the offing, Hal'El had agreed to do as the Queen had commanded. If She kept true to Her word, at least Hal'El might find some future means to avenge himself on Dar'El Shektan. He might even find a way to thwart Suwraith's plans for Ashoka. He still hoped to save the city from the Sorrow Bringer's wrath. Surely if he managed such a monumental feat, his fellow Ashokans would forgive him for his multitude of sins. After all, they'd forgiven Rukh Shektan, and he was every bit as degenerate as Hal'El.

It was this hope for redemption that now drove him. It was the reason why he currently found himself studying the movements of the warriors manning Sunset Gate, the southernmost entrance through the Outer Wall. It was the final obstacle he had to overcome in order to exit Ashoka. There were five guards, all of them Kummas, and the day was late, just past dusk. It was a situation that might work to his advantage.

"I'm talking to you, Fool," Sophy said in a louder tone.

"Quiet," Hal'El hissed to her.

Sophy didn't relent. *"The warriors will capture you, and then what will happen to you, you great, stupid coward? You'll be hung, drawn, and quartered, and your remains will be strewn upon the Isle of the Crows. You'll be forever damned, Fool!"*

"Be silent, or you will be silenced!" Hal'El thundered into the reaches of his mind.

"You can't kill her," a soft voice rasped. Aqua Oilhue. *"You can't kill any of us. We're already dead."* She laughed in black humor.

"And we'll make sure you join us," another voice vowed in an ugly tone. Felt Barnel.

"Don't forget the Knife," Van Jinnu advised in a mocking tone. *"It'll be the death of you."*

Hal'El grimaced even as he stroked the sheath in which the black blade was housed. Even if the Queen hadn't ordered him to bring it with him, there was no chance he would leave it behind in Ashoka. He had lost too much on account of the Withering Knife to be parted from it now.

"You haven't lost everything," Aqua said. *"You have much pain yet to endure."*

"We'll ensure it, Fool," Sophy promised. *"Future generations will wonder at how an overwhelming idiot like you became the ruling 'El of a great House. What a craven jackass you are."*

"Shut up," Hal'El hissed.

"How do you intend to get past those guards?" Sophy persisted.

"I have a plan," Hal'El muttered, knowing it was a mistake to engage her.

"A plan he says?" Sophy scoffed. *"You couldn't plan a trip to the toilet. You'd likely flush yourself down the drain, you imbecile. Are you sure you aren't the get of a donkey, you long-eared jackass."*

Hal'El gritted his teeth. Enough! He imagined his hands on Sophy's throat, choking off her words, choking the life from her. Shockingly, it worked. Sophy gasped once and fell quiet. The other three settled into fitful, uncertain murmurings.

Blessed peace!

While Hal'El suspected Sophy would soon return, at least for now, she and the others were no longer so noisome. He could proceed with the final steps of his plans without their incessant meddling.

Hal'El had managed to get this far by pretending to be a burly Sentya drover, and his disguise should hopefully get him through Sunset Gate. He'd have to be quick about it, though.

He left the shadows of the corn field and returned to the wagon he'd left on a nearby dirt path. He clambered aboard. A strawman sat atop the seat with a set of reins dangling from its hands. Hal'El Blended, and while everyone was now alert for someone hidden in such a fashion, he reckoned it would take the Kummas manning Sunset Gate a precious few seconds to find him. Their task would be made even more difficult by the wagon with its strawman drover charging their position. It should be enough distraction for Hal'El to slip past the guards and manage his escape.

His plan decided, Hal'El set the bullocks to trotting. The fine gelding he'd stolen for the long ride to the camp of the Chimeras was tied off to the side of the wagon, and the horse easily kept pace as Hal'El shortly came upon the Gate. He flicked the reins, and the bullocks were soon at a rumbling gallop. Shouts from the guards ordered him to slow, but Hal'El kept the wagon at a breakneck pace.

He raced past the warriors.

More shouts came to him, this time of a Blend, and arrows were fired at the wagon.

Hal'El had his Shield ready. The arrows bounced off of it. More came. A few pinged close to the gelding, and Hal'El extended his Shield. Fireballs were thrown, but none of them made an impact either.

Except for one. Hal'El let it through just as he mounted the gelding and raced off. The wagon took the brunt of the Fireball, and burst into flames. The bullocks screamed in fear and pain. It was the final distraction Hal'El needed as he raced off into the night.

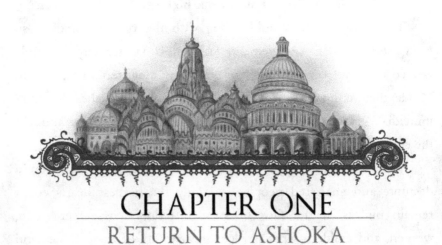

CHAPTER ONE
RETURN TO ASHOKA

'Ware wild, wolf winds and
Hurled lightning from ashen skies.
A bitter rain falls.

—Attribution unknown

"Is the food not to your liking?" Rector asked, breaking into Jaresh's thoughts. "You were frowning," he further said.

"No. The food is fine. I like it," Jaresh replied. The food was actually quite good. It was traditional Duriah fare, served at a bistro in Trell Rue where he and Rector were having lunch. Jaresh wasn't sure what was more surprising, finding something traditional in fashionable, trendy Trell Rue or the fact that it was Rector Bryce who had asked him for a lunchtime meeting. In the past, they hadn't gotten along very well. After a moment's consideration, he decided it was the latter.

"I'm glad to hear it," Rector replied with a half smile. He hesitated then, a question appearing to linger on the tip of his tongue. "What do you think Dar'El will do about the OutCastes?"

Jaresh took a bite of his meal while he formulated his answer.

The Trial to Stronghold, along with the one hundred or so OutCastes who had survived the destruction of their city, had only arrived in Ashoka several days ago, and the Magisterium had yet to decide their ultimate fate. While some people had called for their immediate eviction, the overwhelming majority of Ashokans thought the city should offer the OutCastes sanctuary.

The Strongholders, the descendants of fabled Hammer, were a destitute and shattered people, and only the hardest hearts could remain pitiless in the face of such suffering. These were men, women, and children who had lost the entirety of their homes and hope. They were bereft of everything that gave life meaning, and their haunted, broken eyes reflected the traumas that they had endured.

Nevertheless, though public sentiment favored letting the OutCastes stay, ultimately, it was a decision that would need to be made by the Magisterium. From what Jaresh understood, the Magistrates were struggling to reconcile their compassion with what duty required. They couldn't simply overlook the laws of the city, which were clearly expressed in both *The Word and the Deed* and Ashoka's Constitution.

Allowing the OutCastes sanctuary without finding a basis to do so in the city's statutes would certainly lead to a moral outcome, but the cost might rupture the rule of law. A convenient decision could become a terrible precedent, and a future Magisterium might be tempted to render another such convenient decision, one that might not be so obviously moral. Chaos could ensue, where the plain language of the law could be subverted to mean whatever was needed at the time. It would be a nightmare.

The Magistrates had to render a decision that would stand up to scrutiny, both current and future, and to that end, it was rumored that the Magisterium had contracted with every law firm in the city to find just such a loophole that would allow the OutCastes refuge.

"I'm not sure," Jaresh finally answered to Rector's question. "But I imagine he'll fight to let them stay. After all, Jessira is one of them, and she and Rukh are married."

Rector merely nodded in thought.

His silence once again was surprising, but perhaps it shouldn't have been. Toward the end, Mira had advocated on Rector's behalf. She had insisted that his philosophy had slowly evolved, that he'd grown more compassionate, grown so far as to question the truths he'd once held as unassailable.

Mira.

Jaresh did his best to hide a shudder of grief. He hoped Rector didn't notice. Jaresh had only learned of Mira's death a few days ago. He'd never known that the stabbing knife of bereavement could cut so deep. Mira was dead, but sometimes Jaresh still found it hard to believe that she was truly gone. Sometimes he was certain it would all turn out to be a terrible delusion, that she would walk through the front doors of the Shektan House Seat, wearing a wry grin at his surprise.

And many times, he wondered what might have occurred if he'd stayed behind in Ashoka rather than gone with the Trial to Stronghold. Might Mira still be alive then? Could he have helped protect her? But then, if he hadn't gone to Stronghold, would it have been Rukh who would have died? Had Jaresh's presence at the OutCaste city tipped the scales and somehow preserved his brother's life?

The questions were an endless circle, looping back on themselves and offering no solution or soothing. And they did nothing to distract him from the unalterable truth of Mira's passing, a terrible fact that was like a riptide threatening to pull him under and drown him.

Jaresh shuddered again and took hold of his anger and anguish, mastering them as best he could before turning to study Rector. According to Bree, the man had fought desperately against Hal'El, but in the end, his skills had been overmatched. Afterward, as Mira lay dying on the floor of some dingy flat in Stone Cavern, Rector had chosen that moment to curse Karma that he didn't have Rukh's ability to Heal.

Pity the fool hadn't discovered such wisdom earlier on. Perhaps all the tragedies which had happened to Rukh and Mira might not have come to pass if he had. She might still be alive, and in her place, Hal'El might be the one who was dead.

Nevertheless, Nanna insisted that such wisdom *had* befallen Rector. Of course, the man had likely experienced his new-found knowledge as a chamber pot emptying over his head like a curse. He probably hated his new way of thinking, despised the uncertainty of an uncertain morality.

But it was his to cherish.

Jaresh smiled bitterly, a grimace which left his face a moment later as his brother's words came to him. Rukh had offered his advice when he had learned who Jaresh was having lunch with: *"If Rector truly has changed so much, grown so much that there is no going back to his old ways, then do we not owe him the benefit of the doubt?"*

Perhaps so, but it didn't mean that Rector had earned Jaresh's trust. For instance, the older man certainly hadn't been told about Jaresh's new Kumma Talents. Per Nanna's recommendation, that was a secret known only to Jaresh's immediate family.

"Your nanna's voice carries much weight," Rector said, interrupting Jaresh's thoughts once again.

"It would have carried more if he hadn't revealed the truth about Kuldige," Jaresh replied.

Rector grimaced. "I'm still not sure why he chose to expose such a dangerous secret like that."

"I'm sure he had his reasons."

"Maybe so, but the timing was unfortunate and somewhat suspicious."

"Why was it suspicious?"

"The day before, I'd asked to rejoin the House—"

"Why *did* you want to rejoin House Shektan?" Jaresh challenged. "I thought you considered us only a few steps removed from ghrinas."

"Life and Mira convinced me of the error of my ways," Rector replied with a wistful smile. "I spoke to Dar'El, explaining my reasons for wanting to rejoin House Shektan, and I thought he took me at my word. But on the very morning he accepted my vow of obedience, he also informed the entire city about all the Kummas throughout history that he and all the other 'Els knew had been Sil Lor Kum. Included in the list was Kuldige Prayvar. I can't help—"

"Did my nanna know you knew about Kuldige?" Jaresh interrupted once again. A stray suspicion had come to him.

Rector nodded. "I came across the information when we were taking the Sil Lor Kum apart. It was in a ledger belonging to the Sentya MalDin, Moke Urn."

Jaresh chuckled as his nanna's plan became obvious. His chuckles turned to laughter as Rector's initial confusion turned to annoyance.

"What is so funny?" Rector asked frostily.

Jaresh needed a moment to get his laughter under control, but he still grinned. "Your reappointment into House Shektan and the release of those Sil Lor Kum names was related," he explained. "Nanna didn't want you to have even the smallest weapon by which you could hurt the House."

Rector still appeared confused. "Then why bother letting me rejoin?"

"Nanna has an innumerable list of aphorisms. One of his favorites is this: choose your enemies carefully and keep them near. One day, they may offer you the finest service."

At first, Rector appeared both startled and offended, but a moment later, he threw his head back and laughed. "What greater honor can I have than for your nanna to consider me an enemy worth keeping near?"

———⬤———

"Do you think the Purebloods actually notice any of this?" Sign asked, gesturing out to the city of Ashoka. "Do they still see the beauty all around them?"

She and Jessira shared a table at one of the Shektan House Seat's numerous verandas. Before them, the famed, verdant hills of Ashoka tumbled down to the clear, blue waters of the Sickle Sea, reemerging in the deep bay as peaked, green prominences. The rest of the city was equally lovely with hillside homes painted in brilliant hues of sunshine yellow, summer-sky blue, pale lavender, and salmon-pink. There were also the ornate buildings manning every road and corner with their fanciful lintels and columns. And to the south was the most beautiful jewel in all of Ashoka: Dryad Park, the emerald heart of the city with its lustrous trees, fields, and meadows.

"They see it," Jessira replied. "Why else would they work so hard at maintaining it?"

Sign smiled. "Maybe it's part of their insanity," she suggested. "Make their city beautiful instead of efficient."

Jessira smiled in response, pleased to see her cousin engaged and seemingly happy for once.

The weeks since they'd left the wracked remnants of Stronghold hadn't been easy on any of them. Salvation, much less a future filled with joy, had been an uncertain proposition. There had been the difficult trip down the River Gaunt and the ever-lingering worry of what awaited their journey's end. Would the Purebloods offer them refuge? And if they didn't, then where would the OutCastes go? Thankfully, the answer to the first question had been 'yes', so the second one had never needed considering—at least for now. The people of Ashoka had taken them in, sheltering them in a set of empty flats just south of Mount Crone. Their accommodations had been provided and paid for by the Magisterium.

While the flats were not yet their home—they might never truly be—Jessira was grateful for the refuge the OutCastes had been afforded. Just as important—at least for her—was that Rukh had elected to remain with her and the rest of her people. Early on, he'd asked if Jessira wanted to live at the Shektan Seat rather than the empty flats, but she had told him 'no'. She couldn't leave her people. They needed her. All of them needed one another. Rukh had accepted Jessira's words and without further comment, he had moved their meager belongings into one of the unused flats. Jessira was thankful for his decision. She needed him near and couldn't imagine getting through the day without his steadying presence.

"It *is* efficient," Jessira replied to Sign's earlier statement, "but anything here also has to be lovely."

Sign's smile faded. "I always thought you were exaggerating when you described Ashoka. I just couldn't believe anything could be as amazing as you made this place seem," she said. "But if anything, it's even more beautiful than you described. The Purebloods are lucky to have such a home."

"It's not luck," Jessira said. "It's in their nature to strive for beauty."

Sign shot her a look. "But not in our nature?" her cousin asked, sounding offended. "You don't think our people strive for beauty and elegance as well?"

Jessira bit back an oath. Perhaps she could have phrased what she had said a little better, but Sign didn't have to see it as an insult. She was just looking for an excuse to take offense. It was merely a pretext on her cousin's part to have an argument, something she chose to do with an all-too-regular frequency. Following Stronghold's death, some of the OutCastes had slipped into a dull depression, but Sign had taken a different path. She had responded by lashing out, seeing an affront when none was intended or taking provocation for the slimmest of reasons.

Jessira stared Sign in the eyes, wondering what she could say to mollify the other woman. Pointing out her cousin's flawed thinking and giving her a proper tongue-lashing was tempting but unlikely to be helpful. Patience would be of more use.

"I'm not looking for an argument with you," Jessira said, doing her best to rein in her annoyance. "Or do you really think I'm not proud of our people and our heritage?"

Sign tensed before suddenly deflating. "No." And just like that, her voice had grown meek.

"Then why did you ask the question?" Jessira asked.

Sign's head fell low. "I don't know," she whispered. "I'm just so angry all the time. I don't know how you aren't."

Jessira squeezed Sign's hand. "I am, but I have Rukh. Of all of us, he was the one who was least affected by what happened to Stronghold. He helps keep me sane."

"I haven't been very nice to him," Sign said softly.

"He understands."

"He—everyone here really—are so different from what I expected," Sign continued. "I still can't believe they took us in, especially when their laws forbid them from doing so."

"Laws change, and what was historically thought to be true, doesn't always have to be so," Jessira replied. She remembered her first time in Ashoka when attitudes had gradually transformed as people got used to her presence. Some—thankfully a very small number—had forever hated her on sight, but most folk had simply left her alone, while a blessed few had been kind enough to take the time to say 'hello' when they saw her out and about. In the end, most Ashokans had ended up seeing Jessira as just another woman. They hadn't regarded her as the infectious carrier of sin that *The Word and the Deed* implied.

"You really think people can really change that quickly?" Sign asked, distrust lacing her question.

Jessira sighed. "No. It won't happen immediately," she replied. "It'll take a long time before we're truly accepted, but the Purebloods are trying. Most of them want to let us stay, but they are conflicted. They have to decide between their teachings—the ones that tell them to deny us sanctuary—and their hearts, which tell them to take in those who are suffering. I have faith that they'll make the right choice."

Sign scratched at the tabletop. "You're more trusting than I," she muttered.

Jessira pursed her lips in sympathy. Her cousin simply couldn't see the opportunity their people had before them or accept the generosity the Purebloods had shown them. Then again, it was easier for Jessira. She was used to Ashoka. She wasn't a stranger here, and she also had the support of Rukh's family. "Look around you," Jessira finally said. "Tell me exactly where we are."

Sign glanced around. "The Seat of House Shektan," she said, sounding bewildered and somewhat intimidated.

Good.

"We are in the Pureblood city of Ashoka. Over one hundred ghrinas. You don't find that worthy of trust?" Jessira asked.

Sign's eyes widened with sudden realization, and her face reddened. "Point taken," she muttered. "It's just that I can't see these Ashokans . . ."

"Can't see them doing what?" Jessira asked. "Taking us in? They did that. Finding a way to let us stay? They're working on it. We might even have a chance to earn our way by farming some fallow fields." Jessira leaned forward, and she took Sign's hands in her own. "We can rebuild our lives here," she urged. "Some Shiyens and Duriahs have even spoken of adopting our orphans. How can you continue to doubt a people willing to do something so generous?"

"Because it goes against everything we've been taught about the Purebloods," Sign said with an anguished cry.

"Then what we were taught about the Purebloods is wrong. Just like what they were taught about *us* is wrong. It's time you realized that," Jessira said, her patience finally breaking. "It's also time you showed the strength I know you possess. You've wallowed in self-pity long enough. Our people can't afford any more tantrums on your part."

After she finished speaking, Sign wouldn't look at her. Her cousin stared shame-faced at the table as tears tracked from the corners of her eyes.

Jessira's heart broke for Sign. She was trying. They all were. She again took her cousin's hands. "I know it's not easy for you, or any of us, but if you hope for compassion and sympathy, it helps to be compassionate and sympathetic in return," Jessira advised.

Sign reddened once more and gave a short, choppy nod of agreement before staring off in the distance.

The sounds of the city—rolling wagons, shouted cries, and the echoing undertone of the heaving ocean—filled the silence as a fitful lull fell over their conversation.

Sign picked at the tabletop. "You're being too kind to say it, but you think I'm being a selfish bitch, don't you?"

Jessira gave her cousin's hand another squeeze. "With what we've been through, I think we all have to be understanding, but Sign . . ." She stared her cousin in the eyes. "Our people need us. Some of them forget to eat or drink if they aren't reminded. They don't always remember to care for their children. They need us to be . . ." Jessira searched for the word.

"Strong?" Sign supplied.

"Calm," Jessira corrected. "They need peace. They need quiet. They don't need yelling, and they don't need rage."

Sign nodded, a brief bob of her head. "I'll try," she said. "And thank you for being . . ." Her lips quirked. ". . . strong."

"You're welcome," Jessira said with an answering smile.

Sign turned to look back out over the city. "If the Magisterium allows us to stay, we become Ashokans?"

Jessira nodded. "So it would seem."

Rukh stretched his long legs, trying to work sensation back into them. The small, cramped space of the Cellar in which he and Bree had been spending their time had not been designed for Kummas. It was tight and claustrophobic, and he didn't like it.

The discomfort was worsened by air that was thick with moisture and the smell of moldering paper. Add in the funereal quiet, the reaching shadows in the recesses, and the long, cramped, unlit halls, and the place had an oppressive, almost menacing quality to it. Rukh wasn't ashamed to admit that he couldn't have lasted down here nearly as long as Jaresh and Mira had when the two of them had been searching for information on the Withering Knife. The dark alone would have been enough to drive him away—which was why he and Bree had brought down extra firefly lamps. The lanterns lit their cubicle until it glowed like a vibrant island of warmth in the dismal dark.

Of course, Rukh knew that even if he'd had to work with only the the dim light of the single overhead firefly lamp, he would have still found a way to persevere. He had to. Jessira's life depended on it. Rukh and Bree were searching the Cellar for treatises on the philosophical underpinnings of the city's Constitution. This was the work to which he had devoted himself since his return home, and even though there were already many scholars and attorneys also looking into the matter, none of them had the same intensity that Rukh brought to bear on the subject. Finding a valid reason—one that would stand up to future scrutiny—was the only means by which the OutCastes, and Jessira, would be allowed to stay in Ashoka, and by extension, Rukh as well.

And ultimately, whatever destiny Jessira suffered, he would also endure.

Unsurprisingly, Jaresh and Bree had also taken on the matter of the OutCastes' final fate with nearly the same zealous determination as Rukh himself. The three of them had separated the work. Jaresh was to comb through historical references for when the Constitution might not have been strictly followed while Rukh and Bree focused on finding a means to undercut the primacy of *The Word and the Deed* as the basis for the city's law. So far, their cumulative searches had returned empty as Jaresh quickly discovered that every law and decision in Ashoka's long history had *always* had a basis in the Constitution. There had been no exceptions. Meanwhile Rukh and Bree's quest had proven equally frustrating. There had been nothing to suggest that there had ever been a prior text, such as *The Book of All Souls*, that might have served as the moral basis of the Constitution.

Rukh knew Jaresh was starting to lose hope by their combined lack of success, but their failure had yet to deter Bree. She forged on, still full of grit and resolve as she worked from before sunrise until well after sunset. In this, Bree reminded Rukh of Sophy Terrell, the Hound. Mira's amma had been equally dogged when it came to research that might affect the House's fortune and future.

And for Bree, there might also be another inspiration for her hard work: guilt.

Earlier that evening, Jaresh had explained that for a long time, Bree had blamed herself for Rukh's exile. It had taken her months to forgive herself, but now, with the need to find a means by which Jessira and the rest of the Strongholders could stay in Ashoka, the guilt must have come back full bore.

His sister wore a frown as she bent over an old text, and Rukh placed a hand on one of hers, forcing her to look at him. "I don't blame you," he said. "I never did. I never will."

Bree, always so perceptive, instantly knew what he meant. "Have you told your wife what I did?"

"She knows, and she doesn't care," Rukh answered. "It doesn't matter to her, and it shouldn't matter to you."

Bree smiled. "Good. I wasn't sure how she'd react, and your wife can be . . . formidable. Not scary, but definitely formidable."

Rukh chuckled. "I know what you mean." He'd never been afraid of Jessira, but he always walked warily around her whenever he made her angry. "And I was serious about what I said: I don't blame you for what happened to me."

His first inkling that he might have misread the situation was when Bree laughed at him.

"I heard you, and you don't have to worry about me," Bree said after she was no longer laughing. "I know what happened to you wasn't my fault." She looked him in the eyes. "It was your own." She arched an incredulous eyebrow at him. "Really. Taking Jessira on a late-night stroll through Dryad Park? What were you thinking?"

Rukh felt his face flush with embarrassment. "So you aren't doing this out of guilt?" he asked. Even as he asked the question, he knew the answer.

And he certainly didn't need Bree's head thrown back with laughter to tell him the truth of his stupidity.

"Of course not," she said. "I'm not helping you out of guilt. I'm doing so because . . ." She raised a finger as she ticked off each item. "You're my brother." One finger. "I love you." Two fingers. A third finger went up an instant later. "And if I left this to just you and Jaresh, the OutCastes, including your wife, would be banished from Ashoka." Bree smiled sweetly. "You need my help."

Rukh sat back, abashed and with his mouth agape.

"Are you trying to catch flies?" Bree observed.

Rukh shut his mouth with an audible snap. What an idiot he'd been. How could he have believed that Bree might still feel guilt over something that had never been her fault?

They fell into silence, but something that Bree had said struck a chord with Rukh, and he replayed her words in his mind. "Why do you keep calling Jessira 'my wife' instead of by her name?" he asked.

"I just like calling her your wife." Bree grinned. "It makes her more a part of the family."

"Why don't you call her your vadina, then? It would do the same thing."

"For the same reason, I don't call you Annayya, my older brother. I'm too stubborn." A moment later, a considering look stole across her face. "Given how we both agree that your *wife* can be formidable—"

"But not scary," Rukh said.

"Yes," Bree agreed. "Given that, it might be best if she never learned what Nanna and Amma tricked her into doing."

"It might be," Rukh agreed. "But somehow I imagine she'll figure it out on her own. Nanna and Amma should just tell her themselves."

"She is your wife," Bree said. "I suppose you know her best."

"I'm not going to tell her now," Rukh said with a roll of his eyes. "She's already got too many troubles on her plate."

"Like finding safety for her people if we can't find a way around the Constitution."

"My people, too," Rukh said.

"You'd really leave with them if it came to it?"

"Like you said: she is my wife."

"You know *The Word and the Deed* doesn't actually consider you wed," Bree noted.

"So what. Everyone else thinks we are," Rukh replied. "Besides, it depends on the volume to which you're referring. I saw one version of *The Word and the Deed* in Stronghold, and it specifically discussed 'marriage between a man and a woman of different Castes'. A later edition had that section edited to 'an impure relationship between a man and a woman'." He paused as he startled in sudden insight.

Bree's eyes were lit with enthusiasm as well. "What if earlier editions of *The Word and the Deed* make exceptions for people like the OutCastes?" she suggested. "It would solve everything."

Rukh nodded, trying to tamp down his bubbling excitement. "This could work," he said. "But I don't think we should focus on just this one avenue of research."

"No. Jaresh should continue with what he's doing."

"And I'll continue with what we've been working on here, while you look through the older editions of *The Word and the Deed* and see if there's anything in them that we can use."

Bree gave him an appraising gaze. "You surprise me. I always knew Jaresh was intelligent, but what about you? When did you get so smart?" she asked.

Rukh nodded in solemnity. "I always have been. You simply lacked the wisdom to notice until now."

Bree snorted in derision.

CHAPTER TWO
MAGISTERIAL CHOICES

The life of a Magistrate—to serve the citizens—would be a wondrous life indeed
if not for those same citizens. Why can't they simply leave us in peace?

—From the journal of Magistrate Olive Rue, AF 1833

Rector Bryce sat quietly at his seat and listened as various members of Ashoka vented their thoughts regarding the OutCastes and whether they should be allowed to remain in the city. This was an open meeting of the Magisterium, and as a result, most everyone with an opinion had shown up.

Rector had quickly grown bored with the proceedings. No one was exhuming anything more than emotional pleas based on what they thought was 'right' or 'wrong' with only the most cursory of references to the law. Passion was fine, but the decision before the Magisterium was one that required logic and reason—not merely the lowest common denominator of what was most popular. If the prevailing sentiment was all that was needed, the Magistrates would have long since granted the OutCastes sanctuary.

A year ago, it wouldn't have been the case, but Rukh Shektan's actions in the Chimera breeding caverns had changed many minds about ghrinas and naajas. And when the sad state of the OutCastes themselves was taken into account, who *wouldn't* have been moved to pity? As such, it wasn't surprising how opinions had shifted in such a short period of time.

It also helped that one of the most forceful advocates for the OutCastes was someone well-known to the city. In fact, by now, everyone knew of her. Jessira Shektan had made an unforgettable impression on Ashoka during her initial stay in the city and was doing so now as well.

Rector's stray thoughts were interrupted when a new attestant, a middle-aged Duriah matron, was allowed to speak. He perked up a bit to listen to her.

"I say this without meaning any insult to anyone, but as ghrinas, the OutCastes are beings of sin based upon their very nature. It isn't something that can be corrected," she began. "As such, we must consider the needs of our children. How can they learn what true morality is if the immoral is flaunted before them?" The matron pleaded with utmost earnestness. "They can't. Their young minds can't see the complexity that we can. Therefore, I say the OutCastes can't stay here in Ashoka, but before anyone thinks I'm being cruel, we must also think of *their* children. They are innocent and shouldn't be turned out into the cold night." She nodded with grave self-importance. "We can build them a village just beyond Ashoka's walls and Oasis. They'll live there. We'll live here. Separate but equal."

It was an asinine idea, and Rector rolled his eyes in unconcealed scorn.

She blathered on, and Rector turned his attention to the Magistrates themselves. They appeared as bored as he. Fol Nacket, the Cherid Magistrate, nodded politely at the attestant but his glazed-over eyes spoke the truth about his inattentiveness. The Muran Magistrate, Dos Martel, sat back in her chair and yawned, while Poque Belt and Gren Vos, of Caste Sentya and Caste Shiyen, respectively held demeanors of barely concealed annoyance. Magistrate Krain Linshok of Caste Kumma spoke an aside to Jone Drent, the Duriah Magistrate, and the two of them chuckled over whatever had been spoken. Brit Hule, the uncompromising Rahail, glared sternly at the speaker, causing the poor woman to stumble to an uncertain halt.

When she did, Magistrate Nacket appeared to sigh in relief before calling for the next attestant.

Rector sat up straighter when Bree Shektan stood up and stepped forward. This was why he was here.

A few weeks ago, he had seen Bree researching at the City Library. She had been studying *The Word and the Deed* and had asked for the oldest edition that was available for study. The librarian had brought her a version printed several centuries past, condescendingly insisting it should do for her needs. It hadn't, and Bree had not been pleased. In classic Bree Shektan fashion, she had simply raised an eyebrow and spoke in a clipped manner. *"When I ask for the oldest volume, I expect the oldest volume. Do we have an understanding?"* The librarian had taken one look at her face before scurrying away to fetch the volume she had initially requested.

Rector still couldn't believe how easily Bree could bend people to her will. It was a skill she must have learned from her frightening amma.

At any rate, her actions had piqued Rector's curiosity. It was well-known that Bree and her brothers were trying to find a means by which the Magistrates could allow the OutCastes to remain in

Ashoka. It was what all three of them had been working on ever since Rukh's return to the city.

Rector had watched quietly from afar as Bree had transcribed what seemed to be entire passages from the old volume of *The Word and Deed*. And while she had done so, her countenance had grown steadily more excited. She had finished her work with a satisfied smile and left the Library.

Afterward, Rector had ventured over to her desk. She had returned the borrowed edition of *The Word and the Deed*, but she'd left behind a small stack of blank sheets of papers. Imprinted upon them were whatever notations Bree had busily written down. It had been simplicity itself to use a pencil to highlight the indentations on the blank pages and discover what had her so excited.

A pleased smile had washed across Rector's face when he realized what Bree had been studying. His smile washed away just as quickly as it had arrived when he read her final words: *You aren't as clever as you believe, Rector Bryce. Forget this if you wish any future in Ashoka.*

All along, she'd known he'd been watching her. All along, she'd known that he'd been wondering what she had been up to, but rather than hide her work, she had let him see exactly what she had discovered.

Or had she? Maybe what Rector had rubbed out was merely a ruse. After all, why would Bree have let him see what she'd written?

She wouldn't have.

At that point, Rector could have proceeded down two obvious paths. He could have searched out a way to contest Bree's findings— a difficult proposition even if he could have trusted what she had allowed him to see. Or he could have chosen to do nothing, remained silent and done just as Bree had warned. The latter would have been the simpler path to follow, and the one she likely had expected of him.

Rector had looked long at that scrap of paper with its naked warning before a small grouping of mismatched letters and numbers in the upper right-hand corner had caught his attention. There had been a *C* followed by an illegible number or a *4*, a *V* with an illegible number next to it, and finally an *L3* or *8*. The writing had been faint, likely an imprint of an imprint, and probably something Bree hadn't meant for him to see. As for what it meant, it was probably a verse and a line from *The Word and the Deed*, but what chapter?

Rector had paused as he considered his finding. *The Word and the Deed* was broken down into forty-three chapters, each with a number of verses and lines. But which ones had Bree been studying? With a sigh, Rector had realized that the only way to know would be by reading every chapter number that ended with a four, such as four, fourteen, twenty-four, and thirty-four and all lines three through eight of every verse.

Hours later, he had a faint idea of what Bree might actually be attempting, and if he was right, then the effort was truly inspired. If she managed what he suspected she was going to try, it would overturn several millennia of settled law.

Even as he had stood back and admired the audacity of Bree's plan, he had vacillated over what to do next. Eventually, he came to the realization that a third path had just opened up to him. He had smiled then. No one, least of all Bree Shektan, would expect it of him. It was the trickier route to take, one fraught with risks of misunderstanding, but it was also the one that might allow Rector to make up for some of the wrongs he'd committed in the past few years.

But before he made any final decisions on what to do next, he had needed advice from someone far more clever than he, someone far more cunning. He had needed the input of Dar'El Shektan, the most cunning, clever man that Rector knew.

His faith hadn't been misplaced. Dar'El had seen angles and arguments that Rector had missed. He had found ways to challenge Bree's declarations but to do so in a way that made them even stronger. And Dar'El had impressed upon Rector the need for absolute discretion. No one, not even Bree, was to learn of his secret support.

Her reactions had to be genuine, and no one, especially the Magistrates, could ever become aware of what Rector had done. He took a deep, steadying breath before approaching the attestation stand.

Magistrate Nacket peered down from his raised seat. "You wish to debate Bree Shektan?" he asked.

"Yes, sir," Rector replied. He didn't need to look at Bree to sense the withering scorn on her face.

"You were warned," she whispered.

Bree nodded to the Kumma honor guards as she passed through the open doors of the Magisterium. The guards were dressed in their typical gold-filigreed, bright-red uniforms and stood at parade rest. Their impassive visages gave no hint as to their thoughts regarding the momentous meeting about to take place.

Just past the entrance, a trickle of people made their way through the length of a long hallway, and Bree joined them. She vaguely noted the portraits on the walls. All of them were great Magistrates from Ashoka's history. Another pair of honor guards—again Kummas and dressed identically to the ones outside—flanked a pair of open mahogany doors embossed with the seal of the

Magisterium: a golden eagle clasping a sword and a scythe. The doorway led to the chamber where the Magistrates held their public meetings, and the guards stood at attention, studying those who entered with the same impassive watchfulness as their brethren outside.

Bree entered the large, round chamber where the Magistrates met and searched for her brothers. The room was filling quickly, and people jostled her about, looking for a seat. The deference normally given to a Kumma woman wasn't in evidence today, and the noisome din echoing throughout made for a welter of sight and sound. Bree craned her neck and stood on her tiptoes. A waving hand and her shouted name caught her attention. She relaxed when she saw Rukh and Jaresh gesture her over.

She squeezed in next to them. "Thank you," she said, having to yell in order to be heard over the din. With its high ceiling and stained-glass dome portraying a scene from the life of the First Father, the room was meant to impress, and while it did so, the open and airy nature of the space also meant that sounds reverberated throughout it. Even hushed words could echo into a susurration of sound. And right now with everyone trying to have a conversation at the same time, the chamber groaned with a tide of distant thunder.

Jaresh tried to tell something to Bree, but with the surrounding noise, she couldn't hear a word he said. She shrugged her shoulders in mute apology, and he gave up with a disgusted shake of his head.

The three of them faced forward, staring straight ahead as they waited for the meeting to begin. They didn't have long to wait. A thudding gong quieted the room. The booming note announced the entrance of the Magistrates.

Fol Nacket gaveled the meeting into order. "Let us begin," he said, sounding portentous. "We have before us a decision of utmost importance, and as it is one that affects all of Ashoka, we must ensure that all possible views are heard before the Magisterium renders its verdict."

The Magistrates called forth a number of people who spoke at the attestation stand. They passionately voiced their opinions about what should be done with the OutCastes. Bree was heartened that so many of them supported the notion of allowing Jessira and her people to stay, but throughout the evening, no one offered a suggestion that had a basis in law. All their attestations were simply opinions saturated with emotional pleading but rarely infused with any rational reasoning.

She sighed as a Rahail gentleman meandered at length about how the penumbras and emanations of the Constitution allowed the presence of the OutCastes within Ashoka. Of course, based on his twisted logic, he had somehow managed to turn the straightforward meaning of the text inside out.

Bree shook her head in pity.

"Remember to aim your strongest arguments at Magistrate Belt," Rukh said while the Rahail wound down his inverted dissertation. "He's the fulcrum."

Bree nodded.

"You realize that after tonight, your name will be forever remembered by history?" Jaresh asked. He wore an encouraging smile. "What we've found could transform the entire world."

Bree smiled somewhat sickly at Jaresh's words. "I know you're trying to be inspiring, but I've got enough pressure on me as it is."

"If you're nervous, then let us help you," Rukh said. His face tightened with concentration while Jaresh's grew slack. Lucency from both her brothers—during Stronghold's fall, Rukh and Jaresh had gained one another's Talents—calmed her nerves and settled her mind. She relaxed as her thoughts grew diamond sharp.

During all this, a Duriah matron had been in the midst of meandering rambling, but under the stern glare of Magistrate Brit Hule, she thankfully meandered to a halt. Bree was then called forward to the attestation stand.

Following close behind her was Rector Bryce. She shot him a bemused look, but immediately understood what he meant to do. Her warning to him hadn't taken hold. Rector must have come to realize a small part of what Bree intended and now planned on challenging her.

A cold anger roiled within Bree's mind, thankfully buried too deep to mar her equanimity—the Lucency from her brothers remained with her. Nevertheless, a part of Bree wanted to grind her teeth in fury. This would be Rector's final insult, his final betrayal. When this meeting was over, she would see him raked over the coals. He'd be run out of House Shektan with no hope of ever reclaiming his place in the city. She would see him ruined.

She briefly wondered what could have possessed Rector to go against her like this. According to Mira—and even Jaresh—Rector had grown in wisdom, becoming both more forgiving and understanding. Bree hadn't entirely believed their judgments, and as if to prove her perspicacity, here he was, living down to everything she thought about him.

When Bree reached the attestation stand, Magistrate Nacket peered down at Rector who had kept pace with her and now stood at her side. "You wish to debate Bree Shektan?" he asked.

"Yes, sir," Rector replied.

"You were warned," Bree whispered.

Rector shifted restlessly upon hearing her words.

Bree turned her attention back to the Magistrates. "My name is

Bree Shektan. My brothers are Jaresh Shektan of Caste Sentya and Rukh Shektan, who is married to Jessira Shektan of Stronghold. I believe the OutCastes should be allowed to stay, and I make the case that our Constitution *requires* that they be granted refuge."

"Everyone knows how you feel and why," Rector interrupted before Bree could get into the meat of her discourse. "But the words of the Constitution most certainly do *not* require anything of the sort. In fact, it states the very opposite." He pulled out a slim booklet—the Constitution—and made a show of turning the pages until he found what he was looking for. He theatrically cleared his throat before he began speaking. *"Any Person born within the bounds of Ashoka's Oasis is automatically granted Citizenship. Those Persons who are born elsewhere and are unable to return home, will be offered refuge and granted the choice of Citizenship, with all the attendant rights and responsibilities, if he resides in Ashoka for an uninterrupted period of time of no less than seven years."* He set aside his copy of the Constitution. "I fail to see how the OutCastes fit into either category."

Bree hid a smile. Rector's assertion was easily refuted and doing so now would allow her to build a bridge to her more powerful arguments later on. She wore what she hoped was an introspective expression as she turned to face Rector. "And I don't think anyone would argue that the OutCastes can return to their home since it was destroyed by the Sorrow Bringer," she replied before turning back to the Magistrates. She aimed her next words at Poque Belt. "Thus, by the very words of our Constitution—*Those Persons who are born elsewhere and are unable to return home,* will *be offered refuge.* Not 'might be' or 'possibly', but *'will'*. Therefore, we have a clear obligation of what we must provide. The OutCastes *must* be offered refuge as it is ordered in the Constitution."

Rector wore a condescending smile. "If it were that simple, the

Magisterium would have already ruled on behalf of the OutCastes," he said. "Your assumption is that the OutCastes are Persons," he said. "But the Constitution has a particular comment about the definition of Personhood." He thumbed through his booklet and apparently found a spot he'd earlier marked out. "*For all the purposes of Government and Citizenship, a Person is hereby defined only as an individual Human, whatever his particular Caste. As such, membership in any Caste is not a bar to Personhood. A Person cannot be any grouping of Humans, any type of Animal, or any inanimate object. A Person must be naturally born and is deemed to have Personhood, with all the rights and protections thereof, from the instant of his birth.*" He looked to Gren Vos. "*Whatever his particular Caste,*" he emphasized. "The OutCastes have no Caste. Thus, they cannot have Personhood."

Bree shook her head in disagreement. Although Rector's challenge merited thought, it was also one for which she was well-prepared. "An interesting point," she conceded. "But I think it makes better sense if we break the passage into its component parts. First, the beginning: '. . . *a Person is defined only as an individual Human . . .*' The OutCastes are individual Humans. They petitioned the Magisterium as individual Humans; they seek Personhood as individual Humans. Thus, they meet the first criterion. Next, let us take the rest of the passage. '. . . *whatever his particular Caste.*' It is obvious the OutCastes meet this standard as well." She gathered her thoughts. "The Constitution does not *demand* that a Person be born into a particular Caste. It simply states that a particular Caste is no barrier to Personhood. Therefore, it follows that having no Caste is also no barrier to Personhood since the Constitution is silent on the topic of Personhood with regards to ghrinas. Logically, since there is no evidence to the contrary, it seems obvious that since ghrinas meet the definition of a 'naturally born Human', they must also, therefore, be Persons."

"She has a point," Gren Vos said, leaning forward in her chair.

Rector tilted his head in bare acknowledgment of the Magistrate's words. His gesture could have been construed as a veiled insult. In the least, it was rude, and Bree shook her head in disgust. It was the height of arrogance to show such minimal courtesy to the oldest serving member of the Magisterium, but then again what else was Rector Bryce but arrogant?

"Perhaps this answers the issue of Personhood, but it is the least of the issues facing us," Krain Linshok said. "You wish to allow ghrinas to remain in Ashoka when the law is clear on the matter: they are to either be executed or removed permanently from the city."

"Exactly," Rector said, sounding pleased. "The authors of the Constitution considered the topic of ghrinas to be so important that they devoted several passages to what should be done about them." He held aloft his booklet and this time spoke from memory. "*Those individuals who are judged to have had congress with someone not of his Caste or those born of such a union will henceforth be known as ghrinas. Any such individual must be judged according to the dictates of* The Word and the Deed." He smiled in triumph. "The unchanging verses of *The Word and the Deed*, the basis of all our law and morality, are the reason why ghrinas cannot make a home in Ashoka."

Bree let slip a smile of triumph. This had been her plan all along—dispute the veracity of *The Word and the Deed*. But it would have always been a tricky matter to introduce such a topic in a manner that seemed organic to her presentation rather than merely argumentative. Now she wouldn't have to worry about it. Rector had brought up the topic on his own, and because he had, her statements would merely be explicative.

The weight of her words would fall with greater force, and Bree briefly wondered if this might have been Rector's plan all along: to point out the flaws in traditional theology so she might more easily dispute them. As soon as she considered the notion, she dismissed it. Rector wasn't so subtle. She'd never known him to be. Despite what Mira had thought, Rector was as he'd always been: unduly sure that only his version of dharma led to morality.

Her mind settled, Bree returned to the matter at hand.

But as she realized the true import of what she was about to do, even through Lucency, her heart fluttered. She was about to challenge the very moral basis of Ashoka's laws. There would be many who would find her words heretical. They would be furious with her, and no matter how persuasive her rhetoric, their minds would be closed off by escalating anger. Bree only hoped the Magistrates would not be among those too outraged to listen without prejudice.

"The Constitution does indeed call for judgment of the ghrinas to be based upon what is said in *The Word and the Deed*, and therein lies the problem," Bree began as she held up a sheaf of papers. "A little history first. These are notarized statements from the Head Librarian of the City Library of Ashoka. They confirm what I am about to say next. The first known edition of *The Word and the Deed* was said to have been published shortly prior to the fall of the First World. It is said to be the dictated words of the First Mother and First Father, but the earliest version *we* have only dates back to the Days of Desolation, decades after the Fall. We still have that edition displayed within the atrium of the City Library. I was given an opportunity to study a more recently printed copy of this version, and what I found is truly stunning. *The Word and the Deed* has changed greatly over time."

Shocked intakes and furious conversation met Bree's pronouncement, and Fol Nacket had to gavel for quiet. "Silence!" he thundered. "We will have decorum here! We are the Magisterium of Ashoka, and we will not allow Ashoka to be ruled by a mob!"

When silence reigned once more, Magistrate Nacket gestured for Bree to continue.

She nodded appreciation. "I, too, was surprised by what I found, but here is a quote from that earlier edition from chapter two, verse fourteen, line three: . . . a *marriage between a man and a woman of different Castes is not to be encouraged. It weakens us all.* This is what is now said in our current edition in that same location: . . . *an impure relationship between a man and a woman cannot be allowed. It darkens all our souls.* It's a subtle difference, but nevertheless, it is a significant one." She glanced up from the writing and was heartened to see that the prior boredom of the Magistrates was no longer in evidence. She had their rapt attention, and most of them wore airs of incipient hope.

"I fail to see how this changes the fundamentals of the situation," Rector said, speaking into the hushed quiet. "*The Word and the Deed* is still clear about the nature of ghrinas."

Bree stared at Rector in surprise. So far in his attestation, there had been cadences to his statements, a manner of his phrasing and presentation that had sounded utterly unlike his normal plainspoken self. If anything, his words and delivery reminded her of Nanna, which made absolutely no sense at all.

Bree shook off her confusion and returned to Rector's most recent declaration. "So all of us are taught," she replied, "but after finding this discrepancy, I studied the history of *The Word and the Deed* itself. As I said before, it is reputed to have been written prior to the Fall, but what I, and probably most everyone else, didn't realize is that the version we study and use is actually an edited form of the original. This edition was put into its current form in approximately 350 AF."

"This is old information," Rector declared. "But the *spirit* of the original was kept intact. The editing you cite was simply record-keeping to correct some translational errors."

"It was more than translational errors," Bree snapped. "It was a wholesale changing of the intent of *The Word and the Deed*."

"You have proof of this?" Poque Belt asked.

Bree nodded. "I do. In the Cellar, there are shelves of books documenting when this happened and the reasons for it. Apparently, *our* older version, the one in the City Library's atrium, isn't the same as those found in other cities. There needed to be a single version, and the one we know and use today was the result of a decades-long debate. In fact, one of the most controversial changes was to edit out a single line from *The Word and the Deed*: the first line of the first verse of the first chapter." She read from a sheet of paper. "*Above all else, honor* The Book of All Souls, *the source of all truth and morality, including this, the accumulated insight of the First Father and First Mother.*" Bree set down the paper. "Based on this one missing line, it is obvious that the moral basis of our laws should be *The Book of All Souls*, not *The Word and the Deed*."

More shocked intakes met her statement.

Fol Nacket rapped again for quiet. "Do you have anything to refute this claim?" he asked Rector, who shook his head in negation. Magistrate Nacket turned to Bree. "For the sake of discussion, we'll accept your claims. But what does *The Book of All Souls* say about ghrinas?"

"Very little," Bree answered. "Remember, *The Book of All Souls* is generally pacifist in nature. It emphasizes the importance of service to others, the holiness of understanding, forgiveness, and the universal love of Devesh."

"If that's the case, then the judgments against ghrinas, as

prescribed in *The Word and the Deed* should remain in effect," Rector loudly proclaimed.

"No it should not," Bree proclaimed just as loudly. "Because again, you would be basing your judgment upon the version of *The Word and the Deed* that was edited and compiled from AF 350. However, if you go back to the original book that we have, it says only that ghrinas are unclean, and that they should be kept separate from the rest of society. But *The Book of All Souls* says the following." She reached again for her papers. She shuffled through them until she found what she was looking for. "This is an important passage. *'Devesh sees no Castes, for a man's worth is not measured by the lowness or highness of his birth, but by how well he holds to this simple truth: all those he meets in life are his brothers.'* Devesh sees no Castes," Bree repeated. "Later, *The Book of All Souls* speaks of refuge, and how we are compelled to offer it to our brothers. This is similar to what is described in *The Word and the Deed.* We are compelled to take in the OutCastes because they are our brothers."

A few cheers met her words.

"We need to examine your findings," Poque Belt said, "but if they are accurate, then I know how I will vote."

Similar murmurs from the other Magistrates met the Sentya's words.

"I think we have heard enough," Fol Nacket said. "Please leave that packet of information," he ordered Bree. "We need to further investigate this matter." He rapped his gavel. "This meeting is adjourned."

As Bree turned aside, she caught Rector staring in her direction. Very deliberately, he gave her a brief smile and a wink. For all the world, he looked pleased with himself. "Well done," he whispered as he brushed past her.

Bree frowned. What was that about? Rector had spent the evening trying to sabotage her work, but just now, he'd seemed pleased with himself—and her. She stared at his retreating back in consternation, suddenly caught up in doubt and reconsidering her previous notion: had Rector brought up his questions as he had in order to bolster Bree's testimony and weaken his own? If so, it had been a master work of planning and subtlety.

Once more, as soon as the thought occurred to her, Bree tried to dismiss it. Rector Bryce had never been so canny and cagey and . . . her eyes widened and a grin came to her face.

But Nanna *was* exactly that canny and cagey. Could he have coached Rector and told him what to say? It made sense, and the more she thought about it, the more convinced she was that it had happened in exactly that fashion. Bree chuckled, pleased to have seen through Nanna's clever ploy.

Later in the week, she was even more pleased when the Magisterium rendered its verdict.

The OutCastes had been granted refuge.

CHAPTER THREE
MONTHS AND DAYS

*Time, that unknowable element, ebbs our lives in still waters when the hours are
hard and races us into rushing rapids when the world is rich and sweet.
We would wish it otherwise.*

—*Sooths and Small Sayings* by Tramed Billow, AF 1387

6 Months Later

"Why don't you put it down for now?" Jessira suggested.
Rukh glanced up from what he had been reading, *The
Book of First Movement*. His face was scrunched up in a
mixture of concentration and frustration, but it was mostly the latter.
Ever since their return to Ashoka, he had sought to unlock the
secrets of *The Book*, and while he could still read the first line—
something no one other than Jessira and a few others could
manage—the rest of the pages remained stubbornly blank and
unyielding. In fact, other than the one time in the Wildness when *The
Book* had cast him back into the mind of the First Father, the slim
volume remained closed and indecipherable. Rukh couldn't understand his failure, and Jessira had watched in concern as he gradually

grew more and more frustrated by his lack of success.

"I wish I knew what I was doing wrong," he muttered. "I still remember everything that happened to Linder in those final hours of His life."

"First Father," Jessira corrected. She didn't like it when Rukh referred to the First Father by his first name. It sounded too familiar and somehow disrespectful.

"First Father, then," Rukh said. "Anyway, I remember everything that happened to him. How He discovered the death of the First Mother, His betrayal by His Daughter, and His death at Her hands. I even know what He meant by a Bow and how to make one."

Jessira rose from the couch and crossed the short distance to where Rukh sat at the square, mahogany table at which they had their meals. "You're not doing anything wrong," she said. "Put it away." She took *The Book* from his hands and laid it face down on the table. "Besides, we're supposed to meet the others for dinner in an hour." Jessira's nose wrinkled when Rukh's odor wafted her way. "And you need a shower." Rukh had spent most of the morning and afternoon training and teaching at the House of Fire and Mirrors. Right now, he smelled like an unpleasant mix of oil, sweat, and dirt.

Rukh looked in her direction and a strange gleam lit his eyes. A bowl full of mangoes rested on the table before him, and he popped a slice into his mouth. He grinned around the mouthful of fruit.

Jessira knew what was coming next and she deftly sidestepped his grasping hands before he could pull her into his lap. It was an old trick. Rukh would get smelly and sweaty from teaching at the House of Fire and Mirrors, and when Jessira commented on it, he would try to pull her close and get his stink all over her.

"Not this time," she admonished, using one finger to push him back into his chair as he attempted to rise and follow.

Rukh shrugged, a look of indifference on his face. He slid the bowl of mangoes toward her. "Want some?" he asked.

Jessira loved fruit of any kind, and just as she was about to reach for the bowl, the strange twinkle returned to Rukh's eyes. "Oh no, you don't." She sidestepped away again, this time turning her back on him, trusting him not to give chase. He wouldn't, not after she'd caught him at his trick twice. For some reason, it was his self-imposed limit. "Did you leave a mess in the kitchen?" she called over her shoulder.

"Sure did," he replied, sounding unrepentant.

She shook her head in exasperation at his lighthearted tone. How did he move so easily and seamlessly from overwhelming frustration with deciphering *The Book* to a mood as chipper as the spring morning outside? Part of his charm, she supposed.

Jessira glowered when she saw the kitchen. He *had* left a mess.

"I'll take care of it after I shower," Rukh called over his shoulder as he entered their bedroom.

Jessira knew he would, but there also was no point in waiting for him. She'd take care of the dirty dishes and the mango pit on the cutting board while he cleaned up.

As she stood at the sink, scrubbing the plates and glasses, she glanced through the pass-through window, into the main room of the flat. As Kummas reckoned matters, their flat was modest, and she and Rukh were poor, but Jessira didn't care. Their home was a cheerful space, warm and comfortable. It was more than enough for the two of them, and far more spacious than any home she had ever expected to call home. It was certainly larger than the flat in which she had grown up. Her Amma would have loved it.

Jessira paused in her work and blinked away sudden tears. It was the subtle things that so often reminded her of the enormity of what had happened, that tore her happiness aside like a flower ripped away by a hard wind. It could be as simple as the smell of cold carried on the breeze; a child's glad laughter as she played with her nanna; or the brief glimpse of snow-capped mountains far to the west on a clear winter day. The slightest observation or sensation could set Jessira's thoughts traveling down paths she hated to tread. Even now, many months after the fact, the pain of her loss, the murder of her home and her family, of nearly everyone she loved—the memories still left her with a catch in her throat and eyes shiny with tears. At least the pain wasn't as severe as it had once been. It was a small mercy.

"I said I would clean the dishes," Rukh said, breaking her out of her reverie.

She stared at him helplessly, unable to voice her pain. Wordlessly, he pulled her into his embrace. This time, Jessira didn't try to dodge him. Rukh had showered and donned fresh clothing and smelled of the lavender soap she favored, but even if he had still been as sweaty and dirty as before, she wouldn't have cared. Right now, she needed his warmth and his strength.

It had been his love and devotion that had carried Jessira thus far. It had been his warm presence that had lifted her up, supported her, kept her whole. Even during the times of reticence when Jessira had refused to speak of her pain, when she had shut her heart to the world, he had been there. Or when the toil kept them apart except for a few brief joyless moments at the end of a long day, he had remained a true constant by her side. She might not have survived without him, or if she had, she would likely have been a far angrier, unhappy version of herself, one more like her cousin, Sign.

Jessira held Rukh close, pressing her head against his chest and neck. She grew embarrassed when the sobs started. "Damn it."

Rukh stroked her head, saying nothing.

Jaresh stepped aside for an elderly Kumma grandmother leading a gaggle of children into a nearby park in Jubilee Hills. The grandmother dipped her head in acknowledgment of his courtesy and let the children off their figurative leashes the moment they had entered the park. Their loud peals of laughter rang out, and Jaresh grinned at their joy. How easy it was to be young.

After the children's laughter drifted away, he turned his attention back to the others. Bree was involved in a conversation with Farn, while the final member of their group, Sign Deep, lagged behind and wore a pensive or unhappy countenance. It was a feature Jaresh had come to expect upon the woman's face.

Jaresh could understand her sentiment, at least up to a point, but he did often wonder when Sign might once again start seeing the bright side of life. After all, Jessira seemed, if not happy, then at least content. She certainly wasn't sullen and angry all the time like Sign.

Jaresh listened in on Bree and Farn's conversation.

"Rector is to help with it," Bree said in a tone of disapproval. "I still don't trust him."

Farn shrugged. "I wasn't here when he betrayed Rukh, but hasn't he been helpful since rejoining the House?"

"He certainly helped at the Magisterium," Jaresh interjected.

Bree turned to him. "Yes, he helped at the Magisterium, and I don't know why." She frowned. "It's what has me so bothered," she mused.

Jaresh pretended to stumble and gazed wide-eyed at his sister. "You? Unaware of something? Heavens forfend."

Farn laughed, but Bree rolled her eyes. "I wouldn't think my admission of a fault would cause you to react with so much amusement," she replied.

"It wasn't amusement," Jaresh said with a grin. "It was mockery."

"Leave her alone," Sign said, joining their conversation. "As far as I'm concerned, distrusting Rector Bryce is a wise decision."

"You only say that because either Jessira poisoned you against him or you heard what he supposedly did at the Magisterium last summer," Jaresh said. "But you weren't there. Rector *was* helping your cause. He and Nanna came up with a plan to make it seem like he was trying to sabotage Bree's testimony, but he was really supporting her."

Sign pursed her lips. "But Bree says . . ."

"Bree just doesn't want to admit any of this because of how much she dislikes Rector," Farn interrupted.

"It's not because I don't like Rector," Bree huffed. "I just don't think we should trust him so easily after everything he's done to us in the past."

"Nanna believes otherwise," Jaresh reminded her.

"And everything Nanna says must be the gospel truth?" Bree asked sarcastically. "He isn't always right about everything."

"Maybe so, but after the Magisterium, I think Rector's earned back a large measure of trust," Jaresh said.

"I disagree," Bree replied.

Farn raised a questioning eyebrow at Jaresh, who shook his head in reply.

Bree had badly misjudged Rector Bryce once—they all had—but while the rest of them had seen the change in the man, for his sister, it wasn't enough. Once burned, she was slow to forgive.

"I don't see why the two of you are so intent on having Bree approve of Rector Bryce," Sign commented. "Wasn't he the one who drew a sword on Jessira?"

"The first time he saw Jessira, he had a foot of his blade out of its sheath, but he quickly slammed it home," Jaresh said. "My brother corrected his poor manners, and after that, all he did was make an ass of himself and speak rudely to her."

"And words can't hurt?" Sign argued.

"You're being purposefully dense," Farn said, "Of course words can hurt, but if rude talk was the only reason to dislike someone and never offer them a chance to apologize, then what would you have me say about how I was treated by the OutCastes when I lived in Stronghold?"

"That was different," Sign replied.

"Different how?" Jaresh challenged.

"Because my home is gone. My people are gone. Those who spoke rudely . . . Oh, never mind! It doesn't matter anymore," Sign snarled. Her eyes were shiny with unshed tears.

Jaresh frowned in frustration and confusion, not sure what to make of Sign's words or her demeanor. What was bothering her so badly this time? He shared a glance with Farn and Bree. They looked just as uncertain as he, and Jaresh turned back to Sign. "None of that made the least bit of sense," he said, trying to be diplomatic through his aggravation.

Sign exhaled heavily and mouthed what seemed like a prayer. She turned to Jaresh and ventured a weary smile. "Please forget what I said. I shouldn't have spoken as I did. I'm sorry."

Jaresh still wasn't sure what Sign was talking about, but nevertheless, his irritation with her faded. "Consider yourself forgiven," he said. "Just stop being an ass, and we'll get along fine."

Sign's mouth gaped.

"Now you did it," Bree told Jaresh with a chuckle. "Wait until Amma learns you called a woman an ass."

A sense of dread came over Jaresh. "I don't think she needs to hear about that," he said quickly.

"Or when Jessira learns about Sign's mopey anger," Farn said, coming to Jaresh's rescue.

Now it was Sign who spoke quickly. "Jessira doesn't need to know what happened," she said.

"Then we're agreed. No one else needs to know what was said here tonight," Jaresh said in relief.

"*I'm* not agreed," Bree said, favoring Jaresh and Sign with sunny smiles. "The way I see things, you both owe me something if you want me to keep quiet."

"I wonder what Dar'El would think about how you belittled him earlier," Farn mused as he flashed Jaresh a wink.

"Er . . ." Bree said. Her triumphant grin turned into a sickly smile. "Maybe it *would* be best if we kept this conversation to ourselves."

Farn chuckled. "I thought you might see it that way."

Sign came alongside Jaresh. "Your amma must be a daunting woman."

"You have no idea," Jaresh said. "In some ways, Jessira is a lot like her." A horrifying thought came to him. "Could you imagine what Jessira would do if she knew I upset you?" he asked, trying to keep the mood light.

"You didn't upset me," Sign said.

Jaresh ignored her words. "If Jessira found out I almost made you cry . . ." He shuddered.

"You didn't almost make me cry or anything like that, so stop saying it," Sign warned with a glower.

Jaresh studied her face for a moment before shrugging nonchalantly. "You know, I doubt if Rukh would even protect me from Jessira if she decided to chase me around with a bared sword, screaming like a demented banshee. In his eyes, I doubt your cousin can do any wrong."

Bree laughed. "I'm glad I'm not the only one who's noticed it."

"Noticed what?" Farn asked.

"You've haven't seen how they are around one another?" Jaresh asked in surprise.

"No," Farn said.

Jaresh shook his head in pretend sympathy. "How can you be so brilliant and yet so incomprehensibly dense?" he asked.

Farn glanced around amongst the three of them with deepening ignorance that eventually led to irritation. "Will someone tell me what you're talking about?"

Jaresh clapped Farn on the shoulder. "You'll just have to see it for yourself," he advised. "Just watch them tonight."

Farn growled. "I think you're making fun of me," he muttered. "I liked it better when we were talking about the deficiencies of Rector Bryce."

"I thought we set him aside," Bree observed.

"We had," Sign replied. "And I still think you're right to withhold your trust of him."

Jaresh turned to her. "Rector has already apologized to Jessira, and *she* no longer holds a grudge against him," he noted. "So why do you?"

Sign shrugged. "Maybe he just reminds me of everything I've been taught to fear about the Purebloods."

"And I can understand that fear," Jaresh agreed. "But maybe it won't always be that way. When Jessira first came to Ashoka, she had to go around with her face covered up, but eventually, she decided to make the city acknowledge her." He smiled. "We did, and she still got a lot of ugly looks, but that was it. There was nothing more to it than that. It wasn't like what Rukh and Farn had to put up with in Stronghold. I'm told they were even attacked on several occasions with no justice being brought to bear on the perpetrators."

Sign frowned at Jaresh. "Do you want another apology?" she demanded. "Fine. I'm sorry my people were mean to Rukh and Farn. I'm sure they found it upsetting to their delicate Pureblood constitutions."

Jaresh blinked, both offended and impressed by her outburst. Meanwhile Bree hid a smile, and Farn looked like he wanted to grin as well. Jaresh turned to his cousin. "Why are you laughing?" he asked. "She was making fun of you."

Farn broke into a broad grin. "No, she wasn't," he answered. "She was telling you to shove your opinion somewhere dark and smelly."

Jaresh gave his cousin a pitying look before turning to Sign. There was no chance she would have the last word in this. "I can see I've upset you once again," he said to Sign. "Please don't break down into your womanly tears."

She punched him.

"Ow!"

"Once, I can overlook. Twice, not so much," Sign said.

"What is it with OutCaste women and their temper?" Jaresh asked no one in particular. "I think I liked it better when she was moping along and her eyes were wet with—"

"Be careful," Sign warned.

Farn nudged Jaresh. "Let it go," he advised. "You're not winning."

"Why don't the two of you save your argument for later," Bree suggested. "We're going to a play tonight, remember? Let's enjoy ourselves."

"I'm not arguing," Jaresh said. "I'm being assaulted."

"I'm not sure I remember how to enjoy myself," Sign said, ignoring Jaresh's words. "With everything my people have been through, frivolity just seems—"

"Like exactly what you need," Jaresh interrupted. "A smile won't break your face." He didn't know why he was so intent on irritating her.

Sign threw her hands in the air. "Are you trying to say the *exact* thing that makes me want to punch you?"

"OutCaste women and their temper," Jaresh muttered.

"What was that?" Sign asked.

"Nothing," Jaresh replied.

Sign narrowed her eyes in suspicion.

Jaresh stared back with wide-eyed innocence.

"If you didn't want a night away from the troubles in your life, then why did you come with us?" Bree asked, stepping into the conversation.

"Jessira asked me," Sign responded.

"Well, I doubt she asked you to come along and *not* enjoy yourself," Bree told her.

"I wish it were so easy," Sign answered.

"Life is never easy," Farn countered. "You're a warrior. You should know this. Jessira does."

Sign reddened. "Jessira has much more of a reason to be happy than I."

"Then it's time you found your own reasons to be happy," Bree said. She took Sign by the hand and pulled her into their midst. "We're going to see a play," she continued. "If you can watch it without having your emotions touched, without finding an excuse to smile at least once, then Jaresh will pay for your dinner tonight and clean your flat every day for the next week."

"Wait! What?!" Jaresh squawked.

Sign offered an interested smile and looked Jaresh up and down. "Clean my flat for a week?" she asked. "Is this a wager?"

"Witnessed," Farn said quickly.

"No!" Jaresh protested.

"Seconded," Bree announced.

"I never agreed to it," Jaresh cried.

"Too late," Farn said. "It's been witnessed."

"And seconded," Bree chuckled.

Jaresh gave the two of them a flat look of annoyance. "And what do I get in return?" he asked, turning back to Sign.

Sign tilted her head to the side in consideration. "I'll cook you dinner every night for a week."

"Cook Heltin already does that for me," Jaresh said. "Choose something else."

Sign growled. "Fine. Then you'll have my undying appreciation, and I'll make sure no one learns that you made a weak, little woman like me cry."

"You're not little," Jaresh corrected.

"But I am a weak woman?" Sign asked with an arch of her eyebrows.

"Would you prefer it if I called you a strong man?"

Sign chuckled. "Well played."

"Well, since you just smiled, I think I won the wager," Jaresh said.

"The wager was whether the *play* could make me smile," Sign corrected.

Jaresh scowled at her before turning to Farn and Bree. "What are we seeing tonight?" he asked.

"*Down the Street,*" Farn answered with a sharklike grin.

Jaresh groaned. "A fragging tragedy."

"Why is this bad?" Sign asked.

"It's not bad," Bree said. "At least not for you. A tragedy has lots of drama, and even some death, but very little humor."

Sign smiled in low-lidded pleasure and patted Jaresh's cheek. He was too irritated to notice a woman not of his Caste touching him in public. "Make sure to dust the top of the dresser," she advised.

Rukh held the door open for the others as they entered the restaurant. Jessira was the last in line, and she took his hand, drawing him away from the entrance and leading them outside.

"You don't have to hold the door for me every time," she said. "I'm not helpless."

"I know, but it just feels right," Rukh said with a smile. "I like taking care of you."

"Then thank you," Jessira said with an answering smile. "And if you ever need me to hold the door open, I'll gladly do so."

Rukh gave her hand a brief squeeze. "We better head in before Jaresh starts making fun of us. You know what he says about our being too affectionate?"

"Who cares what he says?" Jessira replied. She reached up and drew him into a kiss that was just short of lingering. "I meant what I said," she added after she'd pulled back. "I'm grateful for all you've done for me and for my people."

She cupped his face, and Rukh stared into her eyes, his breath catching. He might have kissed her again just then, but they'd already drawn a few catcalls from a number of people walking by who had noticed their affectionate display.

Rukh glanced up at one particularly loud whistle and met the sly grins of a group of young Duriah men. Their smiles turned to looks of confusion when they saw Jessira. She was an OutCaste, and though her people had been granted sanctuary in Ashoka, it wasn't the same as acceptance. Too many still thought of Jessira's kind as ghrinas.

Expressions of disgust flitted across the faces of some of the Duriahs, but the more intelligent amongst them must have quickly recognized or realized who Jessira was. It wasn't a difficult deduction to come to. After all, there weren't many OutCastes in Ashoka to begin with, and there was only one who would be held in the arms of a Kumma.

For those men who had ascertained Rukh and Jessira's identities, their grins slid away. They whispered their findings into the ears of those around them, and all the Duriahs swiftly enough wore sickly smiles or expressions of mild alarm. As a group, they gave brief nods to Rukh and Jessira and scurried away.

Jessira chuckled after they had left. "I think they're afraid of you," she noted.

Rukh's head fell low in disappointment. Jessira was likely right. The Duriahs *had* been afraid of him, or if not frightened, then at least intimidated. It was an all-too-common occurrence he'd come to expect ever since his return to Ashoka.

It seemed too much had happened to him in the past few years. First had come his unexpected victory in the Tournament of Hume. Then had come the occurrences of the the failed Trial to Nestle and all he had learned about the Baels, Hume's last years, and the discovery of the OutCastes. Next had followed the expedition to the caverns of the Chimeras. The accounts of what he'd accomplished in those grisly caves varied, but all the stories cast far too much glory on Rukh's role. As far as he saw matters, he'd merely carried out his mission. He'd done as he'd been ordered and as he'd been expected. Nothing more, but Nanna had twisted the truth and managed to raise Rukh's actions to something approaching the mythic. And finally, Rukh's return from a murdered Stronghold. Not only had he come back with the remnants of the OutCastes, he'd also recovered *The Book of First Movement* from lost Hammer.

As a result, strangers no longer knew how to treat him. Whereas in the past, he could walk the streets of Ashoka with no one noticing, he was often recognized now, and when he was, many seemed to view him as some kind of icon, a living legend. Worse, he had a sense that all these people who fixed him with wide-eyed looks of awe hoped that he would reveal something miraculous, something wondrous at any moment. Their expectations were a heavy burden and the reason why Rukh spent most of his days teaching at the House of Fire and Mirrors. There, the Martial Masters, the men who had trained him and remembered him as a boy rather than a hero, treated him as they would any other warrior. Of course the students—even the older ones who knew Rukh from his earlier time at the House—were another matter. They were as bad, or worse, than everyone else in the city.

Rukh hated it. He was just a man, and no man deserved to be worshipped or held in such immeasurable esteem. A life of anonymity was a life of of freedom, and he missed it. His situation left him wondering about those who *did* desire fame. He couldn't understand why they would be so foolish. Or perhaps it was merely their vanity that drove such a needy desire.

Jessira took him by the hand and gave it a gentle squeeze as she offered him a tight-lipped expression of understanding. "I know," she said in sympathy. "And I know how much it bothers you."

He'd long ceased wondering how the two of them so often seemed to know one another's unspoken thoughts.

She gave his hand another squeeze. "Let's go inside."

Rukh nodded and held the door open for her to enter.

"You know, there are some in Ashoka who say that opening a door for a woman is a sign that the man thinks a woman helpless," Jessira said returning to their earlier topic of conversation as she stepped past him.

Rukh rolled his eyes. "And what do these people have to say about a man holding the door open for another man? Like I did earlier for Farn and Jaresh, or when Jaresh did for me when we left the theater?"

Jessira grinned. "Oh, I'm sure they have plenty to say," she replied. "But thankfully, I'm not so shortsighted." She chuckled, low and throaty. "Besides, I like your sense of courtesy."

Rukh smiled wryly. Somehow, his wife always knew what to say to distract him or make him feel better.

They paused inside the entrance to the restaurant and let their eyes adjust to the dim interior. A scattering of tables filled the space. Upon each one rested a single votive candle floating in a wide-mouthed goblet full of water. Shaded firefly lamps served as wall sconces and provided the rest of the lighting. In the back, an open kitchen allowed the patrons to see the cooks at work. The sizzle of grilling meat searing on hot skillets carried throughout the restaurant, along with the sounds and aromas of mustard seeds popping in hot oil, garam masala roasting in a clay oven, and cumin seeds frying in a pan.

Jessira inhaled. "Mmm. Smells good," she said.

Rukh glanced around, looking for the others. Before he could ask for directions, an attendant had already noticed them and directed them to a corner booth where the rest of their group had been seated.

Jaresh exhaled extravagantly at their late arrival. "Let me guess," his brother said in a disgusted tone. "You just *had* to stop and speak of your undying love for one another."

Rukh smiled condescendingly. "One day, maybe you'll understand what it is to be in love." The moment the words left his lips, he wanted to kick himself. His brother *had* known what it was like to be in love. Mira Terrell. "I'm sorry," Rukh said. "I shouldn't have said that."

Jaresh waved aside his apology. "I'm not made of glass," he said. "I'll be fine." The tightening around his eyes exposed the cost of his flippant response.

Farn must have also noticed Jaresh's discomfort. "How about a round of drinks?" he said, changing the subject and trying to lighten the mood. "Rukh's paying."

His suggestion was met with glad cries of agreement, and the matter was dropped.

"Not so smooth," Bree whispered to Rukh as he took a seat next to her.

He was squeezed in by his sister to his left and Sign to his right. "Not my best moment," Rukh agreed.

He looked around the table. Farn and Jaresh were engaged in a conversation, while Sign sipped her water, a faraway look in her eyes. She was likely thinking about the death of her city, and while he understood her pain, her obsession with relieving the past was unhealthy. Rukh hoped she would find a means to regain her once bright, sunny outlook. Back in Stronghold, she'd been a ball of fire, fearless and with nothing to slow her down.

His consideration of her unhappy state was interrupted when something Jaresh said elected a smile from Sign. She set down her glass of water and shifted her attention to the other two men while Rukh sat back in his seat and rubbed his chin. Maybe Sign was doing better than he supposed. If so, he was glad.

"It looks like she's enjoying herself," Bree whispered to him, apparently noticing his quizzical expression.

"I hope so," Rukh whispered back.

Their conversation was cut off when Jaresh laughed loudly at something Farn had just told him. Surprisingly, Sign chuckled as well.

Rukh wondered what Farn could have said that could be so funny. It wasn't in his cousin's dour nature to be humorous or so relaxed and happy. The past few years had sparked a vast change in Farn, and as far as Rukh was concerned, it was for the better. It was good to hear his cousin laugh.

"Poor Farn. Laya's baby bit your finger and it hurt," Jaresh said in a faux-childish voice. "Is it still hurting?"

"Let the baby bite your finger, and we'll see if you're still laughing," Farn replied.

"How did Laya end up staying with you anyway?" Bree asked.

"Amma," Farn answered. "I was just checking in on Laya, doing what I'd promised Cedar before he died. But then Amma asked about it, and somehow she got it in her head that *I* was the father of Laya's unborn baby." He shrugged. "By the time she realized her mistake, she'd already offered up our home to Laya."

"Then it was very generous of your amma to let Laya stay, especially after she found out the truth," Jessira said.

"Yes it was," Farn agreed. "She and little Court—"

"I thought his name was Cedar," Bree interrupted.

"His name is Cedar Court Grey, but Laya calls him little Court," Jessira explained.

"And the two of them will always have a home with us," Farn continued. "Nanna and Amma think of him as another grandson." He sighed. "I just wish the boy wouldn't wake up so often in the middle of the night. Amma and Nanna try to put him back to sleep, but most nights, it's me that ends up taking care of him."

Rukh gave Farn a quizzical look.

"I'm the only one who has the trick of making him go to sleep at night," Farn said in a mix of embarrassment and pride.

"What do you mean?" Bree asked.

"I rock him on my knee, just kind of bounce him up and down on his bottom, and he falls asleep. No one else can keep the right rhythm."

"Not even Laya?" Sign asked. "Where is she during all this?"

"She's there. Little Court sleeps in her bedroom, and I only come in if she can't get him to go back down." Farn wore a put-upon expression. "Which, unfortunately, is most nights."

Sign nodded. "I'm glad she calls him 'little Court,'" she said. "My brother would have appreciated it."

"Court was a wonderful man," Farn agreed. "I'll always be grateful to him."

"I owed him more than I could ever hope to repay," Rukh agreed softly. "I wouldn't be here if it wasn't for his generosity."

"To Court," Jessira said, raising her glass.

After the toast, several conversations broke out as those seated adjacent to one another spoke on various topics.

Rukh turned to Sign. "Did you win your wager?" he asked.

Sign seemed lost in her thoughts again, and he had to repeat his question. She gave a slight head shake before focusing on him and smiling briefly in triumph. "I did," she said.

"You didn't find the scene with the old man looking for his

glasses to be amusing?" Bree asked in surprise.

"I thought it was hilarious," Sign answered as she turned to look at Jaresh. "I just didn't think it was funny enough to laugh out loud and lose our bet."

Jaresh smiled sourly. "I still don't think it was a proper wager since I never agreed to it," he said. "But here's to your victory." He lifted his glass in salute to her triumph.

"What was your favorite part of the play?" Jessira asked Sign.

Her cousin got another faraway expression in her eyes. "All of it," she finally replied. "It was like a dream. I never expected something so silly—people pretending to be someone else—to be so mesmerizing and uplifting, or so sad."

Rukh laughed. "For a moment there, you looked just like Jessira did after she saw her first play."

Jaresh chuckled. "Or her second."

"Or her third and fourth," Bree chimed in. "While you were gone on the expedition to the Chimera caverns, we took her out to a couple more plays, and each time, she'd come out like . . ." She gave a crooked grin. "Well I can't exactly describe her expression—at least not in polite company."

"Say what you want," Jessira replied with a sniff. "You can't cheapen my memory. The plays were bliss."

"That's one word for it," Jaresh muttered.

"Quiet," Jessira ordered.

Jaresh studiously sipped his ale, but his eyes crinkled.

Jessira took a moment to stare him down before turning away. "Anyway, the plays helped me maintain my sanity. My time in Ashoka wasn't always pleasant."

"I thought you loved your time here," Bree said in confusion.

"I did, but I also had plenty of reasons to be unhappy," Jessira answered. "I just wish your parents had trusted me with the truth."

Bree startled. "What do you mean?" she asked.

"She knows," Rukh said to his sister, not bothering to answer the unspoken questions on the faces of the others.

"Knows what?" Farn asked.

"Rukh's parents wanted to make sure I wouldn't leave Ashoka without him, that I'd wait until he returned from the Chimera caverns and take him with me to Stronghold." Jessira explained. "They implied some statements that weren't entirely true."

Rukh gave her hand a squeeze. If their roles had been reversed, he might not have been as forgiving.

Jessira turned to him. "I can't blame them for loving their son," she said. "And they're my parents now, too."

Rukh smiled in gratitude.

"Now they're going to kiss," Jaresh said in disgust.

"What a tragic demise for a once-mighty warrior to be reduced to such a sad, sappy state," Farn agreed solemnly.

"I think it's sweet," Sign said. "My people see little enough happiness as it is."

"Don't backslide," Rukh warned her.

"I'm not backsliding," Sign said with a scowl. "And mind your own business."

"Scowl all you want," Rukh told her, "but I remember the bouncing young woman who was so excited when she tried chocolate for the first time. You were like a child. It's hard to be frightened of someone once you've seen them like that."

"Wait? She had the same reaction as Jessira?" Jaresh asked. "All goofy like she'd just tasted heaven?"

"Was it an expression you can't describe in polite company?" Bree asked.

"Or maybe their reactions have something to do with them being OutCastes," Farn suggested.

"I don't know about that," Rukh said. "But as for Sign, when she ate the chocolate cake, it *must* have been bliss."

"Oh shut up," Sign snapped.

She sounded annoyed, but Rukh noticed her lips twitching with suppressed mirth. "I don't have a bet with you," he said. "You can laugh."

Sign chuckled. "At least now I know why Jessira keeps you around."

"Why's that?" Bree asked. "It's a question we've all wondered about."

"Rukh makes Jessira laugh," Sign explained.

"You mean because he's a fool?" Jaresh asked, his brows furrowed in feigned puzzlement.

———————◆●◆———————

An area south of Mount Crone that directly abutted the Inner Wall of Ashoka was where the OutCastes were now housed. There, a set of fallen-down buildings that no one else wanted had been purchased for a pittance by the Magisterium and with several Kumma Houses and a few other large mercantile concerns to finance the refurbishment. The structures had originally been built during a great pragmatic awakening several centuries prior. It was a time of supposed simplicity, where function ruled form and the lack of adornment in all aspects of life—clothes, furniture, and architecture—had become nothing short of a moral imperative. As a result, buildings from that period had been designed as plain cubes and rectangular structures with flat roofs and narrow windows. It was an efficient but ugly type of design, especially in comparison to the glorious architecture of the rest of the city.

By the time the OutCastes had washed up on Ashoka's shores, most such structures from that late, unlamented period had long since been torn down. The few remaining buildings of that era were now almost always dilapidated and in need of urgent repair, and the ones selected to house the OutCastes had been no different.

Despite her frequent distrust, Sign had been relieved that the Purebloods had allowed their people refuge, but when she'd seen where they were to be housed, she'd initially been taken aback. How would they make these wretched wrecks their homes? It had taken Jessira's explanation to set her mind at ease. Her cousin, who had been instrumental in choosing the buildings, had reasoned that their people needed something to occupy their time and minds, a buffer to give them a chance to forget—however briefly—the terrible tribulations they had all suffered.

Sign had ended up agreeing with Jessira's decision, and every passing day had made her ever more grateful for her cousin's astute vision.

The work needed to bring the buildings back to life had done everything Jessira had said it would. Months of labor had been required and her people had been forced to work hard and fast. Winter had been closing in. But more importantly, the OutCastes had needed to lift one another up. There would always come a time when one of them would reach their limit, ready to give up and set aside the burden of living, when they became ensnared in a wasting weariness and were ready to drift away. In the face of such daunting needs, the OutCastes had to choose between two options: they could have clung to selfishness, or they could have reached out with loving hearts and carry those who couldn't stand.

Sign was proud that in each instance, her people had risen up and chosen the latter path, the better one. Without fail, those who had the strength to spare had generously offered it up to those in need. The OutCastes had created ever-deeper bonds of community and caring, and the ties of fellowship and love that Sign had seen forged—had been a part of—left her humbled and in awe. She had never been more proud to be a daughter of Stronghold.

She was also grateful to the Purebloods who had pitched in to help reclaim the old buildings. Rukh, Jaresh, Bree, and Farn had done what they could, but they weren't skilled at the work that had needed doing. Instead, they had been the loving hearts who had searched out those with the willing hands to help. They had found a number of Duriah master craftsmen to aid Sign's people in their work, and together, the OutCastes and Purebloods had repaired all the damage done by settling foundations and wearing wind, water, and time.

The result was a small cluster of structures that, while not beautiful, were sturdy and weather-tight. More importantly, they were a place of safety, a place where the OutCastes could rebuild their lives.

"I know you think I'm imposing by walking you home," Jaresh said.

Sign startled. They'd walked in silence for so long that she'd forgotten he was there.

After dinner, the others had headed to their respective homes in wealthy Jubilee Hills, and Sign had expected Jaresh to go with them. Instead, he had insisted on walking her to her flat. He had explained that while violence was unlikely to come her way—especially since the immolation of the Sil Lor Kum—given the lateness of the hour, common courtesy dictated that he should accompany her and see her safely home. Farn and Rukh could have done so, but it made more sense for Jaresh to take care of the matter.

"You're not imposing," Sign said, responding to his statement.

"Are you sure?"

"I'm sure," Sign said, flicking him a glance. "But I don't want to take up too much of *your* time. You don't have to walk me all the way to my front door. You can return to your own home if you wish."

"Jessira would not be happy if I did that," Jaresh replied.

Sign's brows lifted in surprised amusement. "Don't tell me you really *are* afraid of her."

"You're not?" Jaresh challenged.

Sign was about to respond with a shake of her head and tell him *'of course not'*, but instead, she paused and truly considered Jaresh's question. She realized a moment later that while she wasn't afraid of Jessira, she did fear disappointing her.

Jaresh nodded. "You see what I mean."

Sign gave a wistful half smile. "My cousin has grown forceful," she said. "She wasn't always so, but after Stronghold's death, any velvet softness around the ironwood mettle of her core seems to have burned off."

"She isn't *quite* that hard, but she's also not a woman I'd want to risk angering," Jaresh agreed. "I think even my nanna treads lightly around her."

"Truly?"

Jaresh smiled disarmingly, a surprisingly winning grin. "No. I was just exaggerating for effect," he answered "But the truth is I think Rukh might be one of the few people who *isn't* the least bit intimidated by Jessira."

"Then he *is* a fool," Sign said, still smiling to take the sting out of her words.

"Maybe love makes him foolishly brave," Jaresh suggested.

Sign chuckled. "Perhaps so," she agreed. They walked in silence before Sign voiced a question that had been bothering her since dinner. "Why did Rukh seem so upset when he spoke to you about loving another?" She realized the question might be impertinent the instant the words left her lips. She put a hand on Jaresh's arm. "You don't have to answer," she said in contrition.

Jaresh gave her a tight-lipped smile. "It's fine. You're likely to hear about it sometime. There was a woman I once loved. Her name was Mira."

"Was?"

Jaresh nodded. He then told Sign a tale of forbidden love, unrequited and unspoken. It was so typical of the Purebloods. If not for the backwardness of their society, there was no reason why Jaresh and this woman he had so deeply loved couldn't have married and lived out a life of joy. Instead, that love had been stillborn, killed before it ever had a chance to flower, and ultimately murdered by an evil that had its origin in the same foul demon that had destroyed Stronghold: Suwraith.

The Queen had much for which to answer.

"I'm sorry," Sign said, somehow feeling closer to him because of his loss.

"You've suffered a lot more than I have," Jaresh noted.

"Should we compare who hurts more severely?" Sign asked, her head tilted in challenge.

Jaresh ventured a smile. "I suppose not," he said. "Grief hurts no matter how seemingly small the cause."

Sign nodded agreement and gestured up ahead. "We're almost there," she noted. The buildings had grown familiar. One more turn, and they would be on her street. "Home," Sign replied. A tingle in her fingers, a dryness in her mouth, and a quickening of her heart let her feel the weight of the word, the longing for it to be true.

"Is it home?" Jaresh asked.

"It's not the home I wanted—that one was destroyed by the Sorrow Bringer—but it is *a* home," Sign replied. She sighed a moment later. "I only wish Jessira could have lived here also. I miss her."

"They had to move back to Jubilee Hills to help the House," Jaresh said. "It was never because of any petty reason to have a bigger flat or separate themselves from the rest of the OutCastes."

Sign had heard this before, and while she vaguely understood the reasons, it wasn't the same as accepting them. "I know. Rukh's marriage to Jessira diminished his status as a Kumma within his Caste. And by extension, it diminishes the status of your parents and House."

Jaresh shrugged apology. "Right now, in some ways, Rukh needs to prove that he's still a Kumma at heart. It was thought that moving back to Jubilee Hills might help him do so."

Sign smiled even as she mentally shrugged off his explanation. There were currents to Ashoka's politics that escaped her, and she reckoned they always would. It was simply too foreign to her way of thinking. "Whatever the reasons, I'm just glad they're happy in their new home," she said before pointing to the building at which they'd arrived. "This is mine," she said. "Good night, Jaresh."

"Good night, Sign."

CHAPTER FOUR
AN EVENTUAL LIFE

The days of a man's life are as the leaves of an autumn tree—bright and bold but finite. And the Lord will shelter you long before the last leaf has fallen.

—*The Book of All Souls*

As Bree travelled along the gravel path, she lightly gripped her scabbarded sword with one hand while her thumb rested on the hilt to keep the weapon in place. It was the proper way of walking with a belted blade, and over time, such a technique had become second nature to her. The swaying of the sword against her left hip and the rise and fall of the sageo-tied-scabbard were now simply a part of who she was.

Of course, it had taken months of hard work and training for Bree to become so comfortable at having a blade by her side. Her ambition had required long hours of tutelage by the Great Duriah, Durmer Volk, with sweltering days under a hot summer sun and chilly afternoons beneath a cool winter wind. All the time spent, though, had achieved its desired outcome. Bree had managed to achieve a certain competence with the sword, and though she strived for more than mere mediocrity, at least now she no longer felt like a helpless weakling. She could defend herself against anyone who was not a Kumma and feel confident that she would survive the encounter.

Some might have wondered why she worked so tirelessly to master such an odd skill for a woman, but the truth was actually quite simple. Never again did Bree want to feel as useless as she had during that terrible conflict when she had almost died. It had been in an otherwise unremarkable alley in the Moon Quarter, and the fight had nearly cost Bree her life. It *would* have—probably should have—if not for Jaresh's swift sword. Bree, on the other hand, had merely watched as a panic-stricken observer. She had stood frozen with fear as her brother had fought for both their lives.

It had been a terrible lesson that she'd learned—of her fragility and inability to protect herself—and it was a mistake she vowed to never repeat or forget. Never again would she allow herself to be caught so defenseless, and Mira's murder had merely steadied and hardened that resolve. Bree would master the blade, and all the other Talents of her warrior Caste, and while she might not ever have the sublime skill of her brother, Rukh, or even Jaresh, at least she would be able to fight if needed. More importantly, no one else would ever again need die because Bree was incapable of protecting herself.

"How much farther?" Jessira asked, interrupting Bree's thoughts of swords and strength.

"Not far," she answered. "We should be there soon."

Bree quickened her pace, and Jessira and Sign, who were accompanying her, increased their stride to keep up. The sound of their feet crunching along the lonely gravel drive sounded vaguely martial.

The three of them marched alongside the fields between Ashoka's Inner and Outer Walls. The wheat and corn had already been planted and showed as thin, green growths while a warm wind blew an earthy aroma of loam and manure. The breeze carried across the fields and bent the crops, causing the shoots and leaves to weave and bob in sinuous waves. It reminded Bree of waves ebbing on the ocean, especially as they broke around the rocky shoals of oaks and maples that grew in the midst of the crops. A small herd of cows lowed from a nearby meadow while songbirds trilled their melodies from their roosts amongst the branches of the trees.

"Do you really think the Murans will let us sharecrop their fallow land?" Sign asked.

"Rukh seems to think they might," Jessira answered. From her tone, Bree could tell she wasn't entirely convinced.

"I hope he's right," Sign replied, doubt also suffusing her voice.

Bree briefly glanced over at the other two women. She, too, had uncertainties about whether an agreement could be obtained with the Murans. Of all the Castes, the Murans were the most religious, and they had also been the ones who had been the most offended by the Magisterium's decision to grant the OutCastes sanctuary. They were especially incensed by the questions raised about validity of the *The Word and the Deed.*

Ultimately, Bree's uncertainties didn't matter, and she set them aside. The decision would be made, and the OutCastes would have their answer one way or another.

"We'll know soon enough," Jessira said, her words an echo of Bree's thoughts.

The gravel road they followed began a slow ascent and on the descent, they had to step aside for a wagon loaded with hay. The Muran drover tipped his hat to them as he passed.

"Do you think we're asking the Ashokans for too much?" Sign asked after the wagon had passed.

"I think you should get used to saying that *you* are Ashokans," Bree answered.

"I think I'll always think of myself as a Strongholder first," Sign replied.

"I can understand that," Bree replied. "But you're also an Ashokan now. And no, I don't think you're asking for too much," she said, hoping her own doubts didn't creep into her voice.

Sign smiled wistfully. "What a wonderful thing if the Murans feel the same way."

"But even if they don't, we have our lives and a chance to give our children a future," Jessira said. "We weren't certain we'd be able to have either a few months ago."

"No we weren't," Sign agreed.

Jessira turned to Bree. "No matter what the Murans say, I want to thank you for convincing them to meet with us. You've done so much for our people."

"Yes. Thank you," Sign said. "I don't know what we would have done without your help."

Bree reddened, touched by the words of both women. "You're welcome," she said.

Jessira chuckled. "I think we've embarrassed you enough."

Bree smiled. "Oh no. Keep going. I have two older brothers who seem to think that teasing me is the height of entertainment. It's good to be appreciated for once."

"Well we definitely appreciate you," Jessira said. She surprised Bree by drawing her into a warm embrace before breaking out into glad laughter and throwing her arms wide. "What a wonderful, fine day it is!"

Bree took in Jessira's display with bemusement.

"Spring fever," Sign explained. "She's always like this when the weather warms up."

Bree nodded in understanding. "Rukh's the same way."

Sign rolled her eyes. "The two of them are bad enough as it is with all their kissing and secret smiles," she said. "Toss in spring fever . . ." She shook her head. "Devesh save us. They'll probably strip naked and bay at the moon."

Jessira laughed when she heard Sign's description of her and Rukh. "Bay at the moon?" she asked.

Sign grinned back at her and howled an example of what she meant.

"You're one to talk," Jessira said with an arch of her eyebrows. "I grew up with you, remember? I know how you made a tradition of swimming naked in Teardrop Lake on the morning of the summer solstice."

Sign wore an air of long-suffering patience. "Yes, but I didn't *bay* at the moon. And I didn't stare lovingly into the eyes of my lover and make everyone around me uncomfortable."

"Husband," Jessira corrected even as she considered Sign's words. She glanced at Bree, who appeared to be trying her best to hide a smile."Rukh and I aren't really like that, are we?" she asked.

Bree held a wide-eyed look of innocence on her face. "Not at all," she answered with a slow shake of her head. "You and Rukh are paragons of quiet reflection when it comes to demonstrating your affection." Her overly slow and deliberate tone left no doubt that she meant the exact opposite of what she was saying.

Jessira frowned. "Do we really make others uncomfortable when we're together?" she asked, repeating her question. "I thought Jaresh was just teasing." She looked them in the eyes. "And I want the truth this time."

Bree hesitated. "It's not so much that we're uncomfortable, but . . . sometimes it feels like everyone else might as well not be there when the two of you are with one another."

"I had no idea," Jessira said. She and Rukh had survived many troubles together, but it didn't excuse the behavior Sign and Bree were describing. It gave Jessira an uncomfortable remembrance of newlyweds she knew, couples who acted like their love was so special that the very sunlight was merely a reflection of their perfect union. It was horribly treacly, and Jessira had always mocked those who behaved in such an absurd fashion.

To find out that she and Rukh were exhibiting those same foolish traits . . . Jessira dropped her head in embarrassment, hoping to hide her blush of humiliation.

"It's not as bad as that," Bree consoled as she laid a hand on Jessira's arm.

"Thank the First Mother for small favors," Jessira muttered.

"The two of you are just unusually close," Bree added.

"You mean more than two people in love?" Jessira asked, forcing droll amusement into her voice, although in her heart she was still mortified.

Bree gave Jessira a squeeze of sympathy. "You and Rukh don't have any reason to be embarrassed. We really were just teasing." She smiled. "A little anyway."

"Or a lot," Sign added with a grin meant to take the sting out of her words. "At least you're not like some of those couples who act like everyone should stand back and admire their love."

Sign's words did little to sooth Jessira's embarrassment. She'd been thinking the exact same thing only moments earlier. Nevertheless, she managed a half-hearted smile.

"I really was joking," Sign said, the teasing grin fading from her face. Now it was she who appeared abashed. "Don't read too much into what I said. You know how I like to tease. Please don't be upset."

Jessira's smile grew less faint.

"Better," Sign said.

"When did you become the one who offers others encouragement?" Jessira asked, her embarrassment fading as amusement took its place.

"It took some time and the patience of a loving cousin," Sign said, offering a surprisingly sweet sentiment. A moment later, her cousin turned away and threw her arms wide. "Just look at those fields," Sign exclaimed, sounding joyful as she changed the subject and gestured all around them. "Compared to them, the Croft was a barren wasteland. Look at how *green* the crops are. I doubt this color even existed back home."

Jessira found herself laughing at Sign's excitement. It was good to see her cousin so enlivened and happy. In the weeks since Sign had gone out with them to see *Down the Street*, more and more often, the carefree woman, the one who had once lived her life with joyous abandon, seemed to be resurfacing. Sign was finally emerging from her angry shell, engaging with the world once again. And while there were crow's feet at the corner of her eyes that hadn't been there last summer, at least the haunted quality Jessira had grown used to seeing on her cousin's face was no longer present so frequently. That sense of heartache might never fully resolve, but at least for now, Sign's smiles were genuine.

"I just can't get over how beautiful this place is," Sign continued.

Jessira smiled wryly. "I hate to say 'I told you so,'" she said, "but I told you so. I'm pretty sure I described Ashoka's beauty on more than one occasion, and you doubted me every time."

Sign shrugged. "I'll admit it. I should have believed you. Ashoka is just as beautiful as you said it was, more beautiful than I ever imagined," she said. "But remember, at the time, you were also going on and on about how Kummas were these otherworldly warriors, but the only ones I knew were Rukh and Farn. One of them couldn't hold a sword, and the other one couldn't walk a straight line without falling over. Given that, I think I can be forgiven for holding some reservations." She sniffed. "Besides, with your taste in men, who can tell what that might mean for your judgment of an entire city."

"And what exactly do you think is wrong with my brother?" Bree asked in a stark tone devoid of any humor.

Sign glanced at her, her smile slithering away. "Er. Nothing. I was just . . ."

"Yes. What *is* wrong with Rukh?" Jessira asked.

Sign looked between the two women, a look of concern on her face.

Bree couldn't hold onto her irritated expression, and she broke into laughter. "You should see your face."

Jessira chuckled with her. "It's so red. Like a—"

"Don't say it," Sign warned.

Jessira disregarded the warning. "—baboon's butt," she finished.

Bree burst out into further laughter while Sign growled a curse. "I hate that joke," she muttered. A look of irritation stole across her face at Bree's ongoing humor. "I've been teased, and so has Jessira," Sign said to Bree. "Just wait until *you're* the object of our mockery."

"Oh no!" Jessira exclaimed, wanting no part of Sign's plan, whatever it might be. "Leave me out of it. She's my sister-in-law. There's no chance I'm helping you make fun of Bree."

"Jessira!" Sign protested.

"We'll have to deal with any planned mockery of me later," Bree said as she pointed to a small lane branching off their gravel road. "We're here."

Sign pulled her attention back to the road and saw the turnoff

Bree indicated. The lane was lined with azaleas blooming in a riot of colors, and the drive took a gradual bend, continuing on toward a large, red barn with cedar shingles. Far out in the distance, workers were busy tilling the land and working the fields.

Sign paused to take in the scene. In Stronghold, where farming was such a challenge given the hard, stony soil of the Privation Mountains high country, the Croft had been regarded with an almost religious reverence. Life began at the fields. Without them, there was no food and without nourishment, there was no life. The farmer was the center of a city.

Bree didn't allow Sign to linger over the lovely, poignant scene as she quickly led them along a brick footpath that branched off the small drive. It curled to the left and deposited them in front of an expansive two-story building, one of Ashoka's famed farmhouses.

A large wraparound porch seemed to beckon weary travelers and farmers to set aside their burdens and rest in one of the green rocking chairs and sip a cool drink on a warm summer evening. Clapboard siding painted a bright sunshine yellow and a roof shingled with cedar shakes continued the sense of welcome as did a set of chimes gently jingling in the breeze.

It was like nothing Sign had ever seen. "It's perfect," she whispered.

"Yes it is," Jessira agreed, her voice also hushed in reverence.

"Come on," Bree said, leading them up the porch steps.

At the top, Sign stumbled to a halt. From inside the home came the most lovely voice she had ever heard. It was raised in song, a paean to moonlight and love. "What *is* that?" Sign asked in a hushed whisper.

"Trellis Weathervine," Bree answered. "She's a student at the Larina."

Sign glanced at her in bewilderment. "What is the Larina?" she asked.

"A school devoted to the art of singing," Bree told her.

Sign shot her a look of incredulity. "You're saying there is a school in Ashoka where all they do is sing?" she asked in disbelief. "Who pays for it?"

"First, they don't just sing. They *learn* to sing. There's a large difference. And second, the school is funded by donations from those who can afford it," Bree said. "People with wealth are expected to support the arts, to voluntarily serve the city in whatever capacity they can. And anyone who hoards their money and does nothing except collect more of it are held in contempt." Bree gave a satisfied nod. "Luckily, not too many do something so selfish."

Sign understood what Bree was telling her. It made sense, but it also didn't make sense. For instance, why should those who accrued wealth be held in contempt if they didn't give it away to the shiftless? Let those without earn their own.

Also, while Trellis Weathervine's voice was certainly beguiling, ultimately what was the point? She could only sing if someone paid her. To Sign's way of thinking, it was a ridiculous notion. The young woman could be doing something far more useful and important with her life, something more productive. Singing didn't build a house or repair the stonework or plow the fields or do the thousand other labors that a city needed in order to prosper. For Ashokans to pay for someone to layabout and do nothing but sing seemed a colossal waste of resources.

"The woman's voice is certainly lovely, but it seems . . . unnecessary. Is there nothing else she can do with her time?" Sign asked, struggling to phrase the question as politely as she could.

"You didn't feel that way on the night we saw the play," Jessira reminded her. "Admit it. It touched you. It made you want to smile and cry at the same time, made you glad to have seen it."

Sign opened her mouth to argue but almost immediately closed it with a click when she realized that Jessira was right. The play *had* touched her. It *had* been wondrous, heart-wrenching, and tragically beautiful at the same time.

With an almost palpable shake, her thoughts twisted into a new way of thinking and questions stirred in her mind. Could it be that the labor of the actors and those who had worked on the production hadn't been in vain? That their creation had been a worthy use of their time and effort? That for Ashoka to afford for its people to do nothing more than perform plays, music, or song was actually *how* the city prospered?

Sign realized that her practical nature would just have to get used to people doing work that had never occurred to anyone back in Stronghold. Singing or storytelling as a profession amongst the OutCastes? Sign mentally scoffed.

Although . . .

Sign furrowed her brows in consideration.

When had any OutCaste actually tried to do such a thing as sing or act as a profession? And just as importantly, what if they had? Maybe such a venture would have been more successful than Sign initially imagined. Maybe there would have been more people in Stronghold than she realized who would have enjoyed seeing such performances—people willing to pay to see the kind of theater performed in Ashoka, or give money to those who could sing like Trellis Weathervine, or offer up coin to hear the wonderful Sentya musicians at the Ahura Temple. After all, look at how much Jessira loved theater and music, or even Sign, herself, for that matter.

"I suppose it's just hard to understand how different our culture is from theirs," Sign reflected after a moment.

"Like I told you before: Ashokans are devoted to beauty in all its forms," Jessira added.

"And like *I* told both of you, you need to get used to being Ashokans," Bree said with a smile. "There will come a time when the OutCastes will be expected to incorporate beauty into *their* creations."

"You keep emphasizing that point," Sign said. "That the OutCastes are now Ashokans. Why is that so important to you?"

"Because it's true, and the only way you'll stop feeling like intruders and make this city your home is if you believe it *is* your home, that you're just as much a part of it as any Pureblood."

"A lot of your people don't believe that," Sign said to Bree. "A lot of them will never believe that."

"And they aren't the ones you need to convince," Bree said. "With time, they'll simply pass on and their old ways with them. The fact that the Magisterium worked so hard to make sure that the OutCastes could stay in Ashoka should tell you something about where popular sentiment lies. You can make Ashoka your home if you push hard enough to demand that you belong here. Hold your heads high. Don't ask for a place at the table. Act like one is already set for you. Most of us would be happy to scoot over and give you a seat."

Jessira chuckled. "I appreciate the sentiment, but what a bunch of mixed metaphors."

"Shut it."

Sign, though, was touched by Bree's words. They had an element of fiery truth to them, the kind that could remake a world. Why *couldn't* her people make a home here? Was that not what many Ashokans had already volunteered? Now, it was up to Sign's people to take that generous offer and make for themselves a life worthy of the Purebloods' altruism. She blinked her eyes at the thought, working to keep the tears from spilling, hoping the other women wouldn't notice.

However, eagle-eyed Jessira did. "What is it?" she asked.

"Dust in my eye," Sign answered.

Bree took Sign's hand and forced her to face her. "In Caste Kumma, as cousins raised in the same house, you and Jessira would be sisters. And once Rukh married Jessira, she became my sister."

Sign looked at her quizzically. "Why are you telling me this?"

"Because as Jessira's sister, you're close family to me as well. In my Caste, you're almost a sister."

Sign smiled, touched once again by Bree's words. "You're saying I have another family if I want one?" she asked.

Bree grinned. "We aren't really all that bad once you get to know us," she said.

"Even Jaresh?" Sign asked.

"*Especially* Jaresh," Jessira said. "He's the most levelheaded one of the entire bunch."

"And there's also Farn and his family and a whole lot of cousins you haven't met," Bree added. "We love Jessira, and we want to love you if you'll give us a chance to get to know you." Bree gave Sign one final squeeze of empathy before swiftly straightening up. An expression of no-nonsense seriousness replaced her look of sympathy "Now, get yourself together," she ordered. "We're about to meet Mistress Shull, and she doesn't like crybabies."

Jessira tried to firm up her features and hoped Sign would be able to do the same. She glanced at her cousin, who was quickly swiping at her eyes and cheeks until they were both dry. Sign gave Jessira a quick nod that she was ready just as the door opened.

The woman who greeted them was a Muran. Like everyone in

that Caste, she had emerald-green eyes like Jessira's and golden-brown skin like Sign. Her once dark hair was now gray and pleated into a braid that hung to the middle of her back. Jessira would have guessed the woman was in her sixties, but she still stood upright and proud, wearing a conservative, dark dress that reached all the way to the floor. She was tall enough to nearly look them in the eyes, and her seamed face was reflective of a life spent outdoors. She studied the three of them with curiosity, her gaze lingering longest on Jessira and Sign. Awareness of what they were stole across her face, and her features grew less welcoming, even wary. "Bree Shektan," the woman said by way of welcome.

"Mistress Shull," Bree replied. "Let me introduce my vadina, Jessira Shektan"—Jessira tilted her head in acknowledgement—"and her cousin-sister, Sign Grey."

Mistress Shull took in their appearance, and if possible, drew herself up even straighter. Her eyes were flinty, and Jessira felt a sinking sensation in her stomach. "How can I help you?" Mistress Shull asked, making no move to allow them entrance into her home.

"We have a business proposition," Bree said, wearing an open, confident smile. "May we come in?"

"No," Mistress Shull said. "It wouldn't be appropriate."

Sign bristled, and Jessira, so often the hothead, found herself in the odd position of calming someone else down. She took her cousin's hand and gave her a slight warning shake of her head.

"Why wouldn't it be appropriate?" Sign asked, her voice level and even.

Mistress Shull turned to her. "You know why," she answered. "The Magisterium might have allowed your kind sanctuary, and you"—she stabbed a finger at Bree—"may have convinced them to do so and even brought *The Word and the Deed* into question, but we

120

still cling to the old ways." She lifted her head proudly.

Though Jessira wanted to smack the smugness from the woman's face, she couldn't afford to submit to her whims. They needed Mistress Shull's help. Instead, she did her best to keep her features calm and relaxed. Sign, on the other hand, had no qualms about letting Mistress Shull see her anger. Her cousin glared at the Muran woman, disregarding Jessira's look of warning.

Meanwhile, Bree's smile slipped away, and she pursed her lips as though in thought. "I see," she said. "I certainly don't hold your faith against you, but when earlier I spoke to you, I made you aware of what I wanted, and yet, this is how you respond? I find it ungracious." Bree wore a stony expression. "Obviously, you must do what you think is right, but so, too, must House Shektan, and those Houses allied with us."

Mistress Shull blanched. "Wait," she said, stepping outside and shutting the door. "I can't let you in." She shrugged in apology. "My amma would likely have an aneurysm if she saw a ghrina in her home." Her face tightened upon seeing Jessira and Sign's flat-eyed glares of anger. "I know you hate the word, but my amma is too old to change. It is what she will always think of you."

The front door opened. "What's going on?" an elderly Muran woman demanded, standing in the doorway. She was hunched over from a dowager's hump that bent her until her head and neck were permanently parallel with the ground.

Mistress Shull stiffened and spun around. "Nothing you need to worry about, Amma," she said, her words hurried. "Just some informal business with House Shektan." Jessira noticed that Mistress Shull had positioned herself so she blocked her amma's view of both Sign and herself. "You remember Bree Shektan?"

"Of course I do," the old woman said, sounding irascible.

"It is good to see you again, Mistress Terras," Bree said.

"You've grown into that sword," the old woman noted before hobbling forward. "Why do those women standing behind you look so strange?" Mistress Terras asked. "They look like a mix . . ." She startled. "What are their kind doing here?" she asked.

Jessira was surprised. Rather than furious, Mistress Terras sounded curious.

"We were discussing a proposal with your daughter," Bree said. She sidestepped Mistress Shull. "This is my vadina, Jessira Shektan, and her cousin-sister, Sign Grey."

Jessira took a risk and offered her hand to the old woman, hoping Mistress Terras would shake it. "It's a pleasure to meet you."

"Mistress Terras," the old woman said, gathering Jessira's hand in her palsied one and giving it a brief shake. "Are you the one married to Rukh Shektan?"

"I am," Jessira replied.

"They say you left your home to be with him, helped him retrieve *The Book of First Movement.*"

"I did," Jessira answered.

Mistress Terras broke into a broad grin. "Then you must come back and tell us all about it one day," she exclaimed. She leaned in and spoke in a conspiratorial whisper. "Did you really befriend a Bael, a Tigon, and a Shylow?"

Jessira nodded.

Mistress Terras cackled. "How wonderful. I never thought I'd live to see the day."

The door opened again. A more youthful version of Mistress Shull stood in the entrance. She was either a younger sister or a daughter.

"Lace," Mistress Shull called out. "Please come and help your ammamma into the house. It's almost time for lunch."

Lace took in the scene before her with remarkable aplomb. "Of course," she said. She took Mistress Terras' hands in her own and drew the old woman inside. "Why don't you help me with the food, Ammamma," she suggested.

Mistress Terras allowed herself to be guided inside. "Did you see the two ghrinas, Shull?" she asked Lace, mistaking her for the older woman. She cackled again. "One of them said she was friends with a Bael. Liars. What's your name again, girl?" The door shut behind her.

Despite Mistress Terras' unpleasant words, Jessira felt a surge of sympathy for the old woman. Her mind was obviously not right. Her thoughts clearly clouded by old age. A tragedy.

"How long has she been like this?" Bree asked, her voice laced with sympathy.

Mistress Shull swallowed heavily. "It started a few years ago, but we always explained away her forgetfulness as being due to age. But over the past six months, it's slowly become worse."

"I'm so sorry," Bree said. "One of Nanna's closest friends, Garnet Bosde, suffers a similar affliction. I know how painful it can be." She dipped her head in apology. "Nevertheless, we have important matters to consider. Will you discuss them with us now?"

Jessira felt a stab of loss at the reminder of Garnet. The old man had always been kind to her, treating her like a granddaughter . But time, that undefeatable enemy, had stolen Garnet's mind and memories. She had visited him once after her return to Ashoka, but he had no recollection of her. He'd quickly grown afraid and upset at seeing her, and she'd been forced to beat a hasty retreat. She hadn't gone back since.

Jessira mentally sighed and turned her attention back to the Muran woman standing before them.

Shull had her dress still clutched in her hands, and she took a deep, shuddering breath. "No. You can stay," she answered in a voice that slowly grew stronger. "But now you see why I didn't want you to come in."

"And do you really think so poorly of us?" Sign asked. She had moved to stand next to Jessira.

Mistress Shull proudly met Sign's gaze before seeming to suddenly deflate. "I do not know," she said with a heavy exhalation. "Sometimes I'm convinced you are an affront to all that is holy, to Devesh's very sight; that the likes of you and your sister are only here in blessed Ashoka because of her"—she pointed at Bree—"blasphemy." She sighed. "And other times, I wish I could be like my daughter and see you as simply being a different kind of people."

"We aren't the ones capable of discussing theology with you," Bree said, "but we are the ones who came here with a business proposal. You can hear us out if you wish."

"And if I say no?" Mistress Shull asked.

Bree gave her a sympathetic smile. "You have to look after your family, and I have to look after mine," she answered. "We would go to Clan Sunhewn."

"Well that won't do," Mistress Shull muttered darkly. She appeared to gather herself up and stood straight once again. "I'll hear you and your friends out," she said.

"Relatives," Bree corrected. "My vadina and her cousin-sister."

Mistress Shull nodded acceptance. "Sit down and let's hear this proposal of yours." She led them to a set of chairs around a low, glass-topped table. All four women took a seat. "So what is your plan?" Mistress Shull asked.

"The OutCastes are farmers, and they would like to sharecrop some of Clan Weathervine's fallow fields," Bree said. "It would profit both of you."

Mistress Shull was shaking her head before Bree had even finished speaking. "You know I can't allow that. No Clan can," she said. "Though what you said to the Magisterium about *The Word and the Deed* caused many to wonder about our beliefs, most of my Caste and Clan remain devoted to what we've always been taught. We would never allow an OutCaste to work alongside our own."

"What if the OutCastes farmed your land but never worked alongside members of Clan Weathervine?" Bree suggested.

Mistress Shull frowned. "I don't see how that's possible," she said. "When would they work? At night when the rest of us have retired from the fields?"

"No," Bree replied. "There is land your Clan has rights to but has never worked. Mount Crone."

"Mount Crone?" Shull's eyes widened in understanding, but again, she shook her head. "That land is too rocky to be properly farmed."

"Not for them. Stronghold was in the Privation Mountains, and so were their farms," Bree explained. "They're used to working land that's stony."

Mistress Shull glanced in Jessira's direction, her face full of skepticism. "Murans are born farmers. It's what we do. You're saying you can work land and cause it to bloom in places we cannot?" she asked in disbelief.

"Not at all," Jessira answered, keeping her voice even and nonconfrontational, which was a challenge for her even in the best of times. "We're not better farmers than Murans, but necessity taught us what you never had to learn. When Stronghold was founded, the surrounding land was far from ideal, but it was all we had to work with. Our choice was to either make the rocky soil bloom or starve." She gestured around them. "For you, it's different. You have these lush lands." She smiled as she gazed about the glorious fields. "Your fields are so bounteous that even a Kumma might bring it to life."

Mistress Shull chuckled. "Let's not get carried away," she said, "but I see your point." She fell silent as she tapped her chin in consideration. "You really think your people can do this?"

"Absolutely," Sign answered.

"And Clan Weathervine will share in the profits?" Shull asked.

Bree nodded. "Which is where I come in. I've been authorized to negotiate on behalf of the OutCastes."

Mistress Shull turned to her. "Then let us begin. But remember: we bargain hard."

Bree smiled, predatory and anticipating. "I wouldn't have it any other way."

CHAPTER FIVE
WHAT HAS PASSED

Before the patient man's hardened heart, even the finest of warriors must quail.

—*The Warrior and the Servant (author unknown)*

The training grounds of the House of Fire and Mirrors were a broad quadrangle of trampled fields that resisted the finest efforts of the Muran groundskeepers to keep them green and vibrant. The memory of generations of warriors had been beaten into the hard-packed dirt, and for some, the continually torn grass was the House's truest sigil. North of the grounds loomed the bulk of the main building of the House of Fire and Mirrors, while to the south rested an array of barracks and barns. East and west, a hedge of ligustrum softened a tall, brick wall upon which were mounted regularly spaced firefly lamps.

With the early spring weather, the scent of cut grass, azalea, and dew mingled in the air while the ground reverberated with the shouts of Martial Masters barking out instructions and critiques to their senior cadets. From a distance, the din and movement of the two hundred or so young men pushed through another round of drills might have seemed purposeless and without pattern, but such was not the case. To the discerning eye, it quickly became clear that the movements of the warriors *did* have purpose. They *did* have a pattern. Their sliding motions were supple, smooth, and focused, informed by years of training and discipline. Today, though, those same fluid movements seemed somewhat forced and frenetic, even frayed. Technique appeared traded for speed, and a few students found themselves slipping head over heels on the slick grass. They cursed loudly before rising to their feet and resuming their matches.

This was the final months-long push for the Trims—the senior cadets—of the House of Fire and Mirrors. This was the training meant to hone them to Ashokan sharpness, to the keen edge needed—not just for their upcoming Trials—but also for something else. It was something seemingly trivial, and yet it was also something the Trims feared to fail. A few months from now would come Hellfire Week. It was held every spring and was the annual competitions and exhibitions in which all the military academies took part.

Hellfire Week began with the Wrath, the competition pitting the finest seniors of the House of Fire and Mirrors against those from their brother Kumma academy, the Fort and the Sword. No one wanted to lose, and it went without saying that the Wrath was bitterly contested. Whoever won the contest would invariably lord their victory over the defeated academy for the entirety of the following year, and for many in Caste Kumma, it was one of the most important competitions of the year.

However, for the rest of the city, the more anticipated contest was what followed after: the Advent Trial. Other than the Tournament of Hume, there was no other event in Ashoka that was more eagerly anticipated. All the Trims from the four military academies: the House of Fire and Mirrors, the Fort and the Sword, the Sarath, and the Shir'Fen—the latter two were the schools in which Rahails and Murans trained as warriors—would take part.

In some ways, the Advent Trial was even more popular than the Tournament of Hume. Since Kummas were utterly dominant in matters of the sword, most martial competitions never had any other entrants other than those from the warrior Caste. Such wasn't the case with the Advent Trial. This wider involvement of other Castes was a large reason for its popularity.

In addition, since the goal of the competition was simple and obvious, it was easy to follow. Two armies, each containing a mix of cadets and commanders from the four military academies, would battle against one another. Their straightforward goal: capture the opposing team's flag and bring it back safely to their own 'Oasis'.

The competition always took place just outside the borders of Ashoka's Outer Wall, and as a result, there were plenty of vantage points by which to view it. But given the contest's popularity, the best places to watch the tournament had already long since been reserved, and a few months from now, the Outer Wall would be thronged with Ashokans cheering on whichever of the two armies caught their fancy.

But first would come the Wrath—and the Prank.

Rukh smiled as he remembered his own participation in the Prank several years ago. In the few short years since, it had already achieved the status of legend. What a fine joke he, Keemo, Farn, and Jaresh had managed to carry out. Keemo had been the instigator and planner while the other three had merely added on some final flourishes to make the Prank come off without a hitch.

His smile became wistful as he remembered the beloved friend he had lost, a man who had been akin to a brother. In a more just world, Keemo should still be with those who loved him. He should be walking the streets of Ashoka, wearing his easy smile and offering his infectious laughter. He should be living out the life he so obviously found so vivacious. In his presence, even Farn hadn't been able to remain dour for long.

Rukh shook his head in sorrow before returning his attention to the here and now. After his return to Ashoka, it had been decided that he had survived six Trials: the failed journey to Nestle, the journey to and from the Chimera caverns, the trip to Hammer and back where he and Jessira had retrieved *The Book of First Movement*, and finally, the return to Ashoka from Stronghold. Therefore, according to the judgment of the Chamber of Lords, Rukh had fulfilled his obligations to his Caste and would never again have to leave Ashoka if he so chose—which he wouldn't. He was a married man after all.

The one obstacle he had yet to overcome, though, was what to do with the rest of his life, and how he would be able to afford it. He had no money. Kummas were given shares in the caravans in which they participated, and through this investment, those with three Trials to their names were generally quite wealthy by that point. However, Rukh was the exception that tested the rule. The Trial to Nestle had ended in disaster with all the men and material destroyed. The expedition to the Chimera caverns had not been for monetary gain, and the journey to Hammer had resulted in the recovery of *The Book of First Movement*, but had yielded nothing in the way of saleable items. And, of course, the return to Ashoka from Stronghold had been due to genocide.

All this meant that Rukh had needed to find a means to earn a living. As a result, he'd applied to become a Martial Master at his alma mater, the House of Fire and Mirrors. He was grateful to Master

Sinngin, the Dean of the academy, for hiring him on, but it was still a challenge finding a balance in his work situation. He was expected to offer instruction and reprimand warriors who he had first known as fellow cadets, and it wasn't easy to make the transition to judging Master.

Farn, however, seemed to have little trouble making just that transition. Farn, like Rukh, had also been deemed to have survived enough Trials to remain in Ashoka with his honor intact. In his case, it was four Trials—to Nestle, the return from Stronghold, and the Trial to and from the OutCaste city. And also like Rukh, he had no wealth to his name, which meant he, too, was an instructor at the House of Fire and Mirrors.

Right now, Farn was working nearby with his own group of seniors, and his voice rose when he saw one of them make a first year error.

Rukh smiled when he saw the chagrined student redden with embarrassment. At least the Trim wouldn't be making that same mistake again.

Rukh turned his attention back to the seniors he'd been tasked to oversee. There were six of them, and he'd split them into two teams of three: the Reds and the Golds. He thought them well-matched, which meant that victory would be achieved by whoever was best able to maintain unit discipline and cohesion since Annexes weren't allowed.

Rukh reckoned he'd given each team enough time to map out their tactics. "Begin!" he shouted.

Immediately, the two teams closed with one another. Rukh measured the placement of each team's warriors. He frowned. Unless there was an unexpected accident, the Reds would lose badly.

Before he'd even finished the thought, a member of the Reds

was down. The teams fought with shokes and the cadet fell to the ground, grunting in pain. He'd taken a figurative disemboweling thrust. With his demise, another of the Reds also fell, and seconds later, it was over. The Golds were the victors, and they stood proudly as they surveyed their handiwork.

Rukh went to the first member of Red Team who had fallen, Lince Chopil, their nominal lieutenant.

The Trim had his jaw clenched in pain, and his hands clutched over his abdomen. He had to be hurting, and while Rukh could have called over one of the Shiyen physicians to Heal the cadet, there was no need. He drew *Jivatma* from his Well and stretched it out as thin as a silken thread before placing his hands on the Trim's abdomen. He let his *Jivatma* empty down into Cadet Chopil, Healing him and removing the senior's pain.

Soon enough, the Trim was breathing easily, and Rukh turned to the other members of the Red Team. He Healed them as well until all of them were moving about without evidence of discomfort. None of them mentioned Rukh's non-Kumma Talents or looked askance or fearful while he had Healed them.

It hadn't always been the case. The first time the members of the House of Fire and Mirrors had witnessed Rukh Healing, an uneasy hush had fallen upon them. The silence had included both his fellow Martial Masters and the cadets who had been involved. All of them had heard the stories about Rukh's non-Kumma Talents, but hearing wasn't the same as experiencing. Thankfully, their discomfiture had faded over time, and now, it was gone entirely. Any who required Rukh's help simply accepted it without comment or concern.

"Why did your unit perform so poorly?" Rukh asked Cadet Chopil.

The Trim stood at attention. "It was my fault, sir! I shouldn't have engaged with Cadet Prind," he replied.

"At ease," Rukh ordered. "Why should you not have engaged Cadet Prind?"

"I underestimated him, sir!" Chopil shouted.

Rukh's lips thinned. It wasn't the answer he had been looking for. He stepped closer to the Trim. "Who took your life?"

"Sir?"

"Are you deaf?" Rukh barked. "I asked who took your life."

Chopil licked his lips. "I believe it was Cadet Dristh."

"So it wasn't Prind?"

Farn arrived just then, and he added his glare to the situation.

Chopil glanced askance at Rukh's cousin and stiffened his spine. "No, sir," he replied.

"Then why do you think your mistake was in engaging Prind?"

Chopil licked his lips again. "I'm not sure what my mistake was."

"Pathetic," Farn said. "Victory is taken by those who deserve it, but even in loss, a wise warrior should be able to understand *why* he was defeated."

Impossibly, Chopil stiffened even further, his face turning red with anger or embarrassment.

"You have something to say?" Farn demanded.

Rukh held his tongue, waiting to hear how the Trim would answer.

Chopil hesitated. "Would the Martial Master be willing to instruct me?"

Rukh smiled. "Of course. You lost because you set your strongest against Gold Team's supposed weakest. In essence, you engaged in one-on-one combat while the Golds fought as a team. Cadet Beol recognized your mistake and exploited it. Your supposed strongest was held up by Gold's weakest just long enough for the other Golds to support him and 'kill' you. After that, with their three to your two, the Reds were doomed."

Chopil frowned. "But in the accounts of your battles in the Chimera caverns and Stronghold, it's how you fought. You stood alone and unbending with your skill and faithful blade against the rage of a horde."

Rukh scowled. Was that truly the lesson the cadets of his martial academy had taken from his battles? And what was it with the manner in which Chopil had just spoken? It sounded like the Trim had recited some bad drama he'd read. It was absolute stupidity.

"If I could have fought with my brothers against the Chimeras, I would have," Rukh growled. "And Stronghold was a massacre. Without the Kesarins, we would have all died. I never fought alone there."

"But, sir, we've watched you train. You defeated two Martial Masters by yourself." Chopil's voice sounded eager, young, and full of awe.

Rukh wanted to shake the Trim loose of his foolishness. How could a senior cadet at the House of Fire and Mirrors be so wrongheaded? Just a few years ago, Rukh had been just another student to these Trims, but all too often, it sounded like some of them harbored some sort of hero worship toward him. It defied reason.

"I was only able to defeat two Martial Masters because I can Blend," Rukh reminded the rest of the Trims, all of whom appeared to be listening intently. "Once they accounted for my Talent, they were able to defeat me."

"But you're still victorious once every third time—"

"Once every third means I'm dead two out of three," Rukh snapped, having heard enough. "Ten laps. Get it done!"

Cadet Chopil rammed back to rigid attention. "Yes, sir!"

Members of Gold Team snickered as the Reds trotted out behind Chopil.

Rukh's attention surged to them. "And you've earned the privilege of joining them," he barked. "Move it!"

Groans met his command, but Gold Team was soon trailing after the Reds.

"I've never seen you get so angry at Trims like that," Farn noted.

"Never had a reason to," Rukh replied.

Jaresh arrived just then and whistled at the swiftly retreating Red and Gold Teams. "What happened to them?" he asked, walking up to join Rukh and their cousin.

"Your brother lost his temper," Farn said in his inimitable, laconic style.

Jaresh did a double take. "Really? Everyone keeps going on and on about his patience, like he's some sort of latter-day Maha Sidtha."

"Don't you have some accounts to receive?" Rukh asked, annoyed by his brother's overly chipper manner.

"Those would be accounts payable, and they've already been paid," Jaresh corrected in a pedantic tone. "So what did the Trims do?"

"They're just filled with all sorts of idiotic ideas," Rukh answered. "Speaking of. What brings you out here?"

Jaresh smirked. "Droll," he said. "Durmer just finished running me and Bree through our paces when Nanna told me to bring you home."

Rukh nodded, understanding what Jaresh meant about Durmer. Ever since the Kesarins—Aia, Shon, and Thrum—had given Jaresh the Talents of a Kumma, he had been training hard under the Great Duriah's tutelage to master his new abilities. Joining him in his practice was Bree.

The last time Rukh had watched them spar, he'd been surprised by how far their sister had come. There were times when she was able to hold her own against Jaresh. Of course her ability to stand against their brother wasn't because of perfect form or technique on her part—in fact, she was relatively raw in the use of a sword—but because she was just that much faster. Just like Rukh couldn't Blend as well as a Muran or a Rahail or Heal like a Shiyen, Jaresh, though he was now much swifter and stronger than most people, still didn't have the speed, endurance, and strength of a Kumma. Most of the time, his excellent technique and form were enough to overcome Bree's advantages, but not always. Her quickness was an undeniable advantage.

"Did Nanna say what he wanted?" Rukh asked.

Jaresh shook his head. "No. But I imagine it has to do with finding the final MalDin."

Rukh grunted in disgust. After Ular Sathin had killed himself, his position as a MalDin of the Sil Lor Kum had come to light. It was still hard to believe. Ular had been both a highly respected Muran—a member of the Society of Rajan, no less—but also the worst kind of scum. How had he managed it? How could any man, evil or otherwise, have so proficiently and consistently betrayed everyone who loved and knew him? Rukh couldn't imagine the self-deception and discipline required to have lived Ular's life of lies.

Regardless, after the man's death, his journal—the one describing his role as a MalDin—had come into Nanna's possession. It had been anonymously mailed to him, and after the code in which it had been written had been deciphered, the Sil Lor Kum had been eradicated. All except for the MalDin representing Caste Duriah, and maybe a few lower-ranking members of the so-called 'Hidden Hand of Justice'.

"What does Nanna want me to do?" Rukh asked.

"He wasn't the one who actually asked for you," Jaresh said. "Bree asked him to ask you—"

"I thought she had her hands full helping out the OutCastes?" Farn interrupted.

"After the contract Bree was able to hammer out on their behalf with Clan Weathervine, they don't really need her assistance any more," Jaresh explained. "Nanna wants her to help the City Watch find the final MalDin and the rest of the Sil Lor Kum." He turned to Rukh. "And Bree wants *your* help."

"Why? What does she think I can do that she can't?"

"Nothing," Jaresh replied. "It's more about Rector Bryce. Nanna asked for his help in finding the rest of the Sil Lor Kum, and when Bree found out who she would have to work with, she said the only person who could keep her from hurting Rector was you."

Rukh snorted. "So she expects me to protect Rector from her?"

Jaresh grinned, clearly enjoying himself. "She says that while others could stop her from hurting Rector, she thinks you're the only one with the skill to do so without killing her in the process." He laughed. "She must really hate him."

Farn chuckled. "She still hasn't forgiven him?"

"I guess not," Rukh said.

"But you have?" Farn asked.

Rukh shrugged. "He was a large part of the reason why I was exiled from Ashoka, but I also remember what he did for Jessira at the Magisterium. After the Magisterium, it wasn't too hard to forgive him."

Farn shook his head. "Not for me. I'd still want to smash his face into the pavement."

Rukh smiled, thinking of something Jessira had once told him.

'You aren't a man made to hate,' she had said.

"I thought you were the one who thought first and fought second," Jaresh said to Farn.

"I guess your stupidity is rubbing off on me," their cousin replied.

"If it's my stupidity rubbing off on you, then you're still gaining in intelligence," Jaresh countered.

"So you're saying that even at your stupidest, you're smarter than me?" Farn said with a scoffing snort. "You must have bathed in an open sewer because I smell bilge water."

"Well you'd know that fragrance better than anyone," Jaresh said before turning to Rukh. "And just what exactly are you smiling about?"

Rukh coughed into his hand, not wanting to admit the truth. It would only set the other two men laughing. To hear them talk, they seemed to think that Rukh believed that the sun rose and set based on Jessira's presence. "I was just thinking how it's nice to be home and hear the two of you bicker," Rukh lied. "I missed it when I was in Stronghold."

"You had a look on your face just then," Jaresh noted, sounding skeptical. His eyes narrowed.

Rukh mentally groaned. "What look?" he asked, trying to keep his features placid and curious rather than guilty.

Jaresh's eyes widened. "You were thinking about Jessira!" He burst into laughter.

"No I wasn't!" Rukh exclaimed.

"Yes, you were," Farn said, joining in Jaresh's laughter.

Rukh sighed. "Why don't we get back on topic?" he suggested.

"You mean you don't want to tell us about the wonderful qualities your wife possesses?" Farn asked with a straitlaced, innocent expression.

"Or maybe we can talk about Laya?" Rukh said, giving his cousin a challenging stare.

Now it was Farn's turn to smother a cough. "So why can't Bree forgive Rector?" he asked in an obvious attempt to change the subject.

Jaresh took a moment to glance between the two men and mutter something about OutCaste women under his breath. Rukh couldn't quite make it out. "I'm not sure why Bree still dislikes Rector so much. I mean, Rukh has already forgiven the man, and I would guess Nanna has as well since he's willing to entrust him with this."

Rukh smiled. "Our sister is a complicated woman."

"Hating someone isn't complicated," Jaresh observed.

Rukh shook his head at his brother's lack of insight. "Bree doesn't hate Rector. She hates how she misjudged him, and now, she isn't sure if she's doing so again with her mistrust."

"It's a conundrum," Farn agreed.

A ia was laid out on her back with her hind limbs stretched out behind her and her front ones tucked up so her paws were under her chin. From her current position, in the distance she could see a row of tall homes made of red brick and cold, dead wood. She sniffed at the sight. There was no beauty to the hard-edged straight lines and stiff stones that made up the city of Ashoka. Even the occasional edging of grass and trees dividing the roads wasn't enough to soften this Human hive of rugged rocks, noxious noises, and strong smells.

She turned away from the view and let her gaze linger upon the place where she was to meet her Human, Rukh. They always met here. This was one of the few places in Rukh's home where she truly felt comfortable. The fields between the city's massive walls would have been fine, but for some reason, the Humans who dug up the land there—farmers were what Rukh called them—always seemed to take offense whenever Aia or her brothers decided to show up and roll about on the ground or dig in the dirt. They would yell and shout, running about and gesticulating wildly like fearful ostriches. It was most annoying. Some even flung dirt at them like a monkey hurling feces.

Aia snorted. How typical. Humans did look a little like monkeys, so maybe it was only natural that they would act like them as well.

Of course back home, if a monkey—or any other animal—had dared disrespect her, Aia would have made sure they never repeated the error. She had been tempted to teach an unforgettable lesson to the rude Human monkeys who had thrown dirt at her, but Rukh had told her in no uncertain terms that harming one of his kind was prohibited. Aia snorted at the thought. She wouldn't have actually hurt any of them. She would have only pretended to, just enough to get the pesky Humans to leave her alone.

Aia sighed. Rukh would probably still have been mad at her.

She set aside her annoyance with her Human and returned to studying this place Rukh had found for her. Dryad Park was what he named it. It was so quiet and subdued here, at least in comparison to the riot that was the rest of Ashoka. In some ways, it even reminded Aia of her own home.

Rolling hills of grass and wildflowers cupped blue lakes and ponds full of delectable, fat fish. And while Aia knew just how succulent those scaled beasties were, once again, Rukh insisted on ruining her fun. He wouldn't let her splash about and try her paws at catching the slippery fish. He said she'd only scare them away.

What foolishness. Fish had no minds by which to feel fear. And they were *so* delicious.

Aia frowned, a flattening of her ears, wishing Rukh could see reason. But he had been steadfast in his refusal.

Once again, Aia set aside her annoyance.

Instead, she glanced at a number of old Humans as they moved rocks of various shapes about on strange, flat piece of wood made of colored squares. What were they doing that was so fascinating? There they sat beneath the arms of a small grouping of oak trees, as still and unmoving as Human-shaped boulders. It looked so pointless. Rukh said it was a game called 'chess', but Aia wasn't sure if he was playing a trick on her.

Kesarin games relied on running, hiding, leaping, and rolling, not staring at pieces of rock and moving them fractionally every few minutes.

Stupidity. Not to mention boring.

Aia then turned her sight to a group of large globes of various colors hanging from the branches of the oaks. She smiled. Finally, a Human creation that made sense. She loved the firefly globes. They were so beautiful, hypnotic even, especially when they waved in the breeze and spooled out bright pinpricks of moving light and shadow. It was like something alive then. Shon and Thrum loved to chase those pinpoints, racing after them, all along the ground and even leaping into the trees. Aia, on the other hand, maintained a dignified air while her brothers played their silly games.

But when her brothers weren't around, she, too, would chase the light and shadows. It was so much fun.

Aia settled herself deeper into the warm ground, lost in pleasant memories.

A cloud passed above her, and she wondered why the sky was

blue. Was it like the nearby sea, but instead of washing about on the ground, was it water floating high above the world? It made sense. After all, where else could rain come from?

Aia mentally shuddered. She loved swimming, but for some reason, she hated the rain. It was a miserable experience, and just imagining the water falling on her head was enough to make her whiskers wilt in imagined melancholy.

Sister, why are you sad? Shon asked, coming up to her and touching her nose with his before he licked the side of her face.

Rain.

Shon pulled up short in startlement. *Where?* he asked in consternation.

Aia laughed. She reached up and grasped her brother's head in her paws. She kept her claws sheathed as she pulled him down until he flopped next to her. He lay beside her, and she groomed the top of his head.

The affection Aia felt for her youngest brother sometimes surprised her. After all, she hadn't always liked Shon, but in the past year, he had grown, not just in size—he was bigger than Aia now and almost as big as Thrum—but also in wisdom. He was no longer the sun-addled pest she had to continually bat on the nose for his silly behavior. It was entirely unexpected, especially since his older brother, Thrum, was still prone to foolishness like galloping about and trying to catch snow in his mouth.

Aia wondered what had caused Shon to change in the ways he had.

Perhaps it was through the influence of Jessira, his Human. She was Rukh's mate—his wife as Humans called things—which meant she had to be someone special. Aia couldn't imagine Rukh settling for anyone ordinary of wit and wisdom. In addition, Jessira was female, and as everyone knew, males were improved through their association with a female.

Why were you sad? Shon asked again.

Aia yawned and rolled to her side. *Why is the sky blue?* she asked. *Is it because the heavens are like the sea? Are they full of water, and rain falls when it slips free of the clouds?*

Shon sat on his hindquarters and tilted his head in thought. *Or maybe the heavens reflect the water.*

Then why don't they reflect the mountains and the grass? Aia challenged.

Shon shrugged. *Do you suppose our Humans could tell us?* he asked.

Aia snorted. *Humans don't know everything,* she said. *They only act like they do.*

Not mine, Shon disagreed. *Jessira is sensible enough to admit when she doesn't know something.*

Rukh is the same, Aia replied, unwilling to concede that Jessira might be better than Rukh in any way. It was simply inconceivable that there was a finer Human than her own. *Which of them do you suppose taught the other humility?* Aia asked.

Her brother cast her a grin. *Whoever it is, I hope they can help Thrum. Ever since he took Jaresh as his Human, our brother has been insufferable.*

Aia nodded. *On this we are agreed,* she said. *Jaresh should teach Thrum proper manners.*

Unlikely. I think it's Jaresh who is feeding our brother's arrogance. Thrum keeps going on about how smart his Human is. How clever he is. How no one can solve puzzles like his Human. How everyone bows before his Human's great intelligence. Shon rumbled in annoyance. *I would like to swipe Thrum across the nose.*

Just be glad he is with his Human and not with us, Aia advised with a smile. *I doubt he would like your notion of swiping him across the nose.*

Shon sniffed. *I'm not afraid of him.*

Aia rubbed her head against his. *Not so long as I'm around,* she said.

Shon rumbled his affection before flopping to the ground and curling up next to Aia.

Soon, both of them were asleep.

———◆———

Rukh approached the drowsing Kesarins as softly as he could. He didn't want to disturb Aia and Shon's slumber. Both cats were the size of an ox and could be as fierce as a raging ice storm. But not when sleeping. Then they appeared as peaceful as newborn kittens.

Jessira walked just as quietly. They were downwind of the cats, and her mild cinnamon scent wouldn't carry. Of course, other than Shon, no one else seemed to be aware of the faint fragrance wafting about her.

"They're so cute when they're asleep," Jessira whispered.

Almost as if on cue, Aia and Shon's eyes opened, and their heads swiveled as they focused on Rukh and Jessira.

Aia uncurled from where she was scooped around her brother, and she arched her back in a shuddering stretch before she reached forward with outstretched paws and lengthened her hind legs as well. When she was done, she sat with her tail demurely curled before her.

Golden-furred Shon mimicked Aia's posture, but the swish of his tail gave away the truth of his budding excitement.

JESSIRA! he shouted, sounding overjoyed. He bounded forward and rubbed his head against her chest, almost knocking her off her feet.

Jessira laughed and rubbed at Shon's ears, forehead, and the corner of his mouth. The last had him trailing after her fingers with his head until he fell over on his side. He quickly stood up, and the entire sequence played out again.

Rukh watched all this with a smile before turning to approach Aia. The calico Kesarin who he had first met in the hills south of Ashoka switched her tail as he stepped closer. She leaned into his hand and rumbled.

You're allowed to act like you enjoy it when I come to see you, Rukh told her.

Aia sat back in confusion. *Why would you think I don't enjoy it?* she asked.

Rukh gestured to Jessira who sat on the ground and had Shon's great head in her lap as she rubbed vigorously at his chin. The tawny Kesarin had his neck arched and his eyes closed as he purred like thunder. *You're always so reserved now,* he said. *You were more like Shon when we first met. Even last summer.*

Aia laughed. *Would you like me to be more kittenish?* she asked. She mewled at him before falling over on her side and pawing ineffectually at the air. *Is that better?*

Rukh chuckled. *I think I prefer the noble version of you.*

Aia righted herself and sat on her belly. It was a thoughtful gesture, which Rukh appreciated since in this position her head was now no higher than his own. *I don't act like Shon because I am his older sister. I have to set an example for him.* she said, somehow sounding regal and self-effacing at the same time.

Rukh stared into her guileless eyes, but a slight widening of them told him that she wasn't being entirely truthful. *That's not true. When we're alone, you're . . . friskier,* he said. There was a moment of strained silence as Aia appeared to dismiss his explanation with a haughty raising of her chin. Rukh studied her for a moment before he broke out in a delighted grin. *You just don't want him to see you as anything other *than his prim and proper sister. You like lording his immaturity over him.*

Quiet, Aia hissed. *Do you want him to hear you?*

Rukh laughed. Strangely, it was nice to see how alike Kesarins and Humans behaved toward their siblings. *He'll never learn your secret from me.* he promised the worried Kesarin.

Do you promise? Aia asked, still appearing concerned.

I promise Rukh replied, knowing how much this meant to her.

Aia seemed to study him for a moment before she smiled with a flicking of her ears and blinking of her eyes. She rubbed her forehead and the corners of her mouth against Rukh, purring when he rubbed her favorite spots: under her chin and the soft space just in front of her ears.

Was there a reason you came back so soon? Rukh asked, still rubbing Aia's chin.

There are important matters we need to discuss, the Kesarin said with a dissatisfied sigh.

We can play some more if you like, Rukh said. His lips twitched. *And when it grows dark, you can even stalk the lights and shadows from the firefly lamps.*

Aia sat back, appearing stricken. *You promised not to tell anyone.*

And I won't, Rukh said with a grin even as he tried to mollify the Kesarin. *I promised, remember?*

Aia rumbled her annoyance.

Shon sat up from Jessira's lap. *What's wrong?* he asked, mistaking Aia's rumble for concern or fear.

Nothing, Aia answered. Rukh tried to keep a straight face as she glowered at him. *We have to tell them what we learned.*

Shon stood up with a sigh. *Why is it that having a Human is so much work?*

Jessira patted him on the shoulder. *I'm sure you'll survive the few minutes of conversation that you'll have to engage in.*

Shon blinked at her. *Can work kill a Kesarin?* he asked in worry.

Jessira laughed. *No,* she replied. *Let me hear what Aia has to tell us, and then we'll go play in the sea.*

Her words seemed to perk the mood of the tawny Kesarin, who now wore a smile of anticipation.

What happened? Rukh asked.

Li-Choke learned of a Human who lives in the Wildness and is protected by the Demon Wind Herself, Aia explained. *He lives just north of our lands, surrounded by a great glaring of the Nocats, the Tigons.*

Rukh shared a look of surprise with Jessira. *Did Choke learn this person's name?*

Aia nodded. *Hal'El Wrestiva.*

Rukh rocked back on his feet. Hal'El was alive? And living amongst the Tigons under the Queen's protection. He scowled. What depravity could have caused a man so honored and exalted to stoop so low?

There's more, Shon said in soft tone.

What else could there be? Rukh asked.

Rather than explaining it, a vision from Aia came to Rukh's mind. It was one where Suwraith's presence had hovered over the western breeding caverns for much of the past winter. In another few months, She would have three Plagues on Continent Ember. Her creatures wouldn't fully mature for another five years, but even now, they could fight.

Does Choke know what She means to do with all those warriors? Jessira asked.

There's more, Shon said instead of answering her question.

Another vision came from Aia. In this one, the Sorrow Bringer had frozen the far northern waters of the Sickle Sea and transported many seasoned warriors—at least half a Plague—from Continent

Catalyst to Continent Ember.

Rukh pinched the bridge of his nose and squeezed shut his eyes. A headache began throbbing at his temples. *How long do we have?*

Aia sent him a soft sense of sympathy. *A few months,* she answered. *Choke says that he and the other Baels have been told to prepare for war. The Demon Wind means to come for Ashoka this summer.*

Jessira managed a smile. *It seems like She's made that threat the past few summers.*

I think this summer She actually means it, Aia replied.

———◆———

S hur Rainfall was a Muran of bland features and bland abilities, but an interesting history. He was originally from Arjun, but relatively late in life, he'd set aside his farmer's plow and replaced it with the sword. It was a holy calling was how he'd explained the sudden change in his fortune to his horrified parents. A younger Shur had been certain that destiny had something momentous in store for him, something majestic, and the only means to discover this wondrous fate was the Trials.

His amma and nanna had tearfully watched as Shur had confidently strode off in service to his city and his Caste.

It would be the last time he ever saw his parents, and his destiny had turned out to be a disaster.

The single Trial in which he had participated had been a horror. The Chimeras had attacked them day and night. They had been merciless, cunning, and cruel. Half the warriors in that single, awful Trial had died before the caravan had finally reached Ashoka's safety.

Fifteen years later Shur could still hear the screams, smell the blood, and see the carnage of men eviscerated. After such a terrifying

Trial, he had wisely chosen to stay in Ashoka. He never returned to his birthplace, rightly judging such an endeavor to be foolhardy. Ashoka became his home, and as all farmers know, the seasons change, life continues, and so too, must a man. As a result, Shur had worked hard to find acceptance into a clan of integrity, diligence, and piety and forge a new life.

He did well for himself, and with every passing year, Shur had grown ever more grateful for the bounty of his life. He'd survived a Trial that so many others had not. He'd prospered in the task to which those of his Caste were best suited: farming. He'd even married, and though his wife had died in childbirth before the physician could reach her, Shur felt no bitterness at her passing.

Devesh had already blessed him in so many other ways. Shur had been arrogant, but the Most High had spared him. Shur had been boastful, but the Lord had granted him safe harbor. Shur had been foolish, but Devesh had guided Shur's footsteps to this special city. Ashoka was a lovely winter rose of enlightenment and justice, and Shur had long ago vowed to protect this wondrous gem of a city with every ounce of his strength and *Jivatma*.

It was why he had joined the High Army, rising to the rank of captain. It was why tonight's meeting was so important. It was the first gathering of the Virtuous, but it would not be their last. These were the men and women who knew the Magisterium had sided with corruption when they had decided to allow the ghrinas sanctuary. These were the pious who knew that truth could not be set aside for the sake of mere convenience. These were the faithful servants who would fight to see Ashoka returned to Devesh's holy grace.

The Virtuous were gathered in a hidden-away cellar that was dank, dark, and musty, but the humbleness of their surroundings didn't matter to Shur. He knew that Devesh's glory shined on them all. He knew there would come a time when the city would see the evil the Magisterium had allowed and hail the Virtuous for their foresight and piety.

But first, there had to be blood. The blood of the ghrinas. They could not be suffered to live.

Shur glanced about at the ten other men and women who had come here in secret. Among them were members of every Caste, but the most heavily represented were Murans. It was unsurprising given the devout nature of Shur's people.

He smiled and rapped his knuckles on the bare wood of the poorly built table around which they had gathered. "Let us begin," Shur said. "This is a momentous occasion. It is the first meeting of the Heavenly Council of the Virtuous." The name was Shur's invention, and he was quite proud of it. His pride was dented a moment later.

"Is that what we really plan on calling ourselves?" a Rahail asked, sounding scornful.

Shur knew the names of all these men and women, but in his mind, he preferred to think of them as 'the Cherid' or 'the Shiyen'. It made it seem like those here were the actual avatars of their Castes, rather than a simple gathering of disparate individuals. It made them all seem more powerful, like they were a manifestation of the divine.

"It's a good name," a Cherid answered, rebuilding some of Shur's lost certainty. "I think its iconic and strong."

The Rahail settled into his chair with a grumble.

Shur gave the Cherid an appreciative nod before turning to the others. "Our first order of business is obvious," he said. "The Magisterium has seen fit to allow the ghrinas a home in our city." He snarled. "We will not allow it. Their wretched wickedness must be banished from Ashoka, and our city's streets washed clean."

"Banished?" a Duriah growled. "I did not come here to merely *banish* the ghrinas."

"They will be banished to Death's domain," Shur said, glad to see that at least one other shared his vision. He was even more heartened to see the understanding nods shared amongst most of the others.

"What do you intend?" a Kumma asked.

Shur glanced the woman's way. "We must begin with a task you will find unpleasant," he said. "The corruption began with one of your own Houses: House Shektan and her iniquitous, Tainted son, Rukh Shektan. As such, that is where the purification must begin."

The Kumma narrowed her eyes, not in anger or distrust, but uncertainty. "What do you mean?"

"I mean House Shektan must be destroyed," Shur replied. "Root and branch. We must kill as many of them as possible."

Gasps and dismayed mumblings met his words.

Shur held back a frown of disappointment. Did they think that they could reshape Ashoka, renew her moral core with a few secret meetings and nothing more? Then they were fools. Renewal required sacrifice, demanded justice, and needed the unflinching zeal of the faithful.

"How?" a Muran finally asked.

"The better question is *why?*" the Kumma countered.

Shur turned back to her. "Because House Shektan has consorted with evil, brought evil to the heart of the city, used sophistry to convince us that perfidy is good and morality is wickedness. They've gone so far as to try and cast doubt on the veracity of *The Word and the Deed*." He snorted derision. "As if their laughable charges can deny that which has guided all the days and years of our lives and those of our ancestors." Shur shook his head. "Nevertheless, their heresy cannot be tolerated. House Shektan must die."

The Kumma pursed her lips. "And how will you go about destroying House Shektan? They are warriors while we are merely conspirators."

Shur nodded. "We aren't warriors, but we will be victorious in this war because we have something House Shektan can never hope to defeat. We have a vision. We share an ideal of what Ashoka should be, a philosophy we can make real, and all of House Shektan's warriors, weapons, and swords will prove useless at trying to destroy our dream."

The Cherid nodded in agreement. "He is right. An idea cannot be killed, and only a better vision can destroy another vision."

The others seemed to accept the Cherid's words and leaned in closer.

"What do you propose?" the Duriah asked.

Shur settled in his chair, satisfied and overjoyed. The first meeting was going better than he had ever dared hope. It was further proof that Devesh guided his movements. Righteousness was with him. "I have a notion of how we can both gain adherents and also strike a blow against the foul Shektans. The upcoming Advent Trial shall be the site of the First Cleansing."

CHAPTER SIX
CHALLENGES

Those who think to thieve from starving wolves are fools.
We know them by their torn-asunder corpses.

—Attribution unknown

Rukh's brows furrowed as he pored over the papers laid out in front of him. In a short time, he was expected to give a full accounting to the Shektan House Council of everything Aia and Shon had related regarding events in the Wildness. There was a lot to cover, and Rukh had written it all down—Hal'El Wrestiva, the increased breeding of the Chimeras, and the supposed summertime attack by the Queen. Everything was included in the papers, even a map revealing the location of western breeding caverns. Rukh just wanted to make sure he hadn't forgotten anything. Even the smallest detail might turn out to be important.

"Are you ready to go?" Jessira asked him. "We're going to be late if we don't leave soon."

Rukh glanced up from where he sat on the couch, looking at the clock on the mantle above the fireplace. "We've got time," he said.

"Only if we run," Jessira replied as she began pacing before the fireplace. "You know it's rude to keep people waiting?"

Rukh exhaled heavily. Jessira hated even the *threat* of being late. Tardiness was one of her pet peeves. "Let me just get these papers together," he said, stuffing the documents he had been studying into a leather satchel.

"Who else will be at the meeting?" Jessira asked.

"The entire House Council," Rukh replied. "I don't think . . ." He trailed off when he looked over at Jessira. Whatever else he was about to say melted from his mind like ice on a hot summer day.

Jessira stood by the dining table with one foot resting on a chair as she laced her sandals. She wore a sleeveless summer dress, pale yellow and made of soft silk, that normally ended a little north of her knees. Right now, though, the dress had hitched itself high up on her thighs, and Rukh found himself tracing the lean, muscular lengths of Jessira's long legs. They were a paler shade of golden-red compared to the rest of her skin but were also softer than the silk dress she wore. He noticed a small mole well up her inner thigh.

"Stop staring," Jessira said without bothering to look his way.

Rukh grimaced. How did she always know when he was looking?

"Because you're a man, and men stare," Jessira replied to his unspoken question.

Rukh shrugged, not bothering to argue the point since she was right.

To his disappointment, Jessira took that moment to straighten up, and her dress settled about her legs and hips, hiding what had been so beautifully displayed only seconds earlier. She walked over to the full-length mirror in the corner near the couch and studied herself from all angles as she smoothed down the dress. When everything met her approval, she turned to Rukh. "Are you ready?" she asked, hands on her hips and an arch to her eyebrows.

Her question had levels of meaning, and Rukh didn't bother answering. Instead, he stepped over to Jessira and cupped her face in both his hands. He kissed his wife briefly but tenderly on the lips. "I'm ready, priya" he said.

As they exited their flat, Jessira took his hand and pressed up against him, and as always Rukh couldn't help but breathe deep her faint cinnamon scent.

Jessira smiled when he did, and she squeezed his hand for a brief instant. "What do you suppose your nanna will do after he hears what we have to say?" she asked as they stepped onto the streets of Jubilee Hills.

Rukh paused to get his bearings before answering.

It was twilight, and the streets were thick with people making their way home or heading out to Semaphore Walk or some other part of Ashoka for an evening of good food and entertainment.

"I imagine he'll hear us out," Rukh said. "He'll want us to verify that Aia and Shon are reliable—which they are—and then pass the information on to the Magisterium."

"And we'll have to prepare for war," Jessira said with a sour grimace. "First Stronghold, and now Ashoka. When will our people finally have peace?"

"Which people are you talking about?" he asked. "Ashokans or the OutCastes?"

"Both," Jessira answered. "As far as I am concerned, we are one people."

Rukh smiled. It was a lovely sentiment, and one he hoped more people would eventually embrace, but right now, it was a faraway fantasy. However, there was also no reason to point out the obvious. Jessira knew it just as well as he did.

"Then I think we'll only have peace when Suwraith no longer

plagues the skies of Arisa," Rukh answered.

Jessira snorted. "We might as well wish away a typhoon."

"Which is another way of saying never," Rukh replied.

"It's a nice dream, though, isn't it?" she asked in a wistful tone.

"Yes it is," he agreed softly.

How fine it would be to live in a world without Suwraith, to live a life without fear, to have a life where only one's hopes and dreams spurred a person forward.

As they walked along a busy boulevard, Rukh inhaled the living night. He imagined himself sparkling from its energy. The city was lit like a firefly from the lamps blazing atop their light posts, and in that moment, Ashoka seemed more vibrant than he could ever recall. It felt exuberant and ready for the impossible as groups of people flocked about with an infectious enthusiasm. Their excitement bubbled over, filling the city's streets with wonder and hope, and in that moment, Rukh realized that while reality might be too hard for his soft desires, tonight, this beautiful place of friendship and fellowship was dream enough.

He pulled Jessira closer to him, avoiding a boisterous group of people who weren't paying attention to those around them.

As the group passed, Jessira remained close and rested her head on his shoulder. She'd braided jasmine blossoms into her honey-blonde hair, and Rukh took in the fragrance. He loved how her natural cinnamon scent interwove with the delicate, sensuous aroma of the flowers. He kissed the top of her head.

Just then, a group of men stared a little too hard at the two of them, likely seeing a Pureblood and an OutCaste. Rukh stared back just as hard. The men quickly dropped their gazes and shuffled on their way.

"They weren't looking for a fight," Jessira murmured after they were out of earshot. "They were just curious."

"How can you tell?"

Jessira looked up into his eyes. "Because whenever I go out, I *always* get plenty of stares. Most of the time, people are just being curious."

"And sometimes they're being jackholes."

Jessira chuckled. "That sounds like something Farn would say," she replied.

"Just because the Magisterium said the OutCastes could remain in Ashoka doesn't mean everyone is going to welcome our people with open arms."

"Our people?"

"I'm an honorary member, remember?" Rukh said.

Jessira smirked. "And I know how hard you fought against liking those of us from Stronghold."

"I think you're not recalling events correctly," Rukh replied. "It was the people of Stronghold who attacked me, not the other way around. And here in Ashoka, we have to be careful that people don't react to you in the same way.

"They haven't so far, but if they did . . ." Jessira gave a tight-lipped smile. "They'd find out my sword isn't just a decoration."

Rukh gave her a disbelieving stare. "How is that different than what I just said?"

"Your way is more cynical," Jessira replied.

"Sometimes the cynical way is the right way," Rukh countered.

"And sometimes it's a cynicism that is based on nothing more than fear, and not on truth," Jessira answered. "Besides, like I said, I can take care of myself, but I also think you need to be more understanding of your—" She corrected herself. "*Our* people. How else can we hope to coexist?"

Rukh blinked as he considered her words and began to chuckle softly. When had Jessira become the voice of reason?

"Your influence must be rubbing off on me," Jessira said in response to his unspoken question.

———•———

"What a Devesh-damned disaster," grumbled Durmer Volk, a blocky, older man in his late sixties. His affected gruff attitude had always amused Jessira, especially when it caused the younger warriors of House Shektan to stumble over themselves in order to avoid insulting 'The Great Duriah'. Even Rukh wasn't immune to the older man's intimidating persona.

Jessira covered a smile when Durmer scowled. While he had always been kind to her, his generosity would likely not extend very far if he saw her amused by his anger. Then would surely come the thunder and growl for which he was famous.

Thankfully, Durmer noticed none of Jessira's silent scrutiny. Instead, he seemed lost in thought as he stroked his thick, luxurious mustache. It was a dull gray now—sometime in the winter, he'd finally stopped coloring it—and he smoothed it along the entirety of its length as it swooped past the corners of his lips before tumbling down to his jaw.

"How can we be sure that what the Kesarins heard is the actual truth?" asked Janos Terrell. "Maybe this is all simply a misinterpretation of what they were told." As had so often become the case, Janos was the hawk-faced voice of logic and patience in the House Council. It was a surprising role for him to have assumed, given that he'd only been elevated to his present position less than six months ago. After the twin murders of his wife, Sophy, and his daughter, Mira, by Hal'El Wrestiva, Janos had thrown himself with abandon into the destruction of the Sil Lor Kum. Given Jaresh's absence with the Trial to Stronghold, more than anyone else, it had been Janos who had decrypted Ular Sathin's slim volume that had described in detail the web of businesses and deceit by which the Hidden Hand had gained their wealth.

Later, when it came time to elect a replacement for an ailing Garnet Bosde, who had formally resigned his post on the House Council a few months earlier, Janos had been the natural choice. He'd accepted the honor, and as before, he'd embraced his new work with the same passion with which he'd hunted down the Sil Lor Kum. Despite the tragedy of a murdered wife and daughter, Janos had never threatened to retreat into a sheltered shell. He had remained vigorous and alive, an example from which many of the OutCastes could benefit.

Jessira found herself wondering where the man found the time or the strength. Beyond tearing down the Sil Lor Kum and becoming one of the hardest working members of the House Council, Janos had also recently adopted an orphaned niece.

"There's no need for alarm until we can verify the facts as they've been presented to us thus far," Janos added.

"I don't see how we can verify any of this information," said Teerma Shole. "We can't go into the Wildness and interrogate the Baels or search amongst the Chimeras for Hal'El Wrestiva. Nor can we send a scouting force to the western breeding caverns to verify that they truly have increased their reproduction." Her voice rose as she finished her statement.

Teerma was the newest member of the House Council. She had been elected a few months ago to replace the fallen Sophy Terrell, but her relative inexperience had never caused her to curb her tongue. She was forceful to the point of being blunt or even abrasive. Perhaps her attitude came from being widowed in her late thirties and having to raise her children on her own. It couldn't have been easy for her.

Of course, Teerma could have made her life simpler if she'd only chosen to marry again. She was young enough and pretty enough to have done so, especially with her ample curves and womanly features, attributes that left Jessira looking on with envy. However, either Teerma hadn't found the right person or she didn't care to look. Regardless, as far as her work on the House Council went, she was said to be diligent and dedicated. In fact, she had already earned a reputation for such devotion to her duty that some were calling her the next Shektan Hound. It was a reference to the late Sophy Terrell, a woman who had been equally admired and loathed by House Shektan's enemies for her unstinting hard work.

"We can verify it," Janos replied, his voice remaining collected in the face of Teerma's passion. "But instead of sending our warriors, we can simply ask the Kesarins to act as our eyes and ears. They can bring back the information we need."

"But do they have the intellect to do as we require?" Teerma challenged. "You're asking us to trust our lives and the lives of our children to what are essentially wild animals."

Her question was met with a reflective quiet by everyone in Dar'El's study. Jaresh and Bree sat at adjoining chairs before the fireplace and shared a brief whispered talk while Satha Shektan and Durmer remained quiet. Dar'El stood behind his desk, arms clasped behind his back and head bent in thought. Rukh, on the other hand, had arisen from his seat on the couch next to Jessira and paced to stand beside his nanna. He stared through the leaded glass windows at the gardens and wore an expression of longing.

Jessira wasn't sure if he'd actually heard Janos and Teerma's debate.

"They can do it," Rukh said, answering her doubts as he turned back to face the others. "The Kesarins. There's a way."

Dar'El took a seat behind his desk and gestured for Rukh to return to his own as well. "Explain," he ordered in his inimitably terse fashion.

"The Kesarins are wild, but they're not simple animals," Rukh began after he had returned to Jessira's side. "They can speak and reason. You've all read my after action reports. They're the reason I can Heal and the OutCaste warriors have the Talents of Caste Kumma. More importantly, some of you have spoken with Aia and her brothers. You know they aren't dull creatures."

"*I* haven't spoken with them," Teerma muttered irritably.

Rukh quirked a half smile. "Then you'll have to trust those of us who have."

"I still think you're asking us to give over too much of our future to creatures whose ultimate motivations we can't know for certain," Teerma replied.

"It *is* a lot to accept," Satha Shektan, Rukh's amma, said in surprising agreement. "But I also think it's a dice roll we'll have to take." She leaned back in her chair. "Do we really dare do nothing if what the Kesarins say is true? Or do we take the least worst measure possible and hopefully find a way to survive Suwraith's rage?"

"I'm not proposing we do nothing, but as Janos said, we don't need to panic either," Teerma said, sounding exasperated and rather impolite.

Rukh's amma turned her gaze to the other woman and arched her eyebrows in a silent, challenging question. Though Satha was a beautiful woman who rarely raised her voice in ire, those same quiet qualities could sometimes lead a person to forget the truth about her. When needed, Rukh's amma could be as intimidating as a bared blade, and right now, when she stared a challenge at Teerma, it was the other woman who looked away first.

"Then what do you propose?" Satha eventually asked Teerma.

"Send out a troop of scouts to the Hunters Flats and learn the truth from the lips of the Baels," Teerma replied. "There won't be as much risk for misinterpretation. And if we send our warriors in the company of the Kesarins, the other great cats of the Flats won't be as likely to attack our scouts."

"The Queen can see through our Blends," Jaresh reminded everyone. "It happened to the warriors of Stronghold. Their scouts had no chance to warn the city."

"We only have the word of one Bael to corroborate such a fantastic claim," Teerma said.

"A Bael who both my sons and Farn Arnicep happen to believe, and the events at Stronghold tend to confirm the Bael's claim," Satha replied before looking to Dar'El. "But how much of what we decide tonight will really matter?"

During most of tonight's meeting, as was usually the case, Rukh's nanna had listened without saying much. He had worn his typically inscrutable expression, occasionally stroking his chin or idly rubbing the ruby earring punched through the scar in his bisected left ear. Now, Dar'El rose to his feet, and while he lacked Rukh's consummate grace, he was still a warrior in the way he moved. He remained in fighting shape, but a different sort of battle, one not involving swords, obviously occupied his mind. It was a concern reflected in his brooding eyes.

Dar'El cleared his throat and seemed to hesitate. "What we decide tonight *may* not matter," he said, couching his words carefully.

"We can shape the decision to come, but ultimately that decision is not ours to make. The Magisterium will be the final arbiter."

"But whatever it is that we decide is something they'll probably go along with," Rukh said, rather than asked.

Jessira nodded understanding as did a few others in the room, but other members of the House Council still appeared unclear. Among them was Janos.

"I had thought we would be presenting our findings to the Chamber of Lords," Janos said. "Our House has a high standing there, so it only makes sense. Now you're saying that we'll present our findings to the Magisterium. Why?"

"Because the Magisterium has ultimate jurisdiction," Dar'El replied.

"True," Janos agreed. "But I still fail to see why they would care what we suggest."

"Because the three Kesarins that have chosen Humans—" Jaresh grimaced. "I hate that they think they own us."

"They know they don't own us," Jessira said with a faint smile as she recalled the one time Shon had tried to order her about. It had ended with him pleading for her to rub his chin.

"At least not in the way you mean," Rukh added. "Depending on the situation, they might treat us like we're an older sibling or a younger one. They can behave like we're a foolish friend who needs their protection and guidance or like an uncle or aunt who must be obeyed."

Bree shook her head. "They sound like giant, domesticated cats," she muttered.

Jessira laughed. "They actually admire domesticated cats," she said. "Domesticated cats live with us and among us, but in their hearts, they're still wild hunters."

"And because the three giant domesticated house cats"—Bree quirked a grin—"the Kesarins with whom we have close contact also happen to have only chosen members of House Shektan as their Humans, it follows that the Magisterium would base their decision on what we recommend."

"And what have we decided?" Janos asked.

"I think we should do as you suggested earlier," Jaresh said. "If the Kesarins will allow it, we should attach a small pouch with paper and pencil to their necks and have the Baels answer *precise* questions of the simple 'yes' and 'no' variety about the nature of the coming attack." He glanced around. "We *do* trust the Baels now, don't we?"

Durmer grumbled into his mustache but finally nodded an assent, and so did Satha.

Dar'El nodded as well. "The Baels will write down their information, but we'll have the Kesarins to confirm those findings. Any objections?" he asked, glancing about the room. Nobody voiced further disagreement. "Then that is what we'll do," he said, bringing the meeting to a close.

Teerma, who had been perched on her chair, grinned in delight as she rose to her feet. Her even, white teeth flashed. "Has it always been this way?" she asked as the others prepared to leave. "Has this House always been on the cusp of history, or is it only a recent occurrence?" She gestured toward Rukh, Jaresh, and Bree. "With everything these three have done in the past few years, is this the type of excitement I can look forward to as a member of the House Council?"

"Beware of a life lived in interesting times," murmured Janos in response.

Teerma threw her head back and laughed. "But what a grand life to live!"

Jessira smiled at the other woman's excitement, amused at how quickly Teerma's mood shifted. A moment ago, she had been agitated and annoyed, but it hadn't taken her long to move on to acceptance and laughter. It was a rare and admirable quality to let go of irritation and anger so easily. Rukh had that same trick, and Jessira wished she did, too.

"You're wrong," Rukh whispered to her. "You and I are both too stubborn to let go of our irritation so easily."

Jessira smiled. "Some might even say I'm hot-tempered," she said.

"Not in my hearing," Rukh replied with a smile. His eyes flicked to Jaresh, who seemed to be listening in on their conversation.

There was a silent entreaty on Rukh's face, and Jessira grinned, understanding his design. She made sure to stare as soulfully as possible into her husband's eyes. She even fluttered her eyelashes. "I don't care what the world thinks of us, so long as we have each other."

Jaresh groaned in abject disgust.

◆

After the House Council concluded its meeting, Satha and Dar'El shared a cup of tea. He brewed it, and she stirred in the milk and sugar. It was a tradition that had developed early on in their relationship. Following any formal gathering, the two of them would afterward share a cup of tea and analyze how they thought the meeting had gone, or just as often, they would simply talk about their family. By now, it had become a decades-old custom.

Satha settled into the couch and took a sip of her tea. "Rukh and Jessira's relationship is odd," she noted.

Dar'El glanced at her over the lip of his cup. "How so?" he asked.

Satha took another sip of tea as she formulated her thoughts. "Have you noticed how they'll say something or make a comment that is utterly nonsensical? It has nothing to do with the topic at hand and most often simply comes across as apropos of nothing. No one else understands what they're talking about, and yet there *is* a meaning to their words. It's just that they're the only ones who know what it happens to be. It's like they have their own private language."

Dar'El smiled. "We have something like that as well."

Satha shook her head. "We have something that *approaches* what Rukh and Jessira share, but it took us years of marriage to get to that point. Those two have only known one another for a couple of years."

"But remember how much time they spent alone together in the Wildness," Dar'El reminded her. "They've been traveling about like no one I've ever heard or read about, journeying from one end of Continent Ember to the other and back again in the space of a year. And most of that time, it was just the two of them. They had to rely on one another for everything. Such shared hardships are bound to form unfathomable bonds between two people." He shrugged. "It was certainly the case between me and my brother warriors during my Trials."

Dar'El's explanation made sense, but it still struck Satha as being incomplete. His words weren't enough to explain what she'd noticed about Rukh and Jessira. "I suppose some of that might be true," Satha finally relented, "but I think Rukh and Jessira's bonds go deeper than what you're describing."

Dar'El nodded. "Their bonds are deeper," he agreed, "but the two of them have something I never had with my brother warriors:

they've loved one another completely and totally almost from the first."

"And it took us years to get to that point as well," Satha reminded him with a half smile.

Dar'El chuckled. "I'm trying to imagine what we would feel for one another if we had also shared the dangers of the Trials," he said. "Words fail."

"Are you jealous?"

"No," Dar'El said with a warm smile. "I have you. What need do I have to be jealous." He drew Satha toward him, and she nestled against his chest. "Does this set your mind at ease about our son and his wife?"

"I was never worried about them," Satha said

"You sounded worried."

"Having interest in something inexplicable isn't the same as worry."

"Then what *were* you worried about?" Dar'El asked. His eyes twinkled.

Satha let him see her eye roll. "I already told you," she said in mild exasperation. "Rukh and Jessira have this innate ability to communicate, one that doesn't require words, and yet, it might even be more accurate than spoken language." She frowned, unaccountably irritated with Dar'El. "You truly haven't noticed?" she asked.

Dar'El shook his head. "I suppose I might have noticed something," he allowed. "But I also didn't pay it as much attention as you seem to have."

"Watch them next time they're together, and you'll see what I mean," Satha urged.

Dar'El nodded. "I will," he promised. "Now tell me what you think about the Kesarins."

Satha's lips thinned. She didn't share Janos and Teerma's uncertainty about the reliability of the Kesarins. She believed they had spoken the truth. "I think we're in trouble."

"And yet, two summers ago, Rukh carried a very similar tale to us of Suwraith planning a strike against Ashoka," Dar'El countered. "How do we know this isn't a similar false alarm?"

Satha snorted. "We both know your question is rhetorical," she replied. "If you truly believed that, you wouldn't have so drastically reduced House Shektan's investments in the upcoming spring Trials. You made those reductions in funding even before the Kesarins came to us with their information."

"It isn't just a decrease in investment," Dar'El said. "We've also been stockpiling supplies."

"You're certain that Suwraith can see a person's *Jivatma*?" Satha asked. "Even through a Blend?" It was a question they had both wrestled with accepting ever since they'd learned of the possibility from Rukh. If true, the information was devastating. Any Trial sent out would face sudden and immediate destruction from the Sorrow Bringer. There would be no chance for the warriors to defend themselves against Her devastating fury.

Satha shivered. If the Queen truly possessed such an ability, then it would mean the end of their way of life. The Trials would be over. The cities would become solitary and isolated with no more sharing of new knowledge and skills. It would be the end of their civilization.

"I am certain enough," Dar'El answered. "You know as well as I that the Magisterium and Chamber of Lords have interviewed many of the OutCastes on the nature of their army in Stronghold. The only means by which the Chimeras could have approached so close without any warning would have been if Suwraith had killed all their scouts. And the only means by which She could have managed *that* is if She could, in fact, see through a Blend."

"Which is also why you think She'll come here."

"Yes."

Satha sighed and kissed Dar'El on the forehead. "What a terrible future our children face."

CHAPTER SEVEN
DISCOVERIES

Mysteries of a man,
His voice a honeyed web.
Entraps you in his truths
Of offered devotion.

—*Daylight and the Moon* by Deside, AF 511

"Why don't we come here more often?" Jessira asked after the hostess had seated them at a small, private booth toward the back of Masala Pull. It was one of their favorite restaurants, and in her mind, it served the finest fare in all of Ashoka: a fusion of Muran and Rahail cuisine. The food at Masala Pull had never disappointed her.

Jessira glanced around. It was still early in the evening, but already the restaurant was alive with young couples and a few families. In this, its popularity, as well as its appearance, Masala Pull was the same as it had been when she'd first visited Ashoka almost two years ago. The walls were a warm terra cotta wash, and a high ceiling with its multitude of chandeliers provided a light, airy feel. The tabletops consisted of vibrantly colored mosaic tiles arranged into various scenes of Ashokan life, but what Jessira appreciated the most were the mouth-watering aromas filling the air.

"We come here often enough," Rukh said. "But I thought tonight could be special. No family. Just the two of us."

"But why tonight?" Jessira asked. "Did I forget an anniversary?" Rukh had a habit of celebrating even the most inconsequential of events. It was a sometimes aggravating habit, but generally Jessira found it sweet and sentimental.

Rukh's eyes tightened for the briefest of instances in response to Jessira's question before he seemed to force a smile. "No. I just wanted some time alone with you. We've both been so busy. Me with getting the Trims ready for the Wrath and Hellfire Week, and you with settling in the OutCastes. I just thought it would be nice if we could have an evening together." He tried to affect a nonchalant expression, but his face appeared pinched and tight.

Jessira's eyes narrowed. Rukh was a terrible liar. She *had* forgotten something. He had brought her here for a specific reason, but for the life of her, she couldn't imagine what it was. And she could tell her lack of understanding was disappointing to Rukh.

Before she could divine what she'd forgotten, dinner arrived. It was cubed chunks of chicken swimming in a spicy, buttery sauce with mustard seeds and served upon a bed of fragrant jasmine rice. A sweet, white wine with a slight hint of lemon zest served as an accompaniment.

Jessira would have enjoyed simply immersing herself in the lush meal, but the reason why she and Rukh were at Masala Pull grated on her thoughts. She couldn't enjoy herself without knowing why tonight was so important to Rukh. It had to be something significant, or he wouldn't have tried so heroically to hide his disappointment.

She tried to see things as he might. His last consequential

anniversary had been a few months ago. He'd gone out with Farn to celebrate the anniversary of the two men's very first Trial, the one to Nestle when they'd marched forth from Ashoka as Virgins, and all their lives had changed forever.

Jessira inhaled sharply. Was that it? Some months after Rukh had left for Nestle, might mean . . . "Tonight is the anniversary of the first night we met," she said.

A brief smile stole across Rukh's face. "And," he prodded.

Jessira glanced at her food, and the rest of the answer came to her. "And this meal—even the wine—is the same as I had the first time you brought me here," Jessira said in a rush.

Rukh's sunbeam smile of happiness was her answer that she had guessed correctly.

Jessira couldn't believe he had remembered the anniversary of their first meeting or had arranged for tonight's wonderful meal at Masala Pull. For a moment, tears threatened to fill her eyes as she was overcome by Rukh's thoughtfulness.

He took her hands in his. "Happy anniversary," Rukh said. He held her gaze with his. "And Jessira?"

He continued to hold her hands and stare into her eyes, and her heart beat faster as Rukh leaned forward. "Yes?" she replied, knowing she sounded a little breathless.

He kissed her, soft and tender before pulling away. "Try not to make those . . . noises you make when you really like your food. We don't want to overwhelm the delicate sensibilities of some nearby matrons."

Jessira's eyes widened with shock. What the—? She remembered what Rukh and Bree had said the first time she'd eaten here. Rukh had leaned back in his chair and was wearing an insufferable smile. Jessira threw her napkin at his grinning face.

Rukh laughed, and Jessira tried to glower at him, but he just laughed harder. Eventually, she couldn't help but laugh with him. "Happy anniversary yourself," Jessira said in mock irritation.

"I'm sorry," Rukh said, sounding not the least bit contrite. "But the look on your face was priceless."

"Well get used to this look," Jessira said, still affecting annoyance. "Especially when we get home and you want to celebrate our anniversary properly."

Rukh took her hands again. "I'd rather take a walk in Dryad Park with you," he said.

His statement was like a douter, snuffing out the last of Jessira's lingering irritation. She found herself smiling. "You're not worried about what people might say?" she teased.

Rukh smiled. "Let them," he said. "I think we can handle anything that might come our way. We have so far."

"And we always will," Jessira promised. When Rukh leaned forward once again, she met him over the middle of the table and kissed him.

After dinner, they left Masala Pull and strolled to Dryad Park. Jessira let Rukh lead the way into Ashoka's green soul. They found themselves cupped within the embrace of low-lying hills on all sides, except to the east where the Adamantine Cliffs plunged to the Sickle Sea. Though it was twilight, there was still a small group of elderly men finishing up a final round of chess. On past them, Jessira and Rukh walked beneath firefly globes hanging from the broad branches of the thick-trunked trees lining the winding walkways. The lights softened the paths with glorious hues of rose, gold, lavender, and violet.

Deeper into the park, the trails were all but empty, except for a few other couples taking an evening stroll. However, a few more twisty turns later, there was no one else about. Jessira exhaled softly in happiness. The setting was romantic and exactly what she needed. Her relationship with Rukh had so often been marked with danger and strife, so much fear and worry. It was good to share a moment where it was just the two of them, and there was no impending danger or incipient terror.

She smiled, remembering the first time Rukh had brought her here. How could he not have realized that showing her this place so late at night would have been interpreted in the worst possible way by everyone else? She glanced at him.

Rukh looked at her with eyebrows raised. "What was I thinking bringing you here?" he asked, guessing her thoughts. "You mean now, or the first time?"

"The first time."

He laughed. "Apparently, not much," he replied. "Otherwise, I might have actually realized what people would say when they learned we'd taken a late night stroll through Dryad Park."

"Do you regret it?"

"Not anymore," he said with a smile.

It was the right answer. Jessira took Rukh's hand, put it on her waist, and pressed herself close to him.

Rukh took her to the center of the park, stopping at the crest of a small bridge spanning a gurgling stream. Lichen-covered stone pillars held up the span, and croaking frogs crooned into the night. A breeze carried the salty scent of the sea.

"This is the same bridge, isn't it?" Jessira asked.

Rukh nodded. "It's the same one I brought you to during our first walk here."

Jessira leaned against the wooden railing. "It's still like a dream," she whispered.

"It took decades to make it look like this," Rukh replied.

"I remember what you told me about this place," she replied with a grin. "I also remember wondering what it would be like to kiss you that night."

"You did?" Rukh asked, sounding surprised.

"I wondered," Jessira clarified. "But only a little. I was engaged, after all," she said primly.

Rukh looked into her eyes. "And now?" he asked.

Jessira laughed and put her arms around his neck. "And now, I'm married."

———◆●◆———

"Can you still hear Aia?" Jessira asked. Rukh cocked his head and sent out a calling to the Kesarin. There was no answer. "No," he said. "Can you hear Shon?"

Jessira shook her head. "The furthest I can hear him is about a half day's travel away."

"I can hear Aia a little further than that," Rukh said. "Closer to a full day's journey."

"Really?" Jessira asked.

Rukh nodded, wondering why Jessira was suddenly eyeing him like he'd said something stupid or offensive. "She and I have been together longer than you and Shon," he explained. And Aia was also smarter and stronger than Jessira's Kesarin.

"You know it's not a competition?" Jessira asked.

"I was just telling you how far away I can hear Aia," Rukh protested. "It's called being accurate."

"Uh huh," Jessira said, not sounding convinced. "I think what you mean to say is that it's called bragging."

"I wasn't bragging. I was just telling you how far my bond with Aia reaches," Rukh continued to protest. Jessira still wore a look of skepticism. "You asked," he said.

Her lips turned down into a frown. "Forget I said anything," she muttered.

Rukh rolled his eyes. What had Jessira so bothered tonight? He was about to return to his fruitless study of *The Book of First Movement*—as usual, the slim tome refused to give up its secrets—but something in Jessira's posture told him that whatever had her upset had little to do with what he had just said. "You're worried about Shon," he guessed.

She nodded. "He's young, and I know he's come far this winter, but I'm worried about him."

"He is a Kesarin. He's one of the deadliest hunters in all of Arisa. He'll be fine. There's nothing he needs to fear."

"He should fear the Queen."

Rukh was about to launch into a series of comforting but meaningless bromides when he realized how asinine and useless they would be. Something more serious was bothering Jessira. "Why would She even notice him?"

"Because of the pouch of papers around his neck," Jessira said. "If it catches the Sorrow Bringer's notice, She'll know some of the Kesarins are allied to Humanity. Who knows what She'll do to them afterward."

Rukh rose from the dining table and walked to where Jessira sat on the couch. He settled next to her. "Aia has an identical pouch," he said softly.

"And you should be just as worried for her."

"I am," Rukh said.

"Then why did you allow her to carry something that could be

176

traced back to Humanity?" Jessira cried, turning to face him.

"If you haven't noticed, the Kesarins have their own minds. They aren't ours to command."

"But we didn't have to tell them what the Magisterium planned," Jessira argued. "It's why I didn't mind when the House Council made the suggestion that they did. I figured we just wouldn't tell the Kesarins, and that would be that."

"But they found out anyway," Rukh said. "Aia and the others speak to us, mind to mind, but I think the bond that each one shares with us is deeper than we realize. It might even be deeper than the Kesarins themselves understand. I think when Aia says I am her Human, there's something much more profound at work."

"What do you mean?" Jessira asked.

"I think when a Kesarin chooses a Human, they bond more closely with us than even they realize. I mean, before Aia, none of them had ever sought out a Human's company."

"What does this have to do with the Kesarins learning about the Magisterium's decision?"

"I think the Kesarins can understand what we're thinking even if we don't 'speak' it to their minds."

"You think Shon knew my thoughts even when I didn't mean to tell him what the Magisterium wanted?"

"I never told Aia, and Jaresh never told Thrum, and if you didn't tell Shon, then it only makes sense that they must have somehow learned it on their own." Rukh answered.

"I'm still worried about them," Jessira said.

"I wouldn't be," Rukh said. "Their kind has hunted the Flats for two thousand years, and the Queen has *never* sought them out before."

"I suppose not," Jessira murmured, sounding somewhat mollified. "What if someone else spoke to them?" she asked, returning to her original area of concern.

Rukh shook his head in negation. "I asked Aia how she knew what the Magisterium wanted, and she just laughed and said something about her silly Human not being able hide anything from her," he replied. "No one else told them."

Jessira leaned back into the couch and frowned. "I don't like the idea of Shon snooping around in my mind without my permission," she said.

"I think it's too late for that," Rukh said with a chuckle. "The first time I met Aia, she said you smelled like my mate. Even then, she apparently knew my heart better than I did."

"Which means she must have chosen you a long time before she actually approached our camp."

"I suppose so."

They settled into a silence. "I'm surprised at you," Jessira said a moment later. "If Aia was right, then after only knowing me for a few weeks, you'd already fallen in love with a ghrina. What would your people say if they knew?"

"Weren't you the one who wanted to kiss me when I first took you to Dryad Park even though you were engaged to someone else?"

Jessira shrugged. "It's not even close to the same," she said. "I just wanted to kiss you, not mate with you."

"That's not *exactly* what Aia said," Rukh corrected.

Jessira arched her eyebrows. "But my interpretation is funnier."

"I don't know if your interpretation is funnier, but given that you're an OutCaste, you're definitely funnier looking."

Jessira hit him in the head with a pillow.

Somehow, they ended up wrestling with Jessira lying on top of him. She had a hold of both his ears. "Say you're sorry," she growled.

Rukh stared into her eyes, getting lost in their green depths. He inhaled her cinnamon scent and leaned closer . . . A tug on his ears returned his attention to the here and now. "I'm sorry," he said. She let go of his ears. "That you're funny looking."

That earned him another pillow smack, but he blocked the second blow and trapped her hands.

"I mean it. I really am sorry this time for what I said," he said with a shameless grin.

Jessira shook her head in disbelief and climbed off of him. "Priya," she said, making the word sound like a curse. "Why did I have to fall in love with such an incorrigible man?"

"I said I'm sorry," Rukh added.

"Well thank you for that," Jessira said, her voice filled with sarcasm.

"And I am sorry that you look—"

"Rukh," she warned.

"—like you'll need to change your clothes if you still plan on going out with my sister, Sign, and Laya."

Jessira groaned. "I forgot."

She made to stand but Rukh pulled her back down on top of him. "You know I think you're beautiful," he said. "Even if you went dressed in those torn up camouflage clothes from when we first met, you'd still be the most beautiful woman I've ever known."

Jessira's annoyance with him seemed to abate, and she smiled. It was like sunshine clearing a cloud. "Why do you spend so much time irritating me and then say something so lovely afterward?"

"It's not intentional," Rukh explained, although it mostly was. "And there's no one else in this world I want to tease and kiss at the same time."

Jessira rolled her eyes. "Incorrigible," she repeated in a mutter before kissing him and sitting up. "Are you sure you don't mind that I'm having dinner with Sign, Bree, and Laya and leaving you alone tonight?" she asked.

Rukh sat up as well. "I don't mind," he answered. "Besides, Jaresh and Farn are coming over, remember?"

"I forgot that," Jessira answered. Her brows furrowed in thought a moment later. "When I first met your cousin, I never thought I'd end up liking him so much," she said. "It's hard to believe how grateful I am to him now, especially with how he's helped with Laya's baby."

"He certainly is devoted to little Court," Rukh said in a careful tone. He didn't add his suspicion that Farn was equally devoted to Laya herself since that was all just a guess on his part. It made sense, though, at least to Rukh. The way Farn talked about Laya, went on about her was in the manner of a man in love with a woman.

"Why *is* he so devoted?" Jessira asked, interrupting his thoughts. "I never would have expected it of him."

"He says that before Cedar died, he asked him to look after Laya," Rukh explained, keeping the majority of his suspicions to himself. "Farn promised he would, and so he has."

Jessira startled. She'd obviously never heard that before. "Why did Cedar ask Farn? Why not ask one of us? His family?"

"Cedar was dying," Rukh said quietly, treading softly. Even though Jessira was the one who had brought up the subject, he didn't want to raise painful memories. "There was no time for him to ask anyone else."

"Well, I'm glad it turned out to be Farn. He's a good man."

Jessira ended up staying out later that she intended with Bree, Sign, and Laya. First, they'd gone to see a play, which was a new experience for Laya, and afterward, they had dinner and a long night of talking at a coffee house. As a result, it was late when Jessira got home, and she was surprised to find Rukh still awake.

He was stretched out on the couch and reading a book. For a wonder it wasn't *The Book of First Movement*.

"I thought you'd be asleep by now," Jessira said when she entered the flat.

"Farn and Jaresh just left a little while ago," Rukh replied. "After I straightened up, I just wasn't ready for sleep." He held up the volume in his hands. "I thought I'd do some light reading."

Jessira studied the book he held. It was a well-worn copy of *Sooths and Small Sayings* by Tramed Billow. She shook her head. Only Rukh would consider *Sooths* light reading.

She sat down next to him and slipped the book from his hands. "Can we talk about something?" she asked.

Rukh eyed her with curiosity. "About what?" he asked, sitting up.

"Sign wants to start training for the Ashokan Guard, maybe even the High Army. She's not the only OutCaste who wants to, either."

"You?" Rukh asked, not sounding surprised.

Jessira nodded.

"Who else?"

"A few others. Men and women alike."

Rukh appeared puzzled. "Why?" he asked.

Jessira sighed. "So that we can have a sense of purpose," she replied. "A life has no meaning without purpose, and not all of us can pick up a new trade or become farmers."

"But why do *you* want to train?" Rukh asked. "You already have a purpose. You're helping the OutCastes settle into Ashoka. You and Bree."

"Maybe so," Jessira replied, "but that part of my life is also coming to an end. I did what I had to for the other OutCastes because there was no one else who could do the task as well as I could. No one else was as familiar with Ashoka or with the politics of the city and the Castes. My people don't need me for that anymore. Most of them have managed to figure out the next step in their lives, and I need to do the same. I want to return to the one profession where I felt like I was doing *exactly* what I'd always been meant to do. I want to go back to being a warrior."

"There are other paths a person can take," Rukh said. He wore a troubled, unhappy expression. "The old stories about how everyone has a single, solitary skill they were meant to exercise just isn't true. It's a lie, and there's so much more you can do with your life other than being a warrior."

Jessira crossed her arms across her chest and tried to hold in her irritation. Why was Rukh so opposed to what she thought was a simple request? "Maybe in the future, I can do those other things," she said, "but right now, I want to be a warrior. Besides, you're like no one I've ever known when it comes to using a sword. Would you really give it up?"

"I am good with a sword, and I do love it," Rukh said, "but I train so hard because duty requires it. It isn't because I want to fight and kill. Not anymore. One of my fondest dreams would be to practice the art of the sword but never have to use the application of the sword." His jaw briefly clenched. "Even more, I would love to see a world where you could do so as well. And with all the death we've seen, I'm surprised you still want to pursue that life when other choices are open to you."

"The Queen is coming," Jessira said. She took his hands in hers and stared him in the eyes, wanting him to understand her meaning and her passion. "You can't shelter me from Her. You can't shelter any of us. Sign and the other OutCastes don't seek out the life of the warrior because of some great desire to kill. None of us do. They do so for the same reason that you do: because duty demands it. Protecting and defending those we love is what gives us the greatest meaning to our lives. We aren't farmers or artisans. We're warriors." Her lips thinned. "Maybe in some happy future, we can be something else, but not now."

"And that's why you want to pick up the sword once again?"

"I never put my blade away," Jessira answered. "Not really. I'm a warrior. It's who I have always wanted to be. Who I still am."

Rukh pulled her close, and she settled against his torso, her back to him. "All right," he said in agreement, although she still heard the doubt in his voice.

They sat quietly, and Rukh idly stroked her forearms. The flat was quiet, as was the world outside.

It was a noiselessness that Jessira ended. "I fight because it is the best way I know how to serve. I don't want to kill," she said, picking up her explanation once again. "I want to defend the people we love, the ones who can't protect themselves against the Chimeras."

"Service," Rukh said. "That's what you're really talking about."

Jessira nodded. "In Stronghold, service to the community was the ideal to which we all aspired, be it as a laborer or as a leader. It's what I believe is true. I'm not as smart as some or as pure-hearted as others, but I can fight. I can protect those who need protection. For me, I can best offer service by wielding my sword in defense of our people."

"I understand," Rukh said with a heavy exhalation.

Jessira was both disappointed and frustrated to sense his lingering reluctance. "And?" she persisted in as patient a tone as she could manage.

"And I'll find out what we can do for any of the OutCastes who want to learn to fight," Rukh answered.

His reluctance seemed to have abated, and Jessira mouthed a silent prayer of gratitude that Rukh was willing to see reason. "And what about those of us who are already trained warriors?" she asked.

"You're trained warriors of Stronghold, but that isn't good enough for Ashokan standards," Rukh answered. "All of you, both the ones who are already warriors and the ones who are new to the sword, will need to be instructed as we would young Kummas. You need to master your new Talents."

"Thank you," she breathed in relief.

"Don't thank me yet. You'll likely have to study alongside the youth of various Kumma Houses." Rukh said. Jessira could sense him smiling. "The individual Martial Masters of each House are *all* very much like Durmer Volk."

Jessira sniffed. There it was again. Rukh and every young Shektan warrior's fear of the so-called Great Duriah. "I don't know why all of you seem to think Durmer is so terrifying," Jessira said, rolling over to face him. "He's nothing but a kind, old man."

Rukh shook his head as if in pity. "Just wait until your technique has to meet his standards. Then tell me then if he's a 'kind, old man'."

"I trained with him before," Jessira said. "Remember? The last time I was in Ashoka."

"That was when he was training an OutCaste. This time he's training a warrior of House Shektan. He won't go nearly as easy on you."

Jessira made of moue of disagreement, certain he was exaggerating.

Rukh held up his hands, suing for peace. "Fine. Learn it on your own, but by the end of a week, you'll be wishing you'd paid more attention to what I warned you about."

Jessira shrugged. It was a worry for another time. "When do you suppose we can get started?"

"I need to ask Nanna to help me arrange it," Rukh answered. "But I imagine it'll be sometime after the Wrath and Hellfire Week."

"About six weeks from now then," Jessira said in satisfaction.

"And what do I get for doing all of this?" Rukh asked, a knowing glint in his eyes.

"The blessed, untroubled sleep of someone who did the right thing," Jessira said with a grin.

CHAPTER EIGHT
NEEDED DECISIONS

Of all of Humanity's various imperfections, the worst by far is betrayal.
A true heart never Heals from such a wound.

—*The Sorrows of Hume*, AF 1789

L i-Choke took a deep breath and breathed in the warm, humid southern wind blowing across the Hunters Flats. The air tasted wet, full of brackish odors like a marsh, while the twinkling lights of a thousand camp fires littered the nearby earth. Muted sounds of crackling wood, hearty hails, and threatening growls murmured like the surge of a far off sea. The entirety of the Eastern Plague surrounded them, but never had Li-Choke felt so alone.

"It appears that the Humans did not fully trust the Kesarins," Li-Choke reported. "They still have their doubts about Mother's intentions toward Ashoka."

The SarpanKum, Li-Shard, merely grunted while his cynical, yet loyal SarpanKi, Li-Brind, grimaced.

A smokey peat fire lit the troubled miens of the three Baels. They shuffled about in uncertainty, unsure how next to proceed. All of them were aware of the precipice upon which they teetered. Of how alone they were even though they stood amidst the company of their eastern brothers. Or more accurately, it was *because* they stood amidst the company of their eastern brothers that they were so alone.

Li-Choke shook his head in disgust. How could the Baels have fallen so far? How had Hume's teachings come to this bitter, barren end of knotted worry and callous selfishness amongst so many of his brothers? He growled in fury.

"Calm yourself," Shard advised. "We need a clear mind for what is to be decided next."

Choke wore a brief, sour expression before nodding agreement. The SarpanKum was right. Choke lifted his head to the night sky above and slowly inhaled and exhaled, working to rid himself of his anger as he considered anew their situation.

He, Shard, and Brind were meeting amidst their brethren, but far enough away to avoid the risk of being overheard. Li-Shard was the SarpanKum, the titular head of the Eastern Plague of the Fan Lor Kum, but he walked a tight line. Mistrust was the true ruler of the Eastern Plague, especially now, after the murder of Stronghold.

Shard's authority hung by a slender thread. The smallest mistake would slice short his command. There was no margin for error, and if their eastern brethren discovered what the three of them were discussing tonight, war would almost certainly break out amongst the Baels. It would be a battle involving tridents, whips, and horns with no quarter to be offered or received.

It was an ugly truth, one that left an ashen taste in Choke's mouth. Once again, he shook his horned head in sad disbelief. His feathers of command rustled softly. It was unthinkable that the SarpanKum could not openly protect Humanity.

During Li-Dirge's time, the previous SarpanKum of the Eastern

Plague—the one who Mother had destroyed several summers ago along with many of the loyal eastern Baels—Choke's brothers had been utterly dedicated to Hume's holy teachings, willing to die for the cause of fraternity. Now, the SarpanKum, the SarpanKi, and a Vorsan had to meet like mice in the dark, hoping to avoid the gaze of the hungry cat, all so they could do what was moral.

Pathetic didn't begin to describe their situation, the genesis of which had begun a year ago when Mother had commanded Li-Shard to take control of the Eastern Plague. In Her orders, the SarpanKum had seen an opportunity. For decades, the western brothers had slowly been losing the faith of their elders, falling further and further away from Hume's teaching. They had begun only paying lip service to the idea of fraternity. Sacrifice, duty, and morality had given way to pliant pragmatism and easy excuses. In fact, it was a miracle that these same apostates had elevated someone as pious as Li-Shard to leadership of the western Baels.

So when Mother had dictated Li-Shard to go east, he had gladly done so and taken with him the majority of the Baels who were weakest in their beliefs. He had wanted them separated from the rest of the brothers left in the west, the ones whose flagging faith might be easily recovered so long as no more words of selfishness and doubt were whispered in their ears. Shard had hoped that with time, proper instruction, and influence, *all* their fallen brethren might be brought back to the light. Or at least that those he took east with him would be so busy reconstituting the Eastern Plague that they would lack the time to sew discord amongst one another.

If not for the memory of Li-Dirge's fate, as well as the terrible risk Li-Choke had taken to save the sad, shattered survivors of Stronghold, Shard's plan might have succeeded. But fear, that faithless friend, had gripped hard on the minds of the eastern brothers. Now those same Baels gritted their teeth with worry, gnawing over every decision and every order for any taste that might indicate a risk to their kind.

"Do you have a suggestion on how we should proceed?" Li-Brind asked.

Choke scuffed his hoof against the ground and stared out into the night. He searched the nearby camp and wondered where the human traitor, Hal'El Wrestiva, was. Which campfire out of the thousands was his?

Choke glanced at the SarpanKum, who had been staring intently into the distance as well but had now turned his eyes back to them. "We continue with our original plan," Li-Shard said decisively. "We will do as the Humans request and send them the answers to their questions."

"Should we send messengers to the other Plagues?" Brind asked. "Let them know of Mother's plans regarding Ashoka?"

"There is no need; nor is there any time," Shard replied. "Our plans will proceed in the manner in which we have already agreed."

"Devesh watch over us then," Choke said with feeling.

⸺⬤⸺

A full moon waxed over the Hunters Flats, lighting up the savannah and the humped and sloped shapes of the Chimeras slumbering all around Hal'El Wrestiva. These were the warriors of the Eastern Plague of the Fan Lor Kum. These were the dread beings spoken of in hushed warnings to misbehaving children. These were Humanity's greatest enemies.

These were Hal'El's only allies.

He bit back an oath at the notion, especially because it was all too true. In all of Arisa, there was no other place where he would find greater safety, where he would be better protected, and where he would find no enemies lurking behind every tree or beneath every bush. The truth of his situation rankled, and his jaw clenched with impotent fury as he remembered the glorious adulation with which he had once been viewed.

Hal'El's had once been a life for others to hold up in admiration and awe, where the young had emulated him, and where his every action had been fêted.

He snorted in self-contempt. Fêted? More like fetid. Others would now judge his life to be a swampy ooze, a sulfurous sludge with all his grand desires and dreams buried in a stink that might never wash away. His glories had been cast aside like wilted flowers and the bloom upon the rose of his life had withered away.

It was all because of Dar'El Shektan and his miserable, low-born House.

Hal'El shivered just then when a mournful wind, warm yet somehow chilling, clutched at his clothes and caused the fire to flare. The breeze brought with it the thick, cloying stench of burning peat and the unwashed odor of the nearby Chimeras. The reek moved about like an ill-winded miasma. It was as foul and malodorous as a barn left festering for unaccounted months. Just being here amongst such a fetor made Hal'El feel dirty. He could almost feel his body and soul imbibing the stink.

"*Fool,*" a hateful voice began speaking from the recesses of Hal'El's mind. "*How can your soul grow more rank when it is already bloated with pus and leaking filth?*" The voice laughed. It was Sophy Terrell.

"*The smell is not nearly as gruesome as the ugliness of your heart,*" another voice added in a silky, smooth whisper. Aqua Oilhue. "*You are nothing more than rotten flesh masquerading as a man.*"

Two other voices laughed in the recesses of Hal'El's mind. Felt Barnel and Van Jinnu.

Idiots.

"It is you who is the idiot," Sophy countered. *"You and your Rahail lover, Varesea Apter, were the jackholes who brought the Withering Knife to Ashoka. Tell me. How has such a decision profited you?"* she asked.

Hal'El grimaced. Of all the people in Ashoka, why had he been stupid enough to kill the Hound with the Withering Knife? Other than rendering her incorporeal, her passing had done nothing to transform the woman. She was the same in death as she had been in life: remorseless, focused, and driven in the pursuit of her goals. And apparently, her goal now was a ceaseless devotion to hectoring Hal'El's every waking moment. The woman was a malignant phantasm, unrelenting in her mocking, grating comments.

And the others—Aqua Oilhue, Felt Barnel, and Van Jinnu—followed her lead. Before Sophy's arrival in Hal'El's mind, the other three had merely shrieked their fury at their fate, yelling and crying at their cruel death. It had been easy enough to ignore their mewling whines, but now they echoed Sophy's actions. They whispered continually in Hal'El's mind, berating him, needling him, deriding his every decision. It left him in a constant state of anxiety.

He waited a breathless moment for one of the four to say something more, to pick up where Aqua had left off. The moment stretched on, but they remained silent, and Hal'El exhaled in relief. He needed quiet in order to think, to plan out his next move, especially now.

Following the disaster in Ashoka, Hal'El had found himself uncharacteristically uncertain of his future and his role in the world. For a time, weeks in fact, his once unwavering self-confidence had been shattered, rendered mute and sterile.

No longer. Time had Healed his concerns and his fears. Once again, Hal'El was filled with surety of his awaiting glory and acclaim.

After all, miraculously he'd managed to make good his escape from the funeral pyre his city had become for him. Then, all alone in the Wildness, he'd survived its dangers and made his way to this place, the Eastern Plague of the Fan Lor Kum where he'd found sanctuary. Who else could have accomplished what he had?

No one.

Which to Hal'El's way of thinking meant that his survival had to have a deeper meaning than the merely personal, that Destiny still had a greater role for him to play.

And while his road to the Eastern Plague had been smoothed by the Sorrow Bringer and he had come here on Her orders, such happenstances were immaterial. All the important decisions had ultimately been his. He was not some meek, little slave or a brainless brute who unquestioningly obeyed the Queen's every command. He was here of his own volition because in this one instance, Suwraith's desires and Hal'El's were in alignment: they both wanted him alive and well.

Of course, their reasons for why they desired his ongoing survival were vastly different. His were obvious, but the Queen claimed Her rationale was because She treasured all who served Her and that She wanted to see Her servants prosper.

It was a farcical lie. The truth was far simpler, far more prosaic, and far more believable. The Sorrow Bringer needed him. She needed his link to the Withering Knife. She needed him to return to Ashoka and find his way to the city's heart. There, he would be expected to stab the source of the city's Oasis and murder his home.

It would never happen.

Hal'El Wrestiva was many things—almost all of them immoral

in the eyes of every Human of Arisa—but Ashoka, the city of his birth, was still the home he loved even more than his own life. He would never betray her.

Thus, came this moment.

The Queen planned on attacking Ashoka this summer. She had said She would, and Hal'El believed Her. She had the bulk of a Plague transporting over from Continent Catalyst to Continent Ember and the western breeding caverns were producing more and more Chimeras with each passing day. Add in the Eastern Plague, and in a few months, the Queen would be able to attack Ashoka with a minimum of two Plagues at Her back. The city might not stand a chance, even if the Oasis remained unharmed.

In addition, there was a hard truth Hal'El had discovered during his time with the Eastern Plague. It was one Ashoka might have forgotten given the soft, seductive fabrications told by Rukh Shektan about the Baels. The horned leaders of the Fan Lor Kum were deceivers. All of them. Since Rukh had first encountered them on the Hunters Flats, they had been lying to him, telling him tales meant to earn the boy's trust, and through him, the open arms of all of Ashoka.

They claimed to honor Hume's teachings, stating that fraternity was their highest ideal, and that brotherhood was a sacrament. They even claimed a secret alliance with Humanity, one so hidden that it had been unknown to anyone else until just a few years ago.

All of what they said were lies.

Hal'El had spoken to the Baels, these so-called pious adherents to Devesh. While they mouthed the proper words, spoke the correct phrases, and even wore expressions of suffering and empathy, their utterances were a sham—nothing more than a wicked pretense. They didn't believe any of their sanctimonious statements. It was something in their bearing, a subtlety to their speech that told Hal'El that all their holy posturing was nothing more than a playact meant to win his confidence.

The truth, as Hal'El was beginning to discover, was that the Baels were very effective commanders of the Fan Lor Kum. He had witnessed their exemplary work this past winter in bringing a chaotic situation to order. The Eastern Plague had been a mess—full of poor discipline, lack of motivation, and lax training, but not anymore. The various breeds of Chimeras would never have the unit cohesion and impeccable skill of Humanity, but they no longer sniped at one another, ready to rend and murder for the mildest of reasons. They were learning to fight as a group.

Hal'El still wasn't sure what had instigated the disintegration of the Eastern Plague in the first place. Perhaps it had been due to Ashoka's strike against their breeding caverns. Maybe the expeditionary force had done more damage to the Chimeras command than they had realized.

It certainly couldn't be this ridiculous fable about the Queen striking down all the eastern Baels all at once. It made no sense. Rukh Shektan had made the claim, but he was an easily misled boy. It was more likely that whatever had occurred to the Eastern Plague was merely part of whatever ruse the Queen had planned for Ashoka's destruction. Rukh Shektan had simply been the unwitting dupe who had fallen for Her scheme and carried the wild tale back to the city.

There was much Hal'El still didn't completely understand, such as why the Baels had hidden their abilities and their intelligence for the centuries since Hammer's fall, but what he did know was this: the Chimeras would come in force against his home, and they would be led with daring and great skill.

Ashoka needed to be warned. His home needed to be rescued.

And Hal'El was the only one who could do it. He knew how the Chimeras fought in a way no warrior in all of history likely ever had. His time here had profited him well, and by extension, Ashoka. He knew how the Chimeras would be arrayed. He knew the strengths of their various formations as well as their weaknesses. They could be exploited. The Fan Lor Kum could be bled and defeated.

All he had to do was find a means to approach the Magisterium and pass on his information. Even after he did so, he likely would still be killed, staked out on the Isle of the Crows, but if that was his fate, then so be it. As long as Ashoka was safe. That's all that mattered.

"What a sly cretin you are," Sophy said. *"You truly believe you can make right that which you've contaminated so thoroughly?"* she asked with a disdainful chuckle.

Hal'El winced. She was back, which meant the others soon would be as well. He did his best to ignore her. Sometimes if he pretended he hadn't heard her words, she would leave him in peace.

"Peace! We should leave you in peace?" Sophy cried, her anger rising higher and higher with every word. *"You murdered us, you fragging coward! You will never know a moment's peace!"*

Hal'El blanched as her diatribe washed over him. She was soon joined by Felt, Van, and Aqua, all of them berating him with vulgar language and coarse comparisons. Eventually, they wound down, and blessedly, his mind was his and his alone once more.

None of what the four fools threatened mattered. None of the falsehoods told by the Baels mattered either. In the end, Hal'El knew he had a chance—a meager one—to recover his standing. People would once again sing his praises. And most importantly, Ashoka would be safe.

But first, he would have to lie to Suwraith. He would have to deceive the Great Deceiver, the Queen Herself. He would have to promise Her his aid and hope She didn't see through his deception. If he was successful, the Sorrow Bringer would be left railing against Ashoka's intact Oasis while Her Fan Lor Kum was slowly whittled to death. She would then have to fight Her own battles.

Just as Hal'El would have to fight his own. But first, Dar'El Shektan had to die.

———————◆———————

Lienna soared high above the Hunters Flats, racing past languid clouds and fleetly flying flocks of birds. The world passed beneath Her steady gaze. To the north were the gray-shouldered Privation Mountains with their shadowed glens and deep lakes of stillness. Directly below and to the south, east, and west was the golden savannah of the Hunters Flats. The fields were decorated with scattered copses of trees lifting their boles skyward like heavenly spires. The young grass was already knee high, and their heads swayed randomly in the breeze.

It was a gentle scene, but Lienna knew better. Down below, a never-ending battle raged between hunter and prey. The thick, bloody streams and rags of meat weren't easily discerned, but they were there. They always were. It was as it should be. Arisa's law was iron: fight for life or be prey.

Lienna shook off her blood-red thoughts. This majestic morning wasn't meant for such morbidity. She focused instead on the glory of the world spread out before Her. From on high, Arisa was serene and lovely, and as was so often the case now that Her mind was clear, Lienna was able to enjoy it. She found Herself laughing, thrilled with the glory of the morning and the joy of flying. Had She a corporal form, She would have embraced the open sky, licked the moisture from the rain-bathed clouds, and ridden the buffeting wind as it whipped across Her skin, through Her hair, and billowed Her clothes. Few experiences would have provided Her greater happiness. To race free and fly would have been to laugh and live without reservation.

But it was not to be.

The world had required a savior. The forests, fens, deserts, and the very sea itself had needed salvation. Arisa couldn't survive Humanity's ever-worsening depredations. The damage done by the pestilence of Lienna's birth race threatened all the growing things, all the animals and all the trees. Lienna could still recall the cries of the forests as the axes cut into their woody flesh. The trees had been amputated, their bodies bisected as roots were severed from trunks and uplifted branches. She could still hear the fearful pleas of innocent animals as they prayed for a great one to rise up and save them and their defenseless children from the murderous arrows of hunters. Who next would feel the piercing chill of cold iron biting into their hearts?

Lienna had walked amongst the murdered trees. She had sorrowed for the small animals who'd lost children to an arrow's flight and had done Her best to ease the suffering of those caught in agony's wasting grip. She'd comforted all She had come across, but in the end, it hadn't been enough. Offering sympathy and condolences had been a near-worthless errand. It had done far too little to soothe Arisa's hurts. Action had been required. Lienna had to save those who couldn't save themselves, give voice to those without speech, and offer Her own life for those whose lives had already been stolen.

Lienna had to surrender Her Humanity, sacrifice all that was good and decent in Her life, murder in the name of peace. She had to do that which was necessary, and She felt a swell of pride in Her accomplishments. To be worthy of the potent power She now possessed, Lienna had first been required to humble Herself through agony, to suffer in ways no one had ever experienced, to live through Her own burning death. It had been a seemingly unending torment, but Lienna had borne it with eyes lifted proudly. To this day, She would do anything to serve the greater needs of Arisa.

"You command and order," Mother said. *"But You have never served."*

"The Baels do not serve You either," Father intoned.

Lienna's good mood faded. After the battle at the city of the UnCasted Humans . . .

"It was a massacre," Mother interrupted in Her typical critical fashion. *"All those murders. How does Your conscience not wrack You with thorns of pain?"*

Lienna didn't bother responding. The shades of Her parents no longer caused Her upset or concern. Now that She could pour Her madness down into the Plagues, Her mind was almost entirely lucid. She could ignore these faded shadows who had once been Her Amma and Nanna, the First Mother and First Father as Humanity reckoned them.

"And You were the wickedness who murdered Us," Mother reminded Her.

"Yours is a lonely, empty existence," Father warned. *"There is no one who loves You."*

Lienna was surprised by Nanna's comments. This was the most He had spoken to Her in the past few months. In fact, in the past half year or more, Nanna had hardly spoken to Her at all. More often, He was quiet now, letting Amma do all the talking for the both of them, including the eternal warnings about the Baels. At times, He almost seemed entirely absent from Her mind.

Strangely, Lienna missed Him. Over the millennia since the death of Her parents, She had grown used to Their continual, if annoying and interfering, presence. Now, Nanna was more often silent than not, and while She had long since grown tired of His perpetual dire predictions, He had been a comforting source of predictability.

Lienna thought back to when His silence had first started. Had it been when She had sensed His *Jivatma* by that small pond in the Privation Mountains? Had that truly been Him come back to life? If it had, then it spelled disaster. When They had worn flesh, Nanna and Amma had both been far more powerful than Lienna. And if Nanna truly had returned, what then? He would almost certainly create His own Withering Knife and become like Lienna, except He would have more power, more knowledge, and more skill in the use of *Jivatma*. Witness the creation of the cursed Oases that still stymied Her will. It must have been Nanna who had breathed life into those wretched constructions even as He had been breaths away from dying.

Lienna shivered in fear.

"Well isn't this just splendid?" a vicious voice whispered.

Lienna's swift passage across the sky came to a sudden stop.

Mistress.

"With all Your power, You are still *a mewling coward."* The voice laughed. *"All things come through Me, You great Idiot, or did You forget that lesson I taught You all those centuries ago? Your power, and that of Your accursed Nanna comes through My blessing. I can take away all that I have given with a simple whim."* Mistress' voice deepened in promise. *"And I tell you this now: Your Nanna will never again be a power upon this world."*

Lienna's mind was filled with panic. After She'd taught two Plagues of Her children to imbibe the poisoned drink of Her insanity, there had been a blessed period of time when She had thought She was rid of Mistress Arisa forever. For months, it had seemed so, and Lienna had rejoiced. But then, during the battle with the UnCasted Humans, Mistress had reappeared, and ever since then, She had remained. Thankfully, not as frequently as She once had, but still, Lienna hated the visitations of this most fearsome of spectres. They terrified Her.

"You think me a product of Your delusions!" Mistress Arisa cried out in shock and outrage.

Lashes lanced into Lienna's mind, shredding it, tearing it apart. She screamed.

"I am who I am! Separate and alive. And I am Your Mistress!" the dread voice thundered. *"And You will obey Me in all things, You mewling Fool."* The rending ended as suddenly as it began.

Lienna whimpered, grateful the torment was over. *"Yes Mistress,"* She whispered. Secretly, in the innermost confines of Her thoughts, She hoped the hated voice would leave and never return. She wished there was a way to kill Mistress.

She gasped. She had said the last sentiment aloud.

But there was no response to Her words. Only dead silence.

"Your pain is a mirror of that which You inflict upon others," Mother said. *"It is well deserved."*

———— • ————

Tell me again why we should allow these Tigons to accompany us? Aia asked. Her tail flicked her annoyance. She didn't like the Nocats, even the ones who claimed friendship with Rukh. They were an abomination, creatures who should never have been brought to life. Their appearance was especially troubling, reminding her of the worst features of her own people mixed in with some other poor creature. What the Demon Wind had done by birthing such twisted beings was a sacrilege on the face of Creation itself. Aia's lip curled in disgust.

Li-Choke sighed. Aia sensed his frustration as he cast his gaze upon her and her brothers, Shon and Thrum. *They are not like their brethren. They have become followers of Hume. They believe in fraternity, of the holiness of all life,* he said, relating thoughts he had already voiced many times now.

Shon yipped his laughter. *And yet both you and these supposedly changed Tigons feast upon the flesh of that which you consider 'holy'.*

It sounds hypocritical, Aia agreed as she gave one of her forepaws a quick swipe with her tongue.

It's not like that, Li-Choke growled in annoyance. *And you both know it. You're just being difficult.*

Aia smiled, a baring of her teeth. Li-Choke had once tried to explain to her the teachings of the Human known as Hume. Aia had done her best to understand, but the supposed philosophies had never struck her as being particularly practical. Why would a Kesarin give her life to save that of a Bael she didn't know? Or why would the Baels risk the existence of their very race in order to defend Humanity? It was nonsense.

Perhaps we are being difficult, Aia's brother, Thrum, said. *But I still have yet to hear a single reason why we should allow these Tigons to journey with us. We generally leave you Chimeras alone when you roam the Flats because we know the Demon Wind will slay us if we kill too many of your kind.* He took a menacing step forward. *But these small numbers of Tigons you have with you—how likely is it that She will truly miss them? I'm tempted to find out.* His russet coat twitched and from deep in his chest came a low-pitched rumble.

Aia switched her tail and flashed Thrum a warning by squinting her eyes and flattening her ears. Violence was unnecessary. Why couldn't Thrum see it? The Baels gathered here, the ones meeting with Aia and her brothers, were numerous. They would assuredly defend the Tigons. It would be tooth and claw against barbed whips, tridents and swords. And worse, the small copse of trees in which the meeting was taking place, with its low-lying shrubs, would do much to negate the Kesarins main advantage: their unmatched speed. Aia, Shon, and Thrum would be lucky to survive a battle against all those assembled here. It would be better to avoid any fighting.

Thrum took the message and the rumble in his chest ceased. His stance remained aggressive, though, and he leaned forward on his forelegs with his eyes alert.

Aia shook her head. Thrum might one day lead the Hungrove Glaring when their father stepped down—or so everyone said—but Aia was not so sure. Her brother was lacking in restraint, and the art of negotiation utterly eluded him. He was too quick to action, unable to sit still and listen quietly while others roared their passions. Too often, he was led by his fervors, hotheaded and full of his maleness, of the lust for tooth and claw. Composed, cool reasoning was the attribute Thrum desperately needed, and right now, he was anything but composed or calm.

Would that Jaresh were here with them now. Perhaps he could have settled her brother down. Ever since Thrum had chosen the Human, some of his tendencies to meet every situation with a leap and scream had abated, and Jaresh's influence had likely been the reason. And right now, Jaresh's influence would be deeply appreciated since Thrum appeared to be an accidental movement away from attacking the Baels and the Tigons.

Aia knew that Rukh would claim that her brother also needed to learn empathy and forgiveness, and, as was often the case, he would have been right. She mentally sighed. She missed her Human and wished that he were here with her also. Instead, Rukh was in far-off Ashoka. It was quite inconsiderate of him.

Chak-Soon, one of the Tigons, stepped forward, and Aia returned her mind to the matter at hand.

I know you find our appearance hideous, the Tigon said. Rukh claimed that Chak-Soon's voice was nearly unintelligible, garbled by his oversized teeth and clumsy tongue, but with his mind, he spoke as clearly as every other sentient being Aia had encountered. *You see us as diseased, as pale shadows of your own power and beauty.* His ears wilted in misery. *And your guess about our origins is correct. Mother created us from your kind. She shaped our ancestors from the Kesarins and another type of creature, twisting us until we wear these—to you—strange, befouled hides. But this isn't what we were meant to be. Our terrible bodies are of Mother's making, but our souls belong to Devesh.* The Tigon licked his lips when he finished speaking, and the copse of trees was quiet with sympathy on the part of the Baels and watchful consideration on the part of Aia and her brothers.

It was a stillness broken by Thrum as he stepped forward. Aia nearly moved to block him, but something in her brother's carriage halted her. *You truly believe this?* Thrum asked, staring Chak-Soon in the eyes from just inches away.

The Tigon didn't blink. He held Thrum's gaze and nodded. *So long my kind have wondered why we anger so easily, why we always answer every challenge with a rage for blood, why we can't remain calm like the Baels. We still don't know, but it likely has something to do with how we were created. We are damaged, but even the lowest can find salvation through Devesh.*

You eat the flesh of your own fallen, Shon said, sounding disgusted.

Aia shared his revulsion. She had seen it. At the Human city of Stronghold, during the battle there, she had seen Tigons leap upon their own injured, killing them, ripping out throats, and tearing out great chunks of flesh, and eating the meat of their own.

Chak-Soon's ears wilted further. *As I said before, we are flawed creations. We are driven to hunt, to desire spilled blood, be it friend or foe. It is an overwhelming urge. And in battle, those urges are impossible to control.* He shuddered. *We have no thought but the need to tear apart any we come across, rend them with tooth and claw. And later, when we once again become aware of ourselves, remorse grips us, but we can never talk about our pain. It is too shameful.*

Once more, silence reigned in the small copse. Li-Choke stared at Chak-Soon as though he had never before seen the Tigon. Grief and amazement warred in equal measures upon the Bael's face.

Aia also found herself impressed by Chak-Soon's words. He knew the entirety of what he was, of what his kind were, and it shamed him. Nevertheless, he sounded determined to somehow overcome those flaws in his forging. There was also something to the manner in which he spoke that touched Aia's fierce Kesarin soul. Rukh would have said that there was poetry trapped in the heart of the Tigon, hidden away behind his disgusting features.

Shon nodded. *You know yourself,* he said. *So you also know why we will always mistrust you. Your hearts were carved with runnels of savagery that we don't possess and can't understand.*

And that is why we will cling even more firmly to the ideals of fraternity, of service rather than mastery, of peace over battle. We—he gestured to the small party of Tigons with him, twenty or so—*have taken up the mantle of brotherhood, and it is a terrible burden and blessing that we will never set aside.*

Aia quirked a smile at Shon and Thrum. *Not all beings are meant to be brothers,* she said. *Some are sisters, and we're generally the more intelligent of the two.*

Shon whoofed in amusement while Thrum flicked his tail in annoyance. Li-Choke grinned.

Are you satisfied now? Shon asked Thrum, giving him a meaningful glance.

Aia's ears perked. It was a strange turn to the conversation, and she wasn't sure what Shon was referring to. Thrum, however, had settled on his haunches and no longer seemed so aggressive, so ready to unsheathe claws and go for the throat. Aia frowned in consternation.

Thrum shrugged, a twitching of his coat. *They needed testing,* he said to Shon.

Realization dawned in Aia's mind. It had all been a pose, a playacting on both their parts, especially that of Thrum. He had never been angry or out of control. It had all been a ploy meant to force the Tigons to reveal their true nature. Shon, apparently, had been aware of it the entire time.

Aia settled on her own haunches, surprised by her brothers' cleverness, especially Thrum's. It seemed she had badly misjudged him. Perhaps Thrum *did* possess the attributes needed to lead the Hungrove Glaring.

By testing them, we now have a better sense of the situation, Thrum continued before turning to Aia. *And you would still be foolish to let them accompany us. You heard what they are. They admitted it with their own voices.*

And you still need to learn to listen without prejudice, Aia said. *Yes, we know who the Tigons are. We have always known this. And now we know they possess the self-awareness to recognize this truth as well.* She tilted her head to the side. *More importantly, are we to refute the evidence from our own eyes and memory? Or do you not remember that it was many of these same Tigons who attacked and destroyed a small glaring of Nosnakes in order to save three Human females? They weren't barbarous in that battle. At no time did any of *them stop to feast upon the Nosnakes.** Aia turned to Li-Choke. *The Tigons can come with us, but first you must tell us everything. What is the true reason behind this sudden desire to go to Ashoka?*

Li-Choke hesitated. His grip tightened on his trident, and he seemed on the verge of refusing Aia's request. All at once, his head stooped low. His hold on his trident loosened, and he stared at the ground, apparently unable to meet her gaze. *We are fleeing,** Choke said, his words a whisper.

Shon startled. *Fleeing? Why? Have you displeased your SarpanKum in some way?*

*We flee on orders of our SarpanKum,** Choke said with a sigh. *I cannot speak of all that will occur, but you know the Queen, the Demon Wind will come for Ashoka?** He glanced at the three Kesarins, waiting for their affirmations before continuing. *We seek to slow down Her plans.*

*How?** Aia asked.

*I cannot tell you,** Choke replied. *I am bound by oaths to my SarpanKum, but understand this: our lives will shortly be forfeit should Mother discover us while we are still in the Wildness.*

Thrum's tail swished in either agitation or sudden insight. *You plan on doing something unwise,** he guessed. *Something dangerous, something that that will earn the Demon Wind's fury. As a result, you seek shelter in Ashoka.*

Li-Choke nodded in answer.

Shon glanced in apparent confusion at the several hundred Bael and score of Tigons. *But what about the other Baels and Tigons? Why were you the only ones chosen to escape?*

Because the SarpanKum thinks we are the best of our two races, the ones most attuned to the teachings of Hume. He believes we are the ones most worthy of saving.

CHAPTER NINE
A TURMOILED TRIAL

Fluxed and foiled are those who marry immorality with selfishness. No matter the riches they earn in this life, their endings are always writ with penury.

—*Our Lives Alone* by Asias Athandra, AF 331

The sun made a brief visitation early on the morning of the Advent Trial, but shortly thereafter, a bank of heavy, cold clouds moved in. They were gray as winter and stretched from horizon to horizon, concealing the world beneath a blanket of dismal dullness and unseasonably chill weather. High up on the Outer Wall, it was even colder. There, a whipping wind raised goosebumps on the skin of those who had dressed for Ashoka's normal springtime warmth. The scent of rain was in the air, and the pennons decorating the Outer Wall in honor of the four military academies clapped loudly in the breeze.

"First Mother, that wind is cold," Bree exclaimed.

Jessira glanced at her sister-in-law and smiled. How similar Bree's words were to what Rukh might have said. The two of them didn't see it, but in many ways, they were very much alike. After all, how many times had Rukh complained of the cold on the way to Stronghold? Then again, perhaps in this—their dislike of weather that was anything less than perfect—maybe Rukh and Bree were merely like the rest of their kind. The Purebloods weren't weak, but they were soft. Or at least they liked to complain a lot about that which was out of their control.

Jessira did feel pity for the warriors of the Advent Trial, though. They would have no cover from the cold. They'd be exposed to the elements out on the wide expanse of relatively open land beyond Ashoka's borders. Jessira turned her gaze to study the terrain. For a distance of several miles, the ground surrounding the Outer Wall had been denuded of all trees and shrubs. It was a bare plain of grass meant to prevent an invading Plague of Chimeras from approaching the Outer Wall unabated. Flocks of wild sheep kept the field thinned and trimmed, and of course, the ovines themselves had to also be periodically trimmed and thinned since no natural predators were allowed near the city limits.

"This view is horrible," Bree said in further complaint to no one in particular. "It's unforgivable what we were offered."

Jessira understood the other woman's frustration, even though she didn't share it.

The women of House Shektan held a portion of the Wall just north of Sunset Gate. It wasn't the finest of vantage points—most of the battles would occur miles further north, in an area closer to the midway point between Sunset and Twilight Gates—but it was all that had been offered to them.

The poor seating was a scandal, a calculated insult on the part of the ticketing brokers. Many of them were devout, and apparently, they were still furious with House Shektan for its role in obtaining sanctuary for the OutCastes. This less than ideal location was their way of expressing that anger and unhappiness.

However, the actions of the brokers had led to further bruised feelings. Many Shektans were determined to seek retribution against them for what they had done.

Jessira, however, wasn't as offended as the rest of the House. She was long-since inured to such insults. She had certainly endured far worse during her time in Ashoka. Most of the city had come to accept the OutCastes, but there were still a thorny few who continued to find their presence anathema. They were certain to still harbor ill will, and Jessira hoped that the reprobates eventually learned reason. Until that happened, such slights were simply part of what it meant to be an OutCaste in Ashoka. This was just another one, and one that Jessira really didn't care much about.

Jessira shivered just then. It wasn't because of the cold, though. Nor was it the wind. It was something else, a foreboding that Jessira couldn't properly name or identify. Perhaps it had something to do with the upcoming Advent Trial.

Rukh would be out there in the midst of it, outside the protections of the Outer Wall. He had been chosen by his fellow Martial Masters of the House of Fire and Mirrors to act as a lieutenant and lead a small group of Trims in the Advent Trial. It was a high honor, and while Jessira was proud of Rukh and happy for him, she also found herself worried for his safety.

She closed her eyes and prayed to the First Mother for him. She also prayed to the First Father and Devesh.

"I'd really be happy if this unholy wind would die down just a bit," Bree complained again.

"If you think this is chilly, you should have tried to take a swim in Teardrop Lake," Jessira said with a chuckle. "Even in the middle of summer, with the air warm and the sun high up in the sky, the water was cold enough to resuscitate the dying. I loved it." She didn't realize she wore a regretful, reflective expression until Sign pointed it out.

Jessira smiled, but her thoughts had turned to Stronghold and remained there. Remembering her fallen home still brought with it a prayerful need and a crying hurt, but more and more often, the pain had become a distant ache, a bittersweet recollection on the happy home she had once known. Jessira sometimes missed the more intense longing and sorrow she had felt immediately after, and for many months following Stronghold's death. Those stronger emotions, no matter how hurtful, more powerfully reminded her of the ones she had loved and who were forever gone now from this world.

Jessira knew the Lord cradled those she loved in His singing light, and it comforted her . . . but still. Just one more time to hug her amma, to be held by her nanna, to tease her nieces and nephews and brothers. Jessira wished she could have done all of that and let them know how much she loved them.

Jessira closed her eyes and sent aloft a prayer to Devesh. She prayed for the souls of her lost loved ones, begging that they be sheltered in the Lord's divine Grace. And she prayed for the life of her husband, Rukh, who stood outside of Ashoka's Oasis. She didn't like it. He was beyond her means to help, but Devesh could see him safe.

<hr>

Rector Bryce pulled his coat close about him in the face of the cold, fitful breeze. His layered clothing kept off the chill, but he still grimaced. A ceiling of gray clouds had banished the early morning sun, and the promise of an icy rain had left the city cold and damp. The day was reminiscent of the endless drab, dreary, and depressing winter of Arjun, an experience he recalled with nothing approaching fondness.

Such weather had no place in Ashoka during the spring.

Rector tugged his coat tighter about him. At least he'd been smart enough to dress warmly. It was a wisdom that many others standing on the Outer Wall likely wished for. Bree Shektan for one. Even now, she was complaining about the unaccountably cold weather.

Rector listened with vague interest as Jessira made a comment about some lake near her home, but he didn't bother concerning himself with any reply that Sign Deep or Bree might have made in return. It was immaterial to his current obligation.

Normally, Rector would have been down by the Sunset Gate—the southwestern egress through the Outer Wall—and watching it in the company of his fellow warriors. It was both an expectation and an honor for the veterans of the Trials to do so. There, down at the Sunset or Twilight Gate, they would stand shoulder to shoulder and welcome this year's Trims as the latest members to their brotherhood. For Rector, it would have been doubly important to be down by the Sunset Gate. As an officer in the Ashokan Guard, he was also required to closely monitor the actions of the Trims and their commanders. It was his duty to search out any possible deficiencies in leadership and execution, to find the fatal flaws that might lead to the defeat of Ashoka's warriors in the field. It was a task that Rector took quite seriously—as did all his fellow officers—but it was a commitment that didn't feel like an unwanted obligation. It was a duty that Rector revered.

In truth, he had always loved the Advent Trial. From his earliest memories as a young boy he had loved it. Later on, Rector had developed a more personal stake in the matter as a student at the House of Fire and Mirrors. And now, he cherished the Advent Trial for what it meant to those young Trims who were even at this moment out beyond Ashoka's Outer Wall. Their banded brotherhood—the lifetime of camaraderie and fellowship that all warriors shared—would have its birth today.

During the Advent Trial, there were no Houses or even Castes. There was no rivalry between the House of Fire and Mirrors, the Fort and the Sword, the Sarath, or the Shir'Fen. All who participated in the Advent Trial were brothers: Kummas, Murans, and Rahails alike.

A possibility came to Rector then. It slipped away, and he had to chase it down and hold it still. He replayed his thoughts, and when he truly understood their import, Rector nearly rocked back on his heels. His ideas were so similar to what Rukh claimed to be in the hearts of the Baels, and their secret alliance with Humanity. Rector wondered if the horned leaders of the Chimeras could truly experience such an exalted emotion as fraternity. It seemed so bizarre, so unlikely.

A moment later, he snorted in self-mockery when he caught sight of Jessira Shektan. Then again, how unlikely was it that a ghrina—over a hundred of them—in fact, would find acceptance in Ashoka? Perhaps there were more unlikely events in this suddenly strange and larger world.

"I know you wish you were down below with the rest of the veterans," Satha Shektan said, coming alongside him, "but you and the others truly were chosen by lots. It wasn't because Dar'El decided to punish you further."

Rector smiled, relieved to hear the news. In truth, he had wondered, even suspected, that the reason he was up here on the

Outer Wall with the women of the House was because Dar'El intended further humiliations on him, that the ruling 'El of House Shektan had yet to truly forgive him. Rector was gratified to learn that it was otherwise.

"At least from up here we'll have a better view," he said, forcing a light tone that he'd didn't necessarily feel.

"I'm sure you will," Satha said. "I'll let you get back to your work." Her message delivered, she turned away and rejoined the rest of the House Shektan women.

Rector watched her retreating back, glad to see that Satha's sharp-tongued aspersions no longer seemed to be aimed in his direction. Life was so much easier without her wickedly barbed words. Of course, Bree could be almost as cutting as her amma, and she remained cool to him. He supposed he deserved her distrust, but he was glad she was at last showing some signs of thawing. Earlier in the morning, she had made a mild quip at his expense. It hadn't been sarcastic or mean-spirited. It had been a simple joke, and then she'd turned away.

Rector shook his head, trying to return his attention to the task to which he had been assigned.

He and nine other warriors of House Shektan had been charged with looking after the women of the House. The ten of them were essentially up here to make sure that no one got too rowdy or forgot themselves in the haze of drunkenness and made inappropriate comments to the women. It was a simple assignment. Even a drunk remembered enough not to cause trouble for a sword-bearing Kumma.

Rector expected today to be no different, but a feeling came over him just then, a sense of a storm. Something filled the air. Hateful. Hidden. Violent.

He studied the crowd, the way it moved, the shifting islands of silence, the loud conversations. He narrowed his eyes, trying to determine what had him so disturbed.

There was nothing obvious. The crowd appeared unchanged. Those nearest to him still laughed and joked with one another as they placed bets on the outcome of the Advent Trial. All seemed utterly normal, and the feeling faded . . . but not entirely.

Rector was worried. His instincts had been honed from his time on the City Watch, and he had learned to trust these niggling suspicions.

There!

It had come again. It was a sensation that he had once known all too well, and one he had almost managed to forget. But here it was again in a setting where it had no place. It was an unappealing energy that he'd prayed to never again experience. It was the electric, nauseating stench that charged the air just prior to a battle.

Rector's brows furrowed in disquiet. This was Ashoka, and such a sensation shouldn't exist here. He shook his head, trying to shake off his suspicious thoughts or at least understand them better. He stared about, trying to discern the source of his ill feelings. He couldn't locate it, but of this he was certain: there was a strangeness to the crowd, a terrible sense of impending violence and promised death. It was invisible and unknowable, but it was there.

Rector glanced at the other Shektan warriors, seeing if they had picked up on his alarm.

They hadn't. They stood behind their charges, relaxed and unworried.

"You feel it, too?" Jessira asked, sidling up next to him.

Rector nodded, unsurprised that Rukh's wife would sense what his brother warriors apparently did not. After all, Jessira had once been a Stronghold scout. She and her kind had survived centuries without an Oasis. Jessira had spent more time in the Wildness than anyone in all of Ashoka, and she had done so with what the Murans and Rahails described as a wholly inadequate Blend. Her instincts were likely as finely tuned as Rector's, and whatever had her bothered had to be taken seriously.

"Keep close," Rector whispered. "Pass the word on to the other women. Do it quietly. I'll fill in the warriors."

"I'll let Sign and Bree know as well," Jessira said. "They're armed."

Rector nodded, but he suddenly found his attention focused upon a Muran. Had the man been frowning at him? Or had he been looking at Jessira? The Muran had already turned away and was laughing heartily at some joke said by a Rahail.

Rector turned aside and continued his study of the crowd even as he maintained part of his focus on the Muran who had laughed too loudly and too obviously.

* * *

"Do you think he saw anything?" the Rahail asked with a false but ready smile even as his pinched eyes betrayed his nervousness.

During the righteous smiting of the First Cleansing, all the men and women of the Virtuous were to be known only by the name of their Caste. It was a carryover from the meetings of the Heavenly Council of the Virtuous, and Shur was convinced that it imbued their purpose with even greater holiness. He was certain that it would make their numbers seem uncountable and strike fear into the hearts of the unholy. The Virtuous would be the anonymous enemy of evil, ready and willing to strike whenever the need arose.

Or so went Shur's dreams, but right now, those dreams had to give way to reality. Right now, he was worried about what he and the rest of the Virtuous were about to do, and his anxiety hadn't been improved after seeing Rector Bryce's slit-eyed scrutiny. Nevertheless, the other Virtuous couldn't be allowed to see his fear. They could only see his courage, and as a result, take heart in it.

Shur Rainfall laughed in the face of the Rahail's question, maintaining his facade of good cheer and joy. "He saw nothing," Shur said. "Let not your heart tremble, for our actions are guided by the First Father and the First Mother. They will be our shield and our sword. We will not fail."

The Rahail gave a terse nod but his worried expression remained.

Shur mentally sighed at the other man's lack of faith before considering his plan once again. He searched out the flaws, anything he might have overlooked. After careful thought, he remained convinced there was nothing he would or could do differently. The plan would work.

And when it did, Ashoka would never again be the same. Everything would change after today when the Virtuous carried out the First Cleansing. It would be like a pebble rushing down a mountain, and as it gathered more and more speed, more and more rocks would follow in its wake until an avalanche was thundering downhill, unstoppable and unpredictable.

What then would happen to the city?

Shur didn't entirely know, nor was he concerned by it. He had faith in the strong arm of Devesh. Whatever would come next would be something better, something wondrous. Of this, he was sure. Therefore, he refused to let fear of the unknown dissuade him from what he knew must be done. The passion of the righteous adherent would guide his actions today. He and those who believed as he did would surely overcome any obstacle. Today would be the start of Ashoka's great purging, when the city would be cleansed of the unclean, when Devesh's light would illuminate the souls of the faithful until they shone like the sun.

Shur could almost feel the holy hands of the First Mother and First Father as They guided him to do what was right. Under Their holy direction, he would push the stone that would start the change to come and the change that was needed.

"Are you sure he isn't looking at us?" the Rahail prodded a moment later.

"He doesn't suspect a thing," Shur replied. "Look. He's already turned away."

The Rahail glanced at Rector—who was looking elsewhere—and his lingering fear seemed to dissipate. "What do you think the ghrina wanted? The two of them looked to be having a serious conversation."

Shur scowled briefly before remembering himself and forced a smile. "It isn't our concern," he admonished. "They could be speaking of their planned evening of fornicatory pleasure for all I care, and it wouldn't matter in the slightest for what we must do. Nothing will save them from the righteous fury of the faithful!"

Shur imagined he could see the other man's eyes grow more fervent upon hearing Shur's inspiring words.

"The Kumma is Rector Bryce," the Rahail said with a false laugh. He must have *finally* caught on that good cheer was the strongest defense against the suspicious gaze of others. "He was one who spoke out against the OutCastes at the Magisterium. Should we not spare someone who believes as we do?"

Shur clapped the Rahail on the shoulder, pretending a camaraderie he didn't feel. "If he believes as we, then why did he rejoin the cursed Shektans?" he asked.

"I'm not sure," the Rahail said. His smile fell away and was replaced by a frown of concern. "The 'cursed Shektans' were the ones who destroyed that Tainted bastard—Hal'El Wrestiva—and the Sil Lor Kum."

Shur scowled again before mastering his emotions once more. He smiled even as he held the Rahail in silent contempt. How like the weak-willed to falter in the face of the enemy, to doubt when the truth was so evident. If they were to succeed on this day, then devotion to duty and unwavering courage would be required. Shur hoped the rest of the Virtuous weren't as cowardly or as faithless as the Rahail.

"House Shektan was founded by a SuDin of the Sil Lor Kum," Shur reminded the Rahail.

"But it was Rukh Shektan who destroyed the Chimera caverns," the Rahail continued to protest. "He is one of our greatest heroes."

"So he is, but it was also Rukh Shektan who contaminated his blood, body, and soul by marrying a ghrina," Shur said in a hiss, tired of the Rahail's ongoing uncertainties and lack of conviction. "And it was Rukh Shektan who desecrated our holy city by bringing the ghrinas to our home. What we do is advocated by Devesh Himself. We purify what Rukh Shektan has polluted."

The Rahail nodded hesitant agreement, and Shur sighed in impatience. "What else?" he asked, wishing the fool Rahail had brought up his unsurety at the last meeting of the Virtuous, instead of now, on the very eve of the First Cleansing.

"The ghrina who spoke to Rector Bryce was Jessira Shektan," the Rahail replied. "She's armed. So are her ghrina cousin, Bree

Shektan, Rector Bryce, and the nine Kumma warriors guarding the women. What if they interfere?" The nervous tic around the Rahail's eyes betrayed his fear.

Shur wanted to throttle the other man, but instead, he throttled his annoyance. "There are fifty of us. Ten Kummas might normally be able to handle such a number, but not in the crowded confines of the Outer Wall." He gestured about them. "Look at all the people," he said. "The Kummas will be hemmed in. Their speed won't count for anything and neither will their Fireballs. If they threw them, they'd end up killing scores of bystanders. They won't risk it."

"What about the women?" the Rahail asked, his voice quavering. The man was apparently bound and determined to behave as meekly as the mouse he resembled.

"What about them?" Shur asked. The contempt in his tone made obvious his view on how well he thought the Shektan women might be able to fight. "They might have paraded around with their swords at one time, acting like they knew the sharp end of a blade from the hilt, but that doesn't make them warriors. They're weak. They're women. They'll break."

The Rahail nodded. "What do we do next?" he asked, his voice firming.

Better. Shur held the other man's gaze, offering strength to the weakling. "We attack in the midst of the Advent Trial. It will be the perfect time to strike. Everyone will be so focused on what's going on beyond the Wall that they'll never see us coming until it's too late."

The Rahail nodded once more, looking more and more certain with each passing second. Suddenly, his head darted up. "Bryce is looking at us again." His face paled with fear as his hardening courage melted like ice in the summer sun.

Shur desperately laughed again and clapped the Rahail on the shoulder as if the two of them were sharing a great jest. It was an effort not to look in the direction of Rector Bryce. "Smile," Shur said to the other man in a jovial tone.

The Rahail laughed shakily, darting glances at Rector Bryce. He fell into the rhythm of his laughter, but even to Shur it sounded maniacal. At least the Rahail had managed to stop his gaze from sneaking back toward Bryce.

———◆———

From a nearby hill, Hal'El Wrestiva observed the city of his birth and the home of his heart with trepidation in his bones. He tried to maintain the confidence that had seen him victorious through so many battles, but an unmanning fear caused doubt to seep into his soul. What if this was the one battle he could not win? What if defeat awaited him on this day? It was certainly possible. After all, this would be the most demanding duty he had ever attempted.

Looming in the distance were the massive, sturdy walls of Ashoka and the equally massive, sturdy gates. Hal'El had to penetrate those sturdy walls and those sturdy gates, but before them stood what looked to be nearly a brigade of well-trained, alert guards. What were so many warriors doing out in force today? The Twilight Gate, the entrance to Ashoka that Hal'El studied so carefully, was typically manned by no more than a single platoon—twenty-three guards—not this uncountable mass of men.

And what about the people milling about atop the Outer Wall? What were they doing up there? What were they staring at with such rapt focus? Was it the young warriors in the fields beyond the Outer Wall, and if so, why? There had to be a reason.

Hal'El turned his spyglass to those young warriors. Their faces were smooth and unlined, and their features vibrant and alive, joyful even. The aging aspect of hardened experience had yet to touch them. There were other men out there in the fields as well. Older men. Men with miens wizened by exposure to wind, rain, sun, and brutal losses. Men who knew what it meant to suffer. Men who had seen their brother warriors die. Men who knew the terrible cost of battle. And these men held the rapt attention of the younger warriors, all of whom stared at the veterans with respect bordering on awe.

Hal'El frowned, trying to discern what he was seeing. There was something to this scene, something familiar.

The answer came to him in an abrupt flash.

It was the Advent Trial. It was the only explanation that made sense. Those young warriors had to be Trims, and the older ones barking orders in their ears had to be their Martial Masters. And the large contingent of guards before the Twilight Gate had to be members of Caste Kumma who wanted the best vantage point possible to view the upcoming contest. As for the crowds of people standing atop the Outer Wall, they were merely spectators—an audience to the Advent Trial, and another obstacle Hal'El had to avoid.

Everyone appeared energetic and enthusiastic, none of which was surprising. The Advent Trial had always been popular, perhaps more so than any other martial competition other than the Tournament of Hume. Hal'El, however, had found the entire contest somewhat pedestrian, especially since the inclusion of Murans and Rahails diluted the true test of a warrior. It was all too easy for even the most brilliant of swordsmen to fail simply due to the weakness or slovenly skill of someone else in his unit. Bad luck it was called, but in Hal'El's mind, bad luck had no place in a rightful contest amongst warriors.

He much preferred the simpler competition wherein one man alone would wage battle against another, and the one with the greater will and skill would walk away victorious. Will and skill. Now *that* was the true test of a warrior. It was what made the Tournament of Hume so gripping.

An instant later, Hal'El sighed in heartache.

All that made his life worth living was in Ashoka, and he wondered: would he ever again be welcome within his home? Could he ever again walk the streets of his city with his face free to the sky and a well-earned pride in his gait? It seemed unlikely, but nevertheless, there was a chance, a small one, but only if Hal'El was able to accomplish the formidable work to which he had set himself.

First, he had to reenter Ashoka undetected, and given the number of warriors assembled down below, that alone would be a riveting risk. Next, he had to traverse the city and reach his safe house with no one the wiser. Following that, he had to arrange a meeting with the Magisterium and negotiate a settlement with them. He would offer them the information he'd gleaned about the Fan Lor Kum and in return, they would offer him clemency. And finally Hal'El had to plan Dar'El Shektan's murder. Or maybe that would be first. Regardless, it had to be done in such a way that his hated enemy knew *exactly* who had arranged his death, but of course, no one else.

If at any point during all of this, Hal'El was found out, especially before the Magisterium absolved him of his crimes, Death would come for him. A mob's justice might be the best he could hope for. He might end up stoned to oblivion before the City Watch could be summoned to arrest him. And if he *were* captured, he would still face certain death.

The Magisterium would have him. The entirety of Hal'El's bargaining position would be negated. The Magistrates could easily compel his knowledge of the Chimeras without offering anything in return. If Hal'El didn't maintain his freedom, he would receive a proper tribunal and a proper judgment followed by a proper punishment for his multitude of supposed sins and crimes. He would receive a slow, lingering death upon the Isle of the Crows.

Who knew how long it would take the black-feathered carrion eaters to pluck out his life? A day? Three? More? It didn't matter. However long it took, it would be a gruesome torment for the entirety of the time.

Hal'El tried to shrug off the negative thoughts, knowing most successes in battle came not from ability, but from desire welded to belief. Right now, he had the desire, but his belief was brittle. He had to shore it up, have faith that success would follow his actions. He breathed more steadily and deeply as adrenaline coursed through his blood. His fists clenched.

He began to believe, fitfully but surely. He could do this.

Hal'El looked to Ashoka's Outer Wall and considered again how best to accomplish his mission.

"What we do here?" a grunting voice asked from behind him.

Hal'El turned. Behind him stood several claws of Tigons. His supposed 'allies' who would somehow see him safe into Ashoka. Or so the Queen promised. Hal'El was dubious of Her claim. No matter how brilliant the Sorrow Bringer's scheme, what could fifty Tigons do against the marshaled might of all the Kumma warriors assembled before the Twilight Gate?

Nothing. The Chimeras might last all of fifteen seconds against even the Trims.

He had made mention of his concerns, but the Queen hadn't deigned to further explain what She intended with the Tigons, only figuratively patting Hal'El on the head and promising him Her aid when the time was needed.

Hal'El scowled. Better if the Queen had allowed Hal'El use of the several hundred Baels and score or so of Tigons he'd seen marching toward Ashoka on a path parallel to his own. From a distance, he'd spied them as he and his Chimeras passed them by a few days ago. They might have lasted a few minutes against the Trims, more than long enough for Hal'El to slip into the city during the ensuing chaos.

"What we do here, Human?" the voice repeated, this time sounding more aggressive.

Hal'El slipped down the crest of the hill, rising only when he was sure he wouldn't be seen by those of Ashoka. He turned and before him stood a sneering, black panther Tigon. Hal'El glared at the Chimera and took a menacing step forward. Early on, he'd learned that Tigons only responded to violence. They needed regular beatings in order to keep them in line.

The Tigon's ears wilted, and he dropped his gaze. "What we do here?" the creature asked, this time his voice timid.

Hal'El glared a moment longer, waiting until he was certain the black-panther had acquiesced to his command. Only then did he deign to answer. "The Queen orders you here. That is all you need know," he growled.

"We wait long time," the Tigon replied, his voice still humble.

"And we will wait for however long it takes Her to arrive!" Hal'El snapped. "Your role is not to question Her judgment."

The black panther appeared suitably chastised, and he drifted back to rejoin the company of the other Tigons.

Hal'El stared at the Tigons, the creatures with whom he was allied, and shook his head in disgust.

Not for the first time did he wonder how he had arrived here as he had. How had his life taken such a crooked path and delivered him to this place and time? So many mistakes made, so many errors in judgment, so many regrets. And the biggest had been accepting the Withering Knife. Two years ago, when the black blade had been delivered into his possession, Hal'El knew he should have turned around and cast it into the Sickle Sea.

CHAPTER TEN
THE NEAR WILDNESS

The cities of Humanity are neutered islands of life within the barren wastes of the
Wildness. Our first home, brutal as decaying death, was a finer place.

—*Mirrors before the First World*, author unknown

R ukh carefully studied his map before looking up to study the
area around which he stood. Again, he dipped his head to
the map before glancing up once more. He needed to make
sure that he and the twenty Trims of his unit were in the right place.
If they weren't, there would be the unholy hells to pay. It would be
an absolutely fragging humiliation. He'd never hear the end of it.

Once more, his head dipped to study the map before he studied
his surroundings again. Was this the right fragging place? He frowned
as he looked for landmarks.

Immediately to his left was the dense tangle of forested hills west
of Ashoka while miles distant to his right was the city itself. From the
imposing Outer Wall snapped a series of pennons, and it was one in
particular that Rukh was looking for. It was the first flag north of
Sunset Gate, and it belonged to the Sarath. It was the marker that

Rukh and Black Platoon, his unit, were supposed to use to find their bearings.

One last time, Rukh looked to the map. There was a slight hollow . . . He glanced around once again and breathed easy when he saw the indicated landmark. They were in the right place.

He rolled away the map and more closely studied the terrain. There wasn't much to see. All around was a wide, flat plain of close-cropped grass and bare dirt. Flocks of wild sheep kept it so, and while no ovines were currently in evidence, the piles of dung littering the plain plainly announced their presence.

Rukh gave a nearby clod of manure a sour look. Centered on the clump was a flattened indentation just the size of his boot. Damn sheep. He scuffed his bootheel on the ground, trying to clean off the dung, but all he managed to do was smear it about. The ripe aroma of sheep droppings rose up to him, and he grimaced in disgust.

He was about to swipe his boots against the grass with more fervor, but a distant roll of thunder caused him to pause in his work. He eyed the gray sky above with the same antipathy with which he had viewed the sheep dung. The day had started out so beautiful. Bright, warm sunshine had filled the sky—perfect weather for the Advent Trial, but then had come this somber curtain of gray clouds. They had hidden away the sun, stolen the warmth of the land, and brought with them a cold, blustery wind. In a matter of minutes, the season seemed to have shifted from a vibrant spring to something akin to a foul late fall or early winter.

Rukh didn't like it. He much preferred the hothouse of summer to this melancholy chill. Of course, Jessira would probably make some remark about him being a thin-blooded Pureblood who couldn't take the cold, but that wasn't it. The weather was just so fragging depressing.

Rukh looked to the Outer Wall, far away in the distance. He

couldn't see Jessira, but he scanned its heights for her anyway. She would be near the Sunset Gate with a less-than-excellent view of the Advent Trial.

From behind Rukh came the sound of a throat clearing, and he turned around.

It was Lince Chopil, the Trim who was the acting corporal of Black Platoon during the Advent Trial.

"Are the warriors ready?" Rukh asked.

"Yes, sir," Chopil answered with a nod.

"Good. Gather them around. We'll have one final briefing before the Trial begins."

"Yes, sir!" Chopil saluted and barked out orders.

Soon, twenty bright, eager, young men with bright, eager, young faces were gathered around Rukh as they waited on his instructions. Suddenly, he was struck by a strange sense of his age. He looked upon the assembled Trims from a distance that felt like decades. It left him with a sense that he was as old as the nannas or even the grandfathers of these young men.

His bones were as old as the hills, his blood as deep as the sea, his heart as eternal as Jivatma.

Rukh startled. Where had *those* thoughts come from? They didn't even make sense. He was only twenty-two, not some ancient relic from the First World.

He cleared his mind, but as he prepared to address his unit, he couldn't help but notice how rapt their focus was, how reverent many of them appeared to be, especially those who didn't know him very well—the Murans and Rahails from the Sarath and the Shir'Fen, and even the Trims from the Fort and the Sword. The warriors of the House of Fire and Mirrors tried manfully to maintain a respectful pose, but the awe was all too evident in their eyes as well.

Nervous claws crawled down the middle of Rukh's back. The Trims looked upon him as though he were the First Father made flesh, and it made him deeply uncomfortable. No man deserved to be looked upon in such a fashion.

Once again, Rukh shook off his bothersome thoughts. Whatever discomfort he might be feeling, he had to set it aside. These men deserved his utmost dedication. They'd worked too hard to have his laxity in attention undo them this late in their training.

Rukh cleared his throat. "When the Advent Trial begins, our platoon will act as the forward western edge of the Southern Cross. We'll march directly west and follow a deer trail about a quarter mile into the forest. From there, we'll strike north. We would normally expect to encounter enemy units of the Northern Star at a point midway between our two locations, but this Advent Trial will be different. We're going into the forest . . ." He paused. ". . . and we're going without Blends. The enemy will never find us or see us coming."

"No Blends, sir?" a Rahail said diffidently. "I don't understand. Without a Blend, won't we be *more* likely to be discovered?"

"No we won't," Rukh said. This part of the strategy had been his. He remembered how easily the Muran and Rahail warriors had been able to pinpoint Blends from even a mile away or more during the battle at Stronghold. The knowledge had left a strong impression. "Remember: Murans and Rahails can sense Blends from a great distance, much farther than they could otherwise see an approaching enemy with their own eyes. With the forest to hide us and no Blends to give away our position, they'll never know we're there."

"Is that why we're wearing the gray-and-green leaf camouflage, sir?" Corporal Chopil asked.

Rukh nodded. "The green-and-brown field camouflage would be

fine if we stayed entirely on the plain," he said, "but we won't be doing that. The gray-and-green leaf is for the forest."

"What happens after that, sir?" a Trim from the Fort and the Sword asked.

"After a certain point, we'll exit the forest. We might get lucky and other units of the Northern Star might think we're one of their own. Regardless, we'll run like hell, straight east toward their flag, which should be just north of Twilight Gate. Depending on how quickly we traverse the forest, at that point, we might be the tip of the spear. More likely, we'll be the latecomers that no one sees coming." He smiled without humor. "We're expected to be devastating, though, no matter when we happen to arrive. We are to strike deep into the heart of the enemy, expend ourselves to soften up his defenses, and whittle them down for other units of the Southern Cross finish off." He paused, staring about him and meeting the gaze of his platoon. "That's what we're *expected* to do, but I say frag that. We *will* strike deep into the heart of the enemy, and we *will* soften up their defenses, but that *won't* be all we'll do," Rukh growled. "I aim to capture the Northern Star's flag and return it to our fortress. We will be the killing Kesarin."

A rousing shout met his words.

———◆———

Li-Choke leaned on his trident as he carefully wended his way down a steep hill. Even with the additional support, his hooves still slipped on the damp dirt.

The sun should have long since burned off the dew that made the ground wet, but clouds had rolled in earlier in the morning and shut away the warmth. With them had come the promise of an icy rain, and while Choke didn't mind the cold, he dreaded the wetness. His fur became uncomfortable and heavy then.

Hopefully, he and the two hundred Baels and twenty or so Tigons following behind him would have reached Ashoka by then. It was unlikely they would be offered immediate refuge within the city itself, but at least many weeks of ceaseless marching with nothing but dry rations to sustain them would soon be over.

The Chimeras had trekked as quietly and as swiftly as they could, traveling from hours before sunrise to hours after sunset. It had been a hard pounding of hooves and padded feet, and Choke looked forward to the journey's end. The haste of their travel, and their decision to forego a fire at night had been a conscious decision meant to prevent the Queen from finding them. At best it was a meager protection since Mother could always sense the presence of Her children, no matter where they hid themselves.

Li-Choke knew this better than most. He and the few brothers who had survived the destruction of Li-Dirge's command had thought themselves safe on the Hunters Flats. They'd been wrong.

Nevertheless, during their current journey, Choke had decided against having a fire at night. It likely made no difference one way or another, but it made him feel better about their chances for survival. Tonight, though, should see them camped right next to Ashoka's proud, obdurate Walls. Then they should be safe enough to have a fire and a warm meal.

Choke glanced at his brothers, the ones strung out behind him. These were the sole members of the Eastern Plague deemed worthy of salvation before the coming battle for Ashoka. It was a pitifully small remnant of those who had once numbered in the thousands. Choke consoled himself, though, with the knowledge that from a seed had once grown the mythical Grove Oak. And just as Hume's teachings had once found fertile soil in the stony hearts of the Baels, so they would again in the future. It would happen when those who were too afraid to accept sacrifice either embraced again that which they were always meant to be or passed on from this world.

Choke twitched his fur, and a cloud of gnats flitted off of him. He twitched again before they could regain their roosts on his ears and nose. He failed, and with a sigh, he did his best to ignore the pests as he walked on.

Eventually, the ground flattened out into a broad hollow west of Ashoka. From here, the ground would rise again into a series of hills that ended at the wide field surrounding the city. It was said that herds of wild sheep kept the vegetation trimmed low, and Choke briefly wondered if the Ashokans would mind if he and the other Chimeras helped themselves to some lamb or mutton. It had been a long time since any of them had tasted fresh meat.

His thoughts distracted by food, he almost ran into Aia who had stopped in the middle of the animal trail they were following. She appeared concerned, and her nose was lifted to the air.

What is it? Choke asked.

Blood, Aia replied. *Lots of blood. Human blood. Fresh.*

Choke held up a fist even as he involuntarily gripped his trident more tightly and shifted about in nervousness. The Humans who patrolled Ashoka's borders were fine warriors. They should have been able to handle any danger out here. What had they run into?

Aia turned to him. *The Humans scout three days out from the borders of Ashoka, and in the past, whenever my brothers and I travelled to or from the city, we were always confronted.* Her tail swished. *Where have they been hiding then? We've yet to run across a single one of their patrols.*

You think something's happened them?

I know something's happened to them, Aia replied with a curl of her lip. *I think the blood I'm smelling belongs to them.*

Choke suspected she was right. Suddenly the forest carried a hidden menace. It was dark here, under the dull, gray sky and the mournful, moaning wind. Trees shook, leaves rattled, and Choke could imagine the acrid, iron-bitter smell of blood.

A nervous shiver passed down his spine. He glanced around in worry, wondering what might be watching them, what might be out in those trees that was deadly enough to kill Human warriors. His heart thudded.

Just then, a hard wind scudded through the forest, furious enough to shake branches. It howled like a nightmare. Choke nearly bit his tongue in fear. For an instant, the wind had sounded like cackling laughter, like sanity torn asunder, like . . . Mother. But where then was the lightning and racing clouds? Mother never was—

The wind faded away and passed.

Choke swallowed heavily and did his best to horn aside his fear and rein in his laboring thoughts. His Chimeras needed him to maintain a clear head. The sound they had all just heard had set the Baels and Tigons to muttering, the fear and—in some cases—abject terror, evident in their tones. But Choke couldn't afford such weakness. He needed to understand what they were facing so he could plan how to defeat it, or failing that, escape it.

Where do you smell the blood? he asked Aia.

She gestured with her nose. *Over there. Deep in the trees. A mile or so in.*

Thrum and Shon padded up to them.

Why are we stopping? And what was that noise? Thrum asked as he paused to lift his nose to the air.

I smell Blood, Shon said. *Close by. And death.*

We need to learn what's happened, Aia said.

I agree, Choke replied, his heart still hammering. He turned to Li-Silt, an older Bael he had grown to know and respect during the battle at Stronghold. "The Kesarins smell blood. They think it's Human, and that they're dead."

"Human?" Silt frowned. "That is not good news," he said in understatement.

"No, it isn't," Choke agreed, taking a measure of courage from the older Bael's calm assessment. "Patrols from Ashoka should have confronted us days ago, and now there's this blood and death." He shook his head in worry, and the feathers on his horns jangled. "We need to investigate this matter and find out what occurred here."

The older Bael nodded. "Who do you want to accompany you?"

Choke considered for a moment. "Just the Kesarins," he answered, although a small, fearful part of him would have been happy to have had all the other Chimeras come along as well. "I want you to lead our brothers on toward Ashoka. We'll catch up once we've learned what's happened."

"Are you certain that's prudent?" Silt asked.

Choke grimaced. "No. But if there's something out there that can kill a troop of Humans *and* three Kesarins, it's unlikely that our brothers would fare much better."

"It stands to reason," Silt said. He turned aside and called out orders to the other Chimeras.

Are you ready? Aia asked.

Choke nodded. *Let's go.*

The Kesarins slid into the forest. Despite their large size, they moved swift and silent. The only sound of their passage was the random brushing aside of low-lying shrubs and the crumpling of leaves on the ground. Choke was hard pressed to keep up with them and walk as quietly as they. His trident wasn't the easiest weapon to maneuver through the closely growing trees of the forest, nor were his horns.

We're getting close, Aia sent as she slowed her pace. She and her brothers moved even more softly now. There was no sound at all to announce their presence.

Choke walked in a hunch, not wanting to disturb any overhanging branches. He held his trident close by his side.

The ground became soft and boggy with the sulfur stink of a swamp.

Beavers, Thrum announced. *The ugly-toothed cretins always try to flood an area,* he muttered in anger.

Choke furled his brow in confusion at Thrum's seeming hatred for the small, furry animals.

One of them bit him on the nose when he was a cub, Aia explained with a chuckle. *Thrum's never forgiven them.* Her words, humorous as they were, momentarily lightened the tension.

Shon paused. *The smell is strongest just past that break in the trees.* He pointed with his nose.

Aia sidled forward. She eased her way through the remaining foliage.

By now, Choke could smell the blood as well. It was rank, overwhelming, and near. He followed on Aia's paws, doing his best to walk as silently as she.

The forest was quiet. No birdsong.

Shon and Thrum followed behind.

I don't like this, one of them muttered.

The trees opened out into a meadow, and Aia crouched even lower. A rumble emanated from her throat, one she quickly silenced.

Choke edged to her side and saw what had her so disturbed.

The meadow was an abattoir. The trees on the far side had been painted with blood, their trunks red. The ground was scarred with burn marks. The Humans must have thrown Fireballs at whatever had attacked them. It had done them no good. Weapons and the shredded bodies of Humans littered the earth. How many, Choke couldn't say. They had been ripped apart. Legs and arms separated from torsos. And where were the heads?

Choke's heart was suddenly in his throat. The scene before him was horrifying enough, but worse, he knew what it portended. A little over a year ago, he had been witness to a similar site of murder. It had been on the Hunters Flats, and the victims had been his brother Baels, the ones who had survived the destruction of Li-Dirge's command.

A movement from up above caught his attention.

A bruised cloud floated low over the trees, ponderously, menacingly heading north. Toward Ashoka.

———●———

In the more than two millennia since Lienna had set for Herself the task of Humanity's destruction, only rarely had She skulked when approaching a battle with Her eternal enemy.

She skulked now. She had to.

For the past few days as Her pet, Hal'El Wrestiva, and his claw of Tigons had made their way to his former home, they had unknowingly required the protection of their Mother. Unbeknownst to them, small groups of Humans had lurked in their path, in places where they hadn't belonged. They had likely been scouts sent by Ashoka and without a doubt, they would have obstructed the progress of Her pet.

It was a shame they had been here.

Following the destruction of the UnCasted Humans, Lienna had hoped that She had so thoroughly frightened *all* their verminous kind that none of them would have ever dared step foot beyond the bounds of their various Oases. She had dared hope that perhaps even the cursed caravans—the wagons of goods that one city sent to another—the so-called Trials, would cease to be a problem. However, with the presence of these patrols, it was clear that Her hopes were misplaced.

Of course, from this unfortunate circumstance had come an unforeseen but welcome opportunity. Lienna had always reveled in the simple pleasure of ending the hideous lives of Arisa's torturers, so with gladness and single-minded fervor, She had torn apart any scouts who might have threatened Her pet Human. Such an occurrence would have been disastrous, and Lienna had worked too hard these past seasons—suffered too much—to see Her plans ruined.

Also, whether Hal'El willed it or not, he *would* be the instrument by which She would smite his unholy home. For this reason, and this reason only—his survival—Lienna couldn't do as She had always done. She had to approach Ashoka unseen and unexpected. She had to subsume the pleasure She derived from wildly lashing out and slaying these Human parasites, these Ashokan scouts. Instead, She had to be quiet, secret, and subtle. She couldn't give in to unthinking rage and allow any of the Humans to somehow escape Her justice. Those who fled might then carry word further afield, to those who would then impede Her pet's progress.

Lienna mentally scowled. Normally, such a situation would have actually been Her preference. In times past, Lienna would sometimes allow a few of the parasites to escape Her righteous wrath, all so they could then fearfully tell their fellow Humans what awful torment they had witnessed. Of course, death was their well-deserved punishment—death was what all Humans merited—and death would find them, but first, Lienna reckoned that the terror of what these supposed survivors had seen and survived would likely haunt them for the remainder of their miserable days. A long life lived in suffering. It was possibly an even more just punishment for the original sin of being born Human. After all, from such a disgraceful beginning, there was no hope of forgiveness.

"All sins are forgiven through Devesh's holy grace," Mother corrected in Her typical pedantic tone.

"Devesh is a myth," Lienna countered. *"All deities are."*

"Are you a myth then as well?" Father asked. *"Your Baels and Chimeras worship You as though You were their Goddess."*

Lienna paused, surprised by Her Father's presence. She hadn't heard His voice in weeks, and as before during His previous long absences, She found Herself missing Him.

However, be that as it may, His question was still irritating. *"I am as I am,"* Lienna said. *"There is nothing more to Me that I need explain."*

"Then with Your own statement, You stand condemned as a murderer," Father challenged.

Lienna figuratively ground Her teeth at his insulting words. She wanted to scream at Him, prove Him wrong, shut Him up for all Time. But She couldn't. That way led to loss of control, and control was needed right now. Lienna grappled with Her anger, and somehow managed to maintain Her grip on patience. *"Insult me however You wish, but mercy can only be offered to those who deserve it,"* Lienna said, proud of how calm and reasonable was Her response.

Father chuckled. It was as horrifying a sound as Lienna had ever heard. Where was the distance and foolish fixation on the Baels that She had come to expect from Him? When had He become so lucid and aware? His response and His laughter were *exactly* how Father might have spoken if He were still alive. Lienna was so distracted by what all this might mean that She almost missed it when He began speaking again.

"Devesh's comfort is all around You," Father said, His words softly spoken and sympathetic. *"His mercy is available with every moment of Your life. Beg His forgiveness, and it shall be given."*

Lienna grimaced in annoyance. Always Devesh. For once, couldn't Father do something other than speak of Devesh? The Simpleton. Lienna disregarded Father's piety and wrapped Herself in the cloak of Her certainty and disdain. Her Parents weren't alive. They couldn't be. She'd personally seen to Their deaths. It had been millennia since They had last breathed Holy Arisa's air, and forever would come before either of Them took another breath.

"Your illusions don't cause Me fear, and Your sophistry won't dissuade Me from My plan," Lienna intoned.

"Your plan?" Mother asked, Her tone dismissive. *"How many innocents will die because of Your plan?"*

"There are no innocents," Lienna snapped. *"And I do what I must because Arisa needs My protection."*

"You think Me so weak then?" Mistress Arisa's voice whispered. Her voice was the dry rustle of a snake's scales gliding across dead leaves.

Lienna pulled up short. *"Of course You aren't weak, Mistress,"* Lienna said. *"You are Glory Incarnate. You are My—"*

Goddess? Father asked with another chuckle. *"I thought such a being was a myth."*

Lienna's mind shuddered. Fear gripped Her by the figurative throat. Only rarely had either of Her Parents spoken in a fashion as to imply that They were aware of Mistress's presence. Now, Father did just that. It was terrifying. What if Father truly *was* still alive?

"Your Father is nothing but a worm, You groveling Idiot!" Mistress Arisa said, interrupting Lienna's thoughts. *"Remember whom You should always fear!"* Her words were spoken in Her typical contemptuous fashion. They cut into Lienna like the ends of a barbed whip. *"I am Your Goddess!"*

Lashes of pain bit into Lienna's mind. She howled for a seeming eternity as the agony went on and on, and She clutched a courage She didn't know She possessed. It slipped through Her grasp, but She reached for it again. This time, She gripped it tight. She held it close and with it, Lienna did something She'd never before accomplished. She threw off Mistress Arisa's torment. She frayed apart the bands of baneful hurt as if they were wispy spiderwebs.

"I refuse to be afraid of You!" She shouted. *"You are not My Goddess, nor are You My Mistress. Begone Shades. All of You!"*

Silence greeted Her rebellious cry. No further voices clamored in Her mind.

Lienna exulted in Her accomplishment, and as distracted as She was by Her sudden freedom, it was with surprise that She came upon a small clump of Humans. Upon seeing Her dread presence, they rightfully howled in fear even as they sought to hide themselves in their Blends.

Lienna grinned lightning.

It wouldn't work. She could see their *Jivatmas*. Little Humans with their little hiding places, but there were no hiding places from Her. Lienna saw all, just as a Goddess should. She laughed when a few even sought to harm Her with their ineffectual arrows and Fireballs. Some sought to run.

That couldn't be allowed.

Lienna lashed out to stop those who fled. With Her actions, all

Her suppressed rage rampaged to the surface of Her mind. Anger overwhelmed thought. Lienna tore apart the vermin, utterly and completely. It was over in moments, and the world was as silent without as it was within Her mind.

Lienna hovered over the forest meadow where She had brought ruination upon the Human parasites, and afterward considered more carefully the meaning of the revelations about Father that had come to Her moments earlier.

She hovered unmoving above the meadow and lost track of time. Her mind circled endlessly, but eventually, She returned to awareness. Whatever the truth about Father's situation, Lienna realized that nothing had truly changed. She still had work to do.

Lienna rose up from the meadow and rolled on toward Ashoka.

———•◦•———

Aia's head unconsciously tilted to the side as she watched the purple-colored cloud move away from the meadow. Her ears were cocked forward in interest, but her eyes were narrowed in confusion. The cloud floated at the level of the treetops and drifted against the wind. A single flicker of lightning lit it up from within. When it did so, eyes, red as fire, appeared to light to life. The lightning faded and the eyes slowly dimmed.

The entire scene before her seemed unreal, like a strange dream or vivid nightmare. There were the torn apart Humans, their caked blood and body parts scattered about like a banquet for a vulture. Then there was the strange cloud in the sky. It didn't move like a real cloud at all.

A scent came off Li-Choke: abject terror.

Aia's eyes widened as she realized what she was seeing. She

crouched low and growled in fear and warning because it felt right to do so. She'd seen this frightful cloud once before. It was a year ago now. This was the being who had murdered Jessira's home.

The Demon Wind, Aia cried out.

Shon and Thrum growled, but they too hunched down. Li-Choke also bent low as fear roiled off all of them.

What is She doing here? Shon asked of the Bael. He sounded a moment away from panic.

Choke didn't answer at first. He absently brushed at Shon's forehead, soothing Aia's brother as the big Bael stared thoughtfully in the direction where the Demon Wind had floated off. The Queen was no longer visible.

What is She doing here, indeed? Choke asked, still appearing thoughtful rather than panic-stricken. Aia was surprised at how calm his voice sounded.

The fear no longer boiled off of the Bael. He'd mastered his terror, and Aia took heart from his courage. Shon apparently did as well. Her brother leaned his head into Choke's hand, rumbling softly like a kitten.

What do we do now? Thrum asked. During all this, he'd crept forward until he was pressed close between Shon and Aia. She licked his forehead, and her brother, so often arrogant and sure of his coming greatness, ducked his head under her chin.

She's heading toward Ashoka, Li-Choke mused. *She must be doing as She did when She killed Jessira's home. She must be murdering all of Ashoka's scouts so they can't expose Her presence.*

But why now? Thrum asked. *If She means to destroy the city, where are Her Nobeasts that would aid in the killing? Shouldn't they be here as well?*

And how could She even get into Ashoka? I thought the Oasis kept Her out, Shon said, right on top of Thrum's words. *Aren't the Nobeasts the *means by which She destroys the Oasis?*

No one knows how She destroys an Oasis, Choke answered, sounding distracted. *But, yes, the Chimeras are meant to help with the sacking of a city. And, no, they aren't here, but they should be if Mother truly meant to destroy Ashoka.*

Perhaps She no longer requires them, Aia said, having a sudden insight. *You said the Demon Wind can now see through the Blends the Humans use. If so, then is it not possible that She can now overcome an Oasis without the help of the Nobeasts?*

Perhaps, Choke said, but his tone was doubtful.

Or maybe She's here because of that claw of Nocats that passed us by a few days ago, Shon suggested.

Aia frowned in thought. *Didn't you say that you smelled a Human amongst them?* she asked Thrum.

Choke's gaze snapped to her. His expression was fierce. *A Human?* He demanded. *Are you certain?*

Thrum has the best nose of any of us, Aia confirmed. *If he says there was a Human, then there was a Human.* She paused. *Why is this so important?*

Choke didn't immediately answer. He kept staring in the direction the Demon Wind had departed. Eventually, he shook his head and rose to his feet. *I don't know if it is important, but of this I am sure: Mother is heading toward Ashoka,* he said. *We have to find a way to warn the city. If nothing else, there may be more Humans beyond the bounds of their Oasis. They will be easy meat for the Queen.*

Just then, Aia gasped with a horrifying realization. *I can feel Rukh,* she said.

Now it was Shon and Thrum whose eyes snapped to her.

That shouldn't be possible, Shon said.

And yet it is, Aia growled, anxiety making her irritable.

But we're so far away, Thrum protested. *How can you feel anything? Ashoka's Oasis has always diminished our sense of our Humans. You shouldn't be able to feel anything from Rukh at this distance. I can't feel anything from Jaresh.*

Nor I from Jessira," Shon added.

Aia had stopped listening. Terror rose. Her ears flattened, and she snarled. *He's outside the Oasis.* Idiot! What was Rukh doing outside the city where it was so dangerous?

She reached for her Human, straining to make her voice heard. *Rukh! Run. The Sorrow Bringer is coming!* Again and again, she shouted her warning, praying to the First Father that Rukh would hear her words. Once more she shouted for his attention.

———◦•◦———

The Advent Trial had begun, and the warriors of Rukh's command, Black Platoon, had struck out into the forest that grew along the slopes of the hills west of Ashoka. As directed, they'd followed a narrow deer trail west for a quarter mile before striking north. Slowly and carefully, five groups of four men eased their way forward. The warriors were alert even though it was unlikely that they would encounter enemy elements in the forest. Typically the Advent Trial was wholly waged on the plains beyond the Outer Wall—but it never hurt to be cautious, especially if units of the Northern Star had come up with a plan similar to that of the Southern Cross.

If they had, then they were likely suffering the same problems as Black Platoon. Rukh glanced around in worry. Their pace was far slower than he had expected, and he couldn't help but wonder if he should have offered up the Blacks for this unproven plan of his. The northward-bearing animal trail upon which they travelled was as thin as a rat's tail. On all sides grew a dense understory—heavy with pine, juniper, and azaleas—and it made for slow going with barely enough room for even a single warrior to pass along it.

When Rukh had scouted out this trail a month ago, he had found that it eventually broadened out. They should be able to move more swiftly then. Hopefully, they'd come across that widening soon.

A little ways to the east, though, things were likely vastly different. There, on the broad plain beyond Ashoka's Outer Wall, platoons were even now racing north. Of course, those other units were Blended, and for those watching from the heights of the Outer Wall, this action—the swift movement of men—would have been invisible. What those watching would have witnessed would be very little. There would be few clues to indicate that anything was untoward on the plain beyond the Outer Wall. The sight of displaced grass and small puffs of dust might be the only signs proving the passage of the platoons.

It had to be deadly dull, at least Rukh remembered it as such. There was nothing to see or sense, and there would be nothing to see or sense for many more hours to come. The forward elements of the two armies had miles to go before they encountered one another. Of course, they eventually would, and when they did, battle would be joined. *Then* there would be something to see.

By convention, when two enemy platoons came in contact with one another, they dropped their Blends. The Kummas would fight with Constrainers and no use of Fireballs allowed, while the Murans and Rahails would fight without Blends. The only weapons the warriors would use during such conflicts would be the blades on their backs and the bows in their hands. It would be skill on skill alone, with little use of *Jivatma* to sway the contest. However, to prevent severe injury or death, the blades were obviously shokes, and the arrows covered by a heavy wad of cloth steeped in a red dye. A strike from one of them would leave an obvious mark and bruise, but they wouldn't kill. For further safety, hundreds of judges patrolled the field of battle, calling out the 'dead' and wounded while Shiyen physicians attended those injured in the mêlée.

"The trail widens out about a hundred yards ahead of us," Corporal Chopil said, breaking Rukh's thoughts. "We should be able to make swifter progress then."

"Thank Devesh," Rukh said with feeling. "Pass the word along to the rest of the warriors. As soon as we're there, I want us picking up our pace. We don't want to miss out on all the fun."

"Yes, sir."

As soon as the trail opened up, there was almost an audible sigh of released tension from the platoon. They hadn't liked their slow progress any more than Rukh. Nevertheless, he was pleased to see them maintain discipline in spite of their relief. They remained alert and serious, but also loose and relaxed enough to grin at quiet complaints or bark hushed laughter at a jest. Rukh smiled when one of the Trims muttered irritated imprecations. A joke had likely been made at the expense of the annoyed warrior. It was how it was done. At least, it had been when Rukh had been a Trim.

Once more came that sense of vast age, similar to what he had experienced earlier in the morning. A long stretch of endless years reached back in time, and the sensation divided Rukh from the men in his command. It left him thinking of them as little more than children even though they were only a few years younger than he.

The weight of years pressed heavier, and ennui sucked at his soul. *He was tired of the long life he had lived. He'd spent too many years in this world, sacrificed too much. It was time to pass on the burden of his duty to someone else.*

Rukh started. Where were these thoughts coming from? He was barely into his twenties. He wasn't an old man with a lifetime of memories. His brow furrowed in puzzlement, but a tremor in the sky caused him to look west. There was nothing there, but he sensed something moving in the clouds. It was familiar. The laughter of a sweet girl . . .

He shook his head, trying to clear his thoughts. He needed to focus on the task before him.

Rukh! A voice, muffled and barely heard, briefly resonated in his mind.

He frowned again. Had that really been a voice in his mind, or had it merely been his imagination?

Rukh!

There. It came again. From the south. Still softer than a whisper. He was still unsure what he was hearing, if anything.

The Sorrow Bringer . . .

Or maybe a shout from a great distance? Rukh slowed, frowning even more deeply as he concentrated on something he wasn't sure was real.

Rukh! Run. The Sorrow Bringer is coming!

Rukh's head snapped up, and he halted. Aia. She was west of him. He bent his head in concentration, listening for her words.

Rukh! Run. The Sorrow Bringer is coming!

Rukh's features went slack. *This couldn't be happening. Not on a day when so many warriors were beyond the protection of Ashoka's Oasis.* The warning repeated, and the blood drained from Rukh's face. *It was happening. Devesh save them.* He took a moment to master his rising tide of fear before turning to Chopil and signaling the corporal. The Blacks stumbled to a jumbled stop.

Rukh turned to the warriors. His thoughts raced as he planned out his next steps. He could hear Aia's thoughts from a maximum of a day's distance. Who knew how quickly the Queen could cover that same journey? An hour? Less. Whatever it was, it couldn't be much. The Blacks—and every other warrior beyond the Outer Wall—would have to drop all their equipment, conduct *Jivatma* without pause, and run to ruination. Only then might they be able to get through this alive.

"Listen up, warriors. Aia, my Kesarin, has just sent me a warning. The Queen is heading toward Ashoka." Rukh spoke in a calm, steady tone. He didn't let his anxiety show. He didn't want the Trims panicking.

It worked. Perplexed murmurings met his words—fear as well—but there was no witless terror. Instead, the Trims appeared alert, ready, and willing. Rukh felt a surge of pride for them.

"This Advent Trial is over," Rukh continued. "Kummas, remove your Constrainers. Everyone discard your weapons. Shokes, bows, and arrows, anything that might slow you down. We're heading back to the city at best speed."

"But how will we defend ourselves against the Chimeras, sir?" a Rahail asked.

"Fireballs will work against them, but otherwise, the weapons we're carrying aren't meant to kill. They're useless," Rukh explained. "And even if we were fully armed, nothing can slow down the Sorrow Bringer." A clatter of weapons hitting the ground met his words. Rukh turned to Chopil. "Send up the emergency arrows."

These were the signal flares, flaming green arrows carried by every platoon. They would relay the message to all the warriors on the plain that enemies were approaching. It would immediately end the Advent Trial. Every platoon would hustle back to the gate closest to them.

And, unfortunately, of all the units, the Blacks would have the hardest, longest run to make.

Rukh took another moment to map out his next decision. The warriors wouldn't like it. He turned to the Kummas. "I want all of you running flat out. Don't slow down for anyone. Get inside the Outer Wall as quickly as you can. That is your only mission."

"But, sir, how will the Murans and Rahails keep up with us?" a Kumma asked.

"They won't," Rukh replied. "But there's also nothing any of you can do for them by being out here. None of us can stop the Sorrow Bringer. And She can likely see through our Blends so you aren't going to be any safer hiding with us behind one of them. If we want to live, we have to run. No slowing down."

"And what about you, sir?" asked Corporal Chopil.

Rukh's jaw briefly clenched. If Jessira were with him, she would have berated his decision even as she understood it. She was a warrior.

"I'm the commander. I'll stay with the Murans and Rahails." He managed to quirk a smile. "Of course, until we break free of this fragging forest, none of us will be doing much running."

CHAPTER ELEVEN
THE COST OF HATE

From the bowels of a sewer seeps the heart of hate.
It pollutes the purest water, dismaying love's longing for belonging.
It is a poisonous slug, so salt it well.

—*To Live Well* by Fair Shire, AF 1842

"What do those red flares mean?" Jessira asked.

"It means the Advent Trial is over," Bree answered with a frown. "Did you see those green arrows from the forest a while back? They were warnings that enemies are approaching. The red arrows are acknowledgment of the warning, and the call for all the platoons to return at once to Ashoka."

"Do we know what kind of enemies?" Jessira asked.

"No. Not yet," Bree said. "All we know is that enemies have been sighted."

The crowd around them shuffled about in unease. The prior lively nature of the jests and conversations had dimmed to muted whispers of worry and uncertainty.

Many minutes later, more green warning arrows fired, this time from the plain itself and sometime later, again from the forest, just in front of it.

Jessira cursed. Rukh was out there. Worrying about him was the last thing she needed, especially with the promise of violence hovering about the Shektans like a wispy fog. She wished it were her own misgivings, but Rector Bryce had also picked up on whatever was in the air. For Jessira, it felt like a bated breath before a battle, of the watchful silence before the storm, of hate and violence waiting to be unleashed. She had passed on her warning to the other women while Rector had done the same with the warriors guarding them.

Once more, Jessira wished that more of the Shektan women were armed. Right now, the only ones who bore blades were her, Sign, and Bree. Following the unmasking of Hal'El Wrestiva as the Withering Knife murderer, safety seemed to have returned to the streets of Ashoka. And since danger no longer lurked, it no longer seemed important to go armed in public. Jessira hoped the decision to forego their swords wouldn't be one that the Shektan women would come to rue.

Just as much, she hoped that her watchful wariness would prove to be unnecessary, that whatever she was sensing would prove illusory, a product of her imagination. She prayed such would be the case because the idea of drawing her sword on another person, hurting them, cutting them, or even killing them . . . she couldn't imagine anything so awful. Such a possibility had her sick at heart.

Bree appeared to share Jessira's misgivings or at least she appeared fearful of something. She circumspectly scanned the crowd with a look of queasy concern on her face. Her hand continually drifted to the hilt of her sword.

Jessira hoped the other woman would be fine. She wasn't a true warrior, but lately, she had worked hard to correct the deficiencies in her training and was actually fairly competent . . . or at least no longer a liability.

"I don't see anything," Sign said as she stepped up to Jessira's side.

"Nor I," Bree added.

"Just stay alert," Jessira warned them.

"Are you sure about what you felt?" Satha asked, coming up alongside them as well. "The Advent Trial has already ended, and I see nothing amiss. Are you certain your feelings aren't directed outward? At whatever enemy might be approaching?"

"What I felt isn't out there," Jessira said, gesturing to the plain beyond the Outer Wall. "What I felt is in here. It's all around us."

Satha exhaled. "And no one else has seen or heard anything out of the ordinary?"

"No one," Jessira confirmed. "But I'm sure of what I felt. I'm feeling it off and on right now. Something bad is about to happen."

"She's right," Rector said. "There *is* something wrong. The other warriors can feel it now, too." He stared Satha in the eyes. "I think it would be best if we simply left."

Satha glanced about at the crowd and made a moue of disgust. "I sense nothing," she said after a moment of study. "And while I trust your judgment, this is the Advent Trial, and this is Ashoka. I can't imagine anything truly dangerous occurring to us here. Not with us guarded by ten Kumma warriors." She hesitated. "But perhaps we should be prudent and do as you suggest. We'll start with the younger women first."

Rector nodded. "We'll make sure they move out in small groups so as to not attract attention." He paused as he was about to turn away. "It would be best if you return to stand amidst the rest of the women," he advised.

Satha nodded agreement and drifted back to where the other women were clustered.

After she had done so, Jessira looked over the crowd once again, trying to find that ineffable source of suppressed violence. Her eyes narrowed. There had been a time when she had been sure the focus of what she was feeling stemmed from the middle-aged Muran who had occasionally flicked his gaze toward her and Rector. Currently, the man stood surrounded by a group of young men—Murans, Duriahs, and Rahails. They stood silent and stared raptly out toward the broad plain surrounding Ashoka. What held their gazes was unclear since there was nothing to see.

The warriors of the Advent Trial were still Blended and nothing could be seen of what was occurring down in the plain beyond the Outer Wall. With the red arrows recalling the platoons, they were all likely sprinting back to the city. Maybe that's what those silent men were looking for: the tell-tale signs of the return of the Advent Trial warriors.

Jessira tried to convince herself that such might be the case, but there was something not quite right about the men. They kept flicking glances at one another, but the bulk of their focus often drifted to the Muran. It was furtive and suspicious, unnoticeable if Jessira hadn't been looking. Some of them shifted about as though nervous, and her certainty that they might be a part of whatever was causing her such unease deepened. There was something about way they stood: the overly conscious casualness, the studiousness in their eyes, and the seriousness that didn't belong, even amidst the quiet worry radiating off the crowd since the firing of the red arrows.

"There," she whispered to Rector.

"I see them," Rector replied. He had already flicked his suspicious gaze in the direction of the suspicious-appearing men. After a moment, his brows furrowed in confusion. "There aren't enough of them to pose us any threat," he said, sounding troubled rather than relieved. "There has to be something more to what we're feeling than just that handful of men."

"Where are all the women?" Bree asked, having overheard their conversation.

"They're right there," Sign said as though she was stating what should have been the most obvious fact possible. She gestured to the Shektan women who huddled together in a large grouping. The House warriors hovered protectively about their charges.

"No," Bree corrected. "Where are the women in the crowd? There used to be a lot more of them, but now there's hardly any."

Jessira suddenly cast her eyes about, looking in all directions. The blood drained from her face. Bree was right. There were hardly any women left in this section of the Outer Wall. It was almost entirely populated by men—men wearing long cloaks. They had the bearing of those who had once served as warriors, and those cloaks could be hiding swords and knives at their hips. There were a lot of them, maybe over fifty.

Jessira struggled to keep her breathing smooth and even, but her heart thudded. The nightmare she had hoped would be an unwonted fear looked like it was about to come true. "I think we're in trouble," she whispered.

"I think you're right," Rector agreed, looking grim-faced but determined. He muttered something under his breath.

"*Now!*" a voice shouted.

Jessira's gaze snapped in the direction of the cry. Of course it had to have been the middle-aged Muran. After that, there was no further time for thought. The cloaked men drew hidden swords and attacked. Screams filled the air.

Shur Rainfall didn't like the eyes of the Shektans upon him. They made him uncomfortable. It was as though a curse were being placed upon his name and that of his family. He especially didn't like it when the filthy ghrina woman stared at him. Jessira Shektan. Her gaze was as soiled as a pus-filled wound. He felt the need to bathe every time she looked his way. As she was doing right now.

He barely restrained a snarl. Even now, it rankled him that an abomination like her had been welcomed so openly into the family of a ruling 'El. What degeneracy could have allowed such evil to gain entrance into the heart of one of Ashoka's great Houses? Or blinded the vision of one of the city's great heroes to the corruption that was in the ghrina's blood. How could Rukh Shektan, slayer of so many Chimeras, have married this woman? It was proof, if any more had been needed, that House Shektan was utterly degenerate and their entire lineage Tainted.

As the ghrina's eyes passed over him once again, the Muran forced himself to turn away and not stare. Instead, he laughed, feigning frivolity even though his blood boiled. Soon enough—today, First Father willing—Jessira Shektan, the ghrinas, and all the Tainted Shektans would pay for their grave sins against nature and Devesh.

"They're looking our way again," one of the Duriahs whispered to him in warning. The man was nervous, and his skin glistened with a sheen of sweat.

"We only need wait a little longer," Shur whispered, wearing a false, toothy grin upon his face. "Our women have almost entirely departed, and the entirety of our warriors will be here soon enough."

"We may not have the time to gather all of our warriors together," the Duriah replied. "They seem to suspect something of us."

Shur bit back his irritation. The Duriah was one of the most devout members of the Virtuous, but also one of the smartest.

"Look at Rector Bryce. He keeps glancing our way," the Duriah noted.

Shur glanced at the City Watchman, the warrior in charge of guarding the Shektan women. The man's eyes were indeed suspicious as he seemed to study the Virtuous. So far, though, his eyes hadn't lingered overlong on Shur and his men. As long as that remained the case, then their attack could still go forward as planned.

"What do you think they're talking about now?" the Rahail asked, stepping forward and interrupting their conversation. He briefly gestured toward Jessira who stood with her cousin—another ghrina—and Bree Shektan. Approaching them was Satha Shektan, matriarch of the House. "Do you think they're talking about us?"

"It doesn't matter," Shur said. "We only need a few more minutes, and their place in this world will be gone." He pretended to laugh. "Look. Satha is already moving off. And they've kindly gathered all their women in one location. It'll make it that much easier to bring Devesh's judgment upon them."

"Some of their women are leaving," the Duriah noted.

Shur nodded. He'd seen it as well. "It's no matter. It's the matrons and the ghrina scum who will taste the severity of our righteousness. With the death of their elders, perhaps the young will be blessed with wisdom and see the error of their ways." Privately, he doubted something like that would ever happen, but it never hurt to show mercy to the weak.

Shur and his men waited in silence for a few more minutes before the Duriah spoke up once more.

"The ghrina is looking our way again," he said. "And so is Rector Bryce."

"So they are," Shur said, "but they're too late. Our warriors are here." He gathered his breath. "*Now!*" he shouted. Shur whipped aside his cloak and drew a sword. The rest of the warriors of the Virtuous did so as well as they leaped into righteous glory.

———————◆●◆———————

R ector wished he could have convinced the women of House Shektan to leave the Outer Wall sooner than he had. Anywhere else would have been safer than here where they were but targets. The small clusters currently evacuating the area were moving too slowly for his liking even as events seemed to be moving too quickly.

Too much was going on, too much that had no explanation. The green arrows followed by the red ones. The early end of the Advent Trial. Were there really enemies approaching the gates of Ashoka? And worst of all, this foreboding sense that something evil lurked nearby, something seeking death.

Rector wished again that *all* the Shektan women were moving off the Outer Wall right now. In fact, he wished many things, but none of it mattered any more. Their time had run out.

Jessira had pointed out the Muran. It was the same man Rector had noticed earlier, and he cursed himself. He should have listened to that niggling voice in back of his mind, the one that told him he should pay attention to the Muran. Rector recognized the man now. He had once been a captain in the High Army of Ashoka. Shur Rainfall was his name. Rector had only had a few interactions with him. It had been a couple of conversations shared shortly after Rector's return from his final Trial a few years ago and just prior to the Muran's retirement from the High Army.

But those brief interactions had left their mark. Ironically, just like Rector had once been, Shur Rainfall had also held an utter certainty of his own moral superiority and judgment. In addition, he had also possessed a self-assurance that bordered on the arrogant and a fervent passion that robbed him of charity for those who studied a problem and came to a different conclusion than he. There had been more than one instance where Shur had dismissively disregarded ideas that didn't stem from his own supposed brilliance, and according to rumor, the subsequent errors in judgment had apparently never done much to harm him with humility. To say that Rector had disliked the man would be an understatement.

"I think we're in trouble," Jessira whispered.

"I think you're right," Rector Bryce replied with a sinking worry. He'd killed a man once before, and the scars from that action still pained him like boils on his soul. All morning he had hoped that he would never need harm another person. That hope was about to be proven futile. And it was all because of Shur Rainfall. "That fragging Muran's face needs a fist," Rector muttered under his breath.

No sooner had the words left his mouth than Shur bellowed out a command. "*Now!*"

Cloaks were flung aside. Swords rasped from scabbards. Cries of hatred filled the air.

The world became chaotic.

Rector Shielded and gut-kicked an attacker. He launched a Fireball, and it screamed through the air.

Rector's soul wilted when two men were incinerated.

———— • ————

Upon the shouted word from the Muran, cloaks were thrown and blades drawn.

"Form a Triad," Bree ordered.

Jessira nodded and conducted *Jivatma*. As always, it was rich like honey and left her feeling connected with the world beyond the shell of her body. She felt a brush against her thoughts. Bree. Jessira reached for her and Sign.

They Annexed, and an unhurried peace stole over Jessira. Her thoughts grew too heavy, too numb to maintain. It was as if she'd taken a swim in winter-cold water. Soon, her mind stilled to silence.

The Triad was born, and it had a single task: survive. It would do so no matter the cost. The Triad Shielded and swords were drawn.

The one known as Rector Bryce stepped forward. He gut-kicked an attacker. His Fireball screamed through the air and incinerated two of the enemy. After that, there was no further room for any weapons other than blades.

The Triad stepped forward. It angled Primary, Secondary, and Tertiary so there were no blind spots. Primary was the swiftest and most powerful of the three, but Secondary was the most skillful warrior. The Triad set her at point.

The enemy held Linked Blends and were effectively invisible. The warriors allied to the Triad were slowed by their inability to see their adversaries. Nevertheless, they persevered. The Triad, however, wasn't hampered in any fashion. Two members could sense Blends. The Triad waited until the time was opportune. Surprise would be devastating. A Link was established with the Blends of the attackers.

Murans, Rahails, and Duriahs suddenly popped into view.

Secondary parried an attacker. Her follow-through was a hard kick to her adversary's knee. It buckled and a diagonal slash ripped the man across the chest. His hands dropped, and a kick to the face put him down.

Primary held off two attackers. She took a blade on her Shield. A quick thrust led to her adversary's gurgling death. Tertiary took the other attacker in the back.

A command came from two of the members: attack. It was immediately rescinded by Secondary.

They were to hold the line. Nevertheless, they were soon surrounded.

Secondary was sent forward. She took the lead and waded into the enemy. She parried slashes and thrusts from all sides, moving faster than the enemy. On her heels came Primary and Tertiary. They dealt death to those Secondary hurled aside.

From all three members came a great horror. Feelings leaked from them: shock, grief, and shame. A bone-deep regret that they had to kill people. Other Humans with life and thought.

The Triad slowed, almost halted. It conducted Jivatma *from all three and from Secondary and Tertiary came Lucency. The thoughts of the members quieted, became sharp as a razor. Purpose was restored.*

The Triad had drifted too far away from allies. It cut a controlled retreat through the middle elements of the enemy. This time Primary led. Her swift sword sang. Tertiary worked to her right. Secondary brought up the rear, defending their backs.

Tertiary took a cut to her thigh. It was deep and immediately began bleeding profusely. Secondary stepped forward to protect her weakened side. Just then, Primary took a stunning blow to the face.

Secondary was left to defend both of them. She blurred, moving even faster than before. She defended against a swarm. The enemy had them surrounded.

———— ● ————

Rector fought without the aid of a Duo, Triad, or Quad. He had to have a clear mind to watch everything that was happening and direct the warriors to where they could better protect the women. As a result, he felt every thrust, every cut, every slice he inflicted upon another living person. He wanted to plead for mercy, to have this weighty burden removed from his shoulders, to cry out at the pain he was inflicting on his very soul. How did these attackers not feel the awfulness of what they were doing? How could they attempt to murder without even the slightest of hesitations?

The questions might have circled in his head, but instead, Rector shoved them down, burying them along with his horror. He did what he had to. The horror could come later.

There came a moment of stillness when the Linked Blends of the adversary simply dissolved. The enemy was suddenly visible. They were a mix of Duriahs, Murans, and Rahails. Nearly a third of their number lay on the ground, unmoving or groaning in pain. As for the warriors of House Shektan—all of them still fought. They remained in the battle, but most were injured. A few gravely. Some of the women who the warriors were meant to protect had taken up swords as well. Their skill was lacking. Unlike Bree, they hadn't spent the last year focused on mastering their martial skills. They were almost more of a hindrance than a help.

Rector cursed when he saw the Triad of Bree, Jessira, and Sign drift away from the main body of House Shektan's warriors. They were too far for the other guards to offer support. He had given permission for those three to fight, but why couldn't they have remained close and hold the line like proper warriors? Maybe a woman in a battle simply couldn't think clearly enough to do what was needed.

He cursed again when Sign took a deep wound and Bree a heavy blow to the face. Jessira blurred, but it was a pace she couldn't maintain for long. Rector called out orders. The other nine guards closed ranks while he stepped forward to rescue the three nits.

<hr/>

Primary shook off the effects of the blow to the face. Secondary was surrounded. Attackers swept around her like water around a boulder. She was immoveable in her determination. It couldn't last forever, though. She would weaken. Tertiary's leg was rapidly failing. A ringing of swords. Secondary was pressed hard. A hard blow was absorbed by her Shield. Primary cut her way to Secondary's side.

Rector Bryce was there as well. He thrust and slashed all about him.

Primary offered distraction to Secondary's main opponent. Rector ran the enemy through.

Another adversary filled the gap, and Primary took a deep cut to the biceps. Her arm immediately weakened.

The Triad followed as Rector acted as the ramming prow and returned them to the thin line of House Shektan's warriors. Triad noted that their numbers were down to eight. Two warriors lay unmoving, and the rest were slowing, all of them injured in some fashion.

The enemy had them hard-pressed on all sides. Their numbers were likely little more than half of what they started with, but they were whittling the Shektans down.

The Triad sensed the worry of its members, but the concern didn't touch it. Purpose was all it knew.

———— ● ————

R ector was growing fearful. The enemy numbers had been cut down—they were down to a little less than half of their original number—but they showed no signs of fatiguing from the fight. They came on, and he distantly wondered what fervor drove them to such evil.

Further rumination had to be put aside. Three of them attacked him just then. Rector slipped past a blow intended to take off his head. He spun with the momentum of his movement. He parried a slash. Still spinning, his upswing took off the third man's sword arm at the elbow. Another blow was taken on his weakening Shield. He thrust forward like a launched arrow. His sword took one of them through the heart. The final opponent was dispatched by Jessira Shektan.

Rector shook his head in disgust. He still didn't like the idea of the three women fighting, but at least they were being useful now that they were holding the line. Not like the City Watch, which had yet to show up. Where in the unholy hells were they! The battle had been going on for seemingly forever, but there was still no sign of relief. If the Watch didn't arrive soon, there might not be anyone of House Shektan left to rescue.

Two more of his warriors were down. Their line contracted further, and despite Rector's distaste with the notion of women as warriors, he was heartened when more of the Shektan women took up fallen weapons to defend themselves. They were the daughters, wives, and mothers of warriors. Rector felt great pride for these women. In their own way, they were warriors as well.

An instant later, that same pride fled. Satha Shektan had taken up a sword.

Rector watched, horrified when he saw her engage an enemy. She had some skill, but if she wasn't supported, she would fall. Rector fought his way to her side. Above all the other women, she had to be preserved.

After a few intense moments of fighting, there came another pause.

"I am capable of defending myself, Rector," Satha said to him in a tart tone. "We would work better as a team."

"I can't form a Duo with you," Rector said. "I have to maintain a clear mind to control the battle."

Jessira, Bree, and a badly limping Sign arrived.

"Form a Quad with us," the Triad said in its inflectionless voice from the mouths of all three women.

Satha did so and a Quad was born.

Rector wasn't sure whether to applaud Satha's courage or cringe with concern at her foolhardiness. In that moment, the most inane concern came to him: Dar'El would be furious that Rector had allowed Satha to risk herself like this.

———◆———

The Triad became the Quad. Its purpose remained unchanged: survive.

Quaternary was the only one uninjured at this point. Her Shield was also the strongest. The other three were straining to conduct Jivatma. Their Wells were rapidly emptying. Quaternary was set at point. Even through the fog of their clouded minds came a rebellion from Primary and Secondary. Quaternary was pulled back. Secondary took point instead.

Rector Bryce fought alongside them. Other Triads, Quads, and Duos, did so as well. All of them were women, except for the six remaining male warriors of House Shektan.

There was a fierceness to the conflict, an escalation as the enemy launched themselves at the Shektans. From Secondary and Tertiary came the sense that this was likely the end of the battle. The enemy would either overwhelm them or be defeated.

The Quad was faced by a constantly moving stream of opponents. They attacked. Blows were exchanged, but the quarters were tight. The enemy would be jostled aside before the Quad could land a telling blow.

Two men stood against Tertiary. Her leg nearly collapsed as she sought to block the closer of the two opponents. The Quad sent Quaternary to support Tertiary. One of the enemy turned to face her. Quaternary slipped a thrust. Her own found a heart.

Tertiary stepped inside the guard of her final opponent. She smashed the hilt of her sword into the man's nose, shattering it. An elbow followed in the same motion. The man stumbled into Secondary's waiting blade.

Primary parried an overhand slash. Her arm buckled. Secondary had already been pulled to guard. Her sword cleaved a deep gash along the flank of Primary's adversary.

Another opponent down. Another filled the gap. And another. For once, Secondary was too slow to act. She took a slash to the ribs. It was deep, and her breathing suddenly came less easily.

A shout came from Rector Bryce to pull back, to fight shoulder to shoulder.

As the Quad did so, another surge came from the enemy. Three of them focused on Tertiary. Quaternary was moved to guard.

Tertiary's leg gave way. Her Shield absorbed one blow. Another. Then it was done. Tertiary's Well could no longer support a Shield. Quaternary was sent to stand before the fallen Tertiary. She fought alone against what was now five opponents. What she was unable to block, she absorbed on her Shield. She would be overwhelmed soon.

But Rector Bryce cut one adversary down. Quaternary took out another. There was a momentary lull.

"Get her out of here!" Rector shouted.

His order was echoed by all four members of the Quad. Quaternary carried out the command. She helped drag and carry Tertiary toward the back, until she was out of immediate danger. Quaternary then rejoined the fray.

Secondary and Primary were both beset by several opponents each. Primary was weakening quickly. Her injured arm hung by her side. She fought one-armed.

Secondary's breathing grew ever more ragged. She didn't have much left in her Well either.

Rector Bryce and another Shektan warrior provided them some relief.

The Quad saw the attack coming. It could do nothing to stop it.

B ree's thoughts, so quicksand slow in the Quad, snapped into racing focus. Her amma was going to die. She faced three Murans. They moved to flank her. There was no one close enough to offer her any support.

The Quad was moving too slowly. Its focus was on keeping as many members alive as possible, even if that meant sacrificing one of them.

Bree severed her ties with the Quad and threw herself forward even as she knew she would never reach Amma in time. She watched in horror as one of the Murans thrust forward. Amma blocked. She parried a slash. Another slash defended. A riposte took one adversary in the throat. Meanwhile, the third Muran—middle-aged and with a face full of hate—had stepped behind her. His blade stabbed out, penetrating Amma's Shield. The sword warped from the impact. Instead of stabbing Amma through the heart, it bent down and took her in the center of her back.

Bree screamed.

Amma collapsed, and her head smacked the ground.

Bree arrived. Hatred and rage rode roughshod over her sorrow. There would be time for tears later. She killed a Muran and felt nothing. The one who had stabbed her Amma took one look at her and ran.

"*Coward!*" Bree shouted at him.

He stopped long enough to gesture rudely in her direction.

Bree realized she had space. There was a cluster of three opponents closing on her. They'd never make it. Her hand glowed but before she could discharge her Fireball, another one impacted the charging enemy first. It had been Rector Bryce's.

His Fireball had punched completely through the lead enemy and also taken his compatriot following on his heels. Both men were launched backward by the blast of the Fireball. They smashed into the third man, who'd been standing behind them. His head hit the ground with the sickening sound of a coconut cracking open.

The rest of the attackers must have taken the sight of Rector's Fireball as a sign. They broke and within seconds, the Shektan section of the Outer Wall was clear.

Bree's anger suddenly drained away, replaced by a desperate fear. She ran to her unconscious amma. Jessira was there also.

"Can you Heal her?" Bree demanded.

Jessira shook her head. "I just used up almost all of my Well, but even if I hadn't . . ." She shrugged helplessly. "Her spinal cord's been severed. Even on my best day, I couldn't help her with something like that."

Bree looked around in desperation. Maybe there was a physician nearby.

Their entire section of the Outer Wall was empty. For yards around where the fighting had taken place, there was no one. Beyond the open space, the crowd which had come to watch the spectacle of the Advent Trial stood still and quiet. They viewed the carnage from the melee with expressions of shocked disbelief. Eventually, they began moving. It was like a dislodged rock allowing the stream to flow once more. The crowd on both sides of the Shektans began moving, running forward. They called out offers of help.

Bree scowled. Where had they been seconds before? What had they been doing while the Shektans had been desperately fighting to survive?

She shook off her angry sense of betrayal. Amma needed help.

Jessira was already yelling. "Is there a physician?" she cried out.

Bree joined her.

Seconds later—an eternity—a Shiyen with a bald pate and a long, pleated beard arrived. "What happened to her?" he asked, brusque and no nonsense.

"Severed spine," Bree answered. She looked to Jessira for confirmation who nodded agreement.

The Shiyen spent no more time on questions. He had his hands by the side of Amma's head. A fierce look of concentration and determination took hold of his features. A glow built up in his hands. It kept building before suddenly draining down into Amma. The shape of the bones in her face became briefly visible.

The Shiyen remained focused and sent another flow of *Jivatma* into Amma. Another flow. One more, and the Shiyen sat back with a sigh. "I've got her stabilized," he said. "It's the best I can do for now. We need to get her to a hospice." He glanced at Jessira. "Let me help with your breathing."

While he did so, Bree's heart eased. Her amma would live. It was over. Relief, sudden and fine like the sweetest water, overwhelmed her. By the barest of margins, she held back the sobs. She feared she'd never get them to stop if she allowed them to start.

Any sense of comfort she felt immediately dissipated when she looked around.

The debris of dead bodies and moaning wounded littered the battlements of the Outer Wall. Too many of that number were of House Shektan.

Jessira was so tired. She wanted to lie down and sleep. She was relieved to know that Satha was going to live, and now she needed to make sure her cousin was safe. "I have to find Sign," she said to

Bree, who nodded mutely.

Jessira squeezed the other woman's arm before standing up and tottering away.

She hadn't been this tired in a long time, and the fatigue wasn't entirely physical. Much of it was emotional as well. Jessira and the other Shektans had been attacked. It had been as violent a clash as anything she could ever remember, and her sense of safety was shattered. She'd almost died today.

Her heart also ached for what she had been forced to do during the battle. She had killed another Human; many of them. Even now, her mind shied away from the memories of what she had done. The finality of death. The smooth parting of flesh. The expression on the faces of those men just before her sword had cleaved the life from their bodies . . .

Jessira bit back a cry. She feared those images would haunt her for the rest of her life. She wished Rukh was with her. If nothing else, his presence would be a comfort, and she needed comforting.

And so, too, would Rukh when he learned what had happened to his amma. Satha would live, but nevertheless, Jessira feared for her. She wasn't sure if Satha would ever again walk. It might be possible—the physicians of Ashoka were almost magical in what they could accomplish—but it seemed unlikely.

Jessira momentarily beat back her fatigue when she saw Sign slowly sitting up. A physician had Healed her cousin and had already moved on to someone else injured in the battle. Sign rose to her feet, tottered, and almost fell.

Jessira rushed to support her. "You know better than to stand up so quickly after a Healing," she chided.

"I'm fine," Sign said irritably. "The Shiyen said I lost some blood and that I should eat some extra meat over the next few weeks. She

Healed the wound, and I hardly even feel it now."

"It still takes a lot out of you," Jessira reminded her.

"I'm fine," Sign insisted.

Jessira was about to reply, but a movement in the sky caught her sight.

Lightning coruscated within a bruise-purple cloud that was moving faster than any cloud had a right to move.

Jessira raced to the edge of the Outer Wall. She gawked at what she was seeing. The fine hairs on her arms stood on end. She knew what was coming. "Rukh," she breathed in terrified horror. He was out there.

CHAPTER TWELVE
RACE THE STORM

The storm beckons the tired warrior.
Blood courses like a blessed, sorrel steed.
Veins burning with fire.
Bones adamantine.
Breathe out unmanning fear and ride the tide.

—*A Romantic Notion* by Anto Jakper, AF 1454

As soon as Black Platoon broke free of the forest, Rukh ordered the firing of their remaining signal arrows. He had to make sure that their message got out. The Blacks had launched their original flares while still deep in the depths of the forest, and though the arrows had climbed up past the upper canopy, what if the other warriors of the Advent Trial had been too far away to see them? Everyone had to be back behind Ashoka's sturdy Walls and even sturdier Oasis if the Sorrow Bringer was truly headed their way.

Black Platoon's final signal flares flashed green fire across the sky, and Rukh's heart unclenched when an answering red blaze climbed heavenward from the Outer Wall. The green arrows had been the call, and the red fire the response that Black Platoon's warning had been seen and heeded.

Rukh turned to the Kummas in his unit. "Run hard. Straight to the Outer Wall. The ladders will be waiting. Don't wait on us. I mean it. If you do, it might be your life. Go!"

As one, the Kummas saluted and broke off. They raced forward in a ground-devouring run. It was *Jivatma* infused and for anyone else, would have been something just short of a dead sprint, but it was a pace the Kummas could keep up for miles.

Rukh turned to the remaining warriors. "Even though Suwraith can see through our Blends, I still want them up. Make them as tight as you can. Now let's run hard like all the hounds of hell are chasing us!"

Rukh led the Murans and Rahails toward Ashoka at a fast trot. As they ran, he did a rough calculation of how long it would take them to reach the city. The plain outside Ashoka was about four miles wide. At their current pace, it would take them a little less than half an hour to cover that distance and reach the Outer Wall. There, rope ladders would have already been lowered so the warriors of the Advent Trial could more quickly gain entrance to the city. It was part of the emergency procedures that allowed those trapped outside the city quicker access into Ashoka beyond just the three main gates or the few scattered sally ports.

Rukh also realized that in their current situation, he and the warriors racing to get back to the city didn't actually have to climb the ladders. They just had to get close enough to touch the Outer Wall. If it was just the Queen coming after them, that's all they would need. The Outer Wall had actually been built ten or fifteen feet *inside* the bounds of the Oasis, a protection She couldn't penetrate.

That was it then. *Get to the Wall, and they'd be safe.* It was a mantra Rukh repeated to himself as he ran.

However, with the passage of time, Rukh fretted over the distance yet to travel. The plain flowed beneath their feet in a slow, painful procession, and the Outer Wall seemed no closer now than it did when they had started their run. How much time did they have before the Sorrow Bringer arrived? Rukh wasn't sure, but it couldn't be much. With every passing moment, he worried that they would be caught out in the open.

Rukh mentally grimaced and pushed aside his worrying thoughts even as he pushed the pace a little faster. Run. That was his only duty. It was the only duty of every warrior still out in the field. Run. That was all that mattered.

And while Rukh could have already made it to the Wall by now—find himself safely atop the Outer Wall—he'd never be able to live with himself. These were Trims. These were young, inexperienced men. They had no one to look after them. Rukh would not simply abandon them out here to be annihilated.

By staying with them, he could push them harder than they likely would have pushed themselves. The pace he set—the pace he expected them to maintain—was likely faster than any they would have managed on their own. It might be the difference between somehow seeing these warriors returned safely to Ashoka or watching them die.

"Sir. There are a number of Blends all around us," panted Lift Toilpeat—a Muran—coming up alongside him. "Both north and south."

Rukh cursed loudly. If those Blends could be sensed, those men couldn't be more than a mile ahead of the Blacks. They should have been a good deal further along than that. "How long have you known of them?" Rukh asked.

"Since before we left the forest, sir."

"Suwraith's spit," Rukh muttered. What were those fragging idiots still doing out here? He scowled. "Link with them."

The Muran didn't answer, but suddenly something like a hundred men sprang into view. Rukh's eyes widened in shock. It was even worse than he had feared. The warriors ran in clusters of twenty—their platoons—in a long, ragged line that stretched more than a mile north and south of the Blacks. Most raced hundreds of yards ahead of Rukh's unit, but some were merely abreast of them. There were even a few laggards who were somehow *behind* Black Platoon.

None of those warriors should still be here. Why hadn't they run for Ashoka as soon as they saw the signal flares? Rukh bit back an oath when he saw Kummas amidst those groups. Those men could have already been to the Wall if they had raced flat out. Instead, they ran with the Murans and Rahails. What were they thinking? Had they thought that the signal flares were for incoming Chimeras? Had they remained with their brother warriors in order to protect them from Suwraith's hordes?

If so, it had been the wrong decision.

Rukh fired a whistling arrow to get the attention of the closest cluster of warriors. When they turned in the direction of the Blacks, Toilpeat used hand signals to message the truth of the situation. There was a momentary startlement before the information was passed down the line of platoons. A wave of surprise greeted the news. Soon enough, the Kummas began separating from their units. They ran more and more swiftly. In just a few seconds, they were many yards ahead of the Murans and Rahails and still pulling away

Good. It was what they should have been doing the moment Black Platoon's warning arrows had gone up in the first place. They might still make it to the city in time.

As for those left behind, the Murans and Rahails . . . all their futures were far less certain. Their fates were unknowable.

Rukh tried to be serene about the situation, to act unmoved by the possibility of the Queen's coming. *If She arrives, She arrives*, was what he told himself, but it was a lie.

Rukh feared the Queen. He feared what She would do to these young warriors by his side. Their lives had been entrusted to his care, and he would be powerless to protect them. His heart thudded, hammering harder than what was needed for this race. Rukh also feared for his own life, especially what would happen to Jessira if he fell.

He could somehow sense her presence. She was on the Outer Wall, just north of Sunset Gate, and he found himself unaccountably worried for her. For a time, it had felt like she had been . . . in a battle? Fighting for her life. It was ludicrous—Jessira was safe in Ashoka—but, still, the sensation hadn't left him. The awareness, the worry had grown, until suddenly, it was gone, disappearing as abruptly as it had begun.

Rukh prayed then to Devesh for peace. It was an appeal that was more fervent than any he could ever recall making. Maybe the prayer even helped, because as he mentally voiced the words, a wisp of calm came to him. He was able to focus on nothing more than the ground before him. The running became hypnotic, meditative.

The flattened grass of the plain blurred beneath his booted feet.

* * *

Had She still Her Human form, Lienna would have gritted Her teeth with impatience. It had taken much longer than She had intended to travel the remaining distance to Ashoka. She'd been slowed by the laborious work that only She could do. Lienna had to make sure that no more of the Humans infested the forested hills west of their pus-filled home. Such searching required careful observation. The parasites could no longer hide from Her sight, but if Lienna passed too swiftly, She might easily miss one or two of them. Thus, a journey that She could have made in minutes had ended up requiring almost an hour.

The one aspect of Her travel that brought Her pleasure was the blessed silence in Her mind. Her parents and Mistress Arisa had remained quiet. Still, Lienna anticipated the end of Her journey. Just a few more hills, and She would be there. She overtopped a rise and found her Human lying atop the peak of a tall hill. Hal'El was hidden behind a humped mound of dirt. He appeared to be scanning the broad plain that began at the base of this crest and led to his once home.

Her children, the Tigons that Lienna had lent Hal'El Wrestiva, crouched down below in a shallow ravine. Upon seeing Her arrival, they fell prostrate upon the ground, quite rightly worshipping the presence of their loving Mother. The soothing sounds of their prayers wafted like rose petals, carried aloft to Her by their devotion rather than the wind.

> *By Her grace are we born*
> *By Her love are we made*
> *By Her will are we shorn*
> *By Her fire are we unmade*
> *And are reborn once more*

When they completed the Prayer of Gratitude, Lienna spoke to them. *"Arise My children,"* She said. *"Know that I am well pleased with you. You have My blessings. Now rest so I may speak to the Human you have so conscientiously served and protected these many weeks."*

Hal'El, of course, offered Her no prayers, nor did he offer Her anything resembling obeisance. But then again, She didn't expect proper behavior from him. The man was a Human. He lacked the ability to act in a civilized fashion. Yes, he was Her devoted follower, but the soul-deep stain of his creation forever marred his being. It could never be washed away. It could never be removed. It would remain with him to the end of his days.

The contrast in comportment between the Human and Her children was striking. The Tigons mouthed the Prayer of Gratitude with heads pressed in humility to the ground while Hal'El haughtily made his way down the hill to the valley where Lienna patiently waited. His unhurried pace betrayed and emphasized his arrogance.

When Hal'El reached the base of the hill, he fell to a single knee and gazed upon the dirt. "My Queen," he said. "What would you have of us?"

Lienna was surprised by his actions. First, by his bended knee, and second by his humble words. Lienna smiled to Herself. Perhaps there was hope for some Humans after all. For a moment, a doubt, a desire to let Humanity live surged through Her.

However, Her hope sprung from Her generous, loving nature, and She immediately snuffed it out.

The truth was that very few of Hal'El's kind had his restraint and wisdom. Her resolve steeled, and Lienna spoke to Her Human. *"You hide here like a slug,"* She said. *"Why have you not done as I commanded and entered Ashoka?"*

"My Queen, You commanded that I enter Ashoka alive, but the plain before the city crawls with their warriors. They would see me and slay me in an instant," Hal'El said. "I have no means by which to evade them."

His words were smooth and even. There had been no hint of fear in them. Lienna appreciated that. She hated when Her children trembled with fear before Her. As such, in this one matter, Lienna had to applaud Hal'El's bearing.

Nevertheless, Humans were sly schemers, even one who was almost moral like Hal'El. In the end, they all lied. Time stretched as Lienna searched the soft words of Her Human for the hidden worm of deceit.

"You mentioned You had intentions for the Tigons You sent with me?" Hal'El asked, breaking into Her thoughts.

Lienna wanted to reply, but, in reality, She had no idea what the Human was talking about. Was this another lie? She couldn't immediately recall what She intended. Eventually, the memory came back to Her. She and the Tigons would provide a distraction while Hal'El snuck back into Ashoka.

"Your 'distraction' will do nothing more than kill all Your so-called children," Her Mother said, speaking from the depths of Lienna's mind. *"They deserve better."*

"Silence," Lienna ordered. *"My children will do as I ask because they love Me."*

"Your children will do as they are told because they fear You," Mother countered.

"They are heroes and martyrs," Lienna said, not sure why She bothered arguing with Her Mother. *"Their sacrifice will be remembered for all time."*

"For all time?" Mother scoffed. *"We once felt the same as You, Your Nanna and I. Our foolish arrogance was proved when You murdered Us and murdered the world We had helped build. And the sacrifice of Your Tigons will simply be another type of murder."*

Again with the charges of murder! Would Mother ever speak of anything other than murder! *"I have no regrets,"* Lienna averred. *"I did what was needed."*

"And You have served Me well," Mistress Arisa said. Her voice was soft as morning dew. *"Kill the Humans on the plain before their foul city, and You will once again offer Me great service just as You have done in the past."*

Lienna didn't want to acknowledge Mistress' presence. It would be easier to pretend She wasn't real. It would be better if Mistress Arisa was simply a figment of Lienna's imagination. It would be simpler to—

"My Queen," Hal'El prodded, ending Lienna's internal conversation and returning Her attention to the matter at hand.

"I will annihilate those warriors on the plains before Ashoka," Lienna said. Her voice grew stronger with every word She spoke. *"They will tremble at My coming and fall on their faces in fear. In the end, they will be grateful when I take their terror from them."*

"And what of the Tigons?" Hal'El asked. He remained on bended knee with a bent head and a penitent voice.

"They will act as My heralds. They will loudly announce My presence," Lienna answered. *"They, too, will serve to raise terror in the hearts of the Humans and fill them with fear of their coming destiny."*

"They are to sacrifice themselves," Hal'El said, sounding thoughtful. "When they attack, warning arrows will be fired. The warriors down on the plain will slowly retreat back to the city since they won't know the nature or number of enemies they face. As they press for Ashoka, if You were to then appear, my Queen, a half an hour or so after the Tigons, they'll flee. It'll be a rout as they seek shelter in Ashoka. I should be able to follow on their panicked heels and enter the city as well. I'll be unknown and unseen."

Lienna paused. With all the excitement of the difficult

conversation with Mother and Mistress Arisa, She'd forgotten that Hal'El was supposed to get into Ashoka. It was the entire reason he was here. How could She have misremembered such an important detail? No matter. The Human's plan would work. Best of all, many of the very worst kind of Humans—their warriors—would die at Her metaphorical hands today.

------●●------

Just a few more minutes and they'd be there. The Outer Wall reared higher and closer. The rope ladders and baskets were clearly visible. Many of them were in use as warriors from earlier-arriving platoons were even now being hauled to the top of the Outer Wall and to safety. Rukh dared to think that he and the other latecomers might make it as well.

No sooner had Hope dared poke Her lovely head past the morose skies above than Rukh caught movement out of the corner of his eyes. A bruise-purple cloud rushed toward them from the south. It smashed Hope straight in the face. Coruscating lightning lit the cloud from within. Thunder pealed a lurid counterpoint.

Everyone glanced back trying to identify what they were seeing, but Rukh already knew what it was. The cloud moved faster than any cloud had a right to move.

"*Run!*" Rukh screamed. "It's Suwraith! Move it!"

His words were passed down in frantic signals. The platoons set off at a dead sprint. The Outer Wall crept closer but not quickly enough. Warriors panted, their faces red with effort as they pushed past pain.

"Don't stop," Rukh urged. "We're almost there."

He glanced to the side.

Suwraith had overtaken a platoon of warriors. Rukh silently urged the men there to greater speed even as She hovered above them. She matched their speeds. Some of the warriors must have kept their bows because arrows sped upward. They sliced through the Queen, but caused no damage. Bolts of lightning sizzled to the ground, and with the rush of a waterfall, the Sorrow Bringer crashed down. When She lifted up again, the mangled bodies of ten or so young men lay unmoving.

Rukh gritted his teeth in fury as Suwraith moved on to another platoon. Their commander must have been a Kumma, and he must have remained with his men. Fireballs erupted toward the Sorrow Bringer. But just like the arrows, they had no effect on the Queen. Within seconds, another ten men lay dead.

Another platoon met a similar fate, and the Blacks were next in line for Suwraith's wrath.

"We aren't going to make it!" Toilpeat cried out.

Rukh knew the Muran was right, but there was no other option except to run. "Keep going," Rukh said. "I'll . . ." The words dried in his throat. He swallowed heavily, hating what he knew he had to do. These men wouldn't die while he did nothing. "Don't wait on me, warrior. Keep running," he commanded. He slapped Toilpeat on the shoulder.

Jessira forgive me.

Rukh broke away from the rest of the Blacks. He took an angle away from them and away from Ashoka. He took an angle toward sacrifice. Toward the Sorrow Bringer. Better that he die than all these others share his fate. His hands glowed. He hurled Fireballs at the Queen, hoping to grab Her attention. She seemed to ignore him at first, but then She paused. Slowly, heavily, Suwraith turned his way.

Rukh might have exulted, but he still had to survive long enough to give his men time to reach the Outer Wall. He had to keep the Queen chasing after him. He had to stay alive long enough for them to find shelter. He would die, but if the cost of his life meant these others could live, it was a sacrifice he was willing to make.

He conducted *Jivatma* and raced away as swiftly as he could. He formed a Shield, held hard to his useless Blend, and even formed a Bow. Why the latter, he didn't know, but it was said that necessity was the Amma of invention. Maybe inspiration would strike him during this forlorn moment of need.

Rukh sensed the Queen rearing overhead, and he twisted aside. A bolt of lightning sizzled directly behind him. Thunder pealed, and the aftershock hurled him forward. Another bolt missed him. Another aftershock hurled him forward. Rukh stumbled but kept to his feet. His ears rang. He felt blood trickle down the side of his face. His ears were bleeding.

Rukh glanced at the Blacks. He only had to hold out a little longer. They were almost to the Wall.

Once again, the Queen overtook him, and Rukh dodged away. The Sorrow Bringer kept after him, floating low over the ground. From Her came the sound of grinding bones, of nails scraping stone, the howl of frustrated anger.

Rukh smiled to himself. Good. The Queen wasn't happy that She hadn't yet killed him.

His pleasure was short-lived. He sensed the Queen pause, as if She were trying to figure out how to smash him down when he refused to stand still. She moved more slowly now, as if to ensure he wouldn't be able to dodge away from Her a third time. She floated lower and rushed toward him from ground level.

There was no way to evade Her. Not this time. Rukh prepared to meet his Creator. Always lacking in faith, in this the final moment of his life, he offered his first heartfelt prayer. *Devesh, if you're there, I commit myself to your care.*

Serenity, so elusive before, came upon him then. Rukh understood he was going to die, that there was no way to avoid it. He accepted his fate, didn't fight it. He simply waited for the end to come.

In that unfathomably long instant, images came to Rukh. Images from his life. Random thoughts and ideas. Notions from childhood. Meeting Jaresh for the first time. Talking to his nanna and amma on the eve of the Tournament of Hume. Touching the WellStone and witnessing the world come to life. Playing with Bree before Jaresh became a part of their family. Seeing his daughter's first smile and watching her first steps. The moment when knowledge of Blending was thrust upon him. Kissing Jessira on their wedding night. Learning the truth about the Baels. Li-Dirge's last words. Touching his wife's pregnant belly. Understanding how to fuse a Shield, Blend, and Bow.

The imagery was a welter of confusing memories, and many of them fled from his mind as soon as he saw them, but Rukh didn't care. Insight had come to him. He knew what was needed. With a desperate lunge, Rukh combined Shield, Blend, and Bow. He was encased in an Oasis.

The Queen lifted skyward as She overtook him. She became a rising mountain before descending like rumbling avalanche.

Rukh barely held onto consciousness as the Sorrow Bringer pounded into him. His Oasis flickered, firmed, and grew stronger as a presence came upon him, ancient, puissant, but so very tired.

Jessira noted that all along the Outer Wall's length, rope ladders and large baskets had been lowered. Warriors from the Advent Trial clambered up on their own or were carried to safety, but there were many more who hadn't yet arrived. Rukh was amongst those who still ran for the security of the Outer Wall.

She could sense him out there, along with a number of other Blends still beyond Ashoka's bounds. When they drew close enough, Jessira was able to Link with them, and a hundred or so warriors suddenly snapped into view. They sprinted for the Outer Wall. Though their features weren't discernible, Jessira imagined the desperation carved into their faces. They were so close. Only a few hundred more yards to go.

Jessira implored them on, urging them to greater speed even as Suwraith surged forward. The Sorrow Bringer aimed unerringly for the closest cluster of warriors.

"Devesh save them," Jessira breathed.

Moments later, the Queen reached the platoon. Arrows were fired into Her and through Her. She paid them no attention. She arched skyward before slamming down. The thunder from Her lightning was nothing compared to the noise when She hammered the ground. A cloud of dirt and grass erupted upward and outward. Even before the debris had settled, ten or so warriors could be seen lying in shattered poses of death.

"Mercy," Sign whispered in a hushed tone.

Another platoon was targeted.

"What's happening out there?" one of the Shektan matrons demanded. "And what's that awful cloud?"

"Suwraith is attacking the remaining platoons on the plain," Jessira answered, keeping her tone as flat and inflectionless as possible. If she allowed the fear surging inside her even the slightest outlet, it would take her. It would do no one any good if she were to panic.

The matron gasped. "Can you see what's happening?"

Jessira nodded.

Another cloud of dust rose heavenward.

"Another platoon has been destroyed," Sign said, her voice also inflectionless.

The entire Outer Wall was silent.

Bree arrived at their side. "Amma has been evacuated," she said. "I wanted to be with her, but she insisted I stay here and find out what's happening to Rukh."

"He's still out there," Jessira said to her.

Another group of warriors died.

"How much farther do the other warriors have?" the matron asked.

"Not far," Jessira replied as Suwraith made Her way to the next set of Trims. She gasped when, from that platoon, a single warrior broke away.

He ran away from the other warriors and away from Ashoka. He ran in the one direction that would lead to his certain destruction. He ran toward the Queen. He threw Fireballs that lit into the Sorrow Bringer. He threw more Fireballs, and just as the warrior must have intended, the Queen altered Her path. She turned and gave chase, racing after the warrior who had challenged Her might.

A hollowness, a pain beyond sorrow, a fear beyond panic, a soul-aching loss took hold of Jessira. She knew the warrior who was sprinting away.

"Are all the warriors safe then?" the elderly matron asked, sounding surprised "Is that why the Queen has turned aside?"

"No," Sign replied. "She's chasing a single warrior. He's leading

Her away from the others. Giving them a chance to win through."

Astonished mutterings arose as Sign's words were passed down the line. Every inch of the Outer Wall was taken up by those watching the drama unfolding down below.

"What courage," someone murmured in awe. "What bravery," added another. Similar sentiments could be heard from many more.

"Whoever it is, he must be a Kumma," the elderly matron standing next to Jessira declared. "He is doing as he was born and bred to do." She gave a proud, satisfied nod. An instant later, her satisfaction fell away as understanding took hold. "A Blended Kumma? Oh no." She shot Jessira a look of pity.

Jessira heard all this as though from a great distance. Her attention was solely dedicated to what was happening to her husband.

Sizzling bolts of lightning chased after Rukh, but somehow, he dodged them. He dodged them again.

The Queen gave a noise of frustration, a sound heard all the way to the Wall. More bolts came but they, too, missed.

Jessira urged Rukh on to greater speed, praying Devesh would give him a chance to survive.

The Queen moved even slower now, barely floating over the ground. She moved languidly, as if She was enjoying the chase. The Sorrow Bringer followed on Rukh's heels, closing the gap by incremental margins. He raced as swiftly as he could, but Suwraith was swifter. She bridged the distance, slowly, steadily, inexorably. In the last twenty feet, She rushed forward, a cloud-shaped tidal wave. She folded over Rukh, hiding him from view. From within Her bruised-colored form, lightning flashed in a seemingly endless discharge.

It was over.

Jessira keened, unable to hold in the agony.

The Oasis held. Somehow, miraculously, it held. Though fragile as gossamer—the puff of a butterfly might have blown it apart—Rukh sustained it with his aching need.

Despite lightning bleeding all around him. Despite the flood of arcing light and rasping hornets. Despite ground melted to glass, it held. Rukh's stubborn core remained resolute and unyielding. He told himself that he would keep ahold of the Oasis for as long as Time's arch stood. He told himself that dissolution wasn't an option. He told himself that he would see this greatest test of his life through to the end.

However, while Rukh's mind was willing, his body was reaching its breaking point. His heart pounded faster than that of a rabbit chased by a wolf. It couldn't go on. And *Jivatma*, too, was finite. Rukh's Well was draining. Despite his desire, even if his body was able, he knew he wouldn't be able to maintain the Oasis for another five minutes, much less all the length of Time.

In that moment, the Queen must have sensed his weakening resolve. She poured forth Her cascading lightning ever more furiously. It was an endless sheet of ragged, white lace mixed with a high-pitched, tortured animal scream. The smell of hair and flesh alight was sickening, and Rukh realized it was his own body burning.

The ground seemed to tremble, and Rukh's vision faded in and out. He panted. Sweat dripped in a waterfall down his back. His heart felt ready to rupture. Muscles became heavy with fatigue. Rukh's will began to crack. The inevitable was about to occur. The Oasis was about to fail.

He had nothing left to give. With his strength fading, Rukh's thoughts turned to Jessira, his family, his love for them. It was those memories that saved him. Remembering them rekindled his will, and Rukh firmed the Oasis just as spears of stone plunged upward. Like stabbing knives, they thrust at him. His will hardened as the granite bones of the earth pressed against the edge of his Oasis. He refused to allow them purchase. They shattered with a sharp crack, and the rubble slid off in the grating scream.

Rukh gasped with the gratefulness of a drowning man reaching air and realized that the strength of the Oasis was a matter of his will. If he was strong enough, he might prolong the battle a few minutes longer. In the end, it might not matter—it likely wouldn't—but for now, every breath was a boon and every heartbeat a gift.

Rukh bit down and gritted his teeth. He would do this. He would hang on for as long as he could. He would last to the very point where his *Jivatma* gave way. His will *would not* be the weak link in the forging of his miraculous Oasis.

Time passed. How long, Rukh didn't know. Life was an agony of blazing, white light from the lightning. It pulsed past his eyelids. Even with both arms shielding them, the light bled through. Thunder pealed, felt and no longer heard. It became a deep-seated rumble of pain. His senses were overwhelmed, and Rukh huddled inside himself. He curled about like a beaten dog waiting for the torment to end. More time passed, and Rukh dared dream that the lightning fell more slowly now. It was almost imperceptible at first, but eventually it became impossible to miss. Seconds later, with a stutter, the lightning failed.

Rukh opened his eyes, hoping they hadn't been burned out. The world was ghostly white. He blinked, over and over again, seeking to clear his sight. He still saw nothing but white. Rukh shut his eyes tight and rubbed them. He blinked some more. This time when he opened his eyes, blurred shapes and colors met his vision. They became recognizable as distinct objects and forms. Rukh blinked again, and the world finally sharpened. Every now and then, though, it blurred, appearing as if seen through a film of water.

Rukh levered himself upright with a groan. His thoughts were a mix of pain and relief that the torment was over. Memory slipped away. He wasn't sure where he was or how he had got here.

Rukh glanced about. Around him was a perfect circle of black glass. Smoke drifted across a broad plain, torn and littered with bodies that flopped like grotesque puppets. Memory started to return. The bodies belonged to the young warriors the Queen had slain. They danced across the ground, caught in the clutches of Suwraith's hurricane wind. More memory came back.

He had been overwhelmed by the Sorrow Bringer, caught in an unending wave of light and sound, pain and madness. Only the thin, invisible shell of his Oasis had kept him safe. The Queen had tried to crack it open, but She had failed. No. That wasn't quite right. Suwraith hadn't failed. She'd simply stopped. Where was She then, and why was She no longer attacking?

Rukh spotted Her roiling twenty or thirty feet above him. She must have drifted upward, spitting him out like the pit of a peach. Her bruise color had turned black, and the snarl of a frustrated wolf pack echoed across the plain.

Rukh watched as She rose even higher.

"Who are you?" a voice like tearing flesh demanded in a booming shout.

In another time, Rukh might have been amazed. Suwraith had actually spoken to him. In all the long years since the Night of Sorrows, two millennia ago, how many times had there been an occurrence like this? Rukh reached for his strength and managed to clamber to his feet. He would not meet such a momentous occasion like a turtle on his back or a coward on his knees. As he swayed about, almost losing his balance more than once, he looked to his home. The Blacks and all the other platoons had made it safely to the city. Even now, they climbed the Outer Wall.

Rukh smiled in joyous disbelief. He'd done it. He'd held out long enough for the others to win through and survive. His eyes narrowed as he realized he himself was only yards away from safety. He began to wonder if he might reach the refuge of the Outer Wall as well.

"Who are you, wretched Human!" the Queen screamed at him. *"Answer Me, or know My unending wrath!"*

Rukh turned back to Suwraith, the enormity of his situation finally breaking through the fog of his fatigue and pain. His mouth was bone dry. He cleared his throat, managing to work some moisture back into it. "No one of consequence," he croaked. He wore a weak, uncertain grin. Why had he chosen to yank the Queen's braids like that? It was foolish.

But then again, what difference would it make? What could the Sorrow Bringer actually do to him? Kill him? Sure She could, but so what? Dead was dead.

Suwraith seemed to inhale sharply. *"You dare mock Me?"*

"Mock You? No," Rukh replied. He reconsidered his words. "Or maybe yes, but I'm too tired and thirsty to care about manners." Rukh was suddenly quite weary of the Queen's presence. Why couldn't She simply leave him in peace? He just wanted to go home. "Now, if you don't mind, I'm going home for a drink and a nap," he added.

The Queen hissed in outrage. *"How dare you speak to Me in such an insolent fashion, ignorant worm,"* Suwraith growled even as She paused for a moment, seemingly collecting Her thoughts. *"You're right,"* She said a moment later, as if She were speaking to someone else. *"A worm is too good for the likes of him. You are nothing more than the entrails of an insect, you miserable cretin, and Insect shall be your name. The world entire shall know of your fate. All will learn of how I ended you, Insect, and men will speak of your passing with hushed breaths of horror for a thousand years!"*

Rukh had long ago stopped listening to the Sorrow Bringer. His fogged thoughts remained, but they had clarified enough for him to make some realizations. He was alive, and though he was far from safe, an opportunity had presented itself. Rukh took deep, controlled breaths. He inhaled through his nose and exhaled through his mouth. His heart settled. His breathing steadied. He needed as much of his remaining strength as possible.

Currently, two paths were open to him. In one, he could continue fighting the Sorrow Bringer. He could match his will to Hers, his fading *Jivatma* against Her seemingly limitless power and hope for the best. The other path . . . not every battle could be won, and the wise warrior knew when to retreat.

The Queen reared back like a striking cobra. *"Die, Insect!"* She cried out.

Rukh didn't bother waiting for Her blow. Instead, he ran. He ran as fast as he could. He headed straight for Ashoka. For some reason, the Queen did not immediately give pursuit. Instead, after he took off running, She remained strangely silent and motionless. Many moments later, She announced Her fury with a scream to tear the bark off a tree.

Rukh silently thanked Her as She gave pause to howl out imprecations and promises of dire retribution. Her threats didn't matter, though. Nothing did but this final race of the day. Hope kindled. He was already halfway to the Outer Wall. *Keep screaming at me*, he urged. Every second the Queen wasted raging at him brought him that much closer to safety. Just a little longer . . .

It was not to be.

The Queen finally got Her wits about Her. She chased after him, screaming like a demented banshee.

Rukh could sense Her pitiless presence rearing closer and closer. She was almost on top of him. His Oasis wouldn't last long against Her power this time. His *Jivatma* was thin as old cotton. He felt Her descent and darted aside. The Queen hammered the earth, barely missing him.

She came at him again, this time from at the same level as his height. There would be no evading Her this time. Rukh wanted to cry out in frustration. The Outer Wall was *so* close.

He looked for something, anything, that might slow the Queen. Fireballs and Blends wouldn't help. With the desperation of a dying man offered a sodden log to hold him aloft, Rukh grasped at the only Talent left to try.

Rukh held onto his Oasis, but drew even more *Jivatma*, almost the last dregs. He formed a Bow. He cupped it in his hands. He had no idea what to do with it, or what it might do. With a shrug, he struck the string that linked the limbs of the Bow. When he did so, a liquid light like quicksilver flew across the intervening space between him and the Queen.

It struck Suwraith, and the most astonishing thing occurred.

Lightning shattered against the Queen. It pierced Her, lanced Her, and the Sorrow Bringer screamed. It wasn't a scream of pain, however. Instead, it was cry of fear and fury.

"You can't be alive!" Suwraith cried out as if She was being tortured. *"You're dead!"* She reared back from Rukh, and the lightning ebbed. *"Who are you, Human?"* the Queen demanded. *"Tell me true this time."*

Rukh didn't answer. There was no need.

"You will *answer Me,"* the Queen cried out, reaching for him again.

Rukh formed another Bow and struck the string. Again, liquid light shot forth and collided with the Queen. Again came the lightning, and again came Her screams of frustrated fury.

Rukh exulted. He had no idea what he was doing to the Queen, but so long as it halted Her progress, he was overjoyed. Only a few more yards to go, and he would be safe.

Rukh steadily worked his way back to Ashoka. He no longer had the energy to run, so, instead, he walked. His Well was almost empty. He could no longer maintain an Oasis *and* imbue his movements with greater speed.

The Queen advanced once more, moving in slow, sinuous lines like a snake. *"You are not who I feared you to be,"* She hissed. *"The one I fear is dead. I saw to it myself."*

Rukh had enough *Jivatma* for one last Bow. With its creation, his Well was tapped out. The Oasis collapsed. The Queen hurled forward. Rukh desperately plucked the string and the quicksilver bolt shot forth.

Again, the Queen was struck. She growled anger and paused momentarily. It was only an instant, but it was long enough to last a lifetime.

Rukh reached for the last of his stamina and sprinted the final fifteen feet to sanctuary. He fell forward, rolling until his face was pressed against the Outer Wall. Salvation was his.

The Queen raged at him from only a few feet away, impotent now since Ashoka's own Oasis utterly halted Her might.

Rukh no longer cared one way or the other.

He was tired, and he hurt. He slumped to his side and fell unconscious.

———●●———

Shur Rainfall gritted his teeth, holding back a scream of frustration and outrage. How could Devesh have allowed such a catastrophic calamity to occur? Even now, it was impossible to accept how completely the Virtuous had been routed. They had lost nearly all their finest warriors. All but a handful had been killed or captured in the disastrous attack on the Shektan women.

Those warriors were irreplaceable. They had been the ones most dedicated to the cause of the Virtuous. They had the truest faith, the greatest heart and finest courage. They had been the only ones willing to deal out death to the naaja bastards of House Shektan.

Now, they were all but exterminated.

Shur wanted to rage at those around him, hurl them off the Outer Wall.

These others were also members of the Virtuous, but their faith was faint. They were as meek as sheep. They were cowards, unwilling to lift swords in defense of Humanity's purity. They lacked the valor needed to deal out death to those who most-assuredly deserved it. Instead, these weak-willed weaklings had only managed a tepid type of assistance. They had stood to either side of the attack and formed a Human barricade around it. By doing so, they had hindered the sight and movement of those who might have helped the Shektan women. Ironically, the sheep amongst the Virtuous had been tasked with guarding the shepherds, the warriors of the faith.

A moment later, Shur grunted reluctant acknowledgement of the work done by those standing around him. In the end, their presence had turned out to be invaluable. If not for them, it was likely that even the handful of warriors who had escaped the disaster of the First Cleansing would have also been captured. Shur would have been amongst that number.

Instead, he'd managed to flee to safety. He could fight on. He wasn't defeated, not now, not ever. The cause of the righteous would prevail. Shur would rally the forces of the Virtuous and restore morality to Ashoka. By Devesh's will, he would keep alive the spirit of the faithful. The Virtuous would learn from the mistakes of today's setback so that next time, those opposed to Humanity's purity would be destroyed.

Cries of horror drew Shur's attention back to the site of the recent battle. His lips curled with scorn at those who were even now weeping over the injured Shektans. Lemmings. They ran pell mell toward the cliff, ignorant and unaware. Let them cry out. Their pitiful mewlings didn't matter. Shur turned his gaze away from them as he considered what next to do. His eyes drifted down toward the plain beyond Ashoka's walls.

Before the beginning of the Cleansing, he had seen the red arrows fired. It was the signal that enemies approached, but wherever Shur looked, he saw nothing to cause such alarm. There were no enemies down there. No Chimeras. Nevertheless, with the red arrows sent up, the Advent Trial was ended. The platoons had been called back to Ashoka. Some had likely already reentered the city.

One of the Virtuous clutched Shur's shirt and gestured frantically at something approaching the city from the south. Shur shook himself free and looked to whatever had the man so excited. It was a large, purple cloud. So what? It was unimportant. Shur frowned in annoyance.

"It's Suwraith," someone shouted in fear.

Shur snorted in scorn. What idiocy. He opened his mouth to mock the nonsensical assertion, but he noticed the purple cloud was picking up speed. It was racing faster than any cloud Shur had ever seen. Lightning lit it from within, leaving an afterglow that suggested glowing red eyes.

Shur's open mouth went dry.

It *was* Suwraith. He watched as She arrived in a storm of horrifying glory. Thunder rumbled on the plains down below. He sensed Blends down there as warriors sprinted at full speed. Shur Linked with them, and a number of platoons sprang into life.

Devesh save them! Shur prayed, even more fervently than he had prior to the Cleansing. The ghrinas stood in opposition to the notion of a pure Humanity, but here was the creature who was the great enemy of *all* Humanity. Here was the author of all evil.

Shur cried out. The Sorrow Bringer had smashed earthward over one of the platoons, and when She lifted off the ground, She made accurate the truth of Her name. A mangled platoon was left in Her wake. The few who hadn't been flattened by Her might had been roasted by Her lightning. Smoke rose from the corpses.

The Queen drifted toward another unit.

Shur joined those lining the Outer Wall in imploring the warriors down below. He shouted as loudly as any, screaming encouragement to the young Trims of the Advent Trial. He urged them on to greater speed. He knew those on the plain couldn't hear him, but it didn't matter. This was all he could do for them, and it was what he did.

The next platoon Suwraith targeted didn't survive any better than the first. The Sorrow Bringer hit them like a falling hill. More men murdered.

Shur shook his head in disbelieving horror. What a day of infamy this was becoming.

Another platoon, this one close by, was next in line. And just like the other two, Suwraith crushed it. The bodies She left behind lay twisted into grotesque parodies of men.

The Queen moved on toward another platoon. Shur was in the midst of screaming for the warriors to run faster when a movement amongst them caused him to trail off. He frowned in consternation. Many others in the crowd did so as well, and it grew quiet on the Outer Wall.

One of the warriors had broken away from the main body of the platoon. Shur didn't know what the man was attempting. Was he a coward, seeking a means by which to save his own life at the cost of his brother warriors? If so, then the man was utterly contemptible. He didn't deserve to live. Banishment was too good for someone so craven. If the Magisterium was wise, it would take this coward and send him straight to the Isle of the Crows if he somehow survived Suwraith's attack.

A moment later, Shur's brow creased further, and his confusion deepened. Fireballs exploded from the man's hands. He was a Kumma then, which meant he shouldn't be a coward. Then why had he abandoned his platoon? And why was he hurling Fireballs?

Shur gasped as understanding came to him. The man was trying to draw Suwraith after him so his brother warriors could escape. Others along the Outer Wall came to the same conclusion. They called out to one another in disbelieving tones. Shur shared their sentiments. What courage! This man was the embodiment of all that it meant to be a Kumma.

Shur yelled out in exultation—he wasn't the only one either—when Suwraith took the man's bait and gave chase.

The rest of the platoons never slowed. They sprinted flat out for the Outer Wall. If the Kumma could survive Her wrath for just a few more seconds, all those Trims down there would live.

The Queen followed on the Kumma's heels. Somehow, he sensed Her oncoming blows. He dodged Her lightning once. Twice. Three times he evaded Her strikes. And still he ran!

"They're going to make it!" someone shouted. His call was excitedly taken up by others.

Shur looked to where they pointed. The other platoons were almost to the Outer Wall. Just a few more yards and . . .

A gasp from the crowd had him return his attention to the deadly chase between Suwraith and the Kumma. The Queen had smashed to the ground, but somehow the Kumma had evaded Her blow. Now, though, She floated after him at head level. She would take him this time.

Shur sensed it as did many others. He glanced back to the platoons and was heartened to see that the Trims had made it. Shur saluted the brave Kumma whose actions had seen those young warriors safely home, and he offered a heartfelt prayer for the Kumma's soul in the life to come. His sacrifice would never be forgotten.

Just then, the Queen overwhelmed the Kumma. She covered him like a purple fog. Lightning pierced the ground with hundreds, if not thousands of strikes. Thunder rolled in an endless bass roll.

Shur's head dropped in regret. It was over. He would have liked to have met that Kumma. His was the type of courage they should all aspire to achieve.

The lightning eventually slowed and stuttered to a halt. The Sorrow Bringer rose and Shur forced himself to look, fully expecting to see the Kumma burnt to a cinder.

What met his vision, though, was entirely unexpected, and he gasped in shock. He wasn't the only one.

The Kumma still lived!

Shur watched with mouth agape as the man stumbled to his feet and toward Ashoka. For some reason, the Sorrow Bringer didn't immediately give chase. Shur found hope rising in his chest. Again, he joined all the others lining the Wall in crying out at the top of his lungs, yelling for the Kumma to reach the Wall.

Finally, the Queen gave chase. The Kumma dodged Her first blow. Her next, he wouldn't. Suwraith floated forward at head level once again.

Bitter disappointment rose up within Shur. The Kumma was *so* close, but he wouldn't make it.

What happened next was a mystery to Shur. The Kumma turned around to face the Sorrow Bringer even as he kept running. And when he did so, a silvery beam of light shot from the Kumma's hands. What it was, Shur didn't know, but when it struck the Queen, She screamed.

Shur was struck dumb by what he was seeing. The Kumma had harmed Suwraith. It was impossible, and yet it had happened!

Again shot forth the silvery beam, and again Suwraith screamed. Once more, and it was over.

The Kumma had reached the wall.

Shur cheered himself hoarse. Tears ran down his cheeks, and he unabashedly hugged a Duriah woman, not caring about sin just then.

———————◦———————

Jessira dug her fingers into the crenellations of the Outer Wall as she cried out her anguish.

Unsurprisingly, it was the elderly matron who was the first to offer Jessira sympathy for her anguish. "I'm so sorry for your loss," the elderly Kumma said.

Jessira nodded numb acceptance of the matron's words, barely hearing them just as she barely felt it when Sign pulled her into a hug. Neither did she register the sympathetic brushes and touches of strangers as word was shared about the name of the brave Kumma who had died so that so many others could live. Jessira heard nothing of their admiring words and felt nothing inside. She was hollowed out, her heart empty.

Rukh was gone. His death was a searing emptiness inside, and Jessira's tearing eyes did nothing to sooth her grief or reflect the enormity of her loss. The world blurred in and out of focus. It was like a nightmare, and Jessira prayed that she would awaken . . . except she never did.

Jessira watched as the Queen continued to spark a flood of lightning and rolling thunder, smothering Rukh like a pestilence. How had this occurred? Just a few hours ago, her husband had been alive and vibrant, his normal happy self as they shared a laugh. Now he was gone? It was surreal, and Jessira felt like she was just witnessing the events unfolding before her instead of actually experiencing them.

The shock of the moment started to wear off, and Jessira realized that she could still sense Rukh's presence. She could still feel his ironwood will. Jessira poked at the sensation, worrying at it as if it were an empty tooth socket. She struggled to believe, to accept an emptiness where a tooth should have been. But Jessira could still feel the tooth. It was still there.

Her eyes had seen the truth of Rukh's demise, but her heart and soul had yet to know it. Rukh lived.

"We should go," Sign suggested softly.

Jessira felt her cousin take her upper arm and give it a gentle tug, urging her to turn away. "No," Jessira said, pulling her arm free from Sign's grasp. "He's still alive. I can feel him," she said in utter certainty.

"Are you sure?" Bree asked, sounding doubtful.

Jessira nodded.

"Jessira, I know—" Sign began.

"He's still alive!" Jessira snarled. Her declaration was heard by those close by, and quiet, disbelieving murmurs arose from them.

Jessira knew what they were likely thinking—that her claim was the desperate hope of someone too distraught to accept the truth, too pained to brave reality.

They were wrong. Their disbelief didn't matter. Jessira knew with utter certainty that Rukh still lived. The link the two of them shared told her so. She could sense her husband down below, struggling with every thread of his will to endure Suwraith's holocaust wrath.

There finally came a time when the lightning lifted, and the Queen drifted up. A fog of black smoke followed Her. It drifted up and parted, revealing a ground baked to glowing glass and fiery embers. Rukh should have been reduced to ashes as well, but somehow, impossibly, he was still alive. He huddled within that circle of fire and death, but after a moment, he shuddered upright and struggled to his feet.

A joyful cry, carrying all of Jessira's love and hope, broke from her throat. He *was* alive! Tears streamed down her face.

Many more people joined Jessira in shouting their gladness. All along the Outer Wall rose cries of stunned disbelief, awe, and unexpected hope. Jessira shared their emotions. She had no idea what providence had allowed Rukh to survive the Sorrow Bringer's fury, but she begged it to deliver her husband home.

An interminable time passed as Rukh seemed to be talking to the Queen. Jessira had no idea what they were saying, but the Queen's purple hue had long since grown black. She was furious. Suddenly, Rukh broke from Her. He was sprinting for the Outer Wall. The Queen remained motionless. Lightning lit the ground, but She held still.

Jessira gripped the crenellations even tighter than before, praying with all her fervency and need, demanding that the Sorrow Bringer remain still for a few more seconds. Seconds were all Rukh needed.

Or at least they would have been if Rukh had been running as fast as he normally could. Right now, he barely moved faster than a stumbling jog. His strength was spent, his Well nearly empty. Jessira wished there were a way she could grace him some of her *Jivatma*. Instead, all she could do was watch as Rukh raced for his life. She urged him on. *Don't stop. Don't look back. Keep going. You're almost there.*

Suwraith finally broke from Her stasis and gave chase.

Jessira swallowed a lump of dismay. She assayed the distance between Rukh and the Sorrow Bringer and realized her husband wasn't going to make it. The Queen would close with him, and he no longer had the strength to fight Her off a second time.

Jessira raged inside. He was so close.

She gasped when a silvery light burst forth from Rukh's hands. When it struck the Sorrow Bringer, a scream echoed across the plain. It was a sound unlike anything Jessira had ever heard. So much hatred and insanity was contained in that cry.

Another silvery bolt shot out. Another demented howl. Rukh was almost to the Outer Wall.

Jessira momentarily lost sight of him. Everyone was leaned over the edge of the parapet, craning to see what would happen. A third bolt shot out.

A roar of triumph rose from the throats of those on the Outer Wall closest to Rukh. It was all the signal Jessira needed. A thrill of relief, joy, and gratefulness ran down her spine. Rukh had made it! She watched Suwraith hurl Herself ineffectually against Ashoka's Oasis. She was repulsed. Again, the Queen tried to breach the Oasis and again was thrust aside. Suwraith screamed Her frustrated rage before swiftly departing.

"First Mother. He defeated Suwraith," Sign said. Her cousin's voice was filled with reverential awe.

Again, it was a sentiment shared by everyone. Strangers hugged one another, uncaring of Caste or custom. Tears streamed down their face as they laughed the life-affirming laughter of those who had witnessed true magic. In the two millennia since the Night of Sorrows, never had there been an account of a Human battling the Sorrow Bringer and living to tell the tale. History had been made this day.

Jessira felt much the same as all those around her, but that sense of reverent wonderment was subsumed by her need to reach Rukh's side. She pushed through the crowd, aided by Sign and Bree who kept to either side of her. The three women linked arms and made their way through the throng.

Snippets of conversation came to Jessira as she struggled to reach where she had last seen her husband as he had approached the Outer Wall.

"He is Hume reborn," one voice proclaimed. "Was he not the one who destroyed the Chimera caverns?"

"He is greater than Hume!" another voice answered. "He destroyed the Chimera caverns *and* defeated the Sorrow Bringer. Not even Hume was so mighty!"

"And what about how he came home with the love of a Shylow, a Kesarin? Or his survival in the Wildness when the Chamber of Lords judged him Unworthy? The shortsighted fools!" someone else declared, his voice throbbing with tones of holy wonder. "He has mastered the Talents of all the Castes, and now he defeats Suwraith. See the Queen retreat from him!"

"He is touched by Devesh! He is holiness made flesh!"

Jessira startled at the stupid statement. Rukh touched by Devesh? What an asinine idea.

"Do you think it's possible?" Sign asked.

"Is what possible?" Jessira replied.

"That Rukh is touched by Devesh?"

Jessira did a double take, thinking at first that Sign was joking. Her cousin's solemn expression indicated that she wasn't. Jessira scowled. Not Sign, too. Her cousin should know better.

"You saw what he did," Sign persisted. "He fought Suwraith and survived. Who else but someone touched by Devesh could do something like that?"

Jessira groaned in dismay.

If someone as levelheaded as Sign wondered whether Rukh was touched by the Lord, what of those with more fervent imaginations? They would likely proclaim Rukh was the First Father reborn. It would be a nightmare for him. He already hated how people viewed him. He hated the hero worship, the easy recognition, the notion that others thought he was someone more special than they. Now it would be a thousand-fold worse. He'd never leave their flat.

"If he is touched by Devesh, I wonder why he didn't he use his power at Stronghold?"

Jessira flashed Sign an angry look. "He did what he could at Stronghold. You saw him save Laya. Whatever happened today is something new. He's never had such an ability before."

"If that's the case, then he can't just be some random Kumma," Sign persisted. "He was chosen for a reason."

"He's who he is," Jessira replied, already tired of the conversation. She just wanted to reach her husband.

"The hand of destiny—"

"Enough!" Jessira barked. "Rukh has no prophecy about him and no destiny before him. He chooses his own path!"

After leading the Tigons onto the plain stretching out from Ashoka's Outer Wall, Hal'El had split them off into groups of ten. During the march north from the Hunters Flats, the Tigons had learned the price of disobedience. As a result, when Hal'El had told them to remain motionless, he knew they would.

An hour of patient work later, they were ready.

While the Tigons crept to their positions, green signal arrows had flared near the forest west of the plain. Answering red flames had risen from the Outer Wall.

Hal'El had no idea why there were platoons in the forest. Nor did he know what they had seen to cause them to pass on the warning of approaching danger. Hal'El had shrugged and grinned. Whatever the reason, he had been grateful for the incompetent commander. The man had likely panicked for some reason. Maybe he'd seen his shadow. At any rate, the green arrows from the forest would cause even more disorder, especially after his Chimeras made their presence known.

Hal'El had cast a signal, and his Tigons had done as Tigons do: they'd mindlessly attacked the Trims. The young warriors had responded with admirable aplomb. They'd turned to face the Tigons, and even with blunted weapons, had annihilated them. None of the Chimeras had survived their attack, but it didn't matter. The Tigons had done their duty.

More green signal flares had been fired from the platoons who had battled the Tigons. Again, answering red flames had burst skyward from the Outer Wall. The Advent Trial was over, and the platoons had raced back to Ashoka.

It had all been to Hal'El's benefit as he had skulked his way closer to Ashoka. In the ensuing chaos, he had managed to dodge past the line of Trims. He had been halfway across the plain when a tingle in his spine had told him to look south. Suwraith had come. Her arrival, a half hour after the attack by the Tigons, had stirred abject panic. The platoons had raced across the plain with the Kummas in the lead and drawing away.

Hal'El had sprinted with them. He would be just another Kumma. The guards at the gates would be too panicked to look closely at the faces of those entering the city.

All had been going according to the plan he and the Queen had devised, but still, Hal'El had felt some measure of grief and even guilt for the dying Trims that Suwraith had destroyed.

Nevertheless, if such sacrifice was the price to be paid for a later, greater victory, then so be it.

Then had come that single Kumma who had dared confront the Queen. He'd thrown his challenge into the teeth of Her storm and come out triumphant. Or at least not dead, which in anyone's estimation was a victory.

Hal'El had watched the man's actions in stunned amazement. After Suwraith had retreated, he realized he hadn't yet reentered Ashoka. With a start he had raced for Sunset Gate. Thankfully, the Kumma's actions had everyone celebrating, and no one was truly warding the entrance to the city. Hal'El passed through with no one giving him a second glance.

Once inside, he'd kept running, wearing a look of dire importance on his face to dissuade any who might think to question him. He had evaded detection and managed to reach a small safe house in a Muran village. It was really just an unused cellar, but it had clothes, provisions, and money. There, he'd changed out of his camouflage and into garb more appropriate for the city.

In the Wildness, he'd allowed his beard free rein. It had grown in thick as a wool rug and gray as dirty snow. As a result, Hal'El Wrestiva, the finest warrior of his generation, one of the finest to ever walk the verdant streets of Ashoka, strode his home as anonymous as a pauper.

In times past, such a lack of recognition would have set his teeth on edge, but this time, his thoughts were taken up by another matter.

Who was the Kumma who had withstood the Sorrow Bringer? And what was the silvery essence he had used to best Her?

Hal'El had to have that knowledge. He needed it. He stroked the Withering Knife, sheathed and hidden next to his heart.

CHAPTER THIRTEEN
INTERCESSIONS

When all seems lost and fear a constant companion, simplistic though it may seem, prayer is often the only solution.

—*Our Lives Alone* by Asias Athandra, AF 331

Li-Choke glanced about his prison and felt a profound sense of gratitude. Being here was certainly better than the alternative, which would have been either dead or left for dead outside of Ashoka's gates. Choke and his brothers had been lucky. He'd always known that their reception in Rukh's home might not end well, especially after Mother's recent killing of so many of Ashoka's young warriors. Choke was just thankful that, upon their arrival, he and his brothers hadn't simply been executed on the spot.

And for the longest time, it seemed like summary execution would be exactly what would occur to the Chimeras. The Baels and Tigons had approached Sunset Gate during the brightest part of the day and had sat down in poses of passivity and meekness. But long before they had settled into place, shouts of challenge had come to them. The cries had been full of hatred, anger, and fear. Several Kummas had even had hands filled with Fireballs, appearing to be only a harsh word or movement away from unleashing their fury.

It had taken many hours to sort out the situation: a long, patient discussion with the captain of the gate guards, then another one with a grizzly general. Finally, a warrior had been dispatched to bring out someone who knew Choke and could verify his words. There came a lengthy wait as the sun progressed across the sky and sank toward the horizon.

Finally, Jessira Shektan had appeared. Choke smiled in remembrance of her warmth and welcome, her unfettered joy upon seeing him. It was she who had vouchsafed Choke's trustworthiness, and by extension, the rest of the Baels and Tigons accompanying him. And it was she who had pleaded for the Chimeras to be allowed entrance into Ashoka. While her words had been eloquent, Choke had still expected her request to be turned down without a second thought. The Ashokans had lost too much, their hatred stoked to a furnace heat by what the Queen had so recently done to them. They would never trust a Chimera—or so Choke reckoned.

Events, though, had worked to surprise him. The general had eyed Jessira with something akin to nervousness and possibly even awe. He had acquiesced to her request, and thus, for the first time in history, a Chimera had been offered open entrance into a Human city.

As Jessira led the Baels and Tigons through the menacing maw of Sunset Gate, she had explained to Choke all that had happened to her and Rukh in the ensuing months since he had last seen her.

To say that he had been stunned would have been a tremendous understatement. Choke had always known that Rukh Shektan was special, but finding out that he had challenged the Queen, fought Her, and might have even caused Her pain or defeated Her, had been a revelation for the ages. His brothers, all of them—Tigons and Baels alike—had been similarly left speechless.

Afterward, Jessira had left, leaving Choke and his brothers penned in a barn near a Muran farm. Days later, they were moved to a structure that looked and felt like a prison. And here they had been ever since, awaiting their final fates. The Magisterium had yet to come to a decision on what do with the Chimeras, and while they dithered, Choke and his brothers had been left in this hastily constructed gaol. However, as a gaol went, it wasn't too uncomfortable.

The prison was a square block with one side composed of the Outer Wall and the other three made of the trunks of ironwood trees, all of them fifteen feet or taller. A single gate allowed entrance and egress with a perimeter catwalk lined with ready and wary Ashokan warriors of various Castes. It went without saying that the Chimeras had been disarmed before being allowed access to the city.

Choke didn't mind any of this, though. He couldn't have asked for any better treatment than what he and the others had thus far experienced.

He smiled again.

He was in Ashoka, and a battle hadn't been required to gain entrance. Instead, it had simply been granted. In the face of something so impossible, what need was there to complain?

Choke took a deep breath, enjoying the heat of the early morning summer sun and the sweet song of cicadas. While the ground making up their prison was a fallow field of ruined grass, the rest of the area encapsulated between the Outer and Inner Walls was lush and verdant. Choke could smell it. The clean scent of dirt and green things growing filled his nostrils. When the Chimeras had been marched into Ashoka, he had seen corn up to his thighs with waving, white tassels. He had seen beans, wheat, barley, and potatoes. So much delectable deliciousness.

Choke rose to his feet and began a series of practiced motions meant to stretch limbs.

"The Tigons talk," Chak-Soon said, joining him in his exercises.

Li-Choke didn't cease his movements, but instead merely offered a glance at the ordinate. He knew Soon would understand his unvoiced question. The Tigon didn't require much to interpret Choke's thoughts—just a tilt of the head, a twist of the horns, or a flick of his ears. It still sometimes surprised Choke how close he and Soon had grown. A year ago, it would have seemed an impossibility.

"They talk about Rukh," Chak-Soon elaborated.

"What about him?" Choke asked.

"They wonder stories about him," Soon replied, his tongue tripping over his oversized, overabundant teeth.

"I don't understand," Choke said as he stretched his arms up to the sky.

"What it means." Soon explained.

"Ah," Choke said with a nod of understanding. "The Baels wonder the same thing," he said. "Jessira says all of Ashoka is struggling with who Rukh is."

Soon frowned in confusion. "He is Rukh," he said, as if the name itself was somehow explanatory.

"Yes, but some think he's more than just Rukh—that he's touched by Devesh or the First Father reborn. They think there is something holy about him."

Soon shook his head. "Not what we think," he said. "We wonder if he defeat Mother. Kill Her forever."

Choke laughed. "What a wonderful world if She were no longer a part of it."

Aia groomed herself from shoulder-to-elbow, shoulder-to-elbow, over and over again, slowly and carefully, until she was satisfied. Next she worked on the other side of her body, still patient and steady. She hoped her bearing was one of nonchalance—lying on the ground grooming herself—but inside, she was almost vibrating with excitement.

For the first time in weeks, she would get to see Rukh. He'd finally have a chance to rub her chin, and she could rub her head against his chest.

It had been several days since her arrival to Ashoka, and Rukh had yet to visit her. It was understandable. His amma had been gravely injured in some fashion—it had been a battle between the Shektans and some unknown foe—and Rukh was torn up with worry for her. In addition, the city was in an uproar—more so than usual for this overturned ant hive. There was the arrival of the Nobeasts to take into account. Choke's kind had been Humanity's implacable enemies ever since their birthing, and now, here they were showing up, begging for sanctuary. And beforehand, the Demon Wind had annihilated scores of Ashoka's warriors. The Queen would have killed even more if not for Rukh's actions.

Aia purred contentment at the thought of what had occurred when the Queen had faced Rukh Shektan. During his battle with the Demon Wind, Aia had heard his thoughts. She had witnessed his bravery as he had lured the the Queen away from his fellow warriors. She had felt his resolve when he had refused to yield to the Demon Wind's might. She had known his triumph when he had survived Her wrath.

It had been a feat no one else could have accomplished. The ferocity of his heart, his courage, his sheer will . . . Rukh was a Human unlike any other, special in a way that neither Jaresh or even

Jessira could ever hope to be. He would have made a mighty Kesarin.

The knowledge left Aia feeling smug, and she knew Thrum thought her insufferable. Yet hadn't he been equally as unbearable in his pride when he had boasted about Jaresh's intellect? Served him right to be humbled.

Be nice, a voice warned.

It was Rukh, and Aia stood up abruptly. He was near. Her ears perked forward, and her gaze shifted about, searching for him. She smiled when she saw him, a flick of her ears and a blink of her eyes. Jessira had accompanied him as well.

Why didn't Jaresh come? Thrum asked.

He had other business to attend to, Jessira replied, *but he promises to come by later.*

Thrum rumbled his disappointment. *Humans and their business,* he muttered in disgust.

Privately, Aia agreed with her brother's assessment, but for now, she was grateful that *her* Human didn't have business to attend to. She stepped forward. *It's good to see you again,* she said. *How is your amma?*

She's being moved back home, Rukh said with a soft smile.

Will she walk again?

His smiled faded, and he didn't answer. Instead, in the way of his kind, he reached up and held her around the neck and hugged her. It was an uncomfortable position for Aia. To have another's mouth and teeth so close to her neck, even if it was Rukh. Mentally, she shuddered. It was too vulnerable a state, but Rukh seemed to take comfort in it, so she allowed his embrace. After a moment, her Human began rubbing her chin and Aia rested her head on his shoulder. Her eyes closed to slits as she purred contentment.

I wish Jaresh were here, Thrum complained.

Aia unshuttered her eyes upon hearing her brother's whining. Shon, as per his usual habit, had rolled over on his back, and Jessira was fiercely rubbing his belly while Thrum looked on in miserable jealousy.

Rukh glanced Aia's way, a questioning look on his face. Over time, she had learned to decipher the myriad expressions on her Human's expressive face.

Go ahead, she said.

Rukh let go of Aia and approached her russet-colored brother. The two of them spoke for a moment before Thrum lowered his head. He regally accepted Rukh's ministrations as Aia's Human rubbed his forehead, the soft areas in front of his ears, and his chin. Just as Aia's ears were flattening in jealousy, Thrum lifted his head away. *Jaresh's fingers are more nimble,* he announced.

But my Human's are stronger, Aia countered.

Jaresh's mind is sharper, Thrum answered.

Rukh's will is mightier. He is the greatest of Humans since the First Father and First Mother, Aia responded. *He fought the Demon Wind and defeated Her. No one else could do that.*

Thrum mumbled something inaudible as he rested his head on his paws and closed his eyes.

What was all that about? Rukh asked.

Aia insists on lauding your accomplishments as though you were the First Father reborn, Shon explained, rolling over on his side. He blinked. *You aren't, are you?*

Rukh laughed. *I'm just me. Just a man. Not a legend.*

But you battled the Demon Wind and defeated Her, Thrum said, raising his head and taking note of the conversation. *My Human says that many in Ashoka wonder if you might be more than just a man.*

Of course he's more than just a man, Aia said with a sniff. *He is my

Human, which means he must be someone who is truly exemplary.

My Human is his mate, so she must be exemplary also, Shon declared.

And mine is his brother, Thrum said. *Anyone related to Rukh must be special.*

Just as long as you understand that mine is the most *special,* Aia replied. She noticed the tightening in her Human's eyes. Her conversation with Shon and Thrum bothered him. Rukh was uncharacteristically annoyed with her. *What did I say that has you so upset?* she asked.

Rukh gave a slight shrug. *It's nothing,* he said. *I'll just have to get used to it.*

Get used to what? Aia asked.

Wherever we go, people seem to expect Rukh to grow wings and fly, to offer up miracles at their need, Jessira explained.

Aia tilted her head in consideration. *You don't like that everyone knows who you are?* she asked.

I don't mind that, Rukh said. *It's the rest that bothers me.*

He is uncomfortable by the expectations others have of him, of how they think he communicates directly with Devesh, Jessira explained. *People have even fallen at his feet and prayed to him. It's hard. I think he's lonely.*

He will never be alone so long as I am here, Aia vowed. *He is my Human.*

And he'll never be alone so long as I am here, either, Jessira said.

Jessira took Rukh's hands in her own, and for a moment, Aia wished she had hands like the two of them. It was fleeting thought. Silly really. What would she do with hands? She certainly couldn't run on them. And a Kesarin who couldn't outrace the wind was no Kesarin at all.

In the dead of night, Ashoka was quiet, hushed and peaceful, something she never was during the day. The furnaces and industry of the Moon Quarter were stifled, and the bustling stores and streets were stilled. It was perfect for Hal'El's purposes. He could travel about the city with no one the wiser. His only company was a light mist, a drizzle that worked to his needs. It allowed him to pull forward the hood of his cloak and further shroud his features with no one to question why. He didn't even have to Blend.

In the near week since his return to Ashoka, Hal'El had learned much. The first piece of information he had desired had to do with the standing of the Wrestivas. Unsurprisingly, the fortunes of the House had been decimated. It was to be expected. After Hal'El's actions had come to light, the scandal had been too hard for the House to bear. Many members, some with ancient ties to House Wrestiva, had quit in disgust. Their abilities and reputations were irreplaceable, and Hal'El doubted the House could survive in the long term. The damage was simply too extensive.

He shrugged a moment later. It was no longer his concern.

There was other information that had also been of interest to Hal'El. For instance, the Sil Lor Kum had been shattered. Their ranks had been ruined when that venomous viper, Ular Sathin, had disclosed everything he knew of them. The man had sent a journal detailing all the works and members of the Sil Lor Kum to Dar'El Shektan, who had quickly acted on the information. Every MalDin but one had been tracked down and executed.

The one who survived, though—her name must not have been in Ular Sathin's journal. Nonetheless, Hal'El knew who she was. Somehow Pera Obbe had escaped the scourging hand of Dar'El Shektan. Somehow, that potato-faced wretch still lived.

Hal'El's jaw clenched at the knowledge. It was said that Karma had a rich sense of humor, but that Justice was more dour. And there could be no Justice in a world where Pera Obbe lived while Varesea Apter was dead. It was almost as revolting as the notion that an imbecile like Pera should escape punishment when others far more clever had become food for the crows.

"But not nearly so revolting as the fact that a cretin like you still breathes when those far worthier do not," Sophy spoke into his mind.

Hal'El shook his head, wishing he could rid himself of the infernal woman. The others began murmuring also, and he tried to ignore their vile mutterings. He had to focus on the here and now, for in the here and now, there was work to be done. In the here and now, there was murder to commit.

Hal'El returned his attention to the streets when he realized he was approaching his destination, a large home sitting on a corner lot. It wasn't the most sizable house in the neighborhood, but there was an elegance about it, one that spoke of subdued, subtle wealth and good taste. It was so unlike its owner.

The house was two stories tall with a large wraparound porch, and a single firefly lamp lit the walkway leading up to it. The dark granite making up the bulk of the home shimmered in the rain as did the slate roof tiles. From memory, Hal'El knew that gardens filled the grounds to the rear. He took a moment longer to study the house. This late, all the windows were darkened. There were no lights on.

Perfect.

Hal'El's footsteps fell soft as a fawn's and carried him swiftly across the street. He glanced about. There was no one about, and no one was watching. He clambered a low compound wall and stepped into the gloom of the gardens in the back. A few seconds of dull scrapings, hushed and barely heard, and he was inside.

The wolf amongst the potato-faced sheep.

S hur Rainfall was glad the room in which the Heavenly Council of the Virtuous met was in a cellar. It was cool down here, which helped prevent nervous sweat from beading on his brow. Had the temperature been even slightly warmer, Shur was certain he would have been covered in a waterfall of sweaty rivulets.

He took a deep breath. Tonight's meeting of the Virtuous wouldn't be easy. It was their first since the disastrous attack on House Shektan almost a week ago now. That they hadn't been able to meet sooner had much to do with the Watch tearing the city apart trying to find them.

So many of their members had been killed in the conflict or captured. And for what? A handful of dead Shektan women? The cost to the Virtuous had been too high. Even worse, the entire reason for the attack was now under question. And who would take the blame for these various disasters but he, the leader of the Virtuous. If he wasn't lynched by the six remaining members of the Heavenly Council, it would be a miracle.

Shur took another steadying breath. "Let us bow our heads and prayer for guidance that we may see Devesh's will more truly."

"His will was easily seen a week ago," said the Rahail. "We need no prayer to give us guidance, not when He sent us as clear a vision as possible last week. We should never have attacked the Shektans."

"Rukh Shektan fought the Queen and lived," said the Cherid. "He bled Her and drove Her away. He is touched by Devesh." Her voice was filled with fervent passion.

"And what of Jessira Shektan?" the Sentya asked. "If Rukh has chosen her to be his wife, and Devesh still showers him with grace and glory, what do we make of her?"

"Nothing has changed," Shur said with utter certainty. "The OutCastes remain ghrina. Their presence pollutes us all."

"Everything has changed. Devesh's touch lingers upon Rukh Shektan's brow," the Rahail avowed. "And if the Lord accepts someone so polluted, someone who has had congress with a ghrina, then what does that mean for us?"

"One battle, and you're willing to disregard millennia of teaching?" Shur asked in disgust.

"You're so sure of yourself that you're willing to disregard something not seen in millennia?" the Cherid sneered. "No one, not even the First Father or the First Mother, the greatest of Devesh's servants, were ever able to oppose the Queen. She slayed Them, and whether They were Her Parents or not, it doesn't matter. We saw a miracle, one that alters everything."

"*The Word and the Deed* has been our guide for all the years of our lives, and those of our forefathers," Shur began, trying to hold rein on his frustration. "And you're willing to cast it aside because of one supposed battle?" He sneered. "You're like a child seeing a pretty bauble and not recognizing the true worth of a humble hammer, a tool that can raise monuments."

"And where has your guidance led us?" the Cherid demanded. "We lost how many of the Virtuous in that disastrous attack?"

"Their martyrdom will see them safe in Devesh's loving embrace," Shur spoke piously.

"Unless the attack wasn't sanctioned by Devesh," the Rahail said.

"It was sanctioned!" Shur disagreed. "We did holy work." He shook his head in disbelief. The splintering of the others' faith was worse than he thought. "When I saw Rukh Shektan defy the Queen, I, too, took it as a sign of Devesh's blessings upon him. But later I realized the truth: it was all a ruse. Think about it. What makes more sense? That Rukh Shektan, a man who is all but a naaja, is touched by Devesh's grace? Or that this same man is secretly of the Sil Lor Kum? That everything we saw was meant to convince us that he was in mortal danger from the Queen? But all along, he knew She wouldn't kill him."

"To what purpose?" the Rahail asked.

"To allow entrance into our city those who are even worse than ghrinas: Chimeras."

A silence met his words.

"You think this might be possible?" the Duriah asked.

Shur nodded, couching his words carefully. The Virtuous couldn't be forced to the truth. They had to arrive at it on their own. "A day after Rukh 'battled' Suwraith, Baels and Tigons suddenly arrive at our doorstep and are granted a place to stay while the Magisterium dithers over their fate. And who was it that spoke so forcefully on their behalf?" He glanced around. "It was none other than Jessira Shektan, a ghrina who must have poisoned Rukh's mind to the foul teachings of her kind. Why, I bet all the ghrinas are secretly of the Sil Lor Kum."

"You're wrong. For reasons known only to Him, Devesh considers Jessira Shektan to be a worthy companion for His Chosen One," the Rahail disagreed. "After the battle, it was she who went down with the basket to haul Rukh to the top of the Outer Wall. She would allow no one else to go in her place. She loves him, and he loves her. I saw it. It was obvious. And such love cannot spring from the minds of evil."

"It is said that Hal'El Wrestiva loved his Rahail consort, Varesea Apter," Shur reminded them. "To love is to be Human, and even those who are evil can love."

"And what of the beams of light?" the Rahail demanded.

"A trick. Something that has no power but is brilliant to look upon. It is no different than the light of a firefly. Likely Rukh Shektan learned it, either from the Queen, or as part of his naaja-born gifts."

"You truly believe everything we saw was a feint?" the Shiyen mused.

Shur nodded. "I think there is more going on here than any of us realize. Something deeper and more dangerous." From their thoughtful expressions, he was relieved that they appeared to be returning to his way of thinking. "Our mission is unchanged."

"If so, then how do we execute it? Many of our warriors are dead or imprisoned," the Duriah said. "And the reason for our grievous losses is on your head. It was your plan that led us to such a calamity."

"I take full responsibility for what occurred," Shur said with a twist of his lips. "But in the middle of a storm, it is foolish to change the captain of the ship."

"Unless the captain is incompetent and threatens to see his crew drowned," the Duriah countered.

Shur gritted his teeth. "You want leadership of the Virtuous?" he asked.

There was a pregnant pause. "No," the Duriah said, "but your own leadership needs to be curtailed. We are the Heavenly Council, and we had little to no input on the plan to attack the Shektans."

"The plan was good," Shur averred, knowing his statement was stupid the moment the words left his lips.

"If *that* was a good plan, then I'd hate to see a poor one," the Shiyen said with a frown.

"Who could have known that so many of the Shektan women would be armed, or that they would take up the swords of our fallen?" Shur asked.

"A canny commander would have known," the Duriah said. "Next time we attack the OutCastes, or the Shektans, or even Rukh Shektan, we need to be better prepared."

The Rahail's chair scraped as he stood. "I am done here," he said. "What you do goes against Devesh's will. Rukh Shektan is touched by the Lord, and we almost killed his wife. And now we think to attack Devesh's Chosen? You will be forever condemned for such a grave sin. I will have no part in it." He stood to leave, as did the Cherid and the Sentya.

A dead quiet commanded the room.

"Let us discuss this," Shur pleaded. He hated the whiny tone of his voice. "Surely we can come to an agreement. We are brothers in seeking righteousness."

"Then you must accept that what we did was wrong. You must accept that Rukh Shektan is the Chosen One of the Lord. You must accept that our true purpose should be helping him with his divine mission."

"Blasphemy!" the Shiyen hissed.

The Duriah called out as well.

The Rahail turned to them. "If you believe so, then we have nothing further to talk about."

"We do have one final thing," Shur said, regretting what he next had to do. He nodded to the guards who drew their swords.

'I would not do that," the Cherid said, speaking swiftly. "My solicitor and others in my employ have damning information about the Virtuous."

Shur held up his hand, halting the guards.

"If I die in suspicious circumstances, they will mail everything I know about all of you to every Watch captain in the city." She paused. "And Dar'El Shektan." She stared Shur in the eyes. "You won't last a day."

322

Shur ground his teeth. He couldn't tell if the woman was bluffing, and if she wasn't, there was nothing he could do to stop her. "You leave us little reason to keep you alive," he said. "When you leave you will likely tell the authorities all about us anyway. Why shouldn't we have our vengeance on you first?"

"You can do as you wish, but I'll promise to give you one week to get your affairs in order before I say anything to anyone." She glanced around the room. "You know we're all marked men and women. The Watch has many of the Virtuous in their custody. The amma of the Chosen One was almost killed. Several members of House Shektan were killed. The Watch and the entire city won't rest until everyone who was responsible is dead."

Angry, fearful mutters met her words.

"Is this true?" the Shiyen asked.

Shur held still, hating to have to answer. "It's true," he finally forced out. "Even with all our precautions to keep our names from those who serve below us, a week—maybe a little more—is all we have left before the Watch learns our names."

The Rahail glanced around the room. "In that week, I plan on making my peace with House Shektan and the Chosen One while I still can." He looked to the guards before turning back to Shur. "Do not go against Rukh Shektan or his family. If you do, our swords will be there to meet you."

He, the Cherid, and the Sentya all left the room.

"One week?" the Duriah muttered. "Our lives have lost all purpose."

Shur couldn't help but believe the man was right.

"They're still out there," Rukh muttered.

Jessira glanced up from the couch where she'd been concentrating on *The Book of First Movement*. Normally, Rukh was loath to allow anyone else to handle it, but ever since the Advent Trial, he had taken to setting it aside. He claimed that he wanted nothing more to do with anything that carried religious overtones.

She could understand why.

Ever since his battle with Suwraith, there was a constant stream of people near their flat. At all hours of the day, they could be seen standing outside, huddling on the street. No matter the weather or the time, they were there. Usually, they remained quiet as they placed mementos of loved ones who had died or garlands of flowers or sweets or fresh fruit on the flat's front stoop. It was almost like they were making offerings to Devesh and the area before the flat was an altar, which was bad enough, but the worst was when one of those outside prayed to Rukh.

It was sacrilege, but it was also a sacrilege that Jessira could comprehend. Rukh had battled the Sorrow Bringer, and in the end, it had been the Queen who had screamed.

Everyone had heard that cry, and it was no wonder that the entire city seemed aflame with religious fervor. Even the normally irreligious Kummas and Cherids had been caught up in the fever of faith.

Jessira set aside *The Book of First Movement* and walked to Rukh's side. She pushed aside the curtain and looked out the window. The crowd was small today. Perhaps people were finally finding the ardor of piety too hard to hold onto. Or maybe it was just the rain. She shook her head at those foolhardy enough to stand outside in the drizzle.

Most of the people out there were Murans, which should have

been odd. As a Caste, they were the most religious, and as a Caste, they had also been the ones most opposed to the presence of the OutCastes. But Rukh's actions had changed many of their hearts. In fact, Jessira had even heard a few of them pray to Devesh in *her* name. Even though she was an OutCaste, simply by being married to Rukh, she had achieved the status of the sacred.

It was a situation that left her flabbergasted and embarrassed. Jessira knew her worth. She was just a wife, a warrior, and a woman. Nothing more. Those people shouldn't be committing sacrilege in her name.

Jessira shook her head. Even while she'd been watching, the gathering had grown. The rain was slackening, and to the west, the skies were clear. The crowd would soon be just as large as on any other day, filled with chanting, praying, or those keeping silent vigil.

"We should move to the House Seat," Jessira suggested. "At least you'll be able to step outside without being mobbed."

"I don't want to bring this . . ." Rukh waved vaguely in the direction on the crowd. ". . . to my parents' doorstep."

"It's already there. You saw them when we visited earlier today," Jessira reminded him. "Besides, they wouldn't consider it trouble. I'm sure they'd understand."

"Or maybe the crowds will eventually go away," Rukh said. "They can't stay here forever."

Jessira didn't need their link to know he didn't believe his words.

"Why don't you want to move in with your parents?" she asked. "What's the real reason?"

Rukh remained quiet for so long that Jessira wasn't sure he'd heard her question.

"I've seen Cook Heltin out in the crowd outside," he finally answered. "She's like family, like an aunt really. I saw Garnet's family out there, too."

"And it bothers you that they'll treat you differently, act differently around you?"

Rukh nodded.

Jessira crossed over to where he'd taken a seat at the dining table. She sat in his lap and leaned into him. From this position, she was taller, and she held his head against her shoulder, stroking his temple. "She likely will treat you differently because you *are* different," Jessira said. Rukh stiffened and she took his face in hands, forcing him to look at her. "I know you want to go back to simply being a Kumma warrior, but it's too late. It's been too late for several years now, and it also isn't the truth, and you know it. You aren't just a Kumma warrior. You're someone who battled the Queen and hurt Her, or at least stopped Her. It *does* make you different. And that doesn't even touch on everything else you've accomplished."

Rukh sighed. "My mind knows that, but my heart doesn't want to accept it."

Jessira tsked in sympathy. Having to deal with a city that insisted on labelling him an iconic figure worthy of worship had to be a heavy burden. Nevertheless, it was one Rukh had to carry, and by extension, she as well. "We can't hide from the truth or wish it away," she said. "Doing so won't change the situation we're in."

"We?"

Jessira turned his head once more so that he was looking at her. "Priya, in case it's escaped your attention, we're married. So, yes, *our* situation."

Rukh smiled at her mild rebuke "And what would moving into the House Seat accomplish?" he asked.

"We'll have time and space to figure out what to do next."

Rukh chuckled. "That's your answer. Time and space to figure out what to do next?"

Jessira grinned. "It's trite. I know, but do you have a better idea?"

---◆---

"How is she? Jaresh asked, having just returned from a meeting with Rector Bryce.

"She's resting," Nanna said. "I expected Bryce. Where is he? I wanted a full report on these so-called Virtuous." His voice held an atypical impatience. "I want to know who they are."

"He got called away," Jaresh answered. "He said he'd come by to give you a report when he was free."

Nanna scowled before turning away. He stared out the window of his study with a look of frustrated anger on his face. "When we find them, we'll send them straight to the unholy hells."

Jaresh understood and shared his nanna's fury. He, too, wanted to find the animals who had attacked the Shektan women. The Virtuous was what they called themselves. It was a patently absurd descriptor, and shortly after the Advent Trial, they had published a manifesto detailing why they had done as they had. But no amount of sophistry or explanation could obviate their heinous crimes. As soon as they were captured, they needed to be fed to the crows. It was how Jaresh reckoned matters. The rest of the family and House felt the same way.

Even now, Rector Bryce, Bree, and many others were out scouring the city for any hint of who the Virtuous might be. Jaresh's sister had been especially outraged over what had occurred, and rightfully so. She'd actually seen the entire attack unfold. She'd seen aunts and lifelong friends cut down. She'd been a few feet away when Amma had nearly been killed. Bree wanted vengeance, and Jaresh hoped she would have it. The truth was that if the Shektans found the Virtuous first, the fragging creatures would be lucky if they weren't torn apart on the spot.

It would justice enough as far as Jaresh was concerned.

Their Amma had a severed spine. She was paralyzed from the chest down, and it was even hard for her to breathe. The physicians reckoned she would always be at risk for pneumonia and that she would never again walk.

"Rukh and Jessira stopped by earlier," Nanna said. "They had to hide in a covered wagon in order to get out, though."

Jaresh understood what Nanna meant. Rukh drew a crowd wherever he went. There would be shouts of need, of prayers, of exhortations for things that Rukh could never do. It was all so idiotic, especially the idea that Rukh was the First Father reborn or even more ludicrously, touched by Devesh. If Rukh held the holy power of the Lord, then why hadn't he simply killed the Queen and been done with it when he'd battled Her?

It was madness, and it was a madness that had driven Rukh away from the House Seat. He and Jessira had wanted to stay here, but they couldn't. The crowds were too loud, and right now, Amma needed quiet.

Of course, what Rukh had done and how he'd done it was still a mystery. He was a Kumma, but he held the Talents of Shiyens and Sentyas, and could also Blend like a Muran or Rahail. But Jaresh held all those Talents, too, and so did Jessira and a number of OutCastes. So what made Rukh different? And what had been that silver light he'd shot from his hands? A new Talent certainly, but how had it come to him?

Rukh didn't know. He claimed to barely remember any of the events of his battle, unable to recall anything of what he'd done. All he could recollect was a burning need to hold on, to fight unto the last, to never surrender. He'd done so and then collapsed in an unmoving heap.

"Am I interrupting?" Sign Deep peeked her head into the study.

Nanna gestured for her to come on in. Since Rukh and Jessira couldn't often come to the House Seat, Sign had taken it upon herself to keep them apprised of Amma's condition.

"Any changes?" she asked.

Nanna turned away and stared out the windows at the drizzly summer day.

"She's stable," Jaresh replied, hating how such shallow words failed to convey the depth and pain of Amma's situation.

"Rukh and Jessira will try to visit again tomorrow," Sign said.

"They ought to just move in," Nanna muttered.

"Rukh says he doesn't want to bring his troubles to the House Seat," Sign replied.

"Those troubles are here whether he is or not," Nanna answered as he turned around to face them. "We are his parents. Anyone who is related to him is felt to be . . . touched by whatever holiness these fools think he possesses. They've been collecting near the gates every day, a few here and there, but always enough to make a ruckus if anyone goes outside."

"You don't believe he's special?" Sign asked, sounding surprised.

"Of course he's special," Nanna said. "But not in the way these others seem to believe. He isn't the First Father reborn and he isn't the way and means through which Devesh's will is known. He is a man, a Kumma whose experiences have changed him."

"But he fought Suwraith," Sign argued. "He survived when She smothered him like a clutching fog of poison. He challenged Her might and smote Her with a silver fire. None of that strikes you as holy?"

Jaresh grimaced in frustration. The words she had used couldn't be her own. Sign was a plainspoken person. Such flowery language had to be the words of someone else. And for her to repeat them might mean that she actually believed them. "I thought you were more levelheaded than that," Jaresh said, not bothering to mask his disappointment.

Sign shrugged. "I don't know what to believe," she replied, "but it's what those other people are saying, the ones gathered by the House Seat's gate. They saw what happened. So did I. So did half of Ashoka, for that matter. And when I saw what I did, I thought I'd witnessed the rebirth of the First Father. I know it sounds ludicrous, but not to them. They don't know Rukh like you do, or even I do."

Jaresh sighed. "I grew up with him. I've seen him at his worst. I've heard him whinge when things didn't go his way in training. He's my brother. It's hard to think of him in any other light."

Sign smiled, looking fond. "And I remember when he came hobbling into Stronghold, when he could barely walk or move his sword arm. He was no hero then. He was just a man barely holding on." She shrugged again. "But like I said—others don't know him like that. They only saw the glory, and they'll only see the glory until Rukh more fully explains what happened to him."

"If they keep pushing him, they'll see his grumpy side," Nanna said with a faint smile. "Maybe then, they won't consider him Devesh-touched."

Jaresh laughed. "Ever since the Advent Trial, he's been as grouchy as a thorn-pawed cat."

"He has reason to be. We all do," Nanna said. "And we have so many decisions to make."

Jaresh nodded. There wasn't just Amma and her injuries to take care of, or whatever it was that Rukh had done, but also the Baels and Tigons who had come to Ashoka begging for asylum.

"We live in interesting times," Sign said.

"A generation cursed," Nanna agreed.

"Or blessed," Jaresh countered.

"Can I see Satha?" Sign asked, changing the subject. "I promised to give Rukh and Jessira a full report."

"They were already here earlier today," Nanna replied. "And Satha just settled down to sleep. She won't awaken for hours."

Sign smiled brightly. "In that case, who wants to play chess?"

"I'll play," Jaresh offered.

"You can play on my board," Nanna said. "I'll do some paperwork while Jaresh works you into a lather and makes you do something stupid."

Sign squawked in outrage as Nanna chuckled.

Several hours later, Rector Bryce was shown into the study. He looked haggard and haunted.

"What is it?" Nanna asked without preamble.

"There's been another Withering Knife murder. Hal'El Wrestiva is back in Ashoka."

CHAPTER FOURTEEN
CHOICES OF SACRIFICE

*Sadly, the future of those bred for battle is often
one walked along a path of loneliness.*

—<u>Sooths and Small Sayings</u> *by Tramed Billow, AF 1387*

L i-Chig, the SarpanKum of the Western Plague of Continent
Ember, wondered what this most momentous of days would
bring to him and his kind. Would it merely bring death or
would it bring extinction?

A crow cried out and Chig frowned. The carrion eater was an ill
omen, always present when death beckoned. The SarpanKum briefly
wondered if the crow could smell blood on the wind. True, that
blood was not yet spilled, but it was sure to come. Perhaps the crow
had prescience about the coming carnage.

Chig exhaled heavily, and his breath misted in the unusually chill
summer weather. A blustery breeze blew, promising an early winter,
but the SarpanKum didn't feel the cold wind or the damp drizzle. His
mind was occupied by other thoughts.

"Are you certain of this?" Li-Sturg, his SarpanKi, asked. "We are about to embark upon the most reckless path any Bael has ever travelled."

Chig smiled. "You mean what we do will forever brand us as traitors?"

"You know that's the least of what we risk," Sturg growled. "What we are about to do could lead to the death of all our brothers."

"Not if Li-Shard's plan works."

Sturg grunted. "Shard seeks to rise to the glory of Li-Dirge."

Chig tested the words of his crèche brother. They didn't taste right. "Glory is not what impels me, nor, I am certain, does it impel Li-Shard," he said.

Sturg's lips twitched. "No. You are right. We do what as we must because we are slaves to those most devious of masters: service and sacrifice."

Chig chuckled a low, gallows-ridden laugh. "Are you ready then?"

Sturg shrugged. "We will know soon enough."

Chig smiled briefly before turning to face his warriors, the ignorant Chimeras he would lead into unwitting treason. He took a deep breath and shouted. "The breeders are the means by which Mother's will is enforced on this world, but word comes that the Chimeras who are meant to guard the eastern breeding caverns of Continent Catalyst have been subverted. Many of you have heard of how the eastern breeding caverns of Continent Ember were eradicated. What you don't know is the truth. Those eastern caverns were overrun through treachery."

Murmurings of shock and disbelief met his words.

Chig stamped his trident on the ground, a single blow demanding silence. "Just as there are righteous Humans who worship

Mother, there are Chimeras who have allowed iniquity to grow in their hearts. They disregard Mother's teachings. They oppose Her will. They seek our destruction." He forced a grimace before drawing himself up. "Their evil cannot be allowed. We must kill these treasonous warriors. We will end their wretched lives, kill them all." He paused. Here was the most dangerous aspect of his plan. "And we must do the same with the breeders."

Silence met his final words. The Chimeras of his Plague turned their eyes to him, questioning and unsure, but not untrusting.

"Yes. The breeders must all be killed," Chig said with a nod of affirmation. "Without their deaths, our mission here will be a failure. Their eradication is the great task set before us. Mother commands it. After what happened to Li-Dirge and the eastern caverns, and now this, She trusts no one, not even the breeders. They are to be extinguished, for just as Mother has always promised us, She will create females of our kind so that we may procreate like all the other natural creatures of Arisa!"

A harsh cry of joy met his words, and Chig smiled. "Follow your Baels. Do as they say. Show the enemy no mercy!"

———◆◆———

Li-Deem sweltered beneath the late afternoon sun and frowned in annoyance. Red sand dunes stretched out in unbroken, sinuous waves for miles in every direction, and a dry wind did nothing to cool off the temperature. Deem irritably wondered why Mother had placed the northern breeding caverns of Continent Catalyst in the midst of the Prayer, the hottest desert in all Arisa. No matter that the caves were buried beneath a series of rocky hills that cupped a large oasis, or that the smell of dirt, dates, and crushed grass softened the bruise-dry air, Deem still hated the heat. He always had, ever since his birth five decades ago. Summer was his bane. It was too hot. Too bright. Too uncomfortable. Deem much preferred the cool sweetness of fall and winter.

He pondered whether he might ever again see those lovely seasons. He pondered whether he might ever again see a sunrise.

It seemed unlikely, and if that turned out to be the case, then he would have no one else to blame but himself. As the SarpanKum of the Northern Plague of Continent Catalyst, ultimately it had been his decision to agree to Li-Shard's plan. It was a proposal that Deem had initially judged foolhardy but over time, found to be more and more intriguing and exciting. His discordant emotions had yet to entirely reconcile.

Following the destruction of the heretofore unknown city of Stronghold last year, Deem had felt a disquiet such as he had never before experienced in his long five decades of life. With the restitution of Her sanity, Mother had grown too powerful. The balance of power had shifted too far in Her favor. She might actually achieve Her ultimate goal of Humanity's extinction. Something had to change, and Li-Shard's plan seemed the most likely means to achieve that change.

Was this the best plan, though? Or even necessary? Those were questions still unanswered, but ones that didn't trouble Deem's crèche-brother and SarpanKi, Li-Feint. He had no doubts about their course, even if such a course might see an end to the Baels.

"The warriors are ready," Feint said, coming to Deem's side. "They only await your command."

Deem smiled faintly, a feeling that didn't reflect his heart's turmoil. "I wish I had your faith, brother," he said softly.

Feint stepped closer and rested a reassuring hand on his

shoulder. "Whatever you lack, lean on me and know that you will not fall," his brother replied. "If you cannot bring yourself to do this, I will still support you."

Deem exhaled softly and gave a tight smile of gratitude. The two Baels, gray-haired and old, should have long ago been retired to the breeding caverns to train the young, but the field was where they felt they could do the most good, where they felt they were the most effective. "I don't fear death," Deem said. "It comes to all of us."

"But you don't want the Baels to die either."

Deem nodded again, unsurprised by his brother's insight. Such had always been their bond. "Mother will see us all dead for what we are about to do."

"We won't be ended." Feint spoke with a steady, unwavering cadence to his voice. "The Baels and Bovars we sent to Hanuman were given sanctuary."

"I hope the Humans weren't lying to us when they gave us their promise," Deem replied. Fear fluttered in his heart for those he had sent to Hanuman.

Feint shrugged. "It will be as it will be," he said enigmatically, "but it helped that the Humans had already heard the story of Rukh Shektan and his friendship with Li-Choke."

"Li-Choke," Deem said with a sigh and shake of his head. "He makes paupers of us all. We've lived so long, but in a sense, not at all, given what that young Bael has experienced."

"Then how would you like to live out the last moments of your life?" Feint asked with a smile. "Would you not want to experience the glory Li-Dirge experienced in his final breaths?"

Deem shook his head. "I have no need for glory," he replied. "It is enough for me to be a servant." His spine stiffened as he replayed the words he had just spoken. They described the heart of who

Deem was: a servant. He chuckled just then as he realized that despite all his stumbling and questioning, all along he'd known the course he would have to take. "We will do as Devesh asks: act as a servant to a greater cause than our own lives," he said in response to the unspoken question in Feint's eyes.

His brother smiled wryly. "Wisdom—decades late—has finally come to you."

Deem chuckled again. "Better late than not," he replied before turning to the Chimeras gathered before him. He drew breath and bellowed. "Warriors. A great challenge lies ahead of us! And should we succeed, a greater prize will be ours!"

Li-Shuk, the SarpanKum of the Southern Plague of the Continent Catalyst, led his warriors through a narrow, shadow-engulfed gorge. A trickle of water rattled over rocks on its way to nearby Lake Corruption, the body of water Mother insisted they call the Chalice of Purity. She claimed it was Her birthplace, which meant it was also the site where She had slaughtered Her Parents, the First Mother and First Father, in Their home at the Palace on the Hill.

As far as Shuk was concerned, everything about Lake Corruption stank of desecration. It was a place pregnant with the stench of mildew and sulfur, of despair and despoilment, of loss and murdered hopes. Shuk only hoped that the cleansing ruin he was bringing to Mother's southern breeders would do much to erase such a foul reek.

Perhaps it would, but even if it did nothing more than hinder Mother's villainous schemes, Shuk reckoned it would be worth the cost. He had heard that Li-Chig and Li-Deem had initially been hesitant to follow Li-Shard's grand scheme, but such doubts had never hindered Shuk's thoughts. He had always known that what he was about to do was just and righteous. Devesh demanded that all His servants oppose evil.

"Do you think Chig and Deem will carry out their roles?" asked Li-Trid, the newly elevated SarpanKi.

The previous one, Li-Kord, had been killed several weeks ago in a failed uprising by less faithful Baels. The traitors had been selfishly attached to their own lives, foolishly believing that a longer life was somehow more meaningful. They were too blinded by their own wants and desires to remember that every breath they took was by Devesh's grace and to His honor should every breath they took be purposed.

"I believe they will," Shuk replied in answer to Trid's question, "but certain knowledge of what they ultimately decided will only come to us on the other side of life."

"I think they will," Trid replied with the hearty assuredness of youth.

Shuk grunted, wishing he still had the young SarpanKi's simple certainty. He had fears about what the other SarpanKums of Continent Catalyst might do. They were of lesser faith than Shuk would have liked, but still, Kord, his fallen crèche-brother, had believed that Deem and Chig would carry out their roles.

Just then, a single tear fell from his eyes. Shuk still grieved over Kord's death. It still hurt, akin to a stabbing pain to the heart. Such a terrible loss. So pointless. His crèche-brother's ending shouldn't have come at the hands of a faithless traitor. And maybe with today's actions, Kord's death wouldn't be in vain.

"Li-Dirge, Li-Shard, and Li-Choke," Trid said, "those are the Baels by which we should measure ourselves. It is how those who follow after us will reckon our standing: as worthy heirs to those great Baels."

Shuk couldn't fail to notice the hopeful expression in the eyes of his earnest SarpanKi. The expression sparked a smile from the SarpanKum. "Gather the warriors. It is time."

<hr />

The day had dawned bright and vibrant. The sun shone, the weather was warm, and the air dry. It was the perfect day to plan the murder of a city.

Lienna soared through the skies, feeling an anticipation and joy that She couldn't ever recall experiencing. Even when approaching Stronghold, knowing that She was about to annihilate a city of Casteless Humans—the very idea of unCasted Humans still left Lienna revolted and feeling dirty—She had not felt this excitement, this tingling, this need to laugh.

The Eastern Plague was almost at the gates of Ashoka. Just another week or so, and they would arrive. Then would come the hammer blows of Her children against the evil walls of evil Ashoka.

"What You intend is evil," Mother interrupted in Her sibilant whisper.

Lienna mentally rolled her eyes in scorn. *"What I do is no more evil than when I threw down Your rule and that of Father's,"* Lienna responded. She let no hint of the worry She felt at Father's ongoing absence enter Her voice. Where *was* Father? Had She really experienced his angry touch outside of Ashoka several weeks ago? It couldn't be. She had seen to His death.

"You murdered Us both," Mother replied. *"How can murder be counted as anything other than evil?"*

Lienna wanted to gnash Her figurative teeth. Mother and Father had died two millennia ago. Why couldn't the foolish woman simply accept it and leave Lienna in peace?

"Peace is only owed to those who are peaceful," Mother said. *"You are anything but peaceful. You are wicked and violent, a murderous plague upon this world."*

"Be silent!" Lienna shouted.

There was a blessed but all-too-brief quiet, one that was broken by Mistress Arisa. *"Ashoka will fall to You, My avenging angel. You will see Humanity's corruption excised from My bosom."*

Once Mistress' voice would have filled Lienna with love and trepidation, but not anymore. At least not as much. *"Yes it will, Mistress,"* Lienna replied.

Better to agree with Arisa rather than to argue with her, or worse, ignore Her. That path often led to terrible pain and still left Lienna wondering how a figment of Her imagination could hurt Her so badly.

"After Ashoka, next to fall will be vain Ajax," Mistress continued.

Lienna held in a sigh. Ajax was dead. She had destroyed the city five centuries ago.

She was about to reply, but She felt the sudden death of thousands of Her children. The sensation came from the east, from the vastness of Continent Catalyst. The deaths continued, even the youngest . . .

Her breeders in the northern caverns!

Lienna shouted outraged thunder and roared eastward in a storm of wind and fury. She raced across the Sickle Sea bent on vengeance when She sensed more of Her children dying. More of Her breeders murdered. This time the southern caverns of Continent Catalyst. Lienna faltered and slowed. The Humans had done this. Somehow they must have discovered Her breeding caverns.

Lienna bled outraged lightning.

When the eastern caverns of Continent Ember had been attacked several years ago, She had been unaware of the evil taking place. Madness had held Her in its cruel grip, and, unlike now, Lienna hadn't sensed the murder of Her children. She had been unable to save them, Her breeders, the most innocent creatures in all creation.

But this time was different. This time Lienna was sane and clear-headed. This time the Humans would pay for this treachery! This time Lienna would tear them apart limb from limb. Rend them and scatter their remnants to the four winds. She would crush their cities; peel the skin off their living children in front of their mothers. She would—

With an anguished cry, Lienna crashed to halt. The western caverns of Continent Ember were also under attack.

<hr />

Within the forests carpeting the hills west of Ashoka, the cool scent of moss and trickling water from a nearby creek struck counterpoint to the trilling of birdsong. Shadows stretched along the ground as the sun set and gloomed the world in gathering, soothing darkness. However, the dimness of the place did little to hide the Fan Lor Kum as they pressed through and amongst the trees. Wherever they went, the soothing sounds of the forest were erased. Taking its place was the mad clapping of wings in flight and small animals scurrying in the undergrowth as they sought to evade the interlopers clattering through their home.

Li-Shard, the SarpanKum of the Eastern Plague of Continent Ember wished he could do the same. He wished he could simply crawl away somewhere and hide from what he knew was coming. It would have been so much easier if others had to make the hard decisions, and not for the first time did he wish that the mantle of leadership had not been his to bear, that someone else could decide what to do about Mother's newfound prowess. She had already destroyed Stronghold, and now Ashoka was in Her sights. And afterward, whatever other city She wished to end would also fall. Such evil could not continue unchallenged.

"The others will do as we've discussed," Li-Brind said in assurance, standing nearby the SarpanKum.

Shard glanced at the hardbitten SarpanKi in surprise. "Since when did you develop such certainty in the actions of others?"

Brind grinned. "When a young SarpanKum came up with a scheme so mad that it had to be the work of a great fool or someone imbued with Devesh's holiness." He shrugged. "And when an even younger Vorsan taught a Tigon the meaning of fraternity and both of them earned the friendship of two Humans."

Shard smiled with the SarpanKi, but his smile quickly faded. "So much rides on the actions of the other SarpanKums. They have to be impeccable in their timing. They have to coordinate their attacks so all the breeders are eliminated in one fell swoop. It has to occur too swiftly for Mother to counter."

"Despite what She claims, Mother is no Goddess," Brind said with a snort. "She cannot be everywhere at once. We do not need impeccable timing. We simply have to have the attacks go off at around the same time. Everything else will take care of itself from that point on."

"I hope you're right," Li-Shard said softly.

"Have faith," Brind said, clapping him on the shoulder.

Shard did a double take upon hearing the SarpanKi's words.

"Faith? You?" he asked in disbelief.

"Faith," Li-Brind averred. "Even me."

Shard studied Brind. The older Bael stared back at him wearing an open, welcoming expression. "When did you find your way back to Devesh?"

"I told you when and why it occurred," Brind said with a shrug. "Besides, I find that with our likely upcoming deaths, my mind is focused like it never has been before."

Shard shook his head, wishing he had Brind's equanimity. His heart thudded fear and his stomach churned uncertainty, both sensations resulting from what would happen should his plan actually succeed.

Once he had asked Brind if Humanity would do the same as the Baels if their respective roles had been reversed. The SarpanKi had felt it unlikely. *"They don't think as we do,"* Brind had said. *"There is a gulf of differences that might mean that we don't always understand one another, but they are still our brothers. And brothers sacrifice for one another."*

"Even unto the end with no hope of a future for our race?" Shard had challenged.

"Even then." Brind had smiled. *"Besides, aren't you the one who's always telling me that our lives belong to Devesh—that in the end, He'll take back that which we have been borrowing? If that's true, then doesn't it stand to reason that the same would hold true for our race as a whole?"*

At the time, the words had been comforting, but now they no longer retained their prayerful tranquility. For himself, Shard was already prepared to encounter his Creator before the day's ending, but he still feared for the collective future of the rest of his kind.

The SarpanKum turned his attention back to the present when he noticed a frown creasing Brind's face.

"What is it?"

"I just wish we were already at Ashoka," the SarpanKi said.

Shard nodded. "It's these accursed trees. These forested hills that stretch for weeks of travel from the city."

"We were to have already rendezvoused with the Shatters that Mother sent from Continent Catalyst, but at the pace we're traveling, they're more likely to be waiting for us at the gates of Ashoka." Brind snorted in disgust.

"Or perhaps they have been similarly slowed by this same forest," Shard observed.

The SarpanKi tilted his head in thought. "Maybe so," he agreed. "The northern approach to Ashoka will be just as hard as ours."

"Hard or easy, we should reach the city in the next few weeks," Li-Shard said. "Then all these months—these worries—will be over. It ends today," he said softly.

"It begins today," Brind replied just as softly. "When Mother discovers our treachery, Her fury will be something this world has never seen." The SarpanKi hardbitten though he was, actually shuddered.

The SarpanKum nodded. "At least we can assume that Li-Choke is safe."

"Why must we assume such a thing?"

"Because if we don't, then everything we're doing somehow seems pointless."

Brind nodded agreement. "Though we will not see another morning, I am grateful that you helped me recover my faith. It allows me to face this terrible future with hope and acceptance."

They both stiffened.

Mother was coming. And She was furious.

———■●■———

Li-Boil heard Mother's call, and his heart quailed. She was incandescent with a rage unlike anything he had ever experienced. It was reminiscent of times past when She had been lost in Her insanity but also different. This time, rather than an inchoate anger at anything and everything—a fury born of Her madness—Her wrath now held a cold, cruel quality; a savagery that was focused and disciplined, icy and sharp like a stiletto blade sliding through the ribs. Mother's fury was always frightening to behold, but this—this was terrifying. Boil could tell that whoever had earned Her wrath would pay a terrible price as She seemed bent on exacting slow, methodical vengeance.

And She was racing in their direction.

Boil's knees trembled and his lips quivered. What had Mother so enraged? He did his best to calm himself by focusing on his breathing. He even prayed, searching for his inner quiet. Eventually he was able to control most of his fear, and his knees stopped knocking so much.

He looked to Li-Shard, the SarpanKum. He and Li-Brind, the SarpanKi. The two of them whispered to one another, but rather than appearing fearful, they seemed unsurprised, or possibly even relieved. It made no sense, and Li-Boil's gaze tightened in mistrusting speculation. Those two knew something, something related to why Mother was so angry. And whatever it was, it likely wasn't good for the Baels.

Shard and Brind were like too many of the brothers who insisted that Hume's teachings required that the Baels sacrifice themselves for the sake of strangers. In this, they were too much like the infamous Li-Dirge who insisted their kind relinquish everything—up to and including their lives—for the protection of Humanity. Boil believed differently. While he considered himself to be just as religious as any

Bael—he prayed daily to Devesh and believed in the truth of fraternity—he wasn't willing to accept that he had to die so someone he had never met should live. He also didn't believe the Baels should suffer and be killed so Humanity could prosper. Where was the justice in such an approach? Boil's vision of fraternity *did not* require that the Baels should impale themselves on their own tridents for the benefit of those who hated them.

"What do you suppose is happening?" asked Li-Torq.

Boil glanced at the smaller Bael who had come alongside him. Torq was his last living crèche-mate. "I don't know," Boil answered, "but it looks like Li-Shard and Li-Brind do."

Torq nodded. "You think they might have betrayed us?"

"Look at their expressions and your question is answered," Boil replied. "Mother is coming, and I've never felt Her so angry." He gestured to the SarpanKum and the SarpanKi. "Yet they show no worry. Only acceptance."

"What do you plan on doing?"

Boil flicked him a sidelong glance. "Whatever is needed to see our kind alive and prosperous."

"I'll speak to the others," Torq said. "Our tridents will be yours if it becomes necessary."

"If Mother doesn't simply kill us outright," Boil muttered after the smaller Bael had left.

"Mother commands us to attend Her. All of us!" the SarpanKum bellowed in that moment. "There is a nearby meadow which should suffice."

"What has happened?" Boil demanded in a tone a VorsanKi should never take with the SarpanKum.

Li-Shard looked his way. "You will learn the answer to your question at the same time that we all do," he said, his tail flicking either annoyance or unease. Given the drooping of his tufted ears, Boil guessed unease.

"Enough delay!" Li-Brind shouted. "We will *not* keep Mother waiting. Now move it!"

Boil didn't miss the look of relief Shard threw to his SarpanKi. Those two *did* know something. Boil looked discreetly in Li-Torq's direction. His crèche-mate nodded back, and the two Baels angled toward one another. Filtering in behind them and to the sides were Boil's supporters, the ones who felt as he did: that the Baels had done enough, given enough, and shouldn't be expected to sacrifice the very existence of their race for Humanity's benefit. They numbered in the several hundreds, and while they were vastly outnumbered by Shard's supporters, they had passion on their side. And passion could carry the day if disaster stalked the Baels.

Boil glanced again at Torq, and they slid in behind Shard and his followers. It was the perfect position from which to watch what might occur and be in a position to do something about it.

They had just entered the broad meadow the SarpanKum had mentioned when Mother's angry roar could be heard. She was still miles away, rushing closer with each passing second, but even from such a vast distance, Her thoughts were clear.

"Betrayal!" Mother shouted out. *"All the breeders for every Caste of Chimeras have been slaughtered by treachery! And it is the Baels who have done this foul deed!"*

The breeders were dead? All of them? No wonder Mother's wrath was so vast and deep. Boil stiffened. And She blamed the Baels for what had happened. His mouth grew dry with terror. Devesh save them. What would Mother do? Her vengeance might strike the Baels even harder than when She had destroyed that pious dullard, Li-Dirge. She might seek to utterly annihilate them.

Boil saw Shard and Brind share a triumphant smile. His fear fled, replaced by a righteous indignation. Those two! They'd known, possibly even helped plan this disaster. An overwhelming sense of outrage came upon Li-Boil, and with an inarticulate cry of hatred, he lifted his trident and uncoiled his chained whip.

All around him, his supporters did the same.

"Your race will rot for this treachery! And it will start here, with the author of this treason. Li-Shard!" Mother screamed, but Boil was no longer listening.

The need to kill those who had brought the Baels to ruin surged through him. His race was about to be destroyed completely and forever, and Li-Shard and Li-Brind dared smile in pleasure? As though they had accomplished something magnificent? Well they would enjoy their triumph for only a few more seconds. Before Mother killed all the Baels, Boil was intent on seeing those two race-traitors dead.

"The Baels will be ended for all time," Mother vowed. *"Even now, Bovars throughout the world are being slaughtered so no new Baels will ever again be born!"*

Upon hearing Mother's promise, Boil's outrage overcame thought, and he shouted. *"Kill the traitors!"* He and his supporters attacked.

———◆———

L i-Shard was on bended knee when he heard the commotion begin. He had lifted his head to search out the trouble when the screams began.

It was the cries of Baels dying at the hands of their brothers.

Brind was already on his feet and moving. The SarpanKi called out orders, but his voice suddenly ended in a gurgle. The tines of a trident had punched through his chest. He slumped over and stared with unseeing eyes at the sky.

Shard shook off his shock and stood. Baels were being slaughtered all about him. They were his closest supporters, the ones who most fervently believed in the ideals of Hume. And those attacking were those who believed otherwise.

Shard's gut clenched with outrage. How could his brothers have debased themselves so?

He uncoiled his whip and set it alight. His trident was ready and steady in his tight grip.

A Bael came at him, his face snarled in blood lust. Li-Torq.

Shard snapped his whip over the other Bael's ear in distraction. He was about to thrust forward with his trident, but pain erupted in his side. He keened.

Torq's crèche-mate, Li-Boil, had stabbed him. Another stab. This time in the chest. It was Li-Torq.

"I am sorry, brother," Li-Boil said.

Shard could barely hear for the pain. He took another thrust to the chest, and Li-Shard relinquished his grip on his weapons. A singing light filled the last moments of his life.

———•———

B oil and his supporters had easily slaughtered Li-Shard's adherents. The SarpanKum and most of those who followed him had been on their knees in prayer. They had been slow to rise and easy to kill, and in the end, their numbers had counted for little since they had been unprepared for the ferocity with which Boil and his supporters attacked them.

Boil panted heavily afterward and felt satisfaction in what he and the others had accomplished, but no joy. It had been a deed that needed doing. Nothing more. Boil had taken no pleasure in killing Li-Shard and his followers. No matter how deluded the SarpanKum had been or how wicked his actions, the Bael had been Boil's brother. His death was to be mourned, not celebrated.

As his panting breath slowed and his heart ceased racing, Boil began to comprehend the enormity of had just occurred. He realized the meadow was unnaturally quiet. It stank of blood and entrails. There was no movement, and all the Baels standing about were mute and in shock. The vast majority had not taken part in the attack on Li-Shard. They had been neutrals, neither supporting nor defending the fallen SarpanKum. They stared at Boil in confusion, and their eyes seemed to beg for direction.

Boil stared back at them in uncertainty. What now? Mother would be here at any moment, and he briefly wondered if by killing Li-Shard, Mother's hideous rage might be turned aside. Might She forgive the Baels? It seemed unlikely, but what other hope did he and the others have?

Thunder heralded Mother's arrival and lightning lashed the sky and ground. A harsh wind howled. It was as unyielding as a moving mountain.

The Baels were forced to fall upon their knees, their heads tucked beneath shielding hands and arms. Almost by rote, Boil began the Prayer of Gratitude. The others fell in with him.

Mother rushed downward. Boil prayed for acceptance in the next life. He waited for the hammer blow, but it never came.

Instead, there came a moment of prolonged relative silence and stillness. Boil dared glance up. Mother had halted. Tendrils of lightning with muted thunder still trailed around Her. *The traitor, Li-Shard, where is he?*

Boil tucked his head back to the ground, impressing it in the blood of his dead brothers. "The traitor is dead," he declared. "By Your words and his expressions, we took justice upon him."

"So you conveniently killed him," Mother jeered. *"And now you hope I will not kill you?"*

"Li-Shard and his SarpanKi were the traitors, but we *have* remained loyal," Boil answered. "Whatever the SarpanKum did, we had no part in it. We killed him, and all who followed him, as soon as we realized they had betrayed You."

"Liar," Mother whispered.

Boil held in his disappointment. It had been too much to expect that Mother might forgive them, and he prepared for his end.

"You have nothing to say in your defense?" Mother asked. *"I called you a liar, and you don't deny it?"*

Boil hesitated, trying to force his mind to think. "Words are easy," he finally answered. "It is deeds that offer proof."

"Indeed," Mother agreed. *"And what deeds do you have to prove your loyalty?"*

"The death of Li-Shard and all who thought as he did."

"And if I require the death of every Bael upon the gates of Ashoka? Will you still remain loyal? And understand this: you will soon be the last of your kind on Arisa. The others will *be ended, just as I promised, unless I am given a reason to change My mind."*

Boil's guts clenched. The Baels were to be wiped out and for what? A Humanity that despised them? He wanted to weep, but instead, he managed to press words past his lips. "Our lives are Yours to spend as You see fit," Boil said. "I only ask . . ." he vacillated at completing the request. What if Mother denied him?

"What do you dare ask?" Mother hissed. *"Quiet, Mother. The dead should remain silent,"* She muttered.

351

Boil froze, unsure to whom She was speaking. Everyone knew Mother was mad. It was a law as certain as the tides. There was an expectant thrill to the air, and Boil realized Mother was still waiting on him. "I only ask that the Bovars are allowed to live. Allow us, the Baels who remained loyal, to instruct the newborn of our kind so there can never be another opportunity for betrayal."

There was an eternity of silence. *"We will see,"* Mother finally said. *"For now, gather My children and make for Ashoka. I will have more instructions for you then."*

CHAPTER FIFTEEN
INTERLUDE ENDED

*When danger beckons, the distance between thought
and action is too short to be measured.*

—*The Warrior and the Servant* (author unknown)

"Another Withering Knife murder," Jessira muttered with a sigh. "I thought Hal'El Wrestiva was gone from our lives for good."

Rukh had hoped for the same thing. "Apparently he's returned," he replied.

"I know *that*," Jessira replied. "What I meant is why is he back?"

Rukh shrugged. "Probably something to do with the coming attack. According to Choke, the Chimeras should only be a week or so away from the city. And everyone saw the Sorrow Bringer flying overhead a few days ago."

Jessira sighed. "I'm so tired of all this. The constant fear and dying. We've had nothing but trouble for the past two years," she said. "A little time without worry would be nice."

"It seems such a gentle fate is not to be our destiny," Rukh replied.

"So it seems," Jessira agreed. "And this next test will likely be our most difficult. We'll be going against the Sorrow Bringer Herself," Jessira said. "And no matter what others might claim, we both know you aren't the First Father reborn."

Rukh winced at her words and glanced around at their surroundings. "How about we keep our voices down," he suggested. "I don't want anyone overhearing us and figuring out who we are."

Jessira rolled her eyes. "There's no one around," she said, pointing out the quiet street on which they walked. "Besides with your false beard and my wig, even your own nanna won't recognize us."

Rukh glanced about one last time just to make sure they were alone. "Since we met, it seems like all we ever do is fight, flee, or pray for deliverance."

"I think I mentioned that already," Jessira said wryly.

"But you forgot to mention how those moments of terror are leavened by our arguing," Rukh said with a smile.

"Oh yes. Mustn't forget that," Jessira replied with a wry grin of her own.

"At least we don't argue nearly as often as we used to," Rukh added, giving her hand a gentle squeeze.

"Sometimes arguing with you is fun. Isn't that what you once said?" Jessira's eyes twinkled.

Rukh quirked a grin. "You just like what happens when we make up."

"You mean when you admit that you were wrong and beg for my forgiveness?" Jessira asked wearing a bland expression of innocence. "I do like that."

Rukh snorted. "Hold that thought," he said. "We're here. Nanna and the others should already be inside."

They paused outside a large, two-story house on a corner lot. Rukh thought it had a quiet grandness to it with its wraparound porch to welcome visitors and its heavy, gray stacked-stone to give it heft. A simple lawn edged with summer flowers beaded under the misty rain while out back there appeared to be even more extensive gardens.

A crowd had already gathered before the house, and the barricades erected by the City Watch held them back. People milled about, sharing rumors and innuendo of what might have happened inside the house, and Rukh and Jessira had to elbow their way forward to reach the front of the crowd. Once they had identified themselves to the guards manning the barricades, they were swiftly ushered past the barriers.

Rukh heard their names whispered in hushed, reverent tones, and he mentally sighed. "I'm fine," he said to Jessira's look of concern.

"They only looked," Jessira said as they climbed the stairs to the front porch. "They . . ."

"I know. I can understand why they think about me the way they do." He shrugged. "It's just hard to get used to it, though."

"If it helps, no one in the family worships you like that. I certainly don't," Jessira said with a wink.

Their conversation was cut short by Nanna, who was waiting at the top of the porch steps. "Go on inside," he said in a no-nonsense tone when they reached him. "Give me a full report when you've had a chance to study the room where the body was found and looked around the house. I need to get home to your amma."

Rukh nodded. "I'm sure she's fine."

"I'm sure she is as well, but . . ." Nanna gave a wan smile. "I just don't like leaving her alone."

With that, he bid them goodbye and hurried on his way.

The front door opened, and in the doorway stood Rector Bryce. "What took you so long?" he demanded. "Jaresh and Bree have already been through here."

"We were at our flat when word reached us," Jessira replied.

"Well, come on in. We were just about to move the body. Her name was Pera Obbe. She owns the house and lives here by herself."

As they stepped into the foyer, Rukh immediately noticed the heavy crystal chandelier hanging up above. It was brightly lit with a number of small, delicate firefly lamps, and Rukh briefly wondered as to Pera Obbe's occupation. Such a luxurious item would have made a fine addition to a Cherid manse.

Rector led them deeper into the house, and the sense of affluence continued. They ascended a wide, floating staircase with carved handrails and balusters that were polished to a high sheen and looked to have been made of an exotic, expensive wood. Maybe teak.

"Whoever lived here was wealthy," Jessira noted. Did you see the furniture downstairs in the sitting room?" She whistled in appreciation.

Rukh nodded. "And look at the paintings on the walls. Those are expensive pieces of artwork."

"You should see her jewelry," Rector said to them. "She had enough gems and gold to make a Kumma woman feel naked."

Rector led them down a long hallway. At the end was a closed door. "She's in there."

"What Caste was she?" Jessira asked.

"Duriah," Rector replied.

Alarm bells pealed in Rukh's mind. "Do we have any idea as to what she did to accrue such wealth?"

"No. There are some notebooks and financial documents

indicating that she was a partner in a number of business ventures, both in the city and in various Trials," Rector answered. "Jaresh already looked through them, but he says they're fairly standard. Apparently, she was just very good at choosing her investments."

Rukh pushed open the door. Inside was a large room with heavy furniture that somehow managed to be both ornate and understated at the same time. On the four-post bed was a shrouded figure. The murdered Pera Obbe.

Jessira stepped forward and exposed the dead woman's face. She gasped. "Why would Hal'El have cut off her face?"

"He did that after stabbing her in the heart, "Rector said, sounding clinical. At Jessira's look of annoyance, he held up his hands. "I'm just telling you what the examining physician said. She said there would have been a lot more blood if he'd cut off her face first and *then* killed her."

"He cut off her face because he hated her," Rukh said. The words sounded right, felt right.

"How do you know?" Rector asked.

Rukh held up a finger. "We have a Duriah woman who is wealthy from remarkably good investing." He held up a second finger. "She is murdered by Hal'El Wrestiva." A third finger went up. "In his journal, Ular Sathin remarked about how much the SuDin despised the Duriah MalDin, how he was offended by her ugliness. Potato-faced was what he called her." Rukh glanced at Rector. "How do the neighbors describe Pera Obbe's appearance?"

"She was ugly," Rector replied before hesitating for a moment. "One of them said her face looked like the get of a potato and a rutabaga."

Rukh looked his way in confusion.

"Her nose looked like a rutabaga," Rector explained.

"You think Pera Obbe was the last MalDin?" Jessira asked.

"I think if Jaresh takes another look at those financial journals, he'll find more than he imagined," Rukh replied.

Rector stroked his chin in thought. "Hal'El killed Pera because he hated her."

"And he wants us to know he's back," Jessira said.

———— • ————

"You look fine," Rukh said.

Jaresh turned away from the mirror where he'd been studying his appearance and looked his brother's way with a raised, questioning eyebrow.

"I know you're taking Sign out tonight," Rukh answered.

"We're just having dinner. I'm not really taking her out in the way you mean. We're just friends," Jaresh replied in a rush. He immediately knew that his words had tumbled out too quickly and made him sound defensive.

Rukh looked on with a knowing grin.

Jaresh rolled his eyes at his brother's amusement. He tried to change the subject and gestured to his pants. "You don't think these pants are too . . . bold, do you?"

"You look good in them," Rukh said. "I'm sure Sign will approve."

Jaresh gave his brother a sardonic expression. "I keep telling you she's just a friend. Nothing more," he repeated. "And with everything going on right now, romance is the last thing on either of our minds."

"With everything going on right now, maybe romance should be on your minds," Rukh countered. "We just had to look over the scene of the latest Withering Knife murder. The Queen and Her Chims should be here any day, so I say you should find happiness whenever you can because you might not have another chance in the days to come."

"Point taken," Jaresh said. "And in the vein of someone who should take his own advice, what do you plan on doing to find happiness?"

Rukh rose to his feet. "I promised to take Jessira out to a play."

Jaresh tilted his head in puzzlement. "How will the two of you leave the House Seat unrecognized."

Rukh gave a crooked grin. "My false beard and her wig," he answered. "And we'll be leaving with a group of servants. None of my faithful followers will recognize us."

Jaresh laughed, happy to see Rukh smiling again. After the Advent Trial, he'd been so downcast and edgy. It was good to see him coming to terms with his situation and accepting it. "Then good luck with your plan," he said.

"Scheme," Rukh corrected, striking a portentous posture.

"Scheme?"

"It sounds sneakier that way."

"Scheme, then," Jaresh agreed.

———•———

"You look nice," Jaresh said when Sign opened the door to her flat. "Is the dress new?"

Sign lifted her arms from her side, giving a better view of the sleeveless dress she was wearing. "It's your sister's. She's letting me borrow it."

"Well you look good in it."

Sign grinned. "Thank you. And you look nice as well. I like those pants."

Jaresh smiled, glad he had taken his brother's advice.

"Let me put on some sandals, and I'll be ready to go."

When Sign turned aside, Jaresh caught a glimpse of a tattoo on her upper arm. It was a ferocious, black cat with webbed batwings tipped in trailing golden light. Tattoos were rare in Ashoka, and Jaresh took a moment to study Sign's. He decided that the mix of a fierce cat and the wingtips fit her.

"I like your tattoo," he said.

Sign straightened with a smile. "Thank you. I got it when I became a scout," she said. "Are you ready?"

Jaresh nodded and led them north, toward Mount Crone. The area where most of the OutCastes lived had come a long way. The buildings were still ugly, unadorned cubes with flat roofs and narrow windows, but the grounds surrounding them were lush with fresh plantings and flowers. In addition, new pathways of colored rocks had been laid in patterns that mimicked water curling around boulders. Several small gazebos with young ivy trailing through trellises were present as well, and the area would be lovely in a couple of years.

If they lived that long, Jaresh thought morosely.

"Where are we going?" Sign asked.

"A place Rector showed me," Jaresh said. "It's in Trell Rue, which isn't too far away, but we can hire a rickshaw if you prefer."

"I'd rather walk." Sign gave him a sidelong glance. "Unless you can't keep up."

Jaresh chuckled. "Ask me that when it's time to walk home."

It was an hour's journey to Trell Rue and the restaurant in question. The crowds were thick at twilight and slowed them, but eventually, they reached their destination. The restaurant was housed in a building made of red brick, and the heat from the roaring fireplace within drove them outside to a table on the patio. Even there the air was heavy with the scent of spiced noodles, dahl, grilled meat, and parathas.

"What do you recommend?" Sign asked.

"It's traditional Duriah fare, so it's a little heavy," Jaresh said. "I'd try the sambar with lamb and a lassi."

Sign took his advice, but also had an order of bhaji and naan to go with her sambar.

Jaresh didn't say anything, but he couldn't imagine she would be able to eat all the food she had ordered.

He was wrong. While they spoke about Sign's life in Stronghold, her impressions of Ashoka, and the training she was undergoing in order to join the High Army, Sign polished off her bhajis. The sambar arrived, and the discussion turned to the health of Jaresh's amma, the Withering Knife murder, and rumors of war. All the while, Sign steadily ate while they spoke, although Jaresh did notice that she was finally slowing down.

"You don't have to eat it all now," he said. "I brought a small pot"— he held up a small, spidergrass container—"for any food we can't finish."

"Thank you," Sign said with a shake of negation. "But right now, this has become a battle between me and the food. I won't let it win."

Jaresh chuckled in bemusement. "As you wish," he said. "I just hope you still feel that way later tonight when your stomach is aching."

Minutes later, Sign finished her meal with an unhappy groan. She pushed her plate away and fell back in her chair. "I think I ate too much," she moaned.

"Really? I would have never guessed."

"Shut up."

Jaresh tried—and failed—not to grin at her misery. "I warned you," he said, knowing his words would earn him another glare. "By the way, do you want that rickshaw now?"

Sign surprised him by offering him a smile. "I'll take the rickshaw, but only if it drops us off at that chocolatier we passed on the way here."

Jaresh chuckled. "You're incorrigible."

Sign shrugged. "I don't know what incorrigible means, but if it means I won't let food defeat me, than I suppose I am."

———— •◆• ————

Rukh wheeled Amma out to her favorite spot in the gardens. It was also his. A copse of trees cupped the space in a leafy embrace and provided a place of seclusion and shelter. A stone bench rested at the edge of a tall drop-off and from it, Rukh could see the aquamarine Sickle Sea. He could almost imagine the cries of the faraway flocks of seagulls squawking for food.

"Right here is fine," Amma whispered in the soft rasp which was all that was left of her voice.

Rukh brought her wheeled chair to a halt and took a seat on the bench.

"I've always loved watching the birds soar," Amma said with a fond smile. "So few worries in their bright lives."

"I was just thinking the same thing," Rukh said with an answering smile.

"*The Book of All Souls* claims that when we are joined with Devesh, we soar higher than the stars." Amma's voice was wistful.

"I didn't know you'd read that book."

"I've read lots of books," Amma replied with a chuckle. "But that particular book is one that your nanna insisted I study when we first married. Over the years, it has brought me a surprising amount of comfort."

Rukh smiled. "Jessira is the same way. She keeps asking me to read it as well."

"I take it you haven't?"

"With everything that's happened, there just hasn't been any time."

"Time washes away all wants," Amma said, her expression faraway.

"Is that a quote?"

"It's from *The Book of All Souls*," Amma said, gracing him with a wry smile. A moment later her smile fell away. "Has there been any word on Hal'El's whereabouts?"

"None," Rukh said with a shake of his head.

"He'll turn up," Amma said. "Vermin always do at the least opportune time." Her blanket slipped from her shoulders, and she pulled it back up, irritably waving off Rukh's offer to help. "I'm an invalid, but I'm not useless. I still have my mind. I can still serve."

Rukh sensed the effort it took for her to get the words out as well as the effort it took for her to infuse those words with a confidence she likely didn't believe. The knowledge had him blinking back tears. It was hard seeing her like this, so broken and weak. He wanted to help her, but he was powerless to do so.

Having nothing else to offer her, he brushed aside a stray lock of her hair and kissed her cheek.

Amma sighed in discontent. "Don't let my frailty fool you," she said in a waspish tone. "I live and I love. My spirit is still strong. Yours should be as well. It has to be, given what's to come, and what you did at the Advent Trial."

Rukh wasn't sure why Amma was bringing up such a conversation now. She needed to rest. That's why he'd brought her out here—not to discuss Hal'El Wrestiva or what Rukh might need to do in the future.

Amma froze him with a glare. "I've been injured, but I meant what I said: I can still serve," she rasped. "Don't pity me. I won't see it from my family. I can still have a purpose, but if you and everyone else insist on taking it away from me, then what reason would I have to live?" she asked. "I need you to talk to me as you did before all this happened." She gestured to her blanket-wrapped body.

Rukh nodded in understanding. Amma had been hurt. She knew it. She'd never again be the woman she had once been. But it didn't mean she was incapable or useless, which Rukh realized is how he had been treating her since her injury. He reddened in shame.

Amma stroked his hair, and he reached for her hand, bending over and kissing it. "I'm sorry," he said.

"No apologies are needed," she whispered, stroking his hair once more. "Now, answer my question. Have you truly considered what your actions from the Advent Trial mean?"

This was a question that Rukh had heard posed many times before and from many different sources, and it still made him uneasy.

"You can't hide from what you did, Rukh," Amma said, likely reading the expression on his face. "What you did was special, and there are gifts you've been given that you have to accept."

"I have accepted them," Rukh said. "But accepting them isn't the same as embracing them, especially when I can't even remember what I did."

"The memory will return," Amma said, sounding certain. "But what of the tasks such gifts imply you are meant to accomplish?"

"I don't know," Rukh said. "I'm a warrior. I always thought duty alone would carry me through my life, but this requires something more."

"And what does it require?"

Rukh wore an appreciative smile as he glanced at Amma. "I know what you're doing."

"And what am I doing?" Amma asked with a twinkle in her eyes.

Rukh grinned. "What you're doing now. You're questioning me, making me come up with the correct answers on my own. It's how you always taught us."

"So you remembered," Amma said with a warm chuckle that was ruined a moment later by a fit of coughing. She waved Rukh off. "I'm fine," she declared. "Now, answer my question. What will carry you through your life?"

Rukh didn't hesitate. "Hope that what I do is in keeping with dharma. And faith that what I do will earn a better life in the next world."

"And what else?" Amma asked.

Rukh's brows creased as he considered Amma's question. What else was there?

His thoughts cleared a moment later, and he smiled. The answer was love. All along love had been the true reason for his actions. Duty and dharma were important, but his truest motivation had always been love. Love for Jessira, for his family, for his city. "Love," Rukh answered.

A pleased expression broke across Amma's face. "In this world, the only true eternals are love and innocence," she quoted.

"And hope and faith will guide you to them," Rukh said, finishing the quote. He smiled. "Jessira loves that saying."

"It is a good saying," Amma said. She closed her eyes and held her face up to the sun as she slept.

———◦●◦———

Jessira sighed impatience as members of the House Council argued over how the House should address the question of the Baels and Tigons. They'd been at it for hours, or at least it felt that way. In reality, it had only been about ten minutes, but for Jessira, the question had an obvious answer: the House should support the Baels and Tigons. Why was it so hard to understand? Especially when there were so many other issues to discuss—issues such as Hal'El Wrestiva's whereabouts or the coming attack by Suwraith and Her Plagues.

Had Rukh's Amma been present, perhaps the decision would already have been made. Unfortunately, she was resting and wasn't expected to make it to today's meeting. Therefore, as it stood, the Council was deadlocked. Janos Terrell and Rukh's Nanna were in favor of adding the House's support to those who believed the Chimeras should be allowed to stay, while Durmer Volk and Teerma Shole, the oldest and newest members of the Council, argued against such a plan.

"We've already stretched out our necks for enough issues others think of as sacrilegious," Durmer said. "Supporting the Chimeras is pointless. It will accomplish nothing but harden hearts against any other advice we might offer."

"I agree," Teerma said. "Enough people are already troubled or even outraged by the changes we've wrought in the past few years. If we support these Baels and Tigons, those feelings will simply change to enmity." She glanced around the room. "And the question has to be asked: what do we truly owe these Chimeras anyway?"

Jessira had heard enough. "We owe them my life. Without them, no OutCaste would have survived Stronghold's destruction." She stared a challenge at Durmer and Teerma. "The same holds true for Rukh, Jaresh, Farn, and every Ashokan who journeyed to Stronghold.

They would all be dead right now if not for the risks taken by Li-Choke and Chak-Soon." Jessira rapped her knuckles on the coffee table. "I think that's plenty owed," she added before settling back into the couch.

Rukh and Bree, also seated on the couch, gave her tight-lipped nods of approval.

"Our House owes these Chimeras a debt. We can't simply wave it away," Janos said in a clear voice.

"Why not?" Durmer grumbled loudly.

The door to the study opened. "Because our House has honor," Rukh's amma rasped into the surprised silence as Jaresh wheeled her inside. "I apologize for my tardiness."

Jessira breathed a sigh of relief. Now maybe this topic could be put to rest . . . with the Council coming to the correct decision, of course.

Rukh's nanna smiled broadly upon seeing his wife. "No need to apologize," he said. "And based on your pronouncement, I take it you are in favor of throwing support to the Chimeras?"

"You would be correct," Satha replied. "We owe them too much, not least of which are the lives of our sons and nephew."

"A point already raised by Jessira," Dar'El said.

"Then why are you still arguing about this?" Satha asked.

"Fear," Rukh said. "No one wants to see the House harmed because we chose to support the Chimeras. I think it's too late for that concern, though. Given how everyone knows of my history with Li-Choke and Chak-Soon, I imagine House Shektan is already linked with the Chimeras in the eyes of most people."

Durmer appeared troubled. "I hadn't considered that," he said.

"Then you think we should support the Chimeras?" Janos pressed the older Kumma.

"I won't go that far, but . . ." Durmer sighed. "Like Rukh said, it may already be too late to salvage the situation. The Baels and Tigons are already within Ashoka's Walls, and as Rukh rightly pointed out, with his connection to Choke and Soon, we will likely be blamed for the matter."

"It looks like I'm the last holdout," Teerma muttered. "I still vote against supporting the Chimeras."

"Your vote doesn't matter," Dar'El said. "The Council offers advice, but the ultimate authority rests with me." He glanced around the room. "We'll support the Chimeras."

Durmer groaned. "I knew you'd say that," he complained.

"The next question is who should stand as our advocate before the Magisterium?" Janos asked.

"I can do it," Bree offered.

"It can't be you," Rukh said to Bree. "You've already spent your credit when you argued on behalf of the OutCastes. The last thing we need is more people angry at you." He winked at his sister. "Though it's easy to understand why they might feel that way."

Bree gave Rukh a playful poke in the ribs as everyone chuckled.

"I think the voice speaking on our behalf should be someone of the highest reputation," Jaresh said. "Someone respected and loved by all." He stared at Rukh the entire time. "Even worshipped by some."

Jessira held back a smile as Rukh groaned.

"A wonderful idea," Durmer said, sounding pleased.

"I thought you were opposed to letting the Chimeras stay," Jaresh said.

"I am," Durmer replied. "But more than that, I can't abide our House losing." He gestured to Rukh. "By sending our holiest member to argue on our behalf, the Magisterium won't have any choice but to rule in our favor." Though he tried to hide it, deep respect for Rukh was obvious in the older man's tone.

Dar'El's lips twitched. "Why, at this moment, do I remember my son playing with mud pies as a child?"

———●———

After the council meeting ended, Nanna asked Bree, her brothers, and Jessira to remain behind. Amma was there as well.

Nanna seemed to study their faces, and Bree got the sense that he was trying to freeze this moment in his memory for all time. A faint smile creased his face, and his eyes appeared touched with longing. "Our family has suffered much turmoil in these past two years," he began. "We've lost many we loved. Sophy Terrell. Mira." He briefly held Jaresh's gaze, who nodded acknowledgement. "And Garnet Bosde, though he still lives, is no longer with us. Bree and Jaresh were attacked, and we almost lost her." He looked at Rukh. "We thought we lost you as well when you were exiled, but somehow you came back to us." He smiled more broadly. "And brought home to us a wonderful daughter." He looked to Jessira.

Bree eyed her nanna in uncertainty. "Why are you telling us this?"

Nanna paced away from his desk and moved to stand behind Amma. He put one hand on Jaresh's shoulder and with the other he gently stroked Amma's hair. "Life is a mystery. Who can tell how many more moments we'll have together as a family? Who knows what the future will bring?" he asked, gazing at the top of Amma's head. "Hal'El Wrestiva has returned to Ashoka. He will want revenge on us. And war is coming—Suwraith is coming."

Amma shifted in her blankets. "Time is not on our side," she said in her soft rasp. "We want you all to know how much we love you. That's all. We don't say these things very often, and perhaps we should."

By the barest of margins, Bree kept her eyes from filling up with tears. Her amma. Her nanna. Her family. She hadn't always appreciated them, but time and hard lessons had taught her wisdom. The people gathered in Nanna's study—she loved them so much.

Jaresh snorted, breaking the mood. "I don't think Rukh and Jessira have that problem."

Nanna chuckled, while Rukh grinned. "It's not a bad thing to love your wife. Or your family," he noted to Jaresh. "And Amma's right. We should say what we feel for one another more often."

This time Bree couldn't stop it. The tears filled her eyes. "Well, I love all of you," she declared.

Jaresh did a double take. "Our formidable sister has a soft heart," he said with a warm smile even as he drew her into an embrace.

"I'll deny it if you tell anyone," Bree vowed with an answering smile and shiny eyes.

"Love should never be denied," Rukh intoned, his voice deep, measured, and powerful.

Bree shot him an uncertain glance. For a moment, Rukh hadn't sounded at all like himself.

———————◆———————

Sign sipped her coffee and pondered the irony of her situation. Here she stood, leaning against the railing of a veranda as she stared out at the glory of the Sickle Sea. The risen sun glowed golden-rose, and the cries of seagulls mingled with the calls of drovers and the songs of early morning buskers. Lifting heavenward were the aromas from Ashoka's myriad restaurants as they competed with and complemented the scent of Sign's fresh-brewed coffee.

It was a lovely way to start the day, one she could have never imagined a year ago, and yet it left her feeling morose.

"What's wrong?" Bree asked, coming up alongside her.

Sign glanced at the taller woman, annoyed as only the tall can be when faced with someone taller. In Stronghold, other than Jessira, there were few women who outstripped Sign in height. In Ashoka, it seemed like every other Kumma did. And their grace and dusky beauty . . . why had Devesh blessed them so abundantly?

Sign mentally shook off the envious thoughts. They were unnecessary. She had her own gifts and her own worth.

"What are you talking about?" Jessira asked, coming to them as well. She held out a cup of coffee for Bree, who gratefully accepted it.

"Nothing," Sign replied. "I was just thinking of what it means to have a home. After Stronghold's destruction, I never thought I could feel that way about a place ever again." She gestured to the broad, beautiful city spread out before them. "This place is so seductive and charming. It's so easy to fall in love with it." She smiled wistfully, sadly.

"And now you fear for its future?" Jessira guessed.

"We all fear for it," Bree said softly. "My parents, my brothers. Everyone."

Sign nodded. "I didn't think that I'd come to like this city and her Purebloods as much as I have." She hesitated. There was one Pureblood—Jaresh—who she liked above all others, but now wasn't the time to bring it up.

"We may yet prevail," Jessira replied.

"Against the Sorrow Bringer?" Sign challenged. "You saw what She did to Stronghold."

"Stronghold didn't have an Oasis. We do," Bree countered.

"I hope it's enough," Sign said.

Jessira smiled. "It's too lovely a day to shed tears over what hasn't yet happened, and by Devesh's grace, may never happen."

Sign looked at her and tilted her head in study. "In the past, you used to ask the First Mother or Father for their favor whenever you prayed. What's changed?"

Jessira's smile retreated. "A personal preference," she said. "I'd just rather ask Devesh directly for His blessings rather than go through an intermediary."

"I've come to feel the same way," Sign said.

"And He blesses us with this glorious summer day," Bree reminded them. "Who knows how many more of them we'll have? We should do our utmost to enjoy it."

"Agreed," Jessira said, lifting her coffee. "To sisters and those like us. May we all live loudly every day of our lives."

Sign and Bree lifted their cups as well.

"To sisters," they all gladly shouted.

CHAPTER SIXTEEN
A TRIAL OF A DIFFERENT SORT

The longing for peace is a desire that never fades.

—The Sorrows of Hume, AF 1789

Shur Rainfall was certain of very few things in his life, but among them was the idea that the OutCastes were a stain upon all Humanity. That Chimeras were unalterably evil was another. And, finally, that only Devesh Himself could bring about the Sorrow Bringer's death.

Rukh Shektan had challenged all those certainties, and now Shur was certain about nothing, but he was comforted by his enduring faith. He still had belief that Devesh had marked him to carry out His word and His deed.

Shur paused as he reconsidered his thoughts. *His word and His deed.* It was a sentiment so like the title to *The Word and the Deed*, the holy text from which he had drawn so much instruction and solace. Shur grimaced a moment later because even there, Rukh Shektan's touch had tainted what he had once believed to be unalterably true.

He paced the brick-walled cellar where the Heavenly Council had first formed. They'd been so innocent then, fierce in their determination to return Ashoka to the path of righteousness. It was odd that here in this dank, dark room, such brilliant truth had been revealed; how in this moldy place, such purity of thought had been birthed.

And this was a place of purity. A fourth certainty.

Shur felt his resolve firm as his doubts fled. He could do what was needed.

"We need to go," one of the Virtuous said, entering the room. It was one of his old lieutenants from when Shur had been in the High Army.

"How many answered the call?"

"Fifty-seven."

"Fifty-seven," Shur repeated in disappointment. He still had trouble believing the Virtuous had been so riven by what Rukh Shektan had supposedly done when he had supposedly battled Suwraith. The Virtuous had once numbered in the hundreds, and even after the disaster against the Shektan women, there still should have been many more than fifty-seven to answer the call to battle.

"After today, I'm certain those who have fallen from the fold will return," his lieutenant said.

"To what shall they return, though?" Shur wondered. "This will be our final battle."

"Fifty-seven against two?" the lieutenant said doubtfully. "Some of our men are warriors."

Shur felt a brief stab of hope. "Kummas?"

"Only a few," the lieutenant replied, dashing away Shur's hopes. "But none of them are too old to fight."

"I suppose we should accept the good news even when it isn't excellent." Shur noted.

"If we fight with everything we have, victory will be ours," the lieutenant averred.

"And everything we have will be needed," Shur replied. "Remember. The ones we seek to kill have Talents sourced in evil."

"It won't save them," the lieutenant said. "And when we kill them, everyone will know that Devesh's touch never graced their souls."

Shur nodded agreement and gathered himself together. He took hold of his faith, gripping it like a line that kept him from drowning. "The Virtuous will ride today," he said, his voice infused with confidence, "and though this will be *our* final ride, the ideals we fight for shall live on."

"We will survive the battle—" the lieutenant began.

"We'll win the battle and the war itself, but the traitors who we once named brethren will betray us. They'll tell the Magisterium who we are. I fear this day will be our last."

"Then we will make sure it is one worth living."

"What do you believe your Magisterium will decide at today's meeting?" Li-Choke asked. He glanced between the three Humans: Rukh, Jessira, and Farn. Their faces, usually so expressive, were now utterly inscrutable, but just then, they shared a knowing glance, and Choke felt his hopes wither. "You think they'll deny us."

"Will we ever not be thought evil?" Chak-Soon asked, his ears drooping in disappointment.

"No one thinks they'll deny you," Rukh said, his face breaking into a look of concern. "We just can't say for certain what will happen."

"This won't be an easy decision for the Magisterium," Farn added, "but as things stand right now, I think we can say that the odds are slightly in our favor."

Jessira squeezed Choke's arm. "We'd rather not see your hopes crushed if we turn out to be wrong," she said.

"Hope is all we have," Choke said softly. "We will never again serve Mother, and we can never go back to the Plague, not after Li-Shard's actions."

Jessira's green eyes suddenly bored into him. "What actions?" she asked.

"It wasn't just him," Choke explained. "It was many others, but ultimately, the plan belonged to Li-Shard."

Chak-Soon's ears perked up, and he shuffled closer, his expression intent and curious.

The Tigon's interest wasn't surprising. In teaching the cat-like Chimeras of fraternity, Choke had also discovered that they loved stories. Who would have guessed such a thing?

"From Mother's reaction, he and the others must have been successful."

Rukh sighed with impatience. "Choke, what did Shard do?"

Choke smiled. "He did what we should have long ago done," he said, drawing himself up. "The SarpanKum redeemed all of us with his masterful plan."

Farn turned to the other two Humans. "Is he always like this?"

Chak-Soon growled in warning. "Let him tell story!"

"Oh, hush," Jessira said to Soon. "We *want* him to tell the story, but he keeps pausing and stalling like he always does."

"Like all Baels do," Rukh added. "Will this help us with the Magisterium? If so, tell us what Li-Shard did. And do it quickly. If it won't help, then just tell us later."

Choke hated when the Humans made him rush his stories. It ruined the flavor of what he was saying. Upon seeing their impatient expressions, he sighed in disappointment. "Fine," he agreed. As quickly as he could, he outlined the plan Li-Shard had urged upon the other SarpanKums. He described the incandescent rage Mother had experienced a few days ago. "I've never felt something like that from Her ever before."

"Even compared to when She destroyed Li-Dirge and his command?" Rukh asked.

Choke nodded. "Even more than then," he said. "Shard's plan must have worked. The attack on the breeders has to be the reason for Mother's fury. Nothing else makes sense."

Farn was frowning. "You're certain of this?" he asked. "Think carefully."

"If we can't prove what actually happened or what caused the Queen's anger, then what difference does it make?" Jessira asked. "It's the plan itself that's important, and what the plan means."

"I agree," Rukh said. "We tell the Magisterium about what Shard and the other SarpanKums tried to do and their likelihood of success given Suwraith's reaction."

"How is this any different than lying?" Choke brought up hesitantly. "Won't the Magisterium be furious with us if we're proven wrong?"

Farn shrugged. "They might be, but I think Rukh and Jessira are right," he said. "We tell them about Li-Shard, and if you're wrong, at least you'll be in Ashoka to beg for forgiveness, rather than camped outside begging to come inside."

"Is there anything else you can tell us about what happened to Li-Shard and the other Baels?" Rukh asked.

"Mother order all Baels killed," Chak-Soon brought up. "Every

Bael but those near Ashoka. She spoke in our dreams like sometimes does."

"He's right," Choke said. "That's why I'm sure Li-Shard's plan must have come to fruition."

"Which means you and your brothers here might be the last Baels left on Arisa," Farn noted.

"But the Bovars in Ashoka and the hundreds wandering outside the city walls—as clear a sign as any that the Fan Lor Kum is coming—can be the means by which my kind do not go extinct. And if the Baels sent to these other cities on Continent Catalyst were also granted sanctuary, then our odds for survival increase even further."

"What about the Tigons and the other Chimeras?" Jessira asked.

"Mother created the original breeders," Choke said. "She can recreate them. But it will take Her many decades to replace what Shard and his fellow SarpanKums destroyed." He grinned, the only joy he could receive from Shard's desperate gambit. "The final part of Shard's plan was to have each Plague positioned around a Human city and attack it. Without Mother's help and the leadership of the Baels, the Plagues will be destroyed."

Farn settled back on his heels. "Well," he began, looking pensive and pleased. "This certainly might change things."

"Suwraith was careless when She birthed Her breeders," Rukh said. "Spawning male mules was a clumsy error. She should have known better."

Choke's ears perked. His Human friend's voice had sounded distant, deep, and powerful. So unlike his usual voice.

"Not the Magisterium, too," Rukh said in exasperation. The self-important air of the Cherid Magistrate, Fol Nacket, was nowhere in evidence. Instead, he stared at Rukh with the head-tilted expression of a dog watching a cat swim. Jone Drent of Caste Duriah, and Poque Belt, the Sentya, studied him with narrow-eyed, unblinking gazes. They appeared worried while Gren Vos, the elderly Shiyen Magistrate—bless her—merely glared at him. Rukh preferred her annoyance to the unalloyed awe shown by Krain Linshok of Caste Kumma, Brit Hule of Caste Rahail, and Dos Martel of Caste Muran.

"What about the Magisterium?" Farn asked.

"Nothing," Rukh said. He hoped that over time, with familiarity to breed some contempt, some of the awe-full attitude—really it was just awful; he smiled at the terrible pun—aimed at him would eventually dissipate.

Jessira flashed him a knowing, sympathetic smile.

"Rukh Shektan," Fol Nacket began, sounding stern. "Why doesn't it surprise me that you come before this body once again, and once again, you mean to upend our way of life."

"My wife would tell you it's part of my charm," Rukh answered. Several years ago, he would have never dared reply to a Magistrate in such a flippant fashion. Time and events had changed him.

"Well, I don't find you charming," Gren Vos groused. "I find you annoying." Krain Linshok and Dos Martel shot the small Shiyen a look of offended disbelief, and Gren noticed. She turned to the other two Magistrates with a waspish expression. "Don't you two eye me like I just spat in your soup," she barked. "You may be in awe of the boy, but that's what he still is to me: a boy." She settled in her seat. "One who should be taken to the woodshed for all the problems he keeps dropping in our laps," she muttered.

Rukh had to suppress a grin at the small Magistrate's fearless display.

Poque Belt cleared his throat. "What would you have us do with the Chimeras in Ashoka?" he asked.

"You're out of order," Fol Nacket said, "but the question remains. What would you have us do with the Chimeras?"

Farn stepped forward. "Perhaps you will allow me to—"

"You will speak when we decide to allow it," Fol Nacket said in an unexpectedly blunt tone. "We know who you are, Farn Arnicep. We also know Jessira Shektan. But of the three of you, only one has driven off Suwraith. He is the one whose voice carries the most weight amongst us, and he is the only one with a chance to convince us to allow Chimeras permanent residence in Ashoka."

"Not true," Dos Martel, the Muran Magistrate said. "Jessira Shektan is his wife. By that reason alone, she has importance amongst my Caste and those who believe as I do."

"I accept that of the three of us, Rukh is the most important," Jessira said. "I love him and am proud of him, but I respectfully ask that you don't assume that my only worth is because I am his wife."

"I didn't mean to offend you," Magistrate Martel said. "If I did, then you have my apology."

"There was no offense taken," Jessira answered.

"Good. Now that everyone's apologized and not taken offense, let's move on," Fol Nacket said curtly. "I still would like to hear Rukh's reasoning regarding the Chimeras." His tone was atypical for him. Usually Fol was smooth and weaselly, even unctuous—not blunt and brusque.

Rukh took in the Cherid Magistrate's impatient expression and mentally shrugged. He explained once again the history of the Baels since the time of Hume Telrest, going over how they had come to believe in fraternity and had secretly aided Humanity all these centuries.

"You're wasting our time," Fol snapped. "We know all this."

"There is no need to be rude," Brit Hule, the Rahail Magistrate admonished. "We might know it, but it doesn't hurt to hear it again given the momentous decision with which we are faced."

Rukh nodded 'thanks' to Magistrate Hule before continuing with his explanation. He reviewed how he had learned of the Baels' secrets. Finally, he described the plan Choke said had been developed by Li-Shard and carried out by the SarpanKums of the other Plagues.

"They killed all the Chimera breeders?" Krain Linshok asked, leaning forward with the intent look of a leopard about to leap.

Rukh nodded. "So we believe."

"Does Choke know whether the plan was successful?" Poque Belt asked.

Rukh scowled. He had hoped no one would ask him that particular question, but he had also known it would be foolish not to expect it.

"Choke believes the plan was successful," Jessira answered.

"You haven't been given the floor," Fol interrupted

"You're being ridiculous," Gren snapped. "Let her continue."

"Thank you." Jessira dipped her head to Gren in acknowledgment. "Li-Choke believes that a few days ago, nearly every Bael in Arisa was killed. Chak-Soon confirms his guess," Jessira said. She went on to explain why Choke believed as he did.

"It's only the word of one Bael and one Tigon," said Jone Drent, the Duriah Magistrate. His heavy features were set in a sneer.

"A Bael and Tigon who saved my life," Farn countered.

"And those of every Ashokan sent to Stronghold and the few OutCastes who escaped Stronghold's destruction," Jessira said.

"They saved my life, too," Rukh added.

Fol sighed heavily. He rested his elbows on the table and his forehead on his fisted hands. He stared downward. "What do you want us to do, Rukh?" he asked without looking up.

Rukh eyed the Cherid Magistrate in concern, unclear why the man was behaving so erratically. "You know what I want," he said. "I want us to offer sanctuary to the Baels, Tigons, and their Bovars."

"Then it will be done," Fol Nacket said, still staring down at him.

Rukh shared a look of elation with Jessira and Farn. This had happened far more quickly and easily than he had ever expected.

"We haven't had a chance to discuss the matter," Poque Belt protested. "And we certainly haven't voted yet."

Fol looked up. "We know how the vote will go," he said, glancing the Sentya's way. "Krain, Dos, Brit, and Gren will vote for the measure. You, Jone, and I will abstain. The measure will pass." He shrugged. "Besides, how can we deny him?" He pointed to Rukh. "He is the Hero of the Advent Trial. The First Father reborn." His voice was full of sarcasm, and his face tightened with anger. "Whatever his wants, we are expected to provide. I only hope this is the last of his demands."

───────●●───────

Jessira motioned to Rukh when she noticed something odd about the crowd in the Plaza of Toll and Toil.

"I know," Rukh whispered to her. "There aren't any women."

Jessira studied the milling people with concern. They were entirely comprised of men who kept glancing about at one another, as if waiting for a signal.

"Get your swords ready," Farn murmured through the side of his mouth.

"We've seen them," Jessira said.

"Who are they?" Farn asked.

"Who knows," Jessira muttered in annoyance. "But I'll tell you this much: I'm tired of being attacked." She held on to her anger, using it to settle the sick sensation in her stomach. She didn't want to do this again. She didn't want to ever again kill another Human. As far as she was concerned, there was nothing worse. During the battle with the Virtuous there hadn't been time to think of such matters. It had all been action and reaction, but now, Jessira knew the horror of what was to come.

"Form a Triad on me," Rukh ordered.

"What's our goal?" Farn asked, also looking ill at ease.

"Survival. All of us," Rukh answered. "It'll be any moment now."

Jessira conducted *Jivatma* from her Well. It pooled like honey in her mind: thick, heavy, and potent with potential. It lifted Jessira, making her believe in the possibility of immortality.

Someone in the crowd shouted a call to battle. "*Take them!*"

Jessira drew her sword. Rukh shifted to her left and Farn to her right. She felt a whispering caress against her mind and stretched her inner senses. She found Rukh and Farn. They Annexed, and Jessira's thoughts slowed, becoming distant and blanketed with a textured fog.

The Triad was born.

———————— ◆ ————————

The Triad Shielded. A searing set of Fireballs were hurled its way. Tertiary bent low and evaded. Secondary allowed a Fireball to strike his Shield.

Primary leapt. A Fireball passed below him. It streaked between Secondary and Tertiary and burned a cluster of the enemy.

Still mid-leap, Primary hurled his own Fireballs. Five of the enemy were down.

The Triad took note of four Kummas coming its way. These others moved smoothly and were well coordinated. They were a Quad. Primary drew back.

Tertiary hurled Fireballs as she incinerated those who threatened to close on them. Secondary glowed brightly. A Fire Shower would thin the ranks of the enemy. Primary moved to cover Secondary until he was ready.

The Triad paused just then.

Another group of men had entered the square. Thirty of them. All armed. They lit into the rear of the enemy. An unexpected ally.

The bulk of the enemy turned to confront these new attackers.

The Fire Shower wasn't necessary.

The Quad raced forward, and Fireballs heralded its approach.

The Triad dodged the blows. Once again, the Fireballs ended up impacting other members of the enemies. The Triad noted their screams. The hosts were horrified by the deaths.

The Quad arrived.

The Triad shifted to meet the enemy.

Tertiary's enemy was a much older Kumma who had the age spots, arthritic hands, and deep wrinkles of a wizened grandfather. However, despite his advanced age, he was still stronger and more skilled than Tertiary. She was immediately hard-pressed. Thankfully, Tertiary was faster. She defended, beating aside several blows. One hard slash left her fingers numb, but her riposte rocked the enemy's Shield. Another set of blows came her way, but she parried them. She slid aside a disemboweling thrust and rolled with the motion before bending to the ground and cupping a hidden handful of dirt. The enemy came forward. Tertiary let him. She stepped into his guard, slipping through his Shield. Too late, he saw his danger. She threw the pebbles in his face, blinding him. He leapt up and back. She kept after him. He partially blocked her powerful blows, but several got through. His Shield shuddered and disintegrated. A slash sliced open his thigh. He crumpled to the ground. Her next thrust took him in the throat.

Secondary faced off against his opponent. They were evenly matched, with neither able to gain the advantage over the other. Thrust and parry. Riposte and block. A hard blow, a punch, got past Secondary's Shield and hit him in the face. Secondary stumbled back on rubbery legs, but still he defended. A kick and punch were turned aside.

Meanwhile, Primary faced off against two members of the Quad. He parried a thrust and slapped down an enemy's blade. A sidekick punched past an opponent's Shield and hurled him ten feet away. Primary stepped into the guard and Shield of the remaining enemy. His elbow leveled a hard crack to the man's head, causing him to stumble away and almost fall. The other opponent returned to the battle before Primary could take advantage of the momentary opening. Another opportunity came, though, and the Triad took it. Primary allowed a blow to scrape against his Shield and ducked a kick to his head. Another parry. Primary's blade spun in his hands. He parried again, and his riposte hammered his opponent's Shield, making it shudder and blink apart.

Both his opponents leapt back to gain distance, and Primary moved to support Secondary. The Kumma facing them twisted to keep them in sight. Secondary feinted, and the enemy responded. Primary took him through the armpit.

The Triad sensed seven new opponents were heading Tertiary's way. They were Blended. The ground shook, hard enough to make Tertiary stumble. Some Murans then and maybe some Rahails as well. The first two Kummas Primary had faced were also back. The Triad shifted its hosts to defend. Primary was sent against the two Kummas while Secondary moved to support Tertiary.

Tertiary had incinerated one Muran with a Fireball. She moved smoothly amidst the remaining six but was taking heavy blows to her Shield. She evaded a thrust to the leg. Parried another aimed at her chest. Her hilt hammered into the forehead of an enemy, dropping him.

Secondary arrived in a blaze of Fireballs. Two Murans screamed their last breaths. Secondary's sword was just as deadly. He hurled into motion. A corpse fell headless. Another took a slash across the chest, nearly cutting him in half. Tertiary disemboweled the final enemy.

Primary faced off against what was now a Duo. Impatience reared within the host. He took the fight to the enemy. He blocked a blow aimed at his head, slithered around a punch, and thrust past an enemy's Shield. He cut his foe deeply across the back of his arm. There was another pass and another parry. Primary checked a kick and spun with the contact. He ducked low, and swords passed overhead. Primary leapt up from his crouch. His sword arrowed through a Shield and took the enemy in the chin. The man dropped.

The final opponent was now just a man. He was a little older than Primary's nanna, and he was scared. The Triad could see it in the man's eyes and sense it from the sudden sweat pouring like a cascade down the man's forehead.

The host didn't want to fight this man, and the Triad stepped back. "Concede, and you will live," the Triad said.

The man licked nervous lips and seemed to steady himself. "No," he pronounced.

The host was disappointed but prepared himself for battle. Secondary and Tertiary, their brief engagement with the Murans over, moved to cover Primary's flanks.

The Kumma they faced licked his lips once again.

Primary moved forward. Hard lethal blows rang out. The Kumma enemy blocked as best he could, but several blows got through. The man's Shield flickered out. Before the Kumma could evade, Primary stepped inside the man's guard. A hard thrust, and it was over.

The Triad gazed around the Plaza of Toll and Toil. Scattered remnants of men still fighting could be seen, but even as it watched, those battles quickly ended. The Plaza had turned into a field of bloody corpses and wounded men, crying or moaning in pain.

The sight made the hosts want to weep.

———————●●———————

Shur looked around the Plaza of Toll and Toil. Men still fought in small clusters. The injured moaned in pain, and blood soaked the ground in pools. The terrible violence that had occurred here was awful enough, but Shur would have reckoned it as a justifiable cost if he'd seen Rukh and Jessira Shektan dead.

It might have even happened just as Shur had intended—it would have occurred just as Shur had intended if not for the untimely intervention of these interlopers. Without their interference, the Virtuous would have won.

A shock of deepest disappointment raced through Shur when he realized that he recognized some of the men who fought in opposition to the Virtuous. He knew them all. They were also members of the Virtuous—or had been—but for some inexplicable reason, they now fought to preserve the life of the ghrinas.

Why?

The answer came to Shur as soon as he asked the question. These once-members of the Virtuous were traitors.

Shur gritted his teeth in fury.

And as if summoned by a treacherous wind, here came the Rahail, the original traitor. The man wore an expression of regret but still managed to look triumphant.

"I promised that I would oppose you if you came against Rukh or Jessira," the Rahail said.

Shur didn't bother responding. He simply attacked the Rahail with an inarticulate cry of fury. He hacked and slashed, taking no care of form or technique. Zealous rage powered his movements.

He never felt the slice across his ribs or the blood soaking his shirt. He never noticed the stab into his biceps or the slash across his shoulder. He never noticed any pain, but he noticed sudden weakness.

The cuts he suffered at the hands of the Rahail made his limbs heavy, made them slow.

Shur Rainfall finally became aware of his imminent death when his hand holding his sword was amputated. Then he became aware of pain, and he screamed.

His scream was blessedly short-lived.

CHAPTER SEVENTEEN
BLURRED MARGINS

Death is both the end and the beginning.
It is the contradiction that orders the world.

—*The Word and the Deed*

S atha awoke from her slumber, confused momentarily as to where she was. It took her longer than she would have liked to recollect her surroundings, but slowly, memory returned.

She had been waiting for Dar'El in the study. She'd been wheeled there a few hours earlier, intending to review some missives and proposals, issues that had piled up since her injury. Beyond needing to be done, the work also helped occupy her mind. It kept her distracted from what she had lost, kept her from lingering on what could never be and also served as a reminder that her life still had a purpose.

Unfortunately, as it so often did, her body had betrayed her. The work had proven fatiguing, and Satha had ended up dozing for most of the time she'd been in the study.

And now, she suspected she had to go to the bathroom. She

couldn't tell for sure. Ever since the attack at the Advent Trial, the sensation that indicated the need to pass water had grown vague and was easily missed. More than once, she'd had an accident when she'd waited too long. It was humiliating. Privately, Satha hated the terrible turn her life had taken, but even more, she hated the whispers about her, the sympathetic glances and the pity.

She had once wondered if it was her pride that made her situation so difficult to accept, but time had taught her that such wasn't the case. Pride had nothing to do with it. Anyone who had experienced what she had would have grieved just as deeply.

Dar'El arrived just then. His expression told her all she needed to know.

"The meeting didn't go well?" Satha guessed.

"Nothing seems to be going well," Dar'El replied with an audible sign of frustration.

"What happened?"

"The Society of Rajan feels that Rukh should turn over *The Book of First Movement*."

"To what end?" Satha asked.

Dar'El gestured to the window. "The Chimeras have come to Ashoka as we've suspected they would. Suwraith has been seen speeding across the skies, and the Society fears Ashoka will fall. They mean to send *The Book* to another city so it will never again be lost as it was when Hammer fell."

"Rukh will never allow himself to be parted with *The Book*. He doesn't see it, but it's become an obsession to him. He thinks himself bound to *The Book*, especially if he truly did share the final thoughts of the First Father."

"I know. But the Society expects me to talk him into doing so anyway."

Satha snorted in derision. "You'd have better luck convincing him to send Jessira away."

"Of course if he was foolish enough to bring up such a suggestion to her, I'm sure she would tell him *exactly* what she thought of such a plan," Dar'El replied.

"Yes she would," Satha agreed with a smile. It was during times like this, when she and her husband discussed their children and their lives, that she once again felt as vital and vibrant as she ever had. "She's like the rest of the women in our family."

Dar'El chuckled at her words.

"Was there anything else?"

"There was some discussion about the so-called Virtuous," Dar'El said.

"What about them? The sooner they're left as food for the crows, the better," Satha said with a curled lip. Those were the men and women who had done this to her, left her hobbled and broken in body. They were the ones who had tried to murder her children. As far as she was concerned, death would be too easy for them.

"They are being questioned first," Dar'El said. "We need to know everything about them, especially since their leader, this Shur Rainfall, died in the attack at the Plaza. Some of the masters and journeymen in the Society are worried that the Virtuous might act as a treasonous column when the battle for Ashoka begins, especially if there are more of them than we know."

"Allow me to question them," Satha said with a snarl. "I'll find out what they know." Being confined to a wheelchair had allowed her to come up with many imaginative ways to exact vengeance on those who had harmed her.

"No need," Dar'El said. "The ones who survived the attack are already telling us everything they can about the Virtuous, and we also have information from those others who defended Rukh, Jessira, and Farn."

Satha frowned. "I still don't understand who these supposed defenders are."

"They were once members of the Virtuous," Dar'El explained. "After the Advent Trial, they became convinced that Rukh and Jessira were touched by Devesh. They are amongst our son's most devoted followers."

Satha shook her head in disbelief. No matter how long she lived, she would never understand how her son could have grown into this man who was touched by the miraculous and holy. Whenever she saw Rukh, she only saw her troublesome little boy.

A sudden pressure from her bladder interrupted her thoughts. She shot a panicked look at her husband.

"Let's get you to the bathroom," Dar'El said.

Devesh bless the man. He had taken in her expression with smooth aplomb and offered her no measure of sorrow, pity, or disgust.

Satha shot him a wordless look of gratitude.

Lienna disregarded Mother's whispered warnings. She paid no heed to the biting exhortations of Mistress Arisa—or at least She tried not to. It wasn't easy. With the betrayal of the Baels, Lienna had lost many of Her children. Even worse, Her Plagues had been left positioned near Human cities, left vulnerable without Lienna to defend them. They would have been utterly destroyed if She hadn't acted swiftly and pulled them back. Even then, many of Her children had still died. It left Lienna with woefully few of Her children to take on Her madness.

Lienna mentally gritted Her teeth at the near disaster. It had been bad enough that Her breeders had been eradicated, but to lose Her Plagues would have also meant the loss of Her sanity. It was a knife's edge Lienna now walked, and on either side lurked Her hungry madness.

"A Knife is what You used to slay Me," Mother said.

Lienna ignored Her, and instead, She wondered again about Father. Where was He? She had heard not a word from Him in weeks, not since She fought the Human outside the gates of Ashoka. As She so often had since that battle, She pondered what had really occurred. Her Father was dead, of this She was certain. But then who had been . . .

She pulled back Her wandering thoughts and chided Herself. She had other matters with which to attend on this auspicious day. Her Chimeras awaited Her command. There stood Her loyal Bael, Li-Boil, the newly installed SarpanKum, piously droning the Prayer of Gratitude along with the rest of Her faithful children.

She allowed the warm love of the words to wash over Her.

> *By Her grace are we born*
> *By Her love are we made*
> *By Her will are we shorn*
> *By Her fire are we unmade*
> *And are reborn once more*

As it always did, the Prayer comforted Her and, in turn, brought comfort to those who spoke it. It was as it should be.

"Are My Children in position?" Lienna asked Her SarpanKum.

Li-Boil rested on his knees in prayerful respect, and he lifted his eyes to look up at Her. His gaze was worshipful and without fear. "Yes, Mother," he answered. "But with the Humans behind their walls, I am not sure how we can overcome them. We will run out of Chimeras before they run out of food."

Lienna nodded to Herself. Her new SarpanKum was not only loyal; he was also astute. *"As to the second, do not worry. I will create more breeders to renew your ranks. As to the first, we will overcome the Humans if you listen closely and attend My instructions."*

Before speaking further, Lienna deliberated on how much to tell Her SarpanKum. What would he do if he knew there were Baels and Tigons in Ashoka? What would he do if he realized that his traitorous brethren had a plan to repopulate their traitorous ranks? Or if he learned that Lienna's plans required that Her pet Human stab the stone with the Withering Knife? If Hal'El didn't do so, the Oasis might never be defeated. Continual worry with stones and rocks might work, but it would take months longer.

The silence stretched on as Lienna considered what next to do.

In the end, She realized She couldn't trust Her SarpanKum. Not yet. Maybe never. Trust lost was not easily won back.

"At last, You show a spark of wisdom," Mistress Arisa sarcastically congratulated Her.

———◆———

Li-Boil listened closely as Mother explained what She wanted. They were to build machines to throw rocks at Ashoka's Wall? Boil glanced at Ashoka's massive fortifications and doubted Mother's plan would work. What could a rock do against Ashoka's stony strength?

Mother paused in Her explanation, and Boil snapped his attention back to her. Lightning coruscated across the sky, and thunder rumbled. Boil swallowed.

"Attend My words," Mother snapped. *"Your one role is to carry out My*

wishes. That is what it means to be the SarpanKum. Am I understood?"

"Yes, Mother," Li-Boil said, bowing low. He remembered to keep the fright from his features. All accounts were clear on this one matter: Mother hated seeing fear in the faces of Her children when they spoke to Her. She also hated being contradicted and expected nothing less than strict obedience. All of these things, Boil knew, but knowing wasn't the same as doing.

Not for the first time did he find himself resenting Li-Shard and the other SarpanKums for putting him in this position. Why couldn't they have done as Baels had since Hammer's Fall: subtly block Mother's will, ruin Her plans through incompetence, and protect Humanity through misdirection? It had worked well for centuries, and such schemes had seen Humanity safe, the Baels alive, and the ideals of fraternity given honorable practice.

Boil scowled to himself.

The works of their forefathers hadn't been enough for Li-Shard, though. The young SarpanKum had desired something more, something to mark his name for all time. The young fool had desired glory, seeking to follow in the footsteps of another fool, Li-Dirge.

And Boil had to be the one to pick up the pieces and keep the Baels alive. He was the one who had saved the Baels from utter ruin.

He smiled as a thought came to him.

Dirge, Shard, and Choke had sought greatness and renown, but if their names were even remembered by future generations of Baels, it certainly wouldn't be with affection. Those three had nearly led their kind to extinction. Instead—ironically—it would be Li-Boil whose name would live on in history. It would be his name that would ring with glory as generations of future Baels would undoubtedly hail him for his wisdom.

As far as Boil was concerned, his acclaim to come was well-deserved.

Mother was still speaking, and Boil quickly returned his attention to what She was saying.

They were to build these things that Mother called 'siege engines'. Boil recognized what they were. Before Hammer, the Baels had created these structures—towers high enough to reach the top of a city's wall, mobile wooden sheds with a large ramming spear, and rock throwers called catapults—to demolish a city's defenses. Knowledge of their construction was no longer taught, and in fact, few—if any—Baels still knew anything of siege engines or their use. However, reports, even entire books of how the Baels had fought when they had been loyal had been archived in the breeding caverns. Mother must have recovered those records. Or perhaps She actually remembered those ancient battles. Maybe Her mind was now clear enough to do so. It certainly hadn't been the case a few seasons ago.

Boil wondered what else Mother might recall, what else She knew, and how aware She truly was because right now, Mother sounded lucid. She sounded cunning. She sounded competent. It was terrifying to consider, and Boil hid a shudder.

"You will need to get close to the city walls," Mother instructed. *"The closer the better. Their Oasis will still block everything you launch at them, but over time, like the slow work of water and wind, you will tear down their mountainous Wall."* A crash of thunder sounded a counterpoint to Mother's sudden irritation. *"The work would go much quicker if the Human would do as I command,"* She muttered.

Boil shivered once at Mother's anger before he managed to master his fear. "Won't the Ashokans simply use their own catapults to destroy our siege engines?" Boil asked, hoping She didn't notice his earlier trepidation.

Mother's lightning and thunder seemed to smile, or at least that was the impression Boil got. *"They can try, but remember, I will be with you,"* She said. *"I will sweep aside anything they use that might hurt My children."*

———————●▬●———————

Rukh wiped the perspiration from his brow and did his best to ignore the rivulets of sweat dripping down his back and chest. He also disregarded the lank hair clinging to his scalp like a wet hat and the sticky shirt and pants pressing on him like a second skin. There was nothing he could do about it. The dog days of Ashoka's summer had come early. The weather had turned hot and humid and the dead air left the world feeling like a warm, wet blanket. Even here atop the Outer Wall it was the same. It was muggy and uncomfortable with no relief to be had, judging by the cloudless sky.

Rukh silently wished for the arrival of autumn's monsoon season even as he pressed a spyglass to an eye. He swore when a bead of stinging sweat dripped into it. As far as he was concerned, the monsoon season—though months away—couldn't arrive quickly enough. Not only would it provide a break from this unholy weather, but the rain would also slow whatever the Chimeras were doing out there on the plain.

Rather than share in the wisdom of all the world's creatures— the ones who were waiting out the day's heat in cool shade—the Chimeras had chosen to spend their hours working as industriously and busily as ants. They chopped, hammered, and sawed a veritable forest of trees into strange structures, and Rukh wondered what they were.

Jessira studied the situation as well and wore an identical expression of puzzlement as she set aside her spyglass. "Do you have any idea what they're doing?" she asked.

Rukh shook his head. "None," he answered.

"Siege engines," Li-Choke grunted.

Rukh looked his way, perplexed. "What are siege engines?"

Choke took the spyglass away from his eye. "Before Hammer, when the Fan Lor Kum attacked a city, we would bring these structures—rams, towers, and catapults—to breach a city's wall. I don't know how it was done—no one does," the Bael said. "We had thought all accounts of how to build such structures—as well as how to attack a city with them—had been lost."

"Apparently someone remembered," Marshal Ruenip Tanhue said. The commander of the expeditionary force against Suwraith's breeders looked relatively unchanged from when Rukh had last seen him. Maybe a little more gray and a few more wrinkles, but otherwise, Marshal Tanhue remained the tall, slim, strong warrior who had commanded the attack on the Chimera caverns two years ago.

Is there any chance we'll get to go swimming soon? Aia complained.

It's too hot up here, and I'm bored, Shon whined.

Rukh glanced at the two Kesarins. Both lounged in the shade of a nearby battlement with tongues lolling out and looking miserable.

We'll be done soon, Rukh replied, feeling pity for the cats. *We can go swimming then.*

You said that an hour ago, Aia grumbled.

Jessira smiled. *Hush,* she admonished.

You hush, Aia huffed. *I'm hot. I'm thirsty. And I'm bored.*

We'll be done soon, Rukh promised once again.

Marshal Tanhue looked his way. "Is there something wrong?" he asked.

Rukh shook his head. "It's just the Kesarins complaining about the heat."

You would complain too if you had fur, Shon muttered.

Marshall Tanhue muttered something under his breath about spoiled, overgrown house cats before turning to Choke. "Do you recognize any of the Baels?" the Marshal asked him. "The one with the red feathers. He should be the SarpanKum, right?"

Choke nodded before looking through his spyglass.

"I thought you said all the Baels had been killed," Jessira said.

Choke shrugged. "I thought so as well, but it seems I was wrong." He hissed a moment later, and his spyglass began darting about, focusing on various Baels.

"What is it?" Tanhue demanded.

"The one with the red feathers, the SarpanKum—he isn't Li-Shard. He isn't even Li-Brind, the SarpanKi. He's Li-Boil, my VorsanKi. He was the second-in-command of my Shatter." Choke frowned in consternation.

"But what does that mean for us?" Rukh asked, trying to make sense of what had Choke so agitated.

"The one wearing the feathers of the SarpanKi is Li-Torq, Boil's crèche-mate," Choke explained.

"How did your VorsanKi become the SarpanKum? Did he kill Shard and take his place?" Jessira asked.

"Would this Boil really be capable of murdering his commanding officer?" Rukh asked, sounding surprised.

Choke didn't answer at first. Instead, his spyglass darted about as he appeared to search out individual Baels. Eventually, he sighed in disappointment and disbelief. He looked crushed. "Yes. He could have killed Li-Shard," he said in answer to Rukh. "Boil barely believed in fraternity. He always sought the easy path for his life's salvation, and too many of the Baels I see down there thought much like him."

"You're sure about this?" Rukh asked.

Choke nodded. "The brothers who were the most faithful to Hume's teachings—none of them are down there," he said with a snarl. Anger replaced his earlier grief. "They're all likely dead because those Baels down there chose the path of evil."

"That's a lot of supposition and guessing," Jessira said.

"It's also likely the truth," Choke replied.

Tanhue stared at the Bael with an enigmatic expression before turning away. He stared out at the field through his spyglass and said nothing.

Rukh knew the Marshal doubted Choke's words.

"He speaks the truth as he knows it," Jessira said into the noiselessness.

The Marshal sighed. "Even if I accept that, it changes nothing."

"It changes everything," Jessira said in disagreement. "If Choke is right about the nature of this Li-Boil, then that is a far different commander we'll be facing compared to a Bael like Li-Shard."

"What do you mean?" the Marshal asked.

"Shard would have led the Chims in a way guaranteed to maximize their losses and minimize ours. If Li-Boil is the kind of Bael Choke describes, he won't. He'll lead the Chimeras with competence."

The Marshal cursed. "Just what we need," he muttered.

"I don't recognize that Bael talking with Boil," Choke said.

———————●———————

Li-Grist gazed upon Ashoka's impressive fortifications and felt hope. Even from a distance, he could see the many catapults and ballistas upon the battlements that were undoubtedly manned by the city's famed warriors. Grist nodded in satisfaction. Even if the two or so Plagues gathered beyond Ashoka's walls were led with competence—which would not be the case—they would not find it easy to penetrate such stout bulwarks. Grist almost grinned. As they had since Hammer's fall, the Baels would maintain morality and justice by subverting Mother's wicked will.

He glanced at the camp of the Eastern Plague. It was a riot of movement, sound, and dust. Balants, Braids, Ur-Fels, and Tigons rushed about in a state of harried hurry. The smell of cut wood overwhelmed all scents, and sawdust clogged the air. Grist's nose itched, and he sneezed.

Just what were the Chimeras constructing? What were they doing with all those strange wooden buildings?

A flash of red caught Grist's attention. It had been the flash of red feathers denoting the SarpanKum. Grist turned to face the Bael he had been expecting to meet, Li-Shard, the brilliant commander who had likely done more to further the ideals of fraternity than any Bael in history. Grist frowned as the SarpanKum came closer. He was older than Grist had expected. Li-Shard was said to be young for his rank, as young as a Levner, but this Bael looked to be as old as a veteran Vorsan. Grist shrugged and disregarded the oddity as Shard arrived.

"It is good to meet the Bael whose plan set Mother's schemes back for decades," Li-Grist offered in greeting.

Shard gave him a cursory examination before breaking into a self-deprecating smile. "I wish I were as brave and honorable as the one of whom you speak," he said. "Sadly, Li-Shard and his SarpanKi, Li-Brind, along with many of our brethren were killed several days past. It was on the day when Shard's plan bore fruit. She knew it had been he who had seen Her breeders destroyed. She came to us in a fury, demanding the death of all our brothers."

401

Grist nodded and his head drooped in sorrow. Shard's end wasn't unexpected, but it still stung to know that such a great Bael had been cut down so young.

"I am Li-Boil," the unfamiliar Bael introduced himself. "And you must be Sarpan Li-Grist, once of the Northern Plague of Continent Catalyst, but now assigned to the Eastern Plague of Continent Ember."

Grist tilted his head in surprise at the other Bael's knowledge of him.

"Your broken horn," Boil explained with a smile. "All of us know the story of your battle with the coral buffalo."

Grist shifted in embarrassment. "It is a story I would rather forget," he said. "The stupid beast thought I meant to steal his cow."

Boil laughed. "Regardless, welcome to the Eastern Plague of Continent Ember." His smile faded. "Your Chimeras are arriving rather later than I expected."

"The hills and forests slowed our progress to a crawl," Grist replied with a grimace.

"We had the same issue," Boil said, "but Mother cleaved a path for us so we could arrive more quickly." The SarpanKum hesitated. "Do you mind if I ask you a question?"

"Please do."

"How did you survive Mother's wrath?" he asked, his expression intense and curious. "We only did so by killing a number of our brothers and pretending we had ferreted out traitors to Mother's cause." Boil shuddered. "She was foolish enough to believe our ruse."

"*You* killed Shard and the others?" Grist asked, confused as to what Boil's admission meant.

Boil wore an unhappy frown. "It was Shard's plan. When we sensed Mother's anger, he told us what he had done and what had to be done. Until then, only he and the SarpanKi knew of the plan to destroy the breeding caverns."

Grist nodded in understanding. "I only knew the vaguest outline of what Li-Deem, my SarpanKum, intended. He planned on destroying the northern breeding caverns while also sending a number of Baels and Bovars to Hanuman and Kush. They were to have begged for sanctuary in the name of this new Human hero, Rukh Shektan."

Boil's eyes narrowed. "Was the plan to send Baels and Bovars to Hanuman and Kush successful?"

Grist shrugged. "I had already arrived on Continent Ember when that portion of the plan was to have been executed." He returned his gaze to Boil, and his hold on his trident involuntarily tightened. "Why did you kill Shard?" he demanded.

"As I said, it was Li-Shard's plan," Boil began. "After what he and the other SarpanKums did, he said that the only way for the Baels to survive Mother's retribution would be to kill all the high-ranking brothers. We were to then tell Her that we had discovered treason amongst the senior commanders and, as a result, had killed them for their betrayal."

A brave, courageous plan from a bold, worthy Bael. Grist lifted his face to the heavens and offered a silent prayer for the fallen SarpanKum.

"Now, what of you?" Boil asked. "How did you survive?"

"Mother came to us, the same day that Shard's plan unfolded," Grist said. "She said that if we didn't level Ashoka, She would eradicate the Baels for all time."

Boil smiled just then, seeming happy. "Then you understand our predicament."

Grist nodded, discomfited by the intense expression worn by the SarpanKum. The older Bael looked . . . hungry. Sweat suddenly broke out on Grist's forehead. It had nothing to do with the humid heat. "We have to help Mother level Ashoka," he began carefully. "But if we do, then we would be authors of the inconceivable. Instead, we should hold tight to what we know is true and pray for Devesh's comfort."

Boil's smile held frozen on his face, and his hungry look faded. "Exactly," he said a moment later.

Grist tried to put the SarpanKum's somewhat odd attitude from his mind and stared toward Ashoka. "Did Shard send Baels and Bovars to the city?" he asked.

"If he did, they likely weren't granted entrance into Ashoka," Boil replied. "Just as the Baels begging for sanctuary in Hanuman were likely cut down, I imagine any of our brothers sent to Ashoka were killed out of hand. The Humans don't believe in fraternity as we do."

Grist hoped the SarpanKum was wrong.

Jessira frowned when she saw the SarpanKum speak to a Bael who had horns festooned with a number of white feathers. It meant he was a Sarpan, the leader of a Dread. Jessira set aside her spyglass and chewed the inside of her cheek. "Do you recognize the Sarpan?" she asked Choke. She pointed him out.

Choke gazed through his spyglass and grunted. "He is likely Li-Grist. Shard told me he had been sent to accompany the Chimeras that Mother sent west from Continent Catalyst."

"Are you sure it's him and not some other Bael who took over like you claim this Li-Boil did?" Marshal Tanhue asked.

"It's him," Choke answered. "His right horn is pitted and the last foot of it is broken off. According to Shard, Grist earned the scar in battle with a coral buffalo." Choke frowned just then.

"What is it?" Rukh asked.

"The postures between Grist and Boil"—Choke gestured to the Baels—"I don't believe they like one another. It's evident in the stiffness of their postures and the angle of their horns."

The marshal rubbed his chin in thought. "If this Sarpan doesn't like Boil, that could be a good thing for us," he noted before turning to Choke. "What do you know about this Grist?"

"He is said to be devout in his piety and a clever commander," Choke replied. "Beyond that . . ." The Bael shrugged.

"If he's devout, then why isn't he dead like the rest of the Baels are supposed to be?" the marshal asked, studying the far-off Bael through his spyglass.

"I couldn't say," Choke said with a huff of frustration.

Rukh turned to Choke. "What was the threat Suwraith used against you when She forced you to go to Hammer?"

"She promised to kill all the Baels and all the Bovars if I disobeyed Her."

Jessira's eyes rounded in speculation. "Then if that *is* Li-Grist the Pious . . ."

"I said he is devout in his piety," Choke complained. "I didn't mean that was his title."

"Of course," Jessira accepted with an amused smile. "At any rate, maybe Grist and his Baels from Continent Catalyst were faced with the exact same threat that you were."

"Then maybe we should show them the Bovars?" Rukh continued, picking up on her thoughts. "Who knows how they'll react if they know their race isn't doomed."

The Marshal smiled in satisfaction. "I like that idea," he said, before calling out orders to a nearby aide.

"The Bovars are penned in a nearby field," Choke said. "It should not take long to bring a few of them up here."

Good. After they're brought up here, can we go swimming in their watering hole while you waste away the afternoon? Aia asked.

Only if you promise to behave, Jessira said.

Shon sighed. *We will,* he replied as he padded over and pressing his forehead against Jessira's chest. *Why don't you ever trust us?*

Jessira chuckled and rubbed her Kesarin's chin.

Aia, on the other hand, rose regally from her lazy, laid-back position with a back-arching stretch. She took a few steps toward Rukh and sat down in front of him with her tail wrapped neatly before her front paws. She blinked.

Rukh rubbed her chin.

Better, Aia murmured, sounding content.

Marshall Tanhue had watched all this with a look of bewilderment before he finally shook his head in disbelief and turned to Li-Choke. "We'll bring up a dozen Bovars, and then we'll send up a signal flare, one that will have every Bael staring up at us."

———————●●———————

Li-Grist walked back to his camp with head bent in disquiet. The Chimeras of the Eastern Plague rushed about raising these weapons of war that Mother had tasked them to build. The use of the structures would take time to master, but it wasn't the challenge ahead that had the Sarpan feeling uneasy.

Instead, it was the off-putting affect of the new SarpanKum, Li-Boil. He had a strangeness to him, an oddness to his demeanor. He smiled too widely when pleased and frowned too deeply when unhappy. Worse, had Grist not known better, he would have guessed that Boil had been happy at the prospect that no Baels had been offered sanctuary in Ashoka.

"What was Shard like?" asked Li-Drill, the SarKi, the second in command of the Dread.

Grist pulled up short. He had been so focused on his thoughts that he hadn't even noticed the approaching Baels of his Dread. With Drill were several of the Vorsans: Li-Jull, Li-Meld, and Li-Cord. They waited expectantly for Grist's response.

"It wasn't Shard," Grist said, going on to explain what had happened to the Baels of the Eastern Plague of Continent Ember.

"And Li-Boil, the new SarpanKum, what do you think of him?" Li-Jull, one of the Vorsans, asked.

Grist worked to keep the frown from his face. The Baels of the Catalyst Dread should form their own opinion of Boil. They shouldn't have it tarnished by his uneasy assessment. Anything less would be unfair to the new SarpanKum. After all, his own opinion of Boil might be tainted by the disappointment of knowing that Shard was dead.

"He is a Bael we will all need to get to know better," Grist answered.

"That's not much of an answer," said Li-Cord, another Vorsan.

"It's the only answer I can give," Grist replied. "You need to form your own opinion of our brother."

The other Baels fell into a thoughtful silence, apparently understanding Grist's unspoken concerns.

The Sarpan mentally sighed. He hadn't intended for his brother commanders to think poorly of the new SarpanKum without first meeting him.

"What about Li-Choke?" asked Li-Meld, the oldest of them.

"Did he survive Mother's wrath?"

Grist shook his head. "Boil believes that the Baels and Tigons—"

Drill barked laughter. "It still defies belief that a Tigon—of all creatures—learned and accepted the beauty of fraternity," he said. "And that both were able to claim the friendship of two Humans."

"It wasn't just one Tigon, either," Cord added. "According to Shard's missives, this Chak-Soon had an entire claw of Tigons who thought as he did."

"It is a miracle," Meld intoned.

"You didn't tell us what happened to Choke," Jull prodded.

"Boil is of the belief that Choke and his Baels and Tigons were denied succor from the city. He believes that the Ashokans killed them," Grist explained.

"But he counted two Humans as friends," Li-Drill said softly in sad disbelief.

A disappointed silence met his words, and to a Bael, they all turned to look at Ashoka's massive fortifications. While they stared at the city, a bright red flare suddenly burned skyward from the Outer Wall, and their conversation stilled as they studied the battlements.

"Who is that tall Human on the battlements?" Cord asked after a moment, pointing to a group of figures on the Wall.

Grist saw who Cord indicated. The man was at least two feet taller than those around him.

Drill handed him a spyglass. "You left it at the camp," he said before pulling out his own.

The Vorsans were similarly equipped, and soon, they all had their spyglasses trained toward the small group on the Outer Wall. Their intense focus earned them mystified stares from the Baels of the Eastern Plague. Many of them looked to Ashoka's Wall, seeking out that which had Drill and the others so interested.

"That is no Human," Grist said, excitement causing his tail to lash as he grinned broadly. "That is a Bael!" he shouted in triumph. "A Bael stands upon the ramparts of Ashoka, and he wears the feathers of a Vorsan."

His words acted as a catalyst, and Eastern Baels up and down the line snapped out their own spyglasses and had them aimed at the Outer Wall. The word soon carried. 'Li-Choke' was the name cried out by many. Their voices were lifted in hope.

Grist turned and thumped Drill on the shoulder. "We live in an age of miracles!" he cried in joy. "Our brother stands with Humanity. Hume's glorious vision is coming to pass."

"There's something else," Meld said, still focused on the group. He gasped an instant later.

Grist whipped his gaze back to the Wall, studying the figure of Li-Choke. There *was* something else. Large beasts shambled along the parapet. They were Bovars.

Drill turned to Grist. The SarKi's eyes were wet with tears. "We are saved."

Grist was too choked up to do anything more than nod in agreement.

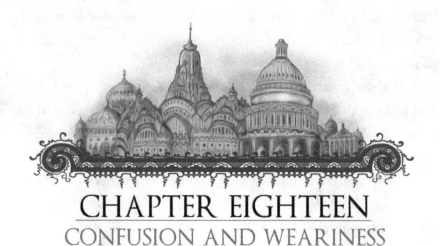

CHAPTER EIGHTEEN
CONFUSION AND WEARINESS

The order of the world becomes simple if external morality and Devesh are decided to be fables. In such a situation, our lives would be rendered immaterial.

—A Wandering Notion by Shone Brick, AF 1784

Li-Dox winced when Mother roared overhead. Back and forth She passed over the columns of Chimeras, crackling lightning and thunder as She soared through the blue heavens. Meanwhile, down in the dirt and dust, the Fan Lor Kum struggled to move Mother's siege engines into position. She expected the Chimeras to run the towers and the turtles—the wheeled, box-like structures with rams—as close to Ashoka's Outer Wall as possible.

It was a difficult task, and Dox sweated along with the rest of his Smash, his one hundred warriors, in accomplishing Her desires. Bovars and Balants had been harnessed to the front of the war engines while Tigons pushed from the rear. It fell to Dox and those like him, lowly Juts—commanders of a Smash—to guide and correct the movement of the heavy, cumbersome siege structures. If close attention wasn't paid, in the blink of an eye, the overladen constructions could easily tip over, something that had already happened to several towers this morning.

Dox glanced up as Mother soared past once again and shook his head in annoyance. If he didn't know better, he would have guessed that Mother was giddy with excitement, as full of vim and vigor as a young Tigon. Dox briefly wondered what Mother had been like as a carefree youngster. She had to have been a young girl at some point in Her long life. After all, Her claim of being the only Child of the First Mother and the First Father was said to be true by none other than Li-Choke.

Dox shivered with excitement at knowing he had actually *seen* the legendary Bael, the one who was the greatest of all of them. Choke, who had defied Mother's will and survived, who had taught Tigons of fraternity, who was the only one of their kind who could claim friendship with a Human.

"Your Balants are pushing too hard on the right," yelled Li-Quill, a fellow Jut, startling Dox back to awareness. "The tower's going to tilt if we don't straighten up their lines."

Dox took one look at his Balants and blanched. Immediately, he began shouting orders, snapping his whip a bare inch above ears to get his point across. More yells were needed to keep the Tigons in order as well. Worrying minutes later, all the Chimeras were eventually back in their proper places, and Dox turned to Quill, nodding his thanks.

"What had you so distracted?" Quill asked once the tower was safely rumbling along again. "You had a faraway expression on your face," he further explained.

"I was thinking about Li-Choke," Dox answered, wanting to hide his face from the embarrassment.

Quill, only a season or two older, grinned in understanding. "I was there when he told us about Rukh Shektan," he said.

Dox blinked. Quill was from the Eastern Plague of Continent Ember, and as a result, he must have actually known Li-Choke, met him, and even spoken to him. Suddenly, all Dox wanted was to corner his fellow Jut and squeeze out every morsel of knowledge Quill knew about the great Bael.

The other Jut chuckled, and Dox's ears wilted in embarrassment.

"No need to be ashamed," Quill said. "As soon as we have our tower in place, I'll tell you all about him."

Dox grinned, but the smile faded as he stared at the massive siege structure. It was almost the height of Ashoka's Wall. "This is an evil thing we'll be doing," he whispered.

Quill turned away, and now it was he who appeared ashamed. "We've already done much evil," he said in a voice hardly above a whisper.

Dox stared at the other Bael in confusion. He wasn't sure what evil it was to which Quill referred. After all, every Bael could be said to have deeply sinned at some point in their lives. Dox mentally shrugged. Perhaps Quill felt the sting of wickedness more acutely than most. "I truly wish Mother's plan will fail," Dox said into the intervening silence.

Quill didn't answer at first, and his expression grew somber. "And sometimes, I truly wish She would allow the Humans to smash us all," he replied.

———◆———

Rukh stood upon the battlements just west of Sunset Gate's barbican. A baking, hot sun and a breezeless, cloudless sky promised no relief from the ongoing unseasonably hot weather. It was another dog day, and Rukh wished for some shade.

The steady drone of thick ropes unwinding like whips, the crack of wooden arms snapping to position, and hurled boulders thudding to the ground was as monotonous as a metronome. The beat was so steady, Rukh could have played his mandolin in time to it if not for the ripped-flesh sound of Suwraith's whirlwind groaning above it all.

Jaresh leaned his back to the merlon. "Their stones bounce off of our Oasis while ours are tossed aside by the Queen," he said. "It's a stalemate."

Just then a cry of Chimeras roaring in pain rose from the plain beyond Ashoka's Oasis.

Rukh tilted his head as he listened to the screams. It was a lovely sound. "I think you mean most of our stones," he said with a smile.

"*Most* of our attacks then," Jaresh agreed. "But my point still holds. The vast majority of the Chimeras are too far away for us to reach, and their siege engines are bunched up enough that the Queen doesn't *have* to be everywhere at once. She can protect most of them without hardly moving. In other words: a stalemate."

Farn responded to Jaresh's statement, but Rukh was only listening with half an ear as he stared out at the plain beyond Ashoka's borders. It teemed with the warriors of the Fan Lor Kum. Not since Hammer's Fall had so many Chimeras been gathered together in one place at one time, tens of thousands of them. It was a daunting sight made worse by the presence of the Sorrow Bringer. She held motionless in the sky, just past the Outer Wall, hanging like a poisonous curtain as erratic lightning lit Her inner reaches. She was suspended so close that Rukh imagined he could almost reach out and touch Her keening winds.

A snort of laughter from Jaresh returned Rukh's attention to the ongoing conversation between his brother and Farn.

"That's what I just said," Jaresh said. "The battle for Ashoka is going to be a long, boring siege."

"Be careful what you wish for," Farn said.

Rukh smiled. "You just might get it," he said, finishing the quote.

"I wasn't wishing for anything," Jaresh protested. "I was just talking about our circumstances." He yawned. "It's so dull; I'm almost tempted to take a nap."

Rukh glanced up and down the Wall. Many of Ashoka's warriors apparently shared Jaresh's sentiments. They stood about, leaning on shields and spears, with the bored expressions of those about to nod off. And truthfully, he felt the same way. There was nothing going on, and there likely wouldn't be, not for a while anyway.

"At least we'll be rotated off the Wall tonight," Jaresh noted hopefully.

Rukh nodded. "Jessira and Sign should be off from Twilight Gate at the same time," he said.

"Laya said she'd bring little Court," Farn said. "It'll be nice seeing the little man."

Not this ridiculous delusion again. Rukh snorted in tired disbelief. "Stop pretending it's just Court you want to see."

Farn's mouth gaped. "What do you mean?" he asked.

"You care for Laya. Just admit it and tell her," Rukh replied. He stared his cousin in the eyes. "She feels the same way, you know."

"And Sign promises to hurt you if you don't speak up soon," Jaresh added helpfully.

Farn continued to gape. "Who else knows?" he asked in a strangled whisper.

Jaresh gave an unsympathetic shrug. "I'm pretty sure everyone does by now."

"Did you really think we hadn't noticed?" Rukh asked at Farn's ongoing discomfiture.

Farn closed his mouth and wore a troubled expression. "She isn't Kumma," he told them. "How will everyone react?"

Rukh rolled his eyes. "You're the stupidest smart person I know." He thumped Farn on the head. "Remember who my wife is."

Farn still appeared uncertain, and he muttered under his breath.

"What's the problem?" Rukh asked, getting annoyed with his cousin. "You like her. She likes you. So tell her."

"What if Laya *doesn't* feel the same way?" Farn asked, sounding worried.

Rukh rolled his eyes once more. "I already told you she does."

"But—"

"Shut up!" a grizzled warrior down the line demanded. "I can't believe you brainless twits are talking about women when we're in the middle of a siege. Maybe you should break out the needlepoint, you stupid gits." He shook his head in disgust and spat over the side of the Wall.

Rukh and the others fell into a chastened quiet after the warrior's outburst.

———◦———

The battle for Ashoka was several weeks old, and from all accounts, it was a deadlock, with no sign that either side would gain the upper hand.

The Queen was not pleased by the state of affairs. Most nights, She hounded Hal'El's dreams, demanding that he thrust the Withering Knife into the heart of the Oasis. Thus far, he had steadfastly ignored Her commands. It would be the end of Ashoka if he did as the Queen ordered. She and Her Chimeras would roll through the city like a terrible tide of swords and death.

Hal'El couldn't allow it, and he refused to be the instrument by which his home was destroyed. The Sorrow Bringer was truly insane if She believed he would allow his people to be slaughtered.

Better to let the battle be decided by whoever had enough stores to outlast the other. Let it become a war of attrition and provisions, of supplies and sustenance, of numbers and accountants. Ashoka's foodstuffs were enough to see the city through a year or more, but what of the Chimeras? Though the Queen appeared fully in control of Her faculties, how much preparation had She really put into this siege? How much time had She allowed for the Baels to ready their warriors for what was shaping up to be a long, drawn-out campaign?

Likely not a lot.

Which meant Ashoka would simply have to wait out the Chimeras until they starved.

A moment later, he grimaced at the thought. If the Chimeras died of hunger, then what information could he offer the Magisterium that would convince them to allow him to live? Precious little.

Hal'El tilted his head as shouts from outside broke through the quiet of his hideaway. He listened intently, trying to make out the words. A moment later, the meaning came clear.

The Chimeras had devised a means to drop their rocks on Ashoka's Outer Wall, and if they had enough rocks, they might actually be able to do some damage to it.

Hal'El smiled in satisfaction. For a time, he'd been worried that his superlative knowledge and skills wouldn't be needed in the defense of his home. For a time, he'd been worried that Ashoka would be safe without his help, but thankfully, that wasn't the case.

The Chimeras would likely find a way to break through the Outer Wall, and if they couldn't, then Hal'El would make sure that they did. He fingered the hilt of the Withering Knife.

The Magistrates needed to learn fear.

If needed, Hal'El could simply use the black blade to scratch the stone upon which Ashoka's Oasis was anchored. He could mar it just enough to weaken the city's protection. A small breach. If he did so, the Magisterium would likely be in a far more accommodating mood toward him and his singular knowledge.

Yes. Perhaps that would be best.

His plan decided, Hal'El returned to the one item that he chewed over like an ugly piece of gristle: how to reach the Shektans. He'd learned that Satha was paralyzed, which was a good start for the punishment that cursed family deserved, but it wasn't nearly enough. Hal'El wouldn't be satisfied until he had Dar'El's head on a pike.

And after that, he would answer Ashoka's cry for a savior. He would rescue his home. Hal'El would ensure that his life's journey didn't end in infamy but in the only manner that truly made sense: as the unconquered hero that saved Ashoka.

But first he needed more abilities than he currently possessed. He needed something only Rukh Shektan possessed.

"You will never *have all that you need,"* Felt Barnel said in his mind. *"You are too great a cretin to even know what you truly require."*

"A jackass dressed as a man," said Aqua Oilhue. *"Thus do we reckon Hal'El Wrestiva."*

"A simpleton, bellowing to his betters about his illusory knowledge. You are an idiot," said Sophy.

Hal'El gritted his teeth in annoyance. The views of the others trapped in his mind were unimportant. He knew what mattered. He knew how he could yet claim his rightful victory. He needed Rukh

Shektan's power. He hadn't forgotten how the young warrior had battled and defeated Suwraith. Hal'El wanted what Rukh had. He needed it. Ashoka needed for him to have it. That kind of Talent melded with what Hal'El knew of the Fan Lor Kum would make him undefeatable, and by extension, the city itself.

Hal'El studied the black blade, the Withering Knife, that had cost him so much but might also provide the salvation he so desperately desired.

———◆———

"The rocks are eventually going to wear down Ashoka's walls," Rukh said. He must have noticed Choke's sudden look of alarm. "Not now, but eventually. Probably many months from now," he further explained.

"How many months?" Choke asked.

"Well into winter, maybe spring," Rukh replied. "But Marshall Tanhue wants to know if you have any ideas on how to slow down the Fan Lor Kum. If nothing else, it would give our people hope."

Li-Choke stroked his chin in thought. "An obvious solution doesn't come to mind," he said, somewhat surprised that the marshall had sought out his advice. He was even more surprised that so early on, Ashoka's warriors thought their Walls might already be at risk. He had been sure it would take many more months, possibly the fall or even winter, to bring down the city's heavy fortifications.

"We have to find a way to hurt the Chims," Rukh said. "Put them on the defensive. We can't just hide here behind the walls while they're pulled down around our ears."

Choke considered the problem anew as he glanced around the prison in which he and the other Chimeras were housed. Though the

Magisterium had allowed them sanctuary, it didn't mean the Baels and Tigons had been given free rein to wander the city. Instead, they were still housed here, in the prison built for them shortly after their arrival to the city.

Right now, most of the Baels and Tigons rested in the shade, doing their best to evade the heat of the afternoon sun. On the catwalk skirting the prison's perimeter, warriors remained vigilant, keeping a close eye on the Baels and Tigons within.

Choke felt no resentment at his ongoing captivity. Why should he? The behavior of the Humans was to be expected. Throughout history, Baels and Tigons had not done nearly enough for Humanity, and yet here were the Ashokans housing and protecting their once mortal enemies. The Humans even fed them regularly. Choke was especially glad for the occasional meat they were offered. Pork, beef, and lamb were a welcome change from the taste of Phed. He . . .

Phed.

An idea came to him.

The Baels, Ur-Fels, and Balants were omnivores. They could feed on grass, but the Tigons and Braids were obligate carnivores. Their primary food source was the Pheds. If the Humans could kill enough Pheds, it wouldn't slow down the Fan Lor Kum, but they would have to hasten their attack or risk starvation for a large number of their warriors.

"What is it?" Rukh asked.

Choke explained what he'd been thinking, but irritatingly, Rukh wouldn't let him reveal his thoughts in the proper manner in which they should be given. Instead, he kept urging Choke to 'hurry up' or 'get to the point'.

Choke found such prompts discourteous, but by now, he'd grown used to the manner in which Humans spoke, and he trudged on with his truncated explanation. When he finished, he gave Rukh a smile. "Kill enough Pheds, and maybe that will give us an opportunity to stop the rest of the Chimeras."

Rukh offered a smile in return and reached up to put his hand on Choke's shoulder.

It was a gesture that left Choke humbled by the camaraderie it indicated.

"I hope so, my friend," Rukh said.

Choke blinked back tears. Even now, it still astonished him when a Human treated him as a brother.

CHAPTER NINETEEN
STRIKE A BLOW

A futile gesture is often the last resort of those with nothing to lose.
Pray never to reach such a sorry state.

—<u>The Warrior and the Servant</u> *(author unknown)*

Jessira shifted the burden on her back and shuffled closer as Rukh went over the plan one final time. Of the nine warriors arrayed around her husband, only Rukh and Jaresh were Purebloods. The rest were OutCastes. These ten were the only warriors in Ashoka who had the Talents of a Kumma and could also Blend. They were about to skulk forth from a postern gate with an aim to wreck ruin upon the Chimeras.

A boulder thudded against the base of the Wall, and everyone flinched. Recently, the Chims had changed the aim of their catapults. Rocks hurled from high in the air were inevitably turned aside by the Oasis. But those launched at a shallow angle and at a slower speed—those could penetrate Ashoka's mystical protection. And while not all the boulders got through, at their current rate of fire, the Chims would eventually do some damage to the Outer Wall. Even worse, according to the Rahails, the continual bombardment and penetration was causing the Oasis itself to weaken somewhat. Not by much, but according to the Rahails, it was certainly a measurable decrease.

Such information had only been intended for the Magistrates, the ruling 'Els, and high-ranking Rahails—such as the Patriarchs—but it had quickly become known to the entire city. Thus, the need for this night's attack. The city needed some hope.

When do we leave? russet-coated Thrum complained.

Hush, Aia ordered. *We'll leave when it's time.*

Thrum subsided with a grumble.

"The Chims have dredged a channel from the Gaunt River that ends in a small pool," Rukh began. "It's where they water their Pheds, the main food source for the Tigons and Braids." He gestured to the packs he and the others wore. "We're going to poison that pool and kill as many Pheds as possible."

"And since the Baels, Ur-Fels, and Balants also drink from that same water, we might get some of them, too," Jessira said.

"Any questions?" Rukh asked.

A murmuring of dissent met his question.

The warriors manning the postern opened a thick ironwood door leading into the tunnel cut into the Wall. The passage was dank and dim with only red-hooded firefly lamps to light the way. Several more ironwood gates lined the throat. They were opened as Rukh's small group approached and shut once they'd passed.

Jessira took a steadying breath before the final gate. All firefly lamps were now put out, and the world was as still and dark as a mountain-hewn cavern.

"Ready?" asked one of the warriors manning the final gate.

Rukh gave a brief nod.

"Good hunting, warriors," the man whispered before easing the door open.

Once outside, Jessira glanced back, but the postern was already closed and hidden by a thick covering of ivy, one that grew in abundance along the entire lower length of the Outer Wall. Sighting the gate was made even more difficult by the lightless night. The moon was hidden behind a bank of clouds, and a drizzly rain had broken the early summer heat. To the south, Jessira could hear the creak and pull of the Chims siege engines as they cranked and released, regular as Clarion Bell, Ashoka's famous clock tower.

Rukh led them into the gloomy night, taking them west. Jessira could sense more than see her fellow warriors arrayed nearby. Their faces were all smeared with soot, and their dark gray camouflage blended perfectly with the night around them. The Kesarins coursed along at their sides on nearly silent paws.

A patrol, Shon said. *Ten lengths to the right.*

Rukh held up a hand, barely seen in the dark, and the small group came to halt, hiding low in the grasses. All the warriors held shallow Blends. They would do little more than mask their scents, but it would have to be enough. Until they understood how the Queen could see through their Blends, they didn't want to risk any that were deeper. Doing so might compromise their positions. For all they knew, the Queen could somehow sense the Blend itself, and the deeper it was, the easier it would be for Her to see it.

Shon was crouched at Jessira's side, steady and ready to leap at a moment's notice. His gaze was focused. It was the poise of a hunter. A rumble came from his chest. Jessira put a hand on his shoulder and quieted him.

They're gone, Aia said.

"Let's go," Rukh hissed.

———— ●◗◖ ————

The mile to the Chimera watering channel was covered in fits and starts as Rukh and the small band with him were forced to skirt around several more Chim patrols. Thankfully, the darkness of the cloudy night with its attendant drizzle kept them well hidden, and the Kesarins' keen senses allowed them to avoid the areas where the Chimeras were congregated. The Blends were hardly needed.

Still, it was nerve-wracking and should have been frightening, but Rukh was too focused to be afraid. His mission might mean the difference between survival and death for his homeland.

"Almost there," Jessira hissed.

Rukh nodded acknowledgement. They had come to a small rise, a landmark to let them know that they neared their destination. The Phed watering hole was supposed to be just a few hundred feet south, and Rukh led them in that direction at a trot. There were no further patrols to impede their progress, and they quickly covered the distance.

The pool was before them, and the warriors lifted leather waterskins off their backs. They emptied their poisonous contents into the small pool, which drank it all in without a burble.

"Don't let any of it touch you," Rukh hissed a reminder.

He shook out the last of the poison, and it was done. Rukh replaced the waterskin on his back. So far, the mission was going well. He offered a brief prayer that it would remain as simple on the return to the postern.

Moments later, a Bovar bolted across their path. Chasing after it was a claw of Tigons. There was no chance to hide. Rukh drew his sword even as the Chimeras shouted in alarm. He prepared to rush forward, but the Kesarins beat him to it. They quickly killed the Tigons, but distant, questioning cries had already been raised.

Rukh cursed their bad luck. "Run," he said without hesitation.

Nodogs and Nosnakes, Shon warned. *Many of them, to our right.*

Nocats, also, Thrum announced. *And Kezins, the horned ones.*

They're already between us and the Wall, Aia said. *More are moving to cut us off. They'll get there first.*

Rukh swore again before turning to the warriors in his unit. "Ashokans"—a few months ago, it would have been utterly incongruous to refer to a band of OutCastes as members of his city—"we've got problems." He quickly passed on the Kesarin's information. "We'll have to run flat out and fight through." He forced a brash confidence into his voice, but inside he was a tight bundle of tension.

The last time he'd sprinted for Ashoka's walls, he'd been leading Trims in the Advent Trial. He had hoped this excursion would be far different. He had hoped none of his brother and sister warriors would die this time. He still hoped that it might happen that way.

"We'll make it," Jessira said to him, making it sound like a promise. She playfully punched him on the shoulder and grinned. "Just don't slow us down."

I'll make sure he keeps up, Aia promised in a voice that sounded like a smile. *Even if I have to carry him.*

Rukh smiled at their teasing, and some of the tension left him. "Let's go," he said. He conducted more *Jivatma* and led the warriors at a fast clip toward the city's walls. Stealth gave way to speed, but they remained somewhat hidden by the soft Blends they all still held. Maybe it would be enough to hide them.

"Shouldn't we tighten our Blends?" Jaresh whispered.

"The Queen might feel it," Sign replied.

"Dead at the hands of a Chim is still dead," Jaresh countered.

"We'll have a better chance surviving the Chimeras then we would the Sorrow Bringer," Sign disagreed.

"Quiet," Rukh snapped. "We're not running a debate club. We're running for the postern. Now shut it."

The band settled down after that, and Rukh did some rough calculations. The Wall was a little more than a mile distant. Just a few minutes away, but only if they avoided any Chimeras. Any delays—even a single nest of Ur-Fels—might see them trapped outside Ashoka's safety. They needed a clear path.

You'll have it, Aia promised. She looked in Rukh's direction. *But my chin will be very itchy when this is all done.* Soundlessly, she and her brothers peeled away from the Ashokans and accelerated forward.

"Where are they going?" Sign asked.

"They're going to clear us a path to the Wall," Jessira answered.

Sounds came: hoots of alarm, snarls of pain, hissing cries of distress, and barks of anger. Over it all was the deep-throated roar of Kesarins in battle. New sounds. This time, the deep-throated bellow of a Bael.

Rukh found himself worrying for Aia and her brothers. There were a lot of Chims out on the plain. The three cats couldn't take them all on. What if they pushed too far ahead for the Ashokans to be able to help them? He was about to call the Kesarins back when Aia spoke.

We aren't stupid, she reminded him. *We won't wander too far.*

Rukh smiled to himself before turning to the others. "We can't go straight for the postern," he told them. "We can't let the Chims know there are any other ways into the city beyond the main gates."

"Then what are we going to do?" Sign asked.

"We'll head for just north of the postern and fire off the signal flares. That'll tell the Rahails and Murans up top to Link to our Blends and toss down scaling ropes," Rukh answered. "And when we

426

reach the Wall, we'll Blend more deeply and climb up to safety."

"What about Suwraith?" an OutCaste warrior questioned.

"If the Sorrow Bringer shows up, we'll have to hope that we're close enough to the Oasis so that even if She does take notice of us, we'll reach the Wall before She can kill us," Rukh explained.

"And the Kesarins?" Jaresh asked.

"Aia, Shon, and Thrum can only enter the city through the postern," Rukh said. "I'll Blend them and bring them in."

"Shon is mine," Jessira said. "I'll stay with him."

"And Thrum's mine," Jaresh announced.

"No you won't," Rukh snapped. Anger bubbled at their obstinance. "All of you *will* go up those ladders. Those are your orders. No more talking."

Jessira looked like she wanted to say more, but a hard shake of his head let her know he didn't want to hear it.

The Kesarins reappeared at their side. *There are a lot of Nobeasts directly ahead of us,"* Aia said.

"Can we cut through them?" Rukh asked.

Aia pondered his question for a moment. *Yes,* she finally said.

But you have to kill them swiftly before others of their kind cut you off from the gate, Thrum added.

We're not going to the gate, Rukh said, quickly explaining the change in plans. *Stay close to us,* he ordered the Kesarins before turning to the others. "When the flares go up, I want you all ready to Annex. Jessira and I will form a Duo. The rest of you form Quads. Your only mission is to get inside."

No arguments came from the others this time, and Rukh breathed out a sigh of relief for small blessings.

Hooting Balants were outlined no more than fifty yards ahead. Beside them crouched growling Tigons, barking Ur-Fels, and hissing Braids.

"Blend as hard as you can," Rukh ordered. He conducted more *Jivatma*, twisting it, thickening his Blend, extending it until it encompassed Aia. Jaresh and Jessira did the same for Thrum and Shon.

The Outer Wall loomed no more than a hundred yards away.

Rukh's heart thudded. "Get the flares ready," he ordered. His jaw was clenched with tension, and he forced himself to relax.

"Ready," Sign said.

"Fire it and Annex!" Rukh ordered. He conducted more *Jivatma*. It tasted like wine and roses, thick as sap, depthless as a mountain's roots. He reached for Jessira. Her answering touch was like a warm caress against his thoughts.

The Balants were close. The Braids closer. Hisses drew his attention to the right.

Hold, he told the Kesarins. They had to remain within the embrace of the Linked Blends. Rukh drew his sword and stretched his inner senses.

His thoughts slowed, flowed away from him like a log on winter-cold water. The wormwood song of his worries faded into the distance. He was gone.

Dimly, he noted a banshee cry from far to the south. It was a hurricane-scream of anger, madness, and retribution. The Queen was coming.

The Annex was enacted.

⊶ ● ⊷

The Duo Shielded. Primary's sword was readied, and he was sent forward. He would be the hammer by which the Duo would punch through the enemy's line. The Kesarin, Aia, flanked Primary, hanging close to his side.

Secondary drifted back. One of her hands glowed, filled with a Fireball waiting to be unleashed. She would protect Primary's back. With her went the Kesarin, Shon.

Hissing sounds came to the Duo. Braids. Hidden in the gloom and tall grass. To the right. The information came from Aia. Even in the quietness of the Annex, the Kesarin had somehow spoken to Primary, and from him the knowledge came to the Duo.

Ur-Fels and Balants were directly ahead. Arrows from the Chimeras thrummed.

Shields were made stronger. The Duo searched the grass. There. A trap of Braids. Primary moved to attack. Parry a thrust. Duck a wild swing, and a sword passed overhead. Primary's return was a slice and disembowelment. A Jivatma-powered elbow smashed a Braid's jaw. Aia took on and killed the other three.

The enemy numbers were considerable. Two claws of Tigons rushed forward. Three nests of Ur-Fels. Two more traps of Braids. Seven Balants. The basso roar of a Bael instructed the Chimeras on where to go.

The Blends had been compromised. Secondary was moved forward. Fireballs scorched into the Chimeras. The Duo noted the casualties. Another volley of Fireballs hurled into a cluster of Balants. This one was from point-blank range. An opening formed as Balants fell back, thrashing in pain.

Primary surged onward, the tip of the spear. Aia kept up, flanking him. Secondary and Shon defended the rear. A hammer blow from a Balant was evaded. Primary leapt upward, a jump that carried him twelve feet into the air. A sword thrust through the Balant's eye finished the Chim.

A Tigon roared, rising directly before Secondary. She swept past a looping swing. A quick slash to the throat, and she moved on. A nest of Ur-Fels charged from the side. Shon instantly cut down three of them. Secondary threw a Fireball and incinerated several more. She took a blow on her Shield, but it didn't slow her down. She snapped a push kick that shattered ribs and flowed into the movement. An arcing slice decapitated another Ur-Fel. A parry and riposte cut deep into the thigh of the final dog-like Chimera. Shon finished him.

A Bael shouted orders. Frenzied Chimeras answered his call. A swarm of them sallied forth. The Duo was suddenly in danger of being overwhelmed.

The Kesarins lashed out in all directions, but still the Chimeras pressed forward. Secondary was taking more and more punishment on her Shield. Primary was hounded on all sides. Arrows from above—the Ashokans on the Outer Wall—thinned the ranks of the attacking Chimeras. The Duo launched Fireballs and gained further breathing space. With it, Primary was set to defend the remaining Ashokans on the ground. They had almost reached the Outer Wall. Aia held ready at his side.

A claw of Tigons, flanked by a trap of Braids on either side, came at Primary. He engaged. Secondary sent Fireballs streaking past him on either side of his head. The Duo drew more Jivatma. Primary leapt over the Tigons. Upon landing, he lopped off the arm of a Braid. He spun and parried a hard smash from a Tigon. A short jab to the throat, and the cat-like Chimera gurgled his last breath. Another parry and a leap carried him straight up. He threw a Fireball while airborne. Two more Braids died. Primary landed again, and with a hard slash, he ripped through the torso of another Tigon. A leap backward, and he evaded frenetic thrusts. A Tigon closed, and Primary took the creature through the eye. The sword hung up on the withdrawal, caught on the skull of the Chim. A Balant suddenly appeared. The sword came loose, but it was too late. The Balant swung his war hammer. Primary had no time to prepare himself. He took the blow on his Shield. It staved in, and the Balant's blow, though cushioned somewhat, still managed to smash Primary in the chest and hurl him yards away. His head hit heavily, and he lay there dazed as he struggled to breathe.

Secondary was there to defend him. So were the Kesarins. More arrows from the Ashokans on the wall threw the Chimeras back.

With the respite, Primary clawed his way to his feet. He swayed a moment before steadying.

The Duo glanced to the Wall. The warriors of Primary's small troop were at the base and some were already scaling upwards. Primary and Secondary raced toward the rest of the unit. The Duo was only yards away from safety with no Chimeras to stop them.

A howl of hate echoed across the plain, and a shower of boulders fell like rain around the Duo. The Queen had come.

Primary exited the Annex.

———— • ————

The Chimeras had scattered upon the Queen's sandstorm approach, but Jessira's eyes were lit with hope. Though Suwraith arrived in a sheet of lightning, arrowing downward like a stooping falcon, She was too late. The Wall was close, only yards away. Thrum already waited there.

Jessira's face fell when she realized Rukh wasn't beside her. He was far behind with a lot of ground to cover. Jessira's mouth went dry. The Sorrow Bringer would block his path. He wasn't going to make it.

"Take the Kesarins inside!" Rukh shouted. "I'll distract Her."

"No! We can both make it." Jessira held back. She wouldn't leave him.

Shon took the choice from her. With his teeth, he grabbed the straps to which her bow and knapsack were tied and lifted her off her feet. He carried her as if she were a kitten, all the while dodging the Queen's boulders, which She hurled like hail.

Put me down! Jessira screamed.

Shon did so, but only when they were an arm's length from the Wall.

Immediately, she turned to see what had become of Rukh.

431

"Vermin! You will not survive My righteous wrath," the Queen vowed. Her voice was jagged like a throat full of splintered glass.

Rukh's ready response for the Sorrow Bringer's promise was a bright beam of quicksilver light that shot forth from his hands. It soared skyward, brightening the plain for yards all around. This close, Jessira saw that the light moved like water, like mirrored glass made liquid.

Suwraith screamed and briefly pulled back. *"It cannot be!"*

Aia, bless her, took the opportunity to pick Rukh up similarly to how Shon had Jessira. She raced for the Wall and reached it well before the Queen could recover.

Aia dropped Rukh to the ground. *I'd really like to get inside and have my chin rubbed now,* she said, sounding anxious.

I never thought I'd hear you say that you want to be inside those walls, Thrum chuckled.

Then stay outside if you wish. Aia snapped with a swish of her tail.

Lighting and thunder tore the sky, and a grating, splintered-glass scream tore the heavens. Suwraith raged. She boiled above, a mindless torrent of lashing wind and lightning. She hammered the ground like an undammed flood.

Rukh shot another beam of light at the Queen. Again, She flinched. "Let's go," he said. "With our Blends, the Chims can't see us, and if we're lucky, the Queen won't think to point out our location."

"And if we're *really* lucky, you'll lose this need to martyr yourself," Jessira said. Her heart was slowing, but her fear for Rukh had yet to subside. He'd been caught in a bad position and had done the only thing that made sense: sacrifice himself so she and the Kesarins could get away. Jessira sent up a silent prayer to Devesh for Aia's intervention. If not for the great cat, Rukh would have died. His bright beams wouldn't have held off the Queen forever, and they would have done nothing against the rocks She had been raining down.

"Trickster! You will not escape My wrath!" Suwraith bellowed.

Rocks peppered the ground before the Oasis: small rocks, large ones, even boulders. Some of them even got through. Stones the size of a hen's egg rattled the ground near Jessira and around her feet. If any of them struck cleanly, it would hurt. Badly.

Jessira quickly conducted *Jivatma* and formed a Shield.

"We have to get inside!" Rukh yelled. "The postern gate should be fifty yards to the south. Blend as hard as you can and run!"

Jessira followed on his footsteps with Aia, Shon, and Thrum trailing behind her. More stones penetrated. A few clipped the Wall. Others bounced off Jessira's Shield. The Kesarins sported several nicks and slunk forward with bellies low and heads stooped down. Rukh managed a crouching run. He looked to be struggling with his breathing.

They quickly came upon the postern, almost bypassing it. With the thick growth of ivy, it was difficult to see. A low whistle caught their attention. The gate stood open, and they darted inside. As soon as they did so, the thick door was slammed shut.

"You're safe now," said the same warrior who had offered them 'good hunting'.

After the words were spoken, the tunnel leading through the Outer Wall fell quiet, except for the hollow sound of rocks bouncing off the ground somewhere close by.

Rukh slid down the wall with a groan and sat on the ground, hunched over in pain.

Jessira tsked in frustration. "You've broken your ribs again," she accused.

"And got a concussion to go with it." Rukh said, managing a lopsided grin. His smile left him. "But you're safe. I'll do anything to see you safe."

Jessira's brows knitted in bafflement. As Rukh had on several other occasions, the words he'd spoken hadn't sounded like his own or even his own voice.

Her thoughts scattered an instant later when a roar came from without, one powerful enough to be heard by all Ashoka. It was the Sorrow Bringer. *"You will pay for your falsehood, false Linder Val Maharj. Next time we meet, I will shred Your soul!"*

CHAPTER TWENTY
OPPORTUNITY AND ENDINGS

When Ajax fell, none knew what had shattered the city.
And none knew what to make of the broken boulders the size
of wagons that were strewn about the streets like pebbles.

—A Concise History of Arisa by Kalthe Mint, AF 1839

Lienna bellowed in fury when She could no longer sense the Humans. A moment before, there had been two of them, a man and a woman, both of them boldly defying Her as they stood before the walls of Ashoka. And in the next, they were gone.

Who were the Humans, and where had they gone?

Lienna lit the sky with a bolt of lightning and the deafening rumble of thunder.

It was the Oasis. Her true sight was blind to anything that existed behind that most cursed of creations. She could see what occurred on the Walls and within the city itself, but of *Jivatma* or Talents used by the denizens of Ashoka , She had no knowledge. It was an unbearable situation.

Lienna growled in frustration. It was the sound of teeth breaking.

Always the Oasis. It interfered with Her plans, stymied Her will, blunted Her justice. If not for the Oasis, Lienna would have long since done away with the blight that was Humanity. This sight-blinding evil was Her Father's most wicked forging, and He would pay for what He had wrought.

Her mind was a haze of red. Something would die this night. Of this, She was certain. It didn't matter that She tasted the scent of Father's *Jivatma* laced through the bolts of Bow that had earlier slammed into Her. She would . . .

Her thoughts trailed off. She had tasted the fragrance of Father's *Jivatma*. It was impossible. Lienna held frozen in the sky. If ever She had doubted that Father might once again walk the hills of Arisa, those bolts of Bow She'd experienced weeks earlier and again tonight, rid Her of all uncertainty. As for the woman . . .

Lienna paused as She considered the implications of what She'd seen tonight.

Father was with a woman. In all his life, there had only been one woman for Him. He had loved no one else. With a sickening realization, Lienna pondered a terrifying notion. Was the woman Mother?

Fear gripped Her heart.

"Shake off Your cowardice before they escape Your grasp," Mistress Arisa grated.

"All that is good in this world will escape Your grasp," Mother commented.

Lienna gave a shiver of relief. Mother wasn't reborn. She couldn't be if She was still trapped here in Lienna's mind. Which meant Father was as well. It had all been a trick then. This Human had sought to make Her believe that Father was alive. He had sought to cause Her fear, to terrify Her.

How dare He!

"Trickster! You will not escape My wrath!" Lienna shouted. In a mindless frenzy, She gathered all the rocks down below Her, every scrap of stone within Her reach, no matter the size. She flung the rocks again and again, tossing them with the force of a whirlwind. And the Oasis redirected every one of Her throws. The boulders broke apart, the stones became pebbles, but still Lienna hurled the rocks. She threw them without direction or aim. Unknowing and uncaring, many She simply cast into the air.

Eventually, Her anger receded enough for rational thought to resume, but one last time, Lienna bellowed. Her fury flattened the grass for yards around. *"You will pay for your falsehood, false Linder Val Maharj. Next time we meet, I will shred Your soul!"* She knew the Human could hear Her, hiding as He was within Ashoka's Oasis.

She turned aside then, prepared to return to the city's southernmost gate where Her Chimeras were slowly whittling down a small portion of the Wall.

But something caught Her attention. There, lying on the ground, were the stones She had thrown a few moments earlier. Many were piled up against the city's wall.

Lienna laughed in triumph as She realized what must have happened. She had breached the Oasis.

The commanders of the Fan Lor Kum met at a distance from the rest of their warriors to discuss what had just transpired. They murmured and muttered as they tried to understood the truth of what they had seen, but few could come to an agreement.

Li-Grist paid little heed to the various conversations taking place around him. His ears still rang with the last of Mother's thunder, but within his mind lingered the memory of the quicksilver light, the liquid beam shot forth from the hands of a Human. It had hurt Mother, or at least it had halted Her progress. Grist wasn't sure exactly what had happened, but of one thing he was certain: this changed everything.

"This changes nothing," Li-Boil announced. "Not yet anyway."

Those from Continent Catalyst shifted about with unhappy murmurs. They weren't pleased with the words of the SarpanKum. However, the Baels of the Eastern Plague appeared to have a different response. They stood with accepting postures, almost as if they had expected Boils' words.

"I know you wish to believe that a Human can truly oppose Mother," Li-Boil began, "that there is a being on this world who can defeat Her —it's the deepest dream of all Baels—but it's too soon to make that determination. We need more information."

While Grist could appreciate the SarpanKum's caution, he remained troubled by Boil's reasoning. In the weeks since he'd first met the Bael, Grist found himself believing ever more strongly that the SarpanKum didn't truly believe in the ideals of fraternity, at least not in the manner he should. Boil spoke the correct words, but from his mouth, they sounded tepid and weak, like the mutterings of the faithless.

"The reports of what actually occurred are still coming in," the SarpanKi, Li-Torq, said. "We have yet to determine exactly how many Humans sallied forth. It might even have been from a hidden gate. One we never suspected might exist." He glanced at the SarpanKum. "Should we search it out?" he asked. "It might ease our entrance into the city."

Grist stiffened in outrage. "We don't *want* an easier entrance into Ashoka," he said from behind gritted teeth as he struggled to hold on to his temper. "We are supposed to do as we always have: the least amount possible to keep Mother appeased. Actively seeking this gate is actively seeking the murder of countless numbers of our Human brothers."

"Torq doesn't intend that we actually use the gate," Boil said. "But what if Mother breaches the Oasis, and the Humans use this gate to try to flee? Would it not make sense for us to know where this hidden gate is located so we can shift our warriors out of the way if the Humans have to use it in order to easily escape their city if it falls?"

Grist's anger slowly ebbed, and he loosened his grip on his trident. He hadn't even realized he'd been clenching it so tightly. Boil's plan made sense, but Grist still had his misgivings. He didn't trust the SarpanKum.

"What do we do about the Human who stood against Mother?" Li-Drill, Grist's SarKi, asked.

"What of him?" Boil asked.

"The accounts may still be coming in on the numbers of Humans who attacked us, but on this matter they are clear: a Human hurt Mother. We should help him."

"I think you exaggerate when you say he hurt Mother—" Boil began.

"He hurt Her," said Li-Cord, one of Grist's Vorsan's. "I was there. I saw."

Boil shrugged. "I don't know what to do," he said. "He may have hurt Her, but then what happened? Mother vanquished him, just as She's vanquished all who oppose Her. I'm not willing to risk the future of our race on the *possibility* that this Human did as you claim. For all we know, he may already be dead."

"He isn't," Li-Drill protested. "If he were dead, then why did

Mother cry out as She did? The words She said at the end—She spoke of this man, this Human. She promised to kill him the next time She met him. She wouldn't have done so unless he still lived."

"The Human may have survived, but you all saw how he scurried to the Outer Wall to escape Mother's wrath," Li-Torq said. "Do you truly wish to bargain the future of the Baels on this man we don't even know?"

"We do know him," said Li-Guile, one of the Vorsans from the Eastern Plague. "Choke told us, and Mother just confirmed it. It's the name of the First Father."

The gathering erupted in tumult.

"Silence!" Li-Boil shouted. "The First Father died two thousand years ago. He is gone. His time is past. He is not suddenly reborn in order to save us. Remember: Mother called him 'false Linder Val Maharj'. He can't be the First Father."

"I heard the terror in Her voice," Drill challenged. "She doesn't believe this man to be Her Father, someone two thousand years dead, but nevertheless, She is fearful of him."

"Only because Mother's mad," Torq said with a dismissive snort. "No matter how sane She may appear, Her insanity still lurks beneath it all."

Boil held up his hands for silence. "All I'm saying is that we should be cautious. We shouldn't pin all our hopes on a hero to come and save us. It's a fool's wish. Instead, we should focus on what we know. There are Baels and Bovars within Ashoka. *They* have to be our first priority. Protecting them. Beyond that, while we will do as little as we can to further Mother's ambitions, never mistake one simple fact: out here we're on our own, as we've always been."

"Devesh walks with us," Grist said. "We shelter in His embrace and love, as we always have. According to our teachings, He is enough to overcome any hardship."

"Of course," Li-Boil said in a soothing, smooth voice. "Devesh is the first and last. His will can achieve anything."

Grist heard the condescension in the SarpanKum's voice.

———◆———

Pebbles mounded against Ashoka's wall like gathered hail. Those were the images cycling through Lienna's mind as She tried to understand how it was that Her storm of stones had penetrated Ashoka's Oasis. As She considered the matter, Her mind bent to the notion of rain and hail. Hail and rain. One a liquid, and the other a solid. Both able to pass unimpeded through Ashoka's Oasis.

How, though? That was the key.

Lienna mentally frowned. Was it something to do with speed alone? She pondered further. Perhaps so. It made sense. After all, the boulders hurled by Her children's siege engines, if launched at a low enough trajectory, were able to roll through the Oasis and batter the wall.

'Batter' was perhaps too fine a word to describe what actually occurred. The Chimeras flung their stones and some struck the wall but rarely did any visible damage. Still, as She'd once told her SarpanKum, Li-Boil, like the slow labor of water and wind, the hurled rocks would tear down Ashoka's Wall. And with Lienna's help, the work would now go quicker—many months rather than many years. But if the Anchoring Stone were damaged, such a time would be measured in days.

Lienna mentally grimaced just then. A few nights back, She'd finally heard from Her treacherous Human, Hal'El Wrestiva. He'd finally agreed to mar Ashoka's Anchoring Stone if Lienna would simply leave him in peace. He didn't want Her reaching into his dreams anymore and tormenting him.

It was an understanding Lienna had grudgingly accepted, been forced to, in fact. Time was slipping away. Her sanity was slipping away. It wouldn't last the years or even months it would take to breach Ashoka's Oasis. Even now, She could sense its dread claws reaching for Her.

But if Hal'El kept his word, then Ashoka's Oasis would fall, and it would likely do so swiftly, suddenly, and unexpectedly.

Lienna sighed, setting aside Her incipient hope. So much relied on the word of a liar. Who knew if Hal'El would actually carry out his promise?

In the meantime, She needed to learn to throw a rock in a manner that would breach Ashoka's Oasis.

Lienna put practice to Her thoughts. She launched boulders and pebbles into the air. Over and over again, She did so, studying the height from which they fell: their movement, their speed. Eventually, She came to understand that it *was* all about speed. If thrown too hard, the rocks rebounded from the protection Her Father had placed around Ashoka. But if the stones were thrown *just* a little lower, a little slower . . .

Had Lienna still a physical form, She would have offered a shark-like grin. How had She not seen it before?

"Because You are a simpleton," Mistress Arisa answered. *"A dullard doesn't begin to describe the depths of Your idiocy."*

"Give over this plan," Mother advised. *"You have murdered far too many as it is. For what You've done, Your soul will never wash away clean."*

"Then You shouldn't care if I dirty it even further," Lienna said in reply.

"Your soul is as bright and pure as the first snow on My highest, holiest mountain," Mistress Arisa declared. *"Though You gall Me with Your lack-*

wit stupidity, Your service cleanses You of all sin."

"*My work is holy,*" Lienna declared to Mother. "*And Your words are empty threats.*"

"So be it," Mother said. "*How could Your Father and I have spawned such evil from the bosom of Our love? You were loved once,*" She continued. "*Now who is there to love You?*"

Lienna smirked. "*I have the love of all who are important: My children, the animals of Arisa, the fish in the sea,*" She declared. "*But what of You? Who is there to love* You? *Where is Father to console Your constant sorrow?*"

"*Where is He indeed,*" was Mother's enigmatic reply.

Lienna felt a stab of concern. She had convinced Herself that the scent She sensed of Father's *Jivatma* had been an illusion, but what if it wasn't?

Before She could ask about it, Mother was speaking again. "*How did We not see how sick was Your mind?*" Mother said, sounding sad. "*Had We known the extent of Your delusions, We would have helped You. So much suffering because of Our ignorance.*"

"*So much suffering amongst the most innocent because of Your lack of compassion,*" Lienna countered. "*Or do the animals not deserve protection from Your Human parasites?*"

"*Is that why You killed Us?*" Mother challenged. "*Is that why You murdered Us and trapped Me here with You? Devesh's singing light summons Me home, and yet I cannot answer His call. What greater evil can there be than that?*"

Lienna was about to reply to Mother's words, but something about them troubled Her. There was a hint in there, something important. A hidden meaning. She pondered them . . .

Understanding came in a flood. Two millennia ago, Lienna had killed Her Mother and Her Father. That was 'Us'. But now Mother asked why She was trapped in Lienna's mind. That was the 'Me'.

Which meant Father was *not* trapped within Lienna's mind any longer. He truly was reborn.

"Where is Father!" Lienna demanded in a shout.

There was no answer.

———— ● ————

"Do you think the SarpanKum is right?" Li-Dox asked. "I don't." In the weeks since the Fan Lor Kum had laid siege to Ashoka, he and Li-Quill had become good friends, and Dox valued the other Bael's judgment. "We both saw the Human battle against Mother, and She *did* cry out in pain. We should find a way to speak to the SarpanKum and let him know. And I also think we should become less competent in our aim at Ashoka's walls. We should be throwing the stones so most of them simply bounce off the Oasis."

Quill didn't reply but instead, he simply stared at Dox with a weighing expression. It was as though the older Bael was deciding whether he should speak or remain silent. The soundlessness stretched, and Dox grew uncomfortable beneath Quill's unblinking gaze.

"Mother did cry out in pain, and we should work less effectively at bringing down Ashoka's walls," Quill finally said in agreement, "but I advise you to be cautious. Do not question the wisdom of the SarpanKum."

Dox stared at Quill in puzzlement. "I don't understand," he began. "The Senzunes teach that we must continually question what we are taught. It is the only way any of us can reach true understanding."

"These aren't the birthing caverns," Quill cautioned, "and the SarpanKum isn't interested in instructing you or hearing your questions. He only wants your loyalty—nothing more, nothing less."

Dox's frown deepened. "But—"

"Don't let anyone else hear your thoughts," Quill hissed. "Only those of whom you are certain."

A tremor of fear worked its way down Dox's spine. It was said amongst the brothers from Continent Catalyst that the Baels of the Eastern Plague of Continent Ember had fallen far from the ideals of fraternity, that they had grown selfish, prideful, and deceitful. It was also said that this overbearing sense of self had in its greatest advocate the SarpanKum himself.

Dox had heard the whispers, the rumors, the innuendo, but he'd always dismissed them. How could the SarpanKum, the one judged to be the finest arbiter of Hume's teachings by his brothers, be himself opposed to the very teachings he was sworn to uphold? It was madness to believe so.

But then there was Quill's warning. Dox trusted the Bael. They were kindred spirits, both young, both Juts, and both the last, living members of their crèches. "Are you someone of whom I can be certain?" Dox asked hesitantly.

Again, Quill was silent, offering that same weighing expression, but after a long period of time, he gave a brief nod.

CHAPTER TWENTY-ONE
BREAKING FIRE

*A clear, dignified mind weathers turmoil more readily
than one that is trapped in panic and stupidity.*

—To Live Well by Fair Shire, AF 1842

Jessira stared in consternation at the giant siege towers lurching
fitfully toward the Outer Wall. There were two of them, and from
atop the structures, at a height that actually overtopped the Outer
Wall, boulders were being launched. Most were turned aside by the
Oasis, but every now and then, a stone would sneak through. Those
would smash onto the Wall walk and splinter into razor-sharp shards
that were flung out in all directions. Most such fragments just caused
deep scrapes and cuts amongst those caught in the blast wave, but
some of the rocks managed to crush a few unlucky warriors beneath
their falling bulk.

Ashoka's response to the attack was, thus far, proving impotent.
Every boulder lofted by the city's catapults at the siege engines was
thrown aside by the Queen, and every fiery bolt meant to set the
rumbling Chimera towers aflame was snuffed out by Her wind.

"Incoming!" someone shouted.

There was a pause in the activity as everyone snapped their attention to the sky. Jessira sighted the large stone as it accelerated through its descent. It impacted many dozens of yards away with a booming crash, but thankfully, no one was injured.

Jessira sighed with relief, and immediately after the debris was cleared away, the crews manning the catapults nearby to where the boulder had struck returned to their work. They continued their frenzied but fruitless assault on the tower while other warriors stood beside them, watching for rocks raining down from the enemy.

Jaresh, Farn, Rukh, and Jessira—after the assault on the Pheds, she'd convinced the commanders to keep her and Rukh together— were amongst the latter. They stood as an island of relative quiet amongst a cacophony of furious sound: the snap of windlassed ropes ripping out to their full length, the Queen's shrieking whirlwind, and rocks cracking like thunder against the obdurate strength of the Outer Wall. Overlaying it was the acrid stench of burning pitch and smoke and a sensation of heart-pounding adrenaline and fear.

"What happens when those things reach the Wall?" Jaresh asked.

Jessira glanced his way. "I imagine a whole bunch of Chims will make our lives very busy," she replied.

"I don't see how we we're supposed to stop those things," Farn complained. "Everything we've tried, the Queen disrupts. The Chims are coming whether we want them to or not."

"That won't be good enough, warrior," Marshall Tanhue said, coming up alongside them. "I don't want to hear talk of defeat before the battle has actually begun. We *have* to find a way to stop those towers. We can't let the Chims gain a foothold on the Wall. Think on it. Or at least hold heart that we'll repel these Chimeras."

Farn flushed at the rebuke. "Yes, sir!" he said.

Meanwhile, Jaresh's brow was furrowed in thought. "Once the forward edge of those towers is within the arc of the Oasis, the Queen won't be able to protect them anymore. And if the catapults can't knock down those towers, we'll have to fight our way into them and figure out a way to destroy them from the inside."

"That's not much of a plan," Jessira noted.

"It'll work," Rukh said, sounding confident. "Like Jaresh said, when the ramp opens, we fight our way in. But we won't just stand there looking for something to do. Instead, I say we toss in as much pitch as possible to the bottom of the tower and set it alight."

Jaresh eyes were suddenly bright with enthusiasm. "The tower will draw the fire up like a chimney."

"It'll burn those fragging things to sticks and ashes," Farn said, looking more confident. "I like it."

Jessira had listened to Jaresh and Rukh's plan, and while it might work, she realized there might be a simpler way to destroy the tower. "What about a stone-splitter?" she asked.

"A what?" the Marshall asked in confusion.

"A stone-splitter. In order to build Stronghold, we—the OutCastes, I mean—had to carve out the heart of a mountain. We learned to carve stone without the need for a chisel and a hammer. A stone-splitter. It's not a common Talent, but if one of them puts his hands on the tower, he could split a large chunk of it—"

"And the other side would simply fall over from the unbalanced weight," Farn finished.

"Is there a stone-splitter amongst the OutCastes?" the Marshall asked.

"Just one." Jessira replied.

"Then send for him," the Marshall ordered.

"Actually, the stone-splitter is a woman," Jessira corrected. She hesitated a moment. "One of the Kummas can reach her more quickly than I," she said. "I can give the messenger her name and description. Perhaps one of them can send word?"

"On a horse, you'll be just as fast," Rukh said.

The Marshall didn't respond at first. Instead, he studied Jessira through judging eyes before nodding shortly thereafter. "So be it," he said, turning aside to one of his aides and snapping out orders.

"You don't want to go and fetch the stone-splitter," Rukh said. "Why?"

"You know why," Jessira replied.

"You think I might do something stupid without you by my side," Rukh said with a faint smile.

"You're *guaranteed* to do something stupid without me by your side," Jessira replied with an answering smile.

Rukh shook his head and laughed.

* * *

The leading edge of the siege towers were little more than an arm's length from the Outer Wall. They were well within the border of the Oasis—beyond the protection of the Queen—and Ashokan weapons fired upon them. Boulders pounded into the structures, fiery bolts set them alight in places, and arrows picked off unwary Chimeras.

Unfortunately, the towers had been stoutly built. They took the impact from the hurled stones without apparent damage and the fires were quickly doused. In addition, now that both siege engines were inside of Ashoka's Oasis, they were able to better utilize their own throwing engines as well. More and more rocks began raining down on the warriors manning the Outer Wall. Some of the stones also fell upon Ashoka's catapults.

All the while, the towers crept closer.

"Where is that stone-splitter?" Farn growled, even as he fired off an arrow before ducking behind a merlon.

"It doesn't matter what's holding her up!" Rukh shouted over the tumult all around them. "We need to form a Quad."

"No!" Jessira disagreed vehemently. "Every time we Annex, you barely survive. You're always the one that the construct sacrifices for the benefit of the others." She gestured to Jaresh and Farn. "They can do what they want, but the two of us are staying out of it!"

"We'll be more effective in a Quad," Rukh protested even as he recognized what she meant. Each time he and Jessira had been Annexed together—at Stronghold, against the Virtuous, and a few days ago, while escaping Suwraith—the construct had always set him at point, the most dangerous position. And he'd almost died in every one of those battles.

"We might be more effective when we're Annexed, but I won't accept one if it means that you're to be sacrificed for everyone else's survival," Jessira said. "We sit it out."

Rukh was prepared to argue further, but a glance at Farn and Jaresh's blank expressions shut his mouth with a click. "You two are already Annexed, aren't you?" he asked.

Both men turned as one to Rukh. *"We are Duo,"* they announced.

Rukh gave a sour grimace to Jessira. "We can still Annex with them."

"We can, but we won't," Jessira said. "And if you're as astute as the rest of the city believes you to be, you won't even *think* of forming a Triad with them."

Rukh was preparing to do exactly that, but a hardening of her expression quickly changed his mind. He knew better than to go against Jessira when her decision was so firmly set.

"Get ready!" Marshall Tanhue shouted, interrupting their conversation. "As soon as their ramp falls, I want whatever's inside filled with arrows and Fireballs."

Of course, it wasn't hard to guess what the inside of the siege tower contained. From the short distance away, calls of nearly every breed of Chimera could be heard: Baels, Tigons, Braids, and Ur-Fels. The only sounds missing were those of the Balants. Rukh reckoned the elephant-sized Chims simply couldn't make the climb up what was likely a narrow set of stairs within the tower.

There came an echoing boom, felt more than heard, from somewhere down below and the tower shivered to a halt. Rukh conducted more deeply from his Well. His heart pounded with adrenaline, and he worked to slow it. *Jivatma* filled his senses. Sights and sounds grew more intense. Possibilities opened up and the world slowed. All along the line, other Kummas looked ready to move in the eye-blurring swiftness that was the hallmark of their Caste.

A few seconds later, with a creaking groan, the tower's ramp thudded heavily onto the Outer Wall. Rukh didn't bother sighting. He fired several Fireballs straight into the maw of the onrushing Chimeras. Jessira did the same.

"Hold the line," the Marshall shouted.

More Fireballs burned the air and were answered by arrows from the Chims in the siege engine. Seconds later, Rukh was forced to draw his sword as a horde of Chimeras boiled past the withering fire of Fireballs and arrows. Jessira stood by his side while Farn and Jaresh moved with the eerie synchronicity of those who were Annexed.

Jessira stepped forward. Her motion caught Rukh off guard. He swore before moving quickly to defend her side. A leopard-spotted Tigon reared before him. A quick thrust finished the cat. A pair of

Braids stepped up to replace the Tigon. Rukh managed to entangle their swords. Before they could disengage, a hard kick to one sent both of them tumbling over the edge of the Wall.

Jessira moved with an economy of motion. She slid past a slice aimed at her chest, and her return thrust took an Ur-Fel through the throat. Rukh reached her side. They stood back-to-back.

Brief impressions came to Rukh as he fought. Fireballs still screamed overhead. The smell of burnt flesh and hair crowded the air. Cries of pain, howls of agony. A bolt from a ballista slammed through a nearby Kumma, punching past the man's Shield and impaling the Tigon he had been fighting. Pockets of Blended Murans and Rahails, hidden and lethal, fought as unseen assassins against the Chimeras.

Jessira stumbled, threatening to go down before a nest of Ur-Fels. A lurch of fear stilled Rukh's heart. An instant later, the fright left him when Jessira regained her balance. Between the two of them, they easily wiped out the nest. A final parry and cut ended the matter, but Rukh's next step forward yielded a hollow sound.

He and Jessira had reached the ramp to the tower. In the front and on both sides, the siege engine was covered with panels of wood layered like shingles, but the back end was open to the sky.

"Push them back!" someone shouted.

"Throw them off their fragging tower!"

A Quad silently swept into position to Rukh's left. It cleaved a claw of Tigons.

A Bael loomed large before Rukh and Jessira. Its whip was alight and its trident held steady and ready. It let loose a basso roar of challenge but moved with an unhappy hesitancy. A feint from Jessira drew the Bael's attention. A slice from Rukh removed the hand holding the trident. Jessira's thrust took the Bael through the armpit.

It fell with a gurgle of pain. "Forgive me," the Bael rasped, staring Rukh in the eyes.

"There is nothing to forgive, brother," Rukh answered with a pang of regret.

It was only a flicker of feeling, though. The battle remained, and he set aside his sadness.

"We need to reach the center of the tower!" Rukh shouted to Jessira.

She nodded understanding.

A wild melee stood between them and their objective. Rukh saw a simpler solution. "Can you make the jump?" he asked Jessira.

Again, she merely nodded.

Rukh caught the attention of Farn and Jaresh's Duo.

"I'm going for the center of the tower. I need you to cover my back."

He didn't wait to see if the Duo would acknowledge his request. He simply took a deep breath and leapt forward. His launch carried him ten feet into the air and twenty feet away. Before landing, he hurled Fireballs, clearing a path in the area where he intended to touch down. Nevertheless, he was soon surrounded on all sides by snarling Tigons, hissing Braids, and barking Ur-Fels. Jessira landed at his back as did the Duo of Jaresh and Farn.

Rukh conducted more deeply from his Well, and *Jivatma* flooded his senses. He needed it all for what he intended. His Shield brightened. "Jump!" he shouted to Jessira and the Duo. A split second later, he released a Fire Shower.

A wave of fiery light swept outward in all directions. Chimeras were tossed aside, slammed into the sturdy frame of the tower or blasted past the wooden shingles on the sides. The lucky ones died instantly. The unlucky ones caught fire, howling in pain as they leapt off the back of the platform and into empty sky in their panic-stricken need to escape the burning.

"Now what?" Jessira asked.

The top of the tower was temporarily cleared, but even now, more Chimeras ascended the ladder leading up to their position. Rukh pointed. "We hold them back," he said.

Four against a horde should have been impossible, but the ladder only allowed two Chimeras to ascend at a time. Rukh moved, slashing, thrusting, kicking, and punching. The Duo stood at his side, moving with mechanical efficiency. Jessira hurled Fireballs, incinerating those still on the ladder.

A Tigon screamed and leapt forward. A parry and thrust, and the creature was done, but the Chim snarled one last time and held tight to Rukh's sword. He struggled to regain control of his blade. The fragging Tigon wouldn't let it go. A kick to the Chim's chest finally allowed Rukh to disengage, but by then the damage had been done. Many more Chimeras had managed to attain the top of the tower. They boiled upward, regaining a foothold on the topmost platform.

Just then, more Ashokans arrived to fill the breach and throw the Chims back. Fireballs burned the air. More Chimeras caught fire or were blasted out the back of the tower.

There then came an ominous creaking. It steadily grew louder.

"We have to get out of here," Jessira shouted to Rukh. "The top of the tower is about to come down. Look at those support beams."

Rukh looked where she pointed. The ceiling rafters had caught fire and many were cracked. They'd break at any moment. "Ashokans! Fall back. The top of the tower is about to come down. Move it!"

He wasn't the senior-most officer present, but nevertheless, his orders were heeded. The Ashokans began a steady retreat out of the tower.

A sharp crack, and several trusses gave way. More followed. The ceiling along the open side of the tower gave way. Heavy beams crashed through the floor. The Ashokans piled out of the tower.

"Run!" someone yelled. "The entire thing is about to fall."

The tower took a series of lurches, first slamming into the Outer Wall and then falling away from it. With a groan, the entire structure slid downward.

A hollow sensation and a feeling of no weight came to Rukh. The tower was falling. He and Jessira were the only two still inside.

They sprinted for the edge. Rukh drew all the *Jivatma* he could hold. They leapt, and in the midst of it, he threw Jessira upward. She sailed over a merlon, while he barely caught hold of the edge of an arrow loop. He slipped, and his heart nearly stopped. Why the frag hadn't anyone pulled him up yet!

He was suddenly gripped hard and hauled over the Wall.

It was Jessira who had pulled him up, and he grinned in relief. The smile faded when he caught sight of her look of irritation. "What did I do this time?" he protested.

"You gave me a push when I didn't need it," she said. "I don't mind your help, but . . ." she shook her head. "You almost didn't make it yourself because of that decision." She sighed a moment later. "Priya, why do you insist on doing such stupid things?"

Rukh didn't know what to say. He would always choose the ones he loved over his own safety.

"I know," Jessira said with faint smile. "But remember what I told you before: '*Guaranteed* to do something stupid.' Looks like I was right."

"Er," Rukh coughed out.

"Er is right," she mocked, putting the lie to her supposed annoyance when she ran her fingers through his hair.

"The stone-splitter managed to break the other tower," the Marshall interrupted. He wore a satisfied smile. "It fell over and must have taken out a thousand or more of the Chims."

Rukh's tension abated, and the tightness in his shoulders and neck eased.

"Now that we know how they're built and how to break them, those towers won't stand a chance," Jaresh said with a cocky grin.

A sharp retort followed by the sound of thunder snapped their attention north. A section of the Outer Wall, at least a hundred feet long, was in the process of crashing to the ground. Rukh stared at the sight in disbelief. He couldn't come to grips with what he was witnessing. The sight was surreal.

A part of the Outer Wall had been broken?

Rukh's mouth went dry with what he saw next. The Sorrow Bringer's whirlwind fury was a shriek of triumph as She slowly pressed forward into Ashoka.

The Marshall was the first to shake off his shock. "Fall back!" he bellowed. "All Kummas, grab hold of a Muran or Rahail or anyone else who can't make the jump. Fall back! Regroup in the fields."

***

The Outer Wall of Ashoka had been blown open. Where once had been unbroken stone, there was now a ragged rent. Mother had been the cause. Her power had ripped a gaping wound, broader at the top than the bottom where it narrowed to a breach that was about fifty feet wide. The breaking of the Outer Wall had occurred with an unexpected swiftness, one that had left Ashoka's defenders unprepared.

When Choke had first seen the Wall tumble down, he had been

left slack-jawed with horror. To see what had seemed an insurmountable obstacle fall so suddenly had been shocking. And to then see Mother loom monstrously large within that entrance had struck him nerveless with fear. Choke had been certain that Mother would erupt through the opening and cast down the entirety of Ashoka.

Instead, She'd merely pushed forward a few yards before pulling back. Choke later learned that the Oasis had been shredded apart only in the portion of the Wall that had fallen. However, it had also quickly been resealed and reformed several yards behind the Outer Wall. As a result, Mother had been unable to fully enter Ashoka's confines. She'd been held at bay, but Her Chimeras had not.

The Oasis had never stymied them. They had raced through the opening in the Outer Wall like a spring flood through a broken dam and pushed deep into Ashoka's farmlands before finally being halted and thrown back. It had required three days of hard fighting.

The result was an uneasy stalemate with the Chimeras on one side of the breach and Humanity holding the other. But the price of such an impasse had been costly: the death or injury of far too many Humans. It was an irreplaceable loss, and one Ashoka couldn't afford. By comparison, while the Fan Lor Kum had lost five times as many of their own, they had the numbers to waste and hardly slow down.

And now, rumor had it that the Rahails might pull the Oasis back even further, all the way to the Inner Wall. Until that happened, though, the Ashokans were determined to harvest as many crops as they could and torch the rest. Even the farm animals would be affected. They were to be sacrificed, killed en masse. It was yet to be determined just how much damage the poisoning of the Fan Lor Kum's water supply had actually done, but if it had somehow killed a large number of the Pheds, then it wouldn't do to have the Fan Lor Kum resupply from Ashoka's own stores.

Chak-Soon lifted his nose to the air. "I smell Bael," he announced.

Choke glanced his way. "You're surrounded by them," he reminded the jaguar-spotted Tigon.

Soon shook his head. "Different. Not us. Other."

Choke straightened in surprise. The Chimeras under his command—both the Tigons and the Baels—currently held a forward position. It was near enough to the break in the Outer Wall to be able to throw a stone and hit it, which wouldn't be hard even now, in the middle of the night.

"Where are they?" Choke asked Soon.

"In opening," the Tigon replied.

Choke frowned consternation. Why hadn't the Humans sensed the approach of the Fan Lor Kum? The Chimeras were not known for subtlety when it came to an approaching battle.

No matter. He quickly called out orders, eventually turning to Li-Silt. "The little ones must be protected at all cost," Choke told the older Bael. "No matter what happens to me or anyone else here, that is the command you must carry out."

Silt gave a solemn nod but said nothing in response.

While the Ashokan farm animals were to be sacrificed, the same would not happen to the Bovars. They were to be transported to empty land within the boundary of the Inner Wall, in Ashoka proper, but the exact location had yet to be agreed upon.

A young Kumma came up to Choke and his small band of Tigons and Baels. "There's a group of your kind in the breach that say they want to talk to you. They came through it yelling for us not to attack them." The Kumma grinned. "Good thing Rukh and Jessira were on the line or we might have killed them before giving them a chance to speak."

Choke felt a stirring hope in his heart. Perhaps those approaching Baels wanted to coordinate a means to end this awful siege. "Please take me to them," he requested.

"Follow me," the Kumma said. When other Baels moved to flank Choke, the Kumma paused. "Just him," he added. "We don't need the Queen wondering why a bunch of Her commanders are having a meeting in the breach."

Li-Choke gestured for his brothers to remain behind before he moved on and followed on the heels of the Kumma. At the edge of the Human encampment, he was passed on to Rukh and Jessira. They were waiting for him, looking relaxed and confident.

"We'll take him the rest of the way," Rukh told the young Kumma, who saluted and turned aside. "Let's go," Rukh said, leading the way to the break in the Outer Wall.

There, hidden in the shadowed depths of the breach were three Baels. They wore feathers of high command.

Rukh and Jessira took positions on either side of Choke. "Come forward slowly," Rukh ordered.

The Baels stepped out of the shadows. "I am Li-Grist," one of them said. "I am the Sarpan of the Dread sent east from Continent Catalyst." He turned to the others and introduced them as well. "Li-Drill, my SarKi, and Li-Jull, a Vorsan."

Li-Choke introduced himself and gestured to Rukh and Jessira, naming them as well.

"The stories *are* true. You do have Human friends," Grist breathed, sounding as if all his deepest prayers had been answered. "Hume's heir is found."

"We need to speak quickly," Jessira said. "The Queen might notice our presence at any moment."

Choke nodded agreement. "What do you wish to discuss?" he asked Grist.

"Our new SarpanKum, Li-Boil—"

Choke hissed. "Exactly what happened to Shard and Brind? I want to know."

"They were killed when Mother discovered that it had been Shard who had planned the destruction of all Her breeding caverns," Grist answered. "Boil says that Shard sacrificed himself so the rest of the Baels of the Eastern Plague would be spared." Grist hesitated. "Those of us here may be the last of our kind."

Choke struggled to understand why Shard would have done as Grist said. "That makes no sense." A moment later, he latched on to something else the Sarpan had said. *The last of our kind.* "What of the Baels sent to Hanuman and Kush?" Choke asked, urgency in his voice.

"We have no way of learning what happened to them," Li-Drill said with a sad shake of his head.

"And we likely will never know," Grist added. "The reason we sought this meeting is because of Li-Boil. He is not very devout in his beliefs."

"No, he is not," Choke agreed.

"He leads the Fan Lor Kum with far too much competence," Grist continued. "It can't go on. Those of us from Catalyst will seek a confrontation with him. We will provoke a civil war if need be." Grist hammered his trident on the ground. "We must do everything we can to end this siege."

Choke nodded. "What can I do to help?"

"I think most of our brothers from the Eastern Plague follow Boil out of fear and uncertainty. It seems to be some infection in their spirits. Even knowing that Baels are present in Ashoka, they obsess over the death of our race. It fills their minds and stills their willingness to serve. Will knowing that you still live, that what is said about you"—Grist gestured to Rukh and Jessira—"that you have Human friends, will that be enough to soothe their terrors?"

Choke mulled over the other Bael's question. "Boil is terrified by what he believes will happen if the Baels continue to go against Mother's will. He is certain that our race will be destroyed. It is what consumes his thoughts and drives his ambitions. Many in the Eastern Plague share that concern to varying degrees, but if they knew that the Bovars we brought with us still live, that they will be kept safe behind the Inner Wall, and even transported to Defiance if need be, perhaps that would ease their worries."

Drill nodded enthusiastically. "When our Eastern brothers learn what you've accomplished, what the Ashokans have offered, they are certain to turn aside from this wicked path they've too long trod."

"There is one other thing," Choke announced with a slow grin. "Something to give our Eastern brothers further hope in these dark times. A miracle."

The other Baels waited expectantly.

"The Bovars in Ashoka are protected, but they've also achieved something wondrous," Choke continued.

"Why does he always stretch out a story?" Rukh muttered to Jessira.

"Must be something in his nature," Jessira said with a shrug. "Or how Dirge trained him."

Choke eyed them askance and rumbled in annoyed embarrassment before turning back to his brother Baels. "The Bovars have birthed three Bael crèches. There are fifteen young ones in Ashoka."

Grist laughed gladly and in triumph. "Our purpose in this world will not end with our passing!"

"Why did you rally an Assembly of the Baels?" Li-Boil asked. "Such meetings are only called to witness the election of a new SarpanKum."

Li-Grist studied the gathered Baels. Those from Continent Catalyst congregated behind him while those from the Eastern Plague stood at Li-Boil's back. Grist shook his head in disgust. It was disgraceful to see the brothers separated in such a fashion. A life truly given over to fraternity could not accept such division. Their ancestors would have been ashamed.

"We also come together when something of grave import that might affect all of us is learned," Grist replied in what he hoped was an even tone. He didn't want any of the nervousness he felt to show through. This was as momentous a meeting as the Baels had ever experienced. And much depended on the reaction and actions of the Eastern Baels. They remained an unknown commodity. Would they behave as Li-Choke hoped they would? Grist wasn't sure, but of his brothers from Continent Catalyst, he *was* confident. They would do what was just. They would hold to morality even at the cost of their own lives.

"And what have you learned that is so important?" Boil asked, not bothering to hide his scorn.

Grist glanced around before answering. He wanted to freeze this moment in his memory. It was not a beautiful setting, but something beautiful could be created tonight. Eastward, the fracture in Ashoka's Wall yawned like a smashed-out tooth and was easily visible in the ivory moonlight. Many fires dotted the plain for miles both north and south, and a warm wind blew, pregnant with the smell of smoke, cooked meat, and the refuse of thousands of Chimeras. As for the

Baels, they stood at a distance from the rest of the Plague, gathering at night when Mother was less likely to see. But even with the moonlight lighting the plain to brightness, She likely wouldn't notice. Ashoka held the entirety of Her attention.

Grist wondered if history would remember what was done here, or would this gathering be forgotten by uncaring future generations of both Baels and Humans?

"I met with Li-Choke and his Human friends, Rukh and Jessira Shektan," Grist began. "Late at night, with Mother none the wiser, deep in the heart of the breach in the Outer Wall. All three of them confirm that the Bovars are safe in Ashoka." He glanced around, heartened to see the hopeful expression in the eyes of his Eastern brothers. "There is more," Grist continued. "Three crèches of Baels have been born from those Bovars."

A murmuring of joyous relief arose from the assembled Baels. Grist noted that the same sense of happiness did not seem to affect Li-Boil or his SarpanKi, Li-Torq. Instead, upon hearing Grist's words, the SarpanKum had grimaced and shifted about on his feet. His tail lashed, and his posture was tense and uneasy. Grist was both saddened and angered by Boil's reaction.

"How do we know Li-Choke speaks the truth?" the SarpanKum asked. "Perhaps the Humans were coercing him."

"It's not possible," Grist answered. "I was there. Everything we were told about Li-Choke and his friendship with Humans is true. I saw them together. Choke wasn't being coerced."

"They even jested at Choke's expense," Li-Drill, Grist's SarKi, said. "It was the type of humor only shared amongst friends."

Still, Li-Boil shook his head. "I am sorry, but you ask us to risk everything based on something only the three of you witnessed. I cannot allow it."

Li-Grist didn't answer. He simply stared at Li-Boil. Anger replaced any lingering regret at what he had to do. Grist saw clearly now. He saw the cowardice at the core of the SarpanKum. How could Boil have fallen so low? It was unfathomable that there might exist a Bael who had never accepted the holy tenets of fraternity, but here before him stood just such an example. It made Grist wonder what had really happened to Li-Shard and Li-Brind. He'd always had his doubts. Boil's explanations regarding the fall of the former SarpanKum had always sounded too self-serving, but Grist had accepted them anyway. No longer.

Grist's anger stoked higher. A rumble, a deep-seated resonance of suppressed fury, rose from his chest. The rest of the gathering remained silent, watching, waiting to see what would happen next. "You are unfit to command us," Grist snarled. "Take up your trident. Your betrayal of all we hold holy ends tonight."

Boil stiffened, pretending outrage, but Grist could see the fear in the smaller Bael's eyes. "You seek to provoke a civil war when Mother's attention might turn to us at any moment?" he accused in disbelief. "Traitor," he spat. "You'll see the death of every one of us."

"I seek no war," Grist replied. "I don't even wish your death, but I cannot allow you to mislead us any longer. Choke already assures us that three crèches were born to the Ashokan Bovars. I believe him, just as I have faith that Kush and Hanuman took in our brethren and more crèches might have been born in those cities as well. Our kind will not die here on the fields of Ashoka. Nor do we need live as slaves to Mother's whims."

"We are not so sanguine," Boil said, anger now filling his eyes as Torq moved to stand in support of him. "My actions have seen us safe. My actions have assured the very existence of our kind." He gestured to the Baels standing behind Grist. "You and a few others may laud Li-Dirge for his piety, but what did that fool's faith truly earn for him and his command?" Boil snorted derision. "Extermination," he said, answering his own question. "And I tell you this: though you may despise me—for what I've accomplished— generations of our brothers will honor me and my brand of fealty." His eyes shone with fervor and pride.

Grist's heart sank. "Is it glory then that impels you?" he asked, appalled by Boil's moral failings.

The SarpanKum grimaced. "You seek to twist my actions into something crass," he answered. "But we saw what Shard and Brind's actions almost led to. I saved us by ending their lives." He stood straight and proud. "And for that alone, yes, I should be held in the highest esteem."

"So Shard and Brind didn't simply step aside for you," Grist noted. "I thought as much. Did you face him, or did you stab him in the back like a coward?"

Torq hissed outrage. "You dare!"

"I dare that and more!" Grist cried out. He didn't want to spill the blood of a brother, even one as craven as Boil, but he would do whatever was needed to see fraternity restored to the Eastern Baels. "Stand down, and I will allow you to leave here with no one to harm you," he promised, giving Boil and his SarpanKi one last chance to live.

"We have not yet fought, and you seek our surrender." Torq sneered. "You and your SarKi will die tonight."

Grist turned to the Eastern Baels, who shuffled about in uncertainty. "You have a reputation of being shallow in your faith, of cowardice," he called out to them. "It is well-known all across Continent Catalyst. Which is why it struck all of us a miracle when one as devout as Shard came to command your Plague. We reckoned

Devesh had touched your hearts and shown you the error of your ways. Were we wrong? Is the raiment of a faithless traitor all you will ever wear?"

Here and there the Eastern Baels began stepping back. They symbolically stamped their tridents, tines down, into the ground. More and more followed until all of them had done so.

Grist nodded approval. They would stay out of the coming fight. Grist sensed when Drill and all his Vorsans move to stand at his back. He smiled. "The two of you are alone. Friendless and without allies," he said. "I am not."

Torq's face had gone slack, while Boil stared about with an assessing gaze.

"What will it be?" Grist asked.

"I will not serve another selfless fool," Boil said. He readied his trident and uncoiled his whip. Torq followed suit.

"So be it," Grist said, as he readied his own weapons. Drill did the same.

"It you survive them, you face us next," said Li-Jull, one of the Vorsans, in dire promise.

"And you will also be put down," Boil vowed.

Grist snapped out his whip and ignited it. Flames dripped. "Come then," he snarled.

Torq took up the challenge. The SarpanKi stepped in front of Boil and twirled his trident.

Grist hid a smile. Perfect.

Torq stabbed out with his trident, and Grist sidestepped it. His return blow also met empty air as Torq twisted out of the way.

But Drill was there. His whip tangled about Torq's neck. Fur burned. A hard jerk by Drill, and Torq was slammed to the ground. The SarpanKi cried out in pain.

Boil rushed forward, slashing at Drill's whip. Even as the SarpanKum's trident slashed downward, Grist was moving. A savage thrust impaled Boil, who slumped to the ground in disbelief.

Grist pulled back his trident. It made a sickening, sticky sound as it withdrew from Boil's gut.

"You'll lead us to oblivion," the SarpanKum rasped. His hands were clasped around his gaping wounds.

"The oblivion of this world leads to Devesh," Grist said. His anger was gone and now only sadness remained. "I wish you had faith in that lesson, brother."

Boil stared up at him. "I hear a song," he said before falling over.

Drill had already finished off Li-Torq.

The Baels on all sides, both the Eastern and those of Continent Catalyst, slammed their tridents, tines down into the ground once more and knelt. They offered obeisance to Li-Grist, the new SarpanKum of the Eastern Plague of Continent Ember.

"I accept the service of leadership," Grist said. "Now. One of you will tell me *exactly* what happened to Li-Shard and Li-Brind."

It was a young Jut named Li-Quill who did so.

CHAPTER TWENTY-TWO
DISPARATE MEASURES

That stillness that bears the grace of peace is either
a blessing or a curse—it can be found in both prayer and in death.

—*Our Lives Alone* by Asias Athandra, AF 331

Three days after the breaching of the Outer Wall, a closed-door, late-night meeting of the Magisterium took place. It was a somber session of fearful voices and hushed discussions. The nature of the gathering made it so, one made even more prominent by the loneliness of a large chamber that was meant to hold hundreds but was currently occupied by only sixteen people. There were the seven Magistrates, Jax'El Tristham—the Liege-Marshall of the High Army—and high-ranking representatives of each of the seven Castes. Dar'El Shektan was amongst the latter group, and unsurprisingly, Rukh had also been asked to attend the meeting.

The two sat next to one another, listening as the leaders of the city discussed the few choices available to them.

"Can we trust the Baels to do as they say they will?" Fol Nacket, the Cherid Magistrate asked.

Jax'El, the Liege-Marshall shook his head. "We would be foolish to believe so."

"I agree," said Krain Linshok, the Kumma Magistrate. "We can't afford to believe that they will suddenly fight with incompetent tactics."

"Then what options do we have?" asked Gren Vos, the elderly Shiyen Magistrate. "We've gone over the status of the Army, but it doesn't seem like the courage of our warriors will be enough to see us through this crisis."

Her question was met by silence.

"Li-Grist, this Sarpan from Continent Catalyst, says that the Fan Lor Kum lost almost a quarter of their Pheds," said Jone Drent, the Duriah Magistrate. "No matter what the Baels do next, that has to count for something."

"They have enough food to remain in the field for a few more months," said Poque Belt, the Sentya Magistrate.

"Not if they ration," muttered Magistrate Linshok.

"Can we expand the Oasis so it covers the Outer Wall once again?" asked Thrivel Nonel, the invited representative of Caste Sentya. Just like Dar'El and several others who had been asked to attend tonight's meeting, he was a member of the Society of Rajan.

"No," said Grain Jola of Caste Rahail and a fellow Rajan. He was a Patriarch, one of the highest-ranking and most knowledgeable members of Caste Rahail."Something happened to the Oasis. Something we don't yet understand. All we know is that it inexplicably weakened all of the sudden. We don't know why or how, but it likely has something to do with the Queen. Her attack maybe."

"And you have no idea how it fell so quickly?" Gren prodded.

It was Brit Hule, the Rahail Magistrate, who answered. " As Patriarch Jola said, it just gave way. We don't know why. And when the Queen penetrated it, we were lucky to firm it up where we did. The Oasis could have contracted much further."

"How much further?" Fol asked.

"To the Inner Wall," Grain replied.

"Why can't the Rahails replenish the Oasis?" the Cherid Magistrate asked. "With all the Synthesis my Caste is making available, you should be able to draw on the untapped *Jivatma* of nearly everyone not directly engaged in the battle and keep the Oasis strong."

"It's still not enough," Brit replied in frustration. "We fill the Oasis with all the *Jivatma* that we have, but it soaks it up like a desert would water."

"Speak plainly," Gren snapped. "What does all this mean?"

"It means we can't hold," Brit stated. "It's this weakness in the Oasis, this flaw. If we had time to figure it out, maybe we could do something about it, but . . ." he shrugged helplessly. "Right now, with any large enough pressure, it's likely that the Oasis will fail once again."

"And with the Oasis' current state of weakness and the Sorrow Bringer's current rate of attack," Jax'El began, "how long do we still have before the Oasis is breached once more?"

"A couple of weeks," Brit said. "No more than four."

Dar'El had a frightening thought. "What if the Queen leveled the Outer Wall and cast it down onto the Oasis?" he asked. "What would be the result?"

"Can She do that?" Magistrate Vos asked in dismay.

"She can," Rukh answered. "When She butchered Stronghold, She punched straight through a mountain."

Grain Jola shuddered. "If She did something like that, the Oasis would snap," he said. "Instantly. It would recoil past the Inner Wall."

"Then rather than expand the Oasis, would it not be more prudent to withdraw it back to the Inner Wall on our own timetable?" Dar'El suggested.

Brit nodded. "And the smaller the area that the Oasis has to protect, the stronger we can make it. Even with this flaw."

"We need another few days to bring in all the crops and sacrifice the rest of the animals," said Dos Martel, the Muran Magistrate. "I don't want to leave anything behind that the Chims can use for food."

"A few days will be an eternity if the Outer Wall is smashed into the Oasis," Dar'El reminded her.

"I agree with Dar'El," Gren Vos said. "We should immediately retreat to the Inner Wall even if it means we have to set fire to the fields we haven't yet harvested. As for the animals, we can run them into the city proper and sacrifice them later." She nodded firmly. "I so motion."

"I second," Poque said.

"All in favor," Fol Nacket asked.

Dar'El was relieved when the vote was unanimous in favor of Gren's motion.

Magistrate Nacket turned to Dos Martel. "Pass the word on to your people. I want everything done by tomorrow night at the latest."

"I still don't understand why the Oasis lets in any of those stones that are thrown at it," Krain Linshok complained.

"The Oasis repels anything fast-moving that comes in contact with it," Grain explained, "but not objects that are moving slowly. Those have no trouble penetrating. It's why rain, hail, and all but the hardest winds have no problem passing through the Oasis. Somehow, the Queen or the Fan Lor Kum deduced this secret."

Fol frowned. "So if the Queen wanted to kill the city with a poisonous fog, like something emitted from a volcano . . ."

"She would have no trouble doing so," Brit Hule said with a nod. "Pray She never comes to such a realization."

"And is there no way to change the nature of the Oasis?" Jone Drent, the Duriah Magistrate demanded. "Make it so that even slow-moving objects are kept out? Perhaps that can provide us the time to find this flaw you mention."

"Or just changing its nature only in the portion facing the Queen and the Chims?" Poque Belt, the Sentya Magistrate asked. "Harden it there."

Grain Jola shook his head. "The truth is that while we of Caste Rahail can maintain the Oasis, there is little we actually know about it," he said. "We can pull it back like we've talked about. We can judge the strength of it, look for weaknesses, but beyond that, we're powerless," he explained. "The Oases were created by the First Father, utilizing Talents only He possessed. In comparison, we are primitives. We simply pour our *Jivatma* into what He constructed, and somehow, that's enough to maintain it. What we're actually doing, though, has always been a mystery. Even two thousand years later, we remain ignorant of all but the basics."

Rukh shifted in his chair. "There is something," he said diffidently. "If an Oasis was tied off to something living, it could probably be manipulated in the way Magistrate Drent wants, but ours is anchored to a boulder at the Plaza of the Martyrs."

Grain frowned. "How do you know about the Stone? Only the Magistrates and Patriarchs know about it."

Rukh shrugged, looking more uncomfortable by the moment. "I learned about it from the memories of Linder Val Maharj, the First Father," he replied, sounding as if he wanted to crawl under his chair and hide. "I also learned that the creation of an Oasis requires a Cohesion of a Bow, a Blend, and a Shield."

Dar'El shot Rukh a look of disbelief. How could he know this? No one else did, including the highest ranking Rahails. And was it even true? There was no way to know, to test what might simply be something stirred from the depths of Rukh's imagination.

However, as soon as the questions were raised in Dar'El's mind, the doubts instantly fell away. This was Rukh, after all—his son who every few months brought forth knowledge that overthrew centuries of received wisdom.

Dar'El shook his head. Wait until Satha heard.

"When you say Cohesion, you mean the Talent of a Duriah?" Magistrate Drent asked.

Rukh nodded. "*The Book of First Movement* was the last testament of the First Father," Rukh continued. "For whatever reason, I was able to . . . experience it once." He went on to explain how he'd lived out the last few moments in the life of Linder Val Maharj when he'd first opened the pages of *The Book of First Movement*. It was a story with which Dar'El was already familiar. "I turned *The Book* over to the Society of Rajan a few days ago."

"Can you form this Bow?" Fol Nacket asked.

"It's the the silvery light I used against the Queen," Rukh answered before hesitating. "I can also Cohese since a Bow is a type of Cohesion in and of itself."

The Cherid Magistrate leaned forward. "And since you can also form a Blend and a Shield, can you then form an Oasis as well?" he asked, his expression intense.

"I can. I have," Rukh replied. "When I fought the Queen during the Advent Trial. My memories of that day are shaky, but parts of it have started to come back. I created an Oasis. It was weak, and if the Sorrow Bringer hadn't been so surprised by what She was facing, She could have easily crushed me."

"Can you make one of these more powerful Oases?" Fol asked, a hawk-eyed look of hope on his face.

"No. An Oasis like what you describe has to be anchored to something living and strong," Rukh said. "A sapling would work best, but until the tree reaches maturity and the fullness of its strength, any Oasis tied to it would be weaker than what we already have. Had Linder the opportunity to do so, that's what he would have wanted. He would have left us with a more effective, flexible Oasis, but He just didn't have enough time. And neither do we."

"Can you teach someone else whatever it is that you can do?" Dar'El asked. A dim idea tickled the back of his thoughts.

"No," Rukh told him. "But Aia and her brothers can. She can transfer my knowledge to anyone."

The notion came clear to Dar'El. "Then we need to teach as many people as possible what you know," he said excitedly, caught up in the fever of his vision.

"Our people will believe themselves Tainted," Krain Linshok said. He looked to Rukh and reddened in embarrassment. "Sorry, but it might be how they view matters."

"Those who wish to die can choose to abstain from what I'm proposing," Dar'El said. "The rest of us will accept whatever is needed. We'll fight to live, and even though what I'm suggesting is an alien way of looking at the world, ultimately it will also lead to a better one."

"How so?" Dos Martel asked.

"Because once others are taught what Rukh knows, they can be sent to other cities," Dar'El explained. "Now. By sea. They can create these new Oases, grow them, understand them, and protect Humanity's cities better than they ever have been so far. We might even be able to establish new cities or resurrect dead ones."

Gren Vos wore an expression of bittersweet longing mingled with satisfaction on her seamed visage. "So even if we fall, Humanity will not."

"I motion we consider this plan," Krain said.

"Second," Dos Martel said, infusing the word with feeling.

"All in favor?" Fol Nacket called out.

Again, the vote was unanimous.

"We'll take a few days to think this matter over before coming to a final decision," Fol said.

Upon hearing Fol's words, hope, so long dimmed, stretched out a tremulous tendril through Dar'El's heart. If the Magisterium decided correctly, the history of Ashoka would not die. Those given Rukh's Talents would remember their first home. They would remember this place of grace and beauty. They would remember from whence they originated. Ashoka's legacy would carry on.

Dar'El knew that for himself, and for many others, such a prayed-for future would have to be enough. In these grim times, this faint dream—expressed as a parent's hopes for the lives of their children—would have to suffice.

"Your plan might be the salvation of all of Humanity," Rukh noted as they left the chamber.

Dar'El nodded. "But only if the Magisterium chooses correctly."

Rukh seemed to hesitate and a faraway expression stole across his face. "I sometimes have odd dreams about the Withering Knife. I have this sense that it might be another means to save Humanity."

Dar'El frowned puzzlement, unsure of the reason for Rukh's troubling words. More than merely nonsensical, they were also antithetical to much of what he believed to be true. "The Withering Knife is evil," Dar'El said carefully. "Salvation can never be born from such wickedness. It can never save us."

Rukh's faraway expression thawed and an embarrassed smile took its place. "As I said, they're odd dreams. Perhaps we can forget that I mentioned them?"

---•---

Jessira tossed a bag of pakoras and samosas to Rukh. "Courtesy of Cook Heltin," she said, flopping down next to him a moment later.

After a furious few weeks, the two of them finally had a few hours alone together. They found themselves sitting near the Inner Wall in a narrow alley. On one end, it opened out into the loud heart of Trell Rue and on the other, a busy street of apartments and stores. The noises, however, never reached very far into the alley. Within its embrace was an island of cool and quiet with dappled sunlight and shadows that was near enough to their posting at Bellary Gate that they could return there in an instant if called back to duty, yet remote and private enough for the two of them to enjoy some time alone. For this reason, Jessira liked the narrow lane. She didn't even much mind the smelly mixture of garbage and spices from Trell Rue's nearby restaurants.

Being together was more than enough to overcome such minor inconveniences.

"I'm almost too tired to eat," Rukh announced just then, resting his head against the wall of a building and closing his eyes.

Jessira shared his fatigue.

The siege had begun almost six weeks ago, and life had become as hard and uneven as a sunbaked rutted road. Following the fall of the Outer Wall there had been the mad dash to evacuate and empty the city's farmlands, and afterward, a long, brutal week of endless rotations for all the warriors upon the Inner Wall. All of them had been working on the vapors of their stamina with too little sleep to sustain them. They'd been asked to stay vigilant and man the Inner Wall in three overlapping rotations as they waited and prepared for the Chimeras to advance.

The Plague never had, though. Despite the fact that the Oasis had been pulled back to the Inner Wall, the Chims and their siege engines had never pressed forward. They had remained stationed past the Outer Wall as the Queen had raced into Ashoka's farmlands, surging like a turmoiled sea. But Her waves weren't made of water. Her waves were a scouring sandstorm. Just like at Stronghold, the Sorrow Bringer had denuded the fertile fields, ripping every green shoot from the ground as She abraded clean the earth, leaving much of it a glassy ruin.

The Ashokans had been unable to do anything but watch as She desecrated their glorious farms.

Rukh sat forward just then. "You realize this is the first time we've been alone together for the past two weeks?" he asked.

Jessira nodded. "Which is why we shouldn't waste this opportunity by just sleeping.

Rukh grinned lecherously, and Jessira made sure he saw her eyeroll.

"I meant by eating," Rukh explained, drawing out a samosa and popping it in his mouth. His face was all innocence.

Jessira rolled her eyes again even as she laughed. She pulled Rukh to her and kissed him. She didn't mind that his unshaved face was filthy with dust, that his hair hung lank, or that he smelled rank as refuse. He was with her, and that was all that mattered.

Besides, Jessira wasn't in much better shape. She was just as grimy, gritty, and gamy.

Rukh passed her the bag of pakoras and samosas. "Who did you send back to the House Seat to get the food?" he asked.

"Shon," Jessira answered.

Rukh's eyebrows lifted in appreciation. "Very clever," he said. "I should have thought of that. Aia wouldn't have minded. Cook Heltin always spoils them with treats anyway."

Yes, you should, Aia, his calico-coated Kesarin, said to him. *I might have even suggested it once or twice.*

I'm trying to talk to my wife, Rukh reminded her in a tart tone.

Talk? Aia asked, sounding confused. *Why waste your time talking when you want to mate?*

Go away, Rukh said.

If you need instructions, I can provide those to you, Aia offered, *just as I did when Jessira needed Healing. Remember when you wanted to look at her . . .*

Aia! Rukh warned, scandalized.

Fine. I'm leaving, Aia said with a chuckle.

Jessira was also laughing. "It's been awhile since we did what Aia suggested," she said.

"You don't have to remind me," Rukh replied with feeling. "It would have been nice if just once, even for one day, we could have lived as husband and wife and all of this fighting for our lives never entered our thoughts."

"We wouldn't have to worry about our families being murdered and our homes destroyed," Jessira said softly, picking up the train of his thoughts. "We could have simply shared our lives with those we love and with one another."

"A dream for another life," Rukh said in a wistful tone, sounding sleepy.

"A beautiful dream, priya," Jessira said. She rested her head against his shoulder and closed her eyes.

Lienna gnashed Her figurative teeth. She had yet to puncture through the final barrier that protected Ashoka, and time was slipping away. She could feel it running through Her figurative fingers like fog. She had to end this. Three times She had felt Father's power. First, by a small pond in the Privation Mountains. Again in the early part of summer when She'd struck down many of the mangy Ashokans. And a third time just a few weeks ago.

Mother refused to fully explain Father's absence, but Her muteness on the matter was answer enough. Lienna knew: Father was reborn.

And with each appearance and confrontation, He had proven Himself to be more sure, more certain, more forceful. His power was still a pale shadow of the puissance He had once possessed—and even more irrelevant compared to what Lienna Herself commanded—but in the end, He was Father. He could not be disregarded.

Lienna had to kill Him before He became a threat. She had to destroy this wretched city, and soon. She had to blast apart the final gates of Ashoka before Father emerged, strong like He once had been.

"The closer You grip murder to Your heart, the more likely you will meet Your own demise," Mother advised. *"As You murdered Me, so to shall that be Your final fate. The world will celebrate."*

Lienna trembled at Mother's words.

"So boastful and proud were You when You recently confronted Me, but now look at what You've become," Mistress Arisa sneered. *"Where is Your great courage now, weakling? You're as fearful as a hen in a room full of tigers."*

Lienna wanted to ignore the voices in Her mind, but she

couldn't. It was too difficult. Too many of Her children were dead, killed when their treacherous commanders had left them helpless before the walls of several of Humanity's cities. There were barely enough of them to hold Lienna's madness at bay.

She worried over what would happen if She again lost Her sanity. She chewed over the possibilities like a hyena would a scrap of meat. No answer sparked in Her thoughts, but an undefined time later, the voices of thousands of Her children raised in prayer eased Her mind's concerns. It was the Prayer of Gratitude, a balm to Her soul. The beautiful, symmetrical lines and cadences of the Prayer filled the heavens. It was a rapturous song that always brought Lienna pleasure.

The Prayer ended, and Lienna descended to where Her Baels had gathered. There were issues for the upcoming battle that needed to be discussed, but as She approached, She broke into a frown. Where was Li-Boil? And his SarpanKi, Li-Torq? Those two had proven trustworthy, unlike the rest of their treacherous brethren.

Lightning lit a counterpoint to Lienna's annoyance. Thunder rumbled. *"Where is My SarpanKum?"* She demanded of a Bael who now wore the red feathers of command.

"The burden of leadership now falls upon my unworthy shoulders," the Bael announced. "I am Li-Grist. The honored Li-Boil and Li-Torq were killed by the Humans in an unexpected attack."

More lightning and growling thunder followed the words of this Li-Grist. Lienna wasn't sure whether to trust him.

"When did this occur?" Lienna demanded.

"Several days ago," Grist answered.

"Their corpses?" Lienna demanded.

"Returned as ashes to holy Arisa's bosom."

Lienna scowled in frustration, and She took on the appearance of a storm cloud. Rain fell. Thunder pealed. She noticed several of Her children flinch in fear, but She was too caught up in Her anger to care.

"Then you will be the one to carry out My commands," Lienna announced. *"We will redouble our efforts on Ashoka's final wall. We will destroy it before the end of the week."*

"It is good You order us to move so quickly," the SarpanKum said. "When the Humans attacked several weeks ago, they poisoned our water supply. We didn't learn of it until the Pheds started dying. Thankfully, we were able to save most of the herd, but it only leaves us with enough food for several more weeks before we will be forced to return to the Hunters Flats and resupply."

Lienna held in Her shock by the barest of margins. How could such an outrage have happened? And why hadn't Boil told Her of it? He should have, no matter that it would have raised questions about his competence. The fact that Boil hadn't told Her but that Grist had, indicated that the new SarpanKum was a more suitable leader of the Eastern Plague.

Lienna grew increasingly irritated, wondering what other setbacks Boil might have kept to himself. More thunder came, and the rain fell more fiercely. An instant later, She put away Her anger as realization lit Her thoughts. Lienna laughed, and Her thunderstorm clouds became a soft, spring drizzle. *"We will not need to resupply,"* She said. *"When we bring down Ashoka's final protection, My children will use the corpses of that foul city's denizens as their meals. It will be the victor's feast."*

"As You command," Grist answered.

Lienna didn't deign any further reply. Her orders had been given, and She rose skyward, heartened to have such competence as evidenced by her new SarpanKum.

And after Ashoka's Oasis fell, She would deal with that traitor

Hal'El Wrestiva. He was no longer listening to Her. He had Her Knife, and She wanted it back, especially before Father found it. It was the one fear that gnawed into Lienna's good cheer. Father with Her Knife. That couldn't be allowed.

CHAPTER TWENTY-THREE
CONSUMING CONSEQUENCES

While blessed Innocence will wear and warp with Time's passage,
Love is otherwise. It need never disappear from a person's life.
Be wise and always choose it.

—*The Book of All Souls*

The battle for Ashoka was one in which Rector Bryce had not yet been allowed to take part. When the Fan Lor Kum had first approached Ashoka, he had not been asked to report to duty and defend his home. Even after the Queen's arrival, he had been denied. The Oasis had been pulled back to the Inner Wall, the fields of Ashoka set afire, and still Rector had not been called forth.

Instead, his superiors had in mind for Rector a somewhat different task, one they felt better suited to his abilities. From the Magisterium itself had come his orders: find Hal'El Wrestiva and kill him. There was no need to offer the traitor a tribunal. One had already been provided him, and Hal'El had been convicted in absentia. He had been found guilty of a long list of crimes, each one worse than the other: treason, membership in the Sil Lor Kum, and finally, murder.

Nevertheless, Hal'El, despite his depravity and evil, was still accounted one of the most skilled warriors of his generation. Just how skilled was something that Rector knew quite well. He had once crossed blades with the man and had lost badly to him. It had been on the night Mira had been murdered.

Of all the defeats he had suffered, that was the one that Rector regretted the most. If he'd only possessed a mite more skill, maybe Mira might still be alive. It was an unknowable, unanswerable regret, but one that still clawed at Rector's heart. It was for this reason that he hadn't argued with his orders. He had gladly accepted them. Who knew what new malevolence Hal'El had planned? The treasonous bastard had to be stopped, and the best service Rector could offer his home would be to destroy Hal'El's evil once and for all.

All this made Rector's progress in finding the former ruling 'El of House Wrestiva all the more frustrating and disheartening. Hal'El had reentered Ashoka—everyone knew it. He'd even murdered one more time, but after that, he seemed to have disappeared. There was no trace of him. He had become a whisper on the wind, a rumor of danger, unseen and unknown, and Rector had been unable to track him down.

Until now.

"This is Solair Tumblewash," Rector said, introducing the bulky Duriah standing beside him. "Tell them what you told me."

The Duriah glanced around the room—Dar'El's study in the Shektan House Seat—and licked his lips. He was obviously nervous, and Rector could understand why. The meeting had to be intimidating for Solair. Here he was, the focus of a gathering attended by none other than Dar'El Shektan, a man of fearsome repute. To make matters worse, also present was the equally redoubtable Satha

Shektan, her children Bree and Jaresh, and her daughter-in-law, Jessira. All of them carried the surname 'Shektan' and all of them had achieved a certain level of fame or infamy in Ashoka.

"You'll be fine," Rector said, urging the Duriah on.

Solair nodded and cleared his throat. "I own a shop down in Hold Cavern," he said. "I'm a bowyer, and early this morning a man came into my store. He was a Kumma, older and looking down on his luck. His clothes were a little worn, not fine like you normally see. Plus, he was dressed like it was cold, with gloves on and his hood thrown forward so I could barely see his face. He told me his name was Vale Driven of House Wrestiva and that he wanted a custom-made bow and quiver of arrows. I told him I couldn't get to it any time soon with all the demands of the High Army." Solair wore a self-deprecating expression. "With the siege, they have me working from sunup-to-sunup. Same with my apprentices," he explained. "Anyway, the Kumma didn't like that, and he said if I had a bow that was close enough to his specifications, he'd take it. I told him that I couldn't be sure without the Army's approval—"

"You keep saying 'the Kumma' instead of referring to him by his name," Dar'El interrupted. "Why?"

Solair nodded. "I was just getting to that part," he explained. "The Kumma gave me the address of where I should deliver the bow if one became available. He gets ready to pay me then, and he takes off his gloves. That's when I saw it," Solair said, giving a pregnant pause and glancing about. "He was wearing a big ring, ironwood with some kind of shiny inlay. It was the ring of an 'El, and it bore the tiger sigil of House Wrestiva."

"You're certain?" Satha whispered in her weak voice.

Solair nodded. "I'm certain. And when I finally caught a good look at his face, I could tell who it was. He's wearing a beard, but it's him. It's that naaja bastard, Hal'El Wrestiva." Solair bobbed his head in apology to Jessira. "No offense intended, miss."

"None taken," Jessira replied.

Dar'El stood. "You have the address?"

Solair slipped him a piece of paper. "Here it is, in his own handwriting."

"Thank you," Dar'El said, offering a faint smile. "You have been most helpful. One of the servants will see you out."

After Solair left, Rector straightened from where he'd been leaning against a wall.

"You think he's telling the truth?" Dar'El asked.

"I do," Rector said. Before bringing Solair to the House Seat, he'd already thoroughly interrogated the Duriah. He had sensed no lies from the man. Rector was certain that this was the opening they needed to bring down Hal'El Wrestiva.

"What about the handwriting from the address," Satha began. "Is it Hal'El's?"

Dar'El nodded.

Jaresh offered a wolfish grin. "Then we have him."

Bree looked to Rector. "Why did you bring Solair and his information here instead of to the City Watch?" she asked.

"Because the Magisterium decided that Dar'El was to have direct oversight of my search for Hal'El," Rector replied. "And I need more warriors to take him down. The men I would have called on are all at the Inner Wall." He looked to Dar'El. "You're the only one who can get them released to my command."

"A number of warriors were given the day off today," Jessira said. "Some were of House Shektan. We should be able to round them up."

Rector smiled in relief. "Excellent. Is Rukh or Kinsu amongst them?" he asked.

"I don't know about Kinsu," Jessira began, "but Rukh's time off begins later in the afternoon, which means he'll arrive too late to join your band."

Rector tried to keep the disappointment from his face. In all of Ashoka, only Kinsu and Rukh were as good as Hal'El Wrestiva with a blade. He would have felt better if one of them were amongst his party.

Dar'El clapped his hands, bringing the meeting to an end. "I'll send runners to gather some warriors," he said to Rector. "Take a few guards from the House Seat as well. I want you ready to go in two hours."

Jaresh stood. "I'll go with you, too."

"Thank you," Rector said in appreciation. Jaresh had the soul of a warrior.

Jaresh moved to Rector's side and studied the stacked-stone exterior of the restaurant to which the Duriah had sent them. A sign above the entrance proclaimed the name of the place: Tranchers. It was likely the surname of the owner. Narrow mullioned windows opened out to the street, and the building shared a wall with a larger structure to the right. A pencil-thin alley ran to the left.

If there was an entrance out back, they'd need to make sure Hal'El didn't escape that way.

Before Jaresh could complete the thought, Rector had gestured to the ten warriors accompanying them, and five of them raced off to the rear of the building.

"Are you sure this is the address?" Jaresh asked dubiously,

glancing at the small, unobtrusive restaurant in Hart's Stand. "This isn't how I would have pictured Hal'El's lair."

"This is the place," Rector said in assurance. "This is the address the bowyer gave us. The owner was likely paid a great deal of money to keep quiet and allow Hal'El to hide out in the cellar."

"The cellar?" Jaresh asked in surprise. "Hal'El never struck me as someone who would allow himself to be humbled enough to sleep in a cellar."

"Desperation drives men to do all manner of things," Rector said, "and Hal'El is desperation personified."

Rector's words sparked an unformed twinge of worry within Jaresh. "Hal'El *would* do anything to gain revenge on those who exposed him as the Withering Knife murderer." He spoke slowly and carefully, speaking aloud his thoughts as he tried to formulate what had him growing increasingly anxious. "He would hate them above anyone else."

Rector bent his head as he considered Jaresh's words. He frowned, and a look of concern replaced his prior surety. "Or the one who led the hunt for him." Rector blanched, and they shared a dawning look of horror. "The Shektan House Seat is all but undefended," Rector said. "Most of the warriors meant to guard it are either with us or at the Inner Wall."

"We're not going to find Hal'El here," Jaresh said. Sweat broke on his brow, and a shiver of fear wormed down his spine. "We have to get back to the House Seat."

Rector nodded. "We'll do a quick sweep first," he said. "Very quick." He gestured to the warriors still with them, and they barreled into the restaurant.

Jaresh entered the building with the others, hoping that his burgeoning suspicion would prove to be a mistake, hoping he was the victim of an overactive imagination. Seconds later, though his fear was realized. The cellar and the other rooms within carried no sign that Hal'El had ever stayed there.

Rector led them back to the House Seat at a dead sprint.

———•———

In all his life, patience was a virtue that Hal'El had never needed to master. He was a man of action and movement, of purpose and drive, of decision and execution. Yet, for what he intended today, patience was what was needed. The waiting and stillness required by that soothing but tepid principle would lead him to what he'd been working toward for so long: revenge upon Dar'El Shektan.

From his vantage point, he could see into the study of his hated enemy. He was too far off to make out much more than a few bland shapes moving about. One figure, though, was unmistakeable—that of the crippled Satha Shektan as she was wheeled about in her chair. Hal'El smiled, knowing her grievous injury had caused Dar'El great anguish.

He shifted about then, relieving an incipient cramp but careful to make no motion that could give away his position. He was secreted away in a tree, unsuspected and unnoticed, upon the very grounds of the Shektan House Seat. He held a Blend, rough and ready—he would never master that Talent—but thus far, it had been enough. No one had seen or sensed him enter the grounds, and no one saw or sensed him now.

He was confident that he remained undetected. He'd scouted this position many times in the past few weeks, always with no one the wiser. No one knew he was here, waiting like a tiger on the unwitting deer.

And from here, he'd memorized the patterns and movements of Dar'El Shektan's day. He knew when and where Dar'El tended to have his meals, when and where Dar'El would break for the morning and the afternoon, and when Dar'El would wheel his crippled wife outside for her daily time in the gardens.

That time was now.

Hal'El had allowed himself to be identified by Solair Tumblewash, the Duriah bowyer. And, of course, Rector Bryce had hustled the man over to the House Seat so he could repeat his testimony. By now, Dar'El had heard it and even now, was likely sending a party of warriors to the address Hal'El had supplied to the bowyer. A surprise would await them when they arrived. The address would take them to a small restaurant in Hart's Stand. It was one Hal'El had once controlled as the SuDin of the Sil Lor Kum but not his true safe house.

The deception was all part of Hal'El's plan to get Dar'El alone. Frustratingly, the man rarely was. There were always other warriors about, more than Hal'El could take on by himself. But with the undeniable lure of finally capturing him, all those others should hopefully be gone by now.

Hal'El's breath came quicker.

Over a year he'd been waiting for this moment. Over a month since the battle for Ashoka had begun. A little less than a week since the fall of the Outer Wall. And two days since his offer to the Magisterium to give them all the information he knew of the Fan Lor Kum in exchange for clemency had been summarily rejected.

Worse, Hal'El had carried out the promise he'd made to the Queen: he'd marred Ashoka's Anchoring Stone—harmed it, in fact, much worse than he had intended. It was supposed to have been a slight slice, nothing more, but the Knife had proved impossible to control. The black blade had slid soundlessly across the misshapen lump that had anonymously protected the city.

That single cut had turned into a deep gash, and while the weapon was biting into the Anchoring Stone, Hal'El had felt something inside him tear. The perfect, crystalline pool of his *Jivatma* had roiled into a whirlpool and grown dark. Terror had filled his mind at the sight, and he felt himself dying. Too late, he had learned the truth. It was the Knife. Murder with the evil weapon had connected it to Hal'El in ways he had never suspected. Priming was what the Queen had labelled it. The blade had stolen *his Jivatma*, tapping into it, corrupting it in order to destroy the Anchoring Stone.

With a harsh cry of effort, Hal'El had managed to withdraw the Knife, but the damage had been done. The Oasis had been weakened. How much, Hal'El didn't know, but events proved it must have been substantial. The Oasis and the Outer Wall had fallen less than a week after Hal'El had cut the Stone.

As a result, the city was now doomed, and it was all Hal'El's fault. He had done this. He had led Ashoka to ruination.

Hal'El wasn't a man to hold on to many regrets, but what he had done to his home, what he had done to this place he loved above all else, was something for which he would never forgive himself.

And now, at this late date, vengeance was all he had left. Vengeance that he had been forced to set aside for weeks while his *Jivatma* recovered. Vengeance that would now finally arrive.

He fingered the Withering Knife sheathed at his side, pondering whether to kill Dar'El with it. It would likely be more painful that way, and Hal'El would also gain the *Jivatma* of his hated enemy, but . . .

With a grimace, Hal'El withdrew his hand from the Withering Knife. The stolen *Jivatma* wouldn't be worth it. Sophy Terrell was already in his mind. How much worse would it be if Dar'El was there as well? It would be a nightmare.

Movement in Dar'El's study snapped Hal'El's attention back to the here and now. The room was emptying, and he sat up straighter. Soon, Dar'El should be wheeling Satha outside. Any moment now . . .

Hal'El waited with bated breath. He prayed this would be the day he could finally avenge Varesea.

A door opened, and out came Dar'El and his wife. Hal'El frowned. With them were two others. Women. His frown deepened as he sought to identify who was with Dar'El and Satha. His brow unfurrowed when he recognized the two women.

Bree and Jessira Shektan.

Even better.

Hal'El would cause Dar'El even greater grief than he had dared hope. This afternoon, he'd kill nearly everyone Dar'El loved, and Dar'El would be forced to watch while he did it.

Hal'El took careful aim with his bow.

⸻ ◆ ⸻

A low whistling sound ended with Nanna stumbling backwards and crying out in pain.

Without thinking, Bree Shielded. She conducted *Jivatma*, using it to heighten her senses. Her body tensed, ready for whatever was to come.

"Someone's Blended in that tree!" Jessira shouted. Even as she pointed, a figure shimmered into view as it released its Blend.

Nanna staggered to his feet. His teeth were clenched in pain and an arrow protruded from his left shoulder. His sword was held steady in his right hand. "Protect your amma," he ordered.

The figure from the tree dropped to the ground. A man. He was shrouded in camouflage clothing with his hood thrown forward to hide his face. He cast aside his bow and quiver of arrows as he sauntered arrogantly toward them.

Bree's mouth went dry. Though she couldn't see his features, she knew who this assassin had to be.

A moment later, her suspicion was confirmed.

The figure pulled back his hood. Hal'El Wrestiva. "Does your shoulder hurt?" the traitor taunted Nanna. "You know what happens next. Or you could simply kill yourself and save me the trouble."

"If I wanted to kill myself, I would scale the heights of your ego and crash down to the depths of your intelligence," Nanna answered.

Hal'El snarled. "Your clever quips won't sound so clever with my sword down your throat," he said. "You'll die at my hands. It is how matters between us were always meant to end."

Bree conducted more *Jivatma* from her Well. Where were the guards? With a sickening realization, she remembered they were gone. They had accompanied Rector to the address supplied by the Duriah bowyer.

Hal'El drew his sword and almost before they could react, he was on them.

He crouched beneath Jessira's swing and spun and leapt. Somehow, he almost ended up *behind* Bree. She twisted about, trying to keep Hal'El in front of her. *Jivatma* fueled her movements, but the fragging traitor shifted too quickly for her to follow. In comparison, she felt like she was moving through mud. He was fast, faster than anyone Bree had ever faced, maybe even Rukh.

Almost lackadaisically, Hal'El slammed an elbow to Bree's jaw. Her eyes rolled up, and she stumbled away from him. Her balance was gone, and her legs wouldn't bear her weight. She fell heavily on her bottom.

Thankfully, Hal'El disregarded her when he sighted Jessira stepping in front of Amma. He smiled sardonically. Bree tried to right herself but couldn't as Hal'El dashed forward. He blocked Jessira's downward swing and snap kicked her in the gut. She flew through the air, and Hal'El was now unimpeded to attack Amma.

But Nanna was there. Bree tried to force her mind to function again. Nanna, weakened and hindered as he was by the arrow in his shoulder, couldn't last long against Hal'El. Bree regained some semblance of composure and surged to her feet. She moved to support Nanna.

Hal'El now faced them both. He moved smoothly, sinuous as a snake, fluid as water. He blocked blows, sliding aside from others, spinning and maneuvering. During it all, Bree never got the sense that he was challenged in any way. He was consummately skilled.

Just then, Jessira arrived back in the fight. Now it was three on one, and Bree felt a surge of hope. She risked a glance at Amma, who was watching the battle with a rapt look of fear.

If possible, Hal'El was now moving even faster. He slipped aside Bree's thrust, and she blocked his return parry. He moved with her motion, flowing out of her range. He smashed aside Nanna's horizontal stroke and delivered a hilt to the forehead in response. Nanna fell back.

Again Hal'El twisted aside and avoided Jessira's thrust, but his own struck straight into her thigh. It was a deep wound and blood flowed freely. Jessira grimaced in pain, but she stayed on her feet until Hal'El kicked her feet out from beneath her.

Hal'El turned away from Jessira and Nanna, and Bree was suddenly faced with the entirety of his focus. She conducted more *Jivatma* and her heart pounded adrenaline even as she sought to relax and fall into the movement of muscle memory that Durmer had so often emphasized. It worked for about seven strokes, but then Hal'El cut past her defenses. His sword sliced a line across her ribs. Another across the back of her arm. Blood dripped to the ground. A kick to the head had Bree nearly poleaxed.

She watched dimly as Nanna attacked then, but Hal'El easily countered him. The traitor moved confidently. He walked Nanna down, stepping through a series of increasingly desperate strokes. Hal'El slipped a reckless swing, punched Nanna in the ribs, and followed up with a thrust to the shoulder that hadn't taken an arrow.

Nanna cried out in pain, and his sword fell from his hand. Hal'El stepped inside, and swept Nanna off his feet. He leveled his sword.

"No!" Amma cried out.

Hal'El towered over Nanna. He seemed to say something, but Bree couldn't hear whatever it was. Her heart hammered a staccato rhythm. She was certain Nanna was about to be murdered before her eyes.

Bree finally managed to right herself. She disregarded the fire burning from where her ribs and arm had earlier been sliced open. She dismissed any pain or fear. There was only need, the desire to protect those she loved. It was hard to hold the sword steady, but she forced herself to do so anyway.

Jessira clawed her way back to her feet at the same time, and together, they faced Hal'El.

He turned to them and laughed in their faces. "I'll kill the ghrina first," he said, sounding clinical as he spoke to Nanna. "Then your wife and finally your daughter. Your death, though, will be the last. I want you to be able to truly appreciate the final, tortured moments of your life as I kill everyone you love." He grimaced in hatred. "You should have never sought me out or murdered Varesea."

Bree tightened the grip on her sword.

Normally the streets of Ashoka would be bustling with business right now. Mid-afternoon should have seen many people out on errands and tasks, talking, gossiping, and laughing. The city had always been alive with optimism and life, but ever since the invasion, especially the fall of the Outer Wall, a pall had settled over Ashoka. Dread had replaced hope, quiet fear had taken the place of hearty boisterousness, and a foreboding sorrow had cloaked even the sunniest of skies. There was a sense that a gloaming hung unmoving over Ashoka, that even in the midst of summer, winter's twilight grasp was reaching for the heart of the city.

Rukh recognized these changes as he and Aia trudged through the traffic on Jain Stoop. The road wasn't especially crowded, but people still stepped aside for him and the Kesarin—mostly for the Kesarin. No matter how often Aia and her brothers were seen wandering through Ashoka, the great cats remained an intimidating sight. People still eyed them askance and moved just a little faster as they passed by or even darted into side streets to evade the presence of the Kesarins.

Rukh mentally shrugged. At least having the traffic move out of the way for him meant that he would get home all that much sooner. His rotation on the Inner Wall had just ended and he had a day off before having to report back for duty. Just a few more turns to make, and he'd be home, able to see his family and spend a few hours with Jessira before she had to report back to her own posting.

Why can't I work on the Wall with you? Aia asked.

Because I'm not working on the Wall right now, Rukh explained.

Aia batted him on the shoulder, causing him to stumble. *I know that,* she said, apparently unamused by his joke. *I mean in general.*

Rukh glanced her way with wry amusement, and Aia grumbled in annoyance. Rukh laughed and reached up to rub her behind the ear. Aia pushed into his hand and purred. Rukh smiled. Nothing soothed or distracted Aia quite as easily as a good rub. *By the way, where are Shon and Thrum?* he asked.

Aia moved away and gave her whole body a shake. It was her way of resettling her fur about her. *During Jessira and Jaresh's day off, they decided to go to Dryad Park and go swimming,* she said. *They're likely lazing away the day.*

Rukh grinned. *Are you jealous?*

Aia's shoulders slumped. *Yes,* she said, sounding dejected.

You'll get to play during my time off, Rukh reminded her.

It won't be the same, Aia said. *There won't be anyone to play with.*

I'll play with you.

Aia's ears perked up. *You will?* she asked, sounding hopeful. *Can we play 'drown the gazelle'?*

Rukh laughed. *You're making that up,* he said. *There's no such game.*

Yes there is! Aia said. *It's so much fun. You'll love it.* She eyed Rukh, looking hungry. *But you have to be the gazelle.*

No chance, Rukh said.

Why? You'd be so good at it, Aia protested. She blinked. *My chin itches, by the way.*

No, Rukh said in exasperation. *I—*

Whatever else he might have said fled from his mind. Something was wrong; something was horribly wrong. A smell came to him. Blood and peril. His nostrils flared. Jessira.

"She needs you," a baritone voice whispered in his mind.

Rukh didn't think to wonder who had spoken to him. Something more important occupied his thoughts. Jessira was at the House Seat.

And she was in danger.

Aia must have picked up on his agitation or his thoughts. *I can run faster than you,* she said.

Then go, Rukh commanded. *Protect her.*

Come with me.

I can't keep up with you, Rukh snapped. He wanted Aia to get moving. Every moment she waited on him, the greater the danger Jessira faced.

I'll carry you, Aia explained.

Shock broke through Rukh's worry. Never in all the time he had known Aia had he ever expected such an offer. Nevertheless, he quickly did as Aia instructed. He clambered onto the Kesarin's back. His heart thudded. Jessira's peril was growing. He settled himself behind Aia's shoulders, clenching her sides with his knees.

Hold on, Aia warned. She broke out into a dead sprint.

The world blurred. It became a confusion of sights and sounds. Shouts of alarm from others on the road came to Rukh, but he paid them no heed. He was too busy struggling to hold on to Aia. While her gait was surprisingly smooth, the speed with which she ran threatened to unseat Rukh with every stride. He settled on lying low across Aia's back and gripping her fine fur as tight as he could. He ended up closing his eyes as well.

<hr />

Hal'El smiled. His long-sought vengeance was about to be completed. Dar'El would finally pay for everything he'd done, everything he'd stolen from Hal'El. All the months of hardships would finally have their answering retribution.

"The world would have been a finer place had you never been born," Sophy

cursed. *"Your mother would have prayed for a miscarriage had she known the degenerate evil she was fated to spawn."*

"Filth! You think we obstruct your will now," Felt Barnel shouted. *"You will never know a moment of silence! Your dreams will be nightmares. We'll strip the very memory of your disgusting lover, Varesea Apter, from your mind."*

"You will pay with pain for what you did to me, pig," the piggish Pera Obbe began.

And as was her nature, the irredeemably stupid Pera shouted the most unimaginative threats and imprecations possible while Sophy's were enough to curdle the soul.

Hal'El had grown used to them, though, and he stopped listening.

There was work to be done. The Shektan women still faced him with swords raised, and privately, Hal'El applauded their bravery. Courage shown in their eyes, but it wouldn't take much effort to disarm them.

"Lay aside your swords," Hal'El urged. "I will make your deaths swift and merciful. Injured or not, you must know by now that you pose no real challenge to me."

An earth-shattering roar distracted him. A giant cat, a furious Kesarin, leapt over the retaining wall that surrounded the Shektan grounds. It was a calico. Rukh's cat. It raced forward.

Hal'El cursed, furious at his fate. He had been seconds away from delivering justice for Varesea. He measured the distance the cat had to cover, trying to reckon if he had enough time to kill the Shektan women before the Kesarin was on him. He wouldn't. He wouldn't even have time to try to escape before the cat was on him.

Wait. There was something, no some*one* on the Kesarin's back. It was Rukh Shektan. It had to be. This was his famous Aia, after all.

Hal'El set the edge of his blade against Dar'El's throat even as bitterness filled his heart. He'd been so close.

The Kesarin roared and bounded forward, almost too quickly to follow. She flanked Hal'El, but he knew the cat wouldn't attack him. Not now. Not with Hal'El's sword pressed against Dar'El's throat.

"You can save your nanna," Hal'El called, "but only if you face me as a man. One warrior against another. No interference. Do I have your word as a Kumma? As a child of Ashoka?"

The figure on the Kesarin's back slid smoothly to the ground. It *was* Rukh Shektan. "You have my word," the younger man said. "But whether you defeat me or not, your evil ends here. Aia will see to it."

The Kesarin growled low and threatening.

Hal'El paid no heed to the great cat. She would kill him if he killed Rukh, but at least this way Hal'El would have a worthy death. He would either kill the finest warrior in Ashoka other than himself or in turn be killed by that warrior. It wasn't ideal, but it would have to do.

Hal'El Shielded and conducted from his Well as Rukh wasted no further time on talk. The younger warrior simply unsheathed his sword and attacked.

Hal'El somersaulted over a white-hot Fireball and landed in a ready position. He barely parried a vertical slash. His riposte met air. Another slash, barely parried. Hal'El leapt backward, covering twenty feet. He needed distance even as he drew more *Jivatma*.

Right now, Rukh was too fast, but Hal'El wasn't worried. He could keep up with the Shektan. Because of the *Jivatma* he'd stolen from the victims of the Withering Knife, he had more than enough strength to outlast the younger man. The world sharpened further. His Shield hardened. Nothing could penetrate it.

Another Fireball screamed toward him, and Hal'El took it on his Shield. Even before the sparks had faded, he answered in kind, and this time it was Rukh who had to dodge. Hal'El followed up with even more Fireballs. Rukh leapt over a few of them and slid aside from others. Fires sprung up throughout the Shektan estate.

Rukh suddenly leapt through the air like a launched spear, straight toward Hal'El. He was moving too fast for further Fireballs. Hal'El gauged the distance, and sprang upward. They met yards above the ground, exchanging blistering strokes. Hal'El could feel them all the way up to his shoulders. His palms stung, but he had no time to rest. Here came Rukh once more. Again they clashed in midair, their bodies parallel to the ground.

With that exchange, Hal'El's confidence was shaken. He'd taken several blows on his Shield. They hadn't gotten through, but they had still been heavy enough to batter him about.

Unholy hells, Rukh was strong. And he was moving faster now than he had at the beginning of their fight.

Hal'El drew more *Jivatma*. He had to if he wanted any hope of keeping up with the younger man. Uncertainty made a presence in his mind. He'd never fought a man with Rukh's skill or power. And how was the younger man moving so fast? It should have been impossible given the amount of *Jivatma* Hal'El was conducting.

The only explanation he could fathom was that Rukh was burning through his *Jivatma* at a prodigious rate, enough to possibly burn out his Well. It was a risky strategy, but it also meant the younger man would soon dramatically slow down. Rukh wouldn't be able to continue this punishing pace for much longer.

Hal'El smiled to himself. And if he pushed the action, Rukh would burn out that much faster.

A Fireball came at him, and Hal'El bent backward at the waist beneath it. Ironically, he'd seen Rukh use that same beautiful move during the Tournament of Hume. More Fireballs came, and Hal'El somersaulted over them while closing the distance.

Once again, it was swords. They fought smooth and swift with no more leaping about. Hal'El breathed easily, still strong and fast. Rukh kept up with him, and no strain was visible on the other man's face. Only concentration.

More strikes thudded against Hal'El's Shield, but some of his struck home as well. More blows were traded, and more blows landed. Both their Shields flickered. Almost as if by silent accord, they stepped away from one another. They stabilized their Shields before once more resuming their battle.

Rukh pressed forward, and Hal'El was forced to give ground. He tried to disengage, but everywhere he went the other man followed.

How was Rukh still drawing so much *Jivatma*? His Well should be nearly dry by now.

Hal'El realized the answer didn't matter. Not really. He bit down and bore forward. He had never tasted defeat in any battle, and today wouldn't be the first. He'd win, one way or another.

Unholy hells, but Hal'El Wrestiva was strong. Not only that, but he was fast enough to impress a Kesarin and skilled enough to put Kinsu Makren to shame.

Rukh was surprised he was able to match such a man. It should not have been possible. And yet, his Well showed no warning that it was waning. It was deeper, richer, and more full than Rukh could ever recall it being.

It was a mystery he would have to examine at another time.

Here came Hal'El again with teeth gritted.

The older Kumma feinted right, but Rukh didn't bite. He held his position. He blocked a horizontal slash, a low angled blow. Rukh took the offensive, but Hal'El was ready. They swept side-to-side, spinning, exchanging positions even as they exchanged heavy strikes. Hal'El grew stronger, faster. Several blows got through and rocked Rukh's Shield. He had to draw further from his Well, trusting that it would hold.

Hal'El must have sensed the momentary weakness. He stepped forward, but Rukh didn't retreat. He held his ground. As Durmer would have described it, he stayed in the pocket. Elbows, knees, fists, and hilts became part of the combat. Rukh checked a kick. A quick vertical slash, delivered too quickly for Hal'El to avoid, punched past the older Kumma's Shield. Blood flowed. It was a shallow cut to Hal'El's chest. But still, it was also the first true blow landed in the engagement.

Hal'El grimaced and stepped back, apparently not wanting to fight in such close quarters. Rukh could understand why. At a distance, with swords alone, the two men were evenly matched, but closer in, Rukh felt like he had the advantage. He pressed forward, determined to deny Hal'El a chance to breathe. He'd stifle the traitor. And then he would end him.

Hal'El sought to separate. He leapt backward, but Rukh followed. He kept pace with the older Kumma, always staying in range. Rukh stepped closer, limiting Hal'El's ability to disengage. Again, it was close in fighting, but this time, it was Hal'El who managed to get in a strike. It opened a shallow cut along Rukh's abdomen. The blow was followed with a knee to the ribs.

Rukh's breath whooshed out, and now it was he who had to disengage. He leapt backward, but Hal'El kept on him. Rukh leapt again. His chest was too tight. He needed time to get his lungs working again. Another leap gave him a bare moment of respite before Hal'El was upon him again. Rukh did his best to block the older man's sword, but mostly he just dodged or took the blows on his Shield. It flickered, and Rukh leapt away once more.

This time, the time and distance gained was enough. His lungs were working again, and his Shield was under control. Still, while both men panted heavily, Rukh knew the fight couldn't go on much longer. His Well was finally emptying. His *Jivatma* was thinning. His stamina, speed, and strength would soon fade.

He took a deep breath and closed the distance with Hal'El. The older Kumma didn't retreat. He, too, was willing to stay in the pocket this time.

Once more, it was fists, knees, and elbows in addition to the sword. Rukh feinted and snuck a foot behind the older Kumma's ankle. A diagonal slash meant to distract allowed a thudding elbow to land on Hal'El's forehead. The traitor stumbled back, and when he did so, he tripped on Rukh's foot and almost fell.

Rukh launched himself into an unprotected Hal'El. His knee thundered into the other man's ribs and abdomen. A liver shot.

Hal'El fell over, curled up around his stomach, gasping in pain.

Rukh leveled his sword and panted heavily. No sense of triumph filled him. Only satisfaction. It was over.

"Kill me," Hal'El begged.

Rukh wanted to. It would be so easy to do and so easy to justify. He'd seen the injuries suffered by Jessira, Bree, and Nanna at the hands of this man. He knew all the evil Hal'El had done, all those who had been murdered at his hands.

If Rukh killed Hal'El right now, no one would care. Vengeance would be a simple and acceptable matter. But vengeance wasn't what drove Rukh. It was justice. All those who had suffered because of Hal'El Wrestiva deserved a chance to face him, force him to acknowledge his wicked actions. It was simply poetic that Hal'El's justice would be far more cruel than vengeance. Drawn and quartered with his remains scattered on the Isle of the Crows was Hal'El Wrestiva's future. It was a sad ending to a once great man.

"Kill me," Hal'El pleaded once more.

Rukh kicked him in the head, knocking him unconscious. "Your death will not be so easy," he said, finding an unexpected welling of pity for the other man.

———◆———

Though the day was late, a time when everyone should be abed, Hal'El Wrestiva found himself awake and unable to sleep. This was his last night on earth, and fear kept him up. It was a terror that pounded through his veins and left him nauseated. Tomorrow would see him drawn and quartered, a brutal death.

He tried to face such a prospect with bravery, but he simply couldn't. Hal'El was a broken man. All his glorious dreams and ambitions had been ripped away just as his life soon would be. He was left with a single hope: Hal'El wanted to die with some small amount of grace and courage. He wanted to die with someone to regret his passing.

"We all suffered what you so greatly fear," Sophy said. *"Now you will join us in pain. Still, I am . . . not sorry for you, but I do pity you."*

"Imbeciles," cackled Pera Obbe. *"I will dance when you scream, Hal'El Wrestiva. I will laugh when they first pull your arms out of their sockets, when your legs are ripped from your torso."*

"Be silent," Aqua Oilhue said. *"Only the degenerate celebrate another person's pain."*

"Go frag yourself," was Pera's witty rejoinder.

"Do not listen to Pera. She is as wicked as you are yourself," Felt Barnel

said. *"Nevertheless, I will pray for you. I will pray that you seek forgiveness and achieve humility, that if Devesh casts you back on the wheel of time, you will be reborn as someone who becomes worthy of your life's gifts."*

"Thank you," Hal'El said, heartfelt and touched in the way only the most truly lonely and desperate can feel.

"I will pray for you as well," Van Jinnu said. *"If you are granted a next life, I pray you don't walk the same paths that led you to this ending. I pray your soul takes lessons from the choices you made in this world. I hope that it does, and I hope that you take a moment to seek Devesh's guidance."*

As the others in his mind settled down to silence, Hal'El found himself thinking about their words. Despite what he'd done to them—he'd murdered them, which was the worst thing one person could do to another—his victims had offered him something he had never expected or deserved. They'd given him warmth and comfort. It was the greatest gift he'd ever been given.

Hal'El had never been a praying man. Like most Kummas, he had little to do with Devesh, but in this, his final night, during those hours when the world rested and those who should have hated him the most had instead offered him their forgiveness, Hal'El prayed. He wasn't sure how to do it, or what he was supposed to do. He simply spoke into the vaults of his mind, uttering whatever came to him. Much of it was nonsense and his words meaningless, but eventually the cadence of prayer reached his heart, and the truth of what he desired was made clear.

Hal'El was too selfish to feel true remorse for what he had done, but nevertheless, he prayed first for those who he had murdered. He prayed that they would not be cast back upon the wheel of time, that Devesh would gather them into His loving embrace, even Pera Obbe. Next, he prayed for Varesea, his one true love, hoping the same for her. And finally, he prayed for himself. He prayed for peace, for calm in the face of fear, to feel Devesh's loving touch even for just an instant before his life was snuffed out.

In the midst of his prayers, the door leading to the small, otherwise empty row of prison cells opened up, and in walked Rukh Shektan.

Hal'El remained seated on the floor. Any hatred he might have once felt for this man who had defeated him was gone. Any bitterness at his life's ruin was drained away. All of it replaced by a hollow ache. As a result, he had no desire to stand and face Rukh as an equal. What difference would it make if he did? Instead, Hal'El simply looked up from his seated position, waiting for the younger man to speak.

The quiet stretched on.

Was Rukh here to gloat? Hal'El would certainly have done so had their roles been reversed. He would have been glad of it, too, but it saddened him to think that Rukh might be just as prone to such a failing as he. Hal'El had hoped the younger man might be made of better moral fiber.

Rukh continued to stare down at him with an unfathomable expression on his face. Finally, he reached into the pocket of his coat and pulled out a small vial. "Tomorrow will be very painful for you, but it need not be." He tossed the vial to Hal'El. "Take enough of this, and it'll stop your breathing."

Hal'El stared at the vial with a burgeoning sense of hope before finally looking up. "Why are you doing this?" he asked, wanting to understand why he was being given this easier way out.

"It isn't because I've forgiven you," Rukh said. "I want to, but I doubt it will happen before you leave this world. I'm bringing this to you because I could have killed you the other day and given you a clean death." Rukh's lips pursed. "But justice demanded that you face those who you so terribly wronged. With your Tribunal before the Magisterium, they finally had the opportunity. And you finally were forced to acknowledge their anguish and feel their anger and hatred. Now you have, and now, I can give you the clean death I wish I could have when we fought."

"Thank you," Hal'El said, clutching the vial to his chest. Tears of gratitude filled his eyes. "Devesh bless you, Rukh Shektan."

The younger man gave a brief bob of his head and turned to leave, but Hal'El called out to him. "What did you do with the Knife?" he asked.

Rukh stiffened. "I have it," he replied. "No one knows what to do with it, so I kept it."

"You should throw it into the deepest water you can find or have a Duriah melt it down to liquid," Hal'El advised. "It's what I should have done."

Rukh nodded agreement. "Yes, you should have," he replied, and Hal'El thought that would be the end of their conversation, but the younger warrior hesitated. "Devesh bless you, Hal'El Wrestiva. I will pray for you if a new life is to be your destiny."

After Rukh's departure, Hal'El settled himself on the ground and a warm peace stole over him. He quickly swallowed the contents of the vial, and his last thoughts were of a distant song.

CHAPTER TWENTY-FOUR
FAREWELL TO HOME

In the midst of tragedy, those with hearts
open to Devesh will find solace and wisdom.

—*The Word and the Deed*

S atha sat alone in Dar'El's study, waiting on the arrival of the rest of the House Council. While she did so, she stared out at the grounds where two days ago, Hal'El Wrestiva had almost murdered her and most of her family. The lawn and shrubbery were a mess with scorch marks all over the place from where Rukh and the traitor had hurled Fireballs at one another. It was miracle they hadn't burned down the House Seat itself.

It was almost as much a miracle that it had been Rukh who had won that battle. Satha shook her head in remembrance. She'd been tight with tension and terror the entire time. No matter what he'd eventually become, Hal'El Wrestiva had once been a legend. He had been the measure by which most every Ashokan warrior for the past twenty years had been compared.

But in the end, it had all worked out. Hal'El was dead, killed by his own hand—someone had snuck him a vial of poison—and his remains were now a feast for the crows.

And Rukh was safe and unharmed, as was Satha's family.

The door to the study opened and Dar'El entered. He moved stiffly, his arms held unmoving at his sides. Both shoulders obviously still pained him. He'd taken an arrow to one and a sword thrust to the other, and both remained heavily bandaged, but her husband was alive. It was blessing enough as far as Satha was concerned.

"How are you feeling?" she asked, still hating the raspy, weak quality to her voice.

"Every day is a little better than the last," Dar'El answered. "How are you?"

"Every day is the same as the one before," Satha replied, trying to keep the bitterness from her voice. Though her children didn't see it—she wouldn't allow them to—her paralysis, her difficulty even drawing a breath, was something that still angered her, consumed her with grief. She hated her weakness, she hated how little she could do for herself, and she mourned her loss of independence.

Dar'El came and stood behind her as he rubbed her shoulders. "I know," he said, understanding her sadness as he kissed the top of her head. "And I'm sorry."

Satha put a hand over his and squeezed, appreciating his support.

The door opened again and in came the others: Janos Terrell, Durmer Volk, and Teerma Shole. As was his wont, Durmer was serious and dour, while Teerma smiled at something the hawk-faced Janos had said. Satha eyed them in consideration. The two newest members of the House Council were known to spend much time together. If it meant something more than friendship had developed between them, Satha reckoned it a good thing. Everyone could use a little brightness in this grim summer.

"Let's get started," Dar'El said, turning Satha around so she faced into the room.

"With the ongoing siege, I'm a little confused as to why we're meeting," Teerma said. "Commercial industry and economy have essentially ground to a halt since everything is needed for the war effort. What new business do we have to discuss?"

"The Magisterium has *finally* come to a decision regarding Rukh's Talents," Dar'El said. "They've decided that what he can do has to be passed on to as many Ashokans as possible and as soon as possible. They want it done in no more than a few days."

Satha had heard all this before, but she forced herself to listen closely anyway.

"The Magisterium thinks our situation hopeless," Durmer guessed.

Dar'El nodded. "Defeat was always the most likely scenario," he said. "In all of history, no city has ever outlasted a siege by Suwraith."

"But why now?" Janos asked. "Why so suddenly?

"It should be obvious," Dar'El explained. "After Rukh almost died battling Hal'El, the Magisterium finally decided that sharing his Talents amongst others is of the utmost importance." His jaw clenched. "They've put it off too long as it is."

"That isn't the only reason," Satha rasped. "The Oasis will fail. The Rahails are certain of it. It is likely to last for only another week or so."

Knowing nods met her statement. It was information the other councilors must have already come to realize.

"And what will become of all those who are given these new Talents?" Teerma asked.

"They will form the nucleus of a new Caste," Dar'El explained. "The first new one since the destruction of the First World."

"And why would we still have Castes to begin with if this new one is going to have the Talents of a Muran, Rahail, Duriah, and a Kumma?" Janos asked.

"Because this new Caste will be sent to Defiance, and from there, members will spread out to every city throughout the world. But until the other cities accept the need to do away with Castes, this is the best first step. The other cities haven't been exposed to the OutCastes, and they haven't experienced what we have. Until they do, they aren't likely to accept *ghrinas* in their midst." He smiled. "But a new Caste, they will."

"What will this new Caste be called?" Teerma asked.

"Caste Maharaj," Dar'El answered. "In honor of the First Father and First Mother's surname. A purposeful misspelling."

All this was the final realization of the Society of Rajan, but Satha wished it could have occurred in better circumstances, one that didn't involve the looming destruction of her home and the death of her children.

Janos narrowed his eyes. "You've thought about this a long time, haven't you?" he asked.

Dar'El nodded. "I have. The Castes are a relic of the past. They hold us back." He glanced at the others. "By now, given what Rukh and the other OutCastes can do, you know this as well. So does the Magisterium, and I would venture to say most of Ashoka."

"You're right," Teerma said, "but it still raises the question: what do you need from us? Why are we here?"

"Because it's been decided that every child and most of the young men and women in *all* the Castes will be given these new Talents, and afterward, they will be sent away from Ashoka. We need to help come up with a plan of evacuation for them, or at least for the children of our House and our Caste."

"Ashoka is to be emptied?" Durmer looked like he'd taken a kick to the gut.

"But only the children and some of the young men and women," Teerma said, trying to sound soothing..

"Which is the same as saying we will send away that which makes our city alive," Durmer replied.

————•————

Jessira read aloud the poem she'd come across, the one that reminded her of Ashoka's present and perhaps its future.

Summer's last light has frayed and faded.
So harvest the wheat with breaths bated,
Whilst the last seritonal heat remains.
Before gilded leaves are semaphore chains.
Before bitter winds, a synecdoche
Of winter's clutching snow and solid sea.

Jessira looked to Rukh, waiting on his response.

They sat on a stone bench in a small garden upon the grounds of the House Seat. A low-lying variegated hedge edged the border, making the space a haven. Birds trilled and butterflies and bumblebees flitted about as the honey scent of flowers filled the air.

Rukh's head had been bent over as he played the mandolin, and he didn't respond at first to what Jessira said. Maybe he hadn't heard.

Jessira recited the poem once again.

Rukh glanced up. "I have no idea what you just said."

Jessira eyebrows rose in surprise. "What do you mean?"

"I don't know what that poem meant," Rukh replied. "Some of

513

those words . . ." He held a teasing smile. "They're pretty large for an uneducated OutCaste."

"It's why this 'uneducated OutCaste' uses a dictionary."

"I think you just like using big words."

Jessira snorted. "You're one to talk." She pushed a stray lock of hair off his forehead. Usually he kept his hair short, but with the siege, he hadn't bothered to have it cut. There were more strands of gray in there as well. They were more easily visible now, a scattering along his temples. She ran her fingers through them, and he leaned into her hand.

"Laya and Sign are going to be a part of the evacuation," he said. "Most every OutCaste and young person will be going, even Farn and Bree."

"I won't go with them," Jessira said.

"You can if you wish," Rukh reminded her. "You were selected."

"Only if you come with me."

"I wasn't chosen for the evacuation," Rukh said. "Those warriors without children who are to leave Ashoka were decided upon by lots. I wasn't one of them."

"The Magisterium would allow it if you asked."

"You know I can't. Someone else would have to stay behind if I did." He stared into her eyes. "But any woman of childbearing years can go . . ."

"Don't," she warned him. "Not again. I'll stay with you, or you can come with me." This was an argument they'd already had more than once, and one she was mightily tired of having. Ever since the decision to create the Maharajs and abandon Ashoka had been made, Rukh had tried to convince her to leave the city without him.

Jessira had steadfastly refused him every time, and every time she kept hoping that maybe he would finally accept her decision.

Perhaps this time he actually had since his head was now bent low over the mandolin again as he plucked an aimless tune.

"I sometimes have strange dreams," Rukh said. "There's always a woman and a girl, but I can't see them. But when I wake up, they're gone. I know they're dead." He looked up from his mandolin. "The dreams leave me feeling like how I would if I were to lose you."

"We don't have a daughter," Jessira noted.

"Not yet, but maybe some day. If we're lucky. Or at least you will."

Jessira mentally sighed as Rukh bent over the mandolin once again. He plucked a slow, melancholy melody. She recognized the song. It was about a man who lost the only woman he ever loved. "That sorrow you're feeling, the fear for me," she began, "how can you believe that I would feel anything less for you? When I thought you had perished during the Advent Trial . . ." She shuddered. "I don't know whether I would have cared if I lived or died."

"I know, priya" Rukh said. His hair had flopped over his eyes, and he didn't look up from the mandolin. "I just want you to live."

Jessira gave his hand a gentle squeeze. "I feel the same way about you."

Rukh's mournful song was the only sound between them then.

"We're to have a farewell gathering for the family tonight," Jessira said when he finished the song. "Cook Heltin said she's using all the available stores she can get her hands on in order to make it a farewell to remember."

"I had hoped it would be our farewell as well," Rukh said. He wore a teasing half smile on his face. "Are you sure you won't go with the ships and leave me in peace?"

Her answer was a playful punch to the shoulder.

"See," Rukh protested. "This is why I want you to go. You're so violent, always pushing and punching. I swear my shoulders are black and blue from all your bruises."

Jessira shut him up by kissing him on the lips. She crossed her arms behind his neck and held him close. The kiss lingered, and his arms went around her as he held her close.

———•———

Jaresh stood upon the ramparts of the Inner Wall and stared out at the ocean of Chimeras camped at the base. They'd finally moved their siege engines closer to the city several days ago and immediately began flinging their stones at the Oasis. However, while their aim remained true, their judgment of velocity was terrible. Most of their stones plowed at high speed into the Oasis, and promptly rebounded off of it.

Jaresh couldn't recall a single one of their rocks penetrating through to worry the warriors on the Inner Wall. Nevertheless, the Chimeras kept up their barrage from sunrise-to-sunset, regular as a clock. Except for today. For some some reason, Suwraith's hordes had quit their bombardment early. Even the Sorrow Bringer was unaccountably quiet.

It didn't make much sense, but it probably didn't mean much either. It certainly didn't mean the siege would soon be lifted. More likely, the Queen was taking a respite for some reason and had ordered Her Chims to do the same. Any moment, though, they would probably get back to volleying their rocks at Ashoka's Inner Wall.

According to Nanna, it wouldn't matter when they resumed their attack. Ashoka couldn't hold out. The city was doomed with only days left before the Oasis was broken.

It was why every child and young person of every Caste had been gifted with Rukh's Talents. There were now thousands who could form a Bow and an Oasis. Jaresh was one of them.

But taking on such a massive project had required a week of non-stop work by the three Kesarins and had left the cats worn out. They were still recovering, and Jaresh wondered what would become of them. They would remain in Ashoka, but after the city's fall and the death of their Humans, what would happen then?

It struck Jaresh just then, all the changes in his life. He was so different from the young warrior who had left for Stronghold a year ago. He was older in a way unmeasured by time and years. He'd seen so much, experienced so much, and now came all these new Talents and knowledge. He couldn't help but wonder what Mira would have thought of the man he'd become, of what the city and her people had become.

He reckoned she would have been proud of them.

Jaresh bent his head in wistful remembrance and drew *Jivatma*. He formed a small Oasis around himself. Only another year, another few months even, and the Sorrow Bringer and all Her hordes could never have destroyed Ashoka.

"You'll be late if you don't get going soon," Sign said to him.

Jaresh turned to her in surprise. He hadn't noticed her arrival until she had spoken. "You aren't coming?"

Sign hesitated. "This is supposed to be a private farewell for your family."

"It won't be that private," he told her. "Jessira will be there, and so will Laya, Farn, and little Court. They're your family, too."

"I don't want to intrude," Sign said, still appearing unsure.

"You won't," Jaresh assured her. "I want you there." He took her hands in his. "My parents want you there."

"Well, since you asked so politely, how can I say 'no'?" Sign asked with a faint smile.

"Plus, it helps that you find me utterly charming and irresistible," Jaresh added with a wiggle of his eyebrows.

"Of course. How could I forget about that?" Sign teased.

Jaresh smiled. "Admit it. You do like me."

"I admit nothing," Sign said. She put the lie to her words a moment later when she kissed him. "I do like you," she added, this time serious. "But why do your parents want me at tonight's party?"

"They want to get to know you as best they can before you leave."

"They know about us?" Sign asked, looking surprised. "I didn't think you'd tell them."

"Of course I would," Jaresh said, perplexed by her demeanor. "Why wouldn't I?"

"I know your parents are open-minded when it comes to the OutCastes, but are you sure they'll want another son of theirs in a relationship with one of my kind?"

Jaresh rolled his eyes. Sometimes Sign's preoccupation about her status as an OutCaste in a city of Purebloods made her overlook the blindingly obvious.

"What?" she asked in protest after seeing his eye roll.

"If you haven't noticed, every child in Ashoka now has Talents not of their birth Caste. We've become a city of OutCastes. We were just smart enough to come up with a better name."

Sign stared at him silently through measuring eyes. "Are you making fun of my people?" she finally asked.

Jaresh held his hands up in surrender at her feigned annoyance. "Never."

7

8

6

"So you don't think your parents would care if they had *two* of my kind as daughters-in-law?"

Jaresh had to laugh at her presumptuous question. "Daughter-in-law? Don't you think you're making a rather large assumption?"

"I don't think I am," Sign replied. She arched a challenging brow. "Am I?"

"You're not," Jaresh said with a sigh, wishing the world were something other than it was. "And if I could go with you to Defiance . . ."

Sign put a finger to his lips. "I'll stay," she said. "I've thought about it. When Stronghold died and I survived, I ended up outliving nearly everyone I love. Jessira is the only family I have left. And now there's you. You're staying, and I can't survive such a loss ever again."

Jaresh gathered her in his arms. He knew there was nothing he could say to change her mind. "We sure picked a lousy time to fall in love."

"There's never a terrible time for love."

Jaresh took her by the hand. "Let's go see my parents."

<hr />

"What happen when the Ashokans leave?" Chak-Soon asked. "Seem cowardly."

Li-Choke didn't answer at first. The setting spread out before him held him entranced.

He and Soon stood within a large field in Dryad Park. Before them grazed a herd of Bovars, munching contentedly on the lush grass. A couple of claws of Tigons dozed in the warm sunlight while the newborn Baels played amongst the tails and hooves of their slumbering, older brethren. A group of old Humans played chess beneath unlit firefly globes as wind chimes rang gently in time to the soft breeze.

Nothing Li-Choke could have ever imagined would have been as graceful as this moment. This sylvan scene perfectly encapsulated all the hopes and aspirations of generations of Baels since the time of Hume, of peace and fraternity amongst those who should have always been brothers.

And this lovely vision would end in a flood of blood and fire.

"No. It's not cowardly," Choke disagreed, finally responding to Soon's earlier words. "It's pragmatic. Whether they stay or go, the Inner Wall *will* come down. It's why the Ashokans created the Maharajs. So their young might live on in some other city."

"An arrogant name," Soon muttered. "Not right. Make sound like . . ." he rambled to a halt, apparently running out of words.

Choke shared the Tigon's distaste for the name given to the new Caste. A memory from several seasons ago came to him, a story he'd once heard, one that left him uneasy. "Li-Dirge told me of the time before the First World," Choke said. "He said that before the coming of the First Father and the First Mother, the world was riven with blood and brutality. Tribes of Humanity warred against one another. They battled for scraps of sustenance scattered throughout the wasteland that was the world. Dirge said that these tribes were vicious and cruel. They tortured their enemies. They fed their weak to wild animals as sport. And their rulers were known as 'Rajs'. I suspect the First Father wasn't always known as Linder Val Maharj. More likely, he changed his name to be some kind of play on words, to make himself something greater than a mere 'Raj'. He was a 'great Raj'." Choke snorted. "Now the Humans return to the names of their amoral ancestors."

"Karma," Chak-Soon pronounced.

"Perhaps," Choke replied. "Or maybe this new Caste can redeem the savage name they were given."

Soon grunted in reply. "What we do when Wall fall?" Soon asked.

"You and I will do as we must," Choke replied, somehow managing a smile.

"Your small ones die?"

Choke shook his head, and his feathers of command rattled. Some of the other Baels had long since removed their symbols of authority, preferring to try to forget their time as slaves to Mother's lust for rampage and ruin. They wanted to wash away any remembrances of the evil they had committed under Her command, but Choke felt otherwise. He didn't want to forget what he'd done. He wanted to remember it all. Such knowledge was what inspired him, impelled him to continue on the path he had chosen.

"The newborn Baels won't die," Choke told Soon. "The Ashokans will allow them passage aboard their ships. Li-Silt will go with them. Of all of us, he is the one most dedicated to Hume's ideals. He is the one best suited to teach them what they need to know."

"And us?"

Choke rested a hand on Soon's shoulder and turned to face the Tigon. "We will fight, my friend. We will protect one another as brothers should. Until the last light fades from our sight"

"And Devesh will welcome us into his warm embrace," Soon answered, for once not mangling the words.

Choke's gaze grew distant. "Yes," he whispered. "And the singing light will call us home."

———————◆———————

Aia stretched out and rested her head on Rukh's lap. He idly scratched at her neck and ran his wonderful fingers through her fur. For some reason, letting Rukh groom her always brought her comfort. She didn't understand why. Perhaps it had to do with the bond she felt for Rukh, a connection which was strongest in these quiet, private moments. It was just the two of them, with her human caring for her as he rightly should.

Thinking back on it, Aia realized that in the past, only as a cub lying between Amma's strong paws had she ever felt this quiet contentment, this serene certainty that the world was *exactly* as it should be. She laughed at the thought. She was no longer a cub, and Rukh was most certainly not her amma.

A breeze blew and carried the scent of blood and ashes. The area where Aia and Rukh rested had once been her favorite place within the lands of the Shektan House Seat. It was hard to remember what it looked like before the burnt bushes and trees, the dead, blackened grass, and the smell of ground steeped in smoke and ruin. This was the place where Rukh's family had almost died, the place where her Human had fought and defeated the wretched Hal-El Wrestiva.

Aia curled her lip in disgust. Hal'El had been a wicked man with a heart full of evil. It was good that he was dead. She growled again.

Rukh must have noticed her anger. *What's wrong?*

I was thinking of Hal'El Wrestiva, Aia answered.

Why?

The smell of this place reminded me of him, Aia said, going on to explain what she noticed. She nosed the black blade sheathed at Rukh's side. *Why don't you get rid of that? It smells wrong.*

I can't just leave it lying around, and the Magisterium made no mention of what they wanted done with it. Rukh said. *It's best if I hold on to it for now.*

Aia huffed. *I don't like it. And I don't like the smoky smell around here.*

Do you want to go somewhere else? Rukh asked, moving as if to rise off his bench.

No, Aia answered quickly. She used a paw to hold one of Rukh's legs in place, careful to keep her claws sheathed.

If they went anywhere else, there would likely be others around, and if there were others around, then Rukh's attention would be diverted. And that just wouldn't do. Right now, Aia wasn't willing to share her Human with anyone else, not even Jessira. Tomorrow would bring great change, and she likely wouldn't see Rukh much afterward. He would be too busy, either seeing off the Ashokan young on their journey across the waters, or manning the Inner Wall. In both cases, Aia couldn't be with him.

Starting tomorrow, their time together would be limited.

The future, generally cloudy and murky, was clear now, and it was bleak. There was a certainty about what was to come. The Demon Wind, Suwraith, would soon breach the final wall around Ashoka. She would pour into the city like a flood of hate and hunger with murder and destruction trailing Her wake. Ashoka would fall, burned even worse than the grounds around the Shektan House Seat. It would happen soon. Aia could sense it. She tasted death on the air. It hovered like a storm cloud whose presence was felt before it was seen.

But before that tragedy occurred, Aia wanted to savor this moment as thoroughly as possible. She wanted to enjoy the few times she had left with Rukh because in that future she sensed, Rukh would almost assuredly die. *She* might die.

You need to leave the city while you still can, Rukh advised.

Aia didn't bother answering. Instead, she merely bumped his forehead with her own. It was a thump that was hard enough to be affectionate but still hurt. He'd gone over the same advice with her several times already.

Females, Rukh muttered.

Jessira said the same thing to you, didn't she? Aia said smugly. She always knew Rukh's mate was special.

She won't see reason, Rukh responded. *And neither will you.*

We are females, which means we are wise, Aia said. *Perhaps you should think on that.*

You mean you're wise enough to stay in danger when safety can be had? Rukh said with a laugh. *Not much wisdom in that.*

Aia switched her tail in annoyance. She had wanted a quiet time with her Human; not an argument or mockery. It was unacceptable. *Quiet,* she ordered.

I will not be quiet, Rukh responded. *I know you think I'm your Human, but you're also my Kesarin . . .* he began.

Aia had heard enough. She belonged to no one, Human or otherwise. She placed a paw on Rukh's forehead, letting the claws out, just enough to put sharp pressure on his skin. *I choose who belongs in my life.*

And when you let me in your life, you put yourself in mine, Rukh said. *You are my Kesarin as much as I am your Human. I will grieve if you die just as much as you would for me if I passed away first. It's how love works.*

Aia eyes slitted in irritation. *You don't own me,* she growled.

I never said I did, Rukh said.

Love means you think you own me or at least a part of me, Aia said, growing steadily more aggravated with him.

No it doesn't, Rukh countered. *Now take your paw off my face.*

Aia didn't like his tone. It was too demanding. Who was he to demand anything of her? Her tail swished, and her ears flattened in annoyance, but still, she did as he asked.

Rukh sighed a moment later and surprised her by pulling her face close to his, touching his forehead to hers. *I wish I could see you *run across the Hunters Flats. I wish I could see Shon and Thrum chase after you and never catch you. I wish I could see you live free, even of this bond we share if that's what it takes to see you safe and alive.* That's *what it means to love.**

Aia tested his words, searching for the flaw that indicated he thought he could control her. She found none. In fact . . . Aia blinked surprise when she realized that she wanted something very similar for Rukh. She loved her Human.

Rukh rested his head against her neck and hugged her tight. Aia had grown to enjoy that expression of his affection, and her eyes closed. She purred, and all was forgiven.

My chin itches, she whispered. *Can you scratch it?*

Always.

———————————◆———————————

Centered within the dining hall of the Shektan House Seat was a long table, easily able to fit the nine people seated about it. It could have managed twice that number. The firefly lamps in the wall sconces and in the chandelier hanging from the coffered ceiling had been turned down. It left the room luminous, soft with a golden light reflected off the almond-colored walls, the wide-paneled mahogany wainscoting, and the teak table. The scents of spiced food filled the space, but the platters from which the aromas originated were all but empty.

The meal was over, and Bree wished this moment could be frozen in candle wax. Her family was gathered here, laughing, teasing, and loving one another. It was likely the last time she would see all these people she loved so much.

Her eyes glistened. She was leaving tomorrow and nearly everyone else in this room was staying, even Sign. Bree wasn't sure she could still go through it and leave them. In some ways, she had trouble accepting that Ashoka was actually in danger of falling. So much about the city was still normal. There were still people going about their work, cooking, cleaning, running their errands, opening their restaurants, and even performing or singing in the playhouses. She wondered if she was making the right decision by leaving.

"You have to go," Nanna said. He sat to her right while Rukh sat to her left and Amma sat directly across the table.

"Is it that obvious?" Bree asked with a smile.

"Only to those who know you," Rukh said.

"We really should have convinced her to play cards with us more often," Jaresh quipped. "She has absolutely no ability to hide her emotions."

Farn grinned like a shark. "We'd have left her penniless every time."

"You're lucky you didn't play me," Jessira said. "I would have taken all *your* money."

Farn eyed her askance. "You never struck me as someone who could . . ." He seemed to run out of words and simply waved his hands in Jessira's general direction.

"You don't think she has the ability to maintain a distant, unreadable focus?" Laya provided for him even while she grinned. "If you truly believe so, then, by all means, please teach her these gambling games."

Sign chuckled as well. "Am I allowed to wager on the outcome?"

Farn looked from one woman to the other, an expression of uncertainty on his face. "Er . . ."

"Just to provide you some perspective," Nanna began, "Jessira often beats me at chess. She does so while wearing the most bland expression imaginable. Most times she doesn't even seem to be paying attention to the game until it's over and she's won."

"Jessira is good at everything," Rukh said in a patently ridiculous, cloying voice. "It's why I love her so."

Bree threw a roll at him.

Amma laughed. It was good to see her enjoying herself. Though she tried to hide her grief, Bree knew how much her paralysis continued to pain her.

Rukh surprised Bree when he reached over and squeezed her hand. He flicked a glance at Amma, who was engaged in a conversation with Sign. "I'll watch out for her," he whispered.

Bree squeezed his hand in return. "Thank you," she whispered back to him.

Nanna must have overheard their brief interaction, and he shook his head in disbelief. "All the arguments the two of you got into when you were children," he said. "Who would have ever thought that you would get along so well as adults?"

"Sign and Jessira were the same way," Laya said. "When they were children, they fought like two cats in a sack."

Bree looked at the two women in surprise. "But you're so close now," she said. "I would have never guessed you didn't always get along."

"We didn't," Sign confirmed. "Growing up, I was always closest to my brother, Court."

"And I was closest to Lure," Jessira said. "We did everything together."

"And now it's you and Rukh who do everything together," Jaresh said.

Bree stared at him, perplexed and unsure as to what he meant. There were so many odd and lurid meanings to what he'd just said.

Jaresh must have replayed the words in his mind because he was reddened with embarrassment. "You know what I meant to say," he said.

The table laughed, while Sign reached over and playfully pushed his head before running her fingers through his hair.

Bree had known Jaresh and Sign had been seeing one another, but until tonight, she hadn't realized just how deep their feelings went. Sign was willing to stay in Ashoka because of Jaresh. Their love had come as a pleasant surprise to her, and she was glad for them.

Bree smiled at a sudden recognition. It seemed both her brothers found OutCaste women irresistible.

She chuckled over the notion before turning her attention back to the discussion at the table.

Rukh was in the midst of describing a conversation featuring the Bael, Li-Choke. "So Jessira tells him that we don't think of one another as brother and sister, and Choke asks us, 'then how do you think of one another?' It took him a moment to figure it out, and then he says in his most solemn surprised tone, 'oh'."

Once again, the table broke out in laughter.

"Well, I'm glad he found you, and that you saved Chak-Soon," Laya said. "I wouldn't be here if not for that Tigon." She smiled fondly.

Farn took her hand. "We both owe those two Chimeras quite a lot," he said.

"They aren't Chimeras," Rukh corrected. "Not anymore. They haven't decided on a name for themselves, but Chimeras isn't it."

"Speaking of the siege," Jaresh said. "Has anyone heard how much longer the Oasis is supposed to hold up?"

"We aren't to talk about the siege tonight," Nanna said. "That topic is banned. Tonight, we're a family having dinner. Nothing more. There will be no talk about death or destruction."

"In that case, to life, family, and love," Jaresh said raising a toast.

CHAPTER TWENTY-FIVE
FALLOW HOPES

Like the dullest of animals,
even after the rope has noosed 'round our necks,
still we struggle vainly for life.

—*Attribution unknown*

Lienna paused in Her work. On the far side of the city, something unusual was happening. Curiosity roused in Her mind, and She rose skyward, extending Her vision. There, along the shores of the Sickle Sea, a thousand boats had been launched into the water.

Lienna's gaze sharpened.

All of them were crammed with the stink of Ashoka's most repellent refuse: Humanity. It seemed the rats hoped to flee the sinking ship by boarding a different one.

Lienna smiled. Their hope was misplaced. She would drown them all, baptize them to death in the pure water.

"There are children aboard those vessels," Mother cried out. For once, She didn't sound distant and distracted but rather all too awake and aware. *"You can't kill them."*

"You must *kill them,"* Mistress Arisa proclaimed. *"Though young, still they are My enemies. Remember, Hume was once a child. You should use the power with which You were gifted and kill them before any of them reach adulthood and become a scourge."*

Lienna didn't need Mistress Arisa's advice. She knew what needed to be done. Child or otherwise, the only good Human was a dead Human. Her mind decided, Lienna disregarded Mother's exhortations and leapt forward. Those on the boats . . . they would all die, from oldest to youngest.

She approached with the speed of a tornado. The vessels disappeared from view. No doubt, the Humans had Blended, but it didn't matter. There was no chance for the ships to escape. She could sense the Humans scurrying about down below. Their Blends didn't hide their *Jivatmas.*

So long as Father wasn't down below, this would be an easy culling.

"Culling implies that You will allow some of them to live," Mistress Arisa said. *"Surely even You aren't so addled as to allow survivors."*

"None will live," Lienna said. *"Now be silent!"*

Needles of pain stabbed Lienna's mind, but She threw them off. It was something She found Herself able to do more and more often, but each instance still filled Her with a thrill. Although Lienna didn't have enough children to altogether banish Mistress from Her mind, there were enough for Her to best Her fearsome, false goddess.

"You grow bold, Girl," Mistress Arisa said in a silky, deadly voice. *"Be cautious of Your arrogance lest it be Your downfall."*

Lienna secretly sneered at Mistress Arisa. Her opinions no longer mattered, if they ever had. However, in this one instance— what to do with the Humans and their ships—She and Mistress were in agreement.

"Set aside this wicked plan," Mother implored. *"Your madness need not drive You to such evil."*

Lienna ignored Mother's unneeded advice. She had an idea on how best to destroy the ships. She would set them alight, burn them to broken spars, before finally swamping them.

As She descended, silvery beams of light lanced into Her. It wasn't painful, but there were so many of them. They hit Her from every ship. Ten thousand feathers had a weight, and Lienna slowed. More lances of light impacted Her.

Were these Bows? And what was it that surrounded the vessels? It tasted like an Oasis—a multitude of them, one for each ship

Lienna slowed to a halt in stunned disbelief. It was impossible. Only Father had the wherewithal to create such a construction. The Humans lacked the knowledge and Talent to do so. What had Father done? And Lienna knew this had to be His work. No one else could have accomplished such a thing.

She came to a halt above the ships and studied the patterns in the beams of light that the Humans sent against Her. They *were* Bows, pitiful and weak, but Bows, nonetheless. And if the vermin persisted with them, at some point, they might even become uncomfortable— which is why they would not. Lienna would destroy these Humans down below. They were different and dangerous. She would kill them all before they could spread their filthy knowledge.

"Those down below will be Your undoing, evil girl," Mother whispered. *"Now Your fate is sealed."*

Lienna paused once again in shock. In that moment, Mother had sounded just like Mistress Arisa.

"You should have never been born," Mother said. *"The world would have been a far better place if I had aborted You."*

"No!" Lienna cried out, outraged and horrified by Mother's

words. How could She say something so awful to Her daughter, Her only child? It was a savage cruelty. And was it not true that Lienna was a goddess? Mother should be proud of all She'd accomplished. Look at Her children, Her Baels—they were the finest of creatures, and they loved Her.

Her mind in turmoil, Lienna slowly became aware of the world once again when the lances of light, the feeble Bows finally began to make Her flinch. They had grown uncomfortable.

It was only then, when awareness had returned to Her, that She came to see that the children She'd left to hound Ashoka's final wall were being decimated. The Humans were attacking, and without Lienna to throw their boulders aside, Her children were being smashed into gory pulps. Worse, a large contingent of Human warriors had left Ashoka's safety and were carving the Chimeras into bloody tatters.

Lienna rumbled thunder. She had to save Her children. With so few of them still alive, She couldn't afford to allow too many to die. The Humans in their ships would have to be dealt with another time.

"Coward. You worm. Always afraid of shades and shadows," Mistress Arisa ridiculed.

"Quiet! I don't need Your distraction right now," Lienna demanded. For a wonder, Mistress actually listened and fell mute.

Lienna raced back to Ashoka, but even as She did, the Human warriors beyond their wall disengaged and raced back for their gate. She smiled grimly. They'd wandered too far from safety. They wouldn't make it back to the walls of their cursed city. Lienna would tear them into red meat and ribbons.

As She thundered toward the helpless Humans, a thousand beams of light lit up from Ashoka's walls, ripping into Her. Again with the feeble Bows! Once more, it wasn't painful, but it was distracting. Lienna screamed in frustration. These Humans also knew Talents they had no business knowing. It was forbidden.

"Your Father taught them," Mother whispered in a voice full of triumph. *"Though You murdered Me, You were unable to kill Him. He has prepared those down below. They are ready for Your evil. You can never defeat them. They will defeat You. And when Your life's grace grows thin, Your Father will come to end Your miserable existence."*

"You're letting the Humans escape," Mistress reminded Her. *"Was it Your intention, or merely another manifestation of Your incompetence?"*

Lienna didn't bother answering. Mother's final words chilled Her.

◆

The ships were two days gone from Ashoka. At first, it hadn't seemed likely that they would survive since, immediately upon their launch, the Sorrow Bringer had charged after the vessels. It was obvious what She would do, but thankfully, the Queen had turned away. The combination of the Bows thrown up by those on the boats and the city's attack on Her Plague must have dissuaded Suwraith's pursuit of the ships.

Whatever the reason, Rukh was grateful. The Maharajs had escaped. Even if the end result meant that the Queen was now perched near the Inner Wall, protecting Her Chimeras as She slung stone after stone at the Oasis, Rukh was . . . well, he wasn't happy, but he was content.

Everyone who remained in the city knew that what would occur next was the best case out of a poor scenario. While they would still defend Ashoka until the last, they knew that ultimately, the city would fall, the city would burn, and the Sorrow Bringer would triumph.

Rukh stood next to Jessira, and from atop the Inner Wall, they gazed out at Chimeras and the desolation of Ashoka's farms. The Murans claimed they could eventually return the soil to health, but they would likely never have the opportunity.

The green farms were prettier, Aia noted.

Rukh glanced at the Kesarin. She and Shon crouched nearby, having earlier decided to disregard any order telling them that they couldn't accompany Rukh and Jessira on the Inner Wall. Thrum felt the same way and was with Jaresh at a position near Kubar Gate.

Rukh noticed Jessira staring out at the ruined fields with a scowl on her face. "There are times I really wish we had taken one of those ships," she said.

"There are many times I also wish we had taken one of those ships," he replied.

"When you say 'we', you really mean 'me', as in just me and not us, don't you?" Jessira asked with a soft smile.

Rukh saw no reason to dissemble. "Yes."

She turned and ran her fingers through his hair. "When will you stop dreaming of the impossible?"

Rukh shrugged. "Probably as long as this Wall lasts," he answered.

Jessira arched an eyebrow. "Only until then?"

Rukh smiled in grim amusement. "Once the Wall falls, we'll likely be dead."

A stone slammed close. Chunks of it broke past the Oasis, and Rukh Shielded, automatically extending his protection to Aia. The Kesarin growled.

Jessira shook off a dusting of stones. "It looks like your wish might come true sooner than you think," she said.

Rukh couldn't help himself. He knew he should just keep quiet, but the words came out anyway. "You're the one who insisted on staying."

Jessira closed her eyes, looking as though she were searching for patience "He just can't stop talking about it," she muttered as she walked off.

I think Jessira is annoyed with you, Aia noted.

She is definitely annoyed with you, Shon confirmed. *She is fiery that way.* He tilted his head to the side. *How could you not know this as her mate?*

Yes. How could you not know this as my mate? Jessira snapped.

Rukh didn't respond, knowing nothing he said would help the situation. This was an old argument, one he knew he could never win, but it was also one he couldn't help but revisit. It was like a loose tooth that wouldn't come free.

I thought your Human was the finest of Humans, Shon said to Aia. *How then can he be so simple?*

He isn't simple, Aia said in outrage. *Rukh is simply looking after the health of those in his glaring. It isn't his fault that your Human is behaving stupidly.*

Rukh was no longer listening. His attention was caught by something else. A huge boulder was hurtling their way. It was massive, almost like a small hill. If it struck the Oasis, it would likely blast its way through and in so doing, annihilate the last of Ashoka's protection from the Sorrow Bringer.

A Spear would split the boulders a voice full of power and command intoned from the depths of Rukh's mind.

He frowned in puzzlement. The voice hadn't belonged to Aia, Shon, or Thrum. Who, then, had spoken? Unexpected knowledge came to him, and any questions he had disappeared. If a Fireball was mixed with a Bow, it would create a Spear. It was another new

Talent. He had no time to think on how such knowledge had come to him.

The huge boulder was tumbling toward the Inner Wall.

Rukh formed a Spear in his hand and thrust it upward. It extended out, a golden bar, further and further, smashing into the hill-sized stone. When the Spear struck, there was a flash and a crack, a high-pitched shriek. It was like bones snapping to shards. The large boulder split, breaking apart into smaller ones that still pounded against the Oasis.

For a moment, Rukh felt a sense of triumph. The Kesarins would have to teach this new Talent to everyone.

His triumph evaporated, and he watched in dismay as the remnant rocks from the large boulder impacted the Oasis. Where they struck, there were shimmers in the air, a ripple like a heat wave. Most of the massive stones were repelled. But one, the largest . . . when it struck the Oasis, it slowed and seemed to hold in place for an interminable instant. Then it was moving again. It thudded with a hollow reverberation against the Inner Wall. A snapping sound came then, like a whip wielded by a giant. It cracked with the force of thunder. Suddenly, more stones were hitting the wall, these from the Chimera siege engines.

The Oasis was down.

A cry arose from the Fan Lor Kum, a low-throated growl of triumph and bloodlust. It would have been a sound to chill the heart but not when compared to the gibbering screams of the Sorrow Bringer. She shrieked madness and conquest.

Rukh's mouth went dry. His stomach felt light. This was it. This was the end of Ashoka. The end of his home. Fear rose, but he quickly mastered it.

Frag it. There was nothing to do but get the work done. More rocks came, and Rukh Shielded. Another huge stone was hurled in their direction, and he formed another Spear, hammering the boulder into pebbles.

Rukh never saw the marble-sized rock that punched through his Shield and hit him in the head.

Jessira had no notion of how Rukh had broken apart the huge boulder that had threatened to flatten them. She didn't know how he had created the golden bar that had thrust up from his hands like a battering ram. She only wished he'd had the time to teach them this latest Talent. The battle for Ashoka's Inner Wall could have been won if he had been able to do so.

A Spear was what it was called, or at least she thought so. That's what Rukh had said anyway. A *Spear would hurl the boulders away.* Those had been the words he'd spoken in that deep, commanding voice, the one that didn't entirely sound like him.

Jessira would have wondered more about what Rukh had said and done, but her questions would have to wait. The Oasis was down. Even now the Chimeras were rushing forward, certain of their imminent victory, while high above, the Sorrow Bringer bellowed Her triumph. Ashoka's warriors along the Wall roared in response. The city wouldn't go down like a lamb before the lion.

Jessira added her shout of defiance to those of her brother warriors. She unsheathed her sword and Shielded, readying herself for what was to come. The Chimeras would attempt to forge a beach head on the Wall. They would try to press into the city under the protection of Suwraith.

Jessira's heart pounded.

It would be just like Stronghold.

She breathed shallow and fast.

Everyone would die.

Jessira' vision grew dim and dark. Sounds became dull. Jessira blinked heavily, trying to will her eyes to clear. She forced herself to take deeper breaths, steady her racing heart, master her panic.

I'm with you, Shon said, his voice comforting as he rubbed against her.

The world snapped back into roaring focus, and Jessira rubbed her Kesarin's shoulder in silent gratitude.

Another large boulder was descending toward them.

Again from Rukh's hands came the dense, golden bar. It was like light made solid. When it struck, the boulder disintegrated with a rapping crack. Stones of every size flew out in every direction, and Jessira hardened her Shield. A number of small rocks rattled against it. Shon yowled, and she extended her coverage, protecting the Kesarin. All along the line, a similar scene played out as the warriors defended themselves against the rocks and boulders that penetrated past the ruptured Oasis.

Jessira turned to Rukh just as a marble-sized stone plunged through his Shield. It impacted against his head with the sickening thud of smashed melon. Rukh went down, limp and lifeless.

For a moment, Jessira was sure he was dead. She rushed to his side, her heart drumming her terror.

Aia reached him first. *He lives,* she said.

Rukh groaned, muttering something unintelligible. "I'm all right," he managed to mumble as he sat up. He tried to stand and stumbled about before falling to the ground once again.

We have to move, Shon said, sounding frightened. *The Demon Wind approaches.*

Jessira glanced heavenward. There, silhouetted against the blue sky was Suwraith, coming on fast. From Her issued a scourge of lightning and a ripping gale. Hail the size of a robin's eggs fell.

Put him on my back, Aia urged. *I'll carry him to safety.*

Jessira quickly did as the Kesarin ordered.

Hold on, Aia told Rukh before she leapt away.

We have to go, Shon said, his voice urgent. *You can't run fast enough.*

He bent low, and Jessira immediately knew what he wanted. She clambered onto his back and settled herself behind his shoulders. She bent low and clutched his fur tight.

The wind rushed against her face as Shon jolted into a dead sprint.

———————●———————

Mother had already crushed the Oasis and hammered a hole in the Inner Wall. The Chimeras poured through the breach. As usual, howling Tigons led the way followed by hissing Braids, barking Ur-Fels, and hooting Balants. The Baels strode amongst their lesser brethren. Their bone-deep bellows carried above the clamor, and their glowing whips cracked out, giving special emphasis to their orders. The Baels were doing their best to slow the progress of the Chimeras, but Mother's warriors were a savage horde. They were an armed and armored tide of weapons and bloodlust that couldn't be held back forever.

Li-Choke noted all this as he led his Baels and Tigons to safety—or at least as much safety as could be found in doomed Ashoka. They were joined in their flight by many others, some of them warriors that Choke's Baels and Tigons had been serving alongside when the Oasis had fallen.

Like Choke, these warriors must have fled before Mother could reach them. Those who had not chosen the wisdom of retreat would already be dead by now. Just as She had at Stronghold, Mother had brought with Her a whipping sandstorm. With it, She had scoured all life from atop the Inner Wall. Any who had stayed to face Her might would be dust in the wind.

"Where we go?" Chak-Soon asked after they'd travelled a mile or so into the city. During their short retreat, he had somehow been able to maintain calm in the face of this unspeakable disaster.

Choke took a measure of courage from the Tigon. While Death would come for them all, the Bael hoped to face that dread gaze with grace and courage. "We'll go to the Shektan House Seat."

Before they could make their way west, a Smash of Chimeras surged out of a narrow lane. There was a lustful cry as the Chimeras took in the fleeing Humans, none of whom happened to be warriors. Balants were in the lead, and they paused long enough to hoot their wrath and smash their clubs against the ground. Their actions only served to clog the lane, and the Jut, the Bael commander, roared for them to press forward.

Choke was about to gesture his Baels and Tigons into a wedge in order to attack the Smash, but he realized a better option was available.

"Halt!" he shouted to the Balants.

The elephant-sized Chimeras shambled to a stop, while Choke led his warriors forward. The rest of the Smash curdled in the alley, and the Humans took the distraction to scatter and escape. Good.

The Jut in command managed to extricate himself past the Balants, and he strode forward, demanding to know why the Smash had come to a stop. He lashed out with his whip, striving to drive the

Balants on, but he pulled up short upon seeing Li-Choke and the other Baels and Tigons. "What is the meaning of this?" he demanded.

Choke merely rattled his rank feathers, the ones that proclaimed his status as a Vorsan. "The meaning of this is that you will offer proper respect to those of higher rank," he said.

The Jut drew himself to attention. "Yes, Vorsan," he said. "No offense was intended."

Choke dipped his head in acceptance of the Jut's apology. "Be cautious with your attitude next time," he advised. "It might not go as easily if you ever again speak to a superior officer with such disrespect."

"I will do as you say, Vorsan," the Jut replied, still standing ramrod straight.

"See that you do," Choke advised. He eyed the Jut through challenging eyes a moment longer. He wanted the younger Bael to fear him too much to even *think* of questioning Choke's order. "Pass on my commands to any others you encounter. They come directly from the SarpanKum," he said. "Mother wishes the pleasure of killing Ashoka Herself. As such, She orders that we are all to return to our places beyond the outskirts of the city's Inner Wall."

The Jut nodded. "Yes, Vorsan," he said. "But what of you?"

"Your role is to obey, not question!" Choke ordered. "We have our own mission. Now go!"

The Jut nodded again and spun on his hooves. He shouted for the Smash to turn about and return in the direction from which they had originally come.

Chak-Soon chuckled as the Jut led his Chimeras away. "Funny lie," the Tigon said. "But is not lie a sin?"

"If a lie saves a life, then how can it be a sin?" Choke asked, momentarily flummoxed that he was arguing philosophy with a Tigon while a city died around them. "Let's get to the Shektan House Seat," he advised while Chak-Soon pondered his words. "You can answer my question there."

———•———

Jaresh sprinted for the end of the alley. Through the warrens of fashionable Trell Rue he raced on, and on his heels chased a claw of Tigons and other Chimeras, all of them braying for his blood. While he ran, hopefully Sign and Rector could escape. Not for the first time, he cursed himself for volunteering to carry out such a stupid plan. Unfortunately, there was no one else who could do what needed to be done.

After the massive boulder had cracked open the Oasis like a hammer would a nut, the Chimeras had flooded forth in a mass of flesh and weapons. They'd been a rolling tide, seemingly unstoppable, claws out and vicious for the kill.

But the Ashokans had been the obdurate dam that held them back. With sword, arrow, Fireballs, and courage, they had held—at least briefly. At least until the Sorrow Bringer had come. She'd descended like Death, and with Her arrival, the Ashokans had been forced to abandon their positions. While most had escaped the Queen's abrading winds, some had not. Of those who hadn't, Jaresh reckoned nothing more than a few chips of bones remained.

Jaresh hoped Rukh and Jessira weren't amongst those who had fallen.

Your brother lives, Thrum said, his voice filled with anxiety. *Reach the end of the alley before the Nocats catch you.*

Jaresh took the Kesarin's advice and ran harder even as he

hardened his Shield. In times past, he would never have stood a chance at outrunning a Tigon, but with his Kumma Talents, he could do so—barely.

"Down!" someone shouted from ahead of him.

Jaresh hurled himself to the ground. From ahead of him came a volley of roaring Fireballs. They blew through the Tigons, leaving them nothing more than incinerated hunks of meat. A greasy smoke filled the narrow passage, and it carried the stench of burnt flesh and hair. Jaresh's ears rang, and he coughed.

Sign appeared before him. Dried blood coated one side of her face, while the other side was covered in soot. Her clothes were equally a mess. They were spattered with blood, dirt, and bits of gore. Her hair had come loose from its tie and haloed around her head in a riot of wild, unkempt strands.

Jaresh knew he looked just as torn up. He certainly felt it, anyway. During the short battle atop the Inner Wall, one of his eyes had been blackened, and he'd suffered a gash across the chest. The cut had stopped bleeding, but it still caused him to flinch in pain with certain movements. Running down the alley had been brutal.

Thrum shouldered past Sign and rubbed his head against Jaresh. *You shouldn't have taken such risks,* the Kesarin said, sounding unhappy.

Sign hauled Jaresh to his feet. He swayed and would have tipped over if Thrum hadn't nosed him upright. Sign looked at him with concern. "Are you all right?" she asked.

"I'll be fine," Jaresh replied. They didn't have time for Sign to bother with Healing him. The Chims would be on them at any moment.

Sign nodded acceptance. "Rector's fine," she said. "A Shiyen physician Healed the wound to his leg."

"What about us?" Jaresh asked. "What are our orders?" He noticed the warriors with Sign were dispersing without any particular organization.

"We have none," Sign answered. "The Sorrow Bringer is moving into the city. She's circling about like She's looking for something."

"Or someone," Jaresh said, thinking of Rukh. The Queen had called him 'Linder Val Maharj' or something like that the last time She had faced him. According to Rukh, it was the name of the First Father; the name of Suwraith's Nanna.

"Whatever the reason, She hasn't done much damage yet, but the same can't be said of the Chimeras. The wide streets are doing nothing to slow them down. And every time we stop to fight them, Suwraith arrives and kills anyone who battles the Chims." Her fists clenched. "It's hopeless. We've been released . . ."

"To be with our families at the end?" Jaresh whispered.

Sign nodded, tears filled her eyes. "It's just like Stronghold."

Aia and Shon are taking their Humans to the home of your parents, Thrum said.

A thunderous boom echoed across the city. Another.

Thrum's ears wilted, and he shrank down in fear.

Jaresh reached for the Kesarin and stroked his shoulder, offering comfort as he turned to the sound. There, hovering above the city was Suwraith. She hurled bolts of lightning. Fires sprung up wherever they touched. They blazed to life with a fiery rush.

"The Queen," Sign explained. "She's tearing the city apart."

Jaresh continued to stare, heartbroken as he heard the cries of pain and fear from people running for their lives.

"We have to go," Sign said, taking his hand and tugging him forward. "Before the Chims cut us off. Rector said he'd meet us at the Shektan House Seat."

"He isn't going to his own family?" Jaresh asked in surprise.

"He said he owes too much to Dar'El. He said he's honor bound to defend him and his family."

Jaresh shook his head in bemused admiration. No matter what, Rector Bryce clung to his honor like a dog did its last bone.

"Let's go," he said.

———•———

Aia hated the risks Rukh took. Her Human was the best of his kind, but it didn't mean he should endanger himself against a creature like the Demon Wind. Against the Queen, no victory was possible. It was better to simply flee from Her baleful gaze and pray something else grabbed Her attention.

It was a wisdom Aia wished Rukh would learn. She doubted it would occur to him, not in the short time they likely had left. Instead, Rukh would rail on against the Queen, fight Her to the end. Aia only hoped that when he fell—and she would grieve terribly when he did—she would have a chance to escape the Demon Wind's wrath.

She wasn't sure such would be the case. Fires blazed throughout the city and battles raged. The crackling sounds of buildings burning filled the air as smoke roiled skyward. It was a black cloud intermixed with the black ravens drawn by the dying. An echoing boom reached Aia. Another one came, and she flinched.

Suwraith's blowing apart some buildings, Rukh said. For minutes after he'd been struck by the stone, he'd been unable to form a coherent sentence. That confusion seemed to be getting better.

I wish we were home amongst our family, Shon whimpered.

Aia noticed her brother settle down under Jessira's gentle touch. It was a touching sight, but one she couldn't help but regret, at least somewhat. If she'd never approached Rukh, she and her brothers wouldn't be in this dire situation. As Shon had said, they would have been at home amongst their family. Safe with no Human to bind them to a path no Kesarin would have ever otherwise chosen. It would have left Aia free of all attachments that could hurt.

And of any attachment that taught of purpose, service, and sacrifice. She, Shon, and Thrum had learned so much from their time with their Humans. Despite the terrible dangers they'd faced and were facing, Aia realized she wouldn't have it any other way.

Aia purred to Rukh, who was holding tight to her fur. She doubted he understood what she was trying to say, but as he so often did, he surprised her with his insight.

I love you, too, Aia, he said, *and I always will.*

Shon says that Thrum, Jaresh, and Sign are heading for the House Seat, Jessira said.

Aia felt Rukh's nod of acknowledgment against her fur. *Take us home,* he said.

CHAPTER TWENTY-SIX
REVELATIONS AND LOSSES

In the deepest hour of need, search for the helping hand,
the soothing embrace, and the forgiving voice. Search for the Lord's Love.

—The Book of All Souls

Rukh's head still ached but the deep-seated throb that made it difficult for him to walk or even see clearly was down to a dull pounding. It was a pain he could ignore—just as he could ignore the blood caked in his eyelashes and on his face, or the small cuts and scrapes on his hands and clothes.

However, he couldn't ignore what was happening to his city. Ashoka burned. Flames engulfed the city as the Sorrow Bringer lashed lightning and set entire districts ablaze. Rukh didn't want to imagine what was happening to those trapped within those areas. Smoke billowed, lofting the scent of burnt wood and flesh. A high-pitched wail came every now and then as the Queen descended to the ground with Her clawing winds.

The fires hadn't yet reached Jubilee Hills, and Rukh hoped Jaresh might make it home so they could see one another a final time. He also hoped his parents were still there to greet them.

They reached the unguarded gatehouse to the Shektan House Seat, and Rukh dismounted Aia. He took a moment to settle his balance—his legs weren't entirely under him—before turning to his Kesarin. *You and Shon should leave,* he said.

Aia blinked. *You no longer wish me in your life?* she asked.

Rukh rubbed his Kesarin between her eyes, one of the places he knew she liked best and swallowed a lump in his throat. Tears filled his vision, and he did his best to blink them away. Aia shouldn't be here. She should be free, back in the Hunters Flats, amongst their own kind. She shouldn't die in Ashoka, not on his account.

I love you, he said. *You know that. But you can't stay. You need to go. Run to safety.*

Aia rubbed her head against his. *I will leave when I know all hope is lost. I will take my brothers with me only then.*

You should leave now, Rukh urged.

Only when all hope is lost, Aia insisted. *Shon feels the same way.*

Rukh hugged Aia. It was the best he could hope for from his stubborn Kesarin.

A deep-voiced hail came to him. "Hold the gate." Striding up the road came Li-Choke and his band of Baels and Tigons. Directly on their heels were Rector, Jaresh, Sign, and Thrum.

Rukh exhaled in relief upon sighting his brother. He pulled him into a brief hug as soon as Jaresh had pulled up and dismounted Thrum. "It's good to see you again," Rukh said.

"Don't get used to it," Jaresh said, managing a strained smile. "We're all likely to be dead in a few hours or even a few minutes from now."

Rukh lightly punched Jaresh's shoulder. "Always the optimist," he said. "Farn could take lessons from you."

"Let me Heal your wounds," Sign said, taking ahold of Rukh's brother. "It's not just his black eye. He's got a wound to the chest also."

"We thought we could stand with your family in these final moments of our lives," Li-Choke said, striding up to join them. "It has been you and yours who were the first to see past prejudice and accept what has always been in our hearts."

"We'd be honored," Rukh said, clasping the Bael's forearm. He did the same with Chak-Soon.

"I will stand with your parents as well," Rector said.

Rukh nodded acceptance. Whatever rationale Rector had for coming to the House Seat rather than going to be with his own family was his own.

As soon as everyone was inside, they closed the gate and barred it as best they could.

The grounds were strangely hushed and empty in comparison to the tumult without. A single swinging barn door was the only lonely sound. Even the birds were quiet. It was an edgy, anticipatory stillness that filled the air, a pregnant pause as if the horrors going on in the rest of the city were simply biding their time before they consumed the House Seat.

Rukh shivered.

Jessira looked his way, a question in her eyes.

"Just nerves," he explained.

She took his hand in hers and gave it a squeeze. "How long is the journey between Ashoka and Defiance?"

"If the weather doesn't turn, about a week."

"Then we have to hope it takes the Queen another three days to finish Ashoka."

"So the ships can reach Defiance before She remembers to go after them," Rukh said, picking up on Jessira's thoughts. "I sure hope they have those three days."

"I hope so as well," she answered.

They trudged hand in hand toward the House Seat when Jessira asked a question that Rukh had been struggling with ever since the Inner Wall had fallen.

"What did you use to break apart that boulder? Is it called a Spear?" she asked.

Rukh looked her way in surprise. "How did you know?"

"Because you said it," Jessira answered. "You said '*A Spear would split the boulders*'. But you didn't say it in your own voice."

Rukh recalled thinking those thoughts, but he hadn't realized he'd spoken them aloud. He frowned when he took in the rest of Jessira's words. "What do you mean it wasn't my voice?"

"Over the past few weeks, you'll say something, but it isn't your voice. It's deeper and the inflections and pronunciations are different, more formal."

"How often does this happen?"

"Not often," Jessira replied. "Only a handful of times."

"I don't know what it means," Rukh said, although the more he thought about the voice, the more familiar it seemed to him.

Jessira quirked a smile. "Don't worry about it," she advised. "None of it matters anymore."

She rested her head on his shoulder, and they walked the rest of the way in silence.

⸻ • ⸻

Jessira followed Rukh into the House Seat while the Chimeras and Kesarins remained outside, retreating to the grounds out back where the battle with Hal'El had so recently occurred.

Jessira startled at how little time had passed since that terrible event. So much had happened since then. Had it really taken place less than two weeks ago? Surely more days had passed than a mere twelve or so. It seemed impossible, but it was true.

Time truly was a wriggling eel, and Jessira wished she could grasp hold of that slippery, sinuous creature and hold it frozen in place, keep Ashoka's death from coming to pass.

Her thoughts turned to other matters as Rukh took them deeper into the House Seat. The soundlessness inside was oppressive with no signs to indicate that the home was occupied. No lights lit the rooms. No conversations or sensations marred the perfect stillness. The servants and their chatty conversations. The delicious foods perfected by Cook Heltin in her kitchen. All were gone now, and their absence left a vacuum, a hollow. The dead might have turned the Shektan House Seat into a mausoleum for all the life to be sensed within it.

Jessira did her best to set aside her macabre thoughts. She didn't want the last moments of her life filled with a gloaming outlook.

Her mind cleared when Rukh brought them to Dar'El's study, and they found his parents waiting within.

Jessira smiled in real joy. Two more people she loved yet lived. Dar'El stood behind his desk and turned to face them as they entered. One of his arms hung in a sling, and he had reached for his sheathed sword when the door opened before relaxing when he saw who it was. Beside him, Satha sat in her wheeled chair. A wool throw lay upon her lap. Even in the heat of summer, she got cold easily.

"Thank Devesh you are all still alive," Dar'El said, breaking into a grateful smile as he came around the desk.

"As Jaresh would say, 'don't get used to it. We'll all likely be dead not too long from now,'" Rukh said with an answering smile. "Or something like that."

"Our optimistic son and his sunny disposition," Satha said with a chuckle.

"Laugh if you like, but someone has to be the voice of reason," Jaresh stated.

"And that someone is on a ship to Defiance," Rukh said. "Her name is Bree."

Dar'El laughed, and the family drew close together, sharing words and holding tight to one another. Sign was also pulled into the embrace.

"Had Devesh allowed, you would have been our daughter," Satha said to Jessira's cousin. "Marriage vows might not have been exchanged, but the heart has already spoken them."

Only Rector Bryce stood silent and apart, and Jessira's heart went out to him.

"Why are you here, Rector?" Dar'El asked. "You should go and be with your family."

"I owe a debt to you and yours. It supersedes my own needs," Rector replied. He drew himself up to attention.

Dar'El circled past his family and walked to Rector, who was rendered speechless a moment later when Dar'El drew him into a warm hug. "In this last hour of our lives, all trespasses are long since forgiven," Dar'El said.

Rukh took Jessira's hand, and together, they approached the man who had once caused them so much grief. "All debts were long since forgiven," Rukh said, clasping Rector's forearm.

Jessira slipped her hand from Rukh's and hugged Rector. "There is no need to be here," she said. "Go home. Be with those you love best."

Rector seemed to deflate as he exhaled heavily. He nodded sharply. "Thank you," he said.

"Devesh's blessings go with you," Satha said as Rector prepared to leave.

Nobeasts are at the gates, Shon said. *They're all over the streets. Li-Choke says the Demon Wind recognized him and called out for Her creatures to kill him and all those with him.* Thunder, likely from the Queen's lightning, and a gale-force howl served to emphasize Shon's final point.

Jessira sighed. "Rector," she called out to him. "Shon says that the Chimeras control the streets beyond the gate. He also says the Queen is close by. You won't make it back to your family. You should stay with us."

Rector's visage fell into an expression of regret.

"I'm sorry," Jessira said softly.

Rector waved aside her words. His eyes were clenched shut, either in regret or sorrow or both. A moment later he had control of his emotions, and he straightened up and took a deep breath.

"We would be grateful if you fought alongside us," Dar'El offered. "As it is said: in a Trial, all warriors are brothers."

"I would be honored," Rector said as he clasped forearms with Dar'El.

The Demon Wind hovers nearby, Aia said. Her voice had been pitched to be heard by Jessira as well as Rukh.

"I can't stay here inside while Aia fights alone out there," Rukh announced, gesturing to the outside grounds. "She'll die trying to protect me. I won't have it."

Jessira felt the same way about Shon, and so did Jaresh about Thrum.

"Inside or out, in the end, none of it will matter," Dar'El said with a shake of his head.

"I can't go outside," Satha said. She gestured to the wheeled chair. "I'll only get in the way."

"Then I'll stay with you," Dar'El declared.

"No," Satha said. "Go outside. Be with our sons. Protect them. Protect me."

Dar'El hesitated.

"Go," Satha urged. "You will always have my love no matter what happens next."

Dar'El kissed her. "And you will always have mine."

———————◦———————

There were many times when Rector wished his sense of honor and duty didn't overcome his good sense. Why in all the unholy hells had he come to the Shektan House Seat? He should have been at the home of his parents, surrounded by those he loved and who, in turn, loved him. Instead, as he'd so often done, he'd chosen the path of supposed righteousness. It was a cold comfort to know his honor was maintained. What good was maintaining dharma if he never again saw those he cared for most, or if they died without him ever able to tell them how much he loved them one last time?

He did his best to ignore his frustration as he waited outside the Shektan House Seat with the others—all but Satha, of course, who remained behind in the study. Crippled as she was, there was nothing she could do to aid them.

Rector glanced at the burned shrubs and ground. The skies above, while sunny in the morning, had turned stormy in the early afternoon. Or maybe it was just the mix of soot and smoke that dimmed the sun. Whatever the reason, Ashoka's demise could be seen in the fires raging throughout the city and heard in the cries of her people as they died by flame or sword. The bitter smell of ash filled the air, and thunder rumbled continuously.

All the desecration was focused on a purple cloud hovering nearby. It moved against the winds. The Sorrow Bringer. Never in Rector's life had he hoped or expected to see the demon who had plagued Humanity for so many centuries. He prayed fervently that Devesh would soon see Her dead.

"Should we form a Quad?" Jaresh asked.

"Not with me," Jessira vowed. "I want to be aware and alive when the end comes. I want to face whatever happens next with all my faculties intact."

Rector found himself in agreement.

"I feel the same way," Dar'El announced a beat later.

Sign shook her head to Jaresh's question.

Jaresh shrugged.

"How should we position ourselves?" Rector asked.

Surprisingly, it was Rukh rather than Dar'El who answered. He pointed to the Baels and Tigons. "They'll protect our flanks while we hold the center along with the Kesarins."

After he spoke, the calico-colored cat—Aia—rubbed her head against Rukh's. The tawny-coated Kesarin—the one called Shon—did the same to Jessira, while Jaresh rubbed the chin of the russet one—Thrum.

"We don't know if the Chims will actually enter the grounds," Sign said.

"Thrum says they just did," Jaresh replied.

Rector didn't need the Kesarin's input to tell him so. Already he could hear a rising tide of barks, growls, and hisses closing fast on their position.

"Get ready," Rukh said.

"When they come, let me try to talk to them first," said the Bael who led the Chimeras. Li-Choke was his name. "I may be able to convince them that you are Mother's servants. They may pass us by."

Rector privately doubted any such miracle would save them, but maybe for once, luck would be on their side. A moment later, he snorted in derision. When had luck ever been with them? Never. And never it would always be.

Rector loosened his sword and conducted *Jivatma*. It swirled in his mind, a mirrored, shimmering pool. His senses heightened. He twitched, ready to race into the eye-blurring motion for which his Caste was known.

"Don't waste your *Jivatma* on a Blend," Rukh advised. "With all the emotions we're feeling, the Chims will be able to see right through them."

Just then, the Chimeras poured around the corner of the house. All kinds of them; Ur-Fels, Braids, Tigons, Balants, and Baels. There were several hundred: a wide grouping of armor, swords, and hatred. Rector set aside all fear when he saw them. Their howls of rage didn't touch him. He stepped forward, ready and willing.

Li-Choke's basso roar lifted above the tumult. "Leave these Humans be," he shouted. His chained whip caught fire. He cracked it. "Mother has placed them under Her protection."

His words were contradicted a moment later when there screeched a vast cry from the storm-wracked sky. It was the Sorrow Bringer. "Kill them all!" She commanded. "Kill every Human you find!" Her voice boomed to all the corners of Ashoka. It was likely a general order to all Her warriors, and the Chims howled in response to Her command. They spurred forward.

Rector took an instant to center himself, to let go of all his regrets and emotions. When he was ready, he filled his hands with Fireballs. He threw them, as swiftly as he could, as many as he could before the Chims reached them. Rukh and the others did the same.

Shouts of triumph turned to cries of dismay and pain as Chims caught fire. Dozens of them died, but even more pressed on. There was no further room for Fireballs, and Rector drew his sword and Shielded.

He parried a thrust. His return cut took off a Tigon's arm. Blood spurted, blinding the Ur-Fel next to the cat. A horizontal slash beheaded the dog-like Chim. A hissing Braid stepped forward. Three of them. Rector dodged a wide swing from one, slipped a thrust from another, and parried a slash. He followed the motion down to the Braid's wrists and cut off both of the snake-like Chim's hands. Rector stepped behind the creature, using the beast as another shield. He kicked it onto the blade of one of its fellows. A thrust and slash and the other two were down.

A hammer blow from behind lifted him off his feet and hurled him to the ground. Rector rolled over with a groan. His Shield had held, but a Balant stood above him. The baboon-like Chim's club was ready to smash him to a pulp, but before the creature could do so, Rukh's Kesarin ripped open the creature's ankles. In the time it took for the Balant to topple, Rector regained his feet. A quick slice across the throat, and the Chim was finished.

Rector scowled and spit blood. He'd bitten his tongue. Fragging Chims.

He roared, and four Tigons took up his challenge. Rector smiled grimly. The fools were bunched up. A Fireball consumed them. Rector shouted defiance again. This time it was five Ur-Fels who answered his call. Rector moved into motion, sliding past slashes and slices. His response always found a home, hacking off legs, arms, and heads.

More Chims came at him, more than he could defend against.

He took blows on his Shield. It bent beneath the strikes but didn't break. Distance was needed. Rector leapt straight up, fifteen feet in the air, even clearing the heads of the Balants. However, when he landed, the fragging Chims were still waiting for him. Rector moved as swiftly as he could, slashing, punching, and kicking. Chims fell all around him, but more came. Always more came.

Rector's Shield buckled. A cut opened on his leg. Another on his arm. On his chest. Still he fought on, remaining in the fray. He firmed his Shield, but his Well was emptying. His *Jivatma* was growing thin. Rector slowed and took more blows. A club to the chest from a Balant crunched into his ribs. Rector felt a number of them break. One went straight into a lung.

He flew through the air and crashed to the ground, unable to breathe. Rector never felt the swords that stabbed into him, over and over again. His mind was elsewhere. A singing light beckoned. It promised to wash away all his repentances, sorrows, and sins. It promised to make pure his *Jivatma*. It promised to take him home.

Rector breathed his last as a singing light took him.

* * *

The Chims would arrive at any moment, and Jaresh worried for his nanna. With only one good arm, and that one his off one, he would have trouble defending himself.

I will protect him, Thrum promised.

Jaresh rubbed the Kesarin's sturdy shoulder in gratitude. *Thank you,* he said. *Just make sure you stay alive. We won't survive them for very long. I want you to run as soon as you know we can't hold them off.*

I could carry you. Sign also. We could flee before they reach us.

*And go where? The Queen can see through a Blend. No matter where we *try to hide, She would find us. She'd kill us and anyone She finds aiding us,** Jaresh answered. **Besides, for now, the Queen cares nothing about the Kesarins. That will change in an instant if She ever discovers one of you helping a Human. Your kind might face extermination, just like Humanity.**

Thrum settled down with an unhappy growl.

Sign glanced his way, an unspoken question in her eyes, and he relayed the conversation he'd had with the Kesarin.

The Nobeasts have entered the grounds, Thrum said.

Jaresh passed on the Kesarin's announcement to everyone else and drew *Jivatma*. His thoughts, previously filled with turmoil, cleared with Lucency. Fear couldn't touch him. His senses heightened. He grew heady with the power that came from his Kumma Talents. He was ready.

Moments later, the Chimeras were there. They surged forward, spurred on by the vile voice of the Queen. She instructed Her Chims to kill everyone they found, and the battle was joined.

Jaresh and Sign fired Fireballs that screamed through the air and detonated into the Chimeras. Many of Suwraith's creatures died, but even more pushed on. Soon, swords were needed, and Jaresh breathed a prayer before drawing his weapon. At his side, Sign was ready to go, too.

The first Chims reached them. As usual, they were Tigons. They raced forward, but in their unthinking rage, some of them cast aside their weapons before leaping into the fray.

Jaresh faced off against one of the cat-like Chimeras. The Tigon roared challenge and swung wildly. Jaresh dropped below the slash aimed at his head. His return blow disemboweled the creature. Another Tigon stepped forward. This one died of a thrust to the heart. Jaresh kneecapped a third Tigon and cleaved an arm. He left the creature to bleed out.

Meanwhile, Sign defended against a large nest of Ur-Fels, and Jaresh moved to protect her. They fought back-to-back, punching, kicking, and cutting. Both were soon covered in unspeakable gore. All around them was chaos.

One of the dog-like Chims snapped at Jaresh's ankles. A kick to the snout threw that one back. Another tried to take a chunk from his calf. Jaresh was able to bring his sword around and slash the creature across the shoulders, nearly decapitating him. Jaresh parried an overhand blow from another Ur-Fel, and his parry ripped across the beast's chest. The Chim fell back with a barking wail. Another took the creature's place and launched a sword strike that Jaresh could neither evade nor block. It tolled against his Shield. Jaresh almost fell to a knee when the blow landed. He steadied himself and countered. The Ur-Fel parried. Jaresh feinted at the beast's head and delivered a thrust to the midsection. The Ur-Fel fell away with a hoarse cry, but here came another. A sword bit through his Shield, and Jaresh took a cut to his stomach. It was shallow, and he paid it no attention. He feinted low and came up high, stabbing the Ur-Fel in the eye and then through the armpit and into the heart.

There came the briefest of pauses when Jaresh realized that the nest was annihilated. He had enough time to realize that he was covered in blood, but then the interlude was over. A pair of Balants reared above them.

Jaresh silently cursed. This would be difficult.

Suddenly, one of the beasts thudded to the ground. Thrum had hamstrung the creature, and Sign quickly finished him off. The other one gawked in surprise. It was the opening Jaresh needed. He drew *Jivatma* and leaped into the air. The Balant had enough time to hoot in alarmed surprise before Jaresh slid three feet of matte-black spidergrass sword through the Chim's throat. The Balant gave a burbling cry and managed to smack Jaresh to the ground before dying.

Jaresh slammed hard and blacked out for a moment. He came back to awareness and shook his head, trying to restore his senses. Slowly, unsteadily, he levered his way back to his feet and swayed.

Before him, a Bael loomed large. His whip glowed, and his trident was ready, but he seemed reluctant to fight. "Forgive me," he said before thrusting out with his trident. It was a half-hearted strike, but, in his current state, it was also one that Jaresh was barely able to avoid.

Sign was there, though. She arrowed forward, her sword leveled and straight. She took the Bael in the heart, and the horned creature stiffened before slumping over.

Sign ripped her sword clear and never noticed the two Braids slither into place behind her.

Even through his Lucency, Jaresh knew fear. He cried out a warning, and thankfully, Sign heard. She reacted quickly but not quickly enough. Though she partially blocked one Braid's strike, it still took her in the shoulder. She grunted in pain. Sign parried another slash aimed at her head and beat back one of the Braids even as she took a deep cut to her calf. Her leg almost buckled, but she held firm. She slid past a thrust, and her answering slash took the Chim in the flank. The creature hissed in pain before falling.

Jaresh, his balance restored, killed the other Braid, hammering his sword through the creature's back and out through its chest.

With the Chim's death, Sign hunched over at the waist and groaned. She had no time to rest, though. Another nest of Ur-Fels came at them, along with a claw of Tigons who shouldered aside their smaller brethren and beat their chests in triumph.

Jaresh scowled. The fragging Chims were certain they had found an easy victory. They'd pay for their misjudgment. Jaresh grinned at the Tigons, baring his teeth as he gestured them forward.

They accepted his wordless invitation.

Jaresh ducked a hard swing. He flowed forward, rolling to his feet and sliced upward. A Tigon was bisected from crotch-to-shoulder. Jaresh parried a strike before ducking and rolling once again. When he rose up, he faced an unarmed Tigon. He took this one's arm at the elbow. The creature keened in pain and spun about, entangling two others of its kind. Jaresh used the distraction to kill both of the encumbered Tigons: a thrust to the chest and a near-decapitating blow to the neck.

Sign had taken another Tigon unawares through the back, and Jaresh moved back to her side. Together, they faced the horde of Chimeras.

———— • ————

Behind you, Aia warned.

Rukh spun about. Sneaking up on him had been a trap of Braids and nest of Ur-Fels. *I can handle them,* Rukh said. *Just cover my back.*

Always, Aia said.

Rukh drew from his Well. He quickened his movements, kept his Shield in place, but left it only strong enough to deflect the weakest of blows. It was all he'd need. Rukh rushed the Braids and Ur-Fels, but just before coming in contact with them, he leapt up and fired a Fireball straight into their midst. At least five were instantly incinerated. Rukh landed in the center of the Chim's confused, pain-filled cries.

Two quick slashes resulted in a dead Braid and a dead Ur-Fel.

Rukh parried a blow, ducked a swing, and kicked in an Ur-Fel's chest, knocking it into its fellows.

He easily swayed away from a Braid's downward strike. A flick of the wrist and a slight lean forward brought his sword angling across the Chim's throat. Another flick of his wrist splattered blood into the eyes of an onrushing Ur-Fel. He grabbed that one by the throat and threw it against two Braids. They all fell to the ground, but before they could recover, Rukh was there. A slash, a downward slice, and a thrust, and they were done.

From the twelve who had come against him, only two Ur-Fels remained. Rukh slid between them and waited what seemed an interminable instant. The Chims barked anger and furiously stabbed at him. But in their frenzy to see him dead, their swords became entangled. Rukh slid aside. He kicked one Ur-Fel onto the other one's sword and decapitated the final one.

Rukh looked about for another foe. He had plenty of fight left.

Aia roared out as a Tigon stabbed at her flank. She spun about. Her claws, already dripping blood, ripped through the Tigon's throat. She kicked back, tearing trenches into the thigh of a Balant. The beast bellowed but didn't fall.

Rukh leapt into the air. He kicked the Balant in the ear, distracting the creature. As the Chim turned to face him, Aia bit the dull creature through his neck.

There was moment of quiet around Rukh and Aia, and he took the brief break to glance around. Jessira and Shon fought together. The wall of corpses about them demonstrated their efficient skill. Thrum defended Nanna, but they were besieged on all sides. Li-Choke and his Chimeras were barely holding their own. And Jaresh and Sign faced a formidable force of Tigons.

Nobeasts taste like gazelle, Aia noted as she savaged an Ur-Fel.

Despite the desperate nature of their situation, Rukh couldn't help but smile at her observation. *You think everything tastes like gazelle.*

Just then, any humor Rukh felt was washed away when his nanna shouted in pain. He'd taken a deep wound to his chest. Blood flooded down Nanna's shirt. It looked to be a mortal injury.

Rukh roared forward, trying to fight his way to his nanna's side, but there were too many Chims. They battled him, bottled him up with numbers too great to overcome.

Moments later, Rector fell beneath a mass of Chims. Rukh watched helplessly, too far away to be of assistance. The Chims surrounding Rector savaged him. Their swords rose and fell, rose and fell. And when they stepped aside, Rector was dead.

Rukh breathed a prayer for the fallen warrior. Strange how easily he'd fallen into the pattern of prayer. In the past few years, it had become so much a part of his life that he sometimes even believed that Devesh actually heard what he had to say.

In his mind, came a thought. *The Lord listens, but His answers are not easily understood.*

What are you talking about? Aia asked.

Rukh shook his head, uncertain where the idea had come from, or why he would have spoken such a notion to his Kesarin. He needed to focus on the battle at hand.

"Destroy them all," a voice from above commanded to all the Chimeras throughout Ashoka. It was Suwraith. *"Let none of them live."*

Her voice created a pause in the fighting as all stared upward.

There, the Queen hovered at a distance, triumphant and unstoppable.

Lienna, a voice within Rukh growled. *Devesh save me, but I cannot forgive what She has become or what She has done.*

Suwraith's mad howl of victory carried across the smoke-stained heavens. From Her madly gyrating storm cloud came a sheaf of lightning. More fires roared to life throughout Ashoka. It was early afternoon, but the sun stood hidden behind the darkness of smoke and the wings of ravens. The world felt like twilight. Thousands were dying. It was as if this was the final day for all of Arisa, as if these were the last hours before death took the entire world.

Despair clawed at Rukh's heart. Never had he felt so powerless, so impotent. There was nothing he could do to stop the carnage. *Devesh see us safe in the life to come*, Rukh prayed.

There is a way to see them safe, a voice said from within the depths of Rukh's mind. It was a deep, powerful voice, one used to obedience.

Rukh frowned. That voice . . . he recognized it. He'd heard it before. He knew it.

But how? And was it even real? Maybe his new Talents or whatever was the source of them was driving him mad? He barked laughter.

"You aren't going mad," the voice said. *"When My Daughter tried to murder Me with Her Knife, part of My Jivatma was thrust into Her being. The rest I preserved within* The Book of First Movement. *With you, the first who was worthy enough to read My last testament, I was finally able to restore My Jivatma, My essence, My soul so that it would reside entirely within you."*

Rukh gaped. This conversation couldn't be happening. Were the last moments of his life to be filled with madness?

"I thought we already established that you aren't mad," the voice said in reproof. *"It is My Daughter who is insane."*

Rukh hesitated. *"Who are You?"* he asked, the words an inadequate expression of his confusion.

"You know Me," the voice answered. *"You witnessed the last moments of My life. Think."*

Rukh's mystification cleared, but the answer that came to him rocked him back on his feet. The voice belonged to the First Father. Rukh thought the First Father was lurking about in his mind? He barked laughter once more. It was an idea too bizarre, too ludicrous, too irrational to be anything but insane. It simply couldn't be true.

"And yet it is true" the voice confirmed. *"I am Linder Val Maharj. When you read The Book and relived My last moments, I was slowly able to leave Lienna's essence and become part of yours. In that time, I've watched and waited, wanting to make sure You truly were worthy of my knowledge."*

"You're why I suddenly have all these new Talents," Rukh said more than asked.

"Yes," Linder said. *"Those Talents are part of My legacy, part of the burdens you need to take up. I wish it were otherwise, but life often isn't as we wish."* His voice throbbed regret. *"Therefore, I leave you with another of My gifts."*

A flash of instruction came to Rukh. It was knowledge that made him want to weep. *"There isn't any other way?"* he asked. Aia might understand what he had to do, but Jessira would never forgive him.

"Not for the likes of us," Linder answered softly, sympathetically. *"It is what it means to serve."*

Rukh blinked back tears as he drew out the Withering Knife.

———◆◆———

Something was wrong. Something horrible was about to happen. It had nothing to do with the freely bleeding cuts that Jessira had taken to both her arms. Nor did it have anything to do with the ache in her ribs from when a Tigon had tried to squeeze the life out of her. Or the pain in her thigh from the glancing blow she'd taken from a

Balant's club. None of that was what had Jessira feeling such a sense of foreboding. It wasn't even the sight of Rector Bryce dying or seeing her cousin, Sign, nearly falling over from her wounds. It wasn't any of those things, not her mortal danger or the battle for survival in which she and Shon were engaged.

Her sudden terror stemmed from something happening to Rukh. Something momentous and awful.

Jessira looked to where she knew Rukh would be. She didn't have to search him out. Her sense of him always told her where he was. There he stood, frozen in place while Aia protected him.

Jessira called to Shon, and together they fought to reach his side.

A Tigon tried to bar her passage. Jessira blocked a strike aimed at her midsection. She kicked the Tigon in the jaw. His head snapped back, and he bit through his own tongue. Shon eviscerated him. Four Braids hissed as they stepped up. They tried to evade Shon, but her Kesarin refused to be denied. He was too fast for the snake-like Chims. They were quickly savaged.

Three Ur-Fels barked opposition.

Jessira faced off against them. She sidestepped a diagonal slash. Her return blow took the Chim in the chest, nearly hewing the beast in half. Another tried to get inside her guard and bite her. Jessira let the Chim come. She ran him through the mouth and kicked him off her sword. The final one took a wild overhand swing at her. She cut through both his forearms and left him to bleed out.

She was almost to Rukh. His head was tilted to the side as though he were listening to something only he could hear. A look of grief and remorse flitted across his face before his face hardened with resolve. He drew a knife.

Jessira was too far away to make out any markings on the weapon, but she knew what it was, what it had to be. It was the

Withering Knife. The sight of the bared black blade chilled her heart.

A single Balant stood between Jessira and Rukh. She drew *Jivatma* and strengthened her muscles. She ducked beneath the Balant's savage blow and rolled to her feet. She bounded up the dull-witted creature's club and leaped higher. Her jump carried her to eye level with the Chim, who hooted fear. He tried to slap her away, but it was too late for him. Jessira thrust her sword through one of the Balant's widened eyes and into the creature's brain. The elephant-sized Chim fell over with a moan and a thud.

The way to Rukh was clear.

Jessira reached him just as he lifted the Withering Knife to his chest.

"Don't do it!" she cried out, knowing what he intended.

Rukh looked her way. "I have to," he said. Once more, regret flitted across his face. "I love you."

He plunged the dagger into his heart.

<hr />

SarpanKum Li-Grist stood beyond the gates of Ashoka's Inner Wall and watched the city burn. He looked into the midday sky where smoke filled the air. It was a black cloud that mingled with the black ravens that had come to feed on the dead.

An unkindness of ravens. That's what they were called. An apropos name.

The crackle and rumble of buildings burning and breaking overcame the cawing of the black birds and even the savage screams of the Fan Lor Kum as they clawed their way into the city.

Mother continued to swoop and soar, lancing the ground with lightning and bands of pounding golden light. She urged Grist to lead the Baels into Ashoka and take part in the massacre, but he refused Her command.

He held back the majority of his Baels, and they stood beside him, outside the Inner Wall. However, some of the Eastern brothers *had* heeded Mother's call and *had* entered the city with the other Chimeras. And what they would do within, possibly aid in the murder of Ashoka, was a stain on their souls that would never wash clean. It was a sin they would have to carry with them all the days of their lives.

Grist felt pity for them, even as their actions angered him to no end. Why had they gone into the city? Did bloodlust truly course so readily through the veins of the Eastern brothers?

"When Mother does away with Ashoka, what will become of us?" asked Li-Quill, a young Jut from the Eastern Plague.

It was Li-Dox, an even younger Jut who answered. "She will do away with us."

Quill's face fell. "Will our kind vanish from the world then?"

"If Ashoka took in Li-Choke, then I would bet the other cities also took in our brothers from Continent Catalyst," Dox said.

"But Choke had the friendship of two Humans," Quill persisted. "The brothers of Catalyst had no one of Rukh Shektan's stature to speak on their behalf."

"Perhaps not," Grist said, "but Devesh speaks to us in the quiet moments when we seek to do what is right. I am sure there were Humans in those other cities who heard the Lord's calling. I feel certain that our brothers were granted asylum there."

Quill still appeared uncertain, even unhappy. He gestured to the city with his trident. "How long do you think it will take Mother to finish destroying the city?"

"No more than a day," Grist said.

"Then if we stay here, we have but one day left on this world." Quill huffed in a mixture of remorse and melancholy. "We should strive for more."

Grist was growing tired of the Eastern Bael's attitude. It reminded him too much of Li-Boil's selfishness. "Do you wish you had gone with your brothers into Ashoka?" Grist asked Quill. "Perhaps you think that Mother will let you live so long as you obey Her commands?"

The Eastern Bael startled upon hearing the question. "No," he replied. "But should we not flee while we have a chance to do so? We may not get very far, but if Mother chases after us, then perhaps those Humans She told us about who left on their boats might yet reach their destination."

Grist wanted to smack himself for not coming up with such an obvious plan himself. Of course they should flee. Those Humans who had recently left Ashoka's imminent destruction were likely still several days travel from their destination. They needed any distraction that would delay Mother's pursuit of them. And chasing after Her traitorous Baels, especially if they sped off in as many directions as possible, might just give those Humans the time they needed to reach safety.

Grist also wanted to smack himself for seeing selfishness in Li-Quill when the Jut was simply thinking aloud on how best to help those who needed it. It was heartening to learn that there were those of the Eastern Baels whose faith in fraternity had not been entirely dimmed by those like Boil or Torq.

"It's a fine suggestion," Grist said to Quill. "One we'll act on immediately." He squeezed the young Jut on the shoulder. "And I am sorry for speaking such ugliness to you."

Quill ducked his head and nodded his acceptance. "I just wish there was a place we could go to be free of Mother's influence," he said.

"As do I," Grist replied. "Such a place will only be found when She finally meets Her demise." It was then that something rising into the heavens caught Grist's attention. "Devesh be praised," he whispered in awe.

———◆●◆———

Jessira gasped with horror. What had Rukh done? Why would he have stabbed himself with the Withering Knife? What could have possessed him to do something so terrible? Questions raced through her shocked mind as she raced to Rukh. She prayed that he was somehow still alive, but in her heart, she knew it wouldn't be true. Her beloved Rukh was dead.

She reached his side, and her grief became a flood when she saw his blood-soaked shirt and the gaping wound in his chest. Her heart broke when she noted his eyes closed in death and his strong, proud body grown as desiccated as a desert. His skin had been pulled taut, and the bones of his face stood prominent.

Jessira fell to her knees. Her sword slipped from her grasp. Rukh was gone. He was dead. Jessira clutched his body to her chest and sobbed with heart-wrenching grief. She no longer heeded the battle raging around her. She disregarded the Chimeras howling all about. None of it mattered. Not without Rukh. Anger made her scream to the heavens. Why had he killed himself? She was furious with him for doing so.

He isn't gone, Aia said to her.

Jessira looked sharply at the Kesarin. It couldn't be true. Rukh's corpse was in her arms.

The Nobeasts understand. It's why they've withdrawn. They're afraid. Aia said.

Jessira glanced around. It was as Aia had described. The Chimeras had withdrawn from Rukh. Their weapons were held low, and they shuffled about, muttering in uncertainty and fear.

Jessira didn't know what to think, what to believe. Rukh was dead. She held his lifeless body. There was no hope for him given the wound inflicted by the Withering Knife.

Your eyes lie, Aia said. *Don't use them.*

Jessira stared at the Kesarin, wanting to believe her.

Trust me, Aia urged. *Trust your heart.*

Jessira slowly closed her eyes and searched for the connection she shared with Rukh.

She gasped.

He was alive. Faint, tentative, and barely present, but there it was, his essence. Jessira didn't care to question the mystery of how it was that he still lived. She was simply grateful that he did. Her next thought was on how to to Heal him.

Before she could work out a solution, Rukh's body twitched, and Jessira's eyes snapped open. He twitched again, and Jessira settled his body back on the ground. She didn't know what was happening. Once more, he twitched and then . . . Jessira blinked, trying to sort out what she was seeing, trying to accept that whatever was happening was really occurring. Rukh's body had floated upward of its own volition. There was nothing above or beneath it. His body rested on a cushion of air, ten or more feet above the ground.

Jessira rose to her feet and dashed away tears. Confusion wracked her mind. She couldn't even form the questions to understand what she was witnessing.

Rukh's body rotated in midair until he was vertical with his feet pointed toward the ground. His eyes snapped open, and they burned with a white-hot fire. His mouth slowly gaped as though he were crying in pain.

Jessira watched all this with her own mouth ajar. She looked sharply when she noticed movement to the side. It was the Chimeras. They had ceased fighting, all of them. Now they were pulling back, many yards away from Rukh. They pulled back once again, even farther.

Jessira turned back to Rukh. His white-hot eyes had cooled. They had became a pure blue, the purest color of the sky in the midst of a perfect summer day. Even the whites were consumed by the blue. A puffy, cotton-white cloud moved across his eyes, from right-to-left. His body twitched once more. Again it twitched, and then it began spinning. The spinning accelerated.

Jessira took a frightened step back as his body *disintegrated*. It was the only word that could imperfectly describe what she was seeing. Small flecks of his body, starting at his extremities, seemed to burn up in a blue flame, but when they did so, those glowing motes rose up to the sky. They didn't fall to the ground. More sparks rose. They flew higher, more of them, cometing into the heavens and disappearing. He was gone. Whatever he had become was now hidden by the smoke greasing the sky.

<hr />

With all the injuries he'd suffered as a warrior, Rukh thought himself inured to pain by now. He had experienced broken bones, bruised organs, and torn muscles. However, nothing in his life could have prepared him for the torment of the Withering Knife. It was an agony unlike anything he could have ever conceived.

Nothing was spared. His body was wreathed in fire and anguish. Every nerve ending screamed. His mind burned in a fit of torture that never ended. The pain was a white-hot, filleting blade. It sliced thin strips off his flesh. It burned the tissue beneath. The agony didn't end there. It gripped his mind in a slowly congealing vice. It squeezed until nothing was left but harrowing misery.

He was torn into two, and those pieces torn into two. The tearing went on and on. He felt every rip, every shred. He became nothing more than a pile of fleshy bits. His *Jivatma* was stripped away. The perfect pool that might have been his soul was gone. Its absence was a wretched hollowing in his mind, an empty space where grace, love, and innocence had once existed. It was gone now. It was the worst suffering of all.

Through it all, Rukh clung to what was foremost in his mind. Jessira. His last vision had been of her terrified visage. His sight had been torn asunder shortly thereafter, and his eyes had boiled away to pus. Blackness ruled. Sound was lost. The world became a quiet place, viable only for the dead. All sensation was gone.

Rukh thought of others. His nanna. Amma. Jaresh. Bree. Aia. His family. His friends. His Caste. His people. Li-Choke. Chak-Soon. All who suffered and merely wanted to live as they wished. For them, he had to endure this pain. For them he had to be the willing sacrifice and serve.

Nothingness existed for an immeasurable amount of time.

But eventually, at the end of all hope, the ache of emptiness slowly filled. His *Jivatma* flickered to life. It slowly replenished, growing deeper, richer, purer . . . transforming. No longer was it a shimmering pond. Now it was a gleaming, depthless ocean. It ebbed with its own tide and waves lapped the shores of his body. The fragments of his flesh fell away, slowly subsumed into those mighty waterless depths until there was nothing left of him but *Jivatma*.

A single pinpoint of light became visible. It grew, becoming a golden glow. Sound came, the echoing notes of a mandolin and his favorite song. The fleeting feel of fog passed through him. He embraced the sensations, and they grew thicker, more weighty.

A rapturous laughter started from within the vaults of his mind. *"You have survived the purification,"* Linder said. His voice echoed louder and louder, becoming separate from him.

The sound merged with that of a singing light. A scent came to Rukh. It held the fragrance of purity and the touch of the sacred. It was a tolling note to which his *Jivatma* pulsed. It was a calling, a yearning that stretched out from the furthest heights—immeasurably distant—yet was close as a prayer. Rukh instinctively knew that the impressions originated from the singing light, and he tried to chase after it.

"It is not yet your time. Your work is not yet complete. Arisa still needs you," Linder said. In their prior, brief conversation, he had sounded heavyhearted and tired, but now he sounded at peace. Rukh watched as the First Father ascended toward the singing light. *"Search yourself, and you will find My final gifts,"* Linder added. His voice grew faint as he quickly became lost to Rukh's senses.

With a pang, Rukh turned away from the singing light. It was one of the hardest things he'd ever done. He had wanted to go to it, to give himself over to it, but he couldn't. Duty came first.

Rukh faced the world. His sight grew clearer. A cloud banked his vision. The haunting strains of the mandolin faded. Harsh cries crowded the skies. The cawing of ravens. He realized that what he'd taken to be a cloud wasn't so. It was smoke, an acrid stench that might have caused him to cough, but he had no lungs. Heat, an updraft from a thousand fires, clawed for him. With the burning he had so recently experienced, the flames were as cold as a winter day.

He mentally inhaled and the world returned in its entirety. With a start, he discovered that he floated far above Ashoka. He witnessed a world that was more vibrant and more clear than Rukh could ever recall it being. Everything held a sharp edge—buildings, trees, roads, people. They all seemed outlined by a stenciling of bright light. Sounds were also more distinct. Cries, shouts, even whispers—Rukh could almost see their reverberations disturb the air. And past the wretched stench of smoke and despoilment, he tasted the sweetness of millions of roses in bloom. The single flutter of a raven's wings flicked across his sight. Time moved slowly. He watched a raindrop form in the heart of a cloud. It floated in the air and dispersed into vapor.

It was how the world appeared when he drew *Jivatma*, but he wasn't drawing *Jivatma* right then. He didn't have to. Not anymore. He was one with his *Jivatma*, and it was vast. His existence was changed. It was then that Rukh came to the final realization that his body . . . he had none. Instead, he had the appearance of a cloud. And lightning coruscated around him.

◆ ● ◆

Jessira had watched Rukh's transformation in open-mouthed astonishment. What had happened to him? What had he become? Had he once again done the unimaginable?

"What just happened?" Jaresh asked, his voice filled with astonishment. He limped over with Sign by his side. Thrum trailed after him carrying an unmoving Dar'El on his back.

"I don't know," Jessira said with a helpless shrug. She looked to Rukh's nanna. "Is he . . ."

"He won't live much longer," Jaresh confirmed with a shudder. A tear leaked down his cheek and Sign held him close.

Shon settled on one side of Jessira and Aia on the other.

It is frightening seeing you in so much danger, Shon said. *I don't like it.* He pushed his head into Jessira's hand, and she stroked his forehead, the area between his eyes.

I'm still with you, Jessira said.

"Set me down," Satha wheezed, arriving just then.

Li-Choke carried her, chair and all. "After the Chimeras left, I felt it only fitting that she be here when her husband is embraced by Devesh's love," the Bael explained.

Lightning crackled, and Jessira's gaze shifted skyward. It wasn't Suwraith. Instead, it was a blue cloud with cotton-white wisps that descended lower. A tendril of its essence hovered over Dar'El. A gentle glow discharged into Rukh's nanna, and he groaned. Dar'El slid off of Thrum's back, but before he could fall, Li-Choke carefully settled him on the ground.

"I'm fine," Dar'El said, waving aside the Bael's assistance. "I can stand on my own."

Satha cried out in relief, and Jaresh carried her to Dar'El's side.

Jessira's attention, though, was caught up with the cloud that hovered over them. She gazed upon it in wonderment. "Rukh?"

From the cloud came a voice. It sounded like Rukh's, but it was so much more vibrant, so much more resonant and powerful. But at the same time, it was also softer and more humble. "*I'm sorry I had to leave you,*" the voice said.

"*You will die!*" a voice of grinding bones and ripping flesh cried out. The Sorrow Bringer, pregnant with puissance and ancient with evil, raced across the skies toward Rukh.

"*This world does not need to be Your prison any longer,*" Rukh said, seeming to entreat the Sorrow Bringer. "*Let it go.*"

The Queen snarled in answer and attacked.

Rukh—though he was transformed into something other than Human, something far more potent and powerful—was yet young to his strength. And even he, in this new, strange state, was but a shade before the Sorrow Bringer's might. She dwarfed him. As the Sorrow Bringer reached for him, Rukh did what was prudent. He fled, racing skyward.

Jessira urged him on as Suwraith gave chase. *Run! Run as fast as you can, as far away as possible!*

However, Rukh was a warrior from birth. He did not flee forever. Nor did he shrink from Suwraith's challenge. Instead, high in the heights above, Rukh halted his flight. He turned to face the onrushing Sorrow Bringer. His blue cloud shape coalesced into the appearance of a man. *"It need not be this way,"* he said, still sounding imploring. *"Your pain can be Healed. The singing light is the way to forgiveness and grace."*

Suwraith laughed at his words. *"There is no light,"* She snarled. *"And you will die like all the others who challenged My might."*

Rukh seemed to sigh. *"So be it,"* he said, sounding regretful. From his hand, he extended a sword, and he gestured to the Sorrow Bringer, motioning Her to come and face him.

The Queen growled acceptance of the challenge. She rose up to meet Rukh. Her bruise-colored cloud slowly congealed, and She took on the shape of a woman, one that was head-and-shoulders larger than Rukh. Lightning haloed Her head, and She held a golden staff in Her hands. *"The sword will not avail you."* Her voice boomed.

Jessira watched the tableau up above in awe, but a flash of reflected light from the ground caught her attention. She bent down and retrieved the Withering Knife.

Rukh stood in a luminescent gulf between flesh and spirit, but there was another who existed in this realm as well. One who had held reign here for far longer. One who was hoary and malevolent. Suwraith. And She was coming for him.

Rukh tried to urge Her away from conflict, to get Her to see the singing light, embrace its love . . . how could She not feel it? See it? Be drawn to it? But for whatever reason, the Sorrow Bringer did not. Instead, the Queen transformed Herself into the image of a young woman. She loomed more than head and shoulders taller than he. She was a giant, and she was old, and likely knew Her abilities in ways that Rukh wouldn't master for many years to come. The Sorrow Bringer forged a golden staff and promised death.

So be it.

Rukh let go of his regrets and firmed his resolve. Had he a chance to make sense of the Talents and knowledge Linder had left for him, perhaps he would have chosen a different weapon, but the sword was what he knew. The sword would be the weapon with which he fought. With a gritting of his figurative teeth, Rukh readied his blade.

The Sorrow Bringer attacked. Rukh raised a hasty Shield just as lightning lit into him. It flowed like a rolling tide of energy, wrapping him in a cocoon of crackling light. The Queen raced in behind it, Her golden staff a whining blur of light.

Rukh blocked once. The power of Her swing nearly disintegrated his sword. He missed Her second blow. It pounded into his Shield. Rukh had to disengage. He pulled back, flowing smoothly, but the Sorrow Bringer followed. He blocked a thrust at his head. Another aimed at his ribs. Rukh's riposte was an angled thrust, but the Queen swept to the side, easily evading his attack. Lightning came for him again, but this time, Rukh was ready. He absorbed the crackling energy into his Shield. He feinted a jab at the Sorrow Bringer. Feinted again, and She reacted with a sweep of Her staff. It left Her open, and Rukh threw a Fireball, white-hot and bleeding lightning.

The Queen let it strike against Her Shield. The Fireball didn't slow Her down in the slightest. She darted forward but at the last instant, rose higher into the air. She now had the heights. Rukh pulled back, but the Sorrow Bringer followed. He tried to keep Her at a distance, and when She descended, he was ready. Or so he thought. She plummeted past him, angling so She was directly beneath him before rocketing straight up. Her staff droned like like a swarm of cicadas and a swing rammed directly at his legs.

Rukh desperately shifted position, moving so he could block Her strike. He basically flung himself to the side. Once more, he was below Her. He barely had time to reestablish his balance before She was on him again.

A flick of Her staff had Rukh defending once again. Another flick came, and he turned away from the swing and blocked the thrust aimed at his chest. Rukh was inside the Queen's reach, but She disengaged before he could go after Her. Suddenly, She lurched toward him, too quick to evade. Her staff whistled as it blurred toward his head, and Rukh blocked it. However, he couldn't avoid the counter-swing aimed at his legs.

He dissipated, taking on the cloud-like form that was his most natural state. He intended to let the staff pass through him, and it would have worked on any being other than the Queen. Instead, Suwraith's staff impacted against his formless form and cut a line of pain through him. It wasn't an injury such as he would have suffered when he still wore flesh—blood certainly didn't flow—but nonetheless, it still felt like he'd been dealt a terrible, ragged wound.

His *Jivatma* roiled, and he cried out in pain. He pulled back, desperate to gain distance. He didn't know what kind of injury he had sustained or how to Heal it. He just knew it hurt. Ironically, it was the Sorrow Bringer who gave him the time to learn how to repair his wounds.

The Queen paused Her attack as he retreated and laughed at him. *"I mastered both the sword and the staff millennia before you were born,"* She sneered.

Rukh didn't pay attention to Her words. Instead, he took the valuable reprieve to search his mind for what to do. It was here that Linder's knowledge proved invaluable. While Suwraith laughed, he was able to Heal his injury. The pain eased and Rukh took the time the Queen had inadvertently given him to try to formulate a better plan.

The staff was a difficult weapon to counter, and the Sorrow Bringer truly was a master. Worse, it had been some time since Rukh had trained against a competent staff wielder. As a result, so far, all he'd been able to do was merely defend. He'd been unable to muster any sort of offense. His approach had to change.

However, the Sorrow Bringer was on him again before he could devise a different strategy. Rukh stepped outside Her range. He blocked a swing aimed at his shoulders. He slid to the side and another blow went wide. She chased after him, but always She was in control. She never overextended. Another swing came too swiftly for him to avoid. It rocked his Shield.

Rukh ground his teeth in frustration. At a distance, Suwraith was simply too fast. He needed to get inside and fight in close quarters.

He stepped past a thrust and attempted to launch a counter. The Queen stifled him. She moved smoothly, effortlessly, turning aside his every strike. During it all, She wore a serene visage, almost as if She were meditating. It was so unlike Her appearances on the other occasions that Rukh had seen Her. Then She had raged, uncontrolled and wild. Rukh needed to fight that version of Suwraith. He had to anger Her so She would lose Her equanimity and perfect technique.

"You are not a goddess." Rukh said, wearing a sneering smile after another disengagement. *"Your Chimeras see You fighting someone who defies You and whom You are unable to immediately punish. They will eventually see the truth, and then what will You do?"* He fired a Fireball, and it struck the Queen head on. *"You are weak,"* he stated in as contemptuous a tone as he could manage. The Sorrow Bringer stumbled away, and Rukh launched another Fireball. This one, She sidestepped. The Fireball detonated in the bay, and a hissing splash over a hundred feet high crashed upward as water boiled.

The Queen didn't bother answering with words. She simply snarled and stepped forward, launching a series of rapid strikes at him. From Her eyes, lightning lanced out. Rukh took it on his Shield, and from his eyes, he fired off a Bow. Suwraith dodged, but Rukh took the distraction to attack. He was briefly inside Her guard, but She brought up a knee, hammering into his essence. He stepped away with a grunt.

"The longer we fight, the more Your Chimeras will abandon You," Rukh managed to say through the pain.

"I know what You are trying to do. You're trying to bait me," Suwraith said with a mocking smile. *"It won't work."* She leveled Her staff at him. *"Now, at the end, understand this: you were never a challenge. You have been tested and found wanting. Prepare yourself."* Her staff blazed into motion.

The Sorrow Bringer chased Rukh across the skies. Wherever he went, so too, did She. Her movements were controlled and fluid. Rukh barely evaded Her swift staff. Their parries rang out over the city like a bell tolling doom. Once more, Her golden staff whipped through the air like a flood of arrows. Rukh couldn't block Her this time. The impact when Her weapon connected with him pealed like thunder and lightning sprayed in all directions.

Just then, Rukh straightened from a crouch and hurled a Bow. The Queen evaded, but Rukh came behind it. He managed to enter Suwraith's guard. A series of swift strikes with his silver sword had the Queen on Her back foot. Rukh followed, keeping the pressure. He blocked a short swing and his own front kick connected. It thudded into the Sorrow Bringer's chest with the force of a rockslide. The Queen quickly drifted out of range, but Rukh leapt after Her. She simply dropped beneath and to the side of an upward-moving slash aimed at Her head.

Rukh spun about to keep Her in front of him. He darted downward to where the Sorrow Bringer had descended, but She rose away from him. Rukh chased after, but the Queen flew backwards. Suwraith gained the distance She needed and settled Herself at the ready once more. Rukh's momentary advantage was gone. They stood at an even height and faced off against one another.

Jessira clenched her fists, watching the battle unfolding in the skies of Ashoka even as she willed Rukh on to greater quickness. He had the skills to defeat the Queen. Of this, she was certain, but he simply lacked the speed. He, who had been the swiftest warrior she had ever seen, was too slow. His parries were often barely made in time. He blocked blows and evaded others but did little more than that. It left him little chance to counter. His movements were all given over to defense. It couldn't go on, not if he wished to survive.

And that's all Jessira wanted. She wanted Rukh to survive. She wanted him to live through this battle. Nothing more.

Victory could be a dream for another day because today, the Queen was simply too fast, too powerful, and too relentless. And as the fight wore on, Her swiftness didn't seem to be abating. She was moving just as quickly now as She had at the beginning of the battle. Rukh, though, was starting to slow down, to weaken. His parries lacked the precision they had early on, and more and more often, he merely threw himself out of the way of Her strikes. He took another battering blow. And another. Another connected and he stepped away from Suwraith, shaking his head as if to clear away the cobwebs.

The Sorrow Bringer walked him down. She no longer bothered with lightning, Bows, Spears, or any other weapon. Her golden staff was all She needed.

Rukh held a look of desperation on his face. He needed help.

Jessira's gaze fell to the Withering Knife. How *had* Rukh transformed into what he had? What was the process? It had been something to do with the Knife, but what? He'd stabbed himself in the chest with it, but was that all there was? To kill oneself with the black blade?

"Do not desire for yourself," a deep, resonant voice said, sounding as though it spoke from a great distance.

Jessira frowned. She'd heard that voice before. It had been during those episodes when Rukh hadn't sounded like himself. It was a voice that had sounded deeper and richer than his own as well as more world weary and fatigued. But this time, the voice had sounded at peace. But was it even real?

"Do not desire power," the voice said, sounding even more distant.

Another peal of thunder. Distractedly, Jessira looked up. Rukh had managed a weak strike against the Queen, but his movements were still too ragged for him to win. He was only delaying the inevitable.

"Desire service with sacrifice," the voice said a final time before growing silent.

Jessira considered the words spoken to her thus far. She still wasn't sure what to do. What the voice had instructed sounded so simple. Was that all there was? In order to become like Rukh, she would have to sacrifice? She would have to desire service rather than power. Was it really so easy?

It seemed wrong for such a transformation to come about with such little cost. After all, this was how Jessira had always lived her life. She had become a warrior so she could protect those who couldn't protect themselves. She was the sheepdog facing down the wolves, even at the cost of her own life.

Another crack of thunder, heavy and rolling, rocked the heavens. Without looking, Jessira knew Rukh had taken another blow. He couldn't take much more. She studied the Knife. *Purity of desire, service and sacrifice. That was it?*

Jessira's decision firmed. In all the other instances she had heard this strange voice, he had always provided wisdom. He had always spoken true.

Jessira would do this to save the people she loved, save Rukh, save Ashoka, save even the poor, deluded Chimeras. All of them deserved a chance to live free of the Sorrow Bringer's evil. She lifted the Knife to her chest and breathed a swift prayer to Devesh, seeking His protection and guidance and forgiveness.

She turned to Dar'El. "The Knife is the key," she said. "It's how Rukh became like Suwraith. But you can only do it if you have nothing in your heart but a desire to serve and sacrifice."

Dar'El shot her a confused stare, but Jessira had no more time for talk. Rukh had taken another series of blows.

Thunder split the skies as Jessira plunged the Knife into her heart.

Pain, like nothing she had ever known, took her.

———————●———————

If Rukh still had a body, he would have been panting in exhaustion by now. He would have been hobbling about, bruised from all the punishing blows the Sorrow Bringer had delivered. Though his *Jivatma* still coursed potently, he was simply taking too much punishment too frequently to give himself time to Heal. New damage occurred before he could care for the old. With a sickening awareness, Rukh knew there would come a point when he would break. Unless something drastic changed, he was doomed.

He even tried to flee the battle, but the Queen was too swift. Every time he tried to retreat, She cut him off.

The worst aspect of his looming defeat and death—the knowledge that made him want to cry out in frustration—was that Rukh finally knew how to fight the Queen. She was fast, but he had Her timing down. She was powerful, but She lacked his precision. She was skilled, but there were stances and movements when Her thrusts and strokes became predictable.

If Rukh only had a few minutes to Heal rather than the paltry few seconds he had been granted so far, he would be refreshed and ready. He would be able to take advantage of his understandings of Suwraith's fighting style. He would finally be able to take the fight to the Sorrow Bringer. Just a little time, and he could take Her.

Rukh snarled.

Then he'd earn that time.

He held tight to his will and poured all his energy into speed and defense. For a time it worked. He parried and blocked. He gave ground. He flew above Suwraith. He flew below Her. All his effort was given over to avoiding Her golden staff. He was able to hold off the Queen, prevent any further injuries, and slowly, he Healed.

Then She launched a seemingly lazy thrust at his midsection, which he easily parried. She slipped to his right. Her staff dipped to the side of his sword, and She swung it up. Rukh never saw it coming until it slammed into his jaw. His head snapped back. He took two more blows before finally gaining space to disengage.

All his Healing was undone.

Suwraith gave him a chilling smile. *"Now comes your end."*

Whatever else She might have said was lost in the flood of Jessira's pain. Something horrific was happening to her. Agony flooded through her, threatening to tear her apart. She burned as if she'd been dipped in molten rock. Her essence was being torn apart, frayed and ripped into ever smaller pieces.

Rukh's figurative heart clenched. The Withering Knife. Jessira must have stabbed herself in the heart with it. It was the only explanation that could account for the terrible pain she was experiencing.

Suwraith hissed. She might have sensed what was happening to Jessira as well. *"Whoever has sheathed the Knife in their flesh won't survive the purification,"* She declared.

"She will survive," Rukh said, more to keep the Queen talking than for any other reason. The longer the Sorrow Bringer let him rest, the more chance he could recover from his latest injuries.

"Only those with the worthiest of hearts can enact the change. You were an aberration, but there won't be two in one day," the Queen sneered. *"And if this woman does survive the purifying fire, still, she will die. I will make certain of it."*

"It is You who will die," Rukh vowed.

Even as he said the words, he knew they sounded asinine. They didn't sound defiant or heroic, but he also didn't care. He would say whatever it took to keep Suwraith distracted. He only needed to stay alive a few moments more. Help *was* coming. Jessira was coming. She would survive the trial with the Withering Knife, and she would be here. He knew it. He had faith.

"I think not," the Sorrow Bringer laughed. *"The woman who sheathed the Knife won't save you. No one will. She will be another I cast down. You'll live to see her dead. This, I promise."* The Queen surged toward him.

But Rukh was ready. Only a few seconds had passed, but it had been enough time for him to somewhat recover.

The Queen attacked, and Rukh's silver sword whistled through the air like a shrieking hawk. He blocked Her strike. A sound like rocks cracking shook Ashoka. Another swing, and Rukh deflected. A tolling echo boomed across the heavens. Rukh stepped back, moving out of range. He rose above the Queen and She followed. He darted down and to the left before moving laterally to the right. She overswept him and had to spin around to keep him in sight. Rukh refused to engage, and this time Suwraith was unable to force the issue.

He had to stay away from the Queen and give Jessira time to complete her transformation. Even now, her pain was slowly fading, and for a time, Rukh couldn't sense her presence. But he held tight to his trust. She would survive.

Eventually, he again became aware of Jessira's essence. She had done it! She had survived the purification.

The Queen bellowed in rage.

This time, he could sense so much more from Jessira than he ever had when they had worn flesh. A luminescent cloud of glowing green motes ascended to the heavens and settled next to Rukh. They coalesced into the shape of a woman that wore Jessira's heart-shaped features.

She smiled at him. *"You look like you could use some help."*

"You have no idea," Rukh said with a laugh. Barely understanding what he was doing or how he was doing it, he passed Linder's knowledge to her.

Jessira nodded in appreciation. *"Thank you,"* she said. *"Let's get to work."* A blue sword extended from her hands, and she turned to the Sorrow Bringer. *"My Queen, I believe You have a date with Death."*

The Sorrow Bringer still towered over both of them. She was a giant, and they were but children in Her presence. But still, She appeared nervous. Suwraith slowly readied Her staff even as She warily eyed them. A moment later, She turned and fled.

Jaresh gaped in awe. He couldn't believe what had just happened. A battle had taken place in the skies above Ashoka, and it had been a battle unlike anything he had ever seen or read about. Thunder had boomed loud enough to tumble buildings, white-hot Fireballs had burned the very air, and lightning had lit the smoke-filled sky, whining like a horde of locusts.

Rukh had become something extraordinary. He had become . . . Jaresh wasn't sure what exactly, but his brother was now like Suwraith, an ethereal being of spirit and might. And while the Queen was old in Her power and had greatly overmatched Jaresh's brother, nevertheless, Rukh had never retreated—he was an Ashokan warrior, a Kumma who understood his duty. But there had come a moment when he had looked moments away from defeat. The hammer strikes heavy enough to level a mountain, the blows from the Sorrow Bringer's golden staff that smacked hard enough to splinter glaciers—they had taken their toll.

But then Jessira had risen up. She had transformed in the same manner as Rukh. Together they'd faced down the Sorrow Bringer, and it had been the Queen who had fled the battle.

"We must rally our warriors before the Chimeras reorganize!" Dar'El shouted, breaking Jaresh out of his amazed reverie.

The Nobeasts are already fleeing in all directions, Thrum said.

Are there any Human warriors about? Jaresh asked.

Shon raised his nose to the air. *There is a large group of a hundred or so just down the hill,* he said. *There are more of them scattered throughout this area.* He turned to Jaresh, his head tilted to the side. *What happened to Jessira?* he asked. *Do Humans ordinarily become like the Demon Wind when faced with danger?*

Aia batted him on the nose. *Foolish kitten,* she chided, fondness taking the sting from her gesture. *Our Humans are not ordinary. They are extraordinary.*

Jaresh set aside their discussion and turned to Nanna. He passed on Thrum and Shon's information.

Nanna nodded. "Good. We'll meet with up with those warriors down below and organize them. Suwraith's creatures no longer have the Queen to defend them from our attacks. If we can rally our forces quickly enough, we can crush the Chimeras before they have a chance to flee the city."

His gaze fell to Sign, who was slumped on the ground. Her wounds had been attended to, and while Jaresh had done his best to Heal her injuries, he'd never been very good at that particular Talent. As a result, they'd taken the expedient of placing heavy bandages over her wounds.

"She should stay here," Amma said. "So should Li-Choke and his Chimeras. They're likely to be attacked if they're seen out on the streets, even if you and Jaresh accompany them."

"We'll also leave Aia and Shon," Jaresh said. "I want to make sure you're protected in case the Chimeras come back."

Jaresh's gaze fell upon Rector's corpse, and a wellspring of grief rose up. Rector and Jaresh hadn't always gotten along, but in the end, he had come to respect the older man's integrity and honesty. In the end, Rector had been a friend, one who had given his life so Jaresh and his family might live. Without his presence here on this day, maybe Rukh and Jessira wouldn't have had the opportunity to do what they had. Without Rector, maybe they all would have been overrun by the tide of Chimeras that had come against the Shektan House Seat. For that reason and so many more, the man deserved to be remembered and his actions celebrated.

"We'll make sure his body is returned to his family," Amma said.

Several days later, a crowd of warriors gathered under a blood red sky. Included with them was a tired and grimy Jaresh. He stood shoulder-to-shoulder alongside the others. They were silent, wary, and watchful as they held the width of Holt Try near Trell Rue in preparation for the final hard push to reclaim the city.

After Nanna had brought order to random, wandering warriors, the broken Ashokan Army had swiftly reorganized. At that point, Marshall Tanhue and his intact brigade had linked up with them. From then on, more and more warriors had gathered, and the Ashokan Army had regrouped. Quickly, running battles had broken out throughout the streets of the city.

The Chimeras had the numbers, but the Ashokans had the will, the hunger, and the skill. They had seen Rukh and Jessira put Suwraith to flight, a scene of salvation that raised the possibility that the Sorrow Bringer's reign of evil might finally come to an end. The

Chimeras had also seen that same battle, but for them, Suwraith's defeat had been a disaster. As a result, while the Queen's creatures still fought, they fought with the half-hearted motions of the broken-willed. The Ashokans, on the other hand, fought with the ferocity of the righteous.

It was ironic. On the day when Ashoka had been invaded by over a Plague of Chimeras—over three hundred thousand of the Fan Lor Kum—a miracle had occurred, transforming the disastrous to the euphoric. The Sorrow Bringer had been defeated and Her creatures decimated, destroyed, and whittled down to less than a quarter of their original number. A terrible morning had yielded a dawn of hope for all Arisa.

And now, two days after that momentous event, gathered in Trell Rue was the final large grouping of Chimeras. It was three Shatters, a little over forty-five thousand. This would be the final reckoning, and afterward, Ashoka—though still aflame—would be reclaimed. The Rahails had already expanded the Oasis back to the Inner Wall, and in another few weeks, they might be able to push it all the way back to the Outer Wall.

Jaresh considered all this as he studied the Chimeras gathered in the distance. Among them strode the Baels, easily differentiated by their height and wide horns. Their whips glowed and their tridents pointed out directions as they barked commands. Somehow, the horned commanders had reestablished control here. In all the other parts of the city, the Chimeras had simply run amok, screaming like rabid dogs until they'd been put down.

There was a stirring amongst the Chimeras, and ten Baels stepped forward from their ranks. They were distinguished by the plethora of feathers dangling from their horns. They had to be senior members of the Plague. In addition, one of them was red-feathered, the SarpanKum. He continued onward while the others waited closer to the lines of their Chimeras.

When the SarpanKum was little more than a bow shot away, he called out. "We surrender," he said in a booming voice. "We will put down our weapons. We won't fight you. We only ask that you let us live until the Queen's final reckoning is determined."

Standing nearby to Jaresh was Marshall Tanhue. He gathered with his officers. One of them gestured for Jaresh to attend them.

Jaresh frowned, not sure why he was being asked to join the High Command.

"You know Rukh and Jessira better than anyone," Marshall Tanhue said. "Can they defeat the Sorrow Bringer?"

"I think they already have," he said. "Before She fled, I could tell that Rukh had Her timing. He was figuring out Her rhythms."

"Then where are they?" growled an older officer. "Why haven't we heard word from them yet if they were victorious?"

Jaresh shrugged again. "I don't know," he said tamping down his worry. "But even if he couldn't defeat Suwraith on his own, with Jessira's help, I'm sure he—or rather they—could."

The Marshall stared off at the remnant of the Eastern Plague through assessing eyes. "We've lost enough warriors these past few days," he finally decided. "And it would be good to lose no one else." His jaw briefly clenched. "We'll accept the Chimeras' surrender, and figure out what to do with them later. For now, we need to take care of our wounded, get these fires under control, and pray that Rukh and Jessira won against the Queen."

Jaresh knew that it went without saying that if the Sorrow Bringer was the one who returned to Ashoka, those same Chimeras would immediately be put to the knife.

<hr />

ienna's confidence was broken. She who had been the death of an entire world. She who was singular and omnipotent. She who had never tasted defeat in all Her long life had been challenged, and for the first time in two millennia, Her might had been found wanting. For the first time in two millennia, Lienna had been forced to flee a battle. For the first time in two millennia, a new Elemental had been birthed, and while he'd proven to be a worthy foe, Lienna had been well on Her way to destroying him. But then had come another Elemental, a woman.

Two beings in one day had become as Lienna. It shouldn't have been possible. Mistress Arisa had promised that only She would—

Lienna halted Her thoughts. Mistress Arisa wasn't real. She had never been real. Mistress Arisa was merely a product of Lienna's delusions, a figment of Her fevered imagination.

"Am I also a delusion then?" Mother asked.

"You are real enough," Lienna growled. *"Just as these new Elementals are also real. But I will destroy them, just as I did You. I will kill them just as I have all the others who dared oppose My immortal will."* Lienna spoke the words with as much confidence as She could muster. She tried to reclaim the focus and self-certainty, the belief that She could carry the day no matter how severe the odds.

"Since You discarded Your flesh, there have been none who could truly be said to have contended with You, Daughter," Mother said with a chuckle. *"And as for immortal . . . I think that on this day, You will learn otherwise."*

"I am immortal," Lienna insisted.

"You lie to Yourself," Mother said, *"but You can no longer lie to Me."*

Lienna tried to ignore Mother's words. They weren't true. They couldn't be true. *"Where's Father?"* She demanded. He usually had some pithy advice She might be able to use.

"With Devesh," Mother replied. *"He ascended today, and if You're truly*

lucky, You may one day be fortunate enough to join Him." Mother seemed to shake Her head. *"However, I fear the circle of birth will spit You out well down the Line of Life before You can again wear a Human's raiment."*

Lienna growled. Those weren't the words She needed to hear. She needed . . .

An idea came to Her. Mistress Arisa. She needed Mistress. After all, every disaster that had occurred in the past few years had been when Lienna had sought to banish Mistress Arisa's presence from Her mind. What if it had been a colossal mistake to do so? What if Mistress Arisa had been the reason for all of Lienna's success? Her victories? Her power?

"Mistress?" Lienna ventured.

"What is it Child?" Mistress Arisa asked.

Lienna shivered in relief. Mistress hadn't abandoned Her. *"I seek Your wisdom. Two Elementals challenge Our might. How should I destroy them?"*

Mistress Arisa laughed in scorn. *"I have no advice to give. Your feeble mind couldn't grasp what is required for victory."*

Lienna gaped. There had to be something Mistress Arisa could tell Her. *"This can't be the end. I am Your chosen vessel, the one who will usher a new age to Your lovely world. Surely You have some words to aid Me in My hour of need."*

Mistress Arisa didn't respond.

"Your ending is coming," Mother said. *"You know it. I warned You. With fire and vengeance You murdered Your way across the world, and with fire and vengeance, You will be cast out from the world."*

Lienna had to put aside further conversation. While She had been busy trying to understand the disaster that had occurred in the skies above Ashoka, while She had been talking to Mother and begging advice from Mistress Arisa, the two new Elementals had chased Her down and overtaken Her.

Their swords were ready, and Lienna was forced to halt Her flight and coalesce into the shape of a woman once more. She prepared Her staff and distantly noted a nearby convoy of ships down below on the Sickle Sea. All of them had the protective shell of an Oasis, and Lienna made a mental note to destroy those ships after She defeated these two Elementals coming for Her.

After that, there was no more time for future plans.

The male Elemental attacked first. He rolled below Lienna's thrust at his head and came up on the other side of Her. She had already set Her staff to block the strike She knew was coming at Her knees. The woman attacked with a horizontal slash at Lienna's midsection. A twirl of the staff blocked that blow as well. Lienna rose higher, gaining separation from the two before they could hem Her in.

A Fireball burned Her way. She batted it aside with Her staff. It smashed into the sea in an explosion of boiling water and thunder. She ducked a Spear. The man pressed Her. He launched a series of strikes that Lienna calmly parried, including a final overhand swing. Her return front kick met empty space as the man stepped out of range. From Lienna's right, the woman feinted. It was a distraction. Lienna didn't bother with it. It would be the man . . . She mentally smiled. He came just as expected, from Her left. She blocked his downward slash at Her knees and stepped back. The woman's thrust at Lienna's shoulder didn't connect.

Lienna laughed. She had always loved sparring. It was a game of position, movement, and moment. There was no time or space needed for distracting thought.

Again came the woman from Lienna's right. Again it was a distraction. Lienna mentally sighed at the repetitive attack. Her opponents should have come up with something more original. She prepared for the man who would come from Her left. Her staff twirled into place, but the man wasn't there.

Tremendous pain erupted from Lienna's back. The man had shifted underneath and behind Her. He'd stabbed Her in the back! His sword extended all the way through Her chest.

Somehow, Lienna managed to pull Herself free of the man's weapon. Pain blotted out Her senses. It felt like She was being torn asunder. She sobbed from the agony. Another blow, this time from the woman, nearly struck off Her arm. Lienna screamed. She had to do something. She would die if She didn't.

One arm hung limp, and Lienna tried to clip the woman in the head with Her staff as She spun about to face the man. But both had already moved beyond the range of Her staff.

"You will die today," the woman vowed in a chilling voice. *"For all the evil You have done to Humanity, death is Your just reward."*

Lienna shuddered. The pain in her back. It made it difficult to focus, but of one thing She was certain. She needed to retreat. She needed time and distance to Heal from the tremendous wounds She had received.

Lienna threw a series of Fireballs at the ships down below. If these two loved Humanity so much, let them save those She had just condemned to death.

As the other two Elementals shouted in outrage, Lienna raced away to safety.

* * *

A cry from high above startled Bree, and her gaze flew to the sky. What she saw caused her mouth to go dry with fear. Suwraith.

There could be no mistaking that stormcloud figure. The Queen had come back. It meant that Ashoka had died. It meant that Bree's home was no more. Everyone she knew was dead, and the Sorrow Bringer had returned to destroy those who had escaped the city's demise.

"Mercy," she whispered.

Farn cursed their luck. "Only two days, and we'd have been safe," he said.

Bree exhaled heavily at the karmic disappointment. Two days might as well have been two years. The two hundred or so ships of the Maharajs extended for miles in every direction, and Bree couldn't help but feel bitter about the days of calm water that had slowed their travel. If not for that, they would have already arrived in Defiance.

She turned away from the swirling vortex and mass of wild lightning that was Suwraith and faced west instead. She wanted to see the sun one last time before she died.

There it stood, bright in the late afternoon sky, but it would soon set. It would be both a literal and figurative setting as the last of Ashoka's hopes would set today as well. The new Caste, the Maharajs, was doomed. They would die out here, far away from home and hearth, unknown and unremembered beneath the waves of the Sickle Sea.

Bree returned her gaze to the Sorrow Bringer. How would Suwraith come at them this time? And would they have any chance of thwarting Her? Bree doubted it. This time she knew that the Queen would annihilate them. This time, there would be no miraculous diversion to distract Her attention.

"What's that?" Farn asked, breaking Bree out of her morose musing. He pointed to two bright blurs that blazed like shooting stars as they streaked in from the west.

Laya held a spyglass to her eyes. "It looks like a man and a woman," she said. "But they're moving too fast for me to focus on them."

Farn held a spyglass to his eyes as well. "It does look like a man and a woman," he agreed, sounding baffled.

Bree no longer needed Farn's confirmation. By now, the streaks—whatever they were—were visible even without a spyglass, and they *did* have the vague appearance of a blue-hued man and a green-colored woman. What were they? Were they new servants of the Sorrow Bringer? And were those swords they held in their hands?

"Look," Laya cried out, pointing to the Queen.

Suwraith's cloud-like form had slowly gathered upon itself and taken on the shape of a bruise-purple woman. A staff slowly extruded from Her hands, and She cried out in defiance.

The man and woman raced straight at Her. That first clash of swords and staff landed with the force of a mountain falling. The sound flattened the air, compressing it and pushing the Ashokan ships deeper into the water. Waves rose and fell in mad abandon.

Bree stared upward with mouth agape. Chills raced up her spine. Rukh had once fought the Sorrow Bringer, and that had been as sublime a sight as she had ever dreamt of seeing, but this . . . this was something else entirely. This was magnificence. The two who battled the Sorrow Bringer were smaller than the Queen, and they likely didn't have Her fearsome power, but they had enough. They fought Her, stood Her off, defied Her will. And She seemed afraid of them.

"What are they?" Laya asked in a voice full of awe.

Bree didn't know, but as the battle progressed, small details became apparent to her. She recognized the sword forms one of them used. It was pure Ashokan, from Caste Kumma and House Shektan. Bree gasped. There was only one man who moved with the fluid grace as the being who battled up above. There was only man who fought with such superlative skill. And there could only be one woman who would fight alongside him.

Bree shouted wordlessly as tears of joy fell from her eyes.

Farn must have figured out who they were at the same. "It's Rukh and Jessira," he cried out. "They're the ones fighting the Sorrow Bringer."

"How can you tell?" someone asked.

Farn explained his reasonings. "It has to be him."

"They'll kill the Queen!" Laya shouted in voice full of joy.

It was a feeling Bree shared. She laughed as Rukh and Jessira hounded the Queen across the sky. To witness the Sorrow Bringer, the demon synonymous with death and suffering, battered about and beaten, was a glorious sight. The thudding of thunder continued to play out with every strike of sword against staff. Lightning lit the clouds in a wild riot.

There came a moment when the Queen missed a parry, and Rukh slipped behind Her. His sword slammed through Her chest. The Sorrow Bringer screamed in pain. She shrieked even as She lifted Herself off of Rukh's blade. Jessira swung, and one of Suwraith's arms nearly came off.

Bree found herself cheering, shouting encouragement. This was it. This was the moment dreamt of by countless generations of Humanity. This was the death of Suwraith. And Bree was blessed enough to be able to watch it happen.

A moment later, her excitement turned to horror. The Sorrow Bringer fired off a series of Fireballs. They blazed hot as the sun. Lightning shredded from each of them as they burned toward the ships.

The Fireballs piled downward, roaring like wide-open furnaces. The air shimmered in the wake of their passage as lightning bled from them, crackling like a thousand whips.

Jessira watched them descend, hating her impotence. There was nothing she could do to stop them. Despite the great power she now possessed, she couldn't destroy them before they reached the ships floating down below.

Rukh fired a Bow, eradicating one Fireball. He quickly destroyed another.

His action sparked an idea. *"Go. We can't let the Queen escape,"* Jessira urged. *"I can take care of the Fireballs."*

Rukh left without seeing what she would do. He trusted her word.

Jessira's ocean-wide *Jivatma* pulsed in time to her need. She stretched her will into a thick, golden bar. The tip glowed like quicksilver. From it streaked lightning, nine different crackling bolts. Each one connected with a Fireball, destroying it on impact.

However, two Fireballs managed to reach their destination. Thankfully, both merely smacked into the sea with an explosive spout of steam and roiling water. The waves raised from the concussive blasts managed to almost capsize a couple of ships. Several people were thrown into the water, and Jessira paused long enough to rescue them.

But as soon as she was sure they were safe, she raced off in the direction Rukh had taken. Jessira had to rejoin the fight against the Sorrow Bringer as quickly as possible. On his own, Rukh couldn't handle the Queen. Suwraith was simply too powerful. Only together could Jessira and Rukh hope to stand a chance of defeating the Sorrow Bringer. Then the Queen would finally be called to account for all the evil She had done.

It took Jessira far longer than she would have liked to finally catch up with Rukh and Suwraith. They had passed over the Sickle Sea and into Continent Catalyst, traveling so far east that it was now twilight in this part of the world. There, deep in a desert—the Prayer—Jessira found them. They warred. Jessira had followed her sense of Rukh's presence to locate them, but she could have just as easily traced the patches of glowing glass that had been created by the violence of their conflict. Jessira had briefly puzzled at those strange, iridescent decorations on the desert floor until she saw a Fireball slam into the the ground. There, at the point of impact, sand burst upward and what was left behind was turned to glass.

The battle broke off when Jessira arrived. Suwraith snapped off a few strokes with Her staff before snarling wordlessly and racing away south. There was no evidence of the injury the Queen had received during their brief battle over the Sickle Sea. Nevertheless, Her expression had been one of fear.

Once again, Rukh and Jessira gave chase. Hills rose, becoming green with stunted grass and shrubs. Trees appeared. The hills grew taller before giving away to foothills and a winding river.

Finally, over a broad body of muddy water—from her study of maps, Jessira realized it had to be Lake Corruption—the Queen turned and faced them. She stood tall, proud and defiant with Her staff held in hand. She beckoned them forth. *"Now you will meet your doom. This is the place where I was birthed into this fallen world, and here is the place where you shall die."*

Jessira's response was a Fireball that burned the short distance to the Sorrow Bringer and slammed against Her Shield. The Queen was hurled back by the force of the impact.

Rukh swept down. He came in below Suwraith. Jessira came in from high. They met in the middle. The Queen twirled Her staff. She blocked Rukh. Jessira's thrust missed. The Queen had bent around it. The Sorrow Bringer pivoted, and Her staff was ready for Rukh's next blow.

Another series of strikes were exchanged before Suwraith swept upward. She taunted them, keeping just ahead of their racing forms. Suddenly, the Queen halted and swung about to face them. Jessira cursed as she went too far. She overswept Suwraith. Rukh, though, had managed to stop in time. He and the Queen traded blows. Neither succeeded in touching the other.

Jessira shot straight up and raced straight down. She aimed another thrust at the Sorrow Bringer. It was the same move she had used only moments before. This time, she pulled her blow. Suwraith's staff met air and passed unencumbered. It left Her briefly out of position. Jessira took the opening. A glancing strike struck the Queen high on one of Her arms.

It wasn't a telling injury, but Suwraith growled in response. She lashed out with a lightning-fast kick and a Bow.

Jessira avoided the first but took the second straight on Her Shield. It melted. Some of the heat and energy of the Bow went straight into her, and Jessira cried out in pain. It was like taking a stab to her heart. Her body felt afire. It wasn't as bad as the Withering Knife, but only barely. Her *Jivatma* boiled.

Jessira pulled back from the battle. She needed to Heal, but Suwraith kept after Her. Meanwhile, Rukh had been thrown aside by a clip of the staff to his temple.

Jessira defended desperately. She tried to keep the Sorrow Bringer in front of her. She blocked a diagonal slash aimed at her head. She backed away from the follow-up swings targeting her knees. A heavy jab pounded into her abdomen, and Jessira gasped. On top of all her other pain, it felt like she'd taken a liver shot. Her body, though it was ephemeral and made of light, locked up. She moved as slow as a slug.

Another blow descended toward Jessira's head. It seemed to fall glacially, but her arms were too heavy to intercept it. They wouldn't respond. Her entire body wouldn't respond. With a tired comprehension, Jessira realized that she couldn't block the blow. However, the Queen's position revealed an unforeseen opening. Just before the Sorrow Bringer's overhand strike connected, Jessira lifted her sword and stabbed the Sorrow Bringer in the abdomen. It was a deep wound, but not a fatal one.

The Queen screamed pain and outrage.

Good. Maybe the injury would allow Rukh to overcome the Sorrow Bringer and end Her for all time.

The Queen's overhand strike connected, and pain erupted in Jessira's mind. She fell to the lake down below and felt herself come apart.

⚬

R ukh watched in horror as Jessira was struck down by a blow to her head. She instantly went limp and plummeted toward the lake. Rukh swooped down, intent on saving her, but he couldn't reach her in time. She plunged into the muddy water of Lake Corruption, and the sparkling green motes of her essence came unglued. The womanly shape Jessira had taken on spread out over the water's surface like a slowly dissipating mist that eventually sank and disappeared.

Rukh could barely sense his wife presence's. Jessira's essence had once been a firm brightness centered within his mind, but now, all that was left was a touch that was softer than a snowflake's kiss and a dim light more faint than a firefly in fog. Rukh wasn't even sure if any of what he was still feeling of his wife was actually real. Maybe the trace sensations were merely a remembrance of her fiery core, like an afterimage from staring at the sun.

It was just as possible that Jessira was gone, and Rukh cried out at the realization. He had been too slow to defend her, too filled with fury at the Queen to fight with clarity. It had been his mistake that had led to Jessira's demise.

He turned to face the Sorrow Bringer.

She seemed to look down at him with the eyes of a vulture. Her ugly mouth stretched into a slow lupine grin. Suwraith's face was the image of cruelty. She gestured for him to come to Her, still wearing that awful smile.

Rukh snarled. He wanted to charge that fragging, evil monster. He wanted to tear Her apart. He wanted to stab out Her eyes, chop Her limb from limb, hurt Her as horribly as it was possible to hurt another being before finally killing Her. He wanted Her to suffer, to feel the agony and anguish he was feeling.

You are not a man made to hate. The words came from his memory. They belonged to Jessira, and grief, a more painful blade than the Withering Knife, stabbed Rukh's heart, replacing some of the anger. Somehow, through it all, a semblance of reason returned.

Rukh had to defeat the Sorrow Bringer. It was his duty, his calling, his purpose. The Queen's death was the long-sought, unfulfilled dream of generations of Humanity. His anger cooled further. Hatred would not win the day, but rational thought and planning might.

Rukh studied his foe. She still floated up above, taunting him with Her cruel smirk. After defeating Jessira, why hadn't Suwraith immediately attacked him? The answer came to Rukh. The Queen was injured. He could see it now that he was looking. It was a deep wound to Her abdomen. Jessira's mark. Suwraith hadn't attacked because She needed time to Heal.

It was time She would not have.

Rukh ascended silently. He sought that glacial stillness that he had first seen manifested by Kinsu Makren when the two of them had fought in the Tournament of Hume in what seemed like another life. Rukh forced the burning hate to flow through him, past him; let it drain it out through his feet.

The Queen cried out challenge and swooped toward him like a falcon.

Rukh twisted away from Her attack. The Sorrow Bringer came again, and Rukh waited on Her. The Queen's staff arced in a blur toward his head. His abdomen. His knees. Rukh parried every blow.

All emotions were set aside except for one, a single focus: the absolute need for victory. It compelled his every movement and thought. Again, the Queen came in a flood of furious motion. Lightning arced toward him. It coruscated as he slapped it away with his sword. He dodged a Fireball, and it detonated in an explosion of steam and mud as it hit the boggy ground.

The Sorrow Bringer came in behind the Fireball. Rukh tried to disengage, but She was too swift. She wasn't as slowed by Her injury as he had hoped. A series of rapid swings and thrusts had Rukh off balance. He took a blow to his Shield, and it keened like a horse screaming in pain. Another blow landed against his Shield. This one punched through, and Rukh's left shoulder ached as though it had been broken. He pulled away, seeking distance to resettle himself.

Once more, Suwraith advanced. Her staff whirled. It buzzed through the air like a nest of angry hornets. It came fast and hard. Rukh was hard-pressed to block Her every blow, but he managed. His shoulder slowly improved. With each passing second, it grew stronger. Rukh circled away, defending, looking for an opening. Again and again, he merely held guard, blocking Her every blow.

Another Fireball burned toward him. She'd launched it too close for him to evade, and he turned to the side. It thudded into his Shield. The echo of the impact thundered out, bending branches in all directions. The water below rocked with heavy waves.

It was an impressive explosion, but more importantly, the impact caused Rukh's Shield to go out. Once again, he desperately sought distance. The Sorrow Bringer kept after him. He blocked and evaded until he could finally reestablish his Shield. On came the Queen.

With Her next pass, Rukh recognized Her stance. He knew what She would do next. A thrust to his head was a feint. Following after came a sweep with Her staff as She attempted to trip him. He rose above Her weapon and snapped out a kick. It thudded against Her face, and She stumbled back.

A grimace replaced Her smile.

Rukh had finally landed a blow against Her, but he didn't let even the slightest sense of success come to him. He held to his calmness.

A darting slash was aimed at Suwraith's head, and She slapped away his sword. Rukh stepped in close and angled a short chop at Her shoulder. She blocked with a smooth motion of Her staff. He ducked Her return swing but continued to pressure Her. He needed to stay inside the circle of Her staff. The Sorrow Bringer tried to rise out of reach, but Rukh kept up with Her. She darted right and left, but he was always there.

Her wound *did* slow Her, and She was unable to escape. Rukh feinted. It was a dangerous plan. With one hand on the hilt of his sword, he thrust up at Her abdomen. She stepped aside, and Her staff twirled. It would slam into his temple. From this distance, there would be no chance for his Shield to hold. It would be the same fearsome blow that had ended Jessira.

But in Rukh's other hand, hidden behind his back, was a Fireball. The Queen's eyes widened in realization. Her staff would strike him, but not before his Fireball struck Her.

Suwraith screamed in agony. Rukh's head exploded in pain. His sword flickered and disappeared. The Fireball had punched through the Queen's Shield. A gaping hole in Her abdomen passed entirely through the glowing violet motes of Her essence. Rukh knew it wasn't over. Though both he and the Queen plunged downward, he knew there was still a chance She might survive Her terrible injury.

He could feel himself coming apart, the same as what Jessira had probably experienced. He held on to his determination. His mission was not yet complete. He forced his essence together. He reformed his sword.

Though his vision had grown dark, he spotted the Queen. She was close. Her mouth gaped in terror and somehow She sensed his regard and his determination. Her own visage steeled, and Her staff reformed.

Rukh managed to halt his freefall at the same time as the Sorrow Bringer. They squared off against one another, both severely injured but neither willing to back down. Rukh leveled his blade. He slashed, a cut that rose from right-to-left. The Queen blocked.

Rukh looked the Sorrow Bringer in the eyes, staring at the being who was the author of so much cruelty. She stared back. Her eyes glowed resoluteness. They locked in place for less than a second, but it was a span of time too long. With his left hand, Rukh grabbed hold of Suwraith's staff. Her eyes widened once again. She understood Her mistake. A fleeting look of regret passed over Her face. His sword was still gripped in his right hand, and Rukh slammed it home.

It punched into Suwraith's chest and out Her back. She screamed. The cry ascended in pitch. More distantly, Rukh noted the glad shout of another woman as she rose to the singing light.

But for the Queen, Her scream endured. It went on and on. It was the sound of fear and fury and mortal agony. Suwraith's essence dissipated into glowing embers. Rukh watched as Her motes rose, not to the singing light, but elsewhere. She went to some far, distant place beyond Arisa, beyond his knowing, up past the sky into an inky sea filled with wrecked islands. Her embers passed from Rukh's sight just as Her echoing cry passed from his hearing.

The Sorrow Bringer was dead.

Rukh would have felt elation, but he hurt too badly to feel anything but regret and grief. Jessira. He couldn't rightly sense her. Rukh slumped toward the muddy water, and his mind stilled.

EPILOGUE

The longing man on a quiet night,
His heart's ease is driven by his need
For the lively woman who makes bright
Music and laughter with the bold reed.
She plays a flute made of warmth and light,
And in divine Rapture comes the creed
From a song of duty and of flight
When the longing man and the lively woman are freed.

—<u>Romance and Love</u> *by Anto Jakper, AF 1456*

A white light burned from somewhere high above him. It shined like a beacon, steady, unblinking, and unmoving. For the longest length of time, a period measured in heartbeats and the absence of memory, he simply watched the orb. He studied it, perplexed as to what it was.

Then again, who was he? It was a more interesting question, and one he considered with as much energy as he could spare. His concentration led him nowhere, and eventually, he gave up. He reckoned hours had passed, but when he returned his attention to the bright orb glowing from an unmeasurable distance away, it hadn't moved at all. Dim memory, as difficult to perceive as the sense of sight in muddy water, came to him. The orb was the sun, and it moved.

How did it move? And did a fire burn within it to cause it to be bright?

He sighed and put away his vision. He was too tired to ponder such difficult questions. His mind stilled.

A white light, the sun, burned like a beacon. Its light barely penetrated whatever it was that surrounded him. The sun stood high in the sky. It might even be noon.

A thrill of pleasure coursed through him at his recognition and remembrance of the measurement of time. He stared up at the sun, wondering why its brilliance did nothing to illuminate the surroundings in which he found himself. Was he buried beneath the ground?

With one question asked, many more followed. Foremost amongst them was this: who was he?

Once again, he had no answer. He tried to force his mind to seek the answer, but instead, an odd sight came to him. Rather than learning the truth about his identity, from a distance, he viewed an ocean of light; it was like the purest of water. It barely moved and from it came the fragrance of innocence and love.

He smiled in wonder, but once more thought and questions had swiftly grown too taxing. He put away his vision, and his mind stilled.

The sun burned dimly from high in the sky. Its light barely lit the murky water in which he found himself.

Rukh—lightning swept through him.

His name was Rukh Shektan. More memories overflowed his thoughts. His childhood. His family. A woman with a heart-shaped face and lovely lips curved into a smile. Jessira. Love filled him. His *Jivatma*, an ocean of purity, pulsed. From an inestimable distance away he heard a singing light.

The water around Rukh shifted and swayed. It glowed in time to the pulsing blue motes that were his essence. More memories came. The Withering Knife and horrific pain. The battle with Suwraith and victory. Any elation he might have felt at the notion of the Sorrow Bringer's demise was quickly washed away. Pain came. Jessira's death. Before Rukh had ended Her life, the Queen had struck Jessira down.

Rukh's mind grew weary once more. His thoughts became as still as the surrounding silence. So it went possibly for days, weeks, months, or maybe even longer.

Strength returned and Rukh rose from the murky waters of Lake Corruption. The setting sun met his emergence. Frogs croaked, and a warm breeze, heavy with humidity and the smell of swamp, rippled the water. In all directions, nothing other than nature stirred.

He floated above the lake, utterly alone. A sense of desolation, of loss and hurt that would never heal poured pain into his heart. He'd come to accept Jessira's absence even as he knew he would never grow used to it. His heart and soul ached at her death. They had yet to heal and perhaps never would.

A green glow emanated from somewhere close by. It was barely visible through the murky water, barely alive.

A tremulous spike of hope shot through Rukh. *"Jessira?"*

Silence met his hopeful query. *"Is that my name?"* came a question from the green glow. *"I'm tired."*

Silence resumed, but Rukh didn't care. His heart overflowed with joy. Jessira's cinnamon-scented presence lived in his mind. She existed. He could sense her down below, weak and faint, but she lived. She would Heal just as he had.

Days later, with halting conversations to mark Jessira's returning strength and memory, she ascended from Lake Corruption in a glory of verdant light filled with the glow of life. She grinned when she saw him. *"You thought I wouldn't come?"* she asked.

Rukh didn't answer. He swept her into his essence and laughed. Glowing blue tendrils shifted about her green form. He breathed in her cinnamon scent, the scent of her spirit. *"Never leave me again,"* he pleaded.

"I won't." Jessira held still in his presence. *"I take it we won,"* she said more than asked.

"We won," Rukh confirmed. *"The Queen is gone from this world."* He swept her into his embrace once again and laughed. Jessira lived.

She smiled at his joy. *"Good,"* she said. *"I'd hate to have to fight Her again."*

"We never will," Rukh promised, still holding onto Jessira and unwilling to let her go.

She settled into him. *"How is it that I can sense your thoughts, your presence, even more than I could when we were Human?"* Jessira asked.

"You already have the answers," Rukh told her.

He felt her shift. *"Why don't you just tell me,"* she said with a smile. *"I just came back to life, after all."*

"We were already growing close when I brought you to Ashoka the first time," Rukh said. *"We became closer when Aia gave me your knowledge of Healing. What the Kesarins do is a type of Annex."*

"And since Healing forms a bridge between patient and Healer, and we had just shared a kind of Annex, our thoughts grew even closer."

"I thought you wanted me to tell you what happened?" Rukh asked.

Jessira laughed. *"Go ahead, then."*

"We grew even closer," Rukh confirmed, *"and we might have only been another couple who were exceptionally close except for Linder Val Maharj, the First Father. When I read* The Book of First Movement, *He experienced my life just as much as I experienced His. And when the Sorrow Bringer came after us later that night, we linked our Blends, and Linder took the opportunity to give us another type of Annex. It was one He and His wife shared."*

"And that's why we could so easily tell what the other was thinking or feeling?"

"And why we always knew where the other one was."

Jessira chuckled. *"I don't mind that Linder did what He did without asking us since things worked out in the end."*

Rukh grinned. *"Yes, they did."*

Jessira cupped his essence. *"Let's go see how Ashoka's doing,"* she suggested.

"Race you home?"

"You'll lose," Jessira said.

"I've never lost a race to you," Rukh reminded her.

"That was when you were a Kumma. Now, you've become something else. I've become something else, and your Kumma Talents won't help you anymore."

Rukh figuratively blinked. She was right. He was no longer a Kumma, and she was no longer an OutCaste. They were no longer Human.

"So what are we?" Jessira asked.

"We've become Elementals," Rukh told her. *"That's what Suwraith said."*

"Elementals," Jessira said as though tasting the word. *"It's as good a name as any."* She kissed Rukh, a warm sensation of her green motes pressing deeply against him. *"And Rukh . . ."*

He could hardly think after that kiss.

"Go," Jessira whispered before darting away.

It took him a while to figure out where she was flying off to in such a hurry, but eventually he remembered. The race. He'd challenged Jessira a race back to Ashoka.

Rukh conducted *Jivatma* and took off after her. As he sped along, it became easier to allow his form to disperse, to become the cloud-like shape he'd so often associated with the Queen. The world below spread out like the finest map as it blurred beneath his speed. Clouds misted against him like fine dew. Birds called out from far below. He arrowed toward the ground, racing along the course of a river. Spray marked his passage. He pulled up, going higher and higher to where the air was thin and cold.

The sensations didn't touch him. He was impervious to them. He was an Elemental. He laughed with sheer joy.

The winds blew harder, and Rukh climbed above them. He went to a place where there was hardly any air. The curve of Arisa became apparent, and darkest blackness beckoned beyond the world's globe. It was an emptiness unlike anything he could have ever imagined. He briefly wondered if even a being such as himself could survive such a void. He wasn't sure, and he didn't want to test his strength.

Just then, he sensed the scrutiny of another and paused to look about. Deep in that vast darkness, somewhere too far away to measure, a pinpoint beam reached for the singing light and then bent away. It was a rainbow, and someone—a man—rode it.

Rukh frowned in uncertainty, and when he looked again, the man and the rainbow were gone.

Rukh shrugged and returned to studying Arisa. He smiled as his regard returned to Jessira. Even from high up here, he could sense her presence. She was nearing the Sickle Sea, far ahead of him, but not too far. She still wore her womanly raiment. It was a much slower mode of travel.

Rukh smiled. He could still beat her to Ashoka.

He plunged downward at an angle. He picked up speed, faster and faster. The wind howled past him, an angry wail. Clouds were shredded as he ripped through them. His glowing blue motes became shot through with lightning.

In the end, Jessira was right. His Kumma Talents did him no good in catching up with her, but nevertheless, he still *did* catch her. The cloud shape was simply that much faster. Rukh adjusted his angle and straightened his flight and ended up passing Jessira somewhere over the Sickle Sea. She squawked in outrage as he swept past her and goosed her with lightning.

He grinned and kept up the speed. There was no chance she would win this race.

As he neared Ashoka, Rukh could see the damage the city had suffered, and his smile faded. The wrecks of many buildings—entire districts—still littered the streets. He would help the city clean up and rebuild, but first, there was somewhere else he needed to be. He needed to go home.

As he approached closer, he sensed the Oasis, rigid and firm once more, shielding the city. It extended all the way to the Outer Wall, and while he could have easily battered it aside, there was an easier way. Once again, Linder's knowledge proved invaluable. Rukh adjusted his form and eased his way through the Oasis.

He waited as Jessira entered Ashoka moments after him. *"You could have gone on,"* she said. *"You didn't have to wait for me."*

Rukh grinned, pleased that he'd beaten her home. *"I know, but . . ."*

He trailed off when Jessira blasted past him. *"The race was to your* home," she said. *"That would be the Shektan House Seat, not just Ashoka. You haven't won yet."*

Rukh gaped. Then he cursed. Then he chuckled. Jessira could still surprise him.

When he arrived at the House Seat, it was to find Jessira floating above the grounds, wearing a smug smile of triumph.

"Congratulations," he said.

Rukh? Aia called out. She stood on the patio outside Nanna's study. With her was Shon.

Rukh and Jessira let out a glad shout and descended. Without discussion, they both shifted and took on the appearance of a man and a woman.

Your family lives, Aia said, sounding as excited as Rukh had ever heard. *All of them. And some of those different Humans, the Maharajs, came home shortly after you left. Your sister and everyone else are inside.*

My sister, Rukh repeated, feeling stupid.

Your sister, Aia confirmed. She almost seemed to bounce from the joy she was emanating. *She said that after she saw you battling the Demon Wind, she and many of the others knew they had to return to Ashoka and help repair the city.*

What if we'd lost to the Queen? Rukh asked, aghast. *They would have all died. Everything we did for them would have been for naught.*

I said some of the Maharajs returned, not all of them, Aia corrected as she gave off an air of smug superiority. *Besides, you are my Human. Your sister knew, almost as well as I, that the Demon Wind would not survive your might.*

Especially as my Human was there to help you as well, Shon said, shoving his nose past Aia. He apparently wanted to get a word in. *And Li-Choke and his Nobeasts and a whole, big glaring of other Nobeasts serve the city as well.*

Aia edged Shon aside. *Our nanna, the Kezin of the Hungrove Glaring, brought a number of Kesarins to Ashoka,* she said. *All of them can speak to your kind, and they all wanted Humans of their own.* She blinked. *It's been a very exciting time since you left.* She blinked again. *My chin itches,* she noted, her tone demanding.

Rukh laughed again, overwhelmed by everything Aia and Shon had told him.

Jessira laughed with him and took his hand. She kissed him again. *"Welcome home."*

THE END

GLOSSARY

Note: Most Arisan scholars use a dating
system based on the fall of the First World. Thus:
BF: Before the Fall of the First World.
AF: After the Fall of the First World.

Adamantine Cliffs: White cliffs, about two hundred feet tall, that form the southern border of Dryad Park.

Advent Trial: An annual competition held in the spring that involves all four military academies in Ashoka.

Ahura Temple, the: One of the schools of song in Ashoka. Open only to Sentyas.

Aia: A young Shylow/Kesarin. Bonded to Rukh Shektan.

Alminius College of Medicine: One of the two Shiyen schools of medicine in Ashoka.

Aqua Oilhue: Caste Cherid. Born AF 2031. Murdered by Hal'El Wrestiva with the Withering Knife.

Arbiter, the: The administrative judge of the Chamber of Lords, interpreting the various rules and points of etiquette. Typically, he is an older Kumma chosen by the 'Els for his wisdom and knowledge. Upon his election, he gives up his House name and takes on the surname of 'Kumma'. The position is a largely ceremonial one, and his vote is only offered in the case of a tie. His social standing is that of a ruling 'El. Current Arbiter is Lin'El Kumma.

Ashok: Caste Unknown. Historical figure who is the reputed author of the *Compact and Binding*, the constitutional basis of all governments in Arisa.

Ashokan Guard, the: A reserve unit of about 25,000 warriors meant to support the High Army in times of crisis. It is composed of veteran Kummas, Murans, and Rahails. A few Duriahs have also joined the Guard over the years.

Attayya: Mother-in-law.

Baels: The commanders of the Fan Lor Kum. They are feared for their intelligence and unwavering commitment to Humanity's destruction as well as their imposing size, chained whips, and tridents. By convention, they are always given a hyphenated name in which Li- makes the first part.

Book of All Souls, the: Sacred text dating from the First World. Author unknown, but said to be Devesh Himself. Over time since the fall of the First World, it has taken on secondary importance to *The Word and the Deed* in the religious life of most people.

Brand Wall: Caste Rahail. Born AF 2041 to Trudire and Simala Wall. Survivor of the Trial between Ashoka and Nestle. Later on was killed by Kesarins.

Bree Shektan: Caste Kumma. House Shektan. Born AF 2044 to Dar'El and Satha Shektan.

Brit Hule: Caste Rahail. Born 2027. He is the youngest Patriarch in living memory as well as the youngest Magistrate in the Magisterium.

Cal Dune: OutCaste. Born AF 2011. Colonel of the Home Army of Stronghold. He was the highest-ranking officer in the Army and only answered only to the Governor-General.

Caravan: Trade expedition meant to maintain contact between the cities. Protection of the caravan—a Trial—has come to be seen as a holy duty, for only through the free exchange of knowledge can Humanity hope to survive Suwraith's unending madness.

Castes, the: The social, moral, and economic organization of all cities on Arisa.

> **Kumma**: The warrior Caste. They are involved in all aspects of defense, supplying the vast majority of warriors to the Ashokan military and the caravans. Their Talents are especially suited for battle.
>
> **Sentya**: Known for their accounting acumen and their skill with musical instruments and compositions. The finest musicians and composers are always Sentya. They possess the Talent of Lucency, which allows them to think with near utter clarity. In such a state, emotions are distant. They can also project this ability onto others.
>
> **Duriah**: Born to build, they are thick and stocky. Their Talent is to Cohese: the ability to take various objects and substances, and from them, forge something different and more useful. Rare individuals can DeCohese, which is the ability to break any object down to its basic components. A master craftsman is known as a Cohesor.
>
> **Rahail**: They maintain the Oasis, sensing where it is growing thin and working to repair and renew it. It is done through their Talent of Sharing wherein they literally give their *Jivatma*, letting it seep into an Oasis and keep it strong. It is an ability they can use but don't really understand, even two thousand years after it first manifested. Their Caste is structured entirely around this Talent, although some join the caravans or the Ashokan Guard.

Muran: Traditionally, they are farmers, although some join the caravans or the Ashokan Guard. Their Talent allows them to bring even a desert to flower. However, the pride of the Caste is their singers.

Cherid: Physically they are the smallest of all the Castes, but Cherids are generally the leaders of a city as a result of their natural intelligence and cunning, as well as their Talent. They possess the ability of Synthesis: they can combine *Jivatmas* and share it out amongst others. Thus, a Rahail can maintain the city's Oasis, not simply with the strength of his own Caste, but that of all Castes if need be.

Shiyen: They all possess the ability to Heal to a certain extent, but only the most gifted amongst them are chosen for one of Ashoka's two medical colleges. The rest are generally craftsmen and merchants.

Cedar Grey: OutCaste. Born AF 2039 to Sateesh and Crena Grey. Lieutenant in the Stronghold Home Guard as a member of the Silversun scouts before his death.

Chamber of Lords: Kumma ruling Council. It consists of all the ruling 'Els and is presided over by the Arbiter. It is involved in decision-making that will affect the Caste as a whole. The Chamber also renders judgment for those charged with being Unworthy or thought to be traitors.

Chak-Soon: A young jaguar-spotted Tigon. He is the first of his kind to learn of fraternity and accept it.

Chimeras, the: Suwraith's created forces who comprise the Fan Lor Kum. There are seven species of Chimeras: Baels, Tigons, Braids, Ur-Fels, Bovars, Balants, and Pheds. All species of Chimeras have some degree of intelligence except for Pheds and Bovars. Pheds are simply a meat source, grown only to feed the Fan Lor Kum. Bovars are beasts of burden, much like oxen, but it is from them that the most intelligent of all Chimeras were birthed: the Baels. The Chimeras are marsupial and born in groups of five, what they label a crèche, and mature to full adulthood within a few years, although the Baels take slightly longer.

City Watch, the: Peacekeeping unit of about three hundred warriors, called upon to maintain the peace and investigate crime in Ashoka.

Compact and Binding: The constitution by which all cities on Arisa are organized. Dated to just after the Night of Sorrows.

Conn Mercur: Caste Shiyen. Born AF 2005. He is the dean of the Verchow College of Medicine.

Constrainers: Leather vambraces used in training or tournaments as a means to suppress the expression of an individual's *Jivatma*.

Council of Rule: Ruling Council of the Sil Lor Kum. It is comprised of the SuDin and the six MalDin.

Court Deep: OutCaste. Born AF 2040. Cousin to Cedar and Jessira Grey and brother to Sign Deep. Died shortly after Stronghold was destroyed.

Crena Grey: OutCaste. Born AF 2007. Married to Sateesh Grey and amma to Kart, Cedar, Jessira, and Lure. Adopted Court and Sign Deep.

Croft, the: Large fertile valley that provides all of Stronghold's food. It was tightly regulated by the Home Senate.

Crofthold: A neighborhood in Stronghold. Each Crofthold is built vertically, each with ten levels and a large atrium in the center. There were ten Croftholds.

Dar'El Shektan: Caste Kumma. House Shektan. Born AF 2006 as Darjuth Sulle to Jarned and Tune Sulle of House Ranthor. Completed four Trials before retiring at age thirty-one. He transferred to House Shektan upon his return to Ashoka after his fourth and final Trial. Married Satha nee Aybar in AF 2039. Later, in AF 2050, he became the ruling 'El of his House.

Days of Desolation: A period of decades where the light of civilization was almost put out. Suwraith raged unchecked throughout the world, and Humanity lay huddled within its cities, hoping to ride out the storm.

Disbar Merdant: OutCaste. Born AF 2035. Plumber and one-time fiancé to Jessira Grey. Died shortly after Stronghold's destruction.

Dos Martel: Caste Muran. Born AF 1998. As well as being the Magistrate representative of her Caste, she is also a singer of great repute.

Dru Barrier: OutCaste. Born AF 2024. Major East of the Home Army of Stronghold. Second highest officer of the Army and only answered to the Colonel and Governor-General. Died during Stronghold's destruction.

Dryad Park: A large, public park known variously as 'the Soul of Ashoka' or 'the green jewel of Ashoka'. It was developed under the auspices of the Magisterium in AF 1363 on an area of boggy, impoverished land full of rundown homes and apartments. The park has gone through several transitions, including a disastrous period of time in the 1600s where the fashion of the day was to return public land to its natural state. The park quickly became a bog once again with swamp gases regularly polluting the air. Thankfully, this idea of 'natural' spaces was swiftly abandoned. In addition, during times of emergency, the park can be converted into arable land.

Durmer Volk: Caste Kumma. House Shektan. Born AF 1990 to Hurum and Kiran Volk. Completed six Trials before retiring at age thirty-five. He is charged with the early training of young Shektans and known as the 'Great Rahail' for how seriously he takes his duties. Member of the Shektan House Council.

East Vineyard Steep: An area of relatively rundown homes and buildings, which barely stand erect. However, the main denizens, the Sentyas, prefer it this way. They would rather not waste money to maintain their homes beyond what's absolutely needed.

Fan and the Reed, the: All-female Kumma academy in Ashoka. Founded AF 343.

Fan Lor Kum: The Red Hand of Justice. Suwraith's forces in the Wildness. Their sole purpose is to kill Humans wherever they find them. They are organized into Plagues, and the commander of each Plague is titled the SarpanKum, a Bael of great cunning and skill. The Fan Lor Kum are sometimes referred to simply as the Chimeras.

Organization of the Fan Lor Kum:

One hundred Chimeras form a Smash, and the commander is labeled a Jut

Ten Smashes form a Fracture, and the commander is labeled a Levner

Fifteen Fractures form a Shatter, and the commander is labeled a Vorsan

Eight Shatters form a Dread, and the commander is labeled a Sarpan

Two Dreads form a Plague, and the commander is titled the SarpanKum

*All commanders at every level are Baels. Of note is the SarpanKi, who does not fit into this hierarchy. The SarpanKi is the special adjunct to the SarpanKum, almost always from his crèche, and outranks the Sarpans.

Farn Arnicep: Caste Kumma. House Shektan. Born AF 2041 to Evam and Midre Arnicep. Survived the Trial between Ashoka and Nestle and lived in Stronghold for a brief time. Later on, he commanded the only Trial to that doomed city.

Felt Barnel: Caste Muran. Born AF 2020. Completed two Trials. A glassblower who was the first person murdered by Hal'El Wrestiva with the Withering Knife.

Fifty-Five, the: The fifty-five survivors of Hammer's Fall. They went on to found the city of Stronghold in AF 1753.

First Father: Along with the First Mother, He was the ruler of the First World, greatly responsible for the peace and fortune of that time. Legends say that the First Father broke the WellStone and was thereby able to gain entrance to the fortress of the First Mother, and together, they were able to bring life to a dead and desolate land. The Baels claim it was the First Father's own Daughter, Lienna, who murdered both of Her Parents.

First Mother: Along with the First Father, She was the ruler of the First World, greatly responsible for the peace and fortune of that time. The Baels claim it was the First Mother's own Daughter, Lienna, who murdered both of Her Parents.

First World: Legendary time of peace and prosperity prior to the arrival of Suwraith. With the death of the First Mother and the First Father, the First World ended with the Night of Sorrows.

Fol Nacket: Caste Cherid. Born AF 2006. He is the Cherid

626

Magistrate and head of the Magisterium.

Fort and the Sword, the: All-male martial academy in Ashoka. Only open to Kummas. Established AF 121.

Fragrance Wall: An area of manses and estates. It is the home to most Cherids.

Garnet Bosde: Caste Kumma. House Shektan. Born AF 1985 to Reoten and Preema Bosde. Completed five Trials before retiring at age thirty-four. One of Dar'El Shektan's earliest supporters and once a member of the Shektan House Council.

Gelan Criatus: Caste Shiyen. Born AF 435 in Hammer. Widely considered the Nanna of modern medicine.

Glory Stadium: Ashoka's main stadium where the Tournament of Hume and other citywide events take place.

Gren Vos: Caste Shiyen. Born AF 1975. She was a highly respected physician in her day, and is currently the longest serving Magistrate, having first been elected in AF 2021.

Gris Holianth: Caste Shiyen. Born AF 2011. Owner of the Long Pull, a pub.

Hal'El Wrestiva: Caste Kumma. House Wrestiva. Born AF 2000 as Halthin Bramer to Suge and Bryni Bramer of House Wrestiva. Completed eight Trials before retiring at age thirty-six. Married to Kilwen nee Asthan in AF 2038 and widowed in AF 2049. Became the ruling 'El of his House Wrestiva in 2046. He was the SuDin of the Sil Lor Kum of Ashoka before being found out by Rector Bryce and Mira Terrell.

High Army of Ashoka: Professional army of Ashoka made entirely of veterans of the Trials. Most of their ranks are filled out by

Kummas, including the post of Liege-Marshall. Currently composed of two legions and a total of approximately 11,000 warriors.

Hold Cavern: A quiet neighborhood of small homes and shops. It is home to many Rahails.

Home Army: The Army of Stronghold.

Home Senate: Highest governmental body in Stronghold with eleven members. There is one senator per Crofthold and the Governor-General. *(All members are deceased)*

> **Senators:**
>
> **Nox Bitter**: Represents Crofthold Babylin.
> **Mix Ware**: Represents Crofthold Primus.
> **Brill River**: Represents Crofthold Jonie. Oldest senator.
> **Gourd Mille**: Represents Crofthold Sharing.
> **Thistle Rub**: Represents Crofthold Lucent.
> **Foil Leak**: Represents Crofthold Ware.
> **Shun Morn**: Represents Crofthold Clannad.
> **Drape Wilt**: Represents Crofthold Cohesed.
> **Frame Seek**: Represents Crofthold Healed.
> **Wheel Cole**: Represents Crofthold Synthesis.

Home Watch: Police force of Stronghold. The members are all veterans of the Home Army, with roughly five of them stationed in each of the ten Croftholds *(all members are deceased)*.

House of Fire and Mirrors, the: All-male martial academy in Ashoka. Generally for Kummas but open to other Castes. Founded AF 216.

Hume Telrest: Caste Kumma. Born AF 1702. He is universally regarded as the finest warrior in the history of Arisa, having completed twenty Trials. It is in his honor that the Tournament of Hume is held in every city throughout the world.

Hungrove, the: A glaring of Shylows/Kesarins led by Aia's nanna.

Insufi **blade**: The sword given to a warrior during his *upanayana* ceremony.

Ironwood: A fast-growing tree known for its lightweight, hardy wood, which has properties similar to iron and is similarly fire resistant.

Isle of the Crows: An island infamous for its black crows in Bar Try Bay. It is where the remains of traitors are left to rot. With the lack of a purifying pyre, such individuals are thought to lose Devesh's grace, and are either punished within the unholy hells or shackled again to the wheel of life to be reborn in a position of impoverishment and suffering.

Jaciro Temult: Caste Shiyen. Born AF 2007. A disreputable Shiyen physician whose addiction to opium and alcohol resulted in the loss of his medical license. He is reputed to offer illicit medical services to those for whom discretion is of utmost importance.

Janos Terrell: Caste Kumma. Born AF 2002. He has completed five Trials. Widower of Sophy Terrell and father to Mira Terrell. Recently appointed to the Shektan House Council.

Jared Randall: Caste Rahail. Born AF 2025. Completed three Trials. Caravan master of the caravan between Ashoka and Nestle. Suspected member of the Sil Lor Kum, although the proof is rather sparse.

Jaresh Shektan: Caste Sentya. House Shektan. Born AF 2042 to Bresh and Shari Konias. His birth parents died in an apartment fire, and he was adopted by Darjuth (later to be Dar'El) and Satha Sulle. He is the only such individual ever adopted into a Kumma House who is himself not a Kumma.

Jessira Shektan (née Viola Grey): OutCaste. Born AF 2042 to Sateesh and Crena Grey. Warrior of the Stronghold Home Army and once a member of the Silversun scouts. Married to Rukh Shektan.

Jivatma: Some believe this to be the body's soul. It springs from a person's Well like a waterfall and can be made richer and more vibrant through discipline and hard work.

Jone Drent: Caste Duriah. Born AF 2005. He has the rare ability to both Cohese and DeCohese. He is the Duriah Magistrate.

Jubilee Hills: An expansive area of rolling hills. It is home to Kummas.

Kart Grey: OutCaste. Born AF 2028 to Sateesh and Crena Grey. Brother to Jessira Grey and Cedar Grey. Cousin to Court Deep and Sign Deep. Died during Stronghold's destruction.

Keemo Chalwin: Caste Kumma. House Dravidia. Born AF 2041 to Loriad and Mishal Chalwin. Survived the Trial between Ashoka and Nestle. Later on was killed by Kesarins.

Kesarin, the: See *Shylows*.

Kezin: See *Slayer*.

Krain Linshok: Caste Kumma. House Flood. Born AF 2003 to Halsith and Jennis Linshok. He has completed five Trials. He is the Kumma Magistrate.

Kuldige Prayvar: Caste Kumma. Born AF 1825. Originally of House Trektim, he went on to found House Shektan in AF 1872. He was thereafter known as Kul'El Shektan. He is also a self-confessed member of the Sil Lor Kum, ruling them for a time as the SuDin.

Larina, the: The only school of singing in Ashoka. Open only to Murans.

Laya Grey: OutCaste. Born AF 2038. Widow of Cedar Grey and vadina to Jessira and Kart Grey, as well as Court and Sign Deep.

Layfind Fish Market: A raucous area of stores and booths near Trell Rue.

Li-Boil: VorsanKi to Li-Choke. Later on, following the murders of Li-Shard and Li-Brind, he becomes the SarpanKum of the Eastern Plague of Continent Catalyst.

Li-Brind: SarpanKi to Li-Shard. He is old and hard-bitten. He was SarpanKi of the Western Plague of Continent Catalyst and followed Li-Shard to the Eastern Plague where he held the same position.

Li-Charn: SarpanKum of the Fan Lor Kum at the time of Hammer's Fall.

Li-Choke: Vorsan and friend to Rukh and Jessira Shektan. Teaches Chak-Soon about the ideals of fraternity.

Li-Dirge: SarpanKum of the Fan Lor Kum during the destruction of the caravan from Ashoka to Nestle. Later on, he and his command were destroyed en masse by Suwraith when She discovered Her betrayal at the hands of the Baels.

Li-Dox: A young Jut ordered west from Continent Catalyst.

Li-Grist: Sarpan from Continent Catalyst who Mother Lienna (Suwraith) orders west, along with his Dread, to join with the Eastern

Plague of Continent Ember.

Li-Quill: A young Jut of the Eastern Plague of Continent Ember.

Li-Reg: SarpanKi to Li-Dirge and his crèche brother. Killed by Suwraith when She discovered Her betrayal at the hands of the Baels.

Li-Shard: Young SarpanKum of the Western Plague of Continent Catalyst. Later he is ordered by Mother Lienna (Suwraith) to take command of the Eastern Plague.

Li-Torq: Crèche brother to Li-Boil. Later on becomes SarpanKi of the Eastern Plague upon the deaths of Li-Shard and Li-Brind.

Lighted Candle, the: Sentya academy given over entirely to the study of finance and accounting.

Lin'El Kumma: Caste Kumma. Born into House Therbal on AF 1980. Completed six Trials and retired at age thirty-four. Elected as the Arbiter of the Chamber of Lords on AF 2051, and thereafter took the surname 'Kumma'.

Lure Grey: OutCaste. Born AF 2044 to Sateesh and Crena Grey. Warrior of the Stronghold Home Army and once a member of the Silversun Scouts. He was killed by Kesarins.

MalDin: The Servants of the Voice. The leaders of the Sil Lor Kum. Along with the SuDin, the six MalDin comprise the Council of Rule.

Mavayya: Father-in-law.

Mesa Reed: Caste Cherid. Born AF 2017. She is one of the wealthiest women in the city, having earned her money through a combination of inheritance from her deceased husband and her own investments. She was executed for her role as a MalDin of the Sil Lor Kum.

Mira Terrell: Caste Kumma. House Shektan. Born AF 2042 to Janos and Sophy Terrell. She exposed Hal'El Wrestiva as the SuDin of the Sil Lor Kum and was murdered by him.

Moon Quarter: Area of wharves, docks, and factories. By law, all manufacturing or industry, which might result in malodorous pollution, must be placed in the Moon Quarter. As such, it is an undesirable residential area.

Moke Urn: Caste Sentya. Born AF 2020. He was born in relative poverty and obscurity but is brilliant when it comes to finances. He was given an opportunity to demonstrate his skills as a member of the Sil Lor Kum. He rose to the rank of MalDin before his execution.

Mon Peace: OutCaste. Born AF 2000. Governor-General of Stronghold at the time of the city's destruction.

Nape Pile: OutCaste. Born AF 2014. Major West of the Home Army of Stronghold at the time of the city's destruction.

Night of Sorrows: The night when Suwraith was born and killed nearly half of all people living at the time.

Nine Hills of Ashoka:
                Mount Creolite
                Mount Walnut
                Mount Channel
                Mount Crone
                Mount Cyan
                Mount Bright
                Mount Auburn
                Mount Equine
                Mount Style

Oasis: A powerful manifestation, supposedly of *Jivatma*, which appeared suddenly and unexpectedly around certain cities of the First World just prior to Suwraith's arrival. Over the ensuing two millennia, they have proven nearly impervious to Suwraith's power. Rahails maintain the Oasis of a city through their Talent of Sharing, but how they manage this is a mystery even to them.

Peddamma: Aunt as father or mother's older brother's wife or father or mother's older sister.

Peddananna: Uncle as father or mother's older brother or father or mother's older sister's husband.

Pera Obbe: Caste Duriah. Born AF 2018. She is stupid, yet she was clever enough to rise to the rank of MalDin of the Sil Lor Kum. Hated by Hal'El Wrestiva.

Plaza of the Martyr: The largest public plaza in Ashoka. Also known as the 'Heart of Ashoka'. It is famous for the Union Fountain.

Plaza of Toll and Toil: The large plaza into which the Magisterium opens. Historically, it was where the contracts of indentured servants were auctioned.

Poque Belt: Caste Sentya. Born AF 2018. He founded a forensic accounting service. Rumor has it he was elected Magistrate for his Caste simply so he could no longer audit the work of other Sentyas.

Rector Bryce: Caste Kumma. House Shektan. Born AF 2029 to Garnet and Maris Bryce. His parents divorced when he was twelve. Completed four Trials before retiring at age thirty-two. Member of Ashokan Guard as a lieutenant of the **Fifth Platoon, Third Company, Second Brigade, Third Legion,** and also a lieutenant in the City Watch.

Ronin: A Kumma warrior expelled from his House. Other than being found Unworthy or given the Slash of Iniquity, nothing is more shameful.

Rose and the Thorn, the: One of the schools of song in Ashoka. Open only to Sentyas.

Rukh Shektan: Caste Kumma. House Shektan. Born AF 2041 to Dar'El and Satha Shektan. He was twenty-one years old at the time of his first Trial. He is the first Virgin to win the Tournament of Hume. Married to Jessira Shektan.

Sarath, the: Rahail academy in Ashoka. Students are instructed in both the maintenance of the Oasis and also trained as warriors.

Sateesh Grey: OutCaste. Born AF 2008. Married to Crena Grey and nanna to Kart, Cedar, Jessira, and Lure. Adopted Court and Sign Deep. Died during the destruction of Stronghold.

Satha Shektan: Caste Kumma. House Shektan. Born AF 2019 to Mira and Rukh Aybar of House Shektan. Married Darjuth Sulle (later to be Dar'El) in AF 2039. She is as responsible for House Shektan's rise in wealth and prestige as her husband. She is admired and loathed in equal measure by the other ruling 'Els.

School of Water, the: All-female Kumma academy in Ashoka. Established AF 153.

Semaphore Walk: Ashoka's theater district.

Shield, the: Rahail academy in Ashoka. Focus is on the training of those sufficiently gifted to maintain the Oasis.

Shir'Fen, the: Rahail military academy in Ashoka. Rigorous admission standards and instructors are a mix of Kummas and Rahails.

Shon: A tawny-coated Kesarin. Bonded to Jessira Shektan.

Shoke: A wooden blade used in training and tournaments. It is blunted and possesses properties that allow it to produce as true a representation as possible of the damage inflicted by an edged weapon without actually causing permanent injury or death.

Shylows: The great cats of the Hunters Flats. They grow to be over seven feet in height and twenty-five feet from nose-to-tail. They are feared for their great speed, power, and ability to see through Blends. The cats are extremely territorial and hunt in glarings, packs of forty-to-fifty. They name themselves the Kesarins.

Shur Rainfall: Caste Muran. Born AF 2012 in the city of Arjun. Completed one Trial. He is the leader of the Virtuous.

Sil Lor Kum: The Hidden Hand of Justice. They are the Human agents of Suwraith and are universally hated and despised. Many consider their existence to be a myth, although inexplicable setbacks are often attributed to the Sil Lor Kum.

Sign Deep: OutCaste. Born AF 2042. Sister to Court Deep and cousin to Kart, Cedar, Jessira Grey.

Slash of Iniquity: A judgment by the Kumma Chamber of Lords in which an individual is found to be deviant and traitorous. Such an individual is either executed with his remains left on the Isle of the Crows or in some instances, merely banished forthwith.

Slayer, the: Leader of a glaring of Shylows. Also known as the Kezin.

Society of Rajan: Legendary society originally founded by Raja, a Cherid in Hammer who discovered *The Book of First Movement*. The Society has come to believe that *The Book* is the key to defeating

Suwraith. Though the Society has failed in its mission of learning the secrets they claim is in *The Book*, nevertheless, they have spread to all the other cities of Arisa, where their influence and reputation is greater than their actual numbers. The Society in each city is comprised of twenty-one active members: three from each Caste with an Apprentice, Journeyman, and Master. Since the Society members are chosen *after* they have proven their worth as influential and moral members of their Castes, they are generally in their thirties before they are first brought into the Society as Apprentices. Some Rajans do resign or retire, but this is rare, and such individuals are no longer allowed to vote on Society business.

Current members:

Caste Kumma:

Master: Silma Thoran
Journeyman: Dar'El Shektan
Apprentice: Bravun Silan

Caste Sentya:

Master: Thrivel Nonel
Journeyman: Krane
Apprentice: Chima Plast

Caste Duriah:

Master: Jaka Moth
Journeyman: Anian Elim
Apprentice: Bove Moth

Caste Rahail:

Master: Grain Jola
Journeyman: Lesur Mint
Apprentice: Olin Treave

Caste Shiyen:

Master: Gren Vos
Journeyman: Rassin Chin
Apprentice: Nisin Mercus

Caste Muran:

Master: Ular Sathin
Journeyman: Walid Greenvole
Apprentice: Alms Soildrew

Caste Cherid:

Master: Sim Chilmore
Journeyman: Diffel Karekin
Apprentice: Minet Jorian

Sophy Terrell: Caste Kumma. House Shektan. Born AF 2014 to Kolt and Versana Drathe of House Primase. Married Odonis Terrell of House Shektan in AF 2035. Once a member of the Shektan House Council and murdered by Hal'El Wrestiva.

Sorrows of Hume, the: Aphorisms attributed to Hume Telrest.

Spidergrass: A type of plant that grows best in temperate climates. It is used in the fashioning of items once made with metal. Duriah smiths claim it has tensile properties identical to the finest steel.

Stone Cavern: A neighborhood of craft shops and manufacturing. It is where most Duriahs live.

Stronghold: City of OutCastes founded in AF 1753 by the fifty-five survivors of Hammer's Fall. The city was hidden in the Privation Mountains, deep within Mount Fort before its destruction by Suwraith.

Stronghold Government: The city was divided into ten Croftholds. Each Crofthold had its own Home Council. Within each Crofthold, the Home Councils had wide discretion in governance. The Home Senate was responsible for citywide issues, such as management of the Croft and defense.

Additionally, each Council chose a Senator to represent their interests in the Home Senate. There were ten Senators.

The Governor-General was the highest elected official, and he was elected every five years in a citywide election.

Stryd Bosna: Caste Kumma. House Andthra. Born AF 2032 to Darjuth and Selese Bosna. Completed four Trials. He is the Captain of the caravan to Nestle that was destroyed by Li-Dirge.

SuDin: The Voice Who Commands. The leader of the Sil Lor Kum. Most recently was Hal'El Wrestiva.

Suge Wrestiva: Caste Kumma. House Wrestiva. Born AF 2040 to Hal'El and Kilwen Wrestiva. He had yet to be chosen for his first Trial at the time of his death when he was killed in a duel by Jaresh Shektan. Known snowblood addict.

Sunpalm Orchard: A wealthy, quiet neighborhood of stately townhomes and small craft shops. It is home to many Shiyens.

Suwraith: A murderous being of wind and storm who suddenly exploded into existence two thousand years ago. Her only desire seems to be the extinction of Humanity. Her origin is a mystery, although the Baels claim that She was the Daughter of the First Mother and the First Father, murdering them on the Night of Sorrows. The Fan Lor Kum name Her Mother Lienna. Humanity also names her the Bringer of Sorrows or the Queen of Madness.

Talents: Skills possessed by individuals of various Castes, each one unique to a Caste.

Tanner's School of Animal Husbandry: Shiyen school of veterinary medicine.

Teerma Shole: Caste Kumma. Born AF 2012. Widow. Recently appointed as a member of the Shektan House Council.

Thrum: A russet-coated Kesarin. Bonded to Jaresh Shektan.

Trial: The holy duty in which warriors leave the safety of an Oasis and enter the Wildness in order to defend a caravan, even if it costs them their lives.

Trell Rue: A fashionable neighborhood of artisan shops and restaurants.

Triumph Court: Plaza surrounding the Glory Stadium.

Ular Sathin: Caste Muran. Clan Balm. Born AF 1989. Completed two Trials before retiring at age twenty-eight. He was a well-to-do farmer before selling his property to other members of his Clan. He was a MalDin of the Sil Lor Kum. After his death, he provided

Dar'El Shektan with a journal that exposed nearly all the members and activities of the Sil Lor Kum.

Unworthy: A designation by which a Kumma is felt to be a coward and/or morally compromised. Such an individual is banished from the city.

Upanayana ceremony: Ceremony that consecrates a boy to his duties as a man. It involves two days and two nights of fasting and praying in solitude and silence. In the case of Kummas and other warriors, it is followed by the granting of the *Insufi* blade at dawn.

Vadina: Sister-in-law (older brother's wife or husband to an older sister).

Van Jinnu: Caste Rahail. Born AF 2018. Completed two Trials. Widower. Murdered by Hal'El Wrestiva with the Withering Knife.

Varesea Apter: Caste Rahail. Born AF 2019. Widowed. Married to Slathtril Apter. MalDin of the Sil Lor Kum and was killed by Mira Terrell.

Verchow College of Medicine: One of the two Shiyen medical colleges in Ashoka.

Virtuous, the: A large group of Ashokans who believe all the OutCastes should be killed. They are led by Shur Rainfall and the Heavenly Council of the Virtuous.

Well: The place within an individual wherein *Jivatma* resides. Some believe the Well is simply another word for consciousness, and from consciousness, *Jivatma* springs forth.

Wildness, the: The vast area beyond the borders of the cities and their Oases.

Withering Knife, the: A black blade rumored to steal *Jivatma* from those it murders.

<u>Word and the Deed, the</u>: Author unknown. It is a sacred text written prior to the fall of the First World. Over time, it has supplanted *The Book of All Souls* as the main source of religious scripture within the world.

Yuthero Gaste: Caste Shiyen. Born AF 2025. He is one of the youngest professors of Surgery at Alminius School of Medicine. He was also a MalDin of the Sil Lor Kum and was executed.

ABOUT THE AUTHOR

Davis Ashura resides in North Carolina and shares a house with his wonderful wife who somehow overlooked Davis' eccentricities and married him anyway. As proper recompense for her sacrifice, Davis unwittingly turned his wonderful wife into a nerd-girl. To her sad and utter humiliation, she knows *exactly* what is meant by 'Kronos'. Living with them are their two rambunctious boys, both of whom have at various times helped turn Davis' once lustrous, raven-black hair prematurely white. And of course, there are the obligatory strange, strays cats (all authors have cats—it's required by the union). They are fluffy and black with terribly bad breath. When not working—nay laboring—in the creation of his grand works of fiction, Davis practices medicine, but only when the insurance companies tell him he can.

He is the author of the semi-award winning epic fantasy trilogy, *The Castes and the OutCastes*, as well as the YA fantasy, *The Chronicles of William Wilde*. Visit him at www.DavisAshura.com and be appalled by the banality of a writer's life.